Paradise Lost
In Plain and Simple English

(A Modern Translation and the Original Version)

John Milton

BookCaps™ Study Guides
www.bookcaps.com

Table of Contents

Paradise Lost

BOOK I

THE ARGUMENT

This first Book proposes, first in brief, the whole Subject, Mans disobedience, and the loss thereupon of Paradise wherein he was plac't: Then touches the prime cause of his fall, the Serpent, or rather Satan in the Serpent; who revolting from God, and drawing to his side many Legions of Angels, was by the command of God driven out of Heaven with all his Crew into the great Deep. Which action past over, the Poem hasts into the midst of things, presenting Satan with his Angels now fallen into Hell, describ'd here, not in the Center (for Heaven and Earth may be suppos'd as yet not made, certainly not yet accurst) but in a

place of utter darkness, fitliest call'd Chaos: Here Satan with his Angels lying on the burning Lake, thunder-struck and astonisht, after a certain space recovers, as from confusion, calls up him who next in Order and Dignity lay by him; they confer of thir miserable fall. Satan awakens all his Legions, who lay till then in the same manner confounded; They rise, thir Numbers, array of Battel, thir chief Leaders nam'd, according to the

This first book introduces, briefly at first, the whole subject of Man's disobedience, and the of Paradise in which he had been placed.Then touches on the main cause of his fall, the or rather Satan disguised as a serpent. He rebelled against God, and with the many regiments of Angels he had drawn to his side he was banished from Heaven by God into the great Deep.Passing over this action, the Poem goes straight to the center of things, showing Satan and his Angels fallen into Hell, which is described here, not in the Center of Earth (for it should be imagined that Heaven and Earth have not yet been made, and certainly not cursed) but in a place of utter darkness which has the appropriate name of Chaos. Here Satan and his Angels lie on the burning lake, astonished and stunned.After a while Satan recovers and calls up his leaders and they discuss their miserable fall. Satan wakes his armies, who had been in the same state. They rise up, and their numbers, battle order and

Original	Modern paraphrase
Idols known afterwards in Canaan and the	*the names of their chief leaders (those by*
Countries adjoyning. To these Satan directs his	*which they were known in Canaan and*
Speech, comforts them with hope yet of regaining	*neighboring lands) are listed. Satan speaks to*
Heaven, but tells them lastly of a new World and	*them and comforts them with the hope of*
new kind of Creature to be created, according to	*recapturing Heaven, but also tells them of a*
an ancient Prophesie or report in Heaven; for that	*a new world and a new kind of Creature*
Angels were long before this visible Creation,	*which will be created according to an ancient*
was the opinion of many ancient Fathers. To find	*prophesy and rumors in Heaven (because the*
out the truth of this Prophesie, and what to	*opinion of many wise men is that Angels*
determin thereon he refers to a full Councel.	*long before the creation of Earth). To find out*
What his Associates thence attempt.	*the truth of this prophesy, and to decide what*
Pandemonium the Palace of Satan rises, suddenly	*to do about it, he calls a full council, which all*
built out of the Deep: The infernal Peers there	*his confederates attend. Pandemonium, the*
sit in Councel.	*palace of Satan, is suddenly built out of the pit, and the Lords of Hell meet there in debate.*
Of Mans First Disobedience, and the Fruit	*Of the first disobedience of Man, and the fruit*
Of that Forbidden Tree, whose mortal tast	*Of the forbidden tree, the taste of which*
Brought Death into the World, and all our woe,	*Brought Death and sorrow into the world*
With loss of EDEN, till one greater Man	*And barred us from Paradise, until a greater Man*
Restore us, and regain the blissful Seat,	*Led us back to the Heavenly lands,*
Sing Heav'nly Muse, that on the secret top	*Sing, sacred Inspiration, you who on the secret mountain*
Of OREB, or of SINAI, didst inspire	*Of Oreb, or in the Sinai Desert, inspired*
That Shepherd, who first taught the chosen Seed,	*The Shepherd who first taught the chosen people*
In the Beginning how the Heav'ns and Earth	*How in the beginning Heaven and Earth*

Rose out of CHAOS: Or if SION Hill	*Was created from disorder.Or if Sion Hill,*
Delight thee more, and SILOA'S Brook that flow'd	*Is your chosen spot, or Siloa's stream which flowed*
Fast by the Oracle of God; I thence	*Swiftly past God's messenger; from there*
Invoke thy aid to my adventrous Song,	*I call you to help me as I sing my ambitious song,*
That with no middle flight intends to soar	*Which I don't intend to take the easy way*
Above th' AONIAN Mount, while it pursues	*Above the mountain of inspiration, while it tries*
Things unattempted yet in Prose or Rhime.	*Things never yet seen in either prose or poetry.*
And chiefly Thou O Spirit, that dost prefer	*And chiefly, Spirit, which values*
Before all Temples th' upright heart and pure,	*More than temples the pure and honest heart,*
Instruct me, for Thou know'st; Thou from the first	*Guide me, for you have the wisdom;from the start*
Wast present, and with mighty wings outspread	*You were there, and with your great wings spread out*
Dove-like satst brooding on the vast Abyss	*Sat like a dove, perched over the great gorge*
And mad'st it pregnant: What in me is dark	*And bred life from it:shine a light*
Illumine, what is low raise and support;	*Into the darkness inside me, lift up what is low,*
That to the highth of this great Argument	*So that I can do justice to this great subject*
I may assert th' Eternal Providence,	*And show the actions of God,*
And justifie the wayes of God to men.	*And explain the ways of God to men.*
Say first, for Heav'n hides nothing from thy view	*Firstly, because you see all that is in Heaven*
Nor the deep Tract of Hell, say first what cause	*And in the deep pit of Hell, say what made*
Mov'd our Grand Parents in that happy State,	*Our grandparents, living that happy existence,*
Favour'd of Heav'n so highly, to fall off	*So much blessed by Heaven, break away*
From their Creator, and transgress his Will	*From their Creator, and disobey his orders,*
For one restraint, Lords of the World besides?	*His one law, apart from which they were Lords of the World.*
Who first seduc'd them to that fowl revolt?	*Who led them into that awful rebellion?*
Th' infernal Serpent; he it was, whose guile	*The hellish snake; it was he whose cunning*

Stird up with Envy and Revenge, deceiv'd
The Mother of Mankinde, what time his Pride
Had cast him out from Heav'n, with all his Host

Of Rebel Angels, by whose aid aspiring

To set himself in Glory above his Peers,

He trusted to have equal'd the most High,

If he oppos'd; and with ambitious aim

Against the Throne and Monarchy of God

Rais'd impious War in Heav'n and Battel proud
With vain attempt. Him the Almighty Power
Hurld headlong flaming from th' Ethereal Skie
With hideous ruine and combustion down

To bottomless perdition, there to dwell

In Adamantine Chains and penal Fire,

Who durst defie th' Omnipotent to Arms.

Nine times the Space that measures Day and Night
To mortal men, he with his horrid crew
Lay vanquisht, rowling in the fiery Gulfe
Confounded though immortal: But his doom
Reserv'd him to more wrath; for now the thought
Both of lost happiness and lasting pain

Torments him; round he throws his baleful eyes
That witness'd huge affliction and dismay
Mixt with obdurate pride and stedfast hate:

At once as far as Angels kenn he views

Driven by envy and revenge, tricked
The Mother of Mankind, after his pride
Caused him to be thrown out of heaven, with his army

Of rebel Angels, with whose help he had planned

To set himself up in heaven as the highest,

Thinking he could even take on the role of God

If he fought Him; and driven by ambition

Against the throne and kingship of God

Started a blasphemous war in heaven and fought proudly
But in vain. The Almighty Power threw him
Down in flames from the skies of Heaven
With terrible flame and destruction, down

To the bottomless pit of hell, to live there

Bound in unbreakable chains, burned with punishing fire,

For having dared challenge the Almighty to battle.

For nine days, as they are measured
By men, he and his terrible gang
Lay beaten, thrashing in the fiery sea,
Defeated though still immortal: But his fate
Raised further anger in him; for now the thought
Of the happiness he had lost and the pain he now faces

Tortures him: he cast around his hate filled eyes
Which showed great pain and terror
Mixed with unyielding pride and unmoving hate:

As far as Angels can see he sees

The dismal Situation waste and wilde,
A Dungeon horrible, on all sides round

As one great Furnace flam'd, yet from those flames
No light, but rather darkness visible

Serv'd only to discover sights of woe,
Regions of sorrow, doleful shades, where peace
And rest can never dwell, hope never comes
That comes to all; but torture without end
Still urges, and a fiery Deluge, fed

With ever-burning Sulphur unconsum'd:

Such place Eternal Justice had prepar'd

For those rebellious, here their Prison ordain'd
In utter darkness, and their portion set

As far remov'd from God and light of Heav'n
As from the Center thrice to th' utmost Pole.

O how unlike the place from whence they fell!
There the companions of his fall, o'rewhelm'd
With Floods and Whirlwinds of tempestuous fire,
He soon discerns, and weltring by his side

One next himself in power, and next in crime,
Long after known in PALESTINE, and nam'd
BEELZEBUB. To whom th' Arch-Enemy,
And thence in Heav'n call'd Satan, with bold words
Breaking the horrid silence thus began.

If thou beest he; But O how fall'n! how chang'd

The terrible place, bleak and wild,
A horrible dungeon, whose walls all around

Burned like one great oven, but from those flames
There is no light, but a visible darkness

Which only showed things of sadness,
Lands of sorrow, miserable shadows, where peace
And rest are unknown, where the hope that comes to all
Never comes; endless torture
Drives on forever, and there is a fiery storm, fed

By sulphur which burns forever and never runs out:

This was the place God's justice had made

For these rebels, here he had ordered their prison built
In total darkness, and their allotted place

Was to be as far away from God and Heaven's light
As three times distance from the equator to the Poles.

Oh, how different it was to their former home!
There those who fell with him, beaten down
With floods and whirlwinds of stormy flames,
He soon makes out, and in turmoil by his side

Is one almost equal in power, as bad in crime,
Who in later times appeared in Palestine, and his name
Was Beelzebub. The Arch Enemy,
Who was now called Satan in Heaven, with bold words
Breaking through the ghastly silence, spoke to him:
"Is that you? How you have fallen, how changed you are

From him, who in the happy Realms of Light
Cloth'd with transcendent brightnes didst outshine
Myriads though bright: If he whom mutual league,
United thoughts and counsels, equal hope,

And hazard in the Glorious Enterprize,

Joynd with me once, now misery hath joynd
In equal ruin: into what Pit thou seest
From what highth fal'n, so much the stronger provd
He with his Thunder: and till then who knew
The force of those dire Arms? yet not for those
Nor what the Potent Victor in his rage

Can else inflict do I repent or change,

Though chang'd in outward lustre; that fixt mind
And high disdain, from sence of injur'd merit,
That with the mightiest rais'd me to contend,
And to the fierce contention brought along
Innumerable force of Spirits arm'd
That durst dislike his reign, and me preferring,
His utmost power with adverse power oppos'd
In dubious Battel on the Plains of Heav'n,

And shook his throne. What though the field be lost?
All is not lost; the unconquerable Will,

And study of revenge, immortal hate,

And courage never to submit or yield:
And what is else not to be overcome?
That Glory never shall his wrath or might

From the one who in the happy Lands of Light,
Dressed in heavenly brightness outshone
So many others, though bright themselves. If it's you
Who joined with me in thought, plans, hope
And risk in our great adventure,

Then now we're joined again in suffering,
In our destruction: you see the pit,
How low we have fallen, which shows how much stronger
God's thunder was: but before we fought Him who knew
Just how strong He was? But for all his strength
And anything else the winner might do in his anger,
I have no regret, I won't change my mind,

Even though my appearance has changed: I am staying
True to my hatred, caused by my sense of injustice,
Which led me to take on the Mighty in battle,
And to bring along to the fight
A numberless force of Spirits
Who also hated His rule, and preferred me.
We took on the ultimate power with the power of our own,
In a hard fought battle on the fields of Heaven
And shook his throne. So what if we lost the battle?
All is not lost: we shall keep our unquenchable ambition,
And look out for revenge, hating forever,
And be brave enough never to give in,
And so what has He truly won?
All His strength and anger will never

Original	Paraphrase
Extort from me. To bow and sue for grace	*Take that away from me.To bow and beg for pardon*
With suppliant knee, and deifie his power	*On bended knee, and worship the power*
Who from the terrour of this Arm so late	*That so recently feared for his rule in the face*
Doubted his Empire, that were low indeed,	*Of my own power, that would be too low,*
That were an ignominy and shame beneath	*That would be a disgrace and shame far worse*
This downfall; since by Fate the strength of Gods	*Than this fall: the Eternal Laws state that our strength*
And this Empyreal substance cannot fail,	*And this stuff we're made of cannot be destroyed,*
Since through experience of this great event	*So our experience in this great battle hasn't*
In Arms not worse, in foresight much advanc't,	*Taken our strength and has increased our cunning,*
We may with more successful hope resolve	*So we can hope for greater success as we set out*
To wage by force or guile eternal Warr	*To fight an everlasting war with strength or cunning,*
Irreconcileable, to our grand Foe,	*Never giving in to our great enemy,*
Who now triumphs, and in th' excess of joy	*Who has won, for now, and with great happiness*
Sole reigning holds the Tyranny of Heav'n.	*Has sole possession of the title of Tyrant of Heaven."*
So spake th' Apostate Angel, though in pain,	*So the rebel Angel spoke, although he was in pain,*
Vaunting aloud, but rackt with deep despare:	*Boasting out loud, but inside torn with despair,*
And him thus answer'd soon his bold Compeer.	*And soon his arrogant comrade replied:*
O Prince, O Chief of many Throned Powers,	*"Oh Prince, the ruler over many thrones,*
That led th' imbattelld Seraphim to Warr	*Who led the Angels in armor to war*
Under thy conduct, and in dreadful deeds	*Under your orders, and with terrible deeds, without*
Fearless, endanger'd Heav'ns perpetual King;	*Fear, challenged the power of Heaven's eternal King,*
And put to proof his high Supremacy,	*And tested his mighty rule.*
Whether upheld by strength, or Chance, or Fate,	*Whether he won through strength, or luck, or fate,*
Too well I see and rue the dire event,	*I can see and regret the terrible result all too well.*
That with sad overthrow and foul defeat	*Our terrible loss and casting down*

Hath lost us Heav'n, and all this mighty Host
In horrible destruction laid thus low,
As far as Gods and Heav'nly Essences
Can Perish: for the mind and spirit remains
Invincible, and vigour soon returns,
Though all our Glory extinct, and happy state
Here swallow'd up in endless misery.
But what if he our Conquerour, (whom I now
Of force believe Almighty, since no less
Then such could hav orepow'rd such force as ours)
Have left us this our spirit and strength intire
Strongly to suffer and support our pains,
That we may so suffice his vengeful ire,
Or do him mightier service as his thralls
By right of Warr, what e're his business be
Here in the heart of Hell to work in Fire,
Or do his Errands in the gloomy Deep;
What can it then avail though yet we feel
Strength undiminisht, or eternal being
To undergo eternal punishment?
Whereto with speedy words th' Arch-fiend reply'd.
Fall'n Cherube, to be weak is miserable
Doing or Suffering: but of this be sure,
To do ought good never will be our task,
But ever to do ill our sole delight,
As being the contrary to his high will
Whom we resist. If then his Providence
Out of our evil seek to bring forth good,
Our labour must be to pervert that end,

Has barred us from Heaven, and all this great army
Has been thrown down in ruin,
As close to death as Gods and Heavenly forms
Can come, for the mind and spirit
Cannot be beaten, and strength will come back, even if
All our light has been extinguished, and our happiness
Is drowned here in this endless suffering.
But what if he who beat us (who I now
Must acknowledge as Almighty in strength, since only
Such a one could have beaten our armies)
Has left our spirit and strength intact
So that we can better feel pain,
So He can go on taking his revenge,
Or carry on serving him as slaves,
His by right of victory: to order us, whatever he's up to,
To work in the fire here in the heart of Hell,
To do his errands in these gloomy depths;
In that case how will it help us to feel
Undiminished strength, or eternal life?
It'll just help us to suffer eternal punishment."
The leader of the demons swiftly replied:
"Fallen Angel, weakness is a miserable thing
In action or in suffering: but I can promise you,
We will never do anything good.
To always do harm will be our only pleasure,
Because it will go against the desires
Of him we are fighting. If God tries create good from our evil
Then we must work to twist his goal

12

And out of good still to find means of evil;	*And make sure that evil comes out of good;*
Which oft times may succeed, so as perhaps	*This might happen often, and perhaps*
Shall grieve him, if I fail not, and disturb	*Cause him grief, if my plans work, and knock*
His inmost counsels from their destind aim.	*His most cherished plans off course.*
But see the angry Victor hath recall'd	*But look, the furious winner has called back*
His Ministers of vengeance and pursuit	*His agents of revenge who chased us,*
Back to the Gates of Heav'n: The Sulphurous Hail	*To the Gates of Heaven: the fiery hail*
Shot after us in storm, oreblown hath laid	*That stormed after us has blown out now.*
The fiery Surge, that from the Precipice	*The wave of fire that followed us*
Of Heav'n receiv'd us falling, and the Thunder,	*As we fell from the edge of Heaven, and the thunder,*
Wing'd with red Lightning and impetuous rage,	*Accompanied by red lightning and furious anger*
Perhaps hath spent his shafts, and ceases now	*Has perhaps been exhausted, and has stopped*
To bellow through the vast and boundless Deep.	*Bellowing through this huge and bottomless pit.*
Let us not slip th' occasion, whether scorn,	*Let's not miss our chance, whether it is contempt*
Or satiate fury yield it from our Foe.	*Or the end of his anger that makes our enemy give it to us.*
Seest thou yon dreary Plain, forlorn and wilde,	*Do you see that miserable plain, abandoned and wild,*
The seat of desolation, voyd of light,	*Desolate, without light*
Save what the glimmering of these livid flames	*Apart from the flicker which these angry flames*
Casts pale and dreadful? Thither let us tend	*Give, pale and horrid? Let us go there,*
From off the tossing of these fiery waves,	*Away from these waves of fire,*
There rest, if any rest can harbour there,	*And rest, if there is any rest to be had there,*
And reassembling our afflicted Powers,	*And gather up our damaged forces,*
Consult how we may henceforth most offend	*Debate how from now on we can do most damage*
Our Enemy, our own loss how repair,	*To our enemy, how we can make up for our loss,*
How overcome this dire Calamity,	*How we can overcome this terrible disaster,*
What reinforcement we may gain from Hope,	*How we can get strength from hope,*
If not what resolution from despare.	*Or at least how we can gain*

13

	determination from despair."
Thus Satan talking to his neerest Mate	*Thus Satan spoke to his lieutentant,*
With Head up-lift above the wave, and Eyes	*With his head lifted above the waves, and his eyes*
That sparkling blaz'd, his other Parts besides	*Burning with fire, the rest of him*
Prone on the Flood, extended long and large	*Laid out on the lake of fire, stretching far and wide*
Lay floating many a rood, in bulk as huge	*Over many acres, as huge*
As whom the Fables name of monstrous size,	*As the one named in legends as being of monstrous size,*
TITANIAN, or EARTH-BORN, that warr'd on JOVE,	*Titan, or "The one born of earth", who battled Jupiter,*
BRIARIOS or TYPHON, whom the Den	*Briaros and Typhon, who lurked in his cave*
By ancient TARSUS held, or that Sea-beast	*By ancient Tarsus, or the sea monster*
LEVIATHAN, which God of all his works	*Leviathan, the biggest thing God created*
Created hugest that swim th' Ocean stream: Him haply slumbring on the NORWAY foam	*Which swims in the oceans' currents: When he might be sleeping in the Norwegian Sea*
The Pilot of some small night-founder'd Skiff,	*The sailors say often the pilot of some small craft,*
Deeming some Island, oft, as Sea-men tell,	*Caught out at night, thinks that he's an island*
With fixed Anchor in his skaly rind	*And fixes an anchor in his scaly skin,*
Moors by his side under the Lee, while Night	*Ties up in the shelter of his side while night*
Invests the Sea, and wished Morn delayes:	*Rules the sea and keeps off the hoped for morning:*
So stretcht out huge in length the Arch-fiend lay	*So the chief demon lay, his great length stretched out,*
Chain'd on the burning Lake, nor ever lay	*Chained to the burning lake from which*
Had ris'n or heav'd his head, but that the will	*He could never have arisen, except that the will*
And high permission of all-ruling Heaven	*And permission of all powerful Heaven*
Left him at large to his own dark designs,	*Left him to carry on his own evil plans,*
That with reiterated crimes he might	*So that by repeating his crimes he might*
Heap on himself damnation, while he sought	*Draw further punishment down on himself as he tried*
Evil to others, and enrag'd might see	*To do wrong to others, and to his fury*

14

How all his malice serv'd but to bring forth
Infinite goodness, grace and mercy shewn

On Man by him seduc't, but on himself

Treble confusion, wrath and vengeance pour'd.
Forthwith upright he rears from off the Pool

His mighty Stature; on each hand the flames
Drivn backward slope their pointing spires, & rowld
In billows, leave i'th' midst a horrid Vale.

Then with expanded wings he stears his flight
Aloft, incumbent on the dusky Air
That felt unusual weight, till on dry Land

He lights, if it were Land that ever burn'd

With solid, as the Lake with liquid fire;

And such appear'd in hue, as when the force
Of subterranean wind transports a Hill

Torn from PELORUS, or the shatter'd side

Of thundring AETNA, whose combustible

And fewel'd entrals thence conceiving Fire,
Sublim'd with Mineral fury, aid the Winds,

And leave a singed bottom all involv'd
With stench and smoak: Such resting found the sole
Of unblest feet. Him followed his next Mate,

Both glorying to have scap't the STYGIAN flood
As Gods, and by their own recover'd strength,
Not by the sufferance of supernal Power.

Is this the Region, this the Soil, the Clime,

he would see
How his evil only brought out
Infinite goodness, grace and mercy given

To the Man he tried to pervert, but on himself

A triple dose of horror, anger and vengeance was poured.
He pulls his great bulk upright from the pool;

On either side the flames,
With their leaping points blown backwards,

Rolled away in waves, leaving a horrid valley in the center.

Then with his wings outstretched he took off
Into the dark air,
Which felt unusually heavy, until he came to dry land

And landed, if it could be called land that burned

With a solid fire just as the lake burned with liquid fire.

In color it was like a hill when
The force of underground winds move it,

Tears it away from Pelorus, or from the broken slopes

Of thunderous Mount Etna, whose burning

And powerful innards kindle fire,
Fuelled by dissolved minerals, and leave

The lands around burnt
And wrapped in stench and smoke; such was the land

The soles of the cursed feet found. His lieutenant followed,

Both of them happy to have escaped the hellish flood
Like Gods, and having done it under their own steam.
Not with the permission of the Divine Power.

"Is this the country, the land, the

<table>
</table>

Said then the lost Arch Angel, this the seat	atmosphere," Said the fallen Archangel, "Is this the place
That we must change for Heav'n, this mournful gloom	That we must swap for Heaven, this mournful gloom
For that celestial light? Be it so, since hee	For that heavenly light? So be it, because he
Who now is Sovran can dispose and bid	Who rules can now order
What shall be right: fardest from him is best	Things as He wishes. It's best to be farthest from Him
Whom reason hath equald, force hath made supream	Whose genius is equal to, and whose force is greater
Above his equals. Farewel happy Fields	Than, others. Farewell to the happy fields,
Where Joy for ever dwells: Hail horrours, hail	Where joy lives forever: welcome horrors, welcome
Infernal world, and thou profoundest Hell	The world of devils, and you, deepest Hell,
Receive thy new Possessor: One who brings	Welcome your new Master: One who brings
A mind not to be chang'd by Place or Time.	A mind that will not be changed by its place or by time.
The mind is its own place, and in it self	The mind is a place in itself, and inside it one
Can make a Heav'n of Hell, a Hell of Heav'n.	Can turn Heaven into Hell or Hell into Heaven.
What matter where, if I be still the same,	Who cares where I am, if I'm still the same,
And what I should be, all but less then hee	And why should I be any different just because
Whom Thunder hath made greater? Here at least	He was made greater by force? Here we will
We shall be free; th' Almighty hath not built	Be free at least: God didn't build this place for himself,
Here for his envy, will not drive us hence:	He won't make us leave:
Here we may reign secure, and in my choice	Here we shall rule undisturbed, and in my opinion,
To reign is worth ambition though in Hell:	To rule is something worth wanting, even in Hell:
Better to reign in Hell, then serve in Heav'n.	It's better to rule in Hell than be a servant in Heaven.
But wherefore let we then our faithful friends,	But why are we letting our trusty friends,
Th' associates and copartners of our loss	Our comrades and sharers in our loss,
Lye thus astonisht on th' oblivious Pool,	Lie so shocked on the uncaring lake,

And call them not to share with us their part	*Why are we not calling them to take their place*
In this unhappy Mansion, or once more	*In this cursed house, and telling them*
With rallied Arms to try what may be yet	*To gather up their strength and see what might still*
Regaind in Heav'n, or what more lost in Hell?	*Be taken back from Heaven, or lost in Hell?"*
So SATAN spake, and him BEELZEBUB	*This was how Satan spoke, and Beelzebub answered him:*
Thus answer'd. Leader of those Armies bright,	*"Leader of those bright armies,*
Which but th' Omnipotent none could have foyld,	*Which only the Almighty could have beaten,*
If once they hear that voyce, their liveliest pledge	*If they could just hear that voice*
Of hope in fears and dangers, heard so oft	*Which gave them hope in fear and danger, heard so often*
In worst extreams, and on the perilous edge	*When things were blackest, and on the fearful edge*
Of battel when it rag'd, in all assaults	*Of the raging battle, in all their attacks*
Their surest signal, they will soon resume	*It was their greatest hope, if they hear it now they will soon*
New courage and revive, though now they lye	*Get new hope and rise up, even though at the moment*
Groveling and prostrate on yon Lake of Fire,	*They're lying groveling on that lake of fire,*
As we erewhile, astounded and amaz'd,	*As we were a short while ago, stunned and shocked,*
No wonder, fall'n such a pernicious highth.	*And no wonder, after falling from such a terrible height."*
He scarce had ceas't when the superiour Fiend	*He'd hardly finished when the senior Devil*
Was moving toward the shore; his ponderous shield	*Started off to the shore, his great shield,*
Ethereal temper, massy, large and round,	*Forged in Heaven, heavy, large and round,*
Behind him cast; the broad circumference	*Slung on his back: the great circle*
Hung on his shoulders like the Moon, whose Orb	*Hung on his shoulders like the Moon, the ball*
Through Optic Glass the TUSCAN Artist views	*Which Galileo watches through his telescope*
At Ev'ning from the top of FESOLE,	*In the evening from the hill town of Fesole,*
Or in VALDARNO, to descry new Lands,	*Or from the Arno Valley, seeking out*

	new lands,
Rivers or Mountains in her spotty Globe.	*Rivers, or mountains in her spotted globe.*
His Spear, to equal which the tallest Pine	*His spear, which was equal in height to the tallest pine*
Hewn on NORWEGIAN hills, to be the Mast	*Cut down in the hills of Norway to make a mast*
Of some great Ammiral, were but a wand,	*For the ship of some great Admiral, was just a stick*
He walkt with to support uneasie steps	*He leaned on to help his cautious steps*
Over the burning Marle, not like those steps	*Over the burning clay, not like the steps he took*
On Heavens Azure, and the torrid Clime	*In the blue of Heaven, and the oppressive atmosphere*
Smote on him sore besides, vaulted with Fire;	*Beat him down as well, surrounded by fire.*
Nathless he so endur'd, till on the Beach	*Nonetheless he suffered it, until upon the shore*
Of that inflamed Sea, he stood and call'd	*Of the burning sea he stood, and called*
His Legions, Angel Forms, who lay intrans't	*His armies, the angelic forms which lay unconscious,*
Thick as Autumnal Leaves that strow the Brooks	*As thick as the leaves of autumn which lie on the streams*
In VALLOMBROSA, where th' ETRURIAN shades	*Of Vallambrosa, where the Tuscan shade*
High overarch't imbowr; or scatterd sedge	*Covers over all; or like the scattered seaweed*
Afloat, when with fierce Winds ORION arm'd	*Floating, when the storms of Orion*
Hath vext the Red-Sea Coast, whose waves orethrew	*Has attacked the Red Sea coast with the waves*
BUSIRIS and his MEMPHIAN Chivalrie,	*Which overthrew the Pharaoh and his Egyptian cavalry,*
VVhile with perfidious hatred they pursu'd	*Who with wicked hatred chased*
The Sojourners of GOSHEN, who beheld	*The Israelites, who saw from the safety of the shore*
From the safe shore their floating Carkases	*Their floating corpses*
And broken Chariot Wheels, so thick bestrewn	*And broken chariot wheels. This was how thick they lay,*
Abject and lost lay these, covering the Flood,	*The pitiful and lost who covered the surface,*
Under amazement of their hideous change.	*Stunned by the terrible thing that had happened to them.*

He call'd so loud, that all the hollow Deep
Of Hell resounded. Princes, Potentates,
Warriers, the Flowr of Heav'n, once yours, now lost,
If such astonishment as this can sieze
Eternal spirits; or have ye chos'n this place
After the toyl of Battel to repose
Your wearied vertue, for the ease you find
To slumber here, as in the Vales of Heav'n?
Or in this abject posture have ye sworn
To adore the Conquerour? who now beholds
Cherube and Seraph rowling in the Flood
With scatter'd Arms and Ensigns, till anon
His swift pursuers from Heav'n Gates discern
Th' advantage, and descending tread us down
Thus drooping, or with linked Thunderbolts
Transfix us to the bottom of this Gulfe.1
Awake, arise, or be for ever fall'n.
They heard, and were abasht, and up they sprung
Upon the wing, as when men wont to watch
On duty, sleeping found by whom they dread,
Rouse and bestir themselves ere well awake.
Nor did they not perceave the evil plight
In which they were, or the fierce pains not feel;
Yet to their Generals Voyce they soon obeyd
Innumerable. As when the potent Rod

He called out so loudly that the whole pit
Of Hell echoed with it: "Princes, Rulers,
Warriors who were once the pride of the Heaven we've lost,
Can this sort of amazement overcome Eternal Spirits? Or have you decided this is the place,
After the efforts of battle, to rest
Your tired strength, as if it was as easy
To sleep here as it was in the Vales of Heaven?
Or have you promised to lie down like this
To worship the one who beat you? The one who now sees
Cherubim and Seraphim rolling around in the flood,
With all their weapons and flags scattered, so that soon
Those who chased us from Heaven's gate will see
They have the upper hand, and coming closer smash us
As we rest here, or with bolts of lightning
Pin us to the floor of this pit.
Wake up, get up, or you'll be lost forever."
They heard and were ashamed, and they leapt up
Into the air, like men on Sentry duty,
Caught sleeping by their Sergeant,
Who get moving before they're properly awake.
It was not as though they were blind to the terrible
Situation they were in, or not feel the awful pains,
But they obeyed their commander's voice,
Flocking in their multitudes. Like when the wand

Of AMRAMS Son in EGYPTS evill day	*Of Moses, in the bad times in Eygpt,*
Wav'd round the Coast, up call'd a pitchy cloud	*Waved round the shores and summoned a dark cloud*
Of LOCUSTS, warping on the Eastern Wind,	*Of locusts, sailing on the east wind,*
That ore the Realm of impious PHAROAH hung	*That hung over the kingdom of the unholy Pharoah*
Like Night, and darken'd all the Land of NILE:	*Like night, and darkened all the lands of the Nile:*
So numberless were those bad Angels seen	*This was how numberless was the crowd of fallen angels,*
Hovering on wing under the Cope of Hell	*Hovering on their wings under the roof of Hell,*
'Twixt upper, nether, and surrounding Fires;	*Between the fires above, below and all around,*
Till, as a signal giv'n, th' uplifted Spear	*Until, like a beacon, the upraised spear*
Of their great Sultan waving to direct	*Of their great ruler led them*
Thir course, in even ballance down they light	*On their journey, and they landed*
On the firm brimstone, and fill all the Plain;	*On the firm brimstone, and covered the plain;*
A multitude, like which the populous North	*Such a crowd the well populated Northern lands*
Pour'd never from her frozen loyns, to pass	*Never poured from her frozen loins,*
RHENE or the DANAW, when her barbarous Sons	*Crossing the Rhine or the Danube, when her barbarian sons*
Came like a Deluge on the South, and spread	*Crashed like a flood upon Southern Europe, spreading*
Beneath GIBRALTAR to the LYBIAN sands.	*From Gibraltar to the Libyan deserts.*
Forthwith from every Squadron and each Band	*At once every platoon and company*
The Heads and Leaders thither hast where stood	*Sent their leaders quickly up to where*
Their great Commander; Godlike shapes and forms	*Their great Commander stood; they were shaped like Gods, princes,*
And Powers that earst in Heaven sat on Thrones;	*These powers that had sat on thrones in Heaven;*
Though of their Names in heav'nly Records now	*Though in the records of Heaven their names*
Be no memorial, blotted out and ras'd	*Were not remembered now, scratched and erased*
By thir Rebellion, from the Books of Life.	*From the Books of Life by their rebellion.*

Nor had they yet among the Sons of EVE
Got them new Names, till wandring ore the Earth,
Through Gods high sufferance for the tryal of man,
By falsities and lyes the greatest part

Of Mankind they corrupted to forsake

God their Creator, and th' invisible

Glory of him, that made them, to transform

Oft to the Image of a Brute, adorn'd
With gay Religions full of Pomp and Gold,

And Devils to adore for Deities:
Then were they known to men by various Names,
And various Idols through the Heathen World.
Say, Muse, their Names then known, who first, who last,
Rous'd from the slumber, on that fiery Couch,
At thir great Emperors call, as next in worth

Came singly where he stood on the bare strand,
While the promiscuous croud stood yet aloof?

The chief were those who from the Pit of Hell
Roaming to seek their prey on earth, durst fix
Their Seats long after next the Seat of God,

Their Altars by his Altar, Gods ador'd

Among the Nations round, and durst abide

JEHOVAH thundring out of SION, thron'd

Between the Cherubim; yea, often plac'd

*Nor had they from Mankind
Yet been given new names, until, as they roamed the Earth,
By great God's allowance, in order to test Mankind,
With lies and deceit they managed, with most
Of Mankind, to corrupt them and persuade them
To abandon God their creator, and the invisible
Glory of the one who made them, to change
Often into animals, dressed up
With bright Religions full of ceremony and luxury,
Worshipping Devils as their Gods:
Then the devils were known to men by various names,
And worshipped as idols throughout the Godless world.
Divine inspiration, what are their names, first and last,
Who awoke from that bed of fire
At the call of their great Emperor and came to him
Where he stood on the bare shore as the next in rank
While the thronging crowd stood back?*

*These were the leaders who, from the pit of Hell,
Roaming the earth to look for their prey on Earth, dared
To set their thrones up next to the throne of God,
Their altars next to his altar and became Gods loved
Amongst all the Nations, and dared defy
Jehovah thundering out of Israel, on his throne
Amongst his angels; they often even put*

Within his Sanctuary it self their Shrines,	*Their shrines within His holy places,*
Abominations; and with cursed things	*Foul objects; and with evil things*
His holy Rites, and solemn Feasts profan'd,	*They polluted His holy ritual and sacred feasts,*
And with their darkness durst affront his light.	*Daring to insult His light with their darkness.*
First MOLOCH, horrid King besmear'd with blood	*First there is Moloch, horrible King covered with the blood*
Of human sacrifice, and parents tears,	*Of human sacrifice and also with parents' tears,*
Though for the noyse of Drums and Timbrels loud	*Who through the noise of the drums and tambourines*
Their childrens cries unheard, that past through fire	*Couldn't hear their children's cries as they were burnt*
To his grim Idol. Him the AMMONITE	*In front of his foul statue. It was him the Ammonites*
Worship in RABBA and her watry Plain,	*Worshipped in Rabba on her flooded plains,*
In ARGOB and in BASAN, to the stream	*In Argob and in Basan, as far as the river*
Of utmost ARNON. Nor content with such	*Of far away Arnon. Not content with such*
Audacious neighbourhood, the wisest heart	*A daring invasion he tricked the wisest man,*
Of SOLOMON he led by fraud to build	*Solomon, into building*
His Temple right against the Temple of God	*His Temple right next to the Temple of God*
On that opprobrious Hill, and made his Grove	*On the Hill of Corruption, and invaded*
The pleasant Vally of HINNOM, TOPHET thence	*The lovely valley of Hinnom, which afterwards was called*
And black GEHENNA call'd, the Type of Hell.	*Tophet and Gehenna, the Valley of the Damned.*
Next CHEMOS, th' obscene dread of MOABS Sons,	*Next came Chemos, the foul curse of the sons of Moab*
From AROER to NEBO, and the wild	*Who stretched his rule from Aroer to Nebo, and the wilds*
Of Southmost ABARIM; in HESEBON	*Of southerly Abarim; to Hesebon*
And HERONAIM, SEONS Realm, beyond	*And Heronaim in the land of Sihon, beyond*
The flowry Dale of SIBMA clad with Vines,	*The fruitful valley of Sibma, dressed in vines,*
And ELEALE to th' ASPHALTICK Pool.	*And from Eleale to the Dead Sea.*
PEOR his other Name, when he entic'd	*He was also called Peor, when he tempted*

ISRAEL in SITTIM on their march from NILE	*The Israelites, stopped in Sittim on the march from the Nile,*
To do him wanton rites, which cost them woe.	*To worship him with obscene ceremonies, for which they were punished.*
Yet thence his lustful Orgies he enlarg'd	*From there he spread his foul orgies*
Even to that Hill of scandal, by the Grove	*Even to the Mount of Olives, next to Moloch's*
Of MOLOCH homicide, lust hard by hate;	*Murderous valley, putting lust next door to hate,*
Till good JOSIAH drove them thence to Hell.	*Until the good man Josiah drove them back into Hell.*
With these came they, who from the bordring flood	*Along with them came the ones known, in the lands*
Of old EUPHRATES to the Brook that parts	*Between the Euphrates and the river which separates*
EGYPT from SYRIAN ground, had general Names	*Egypt and Syria, by the general names*
Of BAALIM and ASHTAROTH, those male,	*Of Baalim and Ashtaroth, the one male,*
These Feminine. For Spirits when they please	*The other female. For when Spirits wish to they can*
Can either Sex assume, or both; so soft	*Be either man or woman, or both; their essential substance*
And uncompounded is their Essence pure,	*Is so soft and moldable,*
Not ti'd or manacl'd with joynt or limb,	*Not chained to joints or limbs*
Nor founded on the brittle strength of bones,	*Or relying on the fragile strength of bones*
Like cumbrous flesh; but in what shape they choose	*And heavy flesh; but choosing whatever shape they wish,*
Dilated or condens't, bright or obscure,	*Expanded or contracted, bright or dark,*
Can execute their aerie purposes,	*They can carry out their supernatural missions,*
And works of love or enmity fulfill.	*Completing their work of love or evil.*
For those the Race of ISRAEL oft forsook	*The people of Israel often rejected*
Their living strength, and unfrequented left	*Him who gave them their power, and left empty*
His righteous Altar, bowing lowly down	*His true altar, bowing down low*
To bestial Gods; for which their heads as low	*To these filthy Gods; as punishment they were bowed down just as low*
Bow'd down in Battel, sunk before the Spear	*In battle, sinking under the spears*
Of despicable foes. With these in troop	*Of despicable enemies. Along with these*
Came ASTORETH, whom the	*Came Astoreth, called by the*

23

Original	Paraphrase
PHOENICIANS call'd	Phoenicians
ASTARTE, Queen of Heav'n, with crescent Horns;	Astarte, Queen of Heaven, with her curved horns;
To whose bright Image nightly by the Moon	Her to whose statue every night under the moonlight
SIDONIAN Virgins paid their Vows and Songs,	Sidonian Virgins gave her their promises and songs,
In SION also not unsung, where stood	Which were also sung in Israel, where she had
Her Temple on th' offensive Mountain, built	Her temple on the Mount of Olives, built
By that uxorious King, whose heart though large,	By the often married King Solomon, who though he had a great heart,
Beguil'd by fair Idolatresses, fell	Was led astray by beautiful idol worshippers and became
To Idols foul. THAMMUZ came next behind,	An idolater himself.Thammuz was the next in line,
Whose annual wound in LEBANON allur'd	Whose death in Lebanon drew, each year,
The SYRIAN Damsels to lament his fate	The Syrian ladies to bewail his fate
In amorous dittyes all a Summers day,	With songs of love on a summer's day,
While smooth ADONIS from his native Rock	While the river Adonis ran from his home mountain
Ran purple to the Sea, suppos'd with blood	To the sea, colored purple, supposedly with the blood
Of THAMMUZ yearly wounded: the Love-tale	Of Thammuz newly wounded each year: the romantic story
Infected SIONS daughters with like heat,	Infected the daughters of Israel with similar desire,
Whose wanton passions in the sacred Porch	And their abandoned behaviour in the sacred doorway of the Temple
EZEKIEL saw, when by the Vision led	Was seen by Ezekiel, when they were under the influence of the vision,
His eye survay'd the dark Idolatries	And he saw with his eyes the evil idolatry
Of alienated JUDAH. Next came one	Of Judah, separated from God.Next came the one
Who mourn'd in earnest, when the Captive Ark	Who mourned deeply when the captured Ark
Maim'd his brute Image, head and hands lopt off	Damaged his brutish statue, with its head and hands broken off
In his own Temple, on the grunsel edge,	In his own Temple, on the edge of the threshold,
Where he fell flat, and sham'd his Worshipers:	Where it fell flat on its face, and embarrassed his worshippers.

DAGON his Name, Sea Monster, upward Man	*Dagon was his name, a sea monster with a man's torso*
And downward Fish: yet had his Temple high	*And a fish's tail: but he had his Temple venerated*
Rear'd in AZOTUS, dreaded through the Coast	*In Azotus, he was feared all along the coast*
Of PALESTINE, in GATH and ASCALON,	*Of Palestine as well as in Gath and Ascalon,*
And ACCARON and GAZA's frontier bounds.	*And in Accaron and on the frontiers of Gaza.*
Him follow'd RIMMON, whose delightful Seat	*Following him came Rimmon, whose beautiful home*
Was fair DAMASCUS, on the fertil Banks	*Was lovely Damascus, on the fertile banks*
Of ABBANA and PHARPHAR, lucid streams.	*Of the shining streams of Abbana and Pharphar.*
He also against the house of God was bold:	*He also was a fighter of the house of God:*
A Leper once he lost and gain'd a King,	*He once lost a leper as a worshipper but gained a king,*
AHAZ his sottish Conquerour, whom he drew	*Ahaz his drunken ruler, whom he persuaded*
Gods Altar to disparage and displace	*To disrespect and replace God's altar*
For one of SYRIAN mode, whereon to burn	*With one of the Syrian type, on which he could burn*
His odious offrings, and adore the Gods	*His revolting sacrifices, and worship the Gods*
Whom he had vanquisht. After these appear'd	*Whom he had beaten. After these came*
A crew who under Names of old Renown,	*A group who, under their ancient famous names,*
OSIRIS, ISIS, ORUS and their Train	*Osiris, Isis, Orus and their followers,*
With monstrous shapes and sorceries abus'd	*With terrible appearances and magic forced*
Fanatic EGYPT and her Priests, to seek	*The raving Egypt and her priests to look*
Thir wandring Gods disguis'd in brutish forms	*For their Gods in brutish characters*
Rather then human. Nor did ISRAEL scape	*Rather than in the shape of a Man. Nor did Israel escape*
Th' infection when their borrow'd Gold compos'd	*Their madness when their borrowed gold was made*
The Calf in OREB: and the Rebel King	*Into the calf idol in Oreb: and Jereboam the rebel King*
Doubl'd that sin in BETHEL and in DAN,	*Made that sin twice as bad in Bethel and in Dan,*

Lik'ning his Maker to the Grazed Ox,	*Comparing his creator to an ox in the field,*
JEHOVAH, who in one Night when he pass'd	*Jehovah, who on one night as he passed*
From EGYPT marching, equal'd with one stroke	*Through Egypt, destroyed with a single bow*
Both her first born and all her bleating Gods.	*Both her first born children and all her bleating Gods.*
BELIAL came last, then whom a Spirit more lewd	*Last came Belial, who had no rival in his obscenity*
Fell not from Heaven, or more gross to love	*In all who fell from Heaven, none had such a disgusting love*
Vice for it self: To him no Temple stood	*Of vice for its own sake: no Temple was built for him, and*
Or Altar smoak'd; yet who more oft then hee	*No fires were lit on altars; and yet who was more often present than him*
In Temples and at Altars, when the Priest	*In Temples and at altars, as when the Priest*
Turns Atheist, as did ELY'S Sons, who fill'd	*Becomes an unbeliever, as Eli's sons did, who filled*
With lust and violence the house of God.	*The House of God with lust and violence.*
In Courts and Palaces he also Reigns	*He also rules in Courts and Palaces,*
And in luxurious Cities, where the noyse	*And in the rich cities, where the noise*
Of riot ascends above thir loftiest Towrs,	*Of the riotous behavior rises above their tallest towers,*
And injury and outrage: And when Night	*As does the sound of fighting and outrages: and when night*
Darkens the Streets, then wander forth the Sons	*Darkens the streets, then the sons of Belial*
Of BELIAL, flown with insolence and wine.	*Come out, driven by arrogance and drunkenness.*
Witness the Streets of SODOM, and that night	*This was seen in the streets of Sodom, and that night*
In GIBEAH, when hospitable Dores	*In Gibeah, when the house which had given hospitality*
Yielded thir Matrons to prevent worse rape.	*Surrendered their women to save the men from rape.*
These were the prime in order and in might;	*These were the main devils, greatest in power;*
The rest were long to tell, though far renown'd,	*There were too many others to name, although they were worshipped far and wide:*
Th' IONIAN Gods, of JAVANS Issue held	*The Greek Gods, believed to be descended from Javan*
Gods, yet confest later then Heav'n and	*And worshipped as Gods in a later*

26

Earth | *time than Heaven and Earth,*
Thir boasted Parents; TITAN Heav'ns first born | *Their alleged parents: Titan, the first child of Heaven*
With his enormous brood, and birthright seis'd | *With his massive offspring, his inheritance stolen*
By younger SATURN, he from mightier JOVE | *By the younger Saturn, who from his own son with Rhea,*
His own and RHEA'S Son like measure found; | *Mighty Jupiter, got the same treatment;*
So JOVE usurping reign'd: these first in CREET | *So Jupiter ruled as the usurper: these Gods were first known*
And IDA known, thence on the Snowy top | *To the Creteans and to Ida, then on the snowy summit*
Of cold OLYMPUS rul'd the middle Air | *Of cold Olympus they ruled the skies,*
Thir highest Heav'n; or on the DELPHIAN Cliff, | *The highest Heaven they knew; and they also ruled in Delphi*
Or in DODONA, and through all the bounds | *And in Dodona and all through the lands*
Of DORIC Land; or who with SATURN old | *Of Greece, and with ancient Saturn*
Fled over ADRIA to th' HESPERIAN Fields, | *Spread over the Adriatic to Italy*
And ore the CELTIC roam'd the utmost Isles. | *And were worshipped by the Celts in the British islands.*
All these and more came flocking; but with looks | *All of these and others gathered round, but they looked*
Down cast and damp, yet such wherein appear'd | *Depressed and damp, though there were some who showed*
Obscure som glimps of joy, to have found thir chief | *Some little signs of happiness, to find that their leader*
Not in despair, to have found themselves not lost | *Was not downcast and to find that all*
In loss it self; which on his count'nance cast | *Was not completely lost, though on his face*
Like doubtful hue: but he his wonted pride | *The same emotion showed: but he soon summoned up*
Soon recollecting, with high words, that bore | *His usual arrogance and with elevated speech which had*
Semblance of worth not substance, gently rais'd | *Apparent value but held no substance, gently encouraged*
Their fainted courage, and dispel'd their fears. | *Their weakened strength, and banished their fears.*
Then strait commands that at the warlike sound | *Then he commands at once that to the warlike sound*
Of Trumpets loud and Clarions be upreard | *Of loud trumpets and bugles they should raise*

His mighty Standard; that proud honour claim'd
AZAZEL as his right, a Cherube tall:
Who forthwith from the glittering Staff unfurld
Th' Imperial Ensign, which full high advanc't
Shon like a Meteor streaming to the Wind

With Gemms and Golden lustre rich imblaz'd,
Seraphic arms and Trophies: all the while

Sonorous metal blowing Martial sounds:

At which the universal Host upsent
A shout that tore Hells Concave, and beyond
Frighted the Reign of CHAOS and old Night.
All in a moment through the gloom were seen
Ten thousand Banners rise into the Air

With Orient Colours waving: with them rose

A Forrest huge of Spears: and thronging Helms
Appear'd, and serried Shields in thick array
Of depth immeasurable: Anon they move

In perfect PHALANX to the Dorian mood
Of Flutes and soft Recorders; such as rais'd

To highth of noblest temper Hero's old

Arming to Battel, and in stead of rage

Deliberate valour breath'd, firm and unmov'd
With dread of death to flight or foul retreat,

Nor wanting power to mitigate and swage
With solemn touches, troubl'd thoughts, and chase

His mighty flag; the honor of doing that was claimed
By Azrael, a tall Cherub, as his right:
Straight away he unfurled from the shining pole
The Emperor's banner, which waving on high
Shone like a meteor, flapping in the wind,

Covered in jewels and embroidered in rich gold
With the Seraph's insignia and signs: all the time

The trumpets were blowing warlike calls:

At these signs the great crowd let out
A shout which tore through the lands of hell, and beyond that
Brought fear to the kingdoms of Chaos and of ancient Night.
Suddenly in the gloom there appeared
Ten thousand banners waving in the air,

Covered in the colors of the Orient: and with them rose up

A great forest of spears: and a great throng of helmets appeared
Alongside ranks of shields so thick
That they could not be counted: soon they move

In perfect drill to the Greek music
Of flutes and soft recorders, the like of which raised

The heroes of old to the peaks of noble purpose

As they armed for battle, and in place of anger

Called them to be brave, firm and steadfast
Fearing surrender or retreat as they feared death,

It had the power to lessen and soften
Troubled thoughts with its touch, and chase away

28

Anguish and doubt and fear and sorrow and pain
From mortal or immortal minds. Thus they

Breathing united force with fixed thought

Mov'd on in silence to soft Pipes that charm'd
Thir painful steps o're the burnt soyle; and now
Advanc't in view they stand, a horrid Front

Of dreadful length and dazling Arms, in guise
Of Warriers old with order'd Spear and Shield,
Awaiting what command thir mighty Chief

Had to impose: He through the armed Files

Darts his experienc't eye, and soon traverse

The whole Battalion views, thir order due,

Thir visages and stature as of Gods,
Thir number last he summs. And now his heart
Distends with pride, and hardning in his strength
Glories: For never since created man,
Met such imbodied force, as nam'd with these
Could merit more then that small infantry

Warr'd on by Cranes: though all the Giant brood
Of PHLEGRA with th' Heroic Race were joyn'd
That fought at THEB'S and ILIUM, on each side
Mixt with auxiliar Gods; and what resounds

In Fable or ROMANCE of UTHERS Son

Begirt with BRITISH and ARMORIC Knights;

Anguish, doubt, fear, sorrow and pain
From the minds of Gods and Men. So they

Breathing as on, being of the same purpose,

Marched on in silence to the soft music of the charming pipes,
Which eased the pain of their steps over the burning ground, and now
They can be seen advanced, a horrible line

Of terrible size and dazzling weaponry, looking like
Ancient warriors arranged with their spears and shields,
Waiting to hear what orders their mighty leader

Had to give them: He ran his experienced eye

Over the armed ranks, and soon has examined

The whole army, lined up in their order,

With the faces and stature of Gods,
And he counts their number. And now his heart
Swells with pride, and he revels in his power;
For since man was created never
Had he raised such a force as this:

Compared to this they were like the pygmies,

Trampled by cranes as they rushed to the sea; even if all the giants
Of Phelgra joined up with the race of Heroes
Who fought at Thebes and Troy, each side having
Lesser Gods fighting with them; and if there were added

What is told in song and story of Arthur, son of Uther,

Surrounded by British and Norman knights;

Original	Paraphrase
And all who since, Baptiz'd or Infidel	*And all of those, Christian or pagan, who had*
Jousted in ASPRAMONT or MONTALBAN,	*Jousted in Aspramont and Montalban,*
DAMASCO, or MAROCCO, or TREBISOND,	*Damascus, or Morocco, or Trebizond,*
Or whom BISERTA sent from AFRIC shore	*And the army sent out from Tunisia, leaving the African shore,*
When CHARLEMAIN with all his Peerage fell	*Which defeated Charlemagne and all his nobles*
By FONTARABBIA. Thus far these beyond	*At Fontarrabia. This was how these were seen,*
Compare of mortal prowess, yet observ'd	*So far beyond any comparison with the armies of men,*
Thir dread Commander: he above the rest	*By their terrible leader: above the rest*
In shape and gesture proudly eminent	*With a great stature and noble gestures*
Stood like a Towr; his form had yet not lost	*He rose like a tower: he had not altogether lost*
All her Original brightness, nor appear'd	*His God-given brightness, and he still looked*
Less then Arch Angel ruind, and th' excess	*Like an Archangel, though ruined, and with some*
Of Glory obscur'd: As when the Sun new ris'n	*Of his Glory hidden, like the sun when it rises*
Looks through the Horizontal misty Air	*Seen through the low misty air*
Shorn of his Beams, or from behind the Moon	*Visible but with no sunbeams, or when it is hidden behind the moon*
In dim Eclips disastrous twilight sheds	*In an eclipse and throws a grim twilight*
On half the Nations, and with fear of change	*Over half the world, and makes Kings fear that*
Perplexes Monarchs. Dark'n'd so, yet shon	*It predicts their overthrow. Darkened in this way, but still shining*
Above them all th' Arch Angel: but his face	*More than the rest was the Archangel: but his face*
Deep scars of Thunder had intrencht, and care	*Was scarred by thunder with deep frown lines, and care*
Sat on his faded cheek, but under Browes	*Showed on his darkened cheek, but these where under brows*
Of dauntless courage, and considerate Pride	*Which showed bravery unbowed, and scheming pride*
Waiting revenge: cruel his eye, but cast	*Plotting its revenge: his gaze was cruel, but showed*
Signs of remorse and passion to behold	*Signs of guilt and feeling when he*

The fellows of his crime, the followers rather

(Far other once beheld in bliss) condemn'd

For ever now to have their lot in pain,
Millions of Spirits for his fault amerc't

Of Heav'n, and from Eternal Splendors flung
For his revolt, yet faithfull how they stood,

Thir Glory witherd. As when Heavens Fire

Hath scath'd the Forrest Oaks, or Mountain Pines,
With singed top their stately growth though bare
Stands on the blasted Heath. He now prepar'd
To speak; whereat their doubl'd Ranks they bend
From Wing to Wing, and half enclose him round
With all his Peers: attention held them mute.

Thrice he assayd, and thrice in spite of scorn,

Tears such as Angels weep, burst forth: at last
Words interwove with sighs found out their way.
O Myriads of immortal Spirits, O Powers

Matchless, but with th' Almighty, and that strife
Was not inglorious, though th' event was dire,
As this place testifies, and this dire change

Hateful to utter: but what power of mind

Foreseeing or presaging, from the Depth
Of knowledge past or present, could have fear'd,

---

looked on
His partners in crime, or rather his followers

(Once seen so different in Paradise), condemned

Now to spend eternity in suffering,
Millions of spirits barred from Heaven for his crime,

Banished from the Eternal Glories
For his rebellion, yet how loyally they stood there,

Their glory destroyed, as when the lightning

Has singed the oaks in the forest, or the mountain pines
With burnt tops still stand tall, though without their greenery,
Upon the blasted heath. He now prepared
To speak, and so they curved their line
From end to end, making a semicircle around him
Of all his comrades: they were silent in anticipation.

Three times he tried to speak, and three times, in spite of his contempt for them,

He wept tears in the way which angels do: at last
He managed to get his words out, mixed with sighs.
"You numberless crowd of immortal spirits, whose power

Has no equal, apart from the Almighty, and in that battle
We were not disgraced, though the results were terrible,
As this place shows us, and the change in our fortunes

Is painful to confess: but how could any mind,

Have had the foresight, using all
The wisdom of the past and the present, could have guessed

How such united force of Gods, how such
As stood like these, could ever know repulse?
For who can yet beleeve, though after loss,
That all these puissant Legions, whose exile
Hath emptied Heav'n, shall faile to re-ascend
Self-rais'd, and repossess their native seat.
For me, be witness all the Host of Heav'n,
If counsels different, or danger shun'd
By me, have lost our hopes. But he who
Monarch in Heav'n, till then as one secure
Sat on his Throne, upheld by old repute,
Consent or custome, and his Regal State
Put forth at full, but still his strength conceal'd,
Which tempted our attempt, and wrought our fall.
Henceforth his might we know, and know our own
So as not either to provoke, or dread
New warr, provok't; our better part remains
To work in close design, by fraud or guile
What force effected not: that he no less
At length from us may find, who overcomes
By force, hath overcome but half his foe.

Space may produce new Worlds; whereof so rife
There went a fame in Heav'n that he ere long
Intended to create, and therein plant
A generation, whom his choice regard

*That such a united force of Gods, such
As I see before me, could ever have been beaten?
Who can believe, even though we have lost,
That all this great army, whose banishment
Has emptied heaven, will fail to go back
And with their power recapture their rightful place?
But all you Host of Heaven can tell me
If a different course should have been taken, or if I avoided some danger
Which has led us to this. But he who reigns
As King in Heaven, up until then safe
On his throne, kept his place through his past reputation,
Through agreement and tradition, and showed his Kingship
In full view, but hid his power,
And this tempted us to rebellion and brought about our downfall.
From now on we know his strength and our own
So that we do not provoke him into a terrible new attack
Or start one ourselves; the best thing we can do
Is to work in secret, and by lies and cunning achieve
What we could not do by force, so he will find
In due course that he who has won
By force has only half beaten his enemy.

There may be new worlds created from space; there was
A rumor in Heaven that he soon intended
To make one, and to place there
A generation who would receive*

Should favour equal to the Sons of Heaven:

Thither, if but to prie, shall be perhaps

Our first eruption, thither or elsewhere:

For this Infernal Pit shall never hold
Caelestial Spirits in Bondage, nor th' Abysse

Long under darkness cover. But these thoughts
Full Counsel must mature: Peace is despaird,
For who can think Submission? Warr then, Warr
Open or understood must be resolv'd.
He spake: and to confirm his words, out-flew
Millions of flaming swords, drawn from the thighs
Of mighty Cherubim; the sudden blaze

Far round illumin'd hell: highly they rag'd

Against the Highest, and fierce with grasped arm's
Clash'd on their sounding shields the din of war,
Hurling defiance toward the vault of Heav'n.
There stood a Hill not far whose griesly top

Belch'd fire and rowling smoak; the rest entire
Shon with a glossie scurff, undoubted sign
That in his womb was hid metallic Ore,
The work of Sulphur. Thither wing'd with speed
A numerous Brigad hasten'd. As when bands
Of Pioners with Spade and Pickaxe arm'd

Forerun the Royal Camp, to trench a Field,

Or cast a Rampart. MAMMON led them on,

affection from him
Equal to that received by the Sons of Heaven:

Even if it's just to spy out the land, maybe

That's where we'll first emerge, which we shall do, either there or elsewhere,

For this terrible pit shall never hold Heavenly spirits imprisoned, nor shall the abyss

Be kept dark for long. But we must allow these plans
Time to mature: there can be no peace,
For which of us would agree to surrender? So we must commit to war,
Either open or secret."
So he spoke, and to greet his words there flew up
Millions of flaming swords, pulled from the waists
Of the great Cherubim; the sudden blaze

Lit up hell all around; they raged furiously

Against God, and with their weapons in a tight grip
They beat them on their shields, making the sound of war,
Screaming their defiance at the sky.
Not far off there was a hill whose grim summit

Belched fire and clouds of smoke; the whole of the rest
Shone with bright specks, a sure sign
That there was metal ore inside,
Made by sulphur. To this hill, quickly,

A large group rushed, as when bands

Of workmen equipped with spades and pickaxes

Run ahead of the King's armies, to dig trenches

Or throw up ramparts. Mammon was

MAMMON, the least erected Spirit that fell
From heav'n, for ev'n in heav'n his looks & thoughts
Were always downward bent, admiring more
The riches of Heav'ns pavement, trod'n Gold,

Then aught divine or holy else enjoy'd

In vision beatific: by him first
Men also, and by his suggestion taught,
Ransack'd the Center, and with impious hands
Rifl'd the bowels of thir mother Earth

For Treasures better hid. Soon had his crew

Op'nd into the Hill a spacious wound
And dig'd out ribs of Gold. Let none admire

That riches grow in Hell; that soyle may best

Deserve the pretious bane. And here let those
Who boast in mortal things, and wondring tell
Of BABEL, and the works of MEMPHIAN Kings,
Learn how thir greatest Monuments of Fame,
And Strength and Art are easily outdone

By Spirits reprobate, and in an hour
What in an age they with incessant toyle

And hands innumerable scarce perform

Nigh on the Plain in many cells prepar'd,
That underneath had veins of liquid fire

Sluc'd from the Lake, a second multitude

With wondrous Art founded the massie Ore,

---

their leader,
Mammon, the least spiritual of all those that fell
From heaven, for even in heaven his looks and thoughts
Were always directed downwards, thinking more
About the richness of Heaven's gold pavement

Than anything else godly or holy which could be found
In heavenly visions.He was the first,
And men followed his example,
To ransack the center, and with blasphemous hands
Go through the innards of their Mother Earth

Looking for treasure that was better left hidden.Soon his gang
Had torn a great gash in the hillside
And were digging out seams of gold. Nobody should be amazed
That there are riches in hell; that earth is the right place
For such cursed things.And let those
Who revere mortal things, and in admiring voices speak
Of the tower of Babel and the pyramids,
See how the greatest works of power
And strength and skill can be easily beaten
By evil spirits, who in an hour
Managed what they could not do in an age of unceasing work
Even if they had an uncountable number of workers.
Many pits were dug on the plain
That had streams of liquid fire running underneath,
Diverted from the lake, and a second group
With amazing skill worked on the

	blocks of ore,
Severing each kinde, and scum'd the Bullion dross:	Separating each kind, skimming off the gold:
A third as soon had form'd within the ground	Just as quickly a third gang dug into the ground
A various mould, and from the boyling cells	A mould, and from the boiling pits
By strange conveyance fill'd each hollow nook,	Through mysterious channels filled each hollow place,
As in an Organ from one blast of wind	Just as in an organ, where one blast of air
To many a row of Pipes the sound-board breaths.	Can be carried to many pipes at once.
Anon out of the earth a Fabrick huge	Soon from the earth came a great construction,
Rose like an Exhalation, with the sound	Rising up as if the earth breathed it out, accompanied by the sound
Of Dulcet Symphonies and voices sweet,	Of melodious music and sweet voices.
Built like a Temple, where PILASTERS round	It was built like a temple, with columns set round it
Were set, and Doric pillars overlaid	And with Doric pillars supporting
With Golden Architrave; nor did there want	Golden beams, and it did not lack
Cornice or Freeze, with bossy Sculptures grav'n,	Moldings or friezes, carved with sculptures in relief
The Roof was fretted Gold. Not BABILON,	And the roof was inlaid with gold. Babylon
Nor great ALCAIRO such magnificence	Nor Cairo could show such magnificence,
Equal'd in all thir glories, to inshrine	For all their glories, when they built shrines
BELUS or SERAPIS thir Gods, or seat	To their Gods Baal and Serapis, or palaces
Thir Kings, when AEGYPT with ASSYRIA strove	For their Kings, when Egypt rivaled Assyria
In wealth and luxurie. Th' ascending pile	For wealth and luxury. The growing building
Stood fixt her stately highth, and strait the dores	Reached the great height intended, and at once the doors
Op'ning thir brazen foulds discover wide	Threw back their bronze leaves to show
Within, her ample spaces, o're the smooth	Within, her great courtyard with smooth
And level pavement: from the arched roof	And level pavements: from the arched roof
Pendant by suttle Magic many a row	Clever tricks were used to hang many rows
Of Starry Lamps and blazing Cressets fed	Of lights like stars and blazing basket

35

	lamps
With Naphtha and ASPHALTUS yeilded light	*Which, fed with oil and sulphur, gave a light*
As from a sky. The hasty multitude	*As bright as day.The rushing crowd*
Admiring enter'd, and the work some praise	*Entered, admiring, and some praised the craftsmanship*
And some the Architect: his hand was known	*And some the designer:his skill was shown*
In Heav'n by many a Towred structure high,	*In Heaven where he had built many tall towers*
Where Scepter'd Angels held thir residence,	*Where high angels had their homes,*
And sat as Princes, whom the supreme King	*Sitting as Princes, whom the highest King*
Exalted to such power, and gave to rule,	*Had promoted to such positions, and gave each one*
Each in his Herarchie, the Orders bright.	*Command of his own order.*
Nor was his name unheard or unador'd	*He was also known and admired*
In ancient Greece; and in AUSONIAN land	*In ancient Greece, and in Italy*
Men call'd him MULCIBER; and how he fell	*Men called him Vulcan, and they told the story*
From Heav'n, they fabl'd, thrown by angry JOVE	*Of his fall from Heaven, thrown by Jupiter*
Sheer o're the Chrystal Battlements: from Morn	*Right over the crystal battlements: from morning*
To Noon he fell, from Noon to dewy Eve,	*To noon he fell, then from noon to the cool evening,*
A Summers day; and with the setting Sun	*A whole summer's day, and as the sun set*
Dropt from the Zenith like a falling Star,	*He fell from the sky like a falling star,*
On LEMNOS th' AEGAEAN Ile: thus hey relate,	*Onto Lemnos in the Aegean Sea. This is what they say,*
Erring; for he with this rebellious rout	*Wrongly; for with this failed rebellion*
Fell long before; nor aught avail'd him now	*He had fallen long before that: nor did it help him*
To have built in Heav'n high Towrs; nor did he scape	*To have built great towers in Heaven, nor did he escape*
By all his Engins, but was headlong sent	*With all his machinery, but was thrown headlong*
With his industrious crew to build in hell.	*With his gang to go and build in hell.*
Mean while the winged Haralds by command	*Meanwhile the winged messengers, ordered*
Of Sovran power, with awful Ceremony	*By the power of their ruler, with terrible procedure*
And Trumpets sound throughout the Host proclaim	*And trumpets ringing throughout the crowd announced*

36

A solemn Councel forthwith to be held	That a solemn meeting was to be held at once
At PANDAEMONIUM, the high Capital	At Pandemonium, the great capital
Of Satan and his Peers: thir summons call'd	Of Satan and his Lords: they summoned, from every
From every Band and squared Regiment	Group and organized regiment,
By place or choice the worthiest; they anon	Those whose rank or election made most worthy; they soon
With hundreds and with thousands trooping came	Came, attended by their troops in their hundreds and thousands;
Attended: all access was throng'd, the Gates	All the entrance was crowded, and the gates and the
And Porches wide, but chief the spacious Hall	Wide porches, but especially the great hall
(Though like a cover'd field, where Champions bold	(Although it was like a covered field, where great champions
Wont ride in arm'd, and at the Soldans chair	Used to ride in their armor, and in front of the Sultan's chair
Defi'd the best of Panim chivalry	Challenged the best of the Paynim nobles
To mortal combat or carreer with Lance)	To mortal combat or to joust with a lance)
Thick swarm'd, both on the ground and in the air,	Was packed, on the ground and in the air,
Brusht with the hiss of russling wings. As Bees	With the rustling hiss of wings. Just as bees
In spring time, when the Sun with Taurus rides,	In the springtime, when the Sun is in Taurus,
Poure forth thir populous youth about the Hive	Send out their many youths around the hive
In clusters; they among fresh dews and flowers	In groups;they go out amongst the fresh dew and flowers,
Flie to and fro, or on the smoothed Plank,	Flying to and fro, or on the smooth plank,
The suburb of thir Straw-built Cittadel,	The edge of their castle of straw,
New rub'd with Baume, expatiate and confer	Freshly cleaned with wool, announce and debate
Thir State affairs. So thick the aerie crowd	The business of the hive.This was how thick the crowd
Swarm'd and were straitn'd; till the Signal giv'n,	Were packed; until a signal was given
Behold a wonder! they but now who seemd	And a miracle was seen!They who had just a moment before
In bigness to surpass Earths Giant Sons	Seemed to be bigger than the Giants
Now less then smallest Dwarfs, in narrow room	Were now smaller than the smallest dwarves, uncounted

Throng numberless, like that Pigmean Race	*Numbers thronging in a narrow room, like the pigmies*
Beyond the INDIAN Mount, or Faerie Elves,	*Who live behind the Indian mountains, or the fairy elves,*
Whose midnight Revels, by a Forrest side	*Whose midnight parties by the edge of the forest*
Or Fountain fome belated Peasant sees,	*Or by a fountain some late travelling peasant sees,*
Or dreams he sees, while over head the Moon	*Or thinks he sees, while above the Moon*
Sits Arbitress, and neerer to the Earth	*Is master of ceremonies, and dips her pale course*
Wheels her pale course, they on thir mirth & dance	*Closer to the earth, and they focus on their dancing and merrymaking*
Intent, with jocond Music charm his ear;	*And with jolly music charm his hearing*
At once with joy and fear his heart rebounds.	*So that his heart thumps with joy and fear all at once.*
Thus incorporeal Spirits to smallest forms	*So these bodiless Spirits reduced their great shapes*
Reduc'd thir shapes immense, and were at large,	*Down to the tiniest forms, so there was space for all*
Though without number still amidst the Hall	*Even though there were still that infinite number in the hall*
Of that infernal Court. But far within	*Of that court of Hell.But deep inside*
And in thir own dimensions like themselves	*And keeping their original shapes*
The great Seraphic Lords and Cherubim	*The great Lords of the Seraphs and the Cherubim*
In close recess and secret conclave sat	*Sat withdrawn in a secret meeting,*
A thousand Demy-Gods on golden seats,	*A thousand demigods on seats of gold,*
Frequent and full. After short silence then	*Filling the space.After a short silence,*
And summons read, the great consult began.	*And the reading of the summons, the great meeting began.*

BOOK II

THE ARGUMENT

The Consultation begun, Satan debates whether another Battel be to be hazarded for the of Heaven: some advise it, others dissuade: A third proposal is prefer'd, mention'd before by Satan, to search the truth of that Prophesie or Tradition in Heaven concerning another and another kind of creature equal or not much inferiour to themselves, about this time to be created: Thir doubt who shall be sent on this difficult search: Satan thir chief undertakes alone the voyage, is honourd and applauded. The Councel thus ended, the rest betake them several wayes and to several imployments, as thir inclinations lead them, to entertain the time till Satan return. He passes on his journey to Hell Gates, finds them shut, and who sat there to guard them, by whom at length they are op'nd, and discover to him the great Gulf between Hell and Heaven; with what difficulty he passes through, directed by Chaos, the Power of that place, to the sight of this new World which he sought.

The debate begins, and Satan asks if they should risk another battle to attempt to Heaven. Some of the demons are for it, some against. A third proposal, mentioned previously by Satan, is chosen; that they should search for the other world and new creature which are supposed to be created about this time. Nobody wishes to take on the mission of looking for this new world, so Satan volunteers himself and is applauded for it. With the Council over the rest start various works and entertainments, according to preference, to pass the time until Satan returns. He travels to the gates of Hell, and finds them locked. He discovers who guards the gates and at length they open them for him. He finds himself on the edge of the great void between Heaven and Hell, which he crosses with difficulty, and Chaos directs him to the location of the new world.

High on a Throne of Royal State, which far

Outshon the wealth of ORMUS and of IND,
Or where the gorgeous East with richest hand
Showrs on her Kings BARBARIC Pearl & Gold,
Satan exalted sat, by merit rais'd
To that bad eminence; and from despair

Thus high uplifted beyond hope, aspires

Beyond thus high, insatiate to pursue

Vain Warr with Heav'n, and by success untaught

*High on a royal throne, which was far
Richer than things found in Ormus or in India,
Or in the palaces of the East where fortune
Rains pearls and gold on the barbaric Kings,
Satan sat on high, raised by right
To that evil prominence; and from despair
Having been lifted far higher than he hoped, dreamed
Of going still higher, with endless greed to continue
His vain war with Heaven, and his defeat had no effect*

His proud imaginations thus displaid.	*On the proud fantasies he built for himself.*
Powers and Dominions, Deities of Heav'n,	*"My powerful rulers, Gods of Heaven,*
For since no deep within her gulf can hold	*As no pit can hold*
Immortal vigor, though opprest and fall'n,	*Immortal strength, even though it may be crushed and thrown down,*
I give not Heav'n for lost. From this descent	*I have not given up Heaven as lost.From our fall*
Celestial vertues rising, will appear	*Heavenly strengths will grow, which will be*
More glorious and more dread then from no fall,	*Even greater and more powerful than if we hadn't fallen,*
And trust themselves to fear no second fate:	*And we won't have to fear the same thing happening again:*
Mee though just right, and the fixt Laws of Heav'n	*I was, through just rights and the laws of Heaven,*
Did first create your Leader, next, free choice,	*Made your leader and you confirmed the choice.*
With what besides, in Counsel or in Fight,	*Leaving aside what good things have been achieved*
Hath bin achievd of merit, yet this loss	*In battle or debate, at least this fall*
Thus farr at least recover'd, hath much more	*Has given us one thing; it has given me*
Establisht in a safe unenvied Throne	*A safe throne that none will try to seize,*
Yeilded with full consent. The happier state	*Given to me with all permission.In heaven, where*
In Heav'n, which follows dignity, might draw	*Things are happier, rank follows birth, and that might*
Envy from each inferior; but who here	*Make the inferior ranks jealous, but who is there*
Will envy whom the highest place exposes	*Who would be jealous of one whose leadership*
Formost to stand against the Thunderers aime	*Places him at the front to bear the brunt of God's thunder,*
Your bulwark, and condemns to greatest share	*As your shelter, and has to take the largest share*
Of endless pain? where there is then no good	*Of eternal pain?When there's nothing good*
For which to strive, no strife can grow up there	*Worth trying to fight for, then there will be no fighting*
From Faction; for none sure will claim in hell	*Through dissent, for surely nobody will claim*
Precedence, none, whose portion is so small	*Higher position in hell, for nobody who only suffers a small share*

Of present pain, that with ambitious mind	*Of the pain we have will scheme*
Will covet more. With this advantage then	*To get himself more. This is our*
	advantage which will give us
To union, and firm Faith, and firm accord,	*Unity, faithfulness and common*
	purpose,
More then can be in Heav'n, we now return	*More than can be found in*
	Heaven. We are reclaiming
To claim our just inheritance of old,	*Our fair inheritance,*
Surer to prosper then prosperity	*And we will get more riches than just*
	staying in Heaven
Could have assur'd us; and by what best	*Would have given us: and we must*
way,	*decide whether*
Whether of open Warr or covert guile,	*Open war or secret cunning is our*
	best weapon.
We now debate; who can advise, may speak.	*This is the question, and any who*
	have advice may speak."
He ceas'd, and next him MOLOC, Scepter'd	*He finished, and next to him Moloch,*
King	*high King,*
Stood up, the strongest and the fiercest Spirit	*Rose, the strongest and fiercest Spirit*
That fought in Heav'n; now fiercer by	*That fought in Heaven, his strength*
despair:	*now reinforced by despair:*
His trust was with th' Eternal to be deem'd	*His ambition was to be equal in*
	strength
Equal in strength, and rather then be less	*To God, and rather than accept a*
	smaller share
Car'd not to be at all; with that care lost	*Chose to have nothing; once he had*
	decided that
Went all his fear: of God, or Hell, or worse	*He lost all fear: he cared nothing*
	about God, or Hell,
He reckd not, and these words thereafter	*Or worse, and these are the words he*
spake.	*spoke.*
My sentence is for open Warr: Of Wiles,	*"I vote for open war: cunning*
More unexpert, I boast not: them let those	*Is not my strength, I don't claim it is:*
	let those
Contrive who need, or when they need, not	*Who want to use cunning use it when*
now.	*it's needed, not now.*
For while they sit contriving, shall the rest,	*Should everyone else, while they sit*
	plotting,
Millions that stand in Arms, and longing	*All these millions waiting armed for*
wait	*battle, longing*
The Signal to ascend, sit lingring here	*For the signal to rise up, sit here,*
Heav'ns fugitives, and for thir dwelling	*Refugees from Heaven, and accept as*
place	*their dwelling*
Accept this dark opprobrious Den of shame,	*This dark shameful pit,*
The Prison of his Tyranny who Reigns	*This prison made by the tyrant who*

By our delay? no, let us rather choose

rules
Because we don't challenge him? No,
let us choose

Arm'd with Hell flames and fury all at once

To arm ourselves with the flames and
fury of Hell

O're Heav'ns high Towrs to force resistless
way,

And straight away force our way up
to the castles of heaven,

Turning our Tortures into horrid Arms

Turning the instruments used to
torture us into terrible weapons

Against the Torturer; when to meet the noise

To use on the torturer; he shall find
the noise

Of his Almighty Engin he shall hear

Of his great weapons are matched

Infernal Thunder, and for Lightning see

By hellish thunder, and against his
lightning he'll see

Black fire and horror shot with equal rage

Horrible black fire thrown with just
as much power

Among his Angels; and his Throne it self

Against his angels, and his throne
itself

Mixt with TARTAREAN Sulphur, and
strange fire,

Will be burned with hellfire,

His own invented Torments. But perhaps

The torture he invented himself. But
perhaps

The way seems difficult and steep to scale

This seems a difficult task to take on

With upright wing against a higher foe.

With our heads held high against a
higher enemy.

Let such bethink them, if the sleepy drench

You can think that, if the drowsy
power

Of that forgetful Lake benumme not still,

Of the lake of forgetfulness is not still
numbing you,

That in our proper motion we ascend

We should go up in our natural way

Up to our native seat: descent and fall

To our rightful place: descent and
fall

To us is adverse. Who but felt of late

Are not fitting for us. Who remembers
recently

When the fierce Foe hung on our brok'n
Rear

As the fierce enemy chased our
fleeing rearguard,

Insulting, and pursu'd us through the Deep,

Insulting us and chasing us through
the pit,

With what compulsion and laborious flight

Who remembers how hard it was

We sunk thus low? Th' ascent is easie then;

To come down so low? That means to
climb up will be easy,

Th' event is fear'd; should we again provoke

But you fear doing it, in case we once
again provoke

Our stronger, some worse way his wrath
may find

God and he finds, in his anger, a
worse way than this

To our destruction: if there be in Hell	*To punish us, if anyone in Hell*
Fear to be worse destroy'd: what can be worse	*Thinks that there can be worse punishment: what's worse*
Then to dwell here, driv'n out from bliss, condemn'd	*Than to live here, driven out of Heaven, condemned*
In this abhorred deep to utter woe;	*To utter sorrow in this revolting pit,*
Where pain of unextinguishable fire	*Where the pain of never ending fire*
Must exercise us without hope of end	*Will work on us eternally,*
The Vassals of his anger, when the Scourge	*Serving his anger, being under the whip forever*
Inexorably, and the torturing houre	*And suffering his tortures*
Calls us to Penance? More destroy'd then thus	*As our punishment? If we were given any greater punishment*
We should be quite abolisht and expire.	*That would be the end of us.*
What fear we then? what doubt we to incense	*So what are we afraid of? Why are we worried about provoking*
His utmost ire? which to the highth enrag'd,	*His strongest anger? When it boils up*
Will either quite consume us, and reduce	*It will either destroy us, and reduce*
To nothing this essential, happier farr	*Us to nothing, which would be far better*
Then miserable to have eternal being:	*Than having to live in misery forever:*
Or if our substance be indeed Divine,	*Or if we are in fact of Godly material*
And cannot cease to be, we are at worst	*And so cannot stop existing, then we have nothing*
On this side nothing; and by proof we feel	*To lose, and we know that we feel we have*
Our power sufficient to disturb his Heav'n,	*The power to disturb Heaven*
And with perpetual inrodes to Allarme,	*And by continual attacks we can shake,*
Though inaccessible, his fatal Throne:	*Even if we can't reach, the throne of God,*
Which if not Victory is yet Revenge.	*Which even if it's not a victory would be some revenge."*
He ended frowning, and his look denounc'd	*He finished, scowling, and his look promised*
Desperate revenge, and Battel dangerous	*Terrible revenge and furious battle*
To less then Gods. On th' other side up rose	*To all. From the other side rose*
BELIAL, in act more graceful and humane;	*Belial, who seemed more graceful and charming,*
A fairer person lost not Heav'n; he seemd	*The most handsome of all those expelled from Heaven, he seemed*
For dignity compos'd and high exploit:	*Made for dignified and noble pursuits,*
But all was false and hollow; though his Tongue	*But it was all an illusion; though his words were*
Dropt Manna, and could make the worse	*Honied, and he could make the bad*

appear
The better reason, to perplex and dash
Maturest Counsels: for his thoughts were low;
To vice industrious, but to Nobler deeds

Timorous and slothful: yet he pleas'd the eare,
And with perswasive accent thus began.

I should be much for open Warr, O Peers,

As not behind in hate; if what was urg'd

Main reason to perswade immediate Warr,

Did not disswade me most, and seem to cast

Ominous conjecture on the whole success:
When he who most excels in fact of Arms,

In what he counsels and in what excels
Mistrustful, grounds his courage on despair
And utter dissolution, as the scope
Of all his aim, after some dire revenge.

First, what Revenge? the Towrs of Heav'n are fill'd

With Armed watch, that render all access

Impregnable; oft on the bordering Deep

Encamp thir Legions, or with obscure wing

Scout farr and wide into the Realm of night,

Scorning surprize. Or could we break our way
By force, and at our heels all Hell should rise

With blackest Insurrection, to confound

Heav'ns purest Light, yet our great Enemie

All incorruptible would on his Throne

appear
Good and confuse and destroy
The best advice: his thoughts were on low things,
And worked hard for vice, but for anything noble

He was weak and slow; but he was pleasing to hear,
And with a persuasive tone he now began.

"I would agree to open war, my lords,

As I hate God just as much, if it wasn't that what's put forward

As the main reason for immediate war

Is what I think is the best reason against it, and makes

The possibility of success remote:
He who is the bravest and best soldier

Seems to be doubtful in his advice,
Basing his courage on his despair,
And seeing complete destruction as
All he can hope for, after he's taken revenge.

Firstly, what revenge will we achieve? The towers of Heaven are packed

With armed watchers, who make any entry

Impossible: they often camp their armies

On the edge of the pit, or on darkened wings

Search far and wide through the lands of Night,

Ruling out a surprise attack. Or we could break in

By force, and take all Hell with us

With the most terrible rebellion, to fight against

Heaven's purest light, but our great enemy would

Sit on his throne, still pure

Sit unpolluted, and th' Ethereal mould	*And undamaged, and the Eternal shape*
Incapable of stain would soon expel	*Which cannot be corrupted would soon be cleansed*
Her mischief, and purge off the baser fire	*Of our mischief and would resist our lower powers*
Victorious. Thus repuls'd, our final hope	*In victory. Beaten in this way*
Is flat despair: we must exasperate	*All we would have left would be despair: we would have to so infuriate*
Th' Almighty Victor to spend all his rage,	*Our great conqueror to vent the full force of his anger,*
And that must end us, that must be our cure,	*And so bring about our death, that must be our cure,*
To be no more; sad cure; for who would loose,	*To not exist. A sad cure, for who would lose,*
Though full of pain, this intellectual being,	*Even though it might be full of pain, his intellect,*
Those thoughts that wander through Eternity,	*His thoughts that wander through eternity,*
To perish rather, swallowd up and lost	*And die, swallowed up and vanished*
In the wide womb of uncreated night,	*In the infertile lands of night*
Devoid of sense and motion? and who knows,	*Having no sense, no motion? And who knows,*
Let this be good, whether our angry Foe	*Even if you think it would be good, do you think our angry enemy*
Can give it, or will ever? how he can	*Can or will give us this release? Whether he can*
Is doubtful; that he never will is sure.	*Is doubtful; that he won't is definite.*
Will he, so wise, let loose at once his ire,	*Will he, with all his wisdom, unleash his anger,*
Belike through impotence, or unaware,	*And perhaps through weakness or ignorance*
To give his Enemies thir wish, and end	*Give his enemies what they want, and finish them*
Them in his anger, whom his anger saves	*Through his anger, when it was his anger that was keeping them*
To punish endless? wherefore cease we then?	*For eternal punishment? Where would it end?*
Say they who counsel Warr, we are decreed,	*Those who vote for war tell us that we are damned*
Reserv'd and destin'd to Eternal woe;	*To carry on suffering for eternity*
Whatever doing, what can we suffer more,	*And that whatever we do we can't suffer*
What can we suffer worse? is this then worst,	*Anything greater than this. Is this the worst of it then,*

Thus sitting, thus consulting, thus in Arms?
What when we fled amain, pursu'd and strook
With Heav'ns afflicting Thunder, and besought
The Deep to shelter us? this Hell then seem'd
A refuge from those wounds: or when we lay
Chain'd on the burning Lake? that sure was worse.

What if the breath that kindl'd those grim fires
Awak'd should blow them into sevenfold rage
And plunge us in the Flames? or from above
Should intermitted vengeance Arme again
His red right hand to plague us? what if all
Her stores were op'n'd, and this Firmament
Of Hell should spout her Cataracts of Fire,
Impendent horrors, threatning hideous fall
One day upon our heads; while we perhaps
Designing or exhorting glorious Warr,
Caught in a fierie Tempest shall be hurl'd
Each on his rock transfixt, the sport and prey
Of racking whirlwinds, or for ever sunk
Under yon boyling Ocean, wrapt in Chains;
There to converse with everlasting groans,
Unrespited, unpitied, unrepreevd,
Ages of hopeless end; this would be worse.
Warr therefore, open or conceal'd, alike
My voice disswades; for what can force or guile

Sitting here, debating, fully armed?
What about when we fled, chased and battered
By God's thunder, and sought out
The pit for shelter? Hell seemed then
A better option; or what about when we lay
Chained on the lake of fire? That was surely worse.

What if the one who lit those grim fires
Was moved to make them seven times greater
And throw us back into the flames? What if above us
His paused vengeance should restart and inspire
His deadly right hand to torment us? What if all
The armory of Heaven were unleashed, and this sky
Of Hell began raining storms of fire,
Terror hanging above us, threatening one day
To come crashing down on us, while we who plan
Or encourage glorious war might be
Caught in a fiery storm and flung away,
Each one stuck on his own rock, the victim
Of torturing winds, or could be sunk forever
Under that boiling ocean, wrapped in chains,
To speak for ever in groans,
Without respite, without pity, without redemption,
For eternity without hope; that would be worse.
And so war, either open or hidden,
Does not get my vote; what can force or cunning do

With him, or who deceive his mind, whose eye
Views all things at one view? he from heav'ns highth
All these our motions vain, sees and derides;
Not more Almighty to resist our might
Then wise to frustrate all our plots and wiles.
Shall we then live thus vile, the race of Heav'n
Thus trampl'd, thus expell'd to suffer here
Chains & these Torments? better these then worse
By my advice; since fate inevitable
Subdues us, and Omnipotent Decree,
The Victors will. To suffer, as to doe,
Our strength is equal, nor the Law unjust
That so ordains: this was at first resolv'd,
If we were wise, against so great a foe
Contending, and so doubtful what might fall.
I laugh, when those who at the Spear are bold
And vent'rous, if that fail them, shrink and fear
What yet they know must follow, to endure
Exile, or ignominy, or bonds, or pain,
The sentence of thir Conquerour: This is now
Our doom; which if we can sustain and bear,
Our Supream Foe in time may much remit
His anger, and perhaps thus farr remov'd
Not mind us not offending, satisfi'd
With what is punish't; whence these raging fires
Will slack'n, if his breath stir not thir flames.

To him, how can you fool him whose eyes
See everything at once? From the heights of heaven
He can see our worthless plans and mock them;
Just as he can resist our forces
He has the same power to block our plots.
Shall we live such a degraded life, the people of Heaven
So downtrodden, thrown out to suffer
These tortures and chains? My advice is,
Better these than worse things, since we are beaten
By unchangeable fate, and the orders of the victor
Are all powerful laws. We are strong enough to live
With this suffering, and the law which says we must
Is not unfair: we should have seen, if we'd had sense,
That this would be what we'd get
For fighting against such a mighty enemy.
I laugh to hear those who are brave with a spear in hand,
When force doesn't work they cringe and are scared
Of that which they know they must come,
Exile, shame, chains or pain,
As sentenced by their conqueror: this is now
Our fate; if we can endure it
Our great enemy may in time lose
His anger, and perhaps as we are so far off
Not mind what we have done and be satisfied
That we have suffered enough; then these raging fires
Would die down if he stops blowing on them.

Our purer essence then will overcome

Thir noxious vapour, or enur'd not feel,

Or chang'd at length, and to the place conformd
In temper and in nature, will receive
Familiar the fierce heat, and void of pain;

This horror will grow milde, this darkness light,
Besides what hope the never-ending flight

Of future days may bring, what chance, what change
Worth waiting, since our present lot appeers

For happy though but ill, for ill not worst,
If we procure not to our selves more woe.

Thus BELIAL with words cloath'd in reasons garb
Counsel'd ignoble ease, and peaceful sloath,

Not peace: and after him thus MAMMON spake.
Either to disinthrone the King of Heav'n

We warr, if warr be best, or to regain
Our own right lost: him to unthrone we then
May hope, when everlasting Fate shall yield
To fickle Chance, and CHAOS judge the strife:
The former vain to hope argues as vain

The latter: for what place can be for us

Within Heav'ns bound, unless Heav'ns Lord supream
We overpower? Suppose he should relent
And publish Grace to all, on promise made

Of new Subjection; with what eyes could we

Stand in his presence humble, and receive

Then our purer substance will overcome

Their poisonous fumes or we will grow used to it.

Maybe in time we will change, and adapt ourselves
To this place in mind and body, so
We'll get used to the fierce heat and not feel its pain;

The terror will lessen and the darkness will grow light,
And besides we don't know what chances

The passage of time may bring, what changes

Worth waiting for may happen, for our present situation seems

Not as bad as it could be,
If we don't bring down more punishment on ourselves".

So Belial, with words dressed up as reason,

Spoke up for dishonored rest and laziness,

Not for peace, and after him Mammon spoke.

"If war is thought best then we will fight
To overthrow the King of Heaven
Or to regain what we have lost: we could hope to dethrone him
When eternal fate gives way
To chance, and chaos decides the result.

If we can't hope to dethrone him we can't hope to regain what's ours:

What place can there be for us in Heaven,

Unless we overthrow its supreme Lord?
Suppose he relents
And gives forgiveness to all, on condition

That we bow before him again; how could we face

Standing humble before him, obeying

49

Strict Laws impos'd, to celebrate his Throne	*His strict laws, celebrating his power*
With warbl'd Hymns, and to his Godhead sing	*By warbling hymns and singing to his magnificence*
Forc't Halleluiah's; while he Lordly sits	*Forced hallejulahs, while he sits in state*
Our envied Sovran, and his Altar breathes	*As our resented ruler, and his altar is scented*
Ambrosial Odours and Ambrosial Flowers,	*With sweet smells and flowers,*
Our servile offerings. This must be our task	*Our humble offerings. This would be our place*
In Heav'n, this our delight; how wearisome	*In heaven, our pleasure; how tiresome*
Eternity so spent in worship paid	*Eternity would be, worshipping*
To whom we hate. Let us not then pursue	*The one we hate. So let's not try and get*
By force impossible, by leave obtain'd	*Either by force, which is impossible, or by permission,*
Unacceptable, though in Heav'n, our state	*Which would be intolerable, even though we were in heaven,*
Of splendid vassalage, but rather seek	*A state of splendid servitude, but get*
Our own good from our selves, and from our own	*What we want for ourselves, and live our own lives.*
Live to our selves, though in this vast recess,	*Even though we would be stuck in this place*
Free, and to none accountable, preferring	*We would be free, answering to nobody,*
Hard liberty before the easie yoke	*And choose uncomfortable freedom over*
Of servile Pomp. Our greatness will appear	*Comfortable slavery. Then our greatness will appear*
Then most conspicuous, when great things of small,	*At its best, when we can make great things from small ones,*
Useful of hurtful, prosperous of adverse	*Useful things from bad ones, get strength through adversity,*
We can create, and in what place so e're	*And wherever we are*
Thrive under evil, and work ease out of pain	*Flourish through evil times, and take pleasure from pain*
Through labour and endurance. This deep world	*Through our work and fortitude. Are we afraid*
Of darkness do we dread? How oft amidst	*Of this darkness? How often did the ruler of Heaven*
Thick clouds and dark doth Heav'ns all-ruling Sire	*Choose to live under thick dark cloud,*
Choose to reside, his Glory unobscur'd,	*Which did not diminish his Glory,*
And with the Majesty of darkness round	*And hid the glory of his power*
Covers his Throne; from whence deep	*In darkness, from which deep thunder*

50

thunders roar	*roared*
Must'ring thir rage, and Heav'n resembles Hell?	*In rage, so that Heaven seemed to be like Hell?*
As he our Darkness, cannot we his Light	*As he imitates our darkness, can we not*
Imitate when we please? This Desart soile	*Imitate his light if we choose? This parched earth*
Wants not her hidden lustre, Gemms and Gold;	*Doesn't lack for hidden treasures, gems and gold;*
Nor want we skill or art, from whence to raise	*Nor are we lacking the skill and knowledge, to bring*
Magnificence; and what can Heav'n shew more?	*Out their glory; what more has Heaven got?*
Our torments also may in length of time	*Our torture may in time*
Become our Elements, these piercing Fires	*Become our proper environment, these stinging fires*
As soft as now severe, our temper chang'd	*Become as soft as they are now harsh as we become*
Into their temper; which must needs remove	*At one with them, which would surely take away*
The sensible of pain. All things invite	*Their power to cause pain. Everything points to*
To peaceful Counsels, and the settl'd State	*The way of peace, the acceptance of things as they are,*
Of order, how in safety best we may	*To work in safety to*
Compose our present evils, with regard	*Adapt to our current evil state, accepting*
Of what we are and where, dismissing quite	*Who and where we are, and putting out of our heads*
All thoughts of Warr: ye have what I advise.	*All thoughts of war. That is what I advise."*
He scarce had finisht, when such murmur filld	*He had hardly finished when there was such a rumble in the hall,*
Th' Assembly, as when hollow Rocks retain	*As when hollow rocks amplify*
The sound of blustring winds, which all night long	*The sound of the howling winds, which had all night*
Had rous'd the Sea, now with hoarse cadence lull	*Whipped up the waves, and the harsh roar*
Sea-faring men orewatcht, whose Bark by chance	*Calms the sailors who have maybe anchored their*
Or Pinnace anchors in a craggy Bay	*Boat within a rocky bay*
After the Tempest: Such applause was heard	*After a storm: this was the sound of applause*
As MAMMON ended, and his Sentence pleas'd,	*Which greeted Mammon's speech, and his advice*
Advising peace: for such another Field	*For peace pleased them, for they*

	dreaded another battle
They dreaded worse then Hell: so much the fear	*Even more than they hated Hell; that was how strong the fear*
Of Thunder and the Sword of MICHAEL	*Of thunder and of Michael's sword*
Wrought still within them; and no less desire	*Still lived within them, and not less was their longing*
To found this nether Empire, which might rise	*To create a lower Empire, which might rise*
By pollicy, and long process of time,	*Through cleverness and the passing of time*
In emulation opposite to Heav'n.	*To be a direct rival to Heaven.*
Which when BEELZEBUB perceiv'd, then whom,	*This was noted by Beelzebub, the one whom*
SATAN except, none higher sat, with grave	*Only Satan was higher than, and with a serious*
Aspect he rose, and in his rising seem'd	*Demeanor he stood, and in standing he seemed to become*
A Pillar of State; deep on his Front engraven	*A great statesman; on his forehead were written the lines*
Deliberation sat and publick care;	*Of great thought and the burden of office,*
And Princely counsel in his face yet shon,	*And noble wisdom still shone in his face,*
Majestick though in ruin: sage he stood	*Majestic even in his ruined state: he stood there wise*
With ATLANTEAN shoulders fit to bear	*With the shoulders of an Atlas, strong enough to support*
The weight of mightiest Monarchies; his look	*The weight of the greatest kingdoms; his appearance*
Drew audience and attention still as Night	*Focused the attention of the listeners who were as still as Night*
Or Summers Noon-tide air, while thus he spake.	*Or the air at noon on a summer's day, while he spoke.*
Thrones and imperial Powers, off-spring of heav'n,	*"You kings and princes, children of heaven,*
Ethereal Vertues; or these Titles now	*Heavenly beings – or are these titles*
Must we renounce, and changing stile be call'd	*We must now give up, and change our titles*
Princes of Hell? for so the popular vote	*To those of Princes of Hell? It seems the popular vote*
Inclines, here to continue, and build up here	*Is for staying here, building up*
A growing Empire; doubtless; while we dream,	*A growing Empire. This is a dream, pretending*
And know not that the King of Heav'n hath doom'd	*That we don't know the King of Heaven has ruled*

This place our dungeon, not our safe retreat
Beyond his Potent arm, to live exempt
From Heav'ns high jurisdiction, in new League
Banded against his Throne, but to remaine
In strictest bondage, though thus far remov'd,
Under th' inevitable curb, reserv'd
His captive multitude: For he, be sure,
In highth or depth, still first and last will Reign
Sole King, and of his Kingdom loose no part
By our revolt, but over Hell extend
His Empire, and with Iron Scepter rule
Us here, as with his Golden those in Heav'n.
What sit we then projecting Peace and Warr?
Warr hath determin'd us, and foild with loss
Irreparable; tearms of peace yet none
Voutsaf't or sought; for what peace will be giv'n
To us enslav'd, but custody severe,
And stripes, and arbitrary punishment
Inflicted? and what peace can we return,
But to our power hostility and hate,
Untam'd reluctance, and revenge though slow,
Yet ever plotting how the Conquerour least
May reap his conquest, and may least rejoice
In doing what we most in suffering feel?
Nor will occasion want, nor shall we need
With dangerous expedition to invade
Heav'n, whose high walls fear no assault or

That this place is our prison, not a safe haven
Out of reach of his power, thinking we can live apart
From the high rule of Heaven, making a new alliance
Against his throne. We would still be Strictly imprisoned, even though far away,
Under his control, put aside As his captives. For it is certain That whether he is on high or down here, he is still always the King,
And he will not lose any part of his Kingdom
By our rebelling, but stretch his rule out over
Hell, and rule with an iron rod Over us here, just as he rules with a golden rod in Heaven.
Why do we sit here then debating peace or war?
We have chosen war, and been beaten with irrecoverable Losses; but none of us have suggested or looked for
A peace treaty, for what sort of peace will be granted
To we slaves, apart from severe imprisonment,
Whippings and other punishments as he chooses?
What peace could we give back When all we feel is hostility and hatred,
Unrepentant reluctance and the desire for revenge,
Always plotting ways to make sure the victor gets the least Possible from his victory, so that we may at least enjoy Letting our feelings have free rein?
We won't lack for opportunity, and we shan't need
To mount a dangerous invasion of Heaven, whose high walls can resist

Siege,	*any attack or siege*
Or ambush from the Deep. What if we find	*Or ambush from the pit. What if we could find*
Some easier enterprize? There is a place	*Some easier undertaking? There is a place,*
(If ancient and prophetic fame in Heav'n	*(If the ancient prophesies of Heaven are correct)*
Err not) another World, the happy seat	*Another world, the happy environment*
Of som new Race call'd MAN, about this time	*Of some new race called Man, who about this time*
To be created like to us, though less	*Is to be made in our image, though less*
In power and excellence, but favour'd more	*Powerful and noble, but dearer to him*
Of him who rules above; so was his will	*Who rules in Heaven; this was his plan,*
Pronounc'd among the Gods, and by an Oath,	*Announced to the Gods, and with an oath,*
That shook Heav'ns whol circumference, confirm'd.	*That shook the foundations of Heaven, confirmed.*
Thither let us bend all our thoughts, to learn	*Let's bend our thoughts in that direction and discover*
What creatures there inhabit, of what mould,	*What sort of creatures live there, how they're made,*
Or substance, how endu'd, and what thir Power,	*What they're made of, what endowments and powers they have,*
And where thir weakness, how attempted best,	*What their weaknesses are, how they're best got at,*
By force or suttlety: Though Heav'n be shut,	*Whether by force or cunning: though Heaven is closed to us*
And Heav'ns high Arbitrator sit secure	*And its high judge sits safe, secure*
In his own strength, this place may lye expos'd	*In his own strength, this place might be exposed*
The utmost border of his Kingdom, left	*At the very edge of his Kingdom, with the defence*
To their defence who hold it: here perhaps	*Left to those who live there: maybe here*
Som advantagious act may be achiev'd	*We can do something productive,*
By sudden onset, either with Hell fire	*With a sudden strike, either taking Hell fire*
To waste his whole Creation, or possess	*And destroying his whole creation, or taking*
All as our own, and drive as we were driven,	*Everything for ourselves, and make the puny inhabitants*

The punie habitants, or if not drive,

Our slaves, and use them as we have been used, or better still

Seduce them to our Party, that thir God

Win them over to our side, so that God

May prove thir foe, and with repenting hand

Becomes their enemy, and repenting his mistake

Abolish his own works. This would surpass

He would have to destroy what he has made.This would be better

Common revenge, and interrupt his joy

Than simple revenge, and would spoil his joy

In our Confusion, and our Joy upraise

At our defeat, and increase our joy

In his disturbance; when his darling Sons

At his torment.When his darling sons

Hurl'd headlong to partake with us, shall curse

Are thrown down to live with us he will curse

Thir frail Originals, and faded bliss,

The first one he made, and paradise shall vanish

Faded so soon. Advise if this be worth

So quickly.Say if you think this is worth trying

Attempting, or to sit in darkness here

Or should we carry on sitting in the darkness,

Hatching vain Empires.

Creating illusory Empires?

Thus BEELZEBUB

This was how Beelzebub

Pleaded his devilish Counsel, first devis'd

Gave his evil advice, that was first thought of

By SATAN, and in part propos'd: for whence,

By Satan, and partly developed by him, for where else

But from the Author of all ill could Spring

But from the author of all evil could

So deep a malice, to confound the race

Such a deep hate spring, to destroy the race

Of mankind in one root, and Earth with Hell

Of Men by striking at the roots, and to mix

To mingle and involve, done all to spite

Earth and Hell together, all done out of spite

The great Creatour? But their spite still serves

For their great Creator?But their spite still

His glory to augment. The bold design

Added to his glory.The bold plan

Pleas'd highly those infernal States, and joy

Was much praised in those Hellish lands, and happiness

Sparkl'd in all thir eyes; with full assent

Shone in all their eyes; they voted for his plan

They vote: whereat his speech he thus renews.

Unanimously, and so he continued his speech.

Well have ye judg'd, well ended long debate,

"You have made a good choice, a good ending to our long discussion,

Synod of Gods, and like to what ye are,

Congress of Gods, and true to your

Great things resolv'd; which from the lowest deep

Will once more lift us up, in spight of Fate,

Neerer our ancient Seat; perhaps in view

Of those bright confines, whence with neighbouring Arms
And opportune excursion we may chance

Re-enter Heav'n; or else in some milde Zone

Dwell not unvisited of Heav'ns fair Light

Secure, and at the brightning Orient beam

Purge off this gloom; the soft delicious Air,

To heal the scarr of these corrosive Fires

Shall breath her balme. But first whom shall we send
In search of this new world, whom shall we find
Sufficient? who shall tempt with wandring feet
The dark unbottom'd infinite Abyss
And through the palpable obscure find out
His uncouth way, or spread his aerie flight
Upborn with indefatigable wings
Over the vast abrupt, ere he arrive

The happy Ile; what strength, what art can then
Suffice, or what evasion bear him safe

Through the strict Senteries and Stations thick
Of Angels watching round? Here he had need
All circumspection, and we now no less

Choice in our suffrage; for on whom we send,

natures
Have committed yourselves to great things; things which will lift us up once again
From the lowest depths, in spite of the blows of fate,
Nearer to our ancient home; perhaps close enough to see
Those shining lands, where with our adjacent armies,
If we wait for our moment, we may get the chance
To re-enter heaven; otherwise in some mild climate
We may live, not completely cut off from the beauty of Heaven's light,
Safe, and with the bright light of the sunrise
We can cast off this gloom; the delicious soft air
Will blow her healing breezes on us and heal the scars
Of these corrosive flames. But first whom shall we send
To look at this new world, who is
Good enough? Who shall walk through
The dark bottomless pit
And through the solid darkness find
His unknown way, or take to the sky,
Rising up on never failing wings
Over the great gap, before he can reach
The happy Island; what strength, what skills will
Be needed, what cunning will carry him safely
Past the sentries and watch posts packed
With angels that keep watch everywhere? He will need
To be prudent, and no less must we be
As we vote for our choice; because whomever we send

The weight of all and our last hope relies.	*Will be carrying the burden of us all, and our last hope."*
This said, he sat; and expectation held	*Having said this he sat down, with a doubtful look*
His look suspence, awaiting who appeer'd	*On his face, waiting to see who would come forward*
To second, or oppose, or undertake	*To agree with him, to oppose him or to volunteer*
The perilous attempt: but all sat mute,	*For the dangerous mission, but all sat silent*
Pondering the danger with deep thoughts; & each	*Thinking deeply about the dangers, and each one*
In others count'nance red his own dismay	*Could see his own fear reflected in the faces of the others:*
Astonisht: none among the choice and prime	*There was none amongst that gathering of the best*
Of those Heav'n-warring Champions could be found	*Of those Knights who fought against heaven who was*
So hardie as to proffer or accept	*Brave enough to volunteer to take on*
Alone the dreadful voyage; till at last	*That terrible journey alone; until at last*
SATAN, whom now transcendent glory rais'd	*Satan, whose glorious power now raised him*
Above his fellows, with Monarchal pride	*Above his comrades, with the pride of a King,*
Conscious of highest worth, unmov'd thus spake.	*Knowing his great worth, and he spoke out unafraid.*
O Progeny of Heav'n, Empyreal Thrones,	*"You children of Heaven, rulers of the sky,*
With reason hath deep silence and demur	*It's natural that silence and doubt should have*
Seis'd us, though undismaid: long is the way	*Come over us, although we are not downcast: it's a long*
And hard, that out of Hell leads up to Light;	*Hard journey that will take us from Hell up to the Light;*
Our prison strong, this huge convex of Fire,	*Our prison is secure, this great bowl of fire,*
Outrageous to devour, immures us round	*Roaring to consume us, is wrapped round us*
Ninefold, and gates of burning Adamant	*Nine times, and the solid burning gates*
Barr'd over us prohibit all egress.	*Barred above us prevent any exit.*
These past, if any pass, the void profound	*Once past these, if they can be passed, the great emptiness*
Of unessential Night receives him next	*Of formless Night is what he'll come*

	to next,
Wide gaping, and with utter loss of being	*Gaping wide, and threatening to completely take away*
Threatens him, plung'd in that abortive gulf.	*His soul, falling into that valley of non-existence.*
If thence he scape into what ever world,	*If he escapes from there into the next world*
Or unknown Region, what remains him less	*Or unknown land, what awaits him there are still*
Then unknown dangers and as hard escape.	*Unknown dangers and an escape just as difficult.*
But I should ill become this Throne, O Peers,	*But I wouldn't deserve this throne, my Lords,*
And this Imperial Sov'ranty, adorn'd	*And my Imperial title, decorated*
With splendor, arm'd with power, if aught propos'd	*With splendid things and armed with power, if any proposal,*
And judg'd of public moment, in the shape	*Thought to be for the good of all, held*
Of difficulty or danger could deterre	*Difficulties and dangers which could put*
Me from attempting. Wherefore do I assume	*Me off making the attempt. How can I take*
These Royalties, and not refuse to Reign,	*These kingly privileges and refuse to be a King,*
Refusing to accept as great a share	*Refuse to accept as large a share*
Of hazard as of honour, due alike	*Of danger as I have been given of honor? Both are the right*
To him who Reigns, and so much to him due	*Of he who rules, and he has a duty to take on*
Of hazard more, as he above the rest	*More of the danger, as he sits above the rest*
High honourd sits? Go therfore mighty powers,	*With honor. So depart, you great powers,*
Terror of Heav'n, though fall'n; intend at home,	*The terror of Heaven, although fallen; stay at home,*
While here shall be our home, what best may ease	*While this is our home, and do whatever's best to ease*
The present misery, and render Hell	*Our current misery, and make Hell*
More tollerable; if there be cure or charm	*More tolerable; if there's any cure or magic*
To respite or deceive, or slack the pain	*Which can ease or trick away or lesson the pain*
Of this ill Mansion: intermit no watch	*Of this foul place; don't neglect to guard*
Against a wakeful Foe, while I abroad	*Against the watchful enemy, while I*
Through all the coasts of dark destruction seek	*Search through the wide shores of dark destruction*

58

Deliverance for us all: this enterprize	*For our deliverance; none shall join with me*
None shall partake with me.	*In this adventure."*
Thus saying rose	*Having said this*
The Monarch, and prevented all reply,	*The King rose, not allowing any reply,*
Prudent, least from his resolution rais'd	*Making sure that none of the chiefs, roused by his*
Others among the chief might offer now	*Bravery, might now offer to undertake*
(Certain to be refus'd) what erst they feard;	*What they had been afraid of, knowing that they would be refused,*
And so refus'd might in opinion stand	*And having been turned down they could look as noble*
His rivals, winning cheap the high repute	*As him, cheaply winning the great reputation*
Which he through hazard huge must earn. But they	*Which he must risk everything to win. But they*
Dreaded not more th' adventure then his voice	*Were as frightened of his dreadful voice as they had been by the mission,*
Forbidding; and at once with him they rose;	*And they all stood to him at once;*
Thir rising all at once was as the sound	*Their all standing together made the sound*
Of Thunder heard remote. Towards him they bend	*Of distant thunder.They bowed to him*
With awful reverence prone; and as a God	*With dreadful respect, and as if he was a God*
Extoll him equal to the highest in Heav'n:	*Praised him as if he was equal to Heaven's highest:*
Nor fail'd they to express how much they prais'd,	*They made sure that they showed their appreciation*
That for the general safety he despis'd	*For the fact that for the safety of all he was ready*
His own: for neither do the Spirits damn'd	*To risk his own; for even damned Spirits do not*
Loose all thir vertue; least bad men should boast	*Lose all their virtues; even good men might praise*
Thir specious deeds on earth, which glory excites,	*Their superficial endeavors on earth, which look glorious,*
Or close ambition varnisht o're with zeal.	*Their secret plans being covered over with a varnish of courage.*
Thus they thir doubtful consultations dark	*So they ended their dark and dreadful planning*
Ended rejoycing in thir matchless Chief:	*Celebrating their unrivalled Chief:*
As when from mountain tops the dusky	*Just as when the dark clouds rise*

clouds	*from the mountaintops*
Ascending, while the North wind sleeps, o'respread	*While the north wind sleeps and spread*
Heav'ns chearful face, the lowring Element	*Across the sun, the lowering weather*
Scowls ore the dark'nd lantskip Snow, or showre;	*Throws snow or rain over the darkened landscape;*
If chance the radiant Sun with farewell sweet	*If by chance the shining sun, with a sweet farewell,*
Extend his ev'ning beam, the fields revive,	*Throws out his evening light, the fields revive,*
The birds thir notes renew, and bleating herds	*The birds start singing again, and the bleating herds*
Attest thir joy, that hill and valley rings.	*Sing out their happiness, so the hills and valleys echo with it.*
O shame to men! Devil with Devil damn'd	*Shame on men! Even damned devils*
Firm concord holds, men onely disagree	*Can agree: only men, of all rational beings,*
Of Creatures rational, though under hope	*Disagree, even though they hope*
Of heavenly Grace: and God proclaiming peace,	*For heavenly redemption and the peace of God,*
Yet live in hatred, enmitie, and strife	*They live in hatred, opposition and fight*
Among themselves, and levie cruel warres,	*Each other, and start cruel wars,*
Wasting the Earth, each other to destroy:	*Destroying the earth so that they can destroy each other:*
As if (which might induce us to accord)	*As if (what should make us join together)*
Man had not hellish foes anow besides,	*Men didn't have enough devilish enemies*
That day and night for his destruction waite.	*Waiting day and night to destroy him.*
The STYGIAN Councel thus dissolv'd; and forth	*And so the Hellish council broke up, and out,*
In order came the grand infernal Peers,	*In order, came the great Lords of hell,*
Midst came thir mighty Paramount, and seemd	*With their great leader in the centre, and it seemed*
Alone th' Antagonist of Heav'n, nor less	*That the opponent of Heaven stood alone,*
Then Hells dread Emperour with pomp Supream,	*No less than the Emperor of hell in high display,*
And God-like imitated State; him round	*Imitating the rank of God; around him*
A Globe of fierie Seraphim inclos'd	*There was a circle of fiery Seraphim,*
With bright imblazonrie, and horrent Arms.	*With shining banners and terrible weapons.*
Then of thir Session ended they bid cry	*Then they ordered, as their council*

With Trumpets regal sound the great result:

Toward the four winds four speedy Cherubim
Put to thir mouths the sounding Alchymie

By Haralds voice explain'd: the hollow Abyss
Heard farr and wide, and all the host of Hell

With deafning shout, return'd them loud acclaim.
Thence more at ease thir minds and somwhat rais'd
By false presumptuous hope, the ranged powers
Disband, and wandring, each his several way
Pursues, as inclination or sad choice
Leads him perplext, where he may likeliest find
Truce to his restless thoughts, and entertain
The irksome hours, till his great Chief return.
Part on the Plain, or in the Air sublime

Upon the wing, or in swift race contend,

As at th' Olympian Games or PYTHIAN fields;
Part curb thir fierie Steeds, or shun the Goal

With rapid wheels, or fronted Brigads form.

As when to warn proud Cities warr appears

Wag'd in the troubl'd Skie, and Armies rush

To Battel in the Clouds, before each Van

Pric forth the Aerie Knights, and couch thir spears
Till thickest Legions close; with feats of Arms

---

was over,
That the royal trumpets should proclaim the great decision:
Four quick Cherubim face each compass point
And putting the horns which copied those of Heaven to their mouths
They transmitted the message: in the hollow pit
It echoed far and wide, and all the citizens of Hell
Gave back their praise with a deafening shout.
And so more easy in their minds and elevated
By a false hope, the gathered armies

Disband, and wandering each one chooses his own path,
As his instinct or a sad choice
Leads him in his confusion, to the place where he is most likely to find
Ease for his troubled mind, and pass
The dragging hours until the return of great leader.
Some are on the plain, some up in the high air
On their wings, or running swift races
As if they were at the Olympic games or on the Pythian fields;
Some control their fiery horses, swerving round the course markers
With their quick chariots, some form into brigades.
As when as a warning to proud cities war
Seems to be being fought in the sky, and armies
Seem to be battling in the clouds, so at the front of every company

There rode out, armed, the Knights, leveling their spears
Until the largest battalions clashed together; with feats of arms

From either end of Heav'n the welkin burns.	*The skies rang from end to end.*
Others with vast TYPHOEAN rage more fell	*Others, with a more monstrous, dangerous rage*
Rend up both Rocks and Hills, and ride the Air	*Tore up rocks and hills and hurled them into the air*
In whirlwind; Hell scarce holds the wilde uproar.	*In a whirlwind; Hell could hardly contain the din.*
As when ALCIDES from OEALIA Crown'd	*It was as when Hercules came from Oealia*
With conquest, felt th' envenom'd robe, and tore	*In triumph and felt the poisoned robe upon him, and tore*
Through pain up by the roots THESSALIAN Pines,	*Up the pines of Thessaly in the rage of his pain,*
And LICHAS from the top of OETA threw	*And threw Lichas from the top of Oeta, down*
Into th' EUBOIC Sea.	*Into the Euboic Sea.*
Others more milde,	*Others, quieter,*
Retreated in a silent valley, sing	*Go to a silent valley and sing*
With notes Angelical to many a Harp	*With angelic music to the accompaniment of harps*
Thir own Heroic deeds and hapless fall	*Of their heroic deeds and their unlucky fall*
By doom of Battel; and complain that Fate	*Caused by battle; they complain that Fate*
Free Vertue should enthrall to Force or Chance.	*Takes their freedom and subjects it to strength or luck.*
Thir song was partial, but the harmony	*They sang in parts, and the harmony*
(What could it less when Spirits immortal sing?)	*(What could one expect when immortal Spirits sing?)*
Suspended Hell, and took with ravishment	*Stilled Hell, and entranced with its sweetness*
The thronging audience. In discourse more sweet	*The gathered crowds.In discussion even sweeter than the music*
(For Eloquence the Soul, Song charms the Sense,)	*(For music charms the senses but eloquence charms the soul)*
Others apart sat on a Hill retir'd,	*Others sat apart on a far off hill,*
In thoughts more elevate, and reason'd high	*With their great thoughts, and discussed*
Of Providence, Foreknowledge, Will, and Fate,	*Providence, Foreknowledge, Will and Fate,*
Fixt Fate, free will, foreknowledge absolute,	*Fate that can't be changed, free will, absolute foreknowledge,*
And found no end, in wandring mazes lost.	*And they could come to no conclusions, lost as if in a maze.*
Of good and evil much they argu'd then,	*They argued much about good and evil,*

Of happiness and final misery,	*Of happiness and the misery that ends it,*
Passion and Apathie, and glory and shame,	*Passion and apathy and glory and shame.*
Vain wisdom all, and false Philosophie:	*It was all corrupted wisdom and false philosophy;*
Yet with a pleasing sorcerie could charm	*It could still, with its trickery, ease*
Pain for a while or anguish, and excite	*Pain and anguish for a while, and summon up*
Fallacious hope, or arm th' obdured brest	*False hopes, or clothe the hardened heart*
With stubborn patience as with triple steel.	*With stubborn patience like triple hardened steel.*
Another part in Squadrons and gross Bands,	*Another group form squads and great mobs*
On bold adventure to discover wide	*To go on a great search right across*
That dismal world, if any Clime perhaps	*That dismal world, to discover if there was any region*
Might yeild them easier habitation, bend	*Which might be easier for them to inhabit, and they set off*
Four ways thir flying March, along the Banks	*On their quick march in four directions, along the banks*
Of four infernal Rivers that disgorge	*Of the four hellish rivers which spew*
Into the burning Lake thir baleful streams;	*Their evil streams into the burning lake;*
Abhorred STYX the flood of deadly hate,	*Horrible Styx, the river of hate,*
Sad ACHERON of sorrow, black and deep;	*Sad Acheron, carrying black deep sorrow;*
COCYTUS, nam'd of lamentation loud	*Cocytus, named for the tearful cries*
Heard on the ruful stream; fierce PHLEGETON	*Coming from its sad stream; fierce Phlegeton*
Whose waves of torrent fire inflame with rage.	*Whose rushing waves whip up the angry flames.*
Farr off from these a slow and silent stream,	*Far away from these the slow and silent stream of*
LETHE the River of Oblivion roules	*Lethe, the river of forgetfulness, rules over*
Her watrie Labyrinth, whereof who drinks,	*Her watery caves; whoever drinks from her*
Forthwith his former state and being forgets,	*Will forget both who and what he was,*
Forgets both joy and grief, pleasure and pain.	*Forget joy and grief, pleasure and pain.*
Beyond this flood a frozen Continent	*Beyond the lake a frozen continent*
Lies dark and wilde, beat with perpetual storms	*Spreads dark and wild, beaten with never ending storms,*

Of Whirlwind and dire Hail, which on firm land	*Whirlwinds and terrible hail, which, landing on solid ground,*
Thaws not, but gathers heap, and ruin seems	*Does not thaw out but gathers in heaps and looks like*
Of ancient pile; all else deep snow and ice,	*The ruins of an ancient building; everything else was deep snow and ice,*
A gulf profound as that SERBONIAN Bog	*A wasteland as great as that Serbian marsh*
Betwixt DAMIATA and mount CASIUS old,	*That lies between Damietta and old Mount Casius,*
Where Armies whole have sunk: the parching Air	*Which has swallowed whole armies; the dry air*
Burns frore, and cold performs th' effect of Fire.	*Burns, frozen, and cold does the work of fire.*
Thither by harpy-footed Furies hail'd,	*Called by claw footed demons,*
At certain revolutions all the damn'd	*At certain points on their journey all damned souls*
Are brought: and feel by turns the bitter change	*Are brought there; and they feel the bitterness of two extremes,*
Of fierce extreams, extreams by change more fierce,	*Extremes which are made worse by contrast,*
From Beds of raging Fire to starve in Ice	*Going from raging fire to freezing ice,*
Thir soft Ethereal warmth, and there to pine	*Their soft heavenly warmth there is tortured, trapped*
Immovable, infixt, and frozen round,	*Unmoving and surrounded by ice,*
Periods of time, thence hurried back to fire.	*For a certain time, and then they are rushed back into the fire.*
They ferry over this LETHEAN Sound	*They are carried over the bay of the Lethe,*
Both to and fro, thir sorrow to augment,	*Both to and fro, to make their suffering worse,*
And wish and struggle, as they pass, to reach	*And they wish, they fight as they pass, to get to*
The tempting stream, with one small drop to loose	*The tempting waters, one drop of which could lose*
In sweet forgetfulness all pain and woe,	*All pain and sorrow in sweet oblivion,*
All in one moment, and so neer the brink;	*It would just take a moment, and they are so near to it;*
But fate withstands, and to oppose th' attempt	*But fate will not allow it, and to block their attempts*
MEDUSA with GORGONIAN terror guards	*Medusa, the terrible Gorgon, guards*
The Ford, and of it self the water flies	*The ford, and the water recedes as*

All taste of living wight, as once it fled	*As living lips come close, just as it once fled*
The lip of TANTALUS. Thus roving on	*From the lips of Tantalus.So marching onwards*
In confus'd march forlorn, th' adventrous Bands	*In sad confusion, the adventurous bands*
With shuddring horror pale, and eyes agast	*Shuddering and pale with horror, with horrified eyes,*
View'd first thir lamentable lot, and found	*Got the first sight of their terrible fate, and*
No rest: through many a dark and drearie Vaile	*Could not rest: through many dark and dreary valleys*
They pass'd, and many a Region dolorous,	*They passed, through many sad regions,*
O're many a Frozen, many a Fierie Alpe,	*Over many frozen mountains, many volcanoes,*
Rocks, Caves, Lakes, Fens, Bogs, Dens, and	*Rocks, caves, lakes, fens, bogs, dens and*
shades of death,	*through the shadows of Death,*
A Universe of death, which God by curse	*It was a whole universe of Death, which by God's curse*
Created evil, for evil only good,	*Was created evil, and evil was all there was,*
Where all life dies, death lives, and nature breeds,	*And there all life dies, Death lives, and nature breeds*
Perverse, all monstrous, all prodigious things,	*Twisted, monstrous, swollen things,*
Abominable, inutterable, and worse	*Terrible, unmentionable, worse*
Then Fables yet have feign'd, or fear conceiv'd,	*Than any story has ever created or fear invented,*
GORGONS and HYDRA'S, and CHIMERA'S dire	*Gorgons, Hydras and terrible Chimeras.*
Mean while the Adversary of God and Man,	*Meanwhile the enemy of God and Man,*
SATAN with thoughts inflam'd of highest design,	*Satan, his thoughts burning with his great plan,*
Puts on swift wings, and toward the Gates of Hell	*Puts on swift wings and takes flight, alone,*
Explores his solitary flight; som times	*Towards the Gates of Hell.Sometimes*
He scours the right hand coast, som times the left,	*He follows the right hand shore, sometimes, the left,*
Now shaves with level wing the Deep, then soares	*Now skims over the depths with gliding wings, then soars*
Up to the fiery concave touring high.	*Up to the height of the bowl of flame.*

65

As when farr off at Sea a Fleet descri'd	*Like a fleet of ships seen far off at sea*
Hangs in the Clouds, by AEQUINOCTIAL Winds	*Which seem to hang in the clouds, sailing from Bengal*
Close sailing from BENGALA, or the Iles	*Blown by the equinocital winds, or coming from the islands*
Of TERNATE and TIDORE, whence Merchants bring	*Of Ternate and Tidore, from where merchants bring*
Thir spicie Drugs: they on the trading Flood	*Their heady spices: on the trade currents*
Through the wide ETHIOPIAN to the Cape	*They sail through the wide Indian Ocean*
Ply stemming nightly toward the Pole. So seem'd	*Guided at night by the pole star. This was how the far off*
Farr off the flying Fiend: at last appeer	*Flying Devil seemed: at last he came*
Hell bounds high reaching to the horrid Roof,	*To the borders of Hell, reaching up to the horrid roof,*
And thrice threefold the Gates; three folds were	*And there were nine gates there; three of them*
Brass	*were brass,*
Three Iron, three of Adamantine Rock,	*Three iron and three were of the hardest rock,*
Impenitrable, impal'd with circling fire,	*Impenetrable, run through with circles of fire*
Yet unconsum'd.	*Though they did not burn up.*
Before the Gates there sat	*In front of the gates on either side*
On either side a formidable shape;	*There sat a forbidding shape;*
The one seem'd Woman to the waste, and fair,	*One looked like a beautiful woman to the waist*
But ended foul in many a scaly fould	*But ended horribly with many scaly coils,*
Voluminous and vast, a Serpent arm'd	*Huge and great, a snake armed*
With mortal sting: about her middle round	*With a fatal sting; round her middle*
A cry of Hell Hounds never ceasing bark'd	*A pack of hellhounds barked unceasingly*
With wide CERBEREAN mouths full loud, and rung	*With their hellish mouths loud, making*
A hideous Peal: yet, when they list, would creep,	*A hideous din: but when they heard anything which*
If aught disturb'd thir noyse, into her woomb,	*Disturbed their racket they would creep into her womb*
And kennel there, yet there still bark'd and howl'd	*And make it their kennel, but they still barked and howled*
Within unseen. Farr less abhorrd then these	*Unseen inside. These were far worse than the ones*
Vex'd SCYLLA bathing in the Sea that parts	*Which tortured Scylla as she bathed*

CALABRIA from the hoarse
TRINACRIAN shore:
Nor uglier follow the Night-Hag, when call'd

In secret, riding through the Air she comes

Lur'd with the smell of infant blood, to dance
With LAPLAND Witches, while the labouring Moon
Eclipses at thir charms. The other shape,

If shape it might be call'd that shape had none
Distinguishable in member, joynt, or limb,
Or substance might be call'd that shadow seem'd,
For each seem'd either; black it stood as Night,
Fierce as ten Furies, terrible as Hell,

And shook a dreadful Dart; what seem'd his head
The likeness of a Kingly Crown had on.
SATAN was now at hand, and from his seat

The Monster moving onward came as fast,

With horrid strides, Hell trembled as he strode.
Th' undaunted Fiend what this might be admir'd,
Admir'd, not fear'd; God and his Son except,

Created thing naught vallu'd he nor shun'd;

And with disdainful look thus first began.

Whence and what art thou, execrable shape,

That dar'st, though grim and terrible, advance
Thy miscreated Front athwart my way

in the sea that separates
Calabria from the harsh shores of
Sicily:
No uglier creatures follow the
goddess of the Underworld

When she's secretly summoned and
comes riding through the air,
Tempted with the smell of child
sacrifice, to dance
With the witches of Lapland, while
the moon
Is forced to eclipse by their spells. The
other shape,

If it can be called a shape that was
formless,
Had no obvious arms, joints or legs,
Nothing that could be called solid nor
shadow,
It might have been either; it stood
black as night,
As fierce as ten demons, terrible as
Hell

And shook a terrible arrow; what
could be called his head
Carried the image of a king's crown.
Satan was now close, and from his
seat
The Monster rose to meet him with
equal speed,

With terrible strides, and Hell shook
to his steps.
The untroubled Devil wondered what
this might be,
Wondered but did not fear, for apart
from God and his Son
There was nothing in creation which
could bother him,
And with a look of contempt he
started to speak.
"What are you, and where do you
come from, you foul shape,
That dares, even if you are grim and
horrible, to place
Your bastardised figure across my
path

To yonder Gates? through them I mean to pass,
That be assur'd, without leave askt of thee:
Retire, or taste thy folly, and learn by proof,
Hell-born, not to contend with Spirits of Heav'n.
To whom the Goblin full of wrauth reply'd,
Art thou that Traitor Angel, art thou hee,
Who first broke peace in Heav'n and Faith, till then
Unbrok'n, and in proud rebellious Arms
Drew after him the third part of Heav'ns Sons
Conjur'd against the highest, for which both Thou
And they outcast from God, are here condemn'd
To waste Eternal daies in woe and pain?
And reck'n'st thou thy self with Spirits of Heav'n,
Hell-doomd, and breath'st defiance here and scorn,
Where I reign King, and to enrage thee more,
punishment,
False fugitive, and to thy speed add wings,
Least with a whip of Scorpions I pursue
Thy lingring, or with one stroke of this Dart
Strange horror seise thee, and pangs unfelt before.
So spake the grieslie terrour, and in shape,
So speaking and so threatning, grew ten fold
More dreadful and deform: on th' other side
Incenc't with indignation SATAN stood
Unterrifi'd, and like a Comet burn'd,

To those gates? I mean to go through them,
You can be certain of that, without your permission:
Step aside or suffer the consequences and learn through experience,
Hell's child, that you should not oppose the Spirits of Heaven."
The Goblin answered him angrily,
"Are you the traitorous angel, is it you,
Who broke the peace of Heaven and Faith, which had
Never been disturbed 'til then, and in arrogant armed rebellion
Led a third of the children of Heaven
To fight against the greatest, for which both you
And they were dismissed by God, and condemned
To spend eternity here in sorrow and suffering?
And you call yourself one of the Spirits of Heaven,
You who is condemned to Hell, and you show your arrogance and anger
Where I am King, and to anger you still more, I am
punishment,
You lying fugitive, and go quickly,
In case I decide to speed you up with a whip
Of scorpions, or with one jab of this arrow,
Cause a strange horror to seize you and make you feel such pain as you have never known."
So the grisly horror spoke, and in its shape,
As it made these threats, grew ten times
More horrible and deformed: opposite,
Furious with indignation, Satan stood
Undaunted, and burned like a comet

That fires the length of OPHIUCUS huge

In th' Artick Sky, and from his horrid hair

Shakes Pestilence and Warr. Each at the Head
Level'd his deadly aime; thir fatall hands
No second stroke intend, and such a frown

Each cast at th' other, as when two black Clouds
With Heav'ns Artillery fraught, come rattling on
Over the CASPIAN, then stand front to front
Hov'ring a space, till Winds the signal blow

To joyn thir dark Encounter in mid air:

So frownd the mighty Combatants, that Hell

Grew darker at thir frown, so matcht they stood;
For never but once more was either like

To meet so great a foe: and now great deeds

Had been achiev'd, whereof all Hell had rung,
Had not the Snakie Sorceress that sat
Fast by Hell Gate, and kept the fatal Key,
Ris'n, and with hideous outcry rush'd between.
O Father, what intends thy hand, she cry'd,

Against thy only Son? What fury O Son,

Possesses thee to bend that mortal Dart

Against thy Fathers head? and know'st for whom;
For him who sits above and laughs the while

At thee ordain'd his drudge, to execute

That crosses the huge length of the constellation Ophicus

In the Arctic skies, that brings in its wake

Pestilence and war. They both aimed deadly blows
At the head; their murderous hands
Didn't intend to need a second blow, and they scowled

At each other, seeming like two black clouds which,
Packed with thunder, come rattling

Over the Caspian Sea, then stand facing each other,

Hovering, until the winds blow the signal

For them to start their battle in the air;

The two mighty fighters scowled so darkly

That it darkened Hell itself as they stood toe to toe;
For there was only one other time that either

Might face such a great enemy: and great things

Would have happened, which would have been heard throughout Hell,
If the snaky witch that sat
Right by Hell's gate, and had the key,
Had not jumped up, and with a hideous screech leapt between them.
"Oh Father, what do you mean to do," she cried,

"To your only son? And Son, what madness

Leads you to want to aim that deadly arrow

At your father's head? Do you know whom you're working for?
It's for the one who sits above and is laughing

To see you become his servant, and carry out

What e're his wrath, which he calls Justice, bids,
His wrath which one day will destroy ye both.
She spake, and at her words the hellish Pest

Forbore, then these to her SATAN return'd:
So strange thy outcry, and thy words so strange
Thou interposest, that my sudden hand

Prevented spares to tell thee yet by deeds
What it intends; till first I know of thee,

What thing thou art, thus double-form'd, and why
In this infernal Vaile first met thou call'st

Me Father, and that Fantasm call'st my Son?

I know thee not, nor ever saw till now

Sight more detestable then him and thee.

T' whom thus the Portress of Hell Gate reply'd;
Hast thou forgot me then, and do I seem

Now in thine eye so foul, once deemd so fair
In Heav'n, when at th' Assembly, and in sight
Of all the Seraphim with thee combin'd

In bold conspiracy against Heav'ns King,

All on a sudden miserable pain

Surpris'd thee, dim thine eyes, and dizzie swum
In darkness, while thy head flames thick and fast
Threw forth, till on the left side op'ning wide,
Likest to thee in shape and count'nance

What his anger, which he calls justice, demands,
That anger which one day will destroy you both."
She spoke, and at her words the hellish beast

Held back, and Satan answered her:
"This is such a strange outburst, and the words are so weird
That you have used, that my quick hand,

Blocked, holds back from what I Intended to do; I'll wait until I know of you,

What sort of thing are you, shaped of two things, and why
When we have met for the first time in this hellish valley you

Call me father and call that phantom my son?

I do not know you, and before now never saw

Anything so revolting as the pair of you."

The guardian of the gate of Hell replied;
"Have you forgotten me then, and do I now seem

So foul to you, me who was once thought so beautiful
In Heaven, when at the meeting, seen by
All the Seraphim who had joined with you

In a bold plot against the King of Heaven,

You were suddenly stunned by a miserable pain

Which surprised you, dimmed your vision, blinded you,
While your head threw out flames

Thick and fast, until its left side opened wide and,
Looking like you in shape and in

bright,
Then shining heav'nly fair, a Goddess arm'd
Out of thy head I sprung: amazement seis'd
All th' Host of Heav'n; back they recoild afraid
At first, and call'd me SIN, and for a Sign
Portentous held me; but familiar grown,
I pleas'd, and with attractive graces won

The most averse, thee chiefly, who full oft
Thy self in me thy perfect image viewing
Becam'st enamour'd, and such joy thou took'st
With me in secret, that my womb conceiv'd
A growing burden. Mean while Warr arose,
And fields were fought in Heav'n; wherein remaind
(For what could else) to our Almighty Foe
Cleer Victory, to our part loss and rout
Through all the Empyrean: down they fell
Driv'n headlong from the Pitch of Heaven, down
Into this Deep, and in the general fall
I also; at which time this powerful Key
Into my hand was giv'n, with charge to keep
These Gates for ever shut, which none can pass
Without my op'ning. Pensive here I sat
Alone, but long I sat not, till my womb
Pregnant by thee, and now excessive grown

shining face,
Which at that time shone with the light of Heaven, I sprang
Out of your head, a Goddess in arms: amazement shook
All the Host of Heaven; they pressed back, afraid
At first and called me Sin, and thought I was a
Bad omen; but when they were used to me
They found me pleasing, and with beauty and grace I won

Those who were against me, especially you, who often
Seeing yourself reflected perfectly in me
Became attracted, and you took me
In secret, and our pleasure resulted in my
Becoming pregnant. Meanwhile the war had begun,
And there were battles in Heaven; from that came
(For what else could have happened?) a clear victory
For our Almighty enemy, and for us loss and chaotic retreat
Right down through the skies; down they fell
Driven headfirst over the side of Heaven, down
Into this pit, and I fell with the rest.
At that time I was given this powerful key
And told to keep
These Gates closed forever, and none can pass through
Unless I open them. I sat here brooding
Alone, but not for long before my womb,
Pregnant from you, and now massively swollen,

Prodigious motion felt and rueful throes.

At last this odious offspring whom thou seest
Thine own begotten, breaking violent way

Tore through my entrails, that with fear and pain
Distorted, all my nether shape thus grew

Transform'd: but he my inbred enemie

Forth issu'd, brandishing his fatal Dart

Made to destroy: I fled, and cry'd out DEATH;
Hell trembl'd at the hideous Name, and sigh'd
From all her Caves, and back resounded DEATH.
I fled, but he pursu'd (though more, it seems,

Inflam'd with lust then rage) and swifter far,

Me overtook his mother all dismaid,
And in embraces forcible and foule
Ingendring with me, of that rape begot

These yelling Monsters that with ceasless cry
Surround me, as thou sawst, hourly conceiv'd

And hourly born, with sorrow infinite

To me, for when they list into the womb

That bred them they return, and howle and gnaw
My Bowels, their repast; then bursting forth

Afresh with conscious terrours vex me round,
That rest or intermission none I find.

Before mine eyes in opposition sits
Grim DEATH my Son and foe, who sets

Felt a great upheaval and painful spasms.

At last this disgusting child you can see,
Your own child, hacked his own violent path,

Tearing through my innards that were twisted
With fear and pain, so that all my lower part

Was transformed; but he, the enemy inside me,

Came out, brandishing his fatal arrow

Created for destruction: I fled, and screamed, 'Death!';
Hell shook at the hideous name, and exhaled
From all her caves came back the echo, 'Death!'
I fled, but he chased me (apparently more burning

With lust than with rage) and being far quicker than me

He caught me, his mother, dismayed,
And with foul and forced embraces
Bred with me, and from that rape were born

These yelling monsters that surround me
With endless wailing, as you saw, conceived

And born every hour, with eternal pain for me,

For when they hear a noise they go back into the womb

That bred them and howl and chew at
My bowels for their meals; then they burst out again
To torture me more with their terrors,

So that there's neither rest nor respite for me.

Opposite me in my sight there sits
Grim Death, my son and enemy, who

them on,
And me his Parent would full soon devour
For want of other prey, but that he knows
His end with mine involvd; and knows that I
Should prove a bitter Morsel, and his bane,
When ever that shall be; so Fate pronounc'd.
But thou O Father, I forewarn thee, shun
His deadly arrow; neither vainly hope
To be invulnerable in those bright Arms,
Though temper'd heav'nly, for that mortal dint,

Save he who reigns above, none can resist.
She finish'd, and the suttle Fiend his lore
Soon learnd, now milder, and thus answerd smooth.
Dear Daughter, since thou claim'st me for thy Sire,
And my fair Son here showst me, the dear pledge
Of dalliance had with thee in Heav'n, and joys
Then sweet, now sad to mention, through dire change
Befalln us unforeseen, unthought of, know
I come no enemie, but to set free
From out this dark and dismal house of pain,
Both him and thee, and all the heav'nly Host
Of Spirits that in our just pretenses arm'd
Fell with us from on high: from them I go
This uncouth errand sole, and one for all

drives them on,
And would soon gladly eat up me, his parent,
When he could get no other prey, except that he knows
That my end and his are intertwined, and he knows
That I would be a bitter tidbit, and his doom,
If he ever tried that; this is what fate has decreed.
But you, father, I warn you, avoid
His deadly arrow, and do not think
That your bright armour will save you from harm,
Even thought it was forged in Heaven, for his mortal blow

None can resist apart from he who rules above."
She finished, and the cunning devil, having heard
The story, was now softer, and smoothly answered.
My dear daughter, since you claim me as Father,
And my fair son here demonstrates evidence
Of the affair I had with you in Heaven, and those joys
Which were sweet then but are now sad to think of
Because of the terrible change which came to us,
Unpredicted, unimaginable, you should know
From this dark and dismal house of pain
Both you and him and the whole Heavenly Host
Of Spirits that took up arms in our just cause
And who fell down with us from above: I am sent from them
Alone on this terrible errand, and for the sake of all

My self expose, with lonely steps to tread

Am risking myself, taking a lonely way

Th' unfounded deep, & through the void immense

Through the bottomless pit, and through the great void

To search with wandring quest a place foretold

I am searching for a place which has been predicted

Should be, and, by concurring signs, ere now

And signs show that already

Created vast and round, a place of bliss

There has been built, vast and round, a region of bliss

In the Pourlieues of Heav'n, and therein plac't

Within the boundaries of Heaven, and in it have been placed

A race of upstart Creatures, to supply

A race of upstart creatures, perhaps

Perhaps our vacant room, though more remov'd,

To fill the gap we have left, though they are farther away

Least Heav'n surcharg'd with potent multitude

In case Heaven should become overrun with a powerful mass,

Might hap to move new broiles: Be this or aught

Who could start new conflicts: whether it's true or not

Then this more secret now design'd, I haste

That this secret plan has been put into action, I'm rushing

To know, and this once known, shall soon return,

To know, and once I've found out I'll soon come back

And bring ye to the place where Thou and Death

And bring you to a place where you and Death

Shall dwell at ease, and up and down unseen

Shall live easy, and you'll be invisible as you

Wing silently the buxom Air, imbalm'd

Glide silently through the air, full

With odours; there ye shall be fed and fill'd

Of scents: there you'll be fed and your hunger satisfied,

Immeasurably, all things shall be your prey.

For all things shall be your prey."

He ceas'd, for both seemd highly pleasd,

He stopped, for both seemed most pleased, and Death

Grinnd horrible a gastly smile, to hear

Grinned a fearful smile, hearing

His famine should be fill'd, and blest his mawe

That his hunger would be fed, and rejoiced that his mouth

Destin'd to that good hour: no less rejoyc'd

Would come to know that happy hour: his evil mother

His mother bad, and thus bespake her Sire.

Was no less happy, and she spoke to her Lord.

The key of this infernal Pit by due,

"The key of this hellish pit I keep by right

And by command of Heav'ns all-powerful King

And by the command of the all powerful King of Heaven.

I keep, by him forbidden to unlock

I am forbidden by him to unlock

74

These Adamantine Gates; against all force	These unbreakable gates; against any attack
Death ready stands to interpose his dart,	Death stands ready to shoot his arrow,
Fearless to be o'rematcht by living might.	Having no fear that he could be beaten by any living strength.
But what ow I to his commands above	But what alliegance do I owe to him above
Who hates me, and hath hither thrust me down	What hates me, and has thrown me down
Into this gloom of TARTARUS profound,	Into this thick Tartarean gloom,
To sit in hateful Office here confin'd,	To sit here chained to a hated task,
Inhabitant of Heav'n, and heav'nlie-born,	A citizen of Heaven, born there,
Here in perpetual agonie and pain,	Now kept in eternal pain and anguish,
With terrors and with clamors compasst round	Wrapped around with terror and the racket
Of mine own brood, that on my bowels feed:	Of my own children, that feed on my bowels.
Thou art my Father, thou my Author, thou	You are my father, my creator, you
My being gav'st me; whom should I obey	Gave me my life, who should I obey
But thee, whom follow? thou wilt bring me soon	And follow but you? You will soon bring me
To that new world of light and bliss, among	To a new world of light and joy, among
The Gods who live at ease, where I shall Reign	The Gods who have an easeful life, where I shall rule
At thy right hand voluptuous, as beseems	Beautiful at your right hand forever,
Thy daughter and thy darling, without end.	As your daughter and your sweetheart should."
Thus saying, from her side the fatal Key,	Saying this, she took from her side the deadly key,
Sad instrument of all our woe, she took;	The sad tool which caused all our sorrow;
And towards the Gate rouling her bestial train,	And dragging her bestial train towards the gate,
Forthwith the huge Porcullis high up drew,	She straight away drew up the great portcullis
Which but her self not all the STYGIAN powers	Which only she, not all the powers of Hell,
Could once have mov'd; then in the key-hole turns	Could move; then in the keyhole
Th' intricate wards, and every Bolt and Bar	The intricate levers turned, and every bolt and bar
Of massie Iron or sollid Rock with ease	Of heavy iron or solid rock unlocked

Unfast'ns: on a sudden op'n flie
With impetuous recoile and jarring sound
Th' infernal dores, and on thir hinges great

Harsh Thunder, that the lowest bottom shook
Of EREBUS. She op'nd, but to shut

Excel'd her power; the Gates wide op'n stood,
That with extended wings a Bannerd Host

Under spread Ensigns marching might pass through
With Horse and Chariots rankt in loose array;
So wide they stood, and like a Furnace mouth
Cast forth redounding smoak and ruddy flame.
Before thir eyes in sudden view appear

The secrets of the hoarie deep, a dark
Illimitable Ocean without bound,
Without dimension, where length, breadth, and highth,
And time and place are lost; where eldest Night
And CHAOS, Ancestors of Nature, hold

Eternal ANARCHIE, amidst the noise
Of endless warrs and by confusion stand.
For hot, cold, moist, and dry, four Champions fierce
Strive here for Maistrie, and to Battel bring

Thir embryon Atoms; they around the flag

Of each his faction, in thir several Clanns,

Light-arm'd or heavy, sharp, smooth, swift or slow,
Swarm populous, unnumber'd as the Sands

Of BARCA or CYRENE'S torrid soil,

Easily: all of a sudden,
With great swing and jarring noise
The Hellish doors flew open,
crashing on their hinges
With a great thunder, which shook Erebus
To its depths. She opened them, but to close again
Was beyond her power; the gates stood open wide,
So that with wings spread a great army
With their flags raised might pass through,
With their cavalry and chariots spread out at ease;
That was how wide they were, and like the mouth of a furnace
Belched rolling smoke and red fire.
Before their eyes there suddenly appeared
The secrets of the deep, a dark Ocean without limits
Without any shape, where length, breadth and height
And time and place mean nothing, where ancient night
And Chaos, the forerunners of nature, rule over
Eternal anarchy, amidst the noise
Of endless battle and confusion.
Four fierce elements, heat, cold, moisture and dryness,
All fight for mastery, and bring their embryonic atoms
To battle; each one gathers around the flag
Of his faction in their different groups,
Lightly or heavily armed, sharp, smooth, swift or slow,
They swarmed in masses, numberless as the sands
Of Barca or the rough ground of Cyrene,

Levied to side with warring Winds, and poise
Thir lighter wings. To whom these most adhere,
Hee rules a moment; CHAOS Umpire sits,

And by decision more imbroiles the fray

By which he Reigns: next him high Arbiter

CHANCE governs all. Into this wilde Abyss,
The Womb of nature and perhaps her Grave,

Of neither Sea, nor Shore, nor Air, nor Fire,
But all these in thir pregnant causes mixt
Confus'dly, and which thus must ever fight,

Unless th' Almighty Maker them ordain
His dark materials to create more Worlds,

Into this wilde Abyss the warie fiend
Stood on the brink of Hell and look'd a while,
Pondering his Voyage; for no narrow frith

He had to cross. Nor was his eare less peal'd

With noises loud and ruinous (to compare

Great things with small) then when BELLONA storms,

With all her battering Engines bent to rase

Som Capital City, or less then if this frame

Of Heav'n were falling, and these Elements

In mutinie had from her Axle torn

The stedfast Earth. At last his Sail-broad Vannes
He spreads for flight, and in the surging smoak
Uplifted spurns the ground, thence many

Ready to sail on the warring winds, raising
Their light wings. The one who can use them best
Rules for a moment; Chaos sits as umpire,
And his rulings further mix up the mob
Over which he rules: next to him the high ruler
Of Chance governs everything. Into this wild abyss,
The womb of nature and perhaps her grave,
Plunge water, earth, air and fire,
All with their potential mixed
In confusion, and they must always fight
Unless the great Creator takes them
And uses his dark materials to create more worlds.
Into this wild abyss the cautious devil
Stood on Hell's edge and watched awhile,
Planning his journey, for this was no narrow channel
Which he had to cross. And his ear was assaulted
With loud and shattering noise, which was no less (to compare
Great things with small), than when the
Goddess of War rages
With all her battering rams lined up to destroy
Some great city, or less than if the structure
Of Heaven collapsed, and these elements
Had mutinied and thrown the solid earth
From her orbit. At last he spreads his wings, wide as sails,
For flight, and in the billowing smoke
He leaves the ground for the air, and

a League	*many miles*
As in a cloudy Chair ascending rides	*Up he travels the thermals as if in a chair of clouds,*
Audacious, but that seat soon failing, meets	*Bold, but that support soon runs out, and he meets*
A vast vacuitie: all unawares	*A great void; caught unprepared*
Fluttring his pennons vain plumb down he drops	*And thrashing his wings in vain he drops*
Ten thousand fadom deep, and to this hour	*Ten thousand fathoms, and he would still*
Down had been falling, had not by ill chance	*Be dropping now, if it wasn't for the unlucky chance*
The strong rebuff of som tumultuous cloud	*Of the explosion of some stormy cloud,*
Instinct with Fire and Nitre hurried him	*Packed with fire and gunpowder, which blew him*
As many miles aloft: that furie stay'd,	*As far back up again: once that storm was blown out*
Quencht in a Boggie SYRTIS, neither Sea,	*He was stranded in a boggy quicksand which was neither sea*
Nor good dry Land: nigh founderd on he fares,	*Nor good dry land: almost stranded he journeys on*
Treading the crude consistence, half on foot,	*Over the filthy substance, half on foot and*
Half flying; behoves him now both Oare and Saile.	*Half flying; now he could do with oars and a sail.*
As when a Gryfon through theWilderness	*Just as the Griffin flies over the hills and valleys*
With winged course ore Hill or moarie Dale,	*Through the wilderness when chasing*
Pursues the ARIMASPIAN, who by stelth	*The Armiaspians, who had cunningly*
Had from his wakeful custody purloind	*Stolen the gold he was guarding*
The guarded Gold: So eagerly the fiend	*From under his nose: that is how eagerly the devil,*
Ore bog or steep, through strait, rough, dense,	*Over bog or climb, through straight or twisted*
or rare,	*paths, thick or bare ground,*
With head, hands, wings, or feet pursues his way,	*Using his head, hands, wings or feet goes on his way,*
And swims or sinks, or wades, or creeps, or flyes:	*And swim or sinks, wades, crawls or flies;*
At length a universal hubbub wilde	*Eventually a great clamor all around*
Of stunning sounds and voices all confus'd	*Of loud noises mixed up with voices*
Born through the hollow dark assaults his eare	*Assaults his hearing, carried through the empty dark*
With loudest vehemence: thither he plyes,	*With shattering volume: he makes his way towards it,*

Undaunted to meet there what ever power	*Unafraid to meet whatever power*
Or Spirit of the nethermost Abyss	*Or Spirit of the deepest pit*
Might in that noise reside, of whom to ask	*Might live within that noise, so that he could ask*
Which way the neerest coast of darkness lyes	*Where the nearest dark coast could be found*
Bordering on light;	*That bordered the edge of the light.*
when strait behold the Throne	*Suddenly he saw the throne*
Of CHAOS, and his dark Pavilion spread	*Of Chaos, with his dark tent spread*
Wide on the wasteful Deep; with him Enthron'd	*Wide on the ruinous waters; with him on his throne*
Sat Sable-vested Night, eldest of things,	*Was dark cloaked Night, the oldest of things*
The consort of his Reign; and by them stood	*And his companion in rule; by them were*
ORCUS and ADES, and the dreaded name	*Orcus and Ades and the terrible*
Of DEMOGORGON; Rumor next and Chance,	*Demogorgon; next to them were Rumor and Chance,*
And Tumult and Confusion all imbroild,	*And Tumult and Confusion all mixed together,*
And Discord with a thousand various mouths.	*And Discord with a thousand voices all speaking at once.*
T' whom SATAN turning boldly, thus. Ye Powers	*Fearlessly Satan turned to them and spoke:*
And Spirits of this nethermost Abyss,	*"You rulers and Spirits of this deepest pit,*
CHAOS and ANCIENT NIGHT, I come no Spie,	*Chaos and ancient Night, I am not a spy,*
With purpose to explore or to disturb	*Come to explore or upset*
The secrets of your Realm, but by constraint	*The secrets of your kingdom, but I am forced*
Wandring this darksome desart, as my way	*To wander this dark desert as my path*
Lies through your spacious Empire up to light,	*Lies through your wide kingdom up to the light.*
Alone, and without guide, half lost, I seek	*I am alone, without a guide, almost lost, and I'm looking*
What readiest path leads where your gloomie bounds	*For the quickest route to the place where your dark borders*
Confine with Heav'n; or if som other place	*Join on to Heaven; or if there is some other place*
From your Dominion won, th' Ethereal King	*Taken from your kingdom which the eternal ruler has*
Possesses lately, thither to arrive	*Recently possessed, that*

I travel this profound, direct my course;
Directed, no mean recompence it brings
To your behoof, if I that Region lost,
All usurpation thence expell'd, reduce
To her original darkness and your sway
(Which is my present journey) and once more
Erect the Standerd there of ANCIENT NIGHT;
Yours be th' advantage all, mine the revenge.
Thus SATAN; and him thus the Anarch old

With faultring speech and visage incompos'd
Answer'd. I know thee, stranger, who thou art,
That mighty leading Angel, who of late

Made head against Heav'ns King, though overthrown.
I saw and heard, for such a numerous host

Fled not in silence through the frighted deep
With ruin upon ruin, rout on rout,
Confusion worse confounded; and Heav'n Gates
Pourd out by millions her victorious Bands

Pursuing. I upon my Frontieres here

Keep residence; if all I can will serve,
That little which is left so to defend
Encroacht on still through our intestine broiles
Weakning the Scepter of old Night: first Hell
Your dungeon stretching far and wide beneath;
Now lately Heaven and Earth, another World
Hung ore my Realm, link'd in a golden Chain
To that side Heav'n from whence your Legions fell:

Is what I'm seeking, tell me the way;
Your help will not go unrewarded:
If I can bring down that land,
Throw out all that grows there,
Return it to darkness and your rule
(and this is why I'm going there) and once again
Raise the banner of Ancient Night;

That will be to your advantage, and it will be my revenge."
So said Satan, and this is how ancient Chaos
With halting speech and disturbed face answered him:
"I know who you are, stranger:

You're that great leader of Angels, who recently
Went to war with the King of Heaven, although you were defeated.
I saw and heard what happened, for such a great band

Did not run through the disturbed depths in silence
In their great ruin and retreat,
Made worse by their confusion; and Heaven's Gates
Poured out in her millions the victorious armies,

Chasing them. I live here on my borders;

I will do all I can to defend
That little which I have left
Which is still further invaded through these wars
Which diminish the power of Ancient Night: first Hell
Your prison took the lands far and wide beneath;
Recently Heaven and Earth, another world
Was placed over my kingdom, linked by a golden chain
To the side of Heaven from which your armies fell:

If that way be your walk, you have not farr;	*If that's the way you're going, you're nearly there;*
So much the neerer danger; goe and speed;	*You are close to the danger now; go and good luck,*
Havock and spoil and ruin are my gain.	*Chaos and damage and ruin shall be my reward."*
He ceas'd; and SATAN staid not to reply,	*He finished, and Satan did not stay to answer,*
But glad that now his Sea should find a shore,	*But glad that his journey would find its end*
With fresh alacritie and force renew'd	*With new speed and renewed energy*
Springs upward like a Pyramid of fire	*He springs upwards like a firework*
Into the wilde expanse, and through the shock	*Into the wild skies, and through the clash*
Of fighting Elements, on all sides round	*Of fighting elements, which were clashing all around,*
Environ'd wins his way; harder beset	*Made his way; he was more oppressed*
And more endanger'd, then when ARGO pass'd	*And in more danger than when Argo sailed*
Through BOSPORUS betwixt the justling Rocks:	*Through the Bosphorous between the jostling rocks,*
Or when ULYSSES on the Larbord shunnd CHARYBDIS, and by th' other whirlpool steard.	*Or when Ulysses sailed Between Scylla and Charybdis.*
So he with difficulty and labour hard	*So with difficulty and hard work*
Mov'd on, with difficulty and labour hee;	*He moved forward,*
But hee once past, soon after when man fell,	*But once he had passed through, soon after the fall of Man,*
Strange alteration! Sin and Death amain	*There was a strange change.Sin and Death*
Following his track, such was the will of Heav'n,	*Had followed on his path, as Heaven had planned,*
Pav'd after him a broad and beat'n way	*And behind him they built a broad and leveled path*
Over the dark Abyss, whose boiling Gulf	*Over the dark chasm, whose boiling waters*
Tamely endur'd a Bridge of wondrous length	*Tamely allowed a bridge of amazing length to be built*
From Hell continu'd reaching th' utmost Orbe	*Stretching from Hell to the farthest planet,*
Of this frail World; by which the Spirits perverse	*This frail world; on this bridge evil Spirits*
With easie intercourse pass to and fro	*Can easily go to and fro*
To tempt or punish mortals, except whom	*To tempt or to punish mortals, apart*

God and good Angels guard by special grace.
But now at last the sacred influence
Of light appears, and from the walls of Heav'n
Shoots farr into the bosom of dim Night

A glimmering dawn; here Nature first begins
Her fardest verge, and CHAOS to retire

As from her outmost works a brok'n foe
With tumult less and with less hostile din,

That SATAN with less toil, and now with ease
Wafts on the calmer wave by dubious light

And like a weather-beaten Vessel holds
Gladly the Port, though Shrouds and Tackle torn;
Or in the emptier waste, resembling Air,

Weighs his spread wings, at leasure to behold
Farr off th' Empyreal Heav'n, extended wide

In circuit, undetermind square or round,

With Opal Towrs and Battlements adorn'd

Of living Saphire, once his native Seat;

And fast by hanging in a golden Chain

This pendant world, in bigness as a Starr

Of smallest Magnitude close by the Moon.
Thither full fraught with mischievous revenge,
Accurst, and in a cursed hour he hies.

from those whom
God and the good Angels guard with special care.
But now at last the holy substance
Of light appears, and from the walls of Heaven
There shoots far into the heart of the dark night

A shimmering dawn; here Nature establishes
Her outer borders, and Chaos has to retreat

From her frontier, a defeated enemy
His storms abated and his savage din quieted,

So that Satan's journey became easier,
And he sailed on calmer waters in the dim light

Like a storm tossed ship that
Is glad to see the port, though her sails and ropes are in tatters;
In the emptier space, which was like air,

He rested his spread wings and was able to see
Far off the empire of Heaven, spread wide around,

Too wide to see if its boundary was square or round,

Decorated with opal towers and battlements

Of shining sapphire, where once he lived;

And close by, hung on a golden chain,

Hung this world, in size like the smallest star

Seen next to the moon.
Full of thoughts of wicked revenge

He cursed it, and in an evil hour he journeyed to it.

BOOK III

THE ARGUMENT

God sitting on his Throne sees Satan flying towards this world, then newly created; shews him to the Son who sat at his right hand; foretells the success of Satan in perverting mankind; clears his own Justice and Wisdom from all imputation, having created Man free and able enough to have withstood his Tempter; yet declares his purpose of grace towards him, in regard he fell not of his own malice, as did Satan, but by him seduc't. The Son of God renders praises to his Father for the manifestation of his gracious purpose towards Man; but God again declares, that Grace cannot be extended towards Man without the satisfaction of divine justice; Man hath offended the majesty of God by aspiring to God-head, and therefore with all his Progeny devoted to death must dye, unless some one can be found sufficient to answer for his offence, and undergo his Punishment. The Son of God freely offers himself a Ransome for Man: the Father accepts him, ordains his incarnation, pronounces his exaltation above all Names in Heaven and Earth; commands all the Angels to adore him; they obey, and hymning to thir Harps in full Quire, celebrate the Father and the Son. Mean while Satan alights upon the bare Convex of this Worlds outermost Orb; where wandring he first finds a place since call'd The Lymbo of Vanity; what persons and things fly up thither; thence comes to the Gate of Heaven, describ'd ascending by staires, and the waters above the Firmament that flow about it: His passage thence to the Orb of the Sun; he finds there Uriel the Regent of that Orb, but first changes him self into the shape of a meaner Angel; and pretending a zealous desire to behold the new Creation and Man whom God had

Sitting on his throne God sees Satan flying towards this world, then just created. He shows him to his Son who sits at his right hand and predicts the success Satan will have in perverting mankind. He clears his own justice and wisdom of any blame for this, having given man free will and the strength to resist if he chose. However he declares that he will forgive Mankind, as he fell due to being led astray, not from his own malice as Satan did. The Son of God praises the Father for his forgiveness, but God says man may not be forgiven until justice has been satisfied. Man has offended God by trying to become like a God himself, and so he and all his descendants must die unless someone stands in for him and accepts Death himself. The Son of God freely offers himself for the task; God accepts, says that he will one day become a man, praises him and orders the Angels to worship him. They obey and celebrate the Father and the Son in song. Meanwhile Satan lands on the bare outer edge of the world and on wandering around it finds a place called the Limbo of Vanities and learns of the type of people who go there. From there he comes to the Gates of Heaven, and the stairs which run up to it, and the waters around it, are described. From there he journeys to the sun and meets Uriel, the Regent of the Sun, having first disguised himself as a lesser angel. Pretending he has a burning desire to see the work of God in his new Creation and the man he has placed in it he gets directions, flies down plac't here, inquires of him the place of his habitation, and is directed; alights first on Mount Niphates.

and lands on Mount Niphates.

Hail holy light, ofspring of Heav'n first-born,
Or of th' Eternal Coeternal beam

*Hail to you, holy light, the first creation of heaven,
Which has forever shone alongside the Eternal one,*

May I express thee unblam'd? since God is light,
And never but in unapproached light

*May I describe you without causing offence? Since God is light
And has never in anything but pure light*

Dwelt from Eternitie, dwelt then in thee,
Bright effluence of bright essence increate.

*Lived for all time, God lived in you,
Bright stream of essential brightness, uncreated.*

Or hear'st thou rather pure Ethereal stream,

Or would you rather I called you pure stream of Heaven,

Whose Fountain who shall tell? before the Sun,
Before the Heavens thou wert, and at the voice
Of God, as with a Mantle didst invest
The rising world of waters dark and deep,
Won from the void and formless infinite.

*Whose spring nobody can know of? You existed
Before the sun, before the heavens, and at God's
Command you covered, like a cloak
The rising world of deep dark waters,
Shaped from empty and shapeless eternity.*

Thee I re-visit now with bolder wing,

I come back to you now with greater strength,

Escap't the STYGIAN Pool, though long detain'd
In that obscure sojourn, while in my flight

*Having escaped the pool of Hell, though I was long
Kept in that dark place, while in my journey*

Through utter and through middle darkness borne
With other notes then to th' ORPHEAN Lyre
I sung of CHAOS and ETERNAL NIGHT,
Taught by the heav'nly Muse to venture down
The dark descent, and up to reascend,

*Through the total and the middle darkness
To other music than the lyre of Orpheus
I sang of Chaos and Eternal Night.
Heavenly inspiration showed me how to risk
The dark journey down, and how to climb back up,*

Though hard and rare: thee I revisit safe,

Though it was difficult and dangerous:I have come back to you safely,

And feel thy sovran vital Lamp; but thou

And can feel the heat of your essential light, but you

Revisit'st not these eyes, that rowle in vain

Cannot be seen by these eyes, that

To find thy piercing ray, and find no dawn;

So thick a drop serene hath quencht thir Orbs,
Or dim suffusion veild. Yet not the more
Cease I to wander where the Muses haunt
Cleer Spring, or shadie Grove, or Sunnie Hill,
Smit with the love of sacred song; but chief
Thee SION and the flowrie Brooks beneath
That wash thy hallowd feet, and warbling flow,
Nightly I visit: nor somtimes forget
Those other two equal'd with me in Fate,
So were I equal'd with them in renown,
Blind THAMYRIS and blind MAEONIDES,
And TIRESIAS and PHINEUS Prophets old.
Then feed on thoughts, that voluntarie move
Harmonious numbers; as the wakeful Bird
Sings darkling, and in shadiest Covert hid
Tunes her nocturnal Note. Thus with the Year
Seasons return, but not to me returns
Day, or the sweet approach of Ev'n or Morn,
Or sight of vernal bloom, or Summers Rose,
Or flocks, or herds, or human face divine;
But cloud in stead, and ever-during dark
Surrounds me, from the chearful waies of men
Cut off, and for the book of knowledg fair

search in vain
For your beams, and cannot see the dawn;

So thick a cataract has covered their lenses
That all light is shaded.But it will not
Stop me from my travels in the lands where the Muses
Haunt the clear springs, the shady groves or the sunny hills,
For I am still in love with holy songs; most of all
Mount Sion and the flowery streams below
That lap around its sacred foot with sweet babbling
I visit nightly:and I never forget
The other two who suffered the same fate as me,
That I hope to be equal to in fame,
Blind Thamyris and blind Homer,
And Tiresias and Phineus, the ancient prophets.
So I will take my inspiration from thought, which naturally
Creates sweet rhythms; I shall be like the nightingale
Which sings in the dark, and hidden in the shadiest woods
Performs her nightly song.So as the year passes
The seasons change, but to me
Day never comes back, nor the sweet approach of morning or dusk,
Or the sight of spring flowers, or the rose of summer,
Or flocks, herds or the beauty of the human face.
But instead there are clouds and eternal darkness
All around me, and I am cut off from the cheerful
Life of man, and instead of the book of the world's beauty

Presented with a Universal blanc
Of Natures works to mee expung'd and
ras'd,
And wisdome at one entrance quite shut
out.
So much the rather thou Celestial light
Shine inward, and the mind through all
her powers
Irradiate, there plant eyes, all mist from
thence
Purge and disperse, that I may see and tell
Of things invisible to mortal sight.

Now had the Almighty Father from above,
From the pure Empyrean where he sits
High Thron'd above all highth, bent down
his eye,
His own works and their works at once
to view:
About him all the Sanctities of Heaven
Stood thick as Starrs, and from his sight
receiv'd
Beatitude past utterance; on his right

The radiant image of his Glory sat,
His onely Son; On Earth he first beheld
Our two first Parents, yet the onely two

Of mankind, in the happie Garden plac't,
Reaping immortal fruits of joy and love,

Uninterrupted joy, unrivald love
In blissful solitude; he then survey'd

Hell and the Gulf between, and SATAN
there
Coasting the wall of Heav'n on this side
Night
In the dun Air sublime, and ready now
To stoop with wearied wings, and willing
feet
On the bare outside of this World, that
seem'd
Firm land imbosom'd without Firmament,

Uncertain which, in Ocean or in Air.

I am given a blank page,
With Nature's works completely
erased for me,
And one source of wisdom is quite cut
off.
So I ask you, heavenly light,
To shine inward, and light up all the
faculties
Of the mind, give me eyes in there,
blow away
All the mist, so I may see and speak
Of things which mortal eyes cannot
see.

Now the great Father in Heaven,
In the pure skies where he sits,
On his high throne that is above all,
looked down
To see his works and the works his
works had made:
Around him all the saints of Heaven
Stood, as many as the stars, and from
his gaze received
Blessing beyond telling; on his right
hand

Sat the shining copy of his glory,
His only son; On Earth he saw first
Our original parents, at that time the
only two

Humans, placed in the happy garden,
Savouring the immortal fruits of joy
and love,

Uninterrupted joy, unrivalled love,
In peaceful solitude; then he looked
over

To Hell and the gulf between, and
saw Satan
Sailing along the walls of Heaven, on
the side that was in darkness,
Suspended in the dull air, and ready
To swoop down on his tired wings
and place his feet
On the empty borders of this world,
that seemed
Solid ground placed in the heavenly
void,

Not obviously in the ocean nor in the

Him God beholding from his prospect high,
Wherein past, present, future he beholds,

Thus to his onely Son foreseeing spake.
Onely begotten Son, seest thou what rage
Transports our adversarie, whom no bounds
Prescrib'd, no barrs of Hell, nor all the chains
Heapt on him there, nor yet the main Abyss
Wide interrupt can hold; so bent he seems
On desperat revenge, that shall redound
Upon his own rebellious head. And now
Through all restraint broke loose he wings his way
Not farr off Heav'n, in the Precincts of light,
Directly towards the new created World,
And Man there plac't, with purpose to assay
If him by force he can destroy, or worse,
By som false guile pervert; and shall pervert;
For man will heark'n to his glozing lyes,
And easily transgress the sole Command,
Sole pledge of his obedience: So will fall
Hee and his faithless Progenie: whose fault?
Whose but his own? ingrate, he had of me
All he could have; I made him just and right,
Sufficient to have stood, though free to fall.
Such I created all th' Ethereal Powers
And Spirits, both them who stood & them

sky.
Seeing him God, from his high seat,
From where he can see the past, the present and the future,
Prophesied thus to His only son:
"My only son, you can see the anger
Which drives our enemy, whom no borders could
Block, neither the bars of Hell, nor all the chains
Loaded on him there, nor the great wide abyss
Can stop him; that shows how desperate
He is for his revenge, that will rebound
Onto his rebellious head. And now
He has broken free of all restraints and is flying
Not far from Heaven, in the lands of light,
Straight towards the newly made world,
And the humans we placed in it, to see
If he can destroy him by force, or worse,
Lead him astray with some trick; and he shall succeed
For Man will listen to his flattering lies
And quickly disobey the one command,
The one pledge of obedience he gave: so down will fall
Him and his faithless children:whose fault will it be?
Whose but his own?Ungrateful man, I gave him
All that he could have; I gave him sufficient wisdom
To have resisted temptation, though he was free to fall.
This is how I made all the heavenly powers
And Spirits, those who were faithful

who faild;
Freely they stood who stood, and fell
who fell.

Not free, what proof could they have
givn sincere
Of true allegiance, constant Faith or Love,

Where onely what they needs must do,
appeard,
Not what they would? what praise could
they receive?
What pleasure I from such obedience paid,

When Will and Reason (Reason also is
choice)
Useless and vain, of freedom both despoild,

Made passive both, had servd necessitie,

Not mee. They therefore as to right
belongd,
So were created, nor can justly accuse

Thir maker, or thir making, or thir Fate;

As if Predestination over-rul'd
Thir will, dispos'd by absolute Decree

Or high foreknowledge; they themselves
decrecd
Thir own revolt, not I: if I foreknew,

Foreknowledge had no influence on their
fault,
Which had no less prov'd certain
unforeknown.
So without least impulse or shadow of Fate,

Or aught by me immutablie foreseen,

They trespass, Authors to themselves in all
Both what they judge and what they
choose; for so
I formd them free, and free they must
remain,

and those who rebelled;
Of their own choice the ones who
stood, stood, and the ones who fell,
fell.

If they had no free will, how could
they have given sincere
Proof of their loyalty, true faith or
love,

If they were only shown what I
ordered them to do,
And they had no choice?How could
they be praised for that?
What pleasure would I get from that
sort of obedience,

If will and reason (reason is also
choice)
Were useless, worthless, stripped of
freedom,

Made passive, doing only what they
were forced to do,

Not serving me freely.So they knew
what was right,
This was how they were made and
they cannot justly complain

About their maker, the way they are
made or their fate

As if predestination had control
Over their will, that they were at the
mercy of high orders

Or knowledge of the future; they
chose themselves
To rebel, I did not cause it; if I knew
it was going to happen,

My knowledge had no influence on
their rebellion,
Which would have happened if I had
known in advance or not.
So without the least influence from
fate

Or anything which I had ordered,
unchangeably, to happen,

They have sinned, their own masters
In what they think and what they do;

I made them free and they must
remain so,

Till they enthrall themselves: I else must change
Thir nature, and revoke the high Decree

Until they make themselves slaves: otherwise I would have
To change their nature, and abolish the unchangeable

Unchangeable, Eternal, which ordain'd
Thir freedom, they themselves ordain'd
thir fall.
The first sort by thir own suggestion fell,

Eternal high law which gave them
Their freedom; they themselves chose to fall.
The first group were led astray by their own ideas,

Self-tempted, self-deprav'd: Man falls deceiv'd

They tempted and perverted themselves; Man will fall

By the other first: Man therefore shall find grace,
The other none: in Mercy and Justice both,

Deceived by the first ones: so Man shall be forgiven,
But not the others: mercy and justice shall both

Through Heav'n and Earth, so shall my glorie excel,
But Mercy first and last shall brightest shine.

Show my glory throughout Heaven and Earth
But mercy shall be brightest, at the start and the finish."

Thus while God spake, ambrosial fragrance fill'd
All Heav'n, and in the blessed Spirits elect

As God spoke these words, a beautiful perfume
Filled all of Heaven, and for the blessed chosen Spirits

Sense of new joy ineffable diffus'd:
Beyond compare the Son of God was seen

A new sense of heavenly joy arose:
They could see the Son of God as glorious beyond compare,

Most glorious, in him all his Father shon
Substantially express'd, and in his face
Divine compassion visibly appeerd,
Love without end, and without measure Grace,
Which uttering thus he to his Father spake.
O Father, gracious was that word which clos'd

For he was the image of his father,
And in his face
Divine compassion could be seen,
And endless love and grace beyond measure.
This is what he said to his father:
"Oh father, that was a gracious thing you said

Thy sovran sentence, that Man should find grace;
For which both Heav'n and Earth shall high extoll
Thy praises, with th' innumerable sound
Of Hymns and sacred Songs, wherewith thy Throne
Encompass'd shall resound thee ever blest.

To end your speech, that Man should be forgiven;
For saying that Heaven and Earth will sing
Your praises with numberless
Hymns and sacred songs, so your throne
Will be forever surrounded with blessings.

For should Man finally be lost, should Man
Thy creature late so lov'd, thy youngest Son

For if Man were to be totally lost,
Should the creature you so loved,

90

Fall circumvented thus by fraud, though joynd
With his own folly? that be from thee farr,
That farr be from thee, Father, who art Judge
Of all things made, and judgest onely right.

Or shall the Adversarie thus obtain
His end, and frustrate thine, shall he fulfil

His malice, and thy goodness bring to naught,

Or proud return though to his heavier doom,
Yet with revenge accomplish't and to Hell

Draw after him the whole Race of mankind,
By him corrupted? or wilt thou thy self
Abolish thy Creation, and unmake,

For him, what for thy glorie thou hast made?
So should thy goodness and thy greatness both
Be questiond and blaspheam'd without defence.
To whom the great Creatour thus reply'd.
O Son, in whom my Soul hath chief delight,

Son of my bosom, Son who art alone
My word, my wisdom, and effectual might,

All hast thou spok'n as my thoughts are, all

As my Eternal purpose hath decreed:
Man shall not quite be lost, but sav'd who will,
Yet not of will in him, but grace in me

Freely voutsaft; once more I will renew

His lapsed powers, though forfeit and enthrall'd
By sin to foul exorbitant desires;

your youngest child,
Be lost through trickery, even if it is joined
With his own error? Do not allow it,
You would not allow it, father, who are the judge
Of all of creation, and always judges correctly.

Will we let the enemy achieve
His aim, and block yours, will he succeed

In his evil and make all your goodness nothing,

Or return to his punishment proud,
With his revenge achieved and dragging back to Hell

All of mankind with him,
Tricked by him? Or will you yourself
Destroy what you have made, and because of him

Unmake that which you made for your own glory?
If that happened your goodness and your greatness
Would both be open to questioning and blasphemy."
The great creator replied to him thus:
"Oh my son, who is the greatest pleasure of my soul,

Son of my heart, my son who alone
Represents my word, my wisdom and my strength,

Everything you have said is what I was thinking,

Everything was what I have ordered:
Man shall not be lost totally, but who wishes shall be saved,
But not through his own actions but from my grace,

Given freely; I shall refresh his lost powers

Once again, although he lost them, letting them
Become slaves through sin to his foul excesses;

Upheld by me, yet once more he shall stand

On even ground against his mortal foe,

By me upheld, that he may know how frail

His fall'n condition is, and to me ow

All his deliv'rance, and to none but me.
Some I have chosen of peculiar grace
Elect above the rest; so is my will:

The rest shall hear me call, and oft be warnd
Thir sinful state, and to appease betimes

Th' incensed Deitie, while offerd grace

Invites; for I will cleer thir senses dark,

What may suffice, and soft'n stonie hearts

To pray, repent, and bring obedience due.

To prayer, repentance, and obedience due,
Though but endevord with sincere intent,
Mine eare shall not be slow, mine eye not shut.
And I will place within them as a guide
My Umpire CONSCIENCE, whom if they will hear,
Light after light well us'd they shall attain,
And to the end persisting, safe arrive.

This my long sufferance and my day of grace
They who neglect and scorn, shall never taste;
But hard be hard'nd, blind be blinded more,

That they may stumble on, and deeper fall;

And none but such from mercy I exclude.

But yet all is not don; Man disobeying,

Raised up by me, he shall once again stand

In a fair fight against his mortal enemy;

Raised up by me, he will know how weak he was,

Having fallen, and he will owe all his redemption

To me and to no other.
I have chosen some of special merits
To be above the rest; this is my order:

The rest will hear me calling, and often be warned
About their sins, and told to quickly appease

Their angered God, who is offering them

Redemption; for I will help them to see clearly

What they should do, and soften stony hearts,

Advising them to pray, repent and obey.

To prayer, repentance and obedience,
As long as it is offered sincerely,
My ears and eyes will be open.

I will give them a guide,
My arbiter Conscience, whom if they follow
Their path shall be well lit for them
And they will arrive safely at their goal.

My great patience and the day of my forgiveness
Will never be enjoyed by those who reject or neglect me:
The hard will become harder, the blind blinder,

So they will continue to stumble and fall down deeper;

These are the only ones I shall exclude from my mercy.

But this is not all; Man, having disobeyed,

Disloyal breaks his fealtie, and sins	*Disloyally broken his oath and rebelled*
Against the high Supremacie of Heav'n, Affecting God-head, and so loosing all,	*Against the high law of Heaven, Disturbing God, and so losing everything,*
To expiate his Treason hath naught left, But to destruction sacred and devote, He with his whole posteritie must die, Die hee or Justice must; unless for him	*Has nothing left to make amends, But to offer his own destruction: He with all of his kind must die: If he does not die then justice will be dead, unless*
Som other able, and as willing, pay The rigid satisfaction, death for death.	*Some other is willing and able to pay The price for him, offering death for death.*
Say Heav'nly Powers, where shall we find such love, Which of ye will be mortal to redeem	*Tell me, powers of Heaven, where shall we find such love? Which one of you will become a mortal to redeem*
Mans mortal crime, and just th' unjust to save, Dwels in all Heaven charitie so deare?	*Man's dreadful crime and so the just will save the unjust: Is there such charity anywhere in Heaven?"*
He ask'd, but all the Heav'nly Quire stood mute, And silence was in Heav'n: on mans behalf	*He asked, but all the Heavenly choir stood speechless And silence reigned in Heaven: no patron or mediator*
Patron or Intercessor none appeerd, Much less that durst upon his own head draw The deadly forfeiture, and ransom set.	*Appeared on man's behalf, None who dared take upon himself The deadly forfeit and the price which was set.*
And now without redemption all mankind	*And so all mankind was going to be lost*
Must have bin lost, adjudg'd to Death and Hell By doom severe, had not the Son of God,	*Without redemption, sentenced to Death and Hell By severe judgment, if the Son of God,*
In whom the fulness dwels of love divine, His dearest mediation thus renewd.	*Who is filled with divine love Had not offered his sweet intervention.*
Father, thy word is past, man shall find grace; And shall grace not find means, that finds her way, The speediest of thy winged messengers,	*"Father, you have decreed that man will have forgiveness; Will that grace not find her way, The quickest of all your winged messengers,*

To visit all thy creatures, and to all

Comes unprevented, unimplor'd, unsought,
Happie for man, so coming; he her aide

Can never seek, once dead in sins and lost;

Attonement for himself or offering meet,
Indebted and undon, hath none to bring:
Behold mee then, mee for him, life for life

I offer, on mee let thine anger fall;
Account mee man; I for his sake will leave

Thy bosom, and this glorie next to thee
Freely put off, and for him lastly die

Well pleas'd, on me let Death wreck all his rage;

Under his gloomie power I shall not long
Lie vanquisht; thou hast givn me to possess

Life in my self for ever, by thee I live,
Though now to Death I yeild, and am his due
All that of me can die, yet that debt paid,

Thou wilt not leave me in the loathsom grave
His prey, nor suffer my unspotted Soule

For ever with corruption there to dwell;
But I shall rise Victorious, and subdue
My Vanquisher, spoild of his vanted spoile;

Death his deaths wound shall then receive, & stoop
Inglorious, of his mortall sting disarm'd.

I through the ample Air in Triumph high

Shall lead Hell Captive maugre Hell, and show
The powers of darkness bound. Thou at the sight

To visit all your creatures, and she comes

Unanticipated, uncalled, unsought,
And it is lucky for man that she comes; he can never ask
For her help, once he has become dead and lost through sin;
He can offer no apology or sacrifice;
Fallen, he has none to give:
See me then, I will offer myself for him, life for life,
Let your anger fall upon me.
Count me as a man; for his sake I will leave
Your side and freely postpone
My glory, and I shall be pleased to die for him;
Let Death's rage fall upon me;

Under his dark rule I shall not suffer
For long; you have given me eternal life,
I live as long as you live,
And though I give myself to death, and pay as his price
All there is of me that can die, but having paid that debt
You will not leave me in the revolting grave
As his prey, nor will you allow my pure soul
To stay rotting there for eternity;
I shall rise victorious and defeat
The one who defeated me and take his prize from him;
Death shall then be killed himself, and fall
To nothing, deprived of his deadly power.
Despite what Hell will try I will lead Hell as my captive
In a triumph through the great skies

And show the powers of darkness subdued. You shall

Pleas'd, out of Heaven shalt look down and smile,
While by thee rais'd I ruin all my Foes,

Death last, and with his Carcass glut the Grave:
Then with the multitude of my redeemd
Shall enter Heaven long absent, and returne,

Father, to see thy face, wherein no cloud

Of anger shall remain, but peace assur'd,

And reconcilement; wrauth shall be no more
Thenceforth, but in thy presence Joy entire.

His words here ended, but his meek aspect

Silent yet spake, and breath'd immortal love

To mortal men, above which only shon

Filial obedience: as a sacrifice
Glad to be offer'd, he attends the will
Of his great Father. Admiration seis'd

All Heav'n, what this might mean, & whither tend
Wondring; but soon th' Almighty thus reply'd:
O thou in Heav'n and Earth the only peace

Found out for mankind under wrauth, O thou
My sole complacence! well thou know'st how dear,
To me are all my works, nor Man the least
Though last created, that for him I spare

Thee from my bosom and right hand, to save,
By loosing thee a while, the whole Race lost.
Thou therefore whom thou only canst

Look out from Heaven and smile at the sight,
While raised up by you I shall defeat all my enemies,
Saving Death 'til last and I shall block up the tomb with his corpse.
Then with all of those I have saved
I shall come back to the Heaven I have left for so long,
And see your face, father, which will retain no trace
Of anger, but hold the promise of peace
And reconciliation; there shall be no more anger
From then on, but only pure joy in your presence."
He stopped speaking, but his gentle face
Still spoke for him in silence, showing immortal love

For mortal men, which only his obedience as a son
Outranked; happy to be offered
As a sacrifice, he obeys the desires
Of his great father.All of heaven was amazed,
Wondering what this could mean and where it would lead,
But soon the almighty replied:
"Oh you have discovered the only redemption
From my anger for mankind, you

My only pleasure!You know how much I love
All my works, and not least Man
Although I made him last, so much that I free you
From my heart and your place next to me to save,
By losing you for a while, the whole of that lost race.
So you, the only one who can win

redeeme,
Thir Nature also to thy Nature joyne;

And be thy self Man among men on Earth,

Made flesh, when time shall be, of Virgin seed,
By wondrous birth: Be thou in ADAMS room
The Head of all mankind, though ADAMS Son.
As in him perish all men, so in thee

As from a second root shall be restor'd,

As many as are restor'd, without thee none.

His crime makes guiltie all his Sons, thy merit
Imputed shall absolve them who renounce

Thir own both righteous and unrighteous deeds,

And live in thee transplanted, and from thee

Receive new life. So Man, as is most just,

Shall satisfie for Man, be judg'd and die,

And dying rise, and rising with him raise

His Brethren, ransomd with his own dear life.
So Heav'nly love shal outdoo Hellish hate,

Giving to death, and dying to redeeme,
So dearly to redeem what Hellish hate

So easily destroy'd, and still destroyes
In those who, when they may, accept not grace.
Nor shalt thou by descending to assume

Mans Nature, less'n or degrade thine owne.

redemption,
Take on their nature along with your own,

And become a man yourself amongst the men of earth.

When the time comes you shall be made flesh, miraculously
Born of a virgin; you shall take Adam's place
As the leader of all men, even though you will be Adam's son.
As he brings death to all men, so from you

New life shall grow like a second shoot;

Many shall be saved, but none that is not through you.

His crime makes all his sons guilty, but they will gain
Your innocence if they renounce all their own deeds

Both the good and the bad

And live their lives through you, and from you

Receive new life. So a man, as is proper,

Shall be tried for man's crimes, be judged and die,

And he shall rise after death, and in rising he shall raise

All his brothers, who have been saved by his sacrifice.
So Heavenly love shall overcome Hellish hate,

Paying Death, and dying to save,
To save at such a cost that which Hellish hate

So easily destroyed, and still destroys
When man does not accept forgiveness when it is offered.
By lowering yourself to the level of the nature of Man

You shall not degrade your own nature.

Because thou hast, though Thron'd in highest bliss	*Because you have, though crowned with highest bliss,*
Equal to God, and equally enjoying	*Equal to my own, and enjoying*
God-like fruition, quitted all to save	*The same life of God, left it all to save*
A World from utter loss, and hast been found	*A world from total damnation, and you have been shown*
By Merit more then Birthright Son of God,	*By your merit more than just your birth to be the Son of God,*
Found worthiest to be so by being Good,	*Shown to be the most worthy of that honor through your goodness,*
Farr more then Great or High; because in thee	*Far more than through your great titles; because in you*
Love hath abounded more then Glory abounds,	*There is more love than there is glory,*
Therefore thy Humiliation shall exalt	*And so your humiliation shall raise you*
With thee thy Manhood also to this Throne;	*Back to the throne with your human nature;*
Here shalt thou sit incarnate, here shalt Reigne	*You shall sit here combined, and rule*
Both God and Man, Son both of God and Man,	*As a God and a Man, as the Son of God and Man,*
Anointed universal King; all Power	*Proclaimed King of the Universe; I give you*
I give thee, reign for ever, and assume	*All power, eternal reign and you shall take*
Thy Merits; under thee as Head Supream	*Your correct titles; I make you the supreme ruler*
Thrones, Princedoms, Powers, Dominions I reduce:	*Of all thrones, princedoms, powers and dominions:*
All knees to thee shall bow, of them that bide	*All shall bow down to you, all who live*
In Heaven, or Earth, or under Earth in Hell;	*In Heaven, on Earth or under Earth in Hell;*
When thou attended gloriously from Heav'n	*When you appear in the sky, gloriously attended*
Shalt in the Skie appear, and from thee send	*By the angels, and you will send*
The summoning Arch-Angels to proclaime	*The summoning archangels to announce*
Thy dread Tribunal: forthwith from all Windes	*The Day of Judgement. At once from all points*
The living, and forthwith the cited dead	*The living and then the named dead*
Of all past Ages to the general Doom	*From all ages gone by will hurry*
Shall hast'n, such a peal shall rouse	*To judgement, woken by the*

thir sleep.
Then all thy Saints assembl'd, thou shalt judge
Bad men and Angels, they arraignd shall sink
Beneath thy Sentence; Hell, her numbers full,
Thenceforth shall be for ever shut. Mean while
The World shall burn, and from her ashes spring
New Heav'n and Earth, wherein the just shall dwell
And after all thir tribulations long
See golden days, fruitful of golden deeds,

With Joy and Love triumphing, and fair Truth.
Then thou thy regal Scepter shalt lay by,

For regal Scepter then no more shall need,

God shall be All in All. But all ye Gods,

Adore him, who to compass all this dies,

Adore the Son, and honour him as me.

No sooner had th' Almighty ceas't, but all

The multitude of Angels with a shout

Loud as from numbers without number, sweet
As from blest voices, uttering joy, Heav'n rung
With Jubilee, and loud Hosanna's fill'd
Th' eternal Regions: lowly reverent

Towards either Throne they bow, & to the ground
With solemn adoration down they cast

Thir Crowns inwove with Amarant and Gold,
Immortal Amarant, a Flour which once

summons.
Then with all your saints you will judge
Bad men and angels, and having been tried
They shall fall before your sentence; Hell will be full
And her doors will be closed forever.

Meanwhile the earth shall burn, and from her ashes there will spring
A new heaven and earth, where the righteous shall live
And after all their long trials they
Shall see golden days, full of golden deeds,

With joy and love triumphant, and beautiful truth.
Then you shall lay aside your royal scepter,

For the royal scepter will not be needed:
God will be himself, totally. But all you Gods here,
Worship him, who is prepared to die to make this happen,
Worship the son as if he were me."

No sooner had God finished than the multitude of angels gave a shout
As loud as if they were an infinite number, as
Sweet as from blessed voices, uttering joy, Heaven rang
With songs of joy, and loud songs of praise filled
The eternal lands: they bow low
With deep reverence to both thrones, and to the ground
In solemn worship they throw

Their crowns, woven with Amarant and gold,
Immortal Amarant, a flower which once
Grew in Paradise, right by the

In Paradise, fast by the Tree of Life

Began to bloom, but soon for mans offence

To Heav'n remov'd where first it grew,
there grows,
And flours aloft shading the Fount of Life,

And where the river of Bliss through
midst of Heavn
Rowls o're ELISIAN Flours her Amber
stream;
With these that never fade the Spirits Elect

Bind thir resplendent locks inwreath'd
with beams,
Now in loose Garlands thick thrown off,
the bright
Pavement that like a Sea of Jasper shon
Impurpl'd with Celestial Roses smil'd.

Then Crown'd again thir gold'n Harps
they took,
Harps ever tun'd, that glittering by their
side
Like Quivers hung, and with Praeamble
sweet
Of charming symphonie they introduce

Thir sacred Song, and waken raptures high;

No voice exempt, no voice but well could
joine
Melodious part, such concord is in Heav'n.

Thee Father first they sung Omnipotent,

Immutable, Immortal, Infinite,
Eternal King; thee Author of all being,
Fountain of Light, thy self invisible
Amidst the glorious brightness where thou
sit'st
Thron'd inaccessible, but when thou shad'st

The full blaze of thy beams, and through

*Tree of life, but due to man's sin it
was soon*

*Removed to Heaven where it first
bloomed and still does,*

*And its petals shade the Spring of
Life,*

*And where the river of Bliss runs
through the middle of Heaven*

*Over the Elysian fields it grows in her
golden waters;*

*With these flowers which never fade
the chosen Spirits*

*Tie their splendid hair which is
plaited with sunbeams.*

*Now that the loose garlands had been
thrown off*

*The bright pavement which shone like
a sea of*

Jasper

*Was beautiful in a cloak of heavenly
roses.*

*Then they put back their crowns and
picked up their golden harps,*

*Harps that were always in tune, that
glittered at their sides*

*Like quivers, and with a sweet
overture*

*Of charming harmonies they
introduced*

*Their sacred song, and caused great
rapture;*

*No voice stayed out, and there was no
voice which could not*

*Join the harmony, such harmony
there is in Heaven.*

*"You, Father," first they sang,
"Omnipotent,*

Unchangeable, Immortal, Infinite,
The eternal King, creator of all,
Fountain of light, you are invisible
*Amidst the glorious brightness where
you sit*

*On your inaccessible throne, but
when you shade*

The full blaze of your beams, and

a cloud
Drawn round about thee like a radiant Shrine,
Dark with excessive bright thy skirts appeer,
Yet dazle Heav'n, that brightest Seraphim

Approach not, but with both wings veil thir eyes.
Thee next they sang of all Creation first,

Begotten Son, Divine Similitude,
In whose conspicuous count'nance, without cloud
Made visible, th' Almighty Father shines,

Whom else no Creature can behold; on thee

Impresst the effulgence of his Glorie abides,

Transfus'd on thee his ample Spirit rests.

Hee Heav'n of Heavens and all the Powers therein
By thee created, and by thee threw down
Th' aspiring Dominations: thou that day
Thy Fathers dreadful Thunder didst not spare,
Nor stop thy flaming Chariot wheels, that shook
Heav'ns everlasting Frame, while o're the necks

Thou drov'st of warring Angels disarraid.

Back from pursuit thy Powers with loud acclaime
Thee only extold, Son of thy Fathers might,

To execute fierce vengeance on his foes,

Not so on Man; him through their malice fall'n,
Father of Mercie and Grace, thou didst not doome
So strictly, but much more to pitie encline:
No sooner did thy dear and onely Son

draw a cloud
Around you like a shining shrine,
Your edges appear, dark in the blaze,
But they still dazzle Heaven, so that the brightest Seraphim

Do not approach, but shade their eyes with both wings.
Next you," they sang, "First of all creation,

Natural born son, copy of God,
In whose visible face, which we can see without cloud
For a shade, the almighty father shines,

That otherwise no creature would be able to see; on you

The splendid radiance of his glory shows,

And his great spirit is transfused into you.

With you he created Heaven and all that's in it,
And with you threw down the Ambitious rebels. That day you
Did not spare your father's dreadful thunder
Or slow the wheels of your fiery chariot, that shook
The eternal frame of Heaven, while you drove

Over the necks of the scattered warring angels.

When you returned from the hunt your powers
Were loudly praised, the son of your father's greatness,

Who takes terrible revenge on his enemies,

Though not on Man; when he has fallen through your enemies' malice,
You, father of mercy and grace, did not judge so harshly,
But leant much more towards pity:
No sooner did your dear and only son

Perceive thee purpos'd not to doom frail Man
So strictly, but much more to pitie enclin'd,
He to appease thy wrauth, and end the strife
Of Mercy and Justice in thy face discern'd,
Regardless of the Bliss wherein he sat
Second to thee, offerd himself to die
For mans offence. O unexampl'd love,
Love no where to be found less then Divine!
Hail Son of God, Saviour of Men, thy Name
Shall be the copious matter of my Song
Henceforth, and never shall my Harp thy praise
Forget, nor from thy Fathers praise disjoine.

Thus they in Heav'n, above the starry Sphear,
Thir happie hours in joy and hymning spent.
Mean while upon the firm opacous Globe
Of this round World, whose first convex divides
The luminous inferior Orbs, enclos'd
From CHAOS and th' inroad of Darkness old
SATAN alighted walks: a Globe farr off
It seem'd, now seems a boundless Continent
Dark, waste, and wild, under the frown of Night
Starless expos'd, and ever-threatning storms
Of CHAOS blustring round, inclement skie;
Save on that side which from the wall of Heav'n

See that you were not intending to punish frail Man
So strictly but wished to show them pity,
To calm your anger and to end the battle
Between mercy and justice that he saw in your face,
Without a thought for the Heaven where he sat
Second only to you, offered himself for death
To pay for man's offence. What matchless love,
Love that can only be found in the divine!
Hail the son of God and savior of men, your name
Will be the great subject of my song
From now on, and my harp shall never stop singing
Your praise, nor praise the Father without praising you."

This was how in heaven, above the stars,
They passed their happy hours in joy and singing.
Meanwhile upon the firm opaque globe
Of this world, whose outer edge is marked
By the smaller stars, fenced off
From Chaos and the entrance of the ancient darkness,
Satan, landed, walks: the globe appeared
Far away, seems a vast continent,
Dark, wasted and wild, exposed under the frown
Of a starless night, with the threatening storms
Of Chaos boiling around the stormy sky;
Except for that side which, though far away,

Though distant farr som small reflection gaines
Of glimmering air less vext with tempest loud:
Here walk'd the Fiend at large in spacious field.
As when a Vultur on IMAUS bred,

Whose snowie ridge the roving TARTAR bounds,
Dislodging from a Region scarce of prey

To gorge the flesh of Lambs or yeanling Kids
On Hills where Flocks are fed, flies toward the Springs
Of GANGES or HYDASPES, INDIAN streams;
But in his way lights on the barren plaines

Of SERICANA, where CHINESES drive

With Sails and Wind thir canie Waggons light:
So on this windie Sea of Land, the Fiend
Walk'd up and down alone bent on his prey,

Alone, for other Creature in this place

Living or liveless to be found was none,
None yet, but store hereafter from the earth

Up hither like Aereal vapours flew
Of all things transitorie and vain, when Sin
With vanity had filld the works of men:

Both all things vain, and all who in vain things
Built thir fond hopes of Glorie or lasting fame,
Or happiness in this or th' other life;

All who have thir reward on Earth, the fruits
Of painful Superstition and blind Zeal,

Gets from the wall of Heaven some small glimpse
Of light air less tortured by the loud storms:
The devil walked free in this region of space.
He was like a vulture bred in the Himalayas,

Whose snowy ridges marked the borders of Ghenghis Khan's territory,
Who leaves his land which is short of prey

To go and feast on the flesh of lambs or baby goats
On the hillsides where flocks are reared, and flies towards the springs
Of the Ganges or the Jhelum, rivers of India,
But on his way crosses the barren plains

Of the Gobi desert, where the Chinese

Drive their cunning light wagons with sails:
So on this windy land-sea, the devil
Walked up and down alone and thought of his prey;

Alone, for there was no other creature,

Living or dead, in this place,
None yet, but afterwards things from the earth

Flew up here like steam,
Worthless things, when Sin
Had made the works of Man full of vanity:

All material things are vain, and it is in vain to hope that things
Will bring glory or lasting fame,

Or happiness in this life or in the hereafter;

All who seek their reward on earth, the gains
Of painful superstition and blind enthusiasm,

Naught seeking but the praise of men, here find	Who look for nothing but the praise of men, here find
Fit retribution, emptie as thir deeds;	Proper punishment, as empty as what they have done;
All th' unaccomplisht works of Natures hand,	All the unfinished works of Nature,
Abortive, monstrous, or unkindly mixt,	Terrible, monstrous, badly mixed
Dissolvd on earth, fleet hither, and in vain,	And dissolved on earth fly here and in vain
Till final dissolution, wander here,	Wander here until the end of time –
Not in the neighbouring Moon, as some have dreamd;	Not on the neighboring moon, as some have dreamed;
Those argent Fields more likely habitants,	Those silver fields are more likely occupied
Translated Saints, or middle Spirits hold	By the spirits of saints or middle Spirits
Betwixt th' Angelical and Human kinde:	Halfway between humans and angels:
Hither of ill-joynd Sons and Daughters born	First we see the Giants from the ancient world,
First from the ancient World those Giants came	Bred from the monstrous coupling of sons and daughters,
With many a vain exploit, though then renownd:	Giants who did many vain things, though they were lauded then:
The builders next of BABEL on the Plain	Next come the builders of Babel on the Plain
Of SENNAAR, and still with vain designe	Of Shinar, and in their vanity they still design
New BABELS, had they wherewithall, would build:	New Babels, which they would build if they had the materials:
Others came single; hee who to be deemd	Others come alone; Empedocles, who voluntarily jumped
A God, leap'd fondly into AETNA flames,	Into the flames of volcanic Etna, to try and prove
EMPEDOCLES, and hee who to enjoy	He was a God, and Cleombrotus who threw himself into the ocean
PLATO'S ELYSIUM, leap'd into the Sea,	Thinking it would get him to Plato's Elysium,
CLEOMBROTUS, and many more too long,	And there were many others too numerous to name,
Embryo's and Idiots, Eremits and Friers	Embryos and idiots, hermits and friars,
White, Black and Grey, with all thir trumperie.	White, Black and Grey, with all their vanities.
Here Pilgrims roam, that stray'd so farr to seek	Here the pilgrims roam who travelled so far

In GOLGOTHA him dead, who lives in Heav'n;
And they who to be sure of Paradise

Dying put on the weeds of DOMINIC,

Or in FRANCISCAN think to pass disguis'd;
They pass the Planets seven, and pass the fixt,
And that Crystalline Sphear whose ballance weighs
The Trepidation talkt, and that first mov'd;

And now Saint PETER at Heav'ns Wicket seems
To wait them with his Keys, and now at foot
Of Heav'ns ascent they lift thir Feet, when loe
A violent cross wind from either Coast
Blows them transverse ten thousand Leagues awry
Into the devious Air; then might ye see

Cowles, Hoods and Habits with thir wearers tost
And flutterd into Raggs, then Reliques, Beads,
Indulgences, Dispenses, Pardons, Bulls,

The sport of Winds: all these upwhirld aloft

Fly o're the backside of the World farr off

Into a LIMBO large and broad, since calld

The Paradise of Fools, to few unknown

Long after, now unpeopl'd, and untrod;

All this dark Globe the Fiend found as he pass'd,
And long he wanderd, till at last a gleame

Looking for Him dead in Golgotha who lives in heaven;
Also here are those who try to get into heaven

By, when they are dying, dressing in the robes of a Dominican,

Or think they will be admitted disguised as a Franciscan;
They pass the seven planets, pass the pole star
And the constellation of Libra whose scale measures
The irregular movements of planets and drives them on;

And now Saint Peter seems to be waiting for them
At Heaven's Gate with his keys, and now they set foot
On the slope up to Heaven, when suddenly
Violent winds from either side
Blow them thirty thousand miles away
Into the deceitful air; then you might see

Cowls, hoods and habits thrown along with their wearers
And torn into rags, then reliquaries, beads,
Indulgences, dispensations, pardons, bulls

Become the toys of the winds; everything is thrown aloft

And flies around the back of the world to

A large and broad Limbo that has been named

The Paradise of Fools, known to most in the future

But for now uninhabited and unexplored;

All this dark world the devil found as he passed,
And he wandered for a long time, until at last

Of dawning light turnd thither-ward in haste
His travell'd steps; farr distant hee descries
Ascending by degrees magnificent
Up to the wall of Heaven a Structure high,

At top whereof, but farr more rich appeerd

The work as of a Kingly Palace Gate

With Frontispice of Diamond and Gold
Imbellisht, thick with sparkling orient Gemmes
The Portal shon, inimitable on Earth

By Model, or by shading Pencil drawn.

The Stairs were such as whereon JACOB saw
Angels ascending and descending, bands

Of Guardians bright, when he from ESAU fled
To PADAN-ARAM in the field of LUZ,
Dreaming by night under the open Skie,

And waking cri'd, This is the Gate of Heav'n.
Each Stair mysteriously was meant, nor stood
There alwaies, but drawn up to Heav'n sometimes
Viewless, and underneath a bright Sea flow'd
Of Jasper, or of liquid Pearle, whereon
Who after came from Earth, sayling arriv'd,

Wafted by Angels, or flew o're the Lake

Rapt in a Chariot drawn by fiery Steeds.
The Stairs were then let down, whether to dare
The Fiend by easie ascent, or aggravate

His sad exclusion from the dores of Bliss.

He saw a gleam of dawning light and turned his steps
Towards it in haste; far off he sees
Climbing in great steps
Up to the wall of Heaven a high structure

At the top of which there was what looked like

A Kingly Palace Gate, though far richer,

With diamonds and gold on its front
And the doorpost shone with eastern jewels
The likes of which could not be copied on earth

By a sculptor, or drawn with a shading pencil.

These were the stairs on which Jacob saw
The angels rising and descending, armies

Of shining guardians, when he fled from Esau
To Padan-Aram in the country of Luz,
When he dreamed at night under the open sky

And when he awoke cried, "This is the Gate of Heaven!"
Each step had a mysterious meaning, and did not
Always stand there but was sometimes pulled up to Heaven
Out of sight, and underneath there was a bright sea
Of Jasper, or of liquid pearl, so that
Those who came afterwards from earth arrived by boat

Blown by angels, or flew over the lake

In a chariot drawn by fiery horses.
Just then the stairs were let down, perhaps
To dare the devil to try the easy way in, or to

Emphasise how he was excluded from the doors of joy.

Direct against which op'nd from beneath,	*Just opposite the doors there opened beneath,*
Just o're the blissful seat of Paradise,	*Just over the blissful land of Paradise,*
A passage down to th' Earth, a passage wide,	*A wide passage down to the earth,*
Wider by farr then that of after-times	*Far wider than that, in times which followed,*
Over Mount SION, and, though that were large,	*Opened over Mount Sion (and that was large)*
Over the PROMIS'D LAND to God so dear,	*Over the Promised Land which was so dear to God,*
By which, to visit oft those happy Tribes,	*Through which, to visit the Tribes of Israel,*
On high behests his Angels to and fro	*On his great errands the angels passed*
Pass'd frequent, and his eye with choice regard	*Frequently to and fro, and he looked with pleasure*
From PANEAS the fount of JORDANS flood	*From Paneas where the Jordan river rises*
To BEERSABA, where the HOLY LAND	*To Beersheba, where the Holy Land*
Borders on AEGYPT and the ARABIAN shoare;	*Has borders with Egypt and the shores of Arabia;*
So wide the op'ning seemd, where bounds were set	*The opening seemed so wide that its edges*
To darkness, such as bound the Ocean wave.	*Were in darkness like the edges of the ocean.*
SATAN from hence now on the lower stair	*Satan now on the lower stair,*
That scal'd by steps of Gold to Heav'n Gate	*That climbed in golden steps to Heaven's Gate,*
Looks down with wonder at the sudden view	*Looks down amazed at seeing*
Of all this World at once. As when a Scout	*All the world at once. He was like a scout*
Through dark and desert wayes with peril gone	*Who has travelled all night on dark and deserted paths, through danger:*
All night; at last by break of chearful dawne	*And at last at the cheerful daybreak*
Obtains the brow of some high-climbing Hill,	*Comes to the summit of some lofty hill*
Which to his eye discovers unaware	*And is surprised to see*
The goodly prospect of some forein land	*The pleasant sight of a foreign land seen for the*
First-seen, or some renownd Metropolis	*First time, or some famous city,*
With glistering Spires and Pinnacles adornd,	*Ornamented with great spires and towers,*
Which now the Rising Sun guilds with his beams.	*Which gleam gold in the rising sun.*

Such wonder seis'd, though after Heaven
seen,
The Spirit maligne, but much more envy
seis'd
At sight of all this World beheld so faire.
Round he surveys, and well might, where
he stood
So high above the circling Canopie
Of Nights extended shade; from Eastern
Point
Of LIBRA to the fleecie Starr that bears
ANDROMEDA farr off ATLANTICK Seas
Beyond th' HORIZON; then from Pole
to Pole
He views in bredth, and without longer
pause
Down right into the Worlds first Region
throws
His flight precipitant, and windes with ease

Through the pure marble Air his oblique
way
Amongst innumerable Starrs, that shon

Stars distant, but nigh hand seemd other
Worlds,
Or other Worlds they seemd, or happy Iles,
Like those HESPERIAN Gardens fam'd
of old,
Fortunate Fields, and Groves and flourie
Vales,
Thrice happy Iles, but who dwelt happy
there
He stayd not to enquire: above them all
The golden Sun in splendor likest Heaven

Allur'd his eye: Thither his course he bends

Through the calm Firmament; but up or
downe
By center, or eccentric, hard to tell,

Or Longitude, where the great Luminarie

Alooff the vulgar Constellations thick,

This was the wonder which seized
(even though he had seen Heaven)
The evil spirit, but his chief emotion
was envy,
At the sight of such a beautiful world.
He looks around, as anyone would, if
they stood in his place
So high above the covering canopy
Of the shades of night; from the
eastern point
Of Libra to the fleecy star that carries
Andromeda far off over the horizons
Of Atlantic seas; then he looks from
pole to pole
And without delay

Throws his rushing flight straight
down
Into the world's first lands, and
glides easily
Through the pure marble air on his
twisting path
Amongst countless stars, that seemed
like stars from a distance
But close up seemed other worlds,

Other worlds or happy islands
Like the legendary Hesperides of old,

Blessed fields and woods and flowery
valleys,
The islands that were thrice blessed,
but who lived there in happiness
He did not stop to ask: above them all
The golden sun, like Heaven in its
splendor,
Had caught his eye: he bends his path
towards it
Through the calm sky; but whether it
was up or down,
Centered or moving it was hard to
tell,
And it was hard to judge positions,
where the sun
Sits above the constellations

That from his Lordly eye keep distance due,
Dispenses Light from farr; they as they move
Thir Starry dance in numbers that compute
Days, months, and years, towards his all-chearing Lamp
Turn swift their various motions, or are turnd
By his Magnetic beam, that gently warms
The Univers, and to each inward part
With gentle penetration, though unseen,
Shoots invisible vertue even to the deep:
So wondrously was set his Station bright.
There lands the Fiend, a spot like which perhaps
Astronomer in the Sun's lucent Orbe
Through his glaz'd Optic Tube yet never saw.
The place he found beyond expression bright,
Compar'd with aught on Earth, Medal or Stone;
Not all parts like, but all alike informd
With radiant light, as glowing Iron with fire;
If mettal, part seemd Gold, part Silver cleer;
If stone, Carbuncle most or Chrysolite,
Rubie or Topaz, to the Twelve that shon
In AARONS Brest-plate, and a stone besides
Imagind rather oft then elsewhere seen,
That stone, or like to that which here below
Philosophers in vain so long have sought,
In vain, though by thir powerful Art they

Which keep a proper distance from his Lordly gaze
As he gives out his light from afar; as they move
Their starry dance measures
The days, the months and the years and they turn
Their orbits around his cheering light, or are turned
By his magnetic beam that gently warms
The universe, and to all the hidden parts
With gentle penetration, even though unseen,
Brings his invisible goodness even to the depths,
This was how he was magnificently set in his bright place.
There the devil landed, a spot which maybe
No astronomer, who looked at the sun's bright ball
Through his telescope, had ever seen.
He found the place bright beyond belief,
Compared to anything on earth, metal or stone;
Not all parts were the same, but they were all glowing
With radiant light, like iron taken from the fire;
If it was metal, some seemed like gold, some like silver;
If it was stone, it seemed to be red or green gemstone,
Ruby or Topaz, like the twelve that shone
In Aaron's breastplate, and also a stone
Which has often been imagined rather than seen anywhere else,
The one which here below,
Philosophers have so long looked for
In vain, even though with their

binde
Volatil HERMES, and call up unbound
In various shapes old PROTEUS from the Sea,
Draind through a Limbec to his Native forme.
What wonder then if fields and regions here
Breathe forth ELIXIR pure, and Rivers run
Potable Gold, when with one vertuous touch
Th' Arch-chimic Sun so farr from us remote
Produces with Terrestrial Humor mixt
Here in the dark so many precious things
Of colour glorious and effect so rare?
Here matter new to gaze the Devil met
Undazl'd, farr and wide his eye commands,
For sight no obstacle found here, nor shade,
But all Sun-shine, as when his Beams at Noon
Culminate from th' AEQUATOR, as they now
Shot upward still direct, whence no way round
Shadow from body opaque can fall, and the Aire,
No where so cleer, sharp'nd his visual ray
To objects distant farr, whereby he soon
Saw within kenn a glorious Angel stand,
The same whom JOHN saw also in the Sun:
His back was turnd, but not his brightness hid;
Of beaming sunnie Raies, a golden tiar
Circl'd his Head, nor less his Locks behind

powerful skills they control
Mercury, and can summon
In various shapes old Proteus from the sea,
Drained through their apparatus to his natural shape.
It is no surprise that the fields and lands here
Breath out pure balm, and the rivers run
With drinkable gold, when one touch
Of the sun, the first doctor, from so far away
Produces, here in our darkness, when mixed
With the things of the earth, so many precious things
With such glorious colors and amazing properties?
Here the devil saw things new to him
And undazzled he casts his gaze far and wide,
For there was no obstacle to sight here, nor shade;
All was sunshine, as when his beams at noon
Shot straight from the equator,
Going straight upwards, with no opaque bodies in the way
To create shadows, and the air,
More clear than anywhere else, sharpened his sight
So that he could see objects far off, and so he soon
Saw within his vision a glorious angel,
The same one St.John saw in his visions:
His back was turned but his brightness was not hidden;
A golden crown of sunbeams
Encircled his head, and his hair behind was no less gleaming

Illustrious on his Shoulders fledge with wings
Lay waving round; on som great charge imploy'd
Hee seemd, or fixt in cogitation deep.

Glad was the Spirit impure as now in hope

To find who might direct his wandring flight
To Paradise the happie seat of Man,

His journies end and our beginning woe.

But first he casts to change his proper shape,
Which else might work him danger or delay:
And now a stripling Cherube he appeers,

Not of the prime, yet such as in his face

Youth smil'd Celestial, and to every   Limb

Sutable grace diffus'd, so well he feignd;

Under a Coronet his flowing haire
In curles on either cheek plaid, wings he wore
Of many a colourd plume sprinkl'd with Gold,
His habit fit for speed succinct, and held

Before his decent steps a Silver wand.
He drew not nigh unheard, the Angel bright,

Ere he drew nigh, his radiant visage turnd,

Admonisht by his eare, and strait was known
Th' Arch-Angel URIEL, one of the seav'n
Who in Gods presence, neerest to his Throne

Stand ready at command, and are his Eyes

That run through all the Heav'ns, or

As it lay waving around on his shoulders
Which sprouted wings; he seemed to be employed
On some great task, or maybe lost in deep thought.

The impure Spirit was now glad, hoping

That he had found one who might direct his path
Down to Paradise, the happy home of Man,

The end of his journey and the beginning of our sorrow.

But first he works to disguise his real shape
Which might otherwise put him in danger or delay him;
And now he looks like a young Cherub,

Not of the highest order, but one in whom

Youth shone like the stars, and he gave every limb

Suitable grace, so well he disguised himself;

Under a coronet his flowing hair
Dropped in curls to his cheeks, and he wore wings
Of multicolored feathers sprinkled with gold,
He was dressed as one who travels fast,

And he carried a silver staff.
He did not approach unheard: the bright angel,

As he drew near turned his shining face,

Warned by his ears, and there stood
The archangel Uriel, one of the seven
Who stand in God's company, nearest to his throne,

Ready to do his bidding, and are his eyes

That run through the heavens or

110

down to th' Earth
Bear his swift errands over moist and dry,

O're Sea and Land: him SATAN thus accostes;

URIEL, for thou of those seav'n Spirits that stand
In sight of God's high Throne, gloriously bright,
The first art wont his great authentic will

Interpreter through highest Heav'n to bring,
Where all his Sons thy Embassie attend;
And here art likeliest by supream decre
Like honour to obtain, and as his Eye

To visit oft this new Creation round;
Unspeakable desire to see, and know
All these his wondrous works, but chiefly Man,
His chief delight and favour, him for whom
All these his works so wondrous he ordaind,
Hath brought me from the Quires of Cherubim
Alone thus wandring. Brightest Seraph tell

In which of all these shining Orbes hath Man
His fixed seat, or fixed seat hath none,

But all these shining Orbes his choice to dwell;
That I may find him, and with secret gaze,

Or open admiration him behold
On whom the great Creator hath bestowd
Worlds, and on whom hath all these graces powrd;
That both in him and all things, as is meet,

The Universal Maker we may praise;

Who justly hath drivn out his Rebell Foes

To deepest Hell, and to repair that loss

---

down to earth,
Doing his errands over wet and dry places,

Over the sea and the land: Satan spoke to him thus:

"Uriel, you are one of those seven who stand
By God's high throne, shining bright,
You are the one who brings his orders

Telling them to all in Heaven,
So that all His sons listen to you;
Most likely you are here at his orders
To do the same thing, and as God's eye

You will often visit this new world;
A burning desire to see and learn
About all these marvelous works, but mainly to know about Man,
His great delight, the one for whom
He made all these wondrous things,
Has brought me wandering alone

From the choirs of the Cherubim. Bright Angel,
Tell me, in which of these glittering balls has Man
Been housed, or has he no fixed abode,

And can take his choice of these glittering balls as his home;
I want to find him and either with a secret look

Or open admiration see the one
The great Creator has given
Planets, and has shown so much favor;
So that we can praise the universal Maker

For making him and all other things, as is suitable;

The one who rightly drove out his rebel enemies

To the depths of Hell, and to replace

Created this new happie Race of Men
To serve him better: wise are all his wayes.

So spake the false dissembler unperceivd;

For neither Man nor Angel can discern
Hypocrisie, the only evil that walks
Invisible, except to God alone,
By his permissive will, through Heav'n and Earth:
And oft though wisdom wake, suspicion sleeps
At wisdoms Gate, and to simplicitie

Resigns her charge, while goodness thinks no ill
Where no ill seems: Which now for once beguil'd
URIEL, though Regent of the Sun, and held

The sharpest sighted Spirit of all in Heav'n;

Who to the fraudulent Impostor foule
In his uprightness answer thus returnd.
Faire Angel, thy desire which tends to know
The works of God, thereby to glorifie
The great Work-Maister, leads to no excess
That reaches blame, but rather merits praise

The more it seems excess, that led thee hither
From thy Empyreal Mansion thus alone,

To witness with thine eyes what some perhaps
Contented with report heare onely in heav'n:

For wonderful indeed are all his works,
Pleasant to know, and worthiest to be all
Had in remembrance alwayes with delight;
But what created mind can comprehend
Thir number, or the wisdom infinite
That brought them forth, but hid thir causes deep.
I saw when at his Word the formless Mass,

them
Created this happy race of men
To serve him better; he is wise in everything."

So the deceitful liar spoke, unrecognized;

For neither man nor angel can see
Hypocrisy, the only evil that is
Invisible, except to God,
Who lets it walk through Heaven and Earth:
And though wisdom is often seen,

The wise are often not suspicious, and often
Are innocent, and the good do not see evil
When there is no reason to: and so was tricked
Uriel, though he had rule over the sun,
And was the most far seeing of all Heaven's spirits;
And he gave the evil impostor
This reply, trusting him.
"Fair Angel, your desire to know
Of God's work, and so to glorify
The great workman, is not something
That should be condemned, but rather should be praised,
The more you desire it, the instinct which led you
To come alone from your heavenly home
To see with your own eyes that which maybe some
Were happy to just hear reports of in Heaven:
All his works are indeed wonderful,
Pleasant to see, and it is right
To enjoy them;
But what mind can understand
Their number, or the infinite wisdom
Which made them, or what his purpose was?
I saw when he made the formless

This worlds material mould, came to a heap: *mass at his command Shape into this world:*

Confusion heard his voice, and wilde uproar *His voice was heard by confusion, and the wild storm*

Stood rul'd, stood vast infinitude confin'd; *Was controlled, the great infinite was tamed;*

Till at his second bidding darkness fled, *Until when he spoke again darkness fled,*

Light shon, and order from disorder sprung: *Light shone, and order came from anarchy:*

Swift to thir several Quarters hasted then *Quickly into their proper places fell*

The cumbrous Elements, Earth, Flood, Aire, Fire, *The clumsy elements of earth, water, air and fire,*

And this Ethereal quintessence of Heav'n *And the ethereal force of heaven*

Flew upward, spirited with various forms, *Made them fly upwards, changed into different shapes,*

That rowld orbicular, and turnd to Starrs *Rolling into balls and forming numberless*

Numberless, as thou seest, and how they move; *Stars, as you can see, and ordered their orbits;*

Each had his place appointed, each his course, *Each was allotted his place and his path,*

The rest in circuit walles this Universe. *To run around the walls of this universe.*

Look downward on that Globe whose hither side *Look down on that planet whose near side*

With light from hence, though but reflected, shines; *Shines with the light from here, though it is only a reflection;*

That place is Earth the seat of Man, that light *That place is Earth, the home of Man, that light*

His day, which else as th' other Hemisphere *Is his day, which otherwise would be covered with night*

Night would invade, but there the neighbouring Moon *As the other half is, but there the moon*

(So call that opposite fair Starr) her aide *(That is the name of the beautiful star opposite)*

Timely interposes, and her monthly round *Gives her help, and in her monthly journey*

Still ending, still renewing, through mid Heav'n; *Keeps waxing and waning through the middle sky;*

With borrowd light her countenance triform *With reflected light her changing shape*

Hence fills and empties to enlighten th' Earth, *Grows and shrinks to light up the earth*

And in her pale dominion checks the night.

That spot to which I point is PARADISE,

ADAMS abode, those loftie shades his Bowre.
Thy way thou canst not miss, me mine requires.
Thus said, he turnd, and SATAN bowing low,
As to superior Spirits is wont in Heaven,

Where honour due and reverence none neglects,
Took leave, and toward the coast of Earth beneath,
Down from th' Ecliptic, sped with hop'd success,
Throws his steep flight with many an Aerie wheele,
Nor staid, till on NIPHATES top he lights.

And with her pale power contains the night.
That place I'm pointing to is Paradise.
The home of Adam, those high trees are his dwelling.
You cannot mistake the path – mine now calls to me."
Having said this he turned away, and Satan bowed low,
Showing the respect to superior Spirits that is the custom in Heaven,
Where all show the reverence that honor deserves,
And left, and down towards the coast of Earth below,
Sped down from the sun, hoping for success,
Spiraling down in his steep flight,

Not stopping until he landed on the summit of Niphates.

114

BOOK IV

THE ARGUMENT

Satan now in prospect of Eden, and nigh the place where he must now attempt the bold enterprize which he undertook alone against God and Man, falls into many doubts with himself, and many passions, fear, envy, and despare; but at length confirms himself in evil, journeys on to Paradise, whose outward prospect and scituation is discribed, overleaps the bounds, sits in the shape of a Cormorant on the Tree of life, as highest in the Garden to look about him. The Garden describ'd; Satans first sight of Adam and Eve; his wonder at thir excellent form and happy state, but with resolution to work thir fall; overhears thir discourse, thence gathers that the Tree of knowledge was forbidden them to eat of, under penalty of death; and thereon intends to found his Temptation, by seducing them to transgress: then leaves them a while, to know further of thir descending on a Sun-beam warns Gabriel, who had in charge the Gate of Paradise, that some evil spirit had escap'd the Deep, and past at Noon by his Sphere in the shape of a good Angel down to Paradise, discovered after by his furious gestures in the Mount. Gabriel promises to find him ere morning. Night coming on, Adam and Eve discourse of going to thir rest: thir Bower describ'd; thir Evening worship. Gabriel drawing forth his Bands of Night-watch to walk the round of Paradise, appoints two strong Angels to Adams Bower, least the evill spirit should be there doing some harm to Adam or Eve sleeping; there they find him at the ear of Eve, tempting her in a dream, and bring him, though unwilling, to Gabriel; by whom question'd, he scornfully answers, prepares resistance, but hinder'd by a Sign from Heaven, flies out of Paradise.

Satan is now in sight of Eden, and the place where he must begin his bold mission against God and Man. He begins to doubt himself and suffers from fear, envy and despair. Eventually he accepts his evil nature, travels on to Paradise, whose outer walls and location are described, leaps over the walls and sits in the Tree of Knowledge like a cormorant to view the Garden. The Garden is described; Satan sees Adam and Eve for the first time. He wonders at their happiness and beauty but resolves that he will overthrow them. He hears them talking and discovers that they are forbidden from eating to the fruit of the Tree of Knowledge, under penalty of Death. He decides that this is how he will bring about their downfall, by tempting them to disobedience. Then he leaves them for a while to find out more about their lands. Meanwhile Uriel descends on a sunbeam and warns Gabriel, who guards the Gates of Paradise, that some evil Spirit had escaped from Hell and at noon had passed by the sun in the shape of a good angel and gone down to Paradise, where Uriel had seen his true nature in his furious gestures on Mount Niphates. Gabriel promises to find him before morning. Night comes and Adam and Eve talk of going to rest; their shelter is described and their evening worship. Gabriel sends his watchmen to patrol the walls of Paradise, and sends two strong angels to Adam's shelter, in case the evil spirit should be there doing them some harm as they sleep. They find him by Eve's ear, tempting her in a dream, and they bring him,

O For that warning voice, which he who saw	*Oh for that voice of warning, which he who saw*
Th' APOCALYPS, heard cry in Heaven aloud,	*The Apocalypse heard cry loud in Heaven,*
Then when the Dragon, put to second rout,	*When the Devil, beaten a second time,*
Came furious down to be reveng'd on men,	*Came down in anger to take revenge on men,*
WOE TO THE INHABITANTS ON EARTH! that now,	*"Sorrow to the inhabitants of Earth!" so that now,*
While time was, our first Parents had bin warnd	*While there was still time, our first parents could have been warned*
The coming of thir secret foe, and scap'd	*Of the coming of their secret enemy and perhaps*
Haply so scap'd his mortal snare; for now	*Might have escaped his deadly trap; for now*
SATAN, now first inflam'd with rage, came down,	*Satan, burning with rage, came down,*
The Tempter ere th' Accuser of man-kind,	*The tempter and the accuser of mankind,*
To wreck on innocent frail man his loss	*To punish innocent weak man for his defeat*
Of that first Battel, and his flight to Hell:	*In that first battle, and his flight to Hell:*
Yet not rejoycing in his speed, though bold,	*But he does not come revelling in his speed, though it is great;*
Far off and fearless, nor with cause to boast,	*Far off and fearless, without a cause,*
Begins his dire attempt, which nigh the birth	*He begins his terrible plan, which since he thought of it*
Now rowling, boiles in his tumultuous brest,	*Has been tumbling, boiling in his stormy heart,*
And like a devillish Engine back recoiles	*And like a Satanic cannon it recoils*
Upon himself; horror and doubt distract	*To harm him; fear and doubt run through*
His troubl'd thoughts, and from the bottom stir	*His troubled mind, and in his depths they stir up*
The Hell within him, for within him Hell	*The Hell within him, for he brings Hell with him,*
He brings, and round about him, nor from Hell	*It is all round him, and he cannot get one step farther*

117

One step no more then from himself can fly	*Away from Hell than he could get away from himself*
By change of place: Now conscience wakes despair	*By changing his location;now his conscience brings*
That slumberd, wakes the bitter memorie	*A despair which had been sleeping and a bitter memory*
Of what he was, what is, and what must be	*Of what he was, what he is and, worse, what he will be;*
Worse; of worse deeds worse sufferings must ensue.	*From worse deeds then worse suffering will follow.*
Sometimes towards EDEN which now in his view	*Sometimes he turned his sad, grieving gaze towards*
Lay pleasant, his grievd look he fixes sad,	*Eden, which he could now see, a pleasant land,*
Sometimes towards Heav'n and the full-blazing Sun	*Sometimes he looked towards Heaven and the blazing sun*
Which now sat high in his Meridian Towre:	*Which had risen up to high noon:*
Then much revolving, thus in sighs began.	*Then, still turning, he began in sadness:*
O thou that with surpassing Glory crownd,	*"Oh sun that is crowned with the greatest glory,*
Look'st from thy sole Dominion like the God	*You look over your kingdom like the God*
Of this new World; at whose sight all the Starrs	*Of this new world; at the sight of you all the stars*
Hide thir diminisht heads; to thee I call,	*Fade away; I'm speaking to you,*
But with no friendly voice, and add thy name	*But not in a friendly way, and I name you,*
O Sun, to tell thee how I hate thy beams	*Oh Sun, to tell you how I hate your light*
That bring to my remembrance from what state	*That reminds me of the place from which*
I fell, how glorious once above thy Spheare;	*I fell, up in glory once above you;*
Till Pride and worse Ambition threw me down	*Until pride and worse ambition overthrew me,*
Warring in Heav'n against Heav'ns matchless King:	*Fighting in Heaven against Heaven's incomparable King:*
Ah wherefore! he deservd no such return	*Ah, he did not deserve such behaviour*
From me, whom he created what I was In that bright eminence, and with his good	*From me, he who created me In that high bright place, and in his goodness*
Upbraided none; nor was his service hard.	*Punished nobody, and nor did he demand hard work.*
What could be less then to afford him,	*The least that one could do would be*

praise	*to praise him,*
The easiest recompence, and pay him thanks,	*The easiest repayment, and to give him thanks,*
How due! yet all his good prov'd ill in me,	*Which he certainly deserved!But all his goodness did not work on me,*
And wrought but malice; lifted up so high	*And only led to hatred; lifted up so high*
I sdeind subjection, and thought one step higher	*I rejected being his subject, and thought I could take just one step up*
Would set me highest, and in a moment quit	*And it would put me in the highest place, and in a moment*
The debt immense of endless gratitude,	*I could lose the debt of endless thanks*
So burthensome, still paying, still to ow;	*Which was so heavy and which one still owed however much one paid;*
Forgetful what from him I still receivd,	*I forgot the good things I was still getting from him,*
And understood not that a grateful mind	*And did not understand that a grateful mind*
By owing owes not, but still pays, at once	*Is cleared of its debt by being grateful, at the same moment*
Indebted and dischargd; what burden then?	*Given a debt and freed from it; what burden is there in that?*
O had his powerful Destiny ordaind	*If his great plan had created me*
Me some inferiour Angel, I had stood	*As some lower angel, I would have been*
Then happie; no unbounded hope had rais'd	*Happy; no great hope would have spurred*
Ambition. Yet why not? som other Power	*My ambition.But it might have happened all the same, some other power*
As great might have aspir'd, and me though mean	*Might have had the same great hopes, and I, though lowly,*
Drawn to his part; but other Powers as great	*Might have been drawn to his side; but the other powers of my rank*
Fell not, but stand unshak'n, from within	*Did not fall, but stand undisturbed, from within themselves*
Or from without, to all temptations arm'd.	*Or from outside, and can withstand all temptation.*
Hadst thou the same free Will and Power to stand?	*Did I have the same free will and the power to resist?*
Thou hadst: whom hast thou then or what to accuse,	*I did; then what can I find to blame?*
But Heav'ns free Love dealt equally to all?	*Only the free love of Heaven which was given equally to us all.*
Be then his Love accurst, since love or hate,	*I curse his love then, since love and*

Original	Modern
To me alike, it deals eternal woe.	*hate alike*
Nay curs'd be thou; since against his thy will	*Bring me eternal sorrow.*
Chose freely what it now so justly rues.	*No, I curse myself, since I chose freely to fight him,*
	The decision that I now so obviously regret.
Me miserable! which way shall I flie	*How miserable I am! Which way shall I go?*
Infinite wrauth, and infinite despaire?	*Shall I be eternally raging or eternally despairing?*
Which way I flie is Hell; my self am Hell;	*Wherever I go, I go to Hell; I am Hell,*
And in the lowest deep a lower deep	*And in the deepest pit another pit*
Still threatning to devour me opens wide,	*Opens wide, threatening to consume me,*
To which the Hell I suffer seems a Heav'n.	*And make the Hell I now suffer seem like Heaven.*
O then at last relent: is there no place	*Then I should give in: is there no chance left*
Left for Repentance, none for Pardon left?	*Of repentance and forgiveness?*
None left but by submission; and that word	*Only if I submit, and to do that I think*
DISDAIN forbids me, and my dread of shame	*Would be unworthy of me, and I could not face the shame*
Among the spirits beneath, whom I seduc'd	*Amongst the Spirits down below, whom I led astray*
With other promises and other vaunts	*With other promises and other boasts,*
Then to submit, boasting I could subdue	*Not by saying we would give in; I told them I could triumph*
Th' Omnipotent. Ay me, they little know	*Over the all powerful. Ah, they do not know*
How dearly I abide that boast so vaine,	*How much I regret that vain boast,*
Under what torments inwardly I groane;	*And how I am tortured inside;*
While they adore me on the Throne of Hell,	*As they worship me on the throne of Hell,*
With Diadem and Scepter high advanc'd	*Showing off my crown and sceptre,*
The lower still I fall, onely Supream	*I fall lower and lower, the only thing I am greatest in*
In miserie; such joy Ambition findes.	*Is misery; this is the happiness which ambition brings.*
But say I could repent and could obtaine	*But what if I could repent and by that act of grace*
By Act of Grace my former state; how soon	*Return to my former state; how quickly*
Would highth recal high thoughts, how soon unsay	*Would a high position bring back those high thoughts, how soon would*

120

What feign'd submission swore: ease would recant
Vows made in pain, as violent and void.

For never can true reconcilement grow
Where wounds of deadly hate have peirc'd so deep:
Which would but lead me to a worse relapse
And heavier fall: so should I purchase deare

Short intermission bought with double smart.
This knows my punisher; therefore as farr

From granting hee, as I from begging peace:
All hope excluded thus, behold in stead

Of us out-cast, exil'd, his new delight,
Mankind created, and for him this World.

So farwel Hope, and with Hope farwel Fear,

Farwel Remorse: all Good to me is lost;

Evil be thou my Good; by thee at least
Divided Empire with Heav'ns King I hold

By thee, and more then half perhaps will reigne;
As Man ere long, and this new World. shall know
Thus while he spake, each passion dimm'd his face
Thrice chang'd with pale, ire, envie and despair,
Which marrd his borrow'd visage, and betraid
Him counterfet, if any eye beheld.

For heav'nly mindes from such distempers foule
Are ever cleer. Whereof hee soon aware,

I go back
On my pretence of swearing submission? In ease I would take back
Promises made under duress, as being invalid, caused by pain.
True reconciliation can never occur,
When the wounds of hate run so deep:
I would rebel, worse than before,

And get a worse punishment: so I would pay dearly
For a short break with double pain.
My punisher knows this, so as far as he is
From granting peace, that's how far I am from asking for it:
So all hope is gone, and I see, instead of we
Whom he has thrown out, his new joy,
Mankind, and the world he has made for him.
So farewell to hope, and with hope farewell to fear,
Farewell regret; all goodness is lost for me,
Evil will be my good; with evil I at least rule over part of the universe,
And with evil maybe I will gain power over the rest,
As Man and this new world will find out very soon."
While he spoke these words, each emotion ran across his face,
Going pale three times with envy, anger and despair,
Spoiling his disguised face and showing
That he was a fake, if there had been anyone to see him.
Heavenly minds are eternally free
Of such disturbances. As soon as he realised what he was doing

Each perturbation smooth'd with outward calme,	*He assumed a calm look,*
Artificer of fraud; and was the first	*That deceitful craftsman; he was the first*
That practisd falshood under saintly shew,	*To practise deceit under a cloak of goodness,*
Deep malice to conceale, couch't with revenge:	*Hiding his great hatred and desire for revenge:*
Yet not anough had practisd to deceive	*But he was not good enough to deceive*
URIEL once warnd; whose eye pursu'd him down	*Uriel, once he had been spotted; his gaze followed him*
The way he went, and on th' ASSYRIAN mount	*As he went down, and on the Assyrian mountain*
Saw him disfigur'd, more then could befall	*He saw him changed, more than a good Spirit*
Spirit of happie sort: his gestures fierce	*Could be: he noticed his fierce gestures*
He markd and mad demeanour, then alone,	*And his raging attitude when he thought*
As he suppos'd, all unobserv'd, unseen.	*He was alone, unobserved.*
So on he fares, and to the border comes	*So he travels on, and comes to the border*
Of EDEN, where delicious Paradise,	*Of Eden, where beautiful Paradise,*
Now nearer, Crowns with her enclosure green,	*Nearer now, wraps a green fence around her,*
As with a rural mound the champain head	*As on a country hill, where there is open ground*
Of a steep wilderness, whose hairie sides	*At the top of a steep wilderness, the hillsides*
With thicket overgrown, grottesque and wilde,	*All overgrown with tangled wild thickets,*
Access deni'd; and over head up grew	*Blocking access; and overhead there grew*
Insuperable highth of loftiest shade,	*To unreachable height great trees,*
Cedar, and Pine, and Firr, and branching Palm,	*Cedar, pine, fir and spreading palm.*
A Silvan Scene, and as the ranks ascend	*A woodland scene, and as the rows climb up,*
Shade above shade, a woodie Theatre	*Tree after tree, they make a forest theatre,*
Of stateliest view. Yet higher then thir tops	*Wonderful to see.But even higher than their tops*
The verdurous wall of Paradise up sprung:	*Rose the green wall of Paradise*
Which to our general Sire gave prospect large	*Which gave Adam a wide view*

Into his neather Empire neighbouring round.
And higher then that Wall a circling row

Of goodliest Trees loaden with fairest Fruit,

Blossoms and Fruits at once of golden hue
Appeerd, with gay enameld colours mixt:

On which the Sun more glad impress'd his
beams
Then in fair Evening Cloud, or humid Bow,

When God hath showrd the earth; so
lovely seemd
That Lantskip: And of pure now purer aire

Meets his approach, and to the heart inspires
Vernal delight and joy, able to drive
All sadness but despair: now gentle gales

Fanning thir odoriferous wings dispense

Native perfumes, and whisper whence
they stole
Those balmie spoiles. As when to them
who saile
Beyond the CAPE OF HOPE, and now
are past
MOZAMBIC, off at Sea North-East
windes blow
SABEAN Odours from the spicie shoare
Of ARABIE the blest, with such delay
Well pleas'd they slack thir course, and
many a League
Cheard with the grateful smell old Ocean
smiles.
So entertaind those odorous sweets the
Fiend
Who came thir bane, though with them
better pleas'd
Then ASMODEUS with the fishie fume,

That drove him, though enamourd, from
the Spouse
Of TOBITS Son, and with a vengeance sent

Around the boundaries of his empire.
Higher than that wall there was an
encircling row
Of the most beautiful trees, loaded
with the loveliest fruit,
Golden flowers and fruits
Appeared, a mixture of bright gay
colors:
The sun devoted to them greater
beams
Than to the fair clouds of evening, or
to the rainbow
When God first gave rain to the
earth, so lovely
That landscape was: and now the air
gets even more pure
As he approaches, and fills the heart
With the joy of Spring, driving out
All sorrow and despair: now soft
breezes,
Fanning their scented wings,
dispense
Native perfumes, and tell of where

They got these sweet scents.As when
those who sail
Beyond the Cape of Good Hope, and
are now
past Mozambique, smell the scents of
Arabia
Carried on the northeast winds
And are pleased to be delayed,
And rest on their journey, and for
many miles
The old Ocean is made beautiful by
the wonderful scent.
This was how the sweet smells came
to the fiend
Who came to destroy them, though
they were pleasing
Than the fishy scent was to
Asmodeus,
Which drove him away, although he
was attracted, from the wife
Of Tobit's son, and sent him with
vengeance

From MEDIA post to AEGYPT, there fast bound.	*From Media to Egypt in chains.*
Now to th' ascent of that steep savage Hill	*Now Satan had travelled, slow and watchful,*
SATAN had journied on, pensive and slow;	*To the climb of that steep hill;*
But further way found none, so thick entwin'd,	*But he could not find a way through, so thick*
As one continu'd brake, the undergrowth	*Was the undergrowth of shrubs and bushes*
Of shrubs and tangling bushes had perplex	*Which seemed to be one solid mass which blocked*
All path of Man or Beast that past that way:	*The way of any Man or beast that tried to journey there:*
One Gate there onely was, and that look'd East	*There was only one entrance, that faced east*
On th' other side: which when th' arch-fellon saw	*On the other side. When the great thief saw*
Due entrance he disdaind, and in contempt,	*The proper entrance he rejected it with contempt*
At one slight bound high overleap'd all bound	*And with one leap cleared the boundaries*
Of Hill or highest Wall, and sheer within	*Of the hill and high walls, and completely inside*
Lights on his feet. As when a prowling Wolfe,	*Landed on his feet. He was like a prowling wolf*
Whom hunger drives to seek new haunt for prey,	*Whose hunger makes him seek out new areas for prey,*
Watching where Shepherds pen thir Flocks at eve	*Watching where shepherds lock up their flocks*
In hurdl'd Cotes amid the field secure,	*In barred pens in walled fields,*
Leaps o're the fence with ease into the Fould:	*And easily leaps the fence into the middle of the flock;*
Or as a Thief bent to unhoord the cash	*Or like the thief who plans to take the cash*
Of some rich Burgher, whose substantial dores,	*Of some rich businessman; his great doors,*
Cross-barrd and bolted fast, fear no assault,	*Barred and bolted, cannot be overcome, and so the thief*
In at the window climbes, or o're the tiles;	*Climbs in at the window, or over the roof;*
So clomb this first grand Thief into Gods Fould:	*This is how the first great thief climbed into God's flock,*
So since into his Church lewd Hirelings climbe.	*Just as later mercenary people climbed into His church.*
Thence up he flew, and on the Tree of Life,	*From there he flew up, and on the*

	Tree of Life,
The middle Tree and highest there that grew,	*The central, highest tree,*
Sat like a Cormorant; yet not true Life	*He sat like a cormorant; he did not regain true life*
Thereby regaind, but sat devising Death	*From the tree, but sat plotting death*
To them who liv'd; nor on the vertue thought	*For the living; nor did he think of the qualities*
Of that life-giving Plant, but only us'd	*Of that life-giving plant, but just used it*
For prospect, what well us'd had bin the pledge	*As a viewpoint, that which was the symbol*
Of immortalitie. So little knows	*Of eternal life. So none*
Any, but God alone, to value right	*Except for God know how to treasure*
The good before him, but perverts best things	*The good things before them, but twist the best things*
To worst abuse, or to thir meanest use.	*And harm them or use them to do evil.*
Beneath him with new wonder now he views	*Beneath him with fresh wonder he sees*
To all delight of human sense expos'd	*Laid out for the delight of Mankind*
In narrow room Natures whole wealth, yea more,	*In that narrow place all of Nature's treasures, and more,*
A Heaven on Earth, for blissful Paradise	*A Heaven on Earth, for the garden was a wonderful*
Of God the Garden was, by him in the East	*Paradise of God, planted by him to the East of Eden;*
Of EDEN planted; EDEN stretchd her Line	*Eden stretched her borders*
From AURAN Eastward to the Royal Towrs	*From Harran east to the royal towers*
Of great SELEUCIA, built by GRECIAN Kings,	*Of great Selucia, built by the kings of Greece,*
Or where the Sons of EDEN long before	*And to where mankind had long ago lived*
Dwelt in TELASSAR: in this pleasant soile	*In Telassar: in this pleasant soil*
His farr more pleasant Garden God ordaind;	*God laid out his far more pleasant garden;*
Out of the fertil ground he caus'd to grow	*From the fertile ground he grew*
All Trees of noblest kind for sight, smell, taste;	*All the best trees for sight, smell and fruit,*
And all amid them stood the Tree of Life,	*And in the middle stood the Tree of Life,*
High eminent, blooming Ambrosial Fruit	*Rising above all, bearing the sweetest golden fruit;*
Of vegetable Gold; and next to Life	*And next to the Tree of Life*
Our Death the Tree of Knowledge grew	*Grew our Death, the Tree of*

fast by, Knowledge of Good bought dear by knowing ill. Southward through EDEN went a River large, Nor chang'd his course, but through the shaggie hill Pass'd underneath ingulft, for God had thrown That Mountain as his Garden mould high rais'd Upon the rapid current, which through veins Of porous Earth with kindly thirst up drawn, Rose a fresh Fountain, and with many a rill Waterd the Garden; thence united fell	Knowledge, Which would bring good at a great price through knowledge of evil. South through Eden there ran a large river, Which did not bend but through the forested hill Passed underneath, for God had thrown That mountain down, as the base for his garden, On top of the swift river, and through the veins Of the porous earth, drawn up by a sweet thirst, There rose a new spring, and with many little streams It watered the garden; then they joined together
Down the steep glade, and met the neather Flood, Which from his darksom passage now appeers, And now divided into four main Streams, Runs divers, wandring many a famous Realme And Country whereof here needs no account, But rather to tell how, if Art could tell, How from that Saphire Fount the crisped Brooks, Rowling on Orient Pearl and sands of Gold, With mazie error under pendant shades Ran Nectar, visiting each plant, and fed Flours worthy of Paradise which not nice Art In Beds and curious Knots, but Nature boon Powrd forth profuse on Hill and Dale and Plaine, Both where the morning Sun first warmly	Running through the steep wood, and met the river On the other side as it emerged from the darkness, And split into four main rivers, Running away into many famous lands, And countries which need no description here; I would rather tell, if my skill could manage it, How from that sapphire spring the sparkling brooks, Rolling on oriental pearls and sands of gold Wandered under the hanging branches, Running with nectar, visiting each plant, feeding Flowers worthy of Paradise, not arranged fussily In beds and curious shapes, but naturally Bursting out thickly on hills, valleys and plains, Both in the open fields where the sun

smote
The open field, and where the unpierc't shade
Imbround the noontide Bowrs: Thus was this place,
A happy rural seat of various view;
Groves whose rich Trees wept odorous Gumms and Balme,
Others whose fruit burnisht with Golden Rinde
Hung amiable, HESPERIAN Fables true,

If true, here onely, and of delicious taste:

Betwixt them Lawns, or level Downs, and Flocks
Grasing the tender herb, were interpos'd,
Or palmie hilloc, or the flourie lap

Of som irriguous Valley spread her store,
Flours of all hue, and without Thorn the Rose:
Another side, umbrageous Grots and Caves

Of coole recess, o're which the mantling Vine
Layes forth her purple Grape, and gently creeps
Luxuriant; mean while murmuring waters fall
Down the slope hills, disperst, or in a Lake,

That to the fringed Bank with Myrtle crownd,
Her chrystall mirror holds, unite thir streams.
The Birds thir quire apply; aires, vernal aires,
Breathing the smell of field and grove, attune
The trembling leaves, while Universal PAN

Knit with the GRACES and the HOURS in dance
Led on th' Eternal Spring. Not that faire field

first touched warm
In the morning and in the dark places amongst the trees
Which are dark even at noon: this was how that place was,
A happy country with many aspects;
Groves whose trees ran with scented gums and ointments,
Others whose fruit, wrapped in golden skin
Hung beautiful, bringing the myths of Hesperus to life,
Even if only in this place, and they had a delicious taste:
Between them were lawns, level downs and flocks
Grazing on the sweet grass,
There were palm covered hills and fertile
Spreading valleys,
Flowers of all colors, and roses without thorns:
On another side there were shady caves and grottoes
Giving cool shelter, round which the vine like a cloak
Lays out her purple grapes, creeping
Abundantly; meanwhile murmuring streams
Fall down the hillsides, spreading or uniting in a lake
That holds her clear mirror to
The myrtle-lined bank.
The birds sing their song; music, spring music,
Imbued with the smell of fields and groves
Runs through the trembling leaves, while Nature
Leads the seasons and fertility in a dance
To bring on the eternal spring. Not the fair field

Of ENNA, where PROSERPIN gathring flours
Her self a fairer Floure by gloomie DIS

Was gatherd, which cost CERES all that pain
To seek her through the world; nor that sweet Grove
Of DAPHNE by ORONTES, and th' inspir'd
CASTALIAN Spring might with this Paradise
Of EDEN strive; nor that NYSEIAN Ile
Girt with the River TRITON, where old CHAM,
Whom Gentiles AMMON call and LIBYAN JOVE,
Hid AMALTHEA and her Florid Son
Young BACCHUS from his Stepdame RHEA'S eye;
Nor where ABASSIN Kings thir issue Guard,
Mount AMARA, though this by som suppos'd
True Paradise under the ETHIOP Line

By NILUS head, enclos'd with shining Rock,
A whole dayes journey high, but wide remote
From this ASSYRIAN Garden, where the Fiend
Saw undelighted all delight, all kind

Of living Creatures new to sight and strange:
Two of far nobler shape erect and tall,

Godlike erect, with native Honour clad

In naked Majestie seemd Lords of all,

And worthie seemd, for in thir looks Divine

The image of thir glorious Maker shon,

Of Enna, where Proserpine was gathering flowers
(Herself a fairer flower) and was kidnapped
To the gloomy underworld, causing Ceres all the labour
Of searching the world for her, nor the sweet gardens
Of Daphne by the Orontes nor the marvellous Castillian Spring
Could compete with this paradise
Of Eden; not the Nyseian Isle,
Surrounded by the river Triton, where old Cham,
Whom the Gentiles call Ammon and Lybian Jove,
Hid Almathea and her ruddy son
Young Bacchus from the sight of his stepmother Rhea;
Nor where the Kings of Abyssinia keep their children
On Mount Amara, even though some think
This is where Paradise is, under the equator
By the head of the Nile, enclosed in a shining rock
Which it takes a day to climb, but that is far
From this Assyrian garden where the devil
Saw without pleasure all these delights, all kinds
Of strange living creatures, never seen before:
There were two who were of noble shape, erect and tall,
As straight as Gods, dressed as Nature intended,
In their naked majesty they seemed Lords of all
And to deserve that title, for in their divine faces
Could be seen the image of their glorious maker,

Truth, Wisdome, Sanctitude severe and pure,
Severe, but in true filial freedom plac't;
Whence true autoritie in men; though both
Not equal, as thir sex not equal seemd;
For contemplation hee and valour formd,
For softness shee and sweet attractive Grace,
Hee for God only, shee for God in him:

His fair large Front and Eye sublime declar'd
Absolute rule; and Hyacinthin Locks
Round from his parted forelock manly hung
Clustring, but not beneath his shoulders broad:
Shee as a vail down to the slender waste
Her unadorned golden tresses wore
Dissheveld, but in wanton ringlets wav'd
As the Vine curles her tendrils, which impli'd
Subjection, but requir'd with gentle sway,
And by her yeilded, by him best receivd,
Yeilded with coy submission, modest pride,
And sweet reluctant amorous delay.
Nor those mysterious parts were then conceald,
Then was not guiltie shame, dishonest shame
Of natures works, honor dishonorable,
Sin-bred, how have ye troubl'd all mankind
With shews instead, meer shews of seeming pure,
And banisht from mans life his happiest life,
Simplicitie and spotless innocence.

Shining with truth, wisdom, strong and pure faith,
Strong but with the freedom of children;
From here come mankind's true powers, though
They were not equal, as their sexes were different;
He was made for thought and action,
She for softness and beautiful grace,
He for God and she for the God in him:

His strapping shape and heavenly eye spoke of
Total rule; and his curling hair
Hung in manly fashion down from his forehead parting,
Thick, but not falling below his broad shoulders:
She wore her unornamented golden tresses
Down to her slender waist like a veil,
Undressed, curled into ringlets
Like the vine curls its branches: it was implied
That she was his subject, but it was asked with gentle persuasion,
And he liked it best when he gave her consent,
Consenting with shy submission, modest pride,
And a sweet loving hesitancy.
Nor were their genitals hidden,
From guilty, impure shame
At the work of nature: dishonourable honor,
Bred from sin, how you have pushed all mankind
Into shows instead, mere shows of being pure,
And taken from man's life his greatest happiness,
Simplicity and spotless innocence.

So passd they naked on, nor shund the sight	So they passed on, naked, and they did not shy at the sight
Of God or Angel, for they thought no ill:	Of God or angels, for they could not imagine evil:
So hand in hand they passd, the lovliest pair	So hand in hand they passed, the loveliest pair
That ever since in loves imbraces met,	That ever met in love's embrace,
ADAM the goodliest man of men since borne	Adam, the best man of all those who came after him,
His Sons, the fairest of her Daughters EVE.	Eve the best of all the women.
Under a tuft of shade that on a green	Under a shady tree that stood rustling softly
Stood whispering soft, by a fresh Fountain side	In a meadow, beside a fresh spring
They sat them down, and after no more toil	They sat down, after having worked
Of thir sweet Gardning labour then suffic'd	At the garden no harder than was needed
To recommend coole ZEPHYR, and made ease	For them to enjoy the cooling breeze, and made rest
More easie, wholsom thirst and appetite	More restful, wholesome thirst and hunger
More grateful, to thir Supper Fruits they fell,	More pleasant to feed, and they started on their meal of fruit,
Nectarine Fruits which the compliant boughs	Nectarines which the bending branches
Yeilded them, side-long as they sat recline	Held out to their sides as they lay
On the soft downie Bank damaskt with flours:	On the soft bank which was embroidered with flowers:
The savourie pulp they chew, and in the rinde	They chew on the tasty flesh, and as they were still thirsty
Still as they thirsted scoop the brimming stream;	Used the skin to scoop up water;
Nor gentle purpose, nor endearing smiles	They were not lacking in gentle conversation and sweet smiles,
Wanted, nor youthful dalliance as beseems	Nor playful joking as is fitting
Fair couple, linkt in happie nuptial League,	For a fair couple, joined in happy marriage,
Alone as they. About them frisking playd	In private as they were. Around them gambolled
All Beasts of th' Earth, since wilde, and of all chase	All the beasts of Earth, which have since turned wild
In Wood or Wilderness, Forrest or Den;	And hunt in the woods and wilderness, forest and dens;
Sporting the Lion rampd, and in his paw	Playfully the lion reared up, and in his paw
Dandl'd the Kid; Bears, Tygers, Ounces,	Rocked a baby goat; bears, tigers,

Pards
Gambold before them, th' unwieldy Elephant
To make them mirth us'd all his might, & wreathd
His Lithe Proboscis; close the Serpent sly

Insinuating, wove with Gordian twine
His breaded train, and of his fatal guile

Gave proof unheeded; others on the grass

Coucht, and now fild with pasture gazing sat,
Or Bedward ruminating: for the Sun

Declin'd was hasting now with prone carreer
To th' Ocean Iles, and in th' ascending Scale

Of Heav'n the Starrs that usher Evening rose:
When SATAN still in gaze, as first he stood,
Scarce thus at length faild speech recoverd sad.
O Hell! what doe mine eyes with grief behold,
Into our room of bliss thus high advanc't

Creatures of other mould, earth-born perhaps,
Not Spirits, yet to heav'nly Spirits bright

Little inferior; whom my thoughts pursue
With wonder, and could love, so lively shines
In them Divine resemblance, and such grace
The hand that formd them on thir shape hath pourd.
Ah gentle pair, yee little think how nigh
Your change approaches, when all these delights
Will vanish and deliver ye to woe,

---

lynx and leopard
Danced before them, and to amuse them the clumsy elephant
Showed off his strength and waved

His flexible trunk; close by the sly serpent
Crept, wove himself into knots
And braided his tail, showing his deadly cunning
But seen by none; others lay on the grass
Filled with grazing and watching the view
Or chewing the cud as they made their way to sleep, for the sun
Was setting, speeding straight down

To the ocean islands, and on the rising side
Of Heaven's balance the evening stars climbed up:
Then Satan, still gazing from where he had first stood,
Could hardly speak for sadness.

"Oh Hell! What do my sad eyes see?

Into our place have come

Creatures of another shape, made of earth perhaps,
Not spirits, but not much inferior to the bright
Heavenly Spirits; I look upon them
With wonder, and I could love them,

They so closely resemble God, and the hand that
Made them has given them such beauty.
Ah, gentle pair, little do you know
The change that is soon coming, when all these joys
Will vanish and be replaced by sorrow,

More woe, the more your taste is now of joy;
Happie, but for so happie ill secur'd

Long to continue, and this high seat your Heav'n
Ill fenc't for Heav'n to keep out such a foe

As now is enterd; yet no purpos'd foe

To you whom I could pittie thus forlorne
Though I unpittied: League with you I seek,

And mutual amitie so streight, so close,

That I with you must dwell, or you with me

Henceforth; my dwelling haply may not please
Like this fair Paradise, your sense, yet such
Accept your Makers work; he gave it me,

Which I as freely give; Hell shall unfould,

To entertain you two, her widest Gates,
And send forth all her Kings; there will be room,
Not like these narrow limits, to receive

Your numerous ofspring; if no better place,

Thank him who puts me loath to this revenge
On you who wrong me not for him who wrongd.
And should I at your harmless innocence

Melt, as I doe, yet public reason just,
Honour and Empire with revenge enlarg'd,

By conquering this new World, compels me now
To do what else though damnd I should abhorre.
So spake the Fiend, and with necessitie,

More sorrow than you have joy at present:
You are happy, but your happiness is not well enough protected
To last for long, and this country, your Heaven,
Heaven did not fence in well enough to keep out an enemy
Such as has now entered; but I am no enemy to you
Whom I could pity in your weakness,
Though nobody pities me: I want a pact with you,
A mutual friendship so strong, so close,
That I must live with you, or you with me
From now on. My home may not please you
As much as this fair Paradise,
But you will have to accept your maker's work: he gave it to me
And I shall just as freely give it to you; hell shall open
For your welcome her widest gates,
And send out all her Kings to greet you.There will be space,
Not like in this narrow space, to welcome
All your children; if you don't like the place,

Blame the one who has made me take this revenge
On you: the fault is his.
I confess that I am touched by your harmless innocence,
But the greater good demands
That we take our revenge by enlarging our empire
By conquering this new world, which makes me now do
Something which otherwise, even though damned, I would hate."
So the fiend spoke, and used

The Tyrants plea, excus'd his devilish deeds.

Then from his loftie stand on that high Tree

Down he alights among the sportful Herd
Of those fourfooted kindes, himself now one,

Now other, as thir shape servd best his end

Neerer to view his prey, and unespi'd

To mark what of thir state he more might learn
By word or action markt: about them round

A Lion now he stalkes with fierie glare,

Then as a Tiger, who by chance hath spi'd
In some Purlieu two gentle Fawnes at play,

Strait couches close, then rising changes oft

His couchant watch, as one who chose his ground
Whence rushing he might surest seise them both
Grip't in each paw: when ADAM first of men
To first of women EVE thus moving speech,
Turnd him all eare to heare new utterance flow.

Sole partner and sole part of all these joyes,

Dearer thy self then all; needs must the Power
That made us, and for us this ample World

Be infinitly good, and of his good

As liberal and free as infinite,
That rais'd us from the dust and plac't us here
In all this happiness, who at his hand

---

necessity, the excuse
Of tyrants, to explain his devilish deeds.
Then from his high perch on that tall tree
He landed amongst the playful throng
Of animals, making himself one

Then another as their shape suited him best
For the purpose of approaching his prey, and unseen
To see what more he could learn about them
By observing their speech and actions: now he stalks
Around them as a lion with a fierce stare,
Then as a tiger who has come across
Two gentle fawns playing in a meadow,
Keeping low to the ground, then rising to often change
His point of view, as one who chooses a position
From which he can be surest of catching them both with a rush,
One in each paw: when Adam, first man,
Spoke to Eve, first woman,
He pricked his ears to hear what was said.

"My only partner and sharer of these joys,
Who is dearer to me than all the rest, the power
That made us, and made this world for us, must be
Infinitely good, and be infinitely generous
With his gifts,
For he made us from the dust and placed us here
In all this beauty, though we

Have nothing merited, nor can performe	*Have done nothing to earn it, nor can we do*
Aught whereof hee hath need, hee who requires	*Any service he might need, and he asks*
From us no other service then to keep	*Nothing from us except that we obey*
This one, this easie charge, of all the Trees	*The one simple rule, that of all the trees*
In Paradise that beare delicious fruit	*Of Paradise that bear delicious fruit*
So various, not to taste that onely Tree	*Of such variety, that we only do not eat from the Tree*
Of knowledge, planted by the Tree of Life,	*Of Knowledge, which is planted by the Tree of Life.*
So neer grows Death to Life, what ere Death is,	*Death grows right next to life, whatever Death is,*
Som dreadful thing no doubt; for well thou knowst	*Something terrible, no doubt, for you know well*
God hath pronounc't it death to taste that Tree,	*That God has proclaimed sentence of Death if we eat from that tree,*
The only sign of our obedience left	*The only symbol of our subjecthood left*
Among so many signes of power and rule	*Amongst so many signs of power and rule*
Conferrd upon us, and Dominion giv'n	*Which he has given us, as well as the mastery*
Over all other Creatures that possesse	*Of all the other creatures*
Earth, Aire, and Sea. Then let us not think hard	*Of the Earth, air and sea. So let us not think it hard*
One easie prohibition, who enjoy	*That he has made one easy to obey rule, we who enjoy*
Free leave so large to all things else, and choice	*So much freedom in everything else, and have*
Unlimited of manifold delights:	*An unlimited choice of so many pleasures:*
But let us ever praise him, and extoll	*But let us always praise him, and give thanks*
His bountie, following our delightful task	*For his bounty, and keep to our sweet task*
To prune these growing Plants, & tend these Flours,	*Of pruning the plants and tending the flowers,*
Which were it toilsom, yet with thee were sweet.	*Which even if it were hard work would be sweet as I do it with you."*
To whom thus Eve repli'd. O thou for whom	*Eve answered him thus: "Oh you for whom*
And from whom I was formd flesh of thy flesh,	*And from whom I was made from your flesh,*

And without whom am to no end, my Guide	*And without whom I have no purpose, my guide*
And Head, what thou hast said is just and right.	*And master, what you have said is right and true.*
For wee to him indeed all praises owe,	*For we do indeed owe all praise to him,*
And daily thanks, I chiefly who enjoy	*And daily thanks, especially me*
So farr the happier Lot, enjoying thee	*Who has the greater fortune, enjoying you*
Preeminent by so much odds, while thou	*Who is so much greater than me, while you*
Like consort to thy self canst no where find.	*Do not have a companion who is equal to you.*
That day I oft remember, when from sleep	*I often remember the day, when I first*
I first awak't, and found my self repos'd	*Awoke from my sleep, and found I was lying*
Under a shade on flours, much wondring where	*In the shade amongst the flowers, wondering where*
And what I was, whence thither brought, and how.	*And what I was, where I had come from and how I was brought here.*
Not distant far from thence a murmuring sound	*Not far away I heard the murmuring sound*
Of waters issu'd from a Cave and spread	*Of waters flowing from a cave which spread*
Into a liquid Plain, then stood unmov'd	*Into a great lake and stood calm,*
Pure as th' expanse of Heav'n; I thither went	*As pure as the sky; I went there,*
With unexperienc't thought, and laid me downe	*Not knowing what I was doing, and laid down*
On the green bank, to look into the cleer	*On the green bank, to look into the clear*
Smooth Lake, that to me seemd another Skie.	*Smooth lake, which seemed to me like another sky.*
As I bent down to look, just opposite,	*As I bent over to look, opposite me*
A Shape within the watry gleam appeerd	*Another shape appeared in the water,*
Bending to look on me, I started back,	*Bending to look at me; I jumped back,*
It started back, but pleasd I soon returnd,	*And it did too, but pleased by it I soon came back*
Pleas'd it returnd as soon with answering looks	*And was pleased that it came back and returned my looks*
Of sympathie and love, there I had fixt	*Of sympathy and love: I would still be looking now,*
Mine eyes till now, and pin'd with vain desire,	*Pining with vain desire,*
Had not a voice thus warnd me, What thou seest,	*If a voice had not warned me, 'What you see*

What there thou seest fair Creature is thy self,
With thee it came and goes: but follow me,

And I will bring thee where no shadow staies
Thy coming, and thy soft imbraces, hee

Whose image thou art, him thou shall enjoy

Inseparablie thine, to him shalt beare

Multitudes like thy self, and thence be call'd

Mother of human Race: what could I doe,

But follow strait, invisibly thus led?

Till I espi'd thee, fair indeed and tall,
Under a Platan, yet methought less faire,

Less winning soft, less amiablie milde,
Then that smooth watry image; back
I turnd,
Thou following cryd'st aloud, Return fair EVE,
Whom fli'st thou? whom thou fli'st, of him thou art,

His flesh, his bone; to give thee being I lent

Out of my side to thee, neerest my heart

Substantial Life, to have thee by my side
Henceforth an individual solace dear;
Part of my Soul I seek thee, and thee claim

My other half: with that thy gentle hand

Seisd mine, I yeilded, and from that time see
How beauty is excelld by manly grace

And wisdom, which alone is truly fair.

There, you fair creature, is yourself,

It comes and goes as you do; but follow me,

And I will take you where no ghost

Awaits you and your soft embraces, to him

In whose image you are made, you shall enjoy him

As your own, inseperable, and you shall bear him

Many like yourself, and you shall be called

The mother of the human race. 'What could I do

But straight away follow my invisible guide?

Then I saw you, beautiful and tall,
Under a plane tree, but I thought you not as lovely,

Less soft and sweetly friendly,
Than that smooth image in the water;
I turned back,

And following me you cried aloud,
'Come back fair Eve,

Who are you running from? The one you run from is the one you were made from,

His flesh and bone; to make you I gave

A rib from my side, by my heart, to give you

Real life, to have you by my side
As my dear comfort;
I look for part of my soul in you, and you have a right

To part of mine.' Saying that your gentle hand

Took mine, I yielded, and since then I have seen
How my beauty is excelled by your manly grace

And wisdom, the only truly beautiful things."

So spake our general Mother, and with eyes
Of conjugal attraction unreprov'd,
And meek surrender, half imbracing leand
On our first Father, half her swelling Breast
Naked met his under the flowing Gold
Of her loose tresses hid: he in delight
Both of her Beauty and submissive Charms
Smil'd with superior Love, as JUPITER
On JUNO smiles, when he impregns the Clouds
That shed MAY Flowers; and press'd her Matron lip
With kisses pure: aside the Devil turnd
For envie, yet with jealous leer maligne
Ey'd them askance, and to himself thus plaind.
Sight hateful, sight tormenting! thus these two
Imparadis't in one anothers arms
The happier EDEN, shall enjoy thir fill
Of bliss on bliss, while I to Hell am thrust,
Where neither joy nor love, but fierce desire,
Among our other torments not the least,
Still unfulfill'd with pain of longing pines;
Yet let me not forget what I have gain'd
From thir own mouths; all is not theirs it seems:
One fatal Tree there stands of Knowledge call'd,
Forbidden them to taste: Knowledge forbidd'n?
Suspicious, reasonless. Why should thir Lord

So our universal mother spoke, and with eyes
Full of innocent wifely attraction
And meek surrender, half embracing leaned
On our first father, and half of her swelling breast
Touched his, naked under the flowing gold
Of her hair; he, delighting
In her beauty and her charming submission,
Smiled with superior love, like Jupiter
Smiles on Juno, when he impregnates the clouds
That rain May flowers; and he covered her womanly lips
With pure kisses: the Devil turned away
In envy, but with a jealous evil leer
Watched them sidelong, and whined to himself:
"Horrible, tormenting sight! So these two lie
Joyful in each other's arms,
That greater Eden, and drink their fill
Of joy on top of joy, while I am thrown into Hell,
Where there is no joy or love, only a fierce desire
Which is not the smallest of our tortures
And which fills us with the pain of unrequited longing.
Don't let me forget what I have learned
From their speech; not everything belongs to them, it seems:
There is one fatal tree, the Tree of Knowledge,
From which they must not eat: knowledge is banned?
That is suspicious and without reason. Why should God

Envie them that? can it be sin to know,

Can it be death? and do they onely stand

By Ignorance, is that thir happie state,

The proof of thir obedience and thir faith?

O fair foundation laid whereon to build

Thir ruine! Hence I will excite thir minds

With more desire to know, and to reject

Envious commands, invented with designe

To keep them low whom knowledge might exalt

Equal with Gods; aspiring to be such,

They taste and die: what likelier can ensue?

But first with narrow search I must walk round

This Garden, and no corner leave unspi'd;

A chance but chance may lead where I may meet

Some wandring Spirit of Heav'n, by Fountain side,

Or in thick shade retir'd, from him to draw

What further would be learnt. Live while ye may,

Yet happie pair; enjoy, till I return,

Short pleasures, for long woes are to succeed.

So saying, his proud step he scornful turn'd,

But with sly circumspection, and began

Through wood, through waste, o're hil, o're dale his roam.

Mean while in utmost Longitude, where Heav'n

Keep that from them? Is it a sin to know things,

Can it cause death? And can they only exist

If they remain ignorant, do they owe their happy state

To this proof of their obedience and faith?

What a good foundation on which I can build

Their downfall! I will excite their minds

With the desire to know more, and to reject

The jaundiced commands, issued with the aim

Of keeping them in their place, when knowledge might lift them up

To be equal to the Gods. Wanting what I offer,

They will taste and die, what else could happen?

But first I must examine this garden closely,

And not neglect any corner of it;

Luck might lead me to meet

Some wandering Spirit from Heaven, by a spring

Or resting in the woods, and from him

I might get more information. Live while you can,

You happy pair; enjoy, until I come back,

Your brief pleasures, for they will be followed by long sorrow."

Saying this he turned his proud steps scornfully away,

Though cautiously, and began his search

Through woods and deserts, hills and valleys.

Meanwhile in the farthest west, where Heaven touches

With Earth and Ocean meets, the setting Sun	*The sky and the sea, the setting sun*
Slowly descended, and with right aspect	*Slowly sank, and facing the right direction*
Against the eastern Gate of Paradise	*Shone his evening beams*
Leveld his eevning Rayes: it was a Rock	*Against the eastern gate of Paradise: it was a rock*
Of Alablaster, pil'd up to the Clouds,	*Of white stone, reaching up to the clouds,*
Conspicuous farr, winding with one ascent	*Visible from far off, with one path winding up*
Accessible from Earth, one entrance high;	*From the earth and one high entrance;*
The rest was craggie cliff, that overhung	*The rest was craggy cliff that leaned outwards*
Still as it rose, impossible to climbe.	*As it rose, impossible to climb.*
Betwixt these rockie Pillars GABRIEL sat	*Between these rocky pillars sat Gabriel,*
Chief of th' Angelic Guards, awaiting night;	*The leader of the Guards of Angels, waiting for night;*
About him exercis'd Heroic Games	*Around him the young of Heaven*
Th' unarmed Youth of Heav'n, but nigh at hand	*Played the games of Heroes, but close by*
Celestial Armourie, Shields, Helmes, and Speares	*Was their heavenly armour, shields, helmets and spears,*
Hung high with Diamond flaming, and with Gold.	*Decorated with diamonds and gold.*
Thither came URIEL, gliding through the Even	*To that place came Uriel, gliding through the evening*
On a Sun beam, swift as a shooting Starr	*On a sunbeam, as quick as a shooting star*
In AUTUMN thwarts the night, when vapors fir'd	*Which crosses the autumn sky when humid lightning*
Impress the Air, and shews the Mariner	*Is in the air, and shows the sailor*
From what point of his Compass to beware	*Where the dangerous winds will come from:*
Impetuous winds: he thus began in haste.	*So he began speaking quickly:*
GABRIEL, to thee thy cours by Lot hath giv'n	*"Gabriel, you have been given the task*
Charge and strict watch that to this happie place	*Of watching this happy place and ensuring*
No evil thing approach or enter in;	*That no evil thing can approach or enter;*
This day at highth of Noon came to my Spheare	*At high noon today a Spirit came to the sun*
A Spirit, zealous, as he seem'd, to know	*Who seemed keen to learn*

139

More of th' Almighties works, and chiefly Man
Gods latest Image: I describ'd his way

Bent all on speed, and markt his Aerie Gate;
But in the Mount that lies from EDEN North,
Where he first lighted, soon discernd his looks
Alien from Heav'n, with passions foul obscur'd:
Mine eye pursu'd him still, but under shade

Lost sight of him; one of the banisht crew

I fear, hath ventur'd from the deep, to raise
New troubles; him thy care must be to find.

To whom the winged Warriour thus returnd:
URIEL, no wonder if thy perfet sight,
Amid the Suns bright circle where thou sitst,
See farr and wide: in at this Gate none pass

The vigilance here plac't, but such as come

Well known from Heav'n; and since Meridian hour
No Creature thence: if Spirit of other sort,

So minded, have oreleapt these earthie bounds
On purpose, hard thou knowst it to exclude
Spiritual substance with corporeal barr.

But if within the circuit of these walks

In whatsoever shape he lurk, of whom

Thou telst, by morrow dawning I shall know.
So promis'd hee, and URIEL to his charge

Returnd on that bright beam, whose point

About more of God's work, and especially about Man,
God's latest creation. I noticed his path,

Hurrying, and followed his angelic flight,
But on the mountain that lies north of Eden
Where he first landed, I saw that his looks
Were not those of Heaven but were covered with foul passions.
My eyes followed him, but under the shadows
I lost sight of him; I fear one of the banished mob
Has risen up from the pit to cause
More trouble: it must be your duty to find him."
The winged warrior answered him:

"Uriel, with your perfect sight
Sitting in the brightness of the sun,
You see far and wide; but only those who come from Heaven
Can pass through this gate and our guard;
Since noon

No creature from Heaven has come. If another sort of spirit
Has chosen to leap over these earthly boundaries,
You know how hard it is to block
Spiritual substance with physical things.
But if, in whatever form he has taken,

He is lurking within the circuit of these walls, the one
You speak of, I shall know by tomorrow morning."
So he promised, and Uriel returned to his post
On that bright beam, which was now

140

now raisd

Bore him slope downward to the Sun now fall'n
Beneath th' AZORES; whither the prime Orb,
Incredible how swift, had thither rowl'd

Diurnal, or this less volubil Earth
By shorter flight to th' East, had left him there
Arraying with reflected Purple and Gold

The Clouds that on his Western Throne attend:
Now came still Eevning on, and Twilight gray
Had in her sober Liverie all things clad;

Silence accompanied, for Beast and Bird,

They to thir grassie Couch, these to thir Nests
Were slunk, all but the wakeful Nightingale;
She all night long her amorous descant sung;
Silence was pleas'd: now glow'd the Firmament
With living Saphirs: HESPERUS that led

The starrie Host, rode brightest, till the Moon
Rising in clouded Majestie, at length

Apparent Queen unvaild her peerless light,

And o're the dark her Silver Mantle threw.

When ADAM thus to EVE: Fair Consort, th' hour
Of night, and all things now retir'd to rest

Mind us of like repose, since God hath set

Labour and rest, as day and night to men

pointing upwards,

And carried him downhill to the sun which had dipped
Below the Azores; either that chief star
Had rolled there with incredible speed
On his daily path, or this stiller Earth
Moved a shorter distance to the east and left him
Gilding with reflected purple and gold
The clouds that surround his western throne.
Now the evening fell, and grey twilight
Had clad everything in her muted colors;
Silence came too, accompanying the beasts
To their grassy beds and the birds to their nests;
All went except for the wakeful nightingale;
She sang her songs of love all night.
Silence reigned; now the sky glowed
With living jewels: the evening star led
All the others, brightest, until the moon,
Rising in majesty from the clouds, at last
Like a queen revealed her matchless light
And threw her silver cloak over the darkness.
Adam said to Eve: "My fair companion,
The nightfall and seeing all other things retiring to rest
Turns our minds to sleep, since God has ordered
Work and rest to follow each other as

Successive, and the timely dew of sleep
Now falling with soft slumbrous weight inclines
Our eye-lids; other Creatures all day long

Rove idle unimploid, and less need rest;

Man hath his daily work of body or mind

Appointed, which declares his Dignitie,

And the regard of Heav'n on all his waies;

While other Animals unactive range,
And of thir doings God takes no account.

Tomorrow ere fresh Morning streak the East
With first approach of light, we must be ris'n,
And at our pleasant labour, to reform
Yon flourie Arbors, yonder Allies green,

Our walks at noon, with branches overgrown,
That mock our scant manuring, and require

More hands then ours to lop thir wanton growth:
Those Blossoms also, and those dropping Gumms,
That lie bestrowne unsightly and unsmooth,
Ask riddance, if we mean to tread with ease;
Mean while, as Nature wills, Night bids us rest.
To whom thus EVE with perfet beauty adornd.
My Author and Disposer, what thou bidst

Unargu'd I obey; so God ordains,

God is thy Law, thou mine: to know no more
Is womans happiest knowledge and her

day and night
For men, and the dew of sleep
Is falling with soft sleepy weight and closing
Our eyelids; other creatures roam idle

All day long, unemployed, and need rest less;

Man has his daily work of body or mind

Appointed to him, which gives him his dignity,

And makes Heaven look favourably on him;

While the other animals drift inactive
And God pays no attention to what they do.

Tomorrow before the first morning light
Appears in the east, we must be up

And about our pleasant tasks, to clip
Those flowery trees and their green companions;

Our noonday paths are overgrown with branches
Which mock our efforts at cultivation, and need

More hands then ours to keep them under control:
Those blossoms too, and those gumtree leaves,

That lie all about, untidy and ugly,
Must be swept up, if we are to walk safely;

Meanwhile, as Nature orders, night invites us to sleep."
Eve, wrapped in perfect beauty, answered:
"My Lord and master, what you order

I will obey without question; this is how God orders it,
You follow God's orders and I follow yours: to be aware of that
Is a woman's happiest privilege.

praise.
With thee conversing I forget all time,

All seasons and thir change, all please alike.

Sweet is the breath of morn, her rising

With charm of earliest Birds; pleasant the Sun
When first on this delightful Land he spreads
His orient Beams, on herb, tree, fruit, and flour,
Glistring with dew; fragrant the fertil earth

After soft showers; and sweet the coming on
Of grateful Eevning milde, then silent Night
With this her solemn Bird and this fair Moon,
And these the Gemms of Heav'n, her starrie train:
But neither breath of Morn when she ascends
With charm of earliest Birds, nor rising Sun

On this delightful land, nor herb, fruit, floure,
Glistring with dew, nor fragrance after showers,
Nor grateful Evening mild, nor silent Night
With this her solemn Bird, nor walk by Moon,
Or glittering Starr-light without thee is sweet.
But wherfore all night long shine these, for whom
This glorious sight, when sleep hath shut all eyes?
To whom our general Ancestor repli'd.

Daughter of God and Man, accomplisht EVE,
Those have thir course to finish, round the Earth,

When talking with you I lose track of the time,
And all the seasons and their changes please me the same.

The morning air is sweet, her coming lovely
With the song of the early birds; the sun is pleasant
When on this delightful land he throws
His light from the east on herbs, trees, fruits and flowers,
All glistening with dew; the earth is fragrant
After the soft showers; the arrival of mild evening
Is also sweet, and so is silent night,
With her solemn bird and beautiful moon,
And her starry train, the jewels of Heaven:
But neither the breath of morning when she rises
With the song of the earliest birds, nor the sun
Rising on this delightful land, not the herbs, fruit, flowers,
Glistening with dew, nor the perfume after the showers,
Nor the mild evening, nor silent night
With her solemn bird, nor walking in the moonlight
Or the glittering starlight can be sweet without you.
But why do these shine all night, who is this
Wonderful sight for, when sleep has closed all eyes?"
To whom our universal father replied:
"Daughter of God and Man, loveliest Eve,
They have to finish their journey round the Earth

By morrow Eevning, and from Land to Land	*By tomorrow evening, going in order from land to land*
In order, though to Nations yet unborn,	*Even though the nations there have not yet risen,*
Ministring light prepar'd, they set and rise;	*With their kindly light they set and rise,*
Least total darkness should by Night regaine	*Lest in the total darkness Night should win back*
Her old possession, and extinguish life	*Her old lands, and put out the life*
In Nature and all things, which these soft fires	*In Nature and all things, which these soft fires*
Not only enlighten, but with kindly heate	*Not only light but with their kind heat*
Of various influence foment and warme,	*In different ways ferment and warm,*
Temper or nourish, or in part shed down	*Strengthen or nourish and throw down*
Thir stellar vertue on all kinds that grow	*Their heavenly blessing on all things that grow*
On Earth, made hereby apter to receive	*Upon Earth, which is thereby made ready*
Perfection from the Suns more potent Ray.	*To receive the perfection of the sun's stronger light.*
These then, though unbeheld in deep of night,	*These then, though they are not seen at dead of night,*
Shine not in vain, nor think, though men were none,	*Are not shining in vain, and do not think that if there were no men*
That heav'n would want spectators, God want praise;	*That there would be none to see them, none to praise God;*
Millions of spiritual Creatures walk the Earth	*Millions of Spirits are walking the Earth*
Unseen, both when we wake, and when we sleep:	*Invisible when we are awake and while we sleep:*
All these with ceasless praise his works behold	*All of them look on his work with ceaseless praise*
Both day and night: how often from the steep	*Both day and night: how often from the slope*
Of echoing Hill or Thicket have we heard	*Of an echoing hill or thicket have we heard*
Celestial voices to the midnight air,	*Angelic voices in the midnight air,*
Sole, or responsive each to others note	*Alone or in harmony with others*
Singing thir great Creator: oft in bands	*Singing to their great creator: often in groups*
While they keep watch, or nightly rounding walk	*As they keep watch, or as they walk through the night,*
With Heav'nly touch of instrumental sounds	*With a heavenly touch on their instruments,*

In full harmonic number joind, thir songs	*They join together in full harmony, their songs*
Divide the night, and lift our thoughts to Heaven.	*Push back the night, and lift our thoughts to Heaven."*
Thus talking hand in hand alone they pass'd	*Thus talking alone, hand in hand, they walked*
On to thir blissful Bower; it was a place	*On to their sweet shelter; it was a place*
Chos'n by the sovran Planter, when he fram'd	*Chosen by the great creator, when he made*
All things to mans delightful use; the roofe	*Everything delightful for the use of Man; the roof*
Of thickest covert was inwoven shade	*Was an interwoven thicket*
Laurel and Mirtle, and what higher grew	*Of laurel and myrtle and their*
Of firm and fragrant leaf; on either side	*Strong and perfumed leaves: the walls were of*
ACANTHUS, and each odorous bushie shrub	*Acanthus, with each scented bush*
Fenc'd up the verdant wall; each beauteous flour,	*Trained up the green walls: all the loveliest flowers,*
IRIS all hues, Roses, and Gessamin	*Irises of all colors, roses and jasmine*
Rear'd high thir flourisht heads between, and wrought	*Were woven into them to make*
Mosaic; underfoot the Violet,	*A mosaic; on the floor were violets,*
Crocus, and Hyacinth with rich inlay	*Crocuses and hyacinths whose rich colors*
Broiderd the ground, more colour'd then with stone	*Decorated the ground, more colourful than*
Of costliest Emblem: other Creature here	*The costliest stonework: no other creature*
Beast, Bird, Insect, or Worm durst enter none;	*Dared enter, beast, bird, insect or worm,*
Such was thir awe of man. In shadier Bower	*Such was their awe of man. In no shadier bower*
More sacred and sequesterd, though but feignd,	*More sacred and secret, even if only in a story,*
PAN or SILVANUS never slept, nor Nymph,	*Pan or Silvanus never slept, nor did Nymphs*
Nor FAUNUS haunted. Here in close recess	*Or Faunus. Here in privacy*
With Flowers, Garlands, and sweet-smelling Herbs	*With flowers, garlands and sweet smelling herbs*
Espoused EVE deckt first her Nuptial Bed,	*Married Eve first made her bridal bed,*
And heav'nly Quires the Hymenaean sung,	*And heavenly choirs sang the wedding song,*
What day the genial Angel to our Sire	*The day the guardian angel brought*

	her to our father
Brought her in naked beauty more adorn'd,	*In the beauty of her nakedness more well endowed,*
More lovely then PANDORA, whom the Gods	*More lovely than Pandora, whom the Gods*
Endowd with all thir gifts, and O too like	*Gave all their gifts, and oh too like, as it sadly transpired,*
In sad event, when to the unwiser Son	*The time the unwiser son*
Of JAPHET brought by HERMES, she ensnar'd	*Of Japhet was brought by Hermes and she trapped*
Mankind with her faire looks, to be aveng'd	*Mankind with her beauty, so that she could be revenged*
On him who had stole JOVES authentic fire.	*On the one who stole the fire of the Gods.*
Thus at thir shadie Lodge arriv'd, both stood,	*So they arrived at their cool shelter and stood*
Both turnd, and under op'n Skie ador'd	*And turned, and under the open sky worshipped*
The God that made both Skie, Air, Earth & Heav'n	*The God who made the sky, the air, the Earth and the Heaven*
Which they beheld, the Moons resplendent Globe	*Which they could see, the great ball of the moon*
And starrie Pole: Thou also mad'st the Night,	*And the shining pole star: "You also made the night,*
Maker Omnipotent, and thou the Day,	*All powerful creator, and the day,*
Which we in our appointed work imployd	*Which we have used to do our appointed work*
Have finisht happie in our mutual help	*And have ended happy in helping each other*
And mutual love, the Crown of all our bliss	*And loving each other, and all our happiness*
Ordain'd by thee, and this delicious place	*Was given to us by you, and this wonderful place*
For us too large, where thy abundance wants	*Which is too large for us, where your generosity needs*
Partakers, and uncropt falls to the ground.	*People to use it, and falls unpicked to the ground.*
But thou hast promis'd from us two a Race	*But you have promised that from the two of us a race*
To fill the Earth, who shall with us extoll	*Will fill the Earth, who shall join us in praising*
Thy goodness infinite, both when we wake,	*Your infinite goodness, both when we are awake*
And when we seek, as now, thy gift of sleep.	*And when we look for, as now, your gift of sleep."*
This said unanimous, and other Rites	*They said this together and did no*

	other rites
Observing none, but adoration pure	*Just giving pure adoration*
Which God likes best, into thir inmost bower	*Which is God's great pleasure, and they went hand in hand*
Handed they went; and eas'd the putting off	*Into their inner room, and not having the task of removing*
These troublesom disguises which wee wear,	*The tiresome disguise which we wear,*
Strait side by side were laid, nor turnd I weene	*Laid down at once side by side, nor do I suppose*
ADAM from his fair Spouse, nor EVE the Rites	*Adam turned away from his beautiful wife, nor did Eve*
Mysterious of connubial Love refus'd:	*Refuse to perform the mysterious rites of married love:*
Whatever Hypocrites austerely talk	*Whatever hypocrites sternly say*
Of puritie and place and innocence,	*About purity and innocence and seemly behaviour,*
Defaming as impure what God declares	*Calling impure what God has declared*
Pure, and commands to som, leaves free to all.	*As pure, and orders some and makes available to all.*
Our Maker bids increase, who bids abstain	*Our maker tells us to multiply, who tells us not to*
But our Destroyer, foe to God and Man?	*Except for our destroyer, the enemy of God and Man?*
Haile wedded Love, mysterious Law, true source	*Salute wedded Love, the mysterious law, the true source*
Of human ofspring, sole proprietie,	*Of human children, the one type of property*
In Paradise of all things common else.	*In Paradise where otherwise all was shared.*
By thee adulterous lust was driv'n from men	*Through you adulterous lust was driven out of men*
Among the bestial herds to raunge, by thee	*And sent off to roam amongst the beasts, by you,*
Founded in Reason, Loyal, Just, and Pure,	*Based on reason, loyal, just and pure,*
Relations dear, and all the Charities	*Dear relationships and all the love*
Of Father, Son, and Brother first were known.	*Of father, son and brother were first known.*
Farr be it, that I should write thee sin or blame,	*Far be it from me to call you a sin,*
Or think thee unbefitting holiest place,	*Or think that you should not be in the holiest place,*
Perpetual Fountain of Domestic sweets,	*The everlasting stream of domestic bliss,*
Whose Bed is undefil'd and chast	*Whose bed is reckoned as pure and*

pronounc't,
Present, or past, as Saints and Patriarchs us'd.
Here Love his golden shafts imploies, here lights
His constant Lamp, and waves his purple wings,
Reigns here and revels; not in the bought smile
Of Harlots, loveless, joyless, unindeard,

Casual fruition, nor in Court Amours

Mixt Dance, or wanton Mask, or Midnight Bal,

Or Serenate, which the starv'd Lover sings

To his proud fair, best quitted with disdain.

These lulld by Nightingales imbraceing slept,
And on thir naked limbs the flourie roof

Showrd Roses, which the Morn repair'd. Sleep on,
Blest pair; and O yet happiest if ye seek

No happier state, and know to know no more.
Now had night measur'd with her shaddowie Cone
Half way up Hill this vast Sublunar Vault,

And from thir Ivorie Port the Cherubim

Forth issuing at th' accustomd hour stood armd
To thir night watches in warlike Parade,

When GABRIEL to his next in power thus spake.
UZZIEL, half these draw off, and coast the South
With strictest watch; these other wheel the North,

chaste,
Now or in the past, as one used by saints or patriarchs.
Here love uses his golden arrows, here he lights
His eternal lamp, and waves his purple wings;
He rules here and enjoys: not in the paid for smile
Of whores, loveless, joyless, without affection,
Casual coupling, nor in the intrigues of Court,
With their dances and masked balls,

Nor the serenade, which the lovesick man sings
To his proud beauty and is paid with contempt.
To the nightingales' lullaby they slept entwined,
And on their naked bodies the flowery roof
Dropped rose petals, which the morning replaced. Sleep on,
Blessed pair; and you will be happiest if you seek
No more happiness, and know you need no more knowledge.
Now night's shadows had crept
Halfway up the hill in this great space under the moon,
And from the ivory doors the Cherubim
Came forward at their usual hour, armed
As soldiers for their nightly guard duty.
Gabriel spoke to his second in command:
"Uzziel, take half this force, and go round the South,
Keeping a strict watch; these others will circle to the North

Our circuit meets full West. As flame they part	And we will meet up at the farthest western point."They parted like a flame,
Half wheeling to the Shield, half to the Spear.	Half following the shield and half the spear.
From these, two strong and suttle Spirits he calld	From each group he called two strong and wise Spirits
That neer him stood, and gave them thus in charge.	That came to him, and he gave them these orders:
ITHURIEL and ZEPHON, with wingd speed	"Ithuriel and Zephon, fly quickly
Search through this Garden, leav unsearcht no nook,	And search through the garden; leave no place unsearched
But chiefly where those two fair Creatures Lodge,	But look especially where those fair creatures live,
Now laid perhaps asleep secure of harme.	Perhaps asleep and safe from harm now.
This Eevning from the Sun's decline arriv'd	This evening someone came from the sun
Who tells of som infernal Spirit seen	And told of some Hellish Spirit
Hitherward bent (who could have thought?) escap'd	Coming this way (who would have imagined it?) having escaped
The barrs of Hell, on errand bad no doubt:	The prison of hell, on an evil errand no doubt:
Such where ye find, seise fast, and hither bring.	When you find such a one hold him fast and bring him here."
So saying, on he led his radiant Files,	Having said this he led on his shining ranks,
Daz'ling the Moon; these to the Bower direct	Outshining the moon; these as directed went to the bower
In search of whom they sought: him there they found	In search of the criminal; they found him there
Squat like a Toad, close at the eare of EVE;	Squatting like a toad by Eve's ear,
Assaying by his Devilish art to reach	Trying with his devilish tricks to reach
The Organs of her Fancie, and with them forge	Her imagination, and to use it to conjure up
Illusions as he list, Phantasms and Dreams,	Illusions, phantoms and dreams,
Or if, inspiring venom, he might taint	Or to inspire hatred and so poison
Th' animal Spirits that from pure blood arise	The essential spirits that live in the blood
Like gentle breaths from Rivers pure, thence raise	And rise up like soft mists from pure rivers, and so he could
At least distemperd, discontented thoughts,	Cause disordered, discontented

	thoughts,
Vain hopes, vain aimes, inordinate desires	*Vain hopes, vain aims, unworthy ambitions*
Blown up with high conceits ingendring pride.	*Inflated with the high thoughts which cause pride.*
Him thus intent ITHURIEL with his Spear	*As he was bent to his work Ithuriel touched him lightly*
Touch'd lightly; for no falshood can endure	*With his spear, for no disguise can withstand*
Touch of Celestial temper, but returns	*The touch of Heavenly metal, but is forced*
Of force to its own likeness: up he starts	*To resume its true shape; he jumps up,*
Discoverd and surpriz'd. As when a spark	*Discovered and surprised.As when a spark*
Lights on a heap of nitrous Powder, laid	*Falls on a heap of gunpowder, collected*
Fit for the Tun som Magazin to store	*Ready to be put in a barrel to stock some armoury*
Against a rumord Warr, the Smuttie graine	*In preparation for war, the sooty grains*
With sudden blaze diffus'd, inflames the Aire:	*Are suddenly full of fire and burn the air:*
So started up in his own shape the Fiend.	*So the Fiend leapt up in his true shape.*
Back stept those two fair Angels half amaz'd	*Those two angels stepped back, astonished,*
So sudden to behold the grieslie King;	*To see the grisly King appear;*
Yet thus, unmovd with fear, accost him soon.	*Yet, unafraid, they challenged him:*
Which of those rebell Spirits adjudg'd to Hell	*"Which of those rebellious Spirits sentenced to Hell*
Com'st thou, escap'd thy prison, and transform'd,	*Are you, escaped from your prison and disguised?*
Why satst thou like an enemie in waite	*Why are you sitting like an enemy in wait*
Here watching at the head of these that sleep?	*At the head of the sleepers' bed?"*
Know ye not then said SATAN, filld with scorn,	*"Do you then not know," said Satan, filled with scorn,*
Know ye not me? ye knew me once no mate	*"Do you not know me? You knew me once, no friend*
For you, there sitting where ye durst not soare;	*Of yours, you sat there because you did not dare to fly;*
Not to know mee argues your selves	*If you don't know me then you don't*

unknown,
The lowest of your throng; or if ye know,

Why ask ye, and superfluous begin
Your message, like to end as much in vain?
To whom thus ZEPHON, answering scorn
with scorn.
Think not, revolted Spirit, thy shape the
same,
Or undiminisht brightness, to be known

As when thou stoodst in Heav'n upright
and pure;
That Glorie then, when thou no more
wast good,
Departed from thee, and thou resembl'st
now
Thy sin and place of doom obscure and
foule.
But come, for thou, be sure, shalt give
account

To him who sent us, whose charge is to
keep
This place inviolable, and these from harm.

So spake the Cherube, and his grave rebuke

Severe in youthful beautie, added grace

Invincible: abasht the Devil stood,
And felt how awful goodness is, and saw

Vertue in her shape how lovly, saw, and
pin'd
His loss; but chiefly to find here observd
His lustre visibly impar'd; yet seemd

Undaunted. If I must contend, said he,
Best with the best, the Sender not the sent,

Or all at once; more glorie will be wonn,

Or less be lost.
Thy fear, said ZEPHON bold,
Will save us trial what the least can doe

know yourselves,
And it shows you are of the lowest
rank, or if you do know
Why are you asking and wasting time
With this worthless talk?"
Zephon answered him with the same
scorn.
"Don't think, you rebellious Spirit,
that your shape is the same,
That your brightness is undiminished,
that you are the same

As when you stood upright and pure
in Heaven;
When you abandoned goodness that
glory left you,
And now you look like

Your sin and your foul dark prison.

But come, you shall give an account
of yourself

To the one who sent us, whose duty is
to protect this place
And keep these creatures from
harm."

So the Cherub spoke, and to his stern
rebuke

His youthful beauty added
unanswerable grace:
The Devil stood ashamed,
And felt the terrible power of
goodness, and saw

How lovely virtue is, and mourned

His loss and most of all the fact that
His brightness was visibly less, but he
seemed

Undaunted. "If I must fight," he said,
"Let it be with the highest, the sender
not his messenger,
Or with all of them at once: more
glory will be gained,
Or less will be lost."
"Your fear," said bold Zephon,
"Will save us finding out what the

151

lowest can do

Single against thee wicked, and thence weak.

Alone against you who are wicked, and so weak."

The Fiend repli'd not, overcome with rage;

The Fiend did not answer, consumed with rage,

But like a proud Steed reind, went hautie on,

But like a proud horse reined in went on haughtily,

Chaumping his iron curb: to strive or flie

Champing at his iron bit; to fight or to fly

He held it vain; awe from above had quelld

He thought was useless; fear of Heaven had subdued

His heart, not else dismai'd. Now drew they nigh

His heart, which nothing else could dismay.Now they came

The western point, where those half-rounding guards

To the western point, where those patrols

Just met, & closing stood in squadron joind

Had just met, and had joined together in a squadron

Awaiting next command. To whom thir Chief

Awaiting the next orders.Their chief Gabriel

GABRIEL from the Front thus calld aloud.

Called aloud to them.

O friends, I hear the tread of nimble feet

"My friends, I hear nimble footsteps

Hasting this way, and now by glimps discerne

Hurrying this way, and now I see glimpses of

ITHURIEL and ZEPHON through the shade,

Ithuriel and Zephon through the dark,

And with them comes a third of Regal port,

And with them comes a third of regal bearing,

But faded splendor wan; who by his gate

But with his brightness faded; by his strut

And fierce demeanour seems the Prince of Hell,

And fierce appearance he seems a Prince of Hell,

Not likely to part hence without contest;

And he is unlikely to go from here peacefully;

Stand firm, for in his look defiance lours.

Stand firm, for his look shows his defiance."

He scarce had ended, when those two approachd

He had hardly finished when those two approached

And brief related whom they brought, wher found,

And quickly told whom they had captured, where they had found him,

How busied, in what form and posture coucht.

What he was doing and what shape he had assumed.

To whom with stern regard thus GABRIEL spake.

Gabriel spoke to him sternly:

Why hast thou, SATAN, broke the bounds prescrib'd

"Why have you, Satan, crossed the boundaries which

To thy transgressions, and disturbd the charge
Of others, who approve not to transgress

By thy example, but have power and right

To question thy bold entrance on this place;
Imploi'd it seems to violate sleep, and those

Whose dwelling God hath planted here in bliss?
To whom thus SATAN with contemptuous brow.
GABRIEL, thou hadst in Heav'n th' esteem of wise,
And such I held thee; but this question askt

Puts me in doubt. Lives ther who loves his pain?
Who would not, finding way, break loose from Hell,
Though thither doomd? Thou wouldst thy self, no doubt,
And boldly venture to whatever place
Farthest from pain, where thou mightst hope to change
Torment with ease, & soonest recompence
Dole with delight, which in this place I sought;
To thee no reason; who knowst only good,

But evil hast not tri'd: and wilt object

His will who bound us? let him surer barr

His Iron Gates, if he intends our stay
In that dark durance: thus much what was askt.
The rest is true, they found me where they say;
But that implies not violence or harme.

Thus hee in scorn. The warlike Angel mov'd,
Disdainfully half smiling thus repli'd.

Your sins set for you, and disturbed the duty
Of others, who did not follow your example

And rebel, but have the power and right

To question your entry to this place;
It seems you have tried to violate the sleep

Of those to whom God has given this place to live in bliss."
Satan answered him with a scornful frown:
"Gabriel, you were called wise in Heaven,
And I thought that you were, but your asking this question

Makes me wonder. Is there anyone who loves pain?
Who would not, if he found a way, break loose from Hell
If he had been sent there? You would do it yourself, no doubt,
And boldly go wherever
You were farthest from pain, where you could hope to exchange
Torture for peace and take compensation
In pleasure, and that's why I came here;
You won't understand this, you who knows only good,

But you have not tried evil, and will you block

The will of the one who imprisoned us? Let him bar

His iron gates, if he means us to stay
In our dark prison, otherwise he'll get what he deserves.
The rest is true, they found me where they say they did,
But that does not prove I meant violence or harm."

So said Satan with scorn. The warlike angel replied,
Half smiling with his disdain:

O loss of one in Heav'n to judge of wise,	*"What a loss to Heaven your wise judgement is,*
Since SATAN fell, whom follie overthrew,	*Since Satan fell, overthrown by his own foolishness,*
And now returns him from his prison scap't,	*And now he comes back, escaped from his prison,*
Gravely in doubt whether to hold them wise	*Saying he doubts that they are wise, the ones*
Or not, who ask what boldness brought him hither	*Who ask him what evil brought him here,*
Unlicenc't from his bounds in Hell prescrib'd;	*Roaming outside the boundaries of hell without permission;*
So wise he judges it to fly from pain	*He says that it is wise to fly from pain*
However, and to scape his punishment.	*And to escape from his punishment.*
So judge thou still, presumptuous, till the wrauth,	*So you still think, arrogant, until the anger*
Which thou incurr'st by flying, meet thy flight	*Which you have brought on yourself by flight*
Seavenfold, and scourge that wisdom back to Hell,	*Rebounds on you sevenfold, and whips your wisdom back to your prison,*
Which taught thee yet no better, that no pain	*Where you failed to learn that no pain is as bad*
Can equal anger infinite provok't.	*As the wrath of God.*
But wherefore thou alone? wherefore with thee	*But why are you alone? Why didn't all Hell*
Came not all Hell broke loose? is pain to them	*Break from the prison with you? Is pain to them*
Less pain, less to be fled, or thou then they	*Not as bad, do they have less desire to escape, or are you*
Less hardie to endure? courageous Chief,	*Less hardy than them? You brave chief,*
The first in flight from pain, had'st thou alleg'd	*The first to run from pain, if you had told*
To thy deserted host this cause of flight,	*Your lost followers why you were fleeing*
Thou surely hadst not come sole fugitive.	*You surely would not have come alone."*
To which the Fiend thus answerd frowning stern.	*To which the Fiend answered with a stern frown:*
Not that I less endure, or shrink from pain,	*"I am no less hardy, and do not shrink from pain,*
Insulting Angel, well thou knowst I stood	*You insulting angel, you well know that I stood*
Thy fiercest, when in Battel to thy aide	*As your fiercest enemy, when in the battle you called*

The blasting volied Thunder made all speed	*The blasting thunder to aid you*
And seconded thy else not dreaded Spear.	*And back up your spear, which did not frighten me at all.*
But still thy words at random, as before,	*But still your drivelling words, as before,*
Argue thy inexperience what behoves	*Show that you have not experienced*
From hard assaies and ill successes past	*The losses and hard trials which go to make*
A faithful Leader, not to hazard all	*A good leader, who would not risk his whole army,*
Through wayes of danger by himself untri'd.	*By sending them through dangerous paths he had not tried himself.*
I therefore, I alone first undertook	*Therefore I undertook alone to be the first*
To wing the desolate Abyss, and spie	*To fly over the terrible abyss, and examine*
This new created World, whereof in Hell	*This newly created world, which has been heard of*
Fame is not silent, here in hope to find	*In Hell, and I hoped to find*
Better abode, and my afflicted Powers	*A better home, and to settle my damaged armies*
To settle here on Earth, or in mid Aire;	*Here on earth, or in midair;*
Though for possession put to try once more	*We are prepared to try another bout*
What thou and thy gay Legions dare against;	*If you and your gaudy armies dare;*
Whose easier business were to serve thir Lord	*It's easier for you to serve your Lord*
High up in Heav'n, with songs to hymne his Throne,	*Up in Heaven, singing hymns around his throne,*
And practis'd distances to cringe, not fight.	*And practice bowing, not war."*
To whom the warriour Angel soon repli'd.	*The warrior angel soon replied:*
To say and strait unsay, pretending first	*"To say and then contradict, pretending*
Wise to flie pain, professing next the Spie,	*You were wisely fleeing pain, then saying that you are a spy,*
Argues no Leader, but a lyar trac't,	*Does not show a leader, but a liar who's been caught out,*
SATAN, and couldst thou faithful add? O name,	*Satan, and could you claim to be faithful? Oh name,*
O sacred name of faithfulness profan'd!	*Sacred name of faithfulness disrespected!*
Faithful to whom? to thy rebellious crew?	*To whom are you faithful? To your rebellious mob?*
Armie of Fiends, fit body to fit head;	*An army of fiends, an appropriate army for such a leader;*
Was this your discipline and faith ingag'd,	*Was this your idea of discipline and*

Your military obedience, to dissolve
Allegeance to th' acknowledg'd Power supream?
And thou sly hypocrite, who now wouldst seem
Patron of liberty, who more then thou

Once fawn'd, and cring'd, and servilly ador'd
Heav'ns awful Monarch? wherefore but in hope
To dispossess him, and thy self to reigne?

But mark what I arreede thee now, avant;

Flie thither whence thou fledst: if from this houre
Within these hallowd limits thou appeer,
Back to th' infernal pit I drag thee chaind,

And Seale thee so, as henceforth not to scorne
The facil gates of hell too slightly barrd.

So threatn'd hee, but SATAN to no threats

Gave heed, but waxing more in rage repli'd.

Then when I am thy captive talk of chaines,

Proud limitarie Cherube, but ere then

Farr heavier load thy self expect to feel
From my prevailing arme, though Heavens King
Ride on thy wings, and thou with thy Compeers,
Us'd to the yoak, draw'st his triumphant wheels
In progress through the rode of Heav'n Star-pav'd.
While thus he spake, th' Angelic Squadron bright
Turnd fierie red, sharpning in mooned

faith,
Of military obedience, to betray
Your oath to the acknowledged highest power?
And you sly hypocrite, who now pretends to be
A great advocate of freedom, who more than you
Once fawned, bowed and worshipped
The terrible King of Heaven? Why else have you come
Except in hope of overthrowing him and taking his throne?
But take note of what I advise you now, depart;
Fly back to where you came from: from now on
If I catch you in this holy place
I shall drag you back to the Hellish pit in chains,
And lock you down so you'll never again
Mock the gates of Hell as being to easy to pass."
So he threatened, but Satan paid no attention
To the threats, but growing in rage answered:
"When I am your prisoner you can talk of chains,
You proud, border guarding Cherub, but before then
Expect to feel a far greater blow
From my fist, even if you have the King of Heaven
On your back, and you and your comrades,
Who are used to slavery, will drag my victorious chariot
In triumph over the starry paths of Heaven."
Whilst he said this, the bright angelic squadron
Flushed fiery red, bringing their lines

hornes
Thir Phalanx, and began to hemm him round
With ported Spears, as thick as when a field

Of CERES ripe for harvest waving bends

Her bearded Grove of ears, which way the wind
Swayes them; the careful Plowman doubting stands
Least on the threshing floore his hopeful sheaves
Prove chaff. On th' other side SATAN allarm'd
Collecting all his might dilated stood,

Like TENERIFF or ATLAS unremov'd:

His stature reacht the Skie, and on his Crest

Sat horror Plum'd; nor wanted in his graspe

What seemd both Spear and Shield: now dreadful deeds
Might have ensu'd, nor onely Paradise

In this commotion, but the Starrie Cope

Of Heav'n perhaps, or all the Elements

At least had gon to rack, disturbd and torne

With violence of this conflict, had not soon

Th' Eternal to prevent such horrid fray
Hung forth in Heav'n his golden Scales, yet seen

Betwixt ASTREA and the SCORPION signe,

Wherein all things created first he weighd,

The pendulous round Earth with ballanc't Aire
In counterpoise, now ponders all events,

round
In a semicircle, and they began to surround him
With lowered spears, as thick as when a field
Of wheat, ripe for harvest, bends down
Her forest of ears whichever way the wind
Blows them; the careful ploughman stands back,
In case his sheaves should prove to be ruined
When taken for threshing. On the other side Satan, alarmed,
Gathered up his faded strength and stood
Solid like the mountains of Tenerife or Atlas;
His height reached up to the sky, and on his helmet
Were horrible plumes, and it seemed as though
He had a spear and a shield in his hands: now dreadful things
Might have been done, and in this commotion
Not only Paradise, but the starry cloak
Of Heaven, perhaps, or all the Elements,
Would have at least been smashed, displaced or torn
By the violence of the battle. But to prevent
Such a terrible fight God
Hung from Heaven his golden scales, which can still be seen
Between the signs of Astrea and the Scorpion,
Which he used to weigh all his creations,
Balancing the heavy round Earth against the air.
Now he thinks of all the events,

Battels and Realms: in these he put two weights
The sequel each of parting and of fight;

The latter quick up flew, and kickt the beam;
Which GABRIEL spying, thus bespake the Fiend.
SATAN, I know thy strength, and thou knowst mine,
Neither our own but giv'n; what follie then

To boast what Arms can doe, since thine no more
Then Heav'n permits, nor mine, though doubld now

To trample thee as mire: for proof look up,

And read thy Lot in yon celestial Sign

Where thou art weigh'd, & shown how light,
how weak,
If thou resist. The Fiend lookt up and knew

His mounted scale aloft: nor more; but fled

Murmuring, and with him fled the shades of night.

Battles and Kingdoms: in these he put two weights,
One representing the consequences of leaving and one those of fighting;
The latter, outweighed, flew up quickly;
Gabriel saw this and so spoke to the Fiend:
"Satan, I know your strength, and you know mine,
Neither of them are our own but are what we have been given; what stupidity
To boast what Arms can do, since you can do no more
Than Heaven allows and nor can I, though my strength is double yours now
And I could trample you like mud: for proof look up,
And see your fate written in that star sign
Where you have been weighed, and see how
light, how weak,
You will be if you resist." The fiend looked up and saw
The scales and argued no more but fled,
Muttering, and the shades of night went with him.

158

BOOK V

THE ARGUMENT

Morning approacht, Eve relates to Adam her troublesome dream; he likes it not, yet comforts her: They come forth to thir day labours: Thir Morning Hymn at the Door of thir Bower. God to render Man inexcusable sends Raphael to admonish him of his obedience, of his free estate, of his enemy near at hand; who he is, and why his enemy, and whatever else may avail Adam to know. Raphael comes down to Paradise, his appearance describ'd, his coming discern'd by Adam afar off sitting at the door of his Bower; he goes out to meet him, brings him to his lodge, entertains him with the choycest fruits of Paradise got together by Eve; thir discourse at Table: Raphael performs his message, minds Adam of his state and of his enemy; relates at Adams request who that enemy is, and how he came to be so, beginning from his first revolt in Heaven, and the occasion thereof; how he drew his Legions after him to the parts of the North, and there incited them to rebel with him, perswading all but only Abdiel a Seraph, who in Argument diswades and opposes him, then forsakes him.

With the coming of morning Eve tells Adam of her troubling dream; he does not like it, but he comforts her. They come out for their day's work and sing their morning hymn at the door of their shelter. To make sure Man has no God sends Raphael to warn him to be obedient, to tell him of his free will and that his enemy is close by, who the enemy is, why he is an enemy, and anything else it might be useful for Adam to know. Raphael comes down to Paradise, his appearance is described. Adam, sitting at the door of his shelter, sees him from far off. He goes out to meet him, brings him to his home and entertains him with the choicest fruits of Paradise, gathered by Eve. Their talk at the table is reported: Raphael passes on his message and reminds Adam of his condition and his enemy. At Adam's request he tells him who the enemy is and how he came to be an enemy, starting with the rebellion in Heaven and its cause. He tells of how he drew his regiments after him to the lands in the north of Heaven, persuading all but the Seraph Abdiel, who tries to dissuade him in debate and then leaves him.

Now Morn her rosie steps in th' Eastern Clime
Advancing, sow'd the Earth with Orient Pearle,
When ADAM wak't, so customd, for his sleep
Was Aerie light, from pure digestion bred,
And temperat vapors bland, which th' only sound
Of leaves and fuming rills, AURORA's fan,

*Now morning with her rosy steps was rising in the east
And covering the earth with dew,*

*When Adam woke, early as he always did, for he slept
Wonderfully light due to his pure diet
And the clear mild climate, in which the only sound
Was rustling leaves and running streams lightly fanned*

Lightly dispers'd, and the shrill Matin Song

Of Birds on every bough; so much the more

His wonder was to find unwak'nd EVE
With Tresses discompos'd, and glowing Cheek,
As through unquiet rest: he on his side

Leaning half-rais'd, with looks of cordial Love
Hung over her enamour'd, and beheld
Beautie, which whether waking or asleep,

Shot forth peculiar Graces; then with voice

Milde, as when ZEPHYRUS on FLORA breathes,
Her hand soft touching, whisperd thus

Awake
My fairest, my espous'd, my latest found,

Heav'ns last best gift, my ever new delight,

Awake, the morning shines, and the fresh field
Calls us, we lose the prime, to mark how spring
Our tended Plants, how blows the Citron Grove,
What drops the Myrrhe, & what the balmie Reed,
How Nature paints her colours, how the Bee
Sits on the Bloom extracting liquid sweet.

Such whispering wak'd her, but with startl'd eye
On ADAM, whom imbracing, thus she spake.
O Sole in whom my thoughts find all repose,
My Glorie, my Perfection, glad I see

By the dawn breezes, and the morning song

Of the birds on every branch; so he had the wonder

Of finding Eve still sleeping,
With her hair disordered and cheeks burning
As if her sleep had been uneasy; lying on his side,

Half raised and leaning over her, with looks of sweet love
He hung over her entranced, and saw
Beauty, which whether asleep or awake

Shot forth unique grace; then with a voice

Soft as when the West Wind blows on his wife Flora,
Softly touching her hand, he whispered,

"Wake up,
My beauty, my wife, what I most recently found,

The last and best gift of Heaven, my constant delight,

Wake up, for morning is here and the fresh field
Is calling us, we're losing the sunrise, the best time to see
How our plants are faring, how the grove of citruses is blooming,
How the myrrh runs from the balsam tree,
How nature paints everything with her colors and how the bee
Sits on the flower taking its sweet nectar.

His whispering woke her, but looking with a startled eye
On Adam she embraced him and spoke:
"Oh soul in whom all my thoughts find rest,
My joy, you who complete me, I am happy to see

Thy face, and Morn return'd, for I this Night,
Such night till this I never pass'd, have dream'd,

If dream'd, not as I oft am wont, of thee,

Works of day pass't, or morrows next designe,
But of offence and trouble, which my mind
Knew never till this irksom night; methought
Close at mine ear one call'd me forth to walk
With gentle voice, I thought it thine; it said,
Why sleepst thou EVE? now is the pleasant time,
The cool, the silent, save where silence yields
To the night-warbling Bird, that now awake
Tunes sweetest his love-labor'd song; now reignes
Full Orb'd the Moon, and with more pleasing light
Shadowie sets off the face of things; in vain,
If none regard; Heav'n wakes with all his eyes,
Whom to behold but thee, Natures desire,
In whose sight all things joy, with ravishment
Attracted by thy beauty still to gaze.

I rose as at thy call, but found thee not;

To find thee I directed then my walk;
And on, methought, alone I pass'd through ways
That brought me on a sudden to the Tree
Of interdicted Knowledge: fair it seem'd,

Much fairer to my Fancie then by day:

And as I wondring lookt, beside it stood

Your face, and the return of morning, for this night,
Such as night as this I have never spent; I have dreamed,

If it was a dream, not of you, as I usually do,

Or of the day's work we have done or the next day's plans
But of offensive, disturbing things, which I never knew of
Before this troubling night; I thought that someone
Close to my ear summoned me to walk,
With a gentle voice which I thought was yours; it said,
'Why are you sleeping, Eve? This is the pleasant time,
Cool and silent except for where the silence gives way
To the nightingale, who has awoken
And is singing his sweetest song of love; now the full moon
Rules over all, and with a more pleasant light
Of shadows displays things at their best; pointlessly,
If nobody is watching; Heaven has opened his eyes,
Just to look at you, Nature's desire,
The sight of whom makes all things rejoice, and with pleasure
Wish to carry on gazing at your beauty.'

I rose as if you had called me, but couldn't find you,
So I walked on to find you,
And on, I dreamed, I went on paths
That brought me suddenly to the tree
Of forbidden knowledge: it looked lovely,
Far more so, I imagined, than during the day:
And as I looked in wonder, beside it

One shap'd & wing'd like one of those from Heav'n

By us oft seen; his dewie locks distill'd

Ambrosia; on that Tree he also gaz'd;

And O fair Plant, said he, with fruit surcharg'd,
Deigns none to ease thy load and taste thy sweet,
Nor God, nor Man; is Knowledge so despis'd?
Or envie, or what reserve forbids to taste?

Forbid who will, none shall from me withhold
Longer thy offerd good, why else set here?

This said he paus'd not, but with ventrous Arme
He pluckt, he tasted; mee damp horror chil'd
At such bold words voucht with a deed so bold:
But he thus overjoy'd, O Fruit Divine,

Sweet of thy self, but much more sweet thus cropt,
Forbidd'n here, it seems, as onely fit

For Gods, yet able to make Gods of Men:

And why not Gods of Men, since good, the more
Communicated, more abundant growes,
The Author not impair'd, but honourd more?
Here, happie Creature, fair Angelic EVE,

Partake thou also; happie though thou art,

Happier thou mayst be, worthier canst not be:
Taste this, and be henceforth among the Gods

there stood
One with the shape and wings of an angel
Such as we have often seen; his glistening hair like distilled
Nectar; he was also looking at the tree;
And he said, 'Oh fair plant, richly loaded with fruit,
Will nobody ease your burden and taste your sweetness,
Not God or man? Is knowledge so hated?
Is it jealousy, or what restriction forbids you tasting?
Whoever forbids it, you will not keep me
From trying your offered goodness, why else were you put here?'
Having said this he didn't hesitate, but reached out an arm
And picked and tasted; a chill horror ran through me
At such bold words backed up with a bold deed:
But he was overjoyed: 'Oh heavenly fruit,
You are sweet anyway, but you are much more sweet taken like this.
You are forbidden here, it seems, as only allowed for
Gods, and yet you can turn men into Gods:
And why shouldn't men be Gods, since the more good
Is spread, the greater it grows,
Not diminishing the author but bringing him honor?
Here you happy creature, fair angelic Eve,
You have some too; though you're happy,
You could be happier, and you could not be more deserving:
Taste this, and become amongst the Gods

Thy self a Goddess, not to Earth confind,
But somtimes in the Air, as wee, sometimes
Ascend to Heav'n, by merit thine, and see
What life the Gods live there, and such live thou.
So saying, he drew nigh, and to me held,
Even to my mouth of that same fruit held part
Which he had pluckt; the pleasant savourie smell
So quick'nd appetite, that I, methought,
Could not but taste. Forthwith up to the Clouds
With him I flew, and underneath beheld
The Earth outstretcht immense, a prospect wide
And various: wondring at my flight and change
To this high exaltation; suddenly
My Guide was gon, and I, me thought, sunk down,
And fell asleep; but O how glad I wak'd
To find this but a dream! Thus EVE her Night
Related, and thus ADAM answerd sad.
Best Image of my self and dearer half,
The trouble of thy thoughts this night in sleep
Affects me equally; nor can I like
This uncouth dream, of evil sprung I fear;
Yet evil whence? in thee can harbour none,
Created pure. But know that in the Soule
Are many lesser Faculties that serve
Reason as chief; among these Fansie next

A Goddess, not tied to the earth,
But sometimes flying as we sometimes do
You may ascend to Heaven, the place which you deserve, and see
What life the Gods live there, and live that life yourself.'
Saying this he came close, and held to my mouth
A part of that fruit
Which he had picked; the pleasant tasty smell of it
Made me so hungry that I thought
I couldn't help myself but taste. Straight away I flew with him
Up to the clouds, and below I saw
The Earth stretched out, massive, a sight both wide
And varied:I was amazed by my flight and my switch
To this exalted height; suddenly
My guide was gone and I thought that I fell down
And fell asleep; but oh how glad I am to wake up
And find it was just a dream!" So Eve told the story
Of her night, and Adam answered her sadly:
"Most beautiful copy of me and my more loved half,
The disturbance of your thoughts in your night's sleep
Disturbs me just as much; and I do not like
This mysterious dream, which I fear comes from evil;
But where could the evil be?There can be none in you,
Who was created pure.But you should know that in the soul
There are many lesser faculties which work
Under the rule of reason; amongst these is imagination;

Her office holds; of all external things,
Which the five watchful Senses represent,
She forms Imaginations, Aerie shapes,
Which Reason joyning or disjoyning, frames
All what we affirm or what deny, and call

Our knowledge or opinion; then retires

Into her private Cell when Nature rests.

Oft in her absence mimic Fansie wakes

To imitate her; but misjoyning shapes,

Wilde work produces oft, and most in dreams,
Ill matching words and deeds long past or late.
Som such resemblances methinks I find
Of our last Eevnings talk, in this thy dream,

But with addition strange; yet be not sad.

Evil into the mind of God or Man
May come and go, so unapprov'd, and leave

No spot or blame behind: Which gives me hope
That what in sleep thou didst abhorr to dream,
Waking thou never wilt consent to do.
Be not disheart'nd then, nor cloud those looks
That wont to be more chearful and serene

Then when fair Morning first smiles on the World,
And let us to our fresh imployments rise
Among the Groves, the Fountains, and the Flours
That open now thir choicest bosom'd smells

Reservd from night, and kept for thee in store.
So cheard he his fair Spouse, and she was

Of all external things
Which the five senses show us,
We see representations,
Which reason, accepting or rejecting,
uses to create
All the we believe or disbelieve, and
we call that

Our knowledge or opinion; then
reason retires

Into her private room when we sleep.

Often in her absence the mimic,
imagination,

Wakes and imitates her; but putting
shapes together wrongly
Often produces crazy work, and this
happens most often in dreams,
Putting together in the wrong order
words or deeds from the past.
I think I can see some resemblance
In your dream to our talk last
evening,

But with some strange additions; but
don't be afraid.

Into the mind of God or man evil
May come and go, and if it is ignored
it leaves

No stain or blame behind: this gives
me hope,
For what you refused to do even in a
dream
You will never consent to do awake.
Don't be downhearted, or have a
frown on that face
Which is more used to being cheerful
and peaceful

When the fair morning first smiles on
the world,
And let us start our new day's work
Amongst the groves, the springs and
the flowers
That now open up their petals to
release their sweetest scent
Which they kept back from the night
and saved for you."
So he tried to cheer his lovely wife,

Original	Translation
cheard,	and she was cheered,
But silently a gentle tear let fall	But a silent tear fell
From either eye, and wip'd them with her haire;	From either eye, and she wiped them with her hair;
Two other precious drops that ready stood,	There were two others ready to fall
Each in thir chrystal sluce, hee ere they fell	But before they could
Kiss'd as the gracious signs of sweet remorse	He kissed them away as the proper signs of sweet regret
And pious awe, that feard to have offended.	And devoted wonder, that was afraid to have sinned.
So all was cleard, and to the Field they haste.	So all was settled, and they hastened to the field.
But first from under shadie arborous roof,	But first, as they left the shady roof of trees,
Soon as they forth were come to open sight	As soon as they came out into the clear light
Of day-spring, and the Sun, who scarce up risen	Of daybreak, and the sun, who had hardly risen
With wheels yet hov'ring o're the Ocean brim,	With its edge just poised on the horizon
Shot paralel to the earth his dewie ray,	Shot his dew soaked rays parallel to the Earth,
Discovering in wide Lantskip all the East	Revealing the great landscape east
Of Paradise and EDENS happie Plains,	Of Paradise and the happy fields of Eden;
Lowly they bow'd adoring, and began	They bowed low in worship, and began
Thir Orisons, each Morning duly paid	Their morning prayers, performed each morning
In various style, for neither various style	In various ways, for they were not lacking ways
Nor holy rapture wanted they to praise	Nor holy joy with which to praise
Thir Maker, in fit strains pronounc't or sung	Their maker, speaking or singing
Unmeditated, such prompt eloquence	Without planning, such eloquence
Flowd from thir lips, in Prose or numerous Verse,	Flowed from their lips, in prose or metered verse,
More tuneable then needed Lute or Harp	Which was so tuneful it needed no instrument
To add more sweetness, and they thus began.	To add sweetness, and so they began:
These are thy glorious works, Parent of good,	"These are your glorious works, parent of good,
Almightie, thine this universal Frame,	The Almighty, this is your universe,
Thus wondrous fair; thy self how wondrous then!	And it is so beautiful and wonderful: how wonderful you are then!

Unspeakable, who sitst above these Heavens	*Indescribable, the one who sits above these skies,*
To us invisible or dimly seen	*Invisible to us, or only dimly seen*
In these thy lowest works, yet these declare	*In your smallest works here, but they show*
Thy goodness beyond thought, and Power Divine:	*Your goodness beyond comprehension, and divine power;*
Speak yee who best can tell, ye Sons of light,	*Speak, for you are the best ones to tell of him, you Sons of Light,*
Angels, for yee behold him, and with songs	*Angels, for you see him and with songs*
And choral symphonies, Day without Night,	*And choral symphonies, in days which have no night,*
Circle his Throne rejoycing, yee in Heav'n,	*Circle his throne rejoicing, you in heaven;*
On Earth joyn all yee Creatures to extoll	*On Earth all creatures should join to praise him*
Him first, him last, him midst, and without end.	*First, last and always, never ending.*
Fairest of Starrs, last in the train of Night,	*Loveliest of stars, the last in the journey of night,*
If better thou belong not to the dawn,	*If it is not the case that you belong to the dawn,*
Sure pledge of day, that crownst the smiling Morn	*The best promise that day is coming, who crowns the happy morning*
With thy bright Circlet, praise him in thy Spheare	*With your bright circle, praise him in your universe*
While day arises, that sweet hour of Prime.	*While day breaks, that lovely first hour.*
Thou Sun, of this great World both Eye and Soule,	*You sun, the eye and the soul of this great world,*
Acknowledge him thy Greater, sound his praise	*Acknowledge him as even greater than you, sing his praise*
In thy eternal course, both when thou climb'st,	*With your everlasting journey, both as you rise*
And when high Noon hast gaind, & when thou fallst.	*And, when you have reached high noon, as you set.*
Moon, that now meetst the orient Sun, now fli'st	*Moon, that now meets the sun in the east, that*
With the fixt Starrs, fixt in thir Orb that flies,	*Now flieswith the stars, fixed in their flying orbit,*
And yee five other wandring Fires that move	*And you five other planets that move*
In mystic Dance not without Song, resound	*In your mystical dance accompanied by heavenly music, sing*
His praise, who out of Darkness call'd up	*His praises, Him who summoned*

Light.	*light from the darkness.*
Aire, and ye Elements the eldest birth	*Air, and you elements that were the first born*
Of Natures Womb, that in quaternion run	*Of Nature, that travel in a fourfold*
Perpetual Circle, multiform; and mix	*Eternal circle, mixing together, and in your mixture*
And nourish all things, let your ceasless change	*Nourish all things, let your neverending changes*
Varie to our great Maker still new praise.	*Vary to give new praise to our great Maker.*
Ye Mists and Exhalations that now rise	*You mists and fogs that rise*
From Hill or steaming Lake, duskie or grey,	*From the hills and steaming lakes, shadowy or grey,*
Till the Sun paint your fleecie skirts with Gold,	*Until the sun touches your fleecy edges with gold,*
In honour to the Worlds great Author rise,	*Rise in honor of the great Creator,*
Whether to deck with Clouds the uncolourd skie,	*Whether to decorate the plain sky with clouds*
Or wet the thirstie Earth with falling showers,	*Or wet the thirsty earth with rain,*
Rising or falling still advance his praise.	*As you rise or fall still give him praise.*
His praise ye Winds, that from four Quarters blow,	*You winds that blow from all four points, give him praise*
Breath soft or loud; and wave your tops, ye Pines,	*As you blow soft or strong; and wave your tops, you pines,*
With every Plant, in sign of Worship wave.	*With all other plants, showing your worship as you wave.*
Fountains and yee, that warble, as ye flow,	*You springs and streams, that murmur harmonious songs*
Melodious murmurs, warbling tune his praise.	*As you flow, praise him with your warbling tune.*
Joyn voices all ye living Souls, ye Birds,	*Join voices all you living souls; you birds,*
That singing up to Heaven Gate ascend,	*That sing as you rise up to the gates of Heaven,*
Bear on your wings and in your notes his praise;	*Carry his praise on your wings and in your song;*
Yee that in Waters glide, and yee that walk	*You that glide through the sea, and you who walk*
The Earth, and stately tread, or lowly creep;	*On land with majestic step or creeping low;*
Witness if I be silent, Morn or Eeven,	*See if I am silent, morning or evening,*
To Hill, or Valley, Fountain, or fresh shade	*The hills, valleys, springs and woods*

168

Original	Modern
Made vocal by my Song, and taught his praise.	Shall ring with my song and shall learn to praise him.
Hail universal Lord, be bounteous still	Hail the ruler of the universe, remain generous
To give us onely good; and if the night	In giving us only good things; and if the night
Have gathered aught of evil or conceald,	Is hiding anything dark or evil,
Disperse it, as now light dispels the dark.	So they prayed in their innocence, and to their minds
Firm peace recoverd soon and wonted calm.	Peace and their accustomed calm soon returned.
On to thir mornings rural work they haste	On to their morning's pastoral work they hurried
Among sweet dewes and flours; where any row	Among the flowers and the sweet dew; where any row
Of Fruit-trees overwoodie reachd too farr	Of overgrown fruit trees reached out too far
Thir pamperd boughes, and needed hands to check	With their well fed branches, they gave needed hands
Fruitless imbraces: or they led the Vine	To check their fruitless growth: or they trained the vine
To wed her Elm; she spous'd about him twines	Around the elm tree; married with him she wraps
Her mariageable arms, and with her brings	Him in her arms, and with her brings
Her dowr th' adopted Clusters, to adorn	Her bounty of bunches of grapes to decorate
His barren leaves. Them thus imploid beheld	His fruitless leaves. So the King of Heaven saw them work,
With pittie Heav'ns high King, and to him call'd	And he pitied them, and to him summoned
RAPHAEL, the sociable Spirit, that deign'd	Raphael, the Spirit friendly to Man, who traveled
To travel with TOBIAS, and secur'd	With Tobias and arranged
His marriage with the seaventimes-wedded Maid.	His marriage to the seven times married maid.
RAPHAEL, said hee, thou hear'st what stir on Earth	"Raphael," he said, "You have heard of what is happening on Earth:
SATAN from Hell scap't through the darksom Gulf	How Satan, escaped from Hell through the dark abyss,
Hath raisd in Paradise, and how disturbd	Has appeared in Paradise, and how he disturbed
This night the human pair, how he designes	In the night this human pair, and how he plans
In them at once to ruin all mankind.	To use them to cause the ruin of all mankind.
Go therefore, half this day as friend with	So go, and spend half the day talking

friend	*with Adam*
Converse with ADAM, in what Bowre or shade	*As friend to friend, in whatever bower or shade*
Thou find'st him from the heat of Noon retir'd,	*You find him sheltering from the noonday heat,*
To respit his day-labour with repast,	*Breaking his work with food*
Or with repose; and such discourse bring on,	*Or rest; and talk to him in a way*
As may advise him of his happie state,	*That will let him know of his happy situation,*
Happiness in his power left free to will,	*With his happiness in the power of his own free will,*
Left to his own free Will, his Will though free,	*Completely his own free will, which although it is free*
Yet mutable; whence warne him to beware	*Is changeable; so warn him to beware thinking*
He swerve not too secure: tell him withal	*That his position is completely safe: tell him about*
His danger, and from whom, what enemie	*The danger he is in, and from who it comes, that the enemy*
Late falln himself from Heav'n, is plotting now	*Who recently fell from Heaven is plotting*
The fall of others from like state of bliss;	*The fall of others from the state of bliss that he once enjoyed.*
By violence, no, for that shall be withstood,	*It will not come from violence, for that can be defended,*
But by deceit and lies; this let him know,	*But from deceit and lies; let him know this,*
Least wilfully transgressing he pretend	*So that if he does choose to disobey he cannot pretend*
Surprisal, unadmonisht, unforewarnd.	*That he is surprised or that he was not warned."*
So spake th' Eternal Father, and fulfilled	*So the eternal father spoke, with the greatest*
All Justice: nor delaid the winged Saint	*Fairness; and the winged saint did not delay*
After his charge receivd, but from among	*Once he had his orders, but from amongst*
Thousand Celestial Ardors, where he stood	*A thousand other angels, where he stood*
Vaild with his gorgeous wings, up springing light	*Wrapped in his gorgeous wings, he sprang up*
Flew through the midst of Heav'n; th' angelic Quires	*And flew through the middle of Heaven; the choirs of angels*
On each hand parting, to his speed gave	*Parted on each side to let him*

way	*through*
Through all th' Empyreal road; till at the Gate	*All along the path of Heaven, until he arrived at the Gate*
Of Heav'n arriv'd, the gate self-opend wide	*Of Heaven, and the gate opened wide by itself,*
On golden Hinges turning, as by work	*Turning on golden hinges, as with his divine craftsmanship*
Divine the sov'ran Architect had fram'd.	*The supreme architect had designed them.*
From hence, no cloud, or, to obstruct his sight,	*From there no stars or clouds blocked his view,*
Starr interpos'd, however small he sees,	*He could see everything however small, and he saw,*
Not unconform to other shining Globes,	*Not unlike the other shining planets,*
Earth and the Gard'n of God, with Cedars crownd	*Earth and the garden of God, with cedars*
Above all Hills. As when by night the Glass	*Crowning the hilltops.As when at nighttime the telescope*
Of GALILEO, less assur'd, observes	*Of Galileo, less far seeing, sees*
Imagind Lands and Regions in the Moon:	*What he believes are lands and continents on the moon:*
Or Pilot from amidst the CYCLADES	*Or a sailor in the Cyclades islands,*
DELOS or SAMOS first appeering kenns	*Delos or Samos sees the first appearance*
A cloudy spot. Down thither prone in flight	*Of a speck of cloud.Straight down, stretched out in flight,*
He speeds, and through the vast Ethereal Skie	*He speeds, and through the vast skies of Heaven*
Sailes between worlds & worlds, with steddie wing	*He sails between the planets, gliding on*
Now on the polar windes, then with quick Fann	*The polar winds, then with quick wings*
Winnows the buxom Air; till within soare	*He beats the supporting air; until he has reached*
Of Towring Eagles, to all the Fowles he seems	*The highest point the eagles can attain, and to all the birds he seems*
A PHOENIX, gaz'd by all, as that sole Bird	*To be a phoenix, watched by all as that solitary bird is*
When to enshrine his reliques in the Sun's	*When he flies to Thebes in Egypt to bury his remains*
Bright Temple, to AEGYPTIAN THEB'S he flies.	*In the bright temple of the sun.*
At once on th' Eastern cliff of Paradise	*At once he lands on the eastern cliff of Paradise,*
He lights, and to his proper shape returns	*And returns to his proper shape*

A Seraph wingd; six wings he wore, to shade
His lineaments Divine; the pair that clad
Each shoulder broad, came mantling o're his brest
With regal Ornament; the middle pair

Girt like a Starrie Zone his waste, and round
Skirted his loines and thighes with downie Gold
And colours dipt in Heav'n; the third his feet
Shaddowd from either heele with featherd maile
Skie-tinctur'd grain. Like MAIA'S son he stood,
And shook his Plumes, that Heav'nly fragrance filld
The circuit wide. Strait knew him all the bands
Of Angels under watch; and to his state,

And to his message high in honour rise;

For on som message high they guessd him bound.
Thir glittering Tents he passd, and now is come
Into the blissful field, through Groves of Myrrhe,
And flouring Odours, Cassia, Nard, and Balme;
A Wilderness of sweets; for Nature here
Wantond as in her prime, and plaid at will

Her Virgin Fancies, pouring forth more sweet,
Wilde above rule or art; enormous bliss.
Him through the spicie Forrest onward com
ADAM discernd, as in the dore he sat
Of his coole Bowre, while now the mounted Sun
Shot down direct his fervid Raies, to warme

Earths inmost womb, more warmth then

Of a winged Seraph: he had six wings, to shade
His heavenly features; one pair came From his broad shoulders and cloaked his chest
With Kingly decoration; the middle pair
Were wrapped around his waist like a starry belt,
And made a skirt for his loins and thighs with golden feathers
Dipped in the colors of Heaven; the third pair
Grew from his heels and covered his feet with feathery armor
The color of the sky. He stood like Maia's son,
And shook his feathers so that a heavenly scent
Spread far and wide. At once all the watching angel guards
Recognised him, and rose to acknowledge his status
And the errandhe was performing,

For they guessed that he was on a mission from God.
He passed their glittering tents, and comes
Into the happy garden, through groves of myrrh,
And the flowering scent of cassia, nard and balm,
A sweet wilderness, for Nature here Flourished innocently, and experimented
With all the things at her disposal, pouring out sweetness,
Wild beyond control; enormous bliss.
Adam saw him approaching through The spicy forest, as he sat in the door Of his cool shelter, while now the ascended sun
Shot his burning rays directly down, to warm
The very heart of Earth with more

ADAM
need;
And EVE within, due at her hour prepar'd

For dinner savourie fruits, of taste to please

True appetite, and not disrelish thirst
Of nectarous draughts between, from milkie stream,
Berrie or Grape: to whom thus ADAM call'd.
Haste hither EVE, and worth thy sight behold
Eastward among those Trees, what glorious shape
Comes this way moving; seems another Morn
Ris'n on mid-noon; som great behest from Heav'n
To us perhaps he brings, and will voutsafe

This day to be our Guest. But goe with speed,
And what thy stores contain, bring forth and poure
Abundance, fit to honour and receive

Our Heav'nly stranger; well we may afford

Our givers thir own gifts, and large bestow

From large bestowd, where Nature multiplies
Her fertil growth, and by disburd'ning grows
More fruitful, which instructs us not to spare.
To whom thus EVE. ADAM, earths hallowd mould,
Of God inspir'd, small store will serve, where store,
All seasons, ripe for use hangs on the stalk;

Save what by frugal storing firmness gains

To nourish, and superfluous moist

*warmth
than Adam needed,
And inside Eve performed her duty of the hour, preparing
A dinner of savory fruit of a taste that would please
The appetite, and to serve thirst
There were sweet drinks like nectar, made from milk,
Berries or grapes; Adam called to her:
"Come quickly, Eve, and look
East amongst those trees, see what a glorious shape
Is coming this way; it seems like another morning
Rising at midday; perhaps he's bringing us
Some great order from Heaven, and will agree
To be our guest today. But go quickly
And bring out the best you have in store,
And lots of it, suited to honor and welcome
Our Heavenly stranger; it is right that we should share
The gifts with the giver, and be generous
Where we have received generosity, where Nature grows and grows,
And where when she sheds her seeds she
Becomes more fruitful, and so we need keep nothing back."
Eve said to him: "Adam, molded from sacred earth,
Created by God, we do not need a store, when
At all times what we need hangs ripe and ready for us;
We only store things that ripen when stored,
Or that need drying out:*

consumes:

Original	Modern
But I will haste and from each bough and break,	But I will hurry and from each branch and bush,
Each Plant & juciest Gourd will pluck such choice	Plant and juicy vegetable I shall pick the best
To entertain our Angel guest, as hee	To entertain our angel guest so that when he sees them
Beholding shall confess that here on Earth	He will admit that God has given us just as good
God hath dispenst his bounties as in Heav'n.	Things on Earth as there are in Heaven."
So saying, with dispatchful looks in haste	Saying this, with a quick farewell glance,
She turns, on hospitable thoughts intent	She turned, thinking of her hospitality
What choice to chuse for delicacie best,	And which delicacies would be the best choice
What order, so contriv'd as not to mix	And what order she should serve them in, arranged not to mix
Tastes, not well joynd, inelegant, but bring	Tastes in a clumsy way, but to bring out
Taste after taste upheld with kindliest change,	Taste after taste, complimenting each other.
Bestirs her then, and from each tender stalk	This was her task, and from each tender stalk
Whatever Earth all-bearing Mother yields	Whatever the fruitful earth gives,
In INDIA East or West, or middle shoare	In India, west or east, or the Mediterranean coast
In PONTUS or the PUNIC Coast, or where	Of Pontus or Africa, or the kingdom
ALCINOUS reign'd, fruit of all kindes, in coate,	Of Alcinous, fruit of all kinds, with skin
Rough, or smooth rin'd, or bearded husk, or shell	Rough or smooth, or hairy coating or shell,
She gathers, Tribute large, and on the board	She gathers, a great offering, and heaps the table
Heaps with unsparing hand; for drink the Grape	With a generous hand; for drink she crushes grapes,
She crushes, inoffensive moust, and meathes	Unfermented juice, and the flesh
From many a berrie, and from sweet kernels prest	Of many berries, and from sweet crushed nuts
She tempers dulcet creams, nor these to hold	She makes sweet creams. She does not lack
Wants her fit vessels pure, then strews the ground	Cups to hold them in, and she covers the floor
With Rose and Odours from the shrub	With the natural perfume of rose

unfum'd.
Mean while our Primitive great Sire, to meet
His god-like Guest, walks forth, without more train
Accompani'd then with his own compleat

Perfections, in himself was all his state,
More solemn then the tedious pomp that waits
On Princes, when thir rich Retinue long
Of Horses led, and Grooms besmeard with Gold
Dazles the croud, and sets them all agape.

Neerer his presence ADAM though not awd,
Yet with submiss approach and reverence meek,
As to a superior Nature, bowing low,

Thus said.
Native of Heav'n, for other place
None can then Heav'n such glorious shape contain;
Since by descending from the Thrones above,
Those happie places thou hast deignd a while
To want, and honour these, voutsafe with us
Two onely, who yet by sov'ran gift possess

This spacious ground, in yonder shadie Bowre
To rest, and what the Garden choicest bears

To sit and taste, till this meridian heat
Be over, and the Sun more coole decline.

Whom thus the Angelic Vertue answerd milde.
ADAM, I therefore came, nor art thou such

Created, or such place hast here to dwell,
As may not oft invite, though Spirits of

petals.
Meanwhile our great forebear, to meet
His Godlike guest, walks out, without any
Adornment except his own complete perfection,
His own body was his robes of state,
Greater than the tedious show that follows
Princes, when with their great train
Of horses and grooms dressed in gold
They dazzle the crowd and sets them all staring.
Adam came nearer to him, not afraid

But with the submission and meek reverence
Due to a superior being, and bowing low

He spoke:
"Native of Heaven, for no other place
Than Heaven could produce such a wonderful form,
Since by descending from the Heavenly thrones
You have agreed to honor these happy places
For a while, stay with us;
We are only two but by the gift of God we own

This wide place: in the shady shelter there
Come and rest, and taste the best things of the garden,
Until this noonday heat
Has passed and the sun gives cooler warmth."
The virtuous angel answered him sweetly:
"Adam, that is why I came, nor are you or
Your dwelling place unfit
To receive guests, even if they are

175

Heav'n	*Spirits of Heaven.*
To visit thee; lead on then where thy Bowre	*Lead on to where your shelter*
	of the day, until sunset,
I have at will. So to the Silvan Lodge	*I have at my disposal." So to the*
	wooded home
They came, that like POMONA'S Arbour smil'd	*They came, that like the house of Pomona smiled*
With flourets deck't and fragrant smells; but EVE	*Decorated with flowers and sweet scents; but Eve*
Undeckt, save with her self more lovely fair	*Was not decorated, she was just herself, more lovely*
Then Wood-Nymph, or the fairest Goddess feign'd	*Than a wood nymph, or than the fairest goddess imagined*
Of three that in Mount IDA naked strove,	*Of the three that fought on Mount Ida.*
Stood to entertain her guest from Heav'n; no vaile	*So she stood to entertain her guest from Heaven, needing*
Shee needed, Vertue-proof, no thought infirme	*No veil, for she was virtuous, and no shame*
Alterd her cheek. On whom the Angel HAILE	*Brought any blush to her cheek. The angel greeted her*
Bestowd, the holy salutation us'd	*With the holy words used long afterwards*
Long after to blest MARIE, second EVE.	*To blessed Mary, the second Eve.*
Haile Mother of Mankind, whose fruitful Womb	*"Hail the Mother of Mankind, whose fruitful womb*
Shall fill the World more numerous with thy Sons	*Shall people the world with a greater number of sons*
Then with these various fruits the Trees of God	*Than the numbers of fruits which the trees of God*
Have heap'd this Table. Rais'd of grassie terf	*Have piled on this table." Their table was made*
Thir Table was, and mossie seats had round,	*Of grassy turf, and had mossy seats around it,*
And on her ample Square from side to side	*And from side to side of its wide top*
All AUTUMN pil'd, though SPRING and	*All the fruits of autumn were piled, although*
AUTUMN here	*spring and autumn*
Danc'd hand in hand. A while discourse they hold;	*Are both present at the same time in that place. They talk for a while,*
No fear lest Dinner coole; when thus began	*Not worrying that their dinner would cool, and then our ancestor*
Our Authour	*Spoke:*
Heav'nly stranger, please to taste	*"Heavenly stranger, please sample*
These bounties which our Nourisher, from	*These gifts which our nourisher, from*

176

whom
All perfet good unmeasur'd out, descends,
To us for food and for delight hath caus'd

The Earth to yeild; unsavourie food perhaps

To spiritual Natures; only this I know,
That one Celestial Father gives to all.

To whom the Angel. Therefore what he gives
(Whose praise be ever sung) to man in part

Spiritual, may of purest Spirits be found
No ingrateful food: and food alike those pure
Intelligential substances require
As doth your Rational; and both contain
Within them every lower facultie
Of sense, whereby they hear, see, smell, touch, taste,
Tasting concoct, digest, assimilate,
And corporeal to incorporeal turn.
For know, whatever was created, needs

To be sustaind and fed; of Elements

The grosser feeds the purer, earth the sea,

Earth and the Sea feed Air, the Air those Fires
Ethereal, and as lowest first the Moon;
Whence in her visage round those spots, unpurg'd

Vapours not yet into her substance turnd.

Nor doth the Moon no nourishment exhale
From her moist Continent to higher Orbes.

The Sun that light imparts to all, receives
From all his alimental recompence
In humid exhalations, and at Even

Sups with the Ocean: though in Heav'n the Trees

whom
All good comes, has sent down to us,
For our food and our enjoyment he has made
The Earth grow them; it may not be the right food
For angels; I only know that
The one Heavenly Father gives to all."

The Angel replied: "And so what he gives
(May it always be praised) to man, who is part
Spirit, even the purest Spirits
Will enjoy: and beings of pure intelligence
Need food just as much
As rational beings like you; they have
The same faculties
Of sense, hearing, seeing, smell, touch, taste,
They taste, digest and absorb
And turn the physical into energy.
For you should know that whatever has been created
Needs to be sustained and fed; with the Elements
The coarser ones feed the purer: earth feeds the sea,
The sea and earth feed the air, the air feeds the fires
Of Heaven, starting with the Moon,
Where you can see those spots on her face

Which are spots of air not yet turned into her fire.

And the moon gives nourishment
From her moist lands to the higher planets.

The sun that gives light to all
Is repaid by all
With humid evaporation, and in the evening

Drinks from the ocean: though in Heaven the trees

177

Of life ambrosial frutage bear, and vines
Yeild Nectar, though from off the boughs each Morn
We brush mellifluous Dewes, and find the ground
Cover'd with pearly grain: yet God hath here
Varied his bounty so with new delights,
As may compare with Heaven; and to taste

Think not I shall be nice.
So down they sat,
And to thir viands fell, nor seemingly
The Angel, nor in mist, the common gloss

Of Theologians, but with keen dispatch
Of real hunger, and concoctive heate

To transubstantiate; what redounds, transpires
Through Spirits with ease; nor wonder; if by fire
Of sooty coal the Empiric Alchimist

Can turn, or holds it possible to turn

Metals of drossiest Ore to perfet Gold
As from the Mine. Mean while at Table EVE
Ministerd naked, and thir flowing cups

With pleasant liquors crown'd: O innocence

Deserving Paradise! if ever, then,

Then had the Sons of God excuse to have bin
Enamour'd at that sight; but in those hearts

Love unlibidinous reign'd, nor jealousie
Was understood, the injur'd Lovers Hell.

Thus when with meats & drinks they had suffic'd,
Not burd'nd Nature, sudden mind arose

Of life bear ambrosial fruit, and vines
Give nectar, through from the branches each morning
We gather sweet dews, and find the ground
Covered with grain like pearls; yet in this place God has
So varied his gifts with new delights
That it may be compared to Heaven; and don't think

I am too fussy to try them."
So they sat down
And started their meal, and the angel,
Who did not seem to be made of mist, as

Theologians often claim, joined in
With real hunger and with real digestion

Turned one thing into another; what remains
Passes from Spirits easily; why should this be surprising,
When with a fire of dirty coal the experimental scientist

Can turn, or thinks it is possible to turn,

The basest metals into gold as perfect
As that from the mine? Meanwhile at the table Eve
Served naked, and filled their flowing cups

With sweet liquids to the brim: oh innocence,

Which deserves Paradise! If there was ever a time

That the sons of God had an excuse to become lustful
It would have been now, seeing the angel; but in those hearts

Love ruled without lust, and jealousy,
The Hell of unhappy lovers, was unknown.

Then when they had had just enough food and drink,
And not overindulged, it suddenly occurred

178

In ADAM, not to let th' occasion pass

Given him by this great Conference to know
Of things above his World, and of thir being

Who dwell in Heav'n, whose excellence he saw
Transcend his own so farr, whose radiant forms
Divine effulgence, whose high Power so far

Exceeded human, and his wary speech

Thus to th' Empyreal Minister he fram'd.
Inhabitant with God, now know I well

Thy favour, in this honour done to man,
Under whose lowly roof thou hast voutsaf't

To enter, and these earthly fruits to taste,
Food not of Angels, yet accepted so,

As that more willingly thou couldst not seem
At Heav'ns high feasts to have fed: yet what compare?
To whom the winged Hierarch repli'd.
 O ADAM, one Almightie is, from whom

All things proceed, and up to him return,

If not deprav'd from good, created all

Such to perfection, one first matter all,

Indu'd with various forms, various degrees

Of substance, and in things that live, of life;
But more refin'd, more spiritous, and pure,

As neerer to him plac't or neerer tending

Each in thir several active Sphears assignd,

To Adam that he should not let the chance pass by
Which this great meeting gave him to learn
Of the things above his world, and what those who
Live in Heaven are like, those whose excellence he could see
Was far greater than his own, whose shining forms
Are made of heavenly light, whose great power was so much
Greater than man's, and so he nervously spoke
To the Minister of Heaven.
"You who live with God, I am very aware
Of the honor you have done us
By agreeing to come into our humble home
And eating our earthly food,
Not the food of angels, but accepted as if it was;
You could not have eaten more willingly
If you were actually at a feast in Heaven; but how does it compare?"
The winged angel replied:
"Oh Adam, there is only one God, from whom
All things come and to whom all returns
If it has not been turned from good. He created all,
With such perfection, all made of the same original material,
Given different forms and different sizes
And in living things different lifespans;
But the more refined, the more spiritual, the purest
Are placed closer to him or attend him more closely,
Each one assigned their position,

Till body up to spirit work, in bounds	*Until the body becomes the spirit, in steps*
Proportiond to each kind. So from the root	*Of appropriate size for each kind. So from the root*
Springs lighter the green stalk, from thence the leaves	*There comes the lighter green stalk, from that come leaves,*
More aerie, last the bright consummate floure	*Still lighter, and at last the bright flower*
Spirits odorous breathes: flours and thir fruit	*Which breathes perfume: flowers and their fruit,*
Mans nourishment, by gradual scale sublim'd	*Man's nourishment, aspire by gradual steps*
To vital Spirits aspire, to animal,	*To rise to the level of Spirits, to be animal,*
To intellectual, give both life and sense,	*Intellectual, to have life and sense,*
Fansie and understanding, whence the soule	*Imagination and understanding, from where the soul*
Reason receives, and reason is her being,	*Receives reason, and reason is what makes her,*
Discursive, or Intuitive; discourse	*Discursive, or intuitive: yours is most often*
Is oftest yours, the latter most is ours,	*Discursive, ours intuitive,*
Differing but in degree, of kind the same.	*Different in strength but of the same kind.*
Wonder not then, what God for you saw good	*Do not be surprised then if I don't refuse*
If I refuse not, but convert, as you,	*What God thought good for you, but convert it, as you do,*
To proper substance; time may come when men	*Into what is needed; there may come a time when men*
With Angels may participate, and find	*Dine with the angels, and find*
No inconvenient Diet, nor too light Fare:	*No food that they cannot eat or is too light for them:*
And from these corporal nutriments perhaps	*And from this physical nourishmentperhaps*
Your bodies may at last turn all to Spirit	*Your bodies might turn at last to Spirits,*
Improv'd by tract of time, and wingd ascend	*Improved by passing time, and fly up,*
Ethereal, as wee, or may at choice	*Heavenly as we are, and may choos*
Here or in Heav'nly Paradises dwell;	*To live here or in the Paradise of Heaven;*
If ye be found obedient, and retain	*This may happen if you remain obedient, and keep*
Unalterably firm his love entire	*Without alteration the full love*
Whose progenie you are. Mean while enjoy	*Of the one whose children you are. Meanwhile enjoy*

Your fill what happiness this happie state	*Your fill of the happiness your current happy state*
Can comprehend, incapable of more.	*Gives you, the most you can understand at this time."*
To whom the Patriarch of mankind repli'd.	*The father of mankind answered him:*
O favourable spirit, propitious guest,	*"You kind Spirit, welcome guest,*
Well hast thou taught the way that might direct	*You have shown us the way*
Our knowledge, and the scale of Nature set	*That we should think, and laid out the whole of Nature*
From center to circumference, whereon	*From end to end, so that*
In contemplation of created things	*In observing the things of creation*
By steps we may ascend to God. But say,	*We may rise up by steps to understanding of God. But tell me,*
What meant that caution joind, IF YE BE FOUND	*What did you mean by that warning,*
OBEDIENT? can wee want obedience then	*'If you are obedient'?*
To him, or possibly his love desert	*How could we lack obedience To him, or turn our backs on his love,*
Who formd us from the dust, and plac'd us here	*Who made us from the dust, and put us here,*
Full to the utmost measure of what bliss	*Enjoying the greatest pleasure*
Human desires can seek or apprehend?	*That humans can ask for or understand?"*
To whom the Angel. Son of Heav'n and Earth,	*The angel replied: "Son of Heaven and Earth,*
Attend: That thou art happie, owe to God;	*Be warned: you owe your happiness to God;*
That thou continu'st such, owe to thy self,	*To remain happy is your responsibility,*
That is, to thy obedience; therein stand.	*For you must always remain obedient.*
This was that caution giv'n thee; be advis'd.	*That was the warning I gave you, take note of it.*
God made thee perfet, not immutable;	*God made you perfect, not unchangeable;*
And good he made thee, but to persevere	*He made you good, but to remain good*
He left it in thy power, ordaind thy will	*He left up to you, giving you free will*
By nature free, not over-rul'd by Fate	*As part of your nature, and you cannot be ruled over by*
Inextricable, or strict necessity;	*Unavoidable fate, or act through complete lack of choice.*
Our voluntarie service he requires,	*He asks us to serve him voluntarily,*
Not our necessitated, such with him	*Not because we are forced: that sort of service*
Findes no acceptance, nor can find, for how	*Will not be accepted, for how*

Can hearts, not free, be tri'd whether they serve	*Can hearts which are not free show if they are serving*
Willing or no, who will but what they must	*Willingly or not, if they can only do what they are forced to*
By Destinie, and can no other choose?	*By destiny, having no other choice?*
My self and all th' Angelic Host that stand	*Myself and all the Host of Angels that stand*
In sight of God enthron'd, our happie state	*In front of God's throne, our happy state*
Hold, as you yours, while our obedience holds;	*Lasts, as yours does, as long as our obedience lasts;*
On other surety none; freely we serve.	*That is all he asks, and we serve through our choice.*
Because wee freely love, as in our will	*Because we choose to love, and have the power*
To love or not; in this we stand or fall:	*To love or not, we stand or fall by our choice:*
And som are fall'n, to disobedience fall'n,	*And some have fallen, through disobedience,*
And so from Heav'n to deepest Hell; O fall	*And been thrown down from Heaven to deepest Hell;*
From what high state of bliss into what woe!	*What a fall, from such ecstasy into such sorrow!"*
To whom our great Progenitor. Thy words	*Our great forefather answered: "I have paid more attention,*
Attentive, and with more delighted eare	*Holy teacher, to your words, and listened with more delight*
Divine instructer, I have heard, then when	*Than when I have heard*
Cherubic Songs by night from neighbouring Hills	*Angel songs sending out airy music*
Aereal Music send: nor knew I not	*From neighboring hills: I did not know*
To be both will and deed created free;	*That we were created to have free will and do as we wish;*
Yet that we never shall forget to love	*But that we could ever forget to love*
Our maker, and obey him whose command	*Our maker, and obey him who has only give us*
Single, is yet so just, my constant thoughts	*One command, and that a fair one,*
Assur'd me and still assure: though what thou tellst	*I am sure that will not happen: though what you tell me*
Hath past in Heav'n, som doubt within me move,	*Has happened in Heaven causes me some doubt,*
But more desire to hear, if thou consent,	*And I would like to hear more, if you are willing,*
The full relation, which must needs be	*The whole story, which must be very*

strange,
Worthy of Sacred silence to be heard;

And we have yet large day, for scarce the Sun
Hath finisht half his journey, and scarce begins
His other half in the great Zone of Heav'n.

Thus ADAM made request, and RAPHAEL
After short pause assenting, thus began.
High matter thou injoinst me, O prime of men,
Sad task and hard, for how shall I relate
To human sense th' invisible exploits

Of warring Spirits; how without remorse
The ruin of so many glorious once

And perfet while they stood; how last unfould
The secrets of another world, perhaps

Not lawful to reveal? yet for thy good

This is dispenc't, and what surmounts the reach
Of human sense, I shall delineate so,

By lik'ning spiritual to corporal forms,

As may express them best, though what if Earth
Be but the shaddow of Heav'n, and things therein
Each to other like, more then on earth is thought?
As yet this world was not, and CHAOS wilde
Reignd where these Heav'ns now rowl, where Earth now rests
Upon her Center pois'd, when on a day

(For Time, though in Eternitie, appli'd

To motion, measures all things durable

strange
And worthy of being listened to with all attention;
And we still have plenty of time, for the sun
Has hardly finished half his journey, and has only just
Begun the other half across the great sky."
So Adam asked, and Raphael,
Agreeing, after a short pause, began.
"You have set me a hard task, first man,
Hard and sad, for how can I explain
To a human mind the invisible actions
Of warring Spirits? How can I tell
Without sorrow of the downfall of so many who were glorious once
And perfect when in Heaven? How can I reveal
The secrets of another world, which perhaps
I am forbidden to do? But for your benefit
It is allowed, and what is beyond
Human understanding I shall describe
By comparing spiritual to physical forms,
In the most understandable way, but it may be that Earth
Is just a reflection of Heaven, and the things in them
Are more similar to each other than is thought on Earth.
This world did not exist, and wild Chaos
Ruled where the skies are now, where Earth rests
Balanced on her center, when one day
(For time, though endless, when joined
To motion measures all physical

By present, past, and future) on such day

As Heav'ns great Year brings forth, th' Empyreal Host
Of Angels by Imperial summons call'd,
Innumerable before th' Almighties Throne

Forthwith from all the ends of Heav'n appeerd
Under thir Hierarchs in orders bright

Ten thousand thousand Ensignes high advanc'd,
Standards, and Gonfalons twixt Van and Reare
Streame in the Aire, and for distinction serve
Of Hierarchies, of Orders, and Degrees;
Or in thir glittering Tissues bear imblaz'd

Holy Memorials, acts of Zeale and Love

Recorded eminent. Thus when in Orbes

Of circuit inexpressible they stood,

Orb within Orb, the Father infinite,

By whom in bliss imbosom'd sat the Son,

Amidst as from a flaming Mount, whose top

Brightness had made invisible, thus spake.

Hear all ye Angels, Progenie of Light,

Thrones, Dominations, Princedoms, Vertues, Powers,
Hear my Decree, which unrevok't shall stand.
This day I have begot whom I declare
My onely Son, and on this holy Hill
Him have anointed, whom ye now behold

At my right hand; your Head I him appoint;

---

things
By present, past and future), on the day
Of the change of Heaven's long year, the Heavenly host
Were summoned by God's angels,
And countless before the Almighty throne
At once from all corners of Heaven there came
Under their leaders with their bright badges
Ten million junior officers with their flags
Held high, and banners between the front and back
Streamed in the air, and marked the boundaries
Of organizations, orders and ranks;
Or on their shining cloth were embroidered
Holy Memorials, with acts of courage and love
Written prominently. So when in circles
Of unmeasurable circumference they stood,
Circles within circles, the Eternal Father,
Next to whom sat the Son, cloaked in bliss,
Spoke, appearing to be a flaming mountain
Whose top was made invisible by its brightness.
'Hear all you angels, children of light,
Thrones, dominions, princedoms, virtues, powers,
Hear my order, which shall not be changed.
Today I have created the one I call
My only son, and on this holy hill
I have anointed him, the one you see now
On my right side; I appoint him your

184

And by my Self have sworn to him shall bow
All knees in Heav'n, and shall confess him Lord:
Under his great Vice-gerent Reign abide
United as one individual Soule
For ever happie: him who disobeyes
Mee disobeyes, breaks union, and that day
Cast out from God and blessed vision, falls

Into utter darkness, deep ingulft, his place

Ordaind without redemption, without end.

So spake th' Omnipotent, and with his words
All seemd well pleas'd, all seem'd, but were not all.
That day, as other solem dayes, they spent

In song and dance about the sacred Hill,

Mystical dance, which yonder starrie Spheare
Of Planets and of fixt in all her Wheeles
Resembles nearest, mazes intricate,

Eccentric, intervolv'd, yet regular
Then most, when most irregular they seem:

And in thir motions harmonie Divine
So smooths her charming tones, that Gods own ear
Listens delighted. Eevning approachd

(For we have also our Eevning and our Morn,
We ours for change delectable, not need)

Forthwith from dance to sweet repast they turn
Desirous, all in Circles as they stood,
Tables are set, and on a sudden pil'd
With Angels Food, and rubied Nectar flows:

chief,
And have sworn that all knees in Heaven
Shall bow to him and acknowledge him as Lord:
Live under his great viceregency,
United as one soul,
Happy forever: if you disobey him
You disobey me, and on that day
You will be cast away from God and my holy sight

And fall into utter darkness, a deep pit, a place

Where you shall stay, unforgiven, forever.'

So spoke the all powerful One, and with his words
All seemed well pleased. All seemed to be, but not all were.
That day, was spent, as other special days were

In singing and dancing around the sacred hill,

A mysterious dance, which that starry realm
Of planets all fixed in their orbits
Closely resembles: intricate wandering,

Strange, intertwined, yet most regular
When they appear to be at their least regular:

And their motions so reflect
The music of Heaven, that God himself
Is delighted to listen. Evening now approached,

(For we also have morning and evening,
Though we change them for pleasure, not because it is needed)

And they turned from the dance to a sweet meal,
Hungry, they all stood in circles,
Tables are set, and suddenly piled
With Angel's food, and deep red nectar flows:

In Pearl, in Diamond, and massie Gold,

Fruit of delicious Vines, the growth of Heav'n.

They eat, they drink, and with refection sweet
Are fill'd, before th' all bounteous King, who showrd
With copious hand, rejoycing in thir joy.

Now when ambrosial Night with Clouds exhal'd
From that high mount of God, whence light & shade
Spring both, the face of brightest Heav'n had changd
To grateful Twilight (for Night comes not there
In darker veile) and roseat Dews dispos'd

All but the unsleeping eyes of God to rest,

Wide over all the Plain, and wider farr

Then all this globous Earth in Plain outspred,
(Such are the Courts of God) Th' Angelic throng
Disperst in Bands and Files thir Camp extend
By living Streams among the Trees of Life,

Pavilions numberless, and sudden reard,

Celestial Tabernacles, where they slept
Fannd with coole Winds, save those who in thir course
Melodious Hymns about the sovran Throne

Alternate all night long:
but not so wak'd
SATAN, so call him now, his former name

Is heard no more Heav'n; he of the first,

In crockery of pearl, of diamond and massive gold
They eat and drink and are filled

With the fruits of delicious vines and the crops of Heaven,
In front of the generous King, who supplied
All with a free hand, rejoicing in their happiness.
Now when sweet night with clouds
Drifted from the high mountain of God, from which
Both light and shade grow, the bright face of Heaven had changed
To a peaceful twilight (for that is as dark as night
Becomes there) and rose colored dews
Soothed all eyes to sleep, except those of God, who never sleeps,
Far and wide across the plains, far wider than
If all this round Earth was spread out flat,
(For this is how it is in Heaven) the angelic throng
Dispersed into groups and stretched their camps
By living streams amongst the trees of life,
With numberless tents and suddenly erected
Heavenly canopies, where they slept
Fanned by cool breezes, apart from those
Who took their turn walking around the Holy throne
Singing hymns all night long;
but this was not
How Satan stayed awake, we'll call him that now, his former name
Is no longer used in Heaven; he was of the first rank,

186

If not the first Arch-Angel, great in Power,	*If not actually the first, of the archangels, great in power,*
In favour and praeeminence, yet fraught	*In favour and position, but torn*
With envie against the Son of God, that day	*With envy against the Son of God who had that day*
Honourd by his great Father, and proclaimd	*Been honored by his great father, declared*
MESSIAH King anointed, could not beare	*Messiah, the anointed King: his pride meant*
Through pride that sight, and thought himself impaird.	*He could not bear the sight, and thought it belittled him.*
Deep malice thence conceiving & disdain,	*With deep hatred and contempt growing within him,*
Soon as midnight brought on the duskie houre	*As soon as midnight brought the dark hour,*
Friendliest to sleep and silence, he resolv'd	*Best suited to sleep and silence, he decided*
With all his Legions to dislodge, and leave	*To decamp with all his legions, and leave*
Unworshipt, unobey'd the Throne supream	*Unworshipped, unobeyed the supreme throne*
Contemptuous, and his next subordinate	*Which he now hated, and waking up his second in command*
Awak'ning, thus to him in secret spake.	*Spoke to him secretly.*
Sleepst thou Companion dear, what sleep can close	*'How can you sleep, my dear companion,*
Thy eye-lids? and remembrest what Decree	*If you remember the order of yesterday,*
Of yesterday, so late hath past the lips	*That which so recently was spoken*
Of Heav'ns Almightie. Thou to me thy thoughts	*By Heaven's greatest. You and I*
Wast wont, I mine to thee was wont to impart;	*Are accustomed to sharing the same thoughts,*
Both waking we were one; how then can now	*We were both as one when awake; how can you now*
Thy sleep dissent? new Laws thou seest impos'd;	*Disagree with sleep? You see the new laws,*
New Laws from him who reigns, new minds may raise	*New laws from the one who reigns, which might inspire*
In us who serve, new Counsels, to debate	*New thoughts in we who serve, new Councils to debate*
What doubtful may ensue, more in this place	*What action should be taken; it's not safe to say more*
To utter is not safe. Assemble thou	*In this place. Assemble all of those*
Of all those Myriads which we lead the	*Numberless armies which are loyal to*

chief;
Tell them that by command, ere yet dim Night
Her shadowie Cloud withdraws, I am to haste,
And all who under me thir Banners wave,
Homeward with flying march where we possess
The Quarters of the North, there to prepare
Fit entertainment to receive our King

The great MESSIAH, and his new commands,
Who speedily through all the Hierarchies

Intends to pass triumphant, and give Laws.
So spake the false Arch-Angel, and infus'd
Bad influence into th' unwarie brest

Of his Associate; hee together calls,

Or several one by one, the Regent Powers,
Under him Regent, tells, as he was taught,

That the most High commanding, now ere Night,
Now ere dim Night had disincumberd Heav'n,
The great Hierarchal Standard was to move;

Tells the suggested cause, and casts between

Ambiguous words and jealousies, to sound

Or taint integritie; but all obey'd

The wonted signal, and superior voice
Of thir great Potentate; for great indeed

His name, and high was his degree in Heav'n;
His count'nance, as the Morning Starr that guides
The starrie flock, allur'd them, and with lyes
Drew after him the third part of Heav'ns Host:

---

us;
Tell them that by my order, before morning
I am going to hurry
With all those who serve under me,
Homeward in double time to our lands
In the North, where we will prepare
An appropriate entertainment for our King,

The great Messiah, and his new commands,
Who intends to speed through the ranks

In triumph, and hand out his laws.'
So the false Archangel spoke, and put
Bad influence into the unguarded heart

Of his comrade; he calls, either in groups

Or singly, the powers of regency,
Who served under him as regent and tells what he has been told,

That the highest had commanded,

That before night had left Heaven,
The great flag of their order was to move;

He tells them the reason, and in between

Throws in ambiguous words and hatred, to test

Or damage their integrity; but all obeyed

The order and superior command
Of their great leader, for his name was indeed great,

And he was of high rank in Heaven;
His face drew them, just as the morning star
Guides all the stars, and with lies
Hedrew away a third of the Host of Heaven:

Mean while th' Eternal eye, whose sight discernes	*Meanwhile the eternal eye, whose sight makes out*
Abstrusest thoughts, from forth his holy Mount	*The deepest thoughts, from his holy mountain*
And from within the golden Lamps that burne	*And from within the golden lamps which burn*
Nightly before him, saw without thir light	*Nightly before him, saw without their light*
Rebellion rising, saw in whom, how spred	*Rebellion rising, saw who had joined it, how it had spread*
Among the sons of Morn, what multitudes	*Amongst the sons of morning, what numbers*
Were banded to oppose his high Decree;	*Had gathered to oppose his high order;*
And smiling to his onely Son thus said. Son, thou in whom my glory I behold	*And smiling he spoke to his only son. 'Son, you in whom I see my glory reflected*
In full resplendence, Heir of all my might,	*'To its highest level, inheritor of all my strength,*
Neerly it now concernes us to be sure Of our Omnipotence, and with what Arms	*Now is the time we must be sure Of our omnipotence, and decide with what arms*
We mean to hold what anciently we claim Of Deitie or Empire, such a foe	*We mean to retain our ancient claims Of Godliness and Empire: there is such an enemy*
Is rising, who intends to erect his Throne Equal to ours, throughout the spacious North;	*Rising, who intends to set up a throne Equal to ours, in the wide northern lands;*
Nor so content, hath in his thought to trie	*He will not stop there, he is planning to fight us*
In battel, what our Power is, or our right.	*In battle and test our powers and our rights.*
Let us advise, and to this hazard draw	*Let us prepare, and to face this danger gather*
With speed what force is left, and all imploy	*Quickly all the armies that are left and use them all*
In our defence, lest unawares we lose	*In our defence, in case we are taken unawares and lose*
This our high place, our Sanctuarie, our Hill.	*This high place, our sanctuary on the hill.'*
To whom the Son with calm aspect and cleer	*The Son, with a calm face*
Light'ning Divine, ineffable, serene, Made answer. Mightie Father, thou thy foes	*And even temper, serene, Answered. 'Mighty father, you rightly*

Justly hast in derision, and secure

Laugh'st at thir vain designes and tumults vain,
Matter to mee of Glory, whom thir hate

Illustrates, when they see all Regal Power

Giv'n me to quell thir pride, and in event

Know whether I be dextrous to subdue

Thy Rebels, or be found the worst in Heav'n.
So spake the Son, but SATAN with his Powers
Farr was advanc't on winged speed, an Host
Innumerable as the Starrs of Night,
Or Starrs of Morning, Dew-drops, which the Sun
Impearls on every leaf and every flouer.
Regions they pass'd, the mightie Regencies

Of Seraphim and Potentates and Thrones

In thir triple Degrees, Regions to which
All thy Dominion, ADAM, is no more

Then what this Garden is to all the Earth,

And all the Sea, from one entire globose

Stretcht into Longitude; which having pass'd
At length into the limits of the North
They came, and SATAN to his Royal seat
High on a Hill, far blazing, as a Mount

Rais'd on a Mount, with Pyramids and Towrs
From Diamond Quarries hew'n, & Rocks of Gold,
The Palace of great LUCIFER, (so call
That Structure in the Dialect of men

Have contempt for your enemies, and being secure
Laugh at their vain plans and rages.

Let me take control of the matter, for it is me
Who has stirred up their hatred, when they saw all their power
Given to me to rein in their pride, and so
Let us find out if I have the skill to crush

Those who rebel against you – if not, I am Heaven's weakest.'
So the Son spoke, but Satan and his armies
Were far away on speeding wings, an army
Numberless as the night stars,
Or the dewdrops which the sun
Places on every leaf and flower.
They passed through territories, the great regencies
Of Seraphim and Potentates and Thrones
In their triple order, territories which
Are greater than all your dominion, Adam,
Just as the Earth and all the sea, if they were stretched
Into one long piece instead of being a globe,
Are bigger than your garden; having passed through these
Eventually they came to the far North
And Satan came to his royal throne,
High on a hill, its glare could be seen from far away, it was like
A mountain on top of a mountain, with pyramids and towers
Made out of diamonds and gold,
The palace of great Lucifer (that is How that place is called, translated

Interpreted) which not long after, hee

Affecting all equality with God,
In imitation of that Mount whereon

MESSIAH was declar'd in sight of Heav'n,
The Mountain of the Congregation call'd;

For thither he assembl'd all his Train,

Pretending so commanded to consult

About the great reception of thir King,

Thither to come, and with calumnious Art

Of counterfeted truth thus held thir ears.
Thrones, Dominations, Princedomes,
Vertues, Powers,
If these magnific Titles yet remain
Not meerly titular, since by Decree
Another now hath to himself ingross't
All Power, and us eclipst under the name

Of King anointed, for whom all this haste

Of midnight march, and hurried meeting here,
This onely to consult how we may best
With what may be devis'd of honours new
Receive him coming to receive from us

Knee-tribute yet unpaid, prostration vile,

Too much to one, but double how endur'd,

To one and to his image now proclaim'd?

But what if better counsels might erect

Our minds and teach us to cast off this Yoke?
Will ye submit your necks, and chuse to bend
The supple knee? ye will not, if I trust

Into the language of Men), which soon after,

Pretending to be equal to God,
He named the Mountain of Congregation,

Imitating that mountain on which
The Messiah was declared in the sight of Heaven;

For there he assembled all his lieutenants,

Pretending he summoned them to consult

As to how they should receive their King

When he came there, and with the lying tricks
Of false truth he held their attention:
'Thrones, dominions, princedoms, virtues, powers,
If these great titles are more
Than just titles, since by order
Another has now awarded himself
All power, and set himself above us under the name

Of the anointed King, for whom all this haste,

This midnight march, this hurried meeting,
Are all to discuss how we may best
Meet him when he comes here to us,
What new type of honors can we give him when he comes?

We have not yet bowed the knee to him, disgusting slavery –

It's too much to give to one, how shall we give it to two,

The first and now the one set up in his image?

What if better thoughts might come to mind

And teach us to cast off this oppression?
Will you bow your heads, and choose to bend your knees?
You will not, if I know you right

To know ye right, or if ye know your selves

Natives and Sons of Heav'n possest before

By none, and if not equal all, yet free,

Equally free; for Orders and Degrees

Jarr not with liberty, but well consist.

Who can in reason then or right assume

Monarchie over such as live by right

His equals, if in power and splendor less,

In freedome equal? or can introduce

Law and Edict on us, who without law
Erre not, much less for this to be our Lord,

And look for adoration to th' abuse

Of those Imperial Titles which assert
Our being ordain'd to govern, not to serve?

Thus farr his bold discourse without controule
Had audience, when among the Seraphim
ABDIEL, then whom none with more zeale ador'd
The Deitie, and divine commands obei'd,

Stood up, and in a flame of zeale severe
The current of his fury thus oppos'd.
O argument blasphemous, false and proud!

Words which no eare ever to hear in Heav'n

Expected, least of all from thee, ingrate

In place thy self so high above thy Peeres.

Canst thou with impious obloquie condemne

As I think I do, or if you know yourselves,

Natives and Sons of Heaven, never before owned

By anyone, and if we are not all equal,

We are all equally free, for orders and ranks

Do not clash with freedom but exist well with it, side by side.

Then who can reasonably or correctly assume

Kingship over those who are by rights

His equals – maybe less in power or splendor, but

Equal in freedom? How can he impose

Laws on us, who do not do wrong Without laws, much less claim to be our Lord,

And expect to be worshipped for abusing

The Imperial Titles which say We are meant to govern, not to serve?'

So far his bold speech was heard without opposition,
When from amongst the Seraphim Abdiel, who up until then had more than anyone
Adored God, and obeyed his divine commands,

Stood up, and in a furious rage Opposed what had been said.
'This is a blasphemous argument, lying and arrogant!

These are words which nobody should expect to hear

In Heaven, least of all from you, ungrateful one,

Who has been given a place so high above your comrades.

Do you dare with blasphemous criticism to reject

The just Decree of God, pronounc't and sworn,
That to his only Son by right endu'd
With Regal Scepter, every Soule in Heav'n
Shall bend the knee, and in that honour due
Confess him rightful King? unjust thou saist
Flatly unjust, to binde with Laws the free,
And equal over equals to let Reigne,
One over all with unsucceeded power.
Shalt thou give Law to God, shalt thou dispute
With him the points of libertie, who made
Thee what thou art, & formd the Pow'rs of Heav'n
Such as he pleasd, and circumscrib'd thir being?
Yet by experience taught we know how good,
And of our good, and of our dignitie
How provident he is, how farr from thought
To make us less, bent rather to exalt
Our happie state under one Head more neer
United. But to grant it thee unjust,
That equal over equals Monarch Reigne:
Thy self though great & glorious dost thou count,
Or all Angelic Nature joind in one,
Equal to him begotten Son, by whom
As by his Word the mighty Father made
All things, ev'n thee, and all the Spirits of Heav'n
By him created in thir bright degrees,
Crownd them with Glory, & to thir Glory nam'd

The fair ruling of God, announced and sworn to,
That to his only Son, given by rights
The power of a King, every soul in Heaven
Should bow down, and in giving him that honor
Accept him as the rightful king? You say
That it is unjust to impose laws upon the free,
And allow one equal to rule over another,
One over all with eternal power.
Are you going to teach God the law, debate
With him the nature of freedom, the one who made
You who you are, and created the powers of Heaven
As he wished, and set out the rules which govern them?
We know from experience how good he is,
And how respectful of our dignity, how
He cares for us, how little he is trying
To diminish us; he is trying to make
Our happy state happier, by uniting us under one leader
Who is closer to us. But you are right to say it is unjust
That an equal shall reign over equals as King;
Do you think that you, though great and glorious,
Or all the angels joined together as one being,
Are equal to the only son of God,
Who was made by the word of God,
Just as he made all things, even you, and all the Spirits of Heaven
In their bright orders,
Crowned them with glory, and to their glory gave them

Thrones, Dominations, Princedoms, Vertues, Powers	*Thrones, dominions, princedoms, virtues, powers,*
Essential Powers, nor by his Reign obscur'd,	*Essential powers, which are not lessened by his Kingship,*
But more illustrious made, since he the Head	*But made more glorious, since as our leader*
One of our number thus reduc't becomes,	*His power is shared by these titles.*
His Laws our Laws, all honour to him done	*His laws become our laws, and all honor done to him*
Returns our own. Cease then this impious rage,	*Is honor for us as well. Stop this blasphemous rage,*
And tempt not these; but hast'n to appease	*And do not tempt these others, but hurry to placate*
Th' incensed Father, and th' incensed Son,	*The angered father and the angered son,*
While Pardon may be found in time besought.	*Whilst there is till time to seek their forgiveness.'*
So spake the fervent Angel, but his zeale	*So the fervent angel spoke, but none seconded*
None seconded, as out of season judg'd,	*His passion, thinking it not right for the time,*
Or singular and rash, whereat rejoic'd	*Or foolhardy and obtuse, and so the rebel*
Th' Apostat, and more haughty thus repli'd.	*Was pleased, and answered with arrogance.*
That we were formd then saist thou? & the work	*'We were made then, is that what you are saying?*
Of secondarie hands, by task transferd	*And we are the work of other hands, now passed down*
From Father to his Son? strange point and new!	*From father to son? This is something strange and new!*
Doctrin which we would know whence learnt: who saw	*We would like to know where you learnt all this: who saw*
When this creation was? rememberst thou	*This creation? Do you remember*
Thy making, while the Maker gave thee being?	*Being made, when the maker brought you to life?*
We know no time when we were not as now;	*We know no time when things were not as they are now;*
Know none before us, self-begot, self-rais'd	*We know of none who came before us, we are self made,*
By our own quick'ning power, when fatal course	*Raised by our own strength, it was inevitable*
Had circl'd his full Orbe, the birth mature	*When time had run round his full course, that*
Of this our native Heav'n, Ethereal Sons.	*Our native Heaven and we its children should be born.*

Our puissance is our own, our own right hand	*Our strength is our own, our own guidance*
Shall teach us highest deeds, by proof to try	*Shall teach us to do great things and by testing*
Who is our equal: then thou shalt behold	*Find who our equal is: then you shall see*
Whether by supplication we intend	*Whether we intend to bow down,*
Address, and to begirt th' Almighty Throne	*And whether we shall approach the almighty throne*
Beseeching or besieging. This report,	*With pleading or with war. Take these words*
These tidings carrie to th' anointed King;	*And this news to the anointed King;*
And fly, ere evil intercept thy flight.	*And fly, before harm comes to you.'*
He said, and as the sound of waters deep	*So he spoke, and like the roar of the sea*
Hoarce murmur echo'd to his words applause	*A rough murmur of applause greeted his words*
Through the infinite Host, nor less for that	*Throughout the great gathering, but in spite of that*
The flaming Seraph fearless, though alone	*The flaming Seraph remained fearless, though he was alone*
Encompass'd round with foes, thus answerd bold.	*And surrounded by enemies, he still answered boldly.*
O alienate from God, O spirit accurst,	*'You are lost from God, you cursed Spirit,*
Forsak'n of all good; I see thy fall	*You have lost all that is good; I can see that*
Determind, and thy hapless crew involv'd	*You will fall, and your unlucky mob involved in this*
In this perfidious fraud, contagion spred	*Deceitful fraud will be infected*
Both of thy crime and punishment: henceforth	*With both your crime and your punishment: from now on*
No more be troubl'd how to quit the yoke	*Don't worry about how you can escape the rule*
Of Gods MESSIAH; those indulgent Laws	*Of God's Messiah; those soft laws*
Will not be now voutsaf't, other Decrees	*Will not now be enacted, other orders*
Against thee are gon forth without recall;	*Against you have been issued and cannot be rescinded;*
That Golden Scepter which thou didst reject	*The golden scepter which you rejected*
Is now an Iron Rod to bruise and breake	*Is now an iron rod which will beat and break*
Thy disobedience. Well thou didst advise,	*Your disobedience. You gave me good advice,*
Yet not for thy advise or threats I fly	*But it's not because of your advice or your threats*

These wicked Tents devoted, least the wrauth
Impendent, raging into sudden flame

Distinguish not: for soon expect to feel

His Thunder on thy head, devouring fire.

Then who created thee lamenting learne,

When who can uncreate thee thou shalt know.
So spake the Seraph ABDIEL faithful found,
Among the faithless, faithful only hee;

Among innumerable false, unmov'd,

Unshak'n, unseduc'd, unterrifi'd
His Loyaltie he kept, his Love, his Zeale;

Nor number, nor example with him wrought
To swerve from truth, or change his constant mind
Though single. From amidst them forth he passd,
Long way through hostile scorn, which he susteind
Superior, nor of violence fear'd aught;

And with retorted scorn his back he turn'd

On those proud Towrs to swift destruction doom'd.

That I flee from this wicked place, but in case the anger
Which is coming, shooting into sudden flame,
Should destroy all here without distinction: expect soon to feel
His thunder crash down on you with his devouring fire.
Then as you wail you will learn who created you,
The one who can unmake you too.'

So the faithful Seraph Abdiel spoke,

The only faithful one amongst all the faithless;
Amongst all the countless false ones he was unmoved,
Unshaken, unseduced, unterrified;
He kept his loyalty, his love, his courage;
Neither weight of numbers nor their example
Could make him swerve from the truth, or change his steadfast mind
Though he was just one.He walked away through the crowd,
A long way through hostile scorn, which he endured
Superior, and did not fear their violence;
And reflecting their scorn he turned his back
On those proud towers which were now marked for destruction.

BOOK VI

THE ARGUMENT

Raphael continues to relate how Michael and Gabriel were sent forth to battel against Satan and his Angels. The first Fight describ'd: Satan and his Powers retire under Night: He calls a Councel, invents devilish Engines, which in the second dayes Fight put Michael and his Angels to some disorder; But, they at length pulling up Mountains overwhelm'd both the force and Machins of Satan: Yet the Tumult not so ending, God on the third day sends Messiah his Son, for whom he had reserv'd the glory of that Victory: Hee in the Power of his Father coming to the place, and causing all his Legions to stand still on either side, with his Chariot and Thunder driving into the midst of his Enemies, pursues them unable to resist towards the wall of Heaven; which opening, they leap down with horrour and confusion into the place of punishment prepar'd for them in the Deep: Messiah returns with triumph to his Father.

All night the dreadless Angel unpursu'd

Through Heav'ns wide Champain held his way, till Morn,
Wak't by the circling Hours, with rosie hand
Unbarr'd the gates of Light. There is a Cave

Within the Mount of God, fast by his Throne,
Where light and darkness in perpetual round
Lodge and dislodge by turns, which makes through

Heav'n

Raphael continues to tell how Michael and Gabriel were sent out to take the battle to Satan and his Angels.The first battle is described and Satan and his powers retire under cloak of night. He calls a council and invents hellish machines, which on the second day of battle cause Michael and the angels some difficulty.Eventually they pulled up the mountains and overwhelmed Stan's machines and his armies.But as the battle was not ended on the third day God sends his son, the Messiah, for whom he had reserved the glory of the victory. He comes to the place with his father's power, and making all his armies stand back he drives into the middle of his enemies with his chariot and thunder, and pursues them towards the wall of Heaven. It opens, and they leap in horror and confusion into the prison prepared for them in the pit. The Messiah returns to his Father in triumph.

"All night the fearless angel, unpursued,
Made his way across the wide plain of Heaven,
Until morning, woken by passage of time, with a rosy hand
Unlocked the gates of light.There is a cave
Inside the mountain of God, near his throne,
Where light and darkness in eternal orbit
Enter and leave in turn, which creates in
Heaven

Grateful vicissitude, like Day and Night;	*A welcome variety, like day and night;*
Light issues forth, and at the other dore	*Light comes out, and at the other door*
Obsequious darkness enters, till her houre	*Obedient darkness comes in and waits until it is time*
To veile the Heav'n, though darkness there might well	*To throw its veil over Heaven; though darkness there*
Seem twilight here; and now went forth the Morn	*Is what you would see as twilight; and now the morning came out*
Such as in highest Heav'n, arrayd in Gold	*As she appears in highest Heaven, dressed in*
Empyreal, from before her vanisht Night,	*Heavenly gold, and night vanished as she came,*
Shot through with orient Beams: when all the Plain	*Shot through with the sunrise; then the whole plain.*
Coverd with thick embatteld Squadrons bright,	*Covered with bright squadrons armed for battle,*
Chariots and flaming Armes, and fierie Steeds	*Chariots and flaming weapons, and fiery horses*
Reflecting blaze on blaze, first met his view:	*All blazing together, appeared before him.*
Warr he perceav'd, warr in procinct, and found	*He could see that all was prepared for war, and found*
Already known what he for news had thought	*That the news he was bringing was*
To have reported: gladly then he mixt	*Already known; so happily he mingled*
Among those friendly Powers who him receav'd	*With his friends who welcomed him*
With joy and acclamations loud, that one	*With joy and loud praise for the fact that one*
That of so many Myriads fall'n, yet one	*Of the great number who had fallen*
Returnd not lost: On to the sacred hill	*Had come back to them: onto the holy hill*
They led him high applauded, and present	*They led him, to great applause, and presented him*
Before the seat supream; from whence a voice	*Before the throne, from where a voice*
From midst a Golden Cloud thus milde was heard.	*From inside a golden cloud spoke softly.*
Servant of God, well done, well hast thou fought	*'Servant of God, well done, you have fought*
The better fight, who single hast maintaind	*The good fight, who alone stood by,*
Against revolted multitudes the Cause	*Against the rebellious masses, the cause*

199

Of Truth, in word mightier then they in Armes;	*Of truth, and your words were greater than their weapons;*
And for the testimonie of Truth hast born	*And for standing by the truth you suffered*
Universal reproach, far worse to beare	*Universal reproach, which is far harder to bear*
Then violence: for this was all thy care	*Than violence: all you cared for*
To stand approv'd in sight of God, though Worlds	*Was to do right in the eyes of God, however much all others*
Judg'd thee perverse: the easier conquest now	*Thought you wrong; now an easier battle*
Remains thee, aided by this host of friends,	*Is left for you, aided by this army of friends.*
Back on thy foes more glorious to return	*You shall return to your enemies with more glory*
Then scornd thou didst depart, and to subdue	*Than the scorn with which you left, to put down*
By force, who reason for thir Law refuse,	*By force those who say they will not accept the law,*
Right reason for thir Law, and for thir King	*Replacing it with their own ideas, and do not accept*
MESSIAH, who by right of merit Reigns.	*Their King Messiah, who reigns on his merits.*
Goe MICHAEL of Celestial Armies Prince,	*Michael, Prince of the heavenly Armies, go,*
And thou in Military prowess next	*And you, the next in military skill,*
GABRIEL, lead forth to Battel these my Sons	*Gabriel, lead out to battle these, my invincible*
Invincible, lead forth my armed Saints	*Sons, lead out my armed saints*
By Thousands and by Millions rang'd for fight;	*Arranged for the fight in their thousands and millions,*
Equal in number to that Godless crew	*Equal in number to that Godless mob*
Rebellious, them with Fire and hostile Arms	*Of rebels, assault them fearlessly with fire*
Fearless assault, and to the brow of Heav'n	*And weapons, and chase them to the edge of Heaven,*
Pursuing drive them out from God and bliss,	*Drive them away from God and bliss*
Into thir place of punishment, the Gulf	*Into their place of punishment, the abyss*
Of TARTARUS, which ready opens wide	*Of Hell, which is open wide with*
His fiery CHAOS to receave thir fall.	*Its fiery chaos ready to receive them. '*
So spake the Sovran voice, and Clouds began	*So the royal voice spoke, and clouds began*
To darken all the Hill, and smoak to rowl	*To darken the hill, and smoke rolled*
In duskie wreathes, reluctant flames, the	*In dusky coils with flickering flames,*

signe
Of wrauth awak't: nor with less dread the loud
Ethereal Trumpet from on high gan blow:

At which command the Powers Militant,
That stood for Heav'n, in mighty Quadrate joyn'd
Of Union irresistible, mov'd on

In silence thir bright Legions, to the sound
Of instrumental Harmonie that breath'd
Heroic Ardor to advent'rous deeds

Under thir God-like Leaders, in the Cause

Of God and his MESSIAH. On they move
Indissolubly firm; nor obvious Hill,
Nor streit'ning Vale, nor Wood, nor Stream divides
Thir perfet ranks; for high above the ground

Thir march was, and the passive Air upbore

Thir nimble tread; as when the total kind

Of Birds in orderly array on wing
Came summond over EDEN to receive

Thir names of thee; so over many a tract

Of Heav'n they march'd, and many a Province wide
Tenfold the length of this terrene: at last
Farr in th' Horizon to the North appeer'd

From skirt to skirt a fierie Region, stretcht

In battailous aspect, and neerer view

Bristl'd with upright beams innumerable

Of rigid Spears, and Helmets throng'd, and Shields
Various, with boastful Argument portraid,

the sign
Of anger aroused; and just as fearsome the loud
Heavenly trumpet began to blow from on high.

At this command the military powers
That represented Heaven joined in a great square formation
Of irresistible strength, moved their bright legions

On, to the sound
Of military music that spoke
Of heroic passion and adventurous deeds

Serving under their Godlike leaders, in the cause

Of God and his Messiah. On they go,
Unbreakably united: no hill,
Nor twisting valley, nor wood, nor stream splits
Their perfect ranks, for they marched high

Above the ground, and the calm air supported

Their soft steps, as when all the species

Of birds, lined up in flight,
Answered the summons to gather over Eden

To receive their names from you, Adam. So over many areas

Of Heaven they marched, and many wide provinces,
Ten times the length of Earth: at last
Far away on the northern horizon there appeared

A fiery region, stretched from edge to edge

In a warlike display, and on closer examination

Was bristling with the countless upright beams

Of great spears, crowds of helmets and shields
Of various types, with boastful slogans on them.

The banded Powers of SATAN hasting on

With furious expedition; for they weend
That self same day by fight, or by surprize
To win the Mount of God, and on his Throne
To set the envier of his State, the proud

Aspirer, but thir thoughts prov'd fond and vain
In the mid way: though strange to us it seemd
At first, that Angel should with Angel warr,

And in fierce hosting meet, who wont to meet
So oft in Festivals of joy and love

Unanimous, as sons of one great Sire

Hymning th' Eternal Father: but the shout
Of Battel now began, and rushing sound

Of onset ended soon each milder thought.

High in the midst exalted as a God
Th' Apostat in his Sun-bright Chariot sate

Idol of Majestie Divine, enclos'd
With Flaming Cherubim, and golden Shields;
Then lighted from his gorgeous Throne, for now
'Twixt Host and Host but narrow space was left,
A dreadful interval, and Front to Front
Presented stood in terrible array

Of hideous length: before the cloudie Van,

On the rough edge of battel ere it joyn'd,

SATAN with vast and haughtie strides advanc't,
Came towring, armd in Adamant and Gold;

The massed powers of Satan rushed on
With furious energy, for they wanted
To fight that very day, or to take
The mountain of God by surprise, and on his throne
To put the one who envied his position, the proud
Would be usurper, but their thoughts proved in vain
Before they had got halfway. It seemed strange to us
At first, that angels should fight with angels,
And meet in fierce battle, those who were used
To meeting so often in festivals of joy and love
United, as the sons of one great father,
Praising eternal god; but the shout
Of battle now went up, and the rushing sounds
Of attack soon banished any softer thoughts.
High in the middle, raised as a God,
The blasphemer in his sun bright chariot sat,
A false copy of divine majesty, circled
With flaming Cherubim and golden shields.
Then he jumped down from his gorgeous throne,
For there was only a narrow gap left between the two armies,
A terrible pause as the two fronts Faced each other in a fearsome display
Of hideous length: ahead of the leading cloud,
On the rough edge of the battle before it began,
Satan advanced with great arrogant strides,
Towering and wearing armor made from adamant and gold;

Original	Modernised
ABDIEL that sight endur'd not, where he stood	Abdiel could not stand that sight, from where he stood
Among the mightiest, bent on highest deeds,	Amongst the mightiest, determined to do the highest deeds,
And thus his own undaunted heart explores.	And so his brave heart spoke.
O Heav'n! that such resemblance of the Highest	'Oh Heaven! That such a resemblance of greatness
Should yet remain, where faith and realtie	Should still remain, where faith and honesty
Remain not; wherfore should not strength & might	Have vanished; why do strength and might
There fail where Vertue fails, or weakest prove	Not fail when virtue fails, or become weakest
Where boldest; though to sight unconquerable?	In the arrogant, even though they appear unbeatable?
His puissance, trusting in th' Almightie's aide,	With the help of God I mean to test
I mean to try, whose Reason I have tri'd	His strength, the one whose reason I have tested
Unsound and false; nor is it aught but just,	And found unsound and false; and it is only right
That he who in debate of Truth hath won,	That he who has won the debate of truth
Should win in Arms, in both disputes alike	Should win in battle, be victorious
Victor; though brutish that contest and foule,	In both; the fight is vicious and horrid,
When Reason hath to deal with force, yet so	When reason has to fight with force, but
Most reason is that Reason overcome.	It is right that reason will triumph.'
So pondering, and from his armed Peers	Thinking this, and stepping out from
Forth stepping opposite, half way he met	His armed comrades, he met his daring enemy
His daring foe, at this prevention more	Halfway, and was more angered by his
Incens't, and thus securely him defi'd.	Arrogance, and so bravely he defied him.
Proud, art thou met? thy hope was to have reacht	'You proud one, is that you? You hoped to reach
The highth of thy aspiring unoppos'd,	The summit of your ambition unopposed,
The Throne of God unguarded, and his side	The throne of God unguarded, with all having
Abandond at the terror of thy Power	Fled his side in terror of your power
Or potent tongue; fool, not to think how vain	Or your tricking tongue; you fool, you cannot see how vain

Against th' Omnipotent to rise in Arms;

Who out of smallest things could without end
Have rais'd incessant Armies to defeat
Thy folly; or with solitarie hand
Reaching beyond all limit, at one blow

Unaided could have finisht thee, and whelmd
Thy Legions under darkness; but thou seest

All are not of thy Train; there be who Faith

Prefer, and Pietie to God, though then

To thee not visible, when I alone

Seemd in thy World erroneous to dissent
From all: my Sect thou seest, now learn too late
How few somtimes may know, when thousands err.
askance
Whom the grand foe with scornful eye

Thus answerd. Ill for thee, but in wisht houre
Of my revenge, first sought for thou returnst
From flight, seditious Angel, to receave
Thy merited reward, the first assay

Of this right hand provok't, since first that tongue
Inspir'd with contradiction durst oppose

A third part of the Gods, in Synod met
Thir Deities to assert, who while they feel

Vigour Divine within them, can allow

Omnipotence to none. But well thou comst

Before thy fellows, ambitious to win

It is to take up arms against the all-powerful,

The one who could from the smallest things forever
Make neverending armies to defeat
Your foolishness, or with one hand
Reaching out wherever you were, with one blow

Could have finished you with no other help, and buried
Your legions in darkness. But you can see

That not all think like you; there are those who prefer

Faith, and devotion to God, though they were not

Visible to you when I seemed to you the only one

In your twisted world who disagreed
With all the rest; you can see my comrades, now learn too late
How a few may sometimes know the truth, when thousands are in error.'

The great enemy, with a scornful sidelong look,
Answered him thus: 'It is bad luck for you, but at this time
Of my revenge, I looked for you first, coming back from
Your flight, seditious angel, to receive
The reward you deserve, the first blow

From this angered right hand, since it was your tongue,
Inspired by error, which dared to oppose

A third of the Gods, called to meeting
To confirm their Godliness, who, while they feel

Godlike power within themselves, can allow

Omnipotence to none. Bt I am glad that you

Have come ahead of your comrades, ambitious to win

From me som Plume, that thy success may show
Destruction to the rest: this pause between

(Unanswerd least thou boast) to let thee know;

At first I thought that Libertie and Heav'n

To heav'nly Soules had bin all one; but now

I see that most through sloth had rather serve,

Ministring Spirits, traind up in Feast and Song;
Such hast thou arm'd, the Minstrelsie of Heav'n,
Servilitie with freedom to contend,

As both thir deeds compar'd this day shall prove.
To whom in brief thus ABDIEL stern repli'd.
Apostat, still thou errst, nor end wilt find

Of erring, from the path of truth remote:

Unjustly thou deprav'st it with the name

Of SERVITUDE to serve whom God ordains,
Or Nature; God and Nature bid the same,

When he who rules is worthiest, and excels

Them whom he governs. This is servitude,

To serve th' unwise, or him who hath rebelld
Against his worthier, as thine now serve thee,
Thy self not free, but to thy self enthrall'd;

Yet leudly dar'st our ministring upbraid.
Reign thou in Hell thy Kingdom, let mee

Some honor from fighting me and with your success
Be raised higher than the rest; this pause between your challenge
And the fight (in case you think you can boast I didn't accept the challenge) is to let you know:
At first I thought that freedom and Heaven
Were the desires of all Heavenly souls; but now
I see that through laziness most would rather be slaves,

Servant Spirits, trained in food and song;
This is your army, the singing servants of Heaven,
Who come to fight freedom with slavery,
And this will be proved by what happens today.'
Abdiel replied, briefly and sternly.
'Blasphemer, still you are wrong and will not find
An end to your error, you have strayed so far from the truth:
Unjustly you pervert with the name of slavery
The act of serving as God orders,
Or Nature; God and Nature have the same rules,
That when the leader is the one who is the most worthy
That raises up those he governs. Slavery
Is to serve the foolish, or one who has rebelled
Against his better, as yours now serve you,
And you are not free, you are a slave to yourself,
But you dare to criticize our service?
You can reign in your Kingdom of

205

serve
In Heav'n God ever blessed, and his Divine
Behests obey, worthiest to be obey'd,

Yet Chains in Hell, not Realms expect: mean while
From mee returnd, as erst thou saidst, from flight,
This greeting on thy impious Crest receive.

So saying, a noble stroke he lifted high,

Which hung not, but so swift with tempest fell

On the proud Crest of SATAN, that no sight,
Nor motion of swift thought, less could his Shield
Such ruin intercept: ten paces huge

He back recoild; the tenth on bended knee

His massie Spear upstaid; as if on Earth

Winds under ground or waters forcing way

Sidelong, had push't a Mountain from his seat
Half sunk with all his Pines. Amazement seis'd
The Rebel Thrones, but greater rage to see

Thus foil'd thir mightiest, ours joy filld, and shout,
Presage of Victorie and fierce desire

Of Battel: whereat MICHAEL bid sound

Th' Arch-Angel trumpet; through the vast of Heav'n
It sounded, and the faithful Armies rung

HOSANNA to the Highest: nor stood at gaze

Hell, let me serve
God in Heaven, forever blessed, and obey
His divine orders, those which most deserve obedience.
But expect chains in Hell, not Kingdoms: meanwhile,
As I am returned, as you first said, from my flight,
Receive this greeting on your blasphemous head.'
Saying this, he drew back a noble blow,
Which did not hesitate, but fell with such a swift storm

On the proud helmet of Satan that no anticipation
Or quick thought, still less his shield,
Could block his downfall; ten great paces
He staggered back; on the tenth his knees buckled
And he was held up by his great spear, as if on Earth
Underground winds or waters pushing along
Sideways had driven a mountain from its place
And half sunk it amongst its forests.Astonishment seized
The rebel powers, but greater than their rage at seeing
Their mightiest foiled was our joy, and we shouted,
With visions of victory and a fierce desire
For battle:at this Michael ordered the archangel's
Trumpet blown; through all of Heaven
It sounded, and the faithful armies rang
With praise to the Highest; the enemy did not

The adverse Legions, nor less hideous joyn'd
The horrid shock: now storming furie rose,

And clamour such as heard in Heav'n till now
Was never, Arms on Armour clashing bray'd
Horrible discord, and the madding Wheeles

Of brazen Chariots rag'd; dire was the noise

Of conflict; over head the dismal hiss

Of fiery Darts in flaming volies flew,
And flying vaulted either Host with fire.

So under fierie Cope together rush'd

Both Battels maine, with ruinous assault

And inextinguishable rage; all Heav'n

Resounded, and had Earth bin then, all Earth
Had to her Center shook. What wonder? when
Millions of fierce encountring Angels fought
On either side, the least of whom could weild
These Elements, and arm him with the force
Of all thir Regions: how much more of Power
Armie against Armie numberless to raise

Dreadful combustion warring, and disturb,

Though not destroy, thir happie Native seat;

Had not th' Eternal King Omnipotent
From his strong hold of Heav'n high over-rul'd
And limited thir might; though numberd

Just stand looking on, and didn't hesitate
To join the horrid clash. A storming fury arose,

And a clamor such as had never been heard before
In Heaven, weapons clashing on armor with
Terrible noise, and the thundering wheels

Of bronze chariots clattered; the noise of battle

Appalling; overhead there was the awful hiss

Of flaming arrows flying in volleys,
And as they flew they set both armies alight.

So under the fiery sky they rushed together,

The main bodies of both armies, with smashing attack

And unquenchable rage; all of Heaven

Shook, and had Earth existed she would have been
Shaken to her core. Is it any wonder? When
Millions of fierce clashing angels fought
On either side, the lowest of whom could use
The elements, and arm himself with the power
Of all the lands; how much more power was there
In two numberless armies raised against each other,
Who fight in a terrible explosion, and disturb.
Though not destroy, their happy native land;
But the eternal omnipotent King
Ruled over from on high and
Limited their strength; though there

such
As each divided Legion might have seemd

A numerous Host, in strength each armed hand
A Legion; led in fight, yet Leader seemd

Each Warriour single as in Chief, expert
When to advance, or stand, or turn the sway

Of Battel, open when, and when to close

The ridges of grim Warr; no thought of flight,
None of retreat, no unbecoming deed

That argu'd fear; each on himself reli'd,
As onely in his arm the moment lay
Of victorie; deeds of eternal fame

Were don, but infinite: for wide was spred

That Warr and various; somtimes on firm ground
A standing fight, then soaring on main wing

Tormented all the Air; all Air seemd then

Conflicting Fire: long time in eeven scale
The Battel hung; till SATAN, who that day

Prodigious power had shewn, and met in Armes
No equal, raunging through the dire attack

Of fighting Seraphim confus'd, at length
Saw where the Sword of MICHAEL smote,

and fell'd
Squadrons at once, with huge two-handed sway
Brandisht aloft the horrid edge came down

Wide wasting; such destruction to withstand

He hasted, and oppos'd the rockie Orb

were such among them
That each divided regiment might have been
A great army, each armed hand as strong
As a regiment; they were led in the fight, but each warrior
Seemed to be a leader, a chief, expert
In when to advance, or stand, or turn the course
Of the battle, when to open and when to close
The grim ranks of war; none thought of flight,
None of retreat, none did anything not suitable for a soldier,
Showing fear; each relied on himself,
As if victory could only be gained
From his arm alone; deeds were done that will have everlasting fame,
An infinite number of them, for that war
Spread far and wide; sometimes a standing fight
On the firm ground, then soaring up on wings
To torment the air; all the sky then seemed
Raging fire; for a long time the battle
Hung in the balance, until Satan, who that day
Had shown great strength, and had not met
His equal in arms, stormed through the terrible throng
Of fighting Seraphim, and finally
He saw where the sword of Michael was
falling,
Dropping whole squadrons at once, with great double handed swings
It was held aloft and then the horrid edge came down
Laying waste all around.He hurried to oppose
This destruction, and held up the

	rocky circle
Of tenfold Adamant, his ample Shield	*Of reinforced diamond, his great shield*
A vast circumference: At his approach	*Of huge size; at his approach*
The great Arch-Angel from his warlike toile	*The great archangel stopped his warlike toil*
Surceas'd, and glad as hoping here to end	*And was glad, seeing a chance to end*
Intestine War in Heav'n, the arch foe subdu'd	*Heaven's civil war, with the arch-enemy crushed*
Or Captive drag'd in Chains, with hostile frown	*Or dragged in chains as a prisoner. With a hostile frown*
And visage all enflam'd first thus began.	*And a face blazing with anger he began.*
Author of evil, unknown till thy revolt,	*'Bringer of evil, which we did not know you were, until your revolt,*
Unnam'd in Heav'n, now plenteous, as thou seest	*No longer mentioned in heaven, you can see how widespread*
These Acts of hateful strife, hateful to all,	*Are these acts of horrible violence, horrible to all*
Though heaviest by just measure on thy self	*Though the worst is, as is only just, falling on you*
And thy adherents: how hast thou disturb'd	*And your followers: how have you disturbed*
Heav'ns blessed peace, and into Nature brought	*The blessed peace of Heaven and brought misery*
Miserie, uncreated till the crime	*Into Nature, which was not created before*
Of thy Rebellion? how hast thou instill'd	*Your rebellion? You have infected*
Thy malice into thousands, once upright	*Thousands with your evil, once upright*
And faithful, now prov'd false. But think not here	*And faithful and now proved false. But do not think*
To trouble Holy Rest; Heav'n casts thee out	*That you can disturb the Holy Peace; Heaven banishes you*
From all her Confines. Heav'n the seat of bliss	*From all her lands. Heaven, the seat of bliss,*
Brooks not the works of violence and Warr.	*Will not tolerate acts of violence and war.*
Hence then, and evil go with thee along	*Go from here, and take your child, evil,*
Thy ofspring, to the place of evil, Hell,	*With you, to the place of evil, Hell,*
Thou and thy wicked crew; there mingle broiles,	*You and all your wicked army; go and boil there*
Ere this avenging Sword begin thy doome,	*Before this avenging sword seals your fate,*

Or som more sudden vengeance wing'd from God
Precipitate thee with augmented paine.
So spake the Prince of Angels; to whom thus
The Adversarie. Nor think thou with wind
Of airie threats to aw whom yet with deeds
Thou canst not. Hast thou turnd the least of these
To flight, or if to fall, but that they rise
Unvanquisht, easier to transact with mee
That thou shouldst hope, imperious, & with threats
To chase me hence? erre not that so shall end
The strife which thou call'st evil, but wee style
The strife of Glorie: which we mean to win,
Or turn this Heav'n it self into the Hell
Thou fablest, here however to dwell free,
If not to reign: mean while thy utmost force,
And join him nam'd ALMIGHTIE to thy aid,
I flie not, but have sought thee farr and nigh.
They ended parle, and both addrest for fight
Unspeakable; for who, though with the tongue
Of Angels, can relate, or to what things
Liken on Earth conspicuous, that may lift
Human imagination to such highth
Of Godlike Power: for likest Gods they seemd,
Stood they or mov'd, in stature, motion, arms
Fit to decide the Empire of great Heav'n.

Now wav'd thir fierie Swords, and in the

Or some quicker vengance sent by God
Throws you down with added pain.'
So the prince of angels spoke, and the enemy
Replied: 'Don't think that with your talk
Or empty threats you can frighten one whom you cannot
Frighten with deeds. Have you managed to make the weakest of my army
Fly? And if you have made any fall, they
Rise again, unbeaten,
And you thought, arrogant, that you could drive me from here
With your threats? Don't think that will end
This battle which you call evil but we
Call glory; we intend to win,
Or else turn this Heaven into the Hell
You tell stories of, and live free here
Even if we do not rule: meanwhile from your best efforts,
Even if you summon the one you call Almighty to help you,
I do not run, but have sought you far and wide.'
They ended their talk, and both set themselves for a fight
Which cannot be described; for who, even if he speaks the language
Of angels, can tell in a way, or find comparisons
On Earth, that might lift
The human imagination up so they could understand
Such Godlike power: for they seemed like Gods,
As they stood or moved, in stature, movement and military skill
They were fit to decide the fate of Heaven.

Now they waved their fiery swords,

Aire	*and in the air*
Made horrid Circles; two broad Suns thir Shields	*They made two horrid circles; like two great suns their shields*
Blaz'd opposite, while expectation stood	*Blazed at each other, while all stood expectant*
In horror; from each hand with speed retir'd	*In horror; all around, wherever the fight was thickest,*
Where erst was thickest fight, th' Angelic throng,	*The angelic throng quickly retired,*
And left large field, unsafe within the wind	*And left a large field, for all were unsafe if near*
Of such commotion, such as to set forth	*Such a fight, which was as though, to compare*
Great things by small, If Natures concord broke,	*Great things with small, the peace of Nature broke,*
Among the Constellations warr were sprung,	*And the constellations started to fight each other,*
Two Planets rushing from aspect maligne	*And two planets, bent on harm,*
Of fiercest opposition in mid Skie,	*Rushed to fight in the middle of the sky,*
Should combat, and thir jarring Sphears confound.	*And clashed their shuddering spheres together.*
Together both with next to Almightie Arme,	*They both, with arms which were second only to God's,*
Uplifted imminent one stroke they aim'd	*Lifted their swords for a single stroke*
That might determine, and not need repeate,	*That might settle everything, and not need repeating,*
As not of power, at once; nor odds appeerd	*Because the first was of such power; and none could guess*
In might or swift prevention; but the sword	*Which blow might triumph; but the sword*
Of MICHAEL from the Armorie of God	*Of Michael was from the armory of God*
Was giv'n him temperd so, that neither keen	*And was so made that nothing, sharp*
Nor solid might resist that edge: it met	*Or blunt, might resist its edge; it came*
The sword of SATAN with steep force to smite	*Down steeply on the sword of Satan*
Descending, and in half cut sheere, nor staid,	*And cut it completely in half, and did not stop*
But with swift wheele reverse, deep entring shar'd	*But with a quick change of direction cut off*
All his right side; then SATAN first knew pain,	*All of his right side; then Satan first knew pain,*
And writh'd him to and fro convolv'd; so	*And thrashed to and fro, convulsed;*

sore
The griding sword with discontinuous wound
Pass'd through him, but th' Ethereal substance clos'd
Not long divisible, and from the gash

A stream of Nectarous humor issuing flow'd
Sanguin, such as Celestial Spirits may bleed,
And all his Armour staind ere while so bright.
Forthwith on all sides to his aide was run

By Angels many and strong, who interpos'd

Defence, while others bore him on thir Shields
Back to his Chariot; where it stood retir'd

From off the files of warr; there they him laid
Gnashing for anguish and despite and shame
To find himself not matchless, and his pride

Humbl'd by such rebuke, so farr beneath

His confidence to equal God in power.
Yet soon he heal'd; for Spirits that live throughout
Vital in every part, not as frail man

In Entrailes, Heart or Head, Liver or Reines,

Cannot but by annihilating die;

Nor in thir liquid texture mortal wound

Receive, no more then can the fluid Aire:
All Heart they live, all Head, all Eye, all Eare,
All Intellect, all Sense, and as they please,

so deep
Had the cutting sword slashed through him
That his ethereal substance

Could not close around the wound, and from it
A stream of fluid like nectar ran

Like blood, for this is how Heavenly Spirits bleed,
And all his bright armor was stained with it.
Straight away, on all sides, many strong angels

Ran to help him and surrounded him defensively,

Whilst others carried him on their shields
Back to his chariot where it stood apart

Out of the ranks of battle; there they laid him,
Thrashing with pain and hate and the shame
Of not finding himself unbeatable, and his pride

Was wounded by this setback to his belief
That he was equal in power to God.
But he soon healed, for Spirits, whose life
Runs all through them, not like frail man

Where it lives in the stomach, heart, head, liver or kidneys,
Can only die if they are completely dissolved;
Nor can their liquid texture suffer a mortal wound,
Any more than the air could;
They are all heart, all head, all eye, all ear,
All intellect, all senses, and they choose

They Limb themselves, and colour, shape or size	*Their own limbs, and assume the color, shape and size*
Assume, as likes them best, condense or rare.	*That best pleases them, small or large.*
Mean while in other parts like deeds deservd	*Meanwhile in other places other deeds were done which deserve*
Memorial, where the might of GABRIEL fought,	*To be remembered, where mighty Gabriel fought,*
And with fierce Ensignes pierc'd the deep array	*And with his fierce officers charged deep into the army*
Of MOLOC furious King, who him defi'd,	*Of Moloch, the furious King, who defied him*
And at his Chariot wheeles to drag him bound	*And threatened to drag him, bound, behind his chariot,*
Threatn'd, nor from the Holie One of Heav'n	*And he did not refrain from uttering blasphemy*
Refrein'd his tongue blasphemous; but anon	*Against the holy one of Heaven, but soon,*
Down clov'n to the waste, with shatterd Armes	*Split right down to the waist, he fled with shattered weapons*
And uncouth paine fled bellowing. On each wing	*And bellowing with terrible pain. On each side*
URIEL and RAPHAEL his vaunting foe,	*Uriel and Raphael took on their bragging enemies,*
Though huge, and in a Rock of Diamond Armd,	*And even though each one was huge and wearing diamond armor*
Vanquish'd ADRAMELEC, and ASMADAI,	*They beat Adramelec and Asmadi,*
Two potent Thrones, that to be less then Gods	*Two great powers who thought it beneath them to be*
Disdain'd, but meaner thoughts learnd in thir flight,	*Less than Gods, but they learned differently as they fled,*
Mangl'd with gastly wounds through Plate and Maile.	*Torn with ghastly wounds through their armor.*
Nor stood unmindful ABDIEL to annoy	*Nor did Abdiel cease to torment*
The Atheist crew, but with redoubl'd blow	*The atheist mob, but with his strength redoubled,*
ARIEL and ARIOC, and the violence	*Scorched and overthrew the violence*
Of RAMIEL scorcht and blasted overthrew.	*Of Ariel, Arioc and Ramiel.*
I might relate of thousands, and thir names	*I could tell of thousands, and make their names*
Eternize here on Earth; but those elect	*Eternal here on Earth; but those favored*
Angels contented with thir fame in Heav'n	*Angels are happy with their fame in Heaven*
Seek not the praise of men: the other sort	*And do not want the praise of men;*

In might though wondrous and in Acts of Warr,
Nor of Renown less eager, yet by doome

Canceld from Heav'n and sacred memorie,

Nameless in dark oblivion let them dwell.

For strength from Truth divided and from Just,
Illaudable, naught merits but dispraise

And ignominie, yet to glorie aspires
Vain glorious, and through infamie seeks fame:
Therfore Eternal silence be thir doome.
And now thir mightiest quelld, the battel swerv'd,
With many an inrode gor'd; deformed rout

Enter'd, and foul disorder; all the ground

With shiverd armour strow'n, and on a heap

Chariot and Charioter lay overturnd

And fierie foaming Steeds; what stood, recoyld
Orewearied, through the faint Satanic Host

Defensive scarse, or with pale fear surpris'd,

Then first with fear surpris'd and sense of paine
Fled ignominious, to such evil brought

By sinne of disobedience, till that hour

Not liable to fear or flight or paine.

Far otherwise th' inviolable Saints

In Cubic Phalanx firm advanc't entire,
Invulnerable, impenitrably arm'd:

---

the other sort,
Though they were mighty and great in the acts of war,
And are no less eager for fame, they are sentenced
To be struck off Heaven's rolls and from the holy memory,
Let them live nameless in dark oblivion.
For strength, separated from truth and justice,
Cannot be praised, it only merits censure
And shame, but it seeks glory
In its boastfulness, and seeks to be famous through its evil;
So let their fate be to be unnamed.
And now, with their mightiest crushed, the battle changed,
And many an inroad was cut out; disorderly retreat
Began, and there was foul disorder; all the ground
Was covered in shattered armor, and in a heap
Chariots and their drivers were overturned
With their fiery foaming horses. Those who stood, retreated,
Exhausted, and the pale Satanic Host could hardly
Defend itself, and now they felt fear for the first time,
Fear, and pain as well,
And they fled in shame, reduced to such a state
By their sin of disobedience: until that time
They had never known fear or pain or retreat.
It was very different for the sacred saints
Who advanced as one solid body,
Invulnerable, with impenetrable

Such high advantages thir innocence

Gave them above thir foes, not to have sinnd,
Not to have disobei'd; in fight they stood

Unwearied, unobnoxious to be pain'd
By wound, though from thir place by violence mov'd.
Now Night her course began, and over Heav'n
Inducing darkness, grateful truce impos'd,

And silence on the odious dinn of Warr:
Under her Cloudie covert both retir'd,

Victor and Vanquisht: on the foughten field
MICHAEL and his Angels prevalent
Encamping, plac'd in Guard thir Watches round,
Cherubic waving fires:
on th' other part
SATAN with his rebellious disappeerd,
Far in the dark dislodg'd, and void of rest,

His Potentates to Councel call'd by night;

And in the midst thus undismai'd began.
O now in danger tri'd, now known in Armes

Not to be overpowerd, Companions deare,

Found worthy not of Libertie alone,
Too mean pretense, but what we more affect,
Honour, Dominion, Glorie, and renowne,
Who have sustaind one day in doubtful fight,
(And if one day, why not Eternal dayes?)

What Heavens Lord had powerfullest to send
Against us from about his Throne, and judg'd
Sufficient to subdue us to his will,

---

armor;
These were the great advantages their innocence

Gave them over their enemies, by not sinning
And not disobeying, in the fight they stood

Unwearied, unable to be hurt
By wounds, even if they were subject to violence.
Now night fell, and over Heaven

Brought darkness, which caused a welcome truce,

And silenced the terrible din of war.
Under her cloud cover both victors and vanquished

Retired: on the battlefield
Michael and his angels pitched
Their tents and placed their guards on watch,
Cherubs with fire.
For the other side,
Satan and his rebels disappeared,
Driven far into the dark, allowed no rest.

He called his leaders to a night council,

And undismayed he spoke to them:
'Now we have been tested by danger, now we have shown we cannot

Be overcome by force, dear comrades,

We deserve not just freedom,
That is too little to ask, what more do we want?
Honor, power, glory and fame.
We have endured one day in an inconclusive fight
(And if we can endure one day, why not eternal days?)
The Lord of Heaven sent his greatest warriors
To fight us, and thought

They would be enough to bend us to

Original	Modern
	his will,
But proves not so: then fallible, it seems,	*But this was not the case; then it seems that in future*
Of future we may deem him, though till now	*We may regard him as fallible, even though to date*
Omniscient thought. True is, less firmly arm'd,	*We thought him all powerful. It's true*
Some disadvantage we endur'd and paine,	*That we suffered some setbacks, and pain,*
Till now not known, but known as soon contemnd,	*Which we did not know until now, but knowing it we can now discount it,*
Since now we find this our Empyreal forme	*Since we have discovered that our Heavenly forms*
Incapable of mortal injurie	*Cannot suffer mortal wounds,*
Imperishable, and though peirc'd with wound,	*And are everlasting, even if pierced with wounds;*
Soon closing, and by native vigour heal'd.	*They soon close, and are healed by our own strength.*
Of evil then so small as easie think	*Something so easy to cure is of*
The remedie; perhaps more valid Armes,	*Little importance; perhaps stronger armor*
Weapons more violent, when next we meet,	*And more violent weapons, next time we meet,*
May serve to better us, and worse our foes,	*Might serve to make us greater and weaken our enemies,*
Or equal what between us made the odds,	*Or at least equal the difference between us,*
In Nature none: if other hidden cause	*Because in nature we are as strong; if some other hidden cause*
Left them Superiour, while we can preserve	*Made them stronger than us, while we can keep*
Unhurt our mindes, and understanding sound,	*Our minds undamaged and our reasoning sound*
Due search and consultation will disclose.	*We will be able to discover what it is.*
He sat; and in th' assembly next upstood	*He sat, and the next one to address the meeting*
NISROC, of Principalities the prime;	*Was Nisroc, the leader of the Principalities;*
As one he stood escap't from cruel fight,	*He stood as one who has escaped a cruel fight,*
Sore toild, his riv'n Armes to havoc hewn,	*Exhausted, his weapons smashed,*
And cloudie in aspect thus answering spake.	*And frowning he answered:*
Deliverer from new Lords, leader to free	*'Savior from new Lords, you lead us to free*

Enjoyment of our right as Gods; yet hard

For Gods, and too unequal work we find
Against unequal armes to fight in paine,

Against unpaind, impassive; from which evil
Ruin must needs ensue; for what availes

Valour or strength, though matchless, quelld with pain
Which all subdues, and makes remiss the hands
Of Mightiest. Sense of pleasure we may well
Spare out of life perhaps, and not repine,
But live content, which is the calmest life:

But pain is perfet miserie, the worst
Of evils, and excessive, overturnes
All patience. He who therefore can invent

With what more forcible we may offend
Our yet unwounded Enemies, or arme

Our selves with like defence, to mee deserves
No less then for deliverance what we owe.
Whereto with look compos'd SATAN repli'd.
Not uninvented that, which thou aright

Beleivst so main to our success, I bring;

Which of us who beholds the bright surface

Of this Ethereous mould whereon we stand,

This continent of spacious Heav'n, adornd

With Plant, Fruit, Flour Ambrosial, Gemms & Gold,
Whose Eye so superficially surveyes
These things, as not to mind from whence they grow
Deep under ground, materials dark and

Enjoyment of our rights as Gods; but it is hard
For Gods, we find it too one-sided,
To have to fight greater opposition while suffering pain,
Against those who feel no pain and are unmoved; from this
Our downfall must come, for what use
Is bravery or strength? Even if it is matchless, it can be beaten with pain,
Which overcomes all, and leads the hands of even the greatest
Astray. We may well be able to leave a sense of pleasure
Out of our lives, and not suffer,
But live contented, which is the calmest life.
But pain is total misery, the worst Evil, and if you suffer too much of it
It overthrows the mind. Anyone who can devise
A better way of harming
Our as yet unwounded enemies, or give us
Defense equal to theirs, will

Get fully paid by me.'
With a calm face Satan replied:

'It has been invented, that which you rightly
Believe is essential for our success: I will show you;
Which of us who sees the bright surface
Of this ethereal land we stand on,

This spacious continent of Heaven, covered
With plants, fruits, ambrosial flowers, jewels gold,
Only sees these things
And doesn't think about what they grow from
Deep under ground, dark and rough

217

crude,	*materials*
Of spiritous and fierie spume, till toucht	*Of volatile fiery smoke, which when touched*
With Heav'ns ray, and temperd they shoot forth	*By the sun of heaven shoot up*
So beauteous, op'ning to the ambient light.	*So lovely, opening to the light.*
These in thir dark Nativitie the Deep	*These we shall get from the deep, unformed,*
Shall yeild us, pregnant with infernal flame,	*Pregnant with Hellish fire,*
Which into hallow Engins long and round	*Which we shall ram into hollow machines, long and round,*
Thick-rammd, at th' other bore with touch of fire	*Pack them in tight, and at the other end we shall touch a flame,*
Dilated and infuriate shall send forth	*Which compressed and angry will send out*
From far with thundring noise among our foes	*From a distance, with a thundering din, amongst our enemies*
Such implements of mischief as shall dash	*Such tools of mischief as will dash*
To pieces, and orewhelm whatever stands	*Them to pieces, and overwhelm whatever stands*
Adverse, that they shall fear we have disarmd	*Against them, so they will think we have disarmed*
The Thunderer of his only dreaded bolt.	*The thunderer, God, of his only dreaded weapon.*
Nor long shall be our labour, yet ere dawne,	*They won't take long to make; before dawn*
Effect shall end our wish. Mean while revive;	*Or dreams will be reality. Meanwhile cheer up,*
Abandon fear; to strength and counsel joind	*Forget your fear; strength and wisdom joined*
Think nothing hard, much less to be despaird.	*Fear nothing, and see no need for despair.'*
He ended, and his words thir drooping chere	*He finished, and his words lifted their low mood*
Enlightn'd, and thir languisht hope reviv'd.	*And raised their fallen hopes.*
Th' invention all admir'd, and each, how hee	*They all admired the invention, and each wondered how*
To be th' inventer miss'd, so easie it seemd	*He did not invent it himself, it seemed so obvious*
Once found, which yet unfound most would have thought	*Once described; but undescribed most would have thought it*
Impossible: yet haply of thy Race	*Impossible; but maybe with your race, Adam,*
In future dayes, if Malice should abound,	*In the future, if evil flourishes,*
Some one intent on mischief, or inspir'd	*Someone set on mischief or inspired*

With dev'lish machination might devise	*With devilish purpose might invent*
Like instrument to plague the Sons of men	*The same sort of machine to curse the Sons of men*
For sin, on warr and mutual slaughter bent.	*For their sin, causing war and mutual slaughter.*
Forthwith from Councel to the work they flew,	*After the council they set straight to work,*
None arguing stood, innumerable hands	*None stood debating, numberless hands*
Were ready, in a moment up they turnd	*Were ready, and in an instant they had dug*
Wide the Celestial soile, and saw beneath	*A great hole in the soil of Heaven, and saw underneath*
Th' originals of Nature in thir crude	*Nature's raw materials in their crudest*
Conception; Sulphurous and Nitrous Foame	*State; they found sulphur and nitrate*
They found, they mingl'd, and with suttle Art,	*And mixed it, and with cunning skill*
Concocted and adusted they reduc'd	*Heated and dried it, reducing it*
To blackest grain, and into store conveyd:	*To a black powder, and stored it away;*
Part hidd'n veins diggd up (nor hath this Earth	*Some of them dug up hidden seams (this Earth*
Entrails unlike) of Mineral and Stone,	*Has innards quite similar) of mineral and stone*
Whereof to found thir Engins and thir Balls	*With which to make their machines and projectiles*
Of missive ruin; part incentive reed	*Of great destruction; some found*
Provide, pernicious with one touch to fire.	*Fuse material, ready to flame at a touch.*
So all ere day spring, under conscious Night	*So they had finished all before daybreak,*
Secret they finish'd, and in order set,	*Throughout night they secretly set everything up*
With silent circumspection unespi'd.	*With silent caution, unseen.*
Now when fair Morn Orient in Heav'n appeerd	*When the fair morning came to Heaven*
Up rose the Victor Angels, and to Arms	*The victorious angels arose, and the morning trumpet*
The matin Trumpet Sung: in Arms they stood	*Called them to arms: fully armed they stood*
Of Golden Panoplie, refulgent Host,	*A golden display, a shining army*
Soon banded; others from the dawning Hills	*Quickly gathered. Others looked out*
Lookd round, and Scouts each Coast light-armed scoure,	*From the hills, and on all the borders lightly armed scouts checked*
Each quarter, to descrie the distant foe,	*Each point, to try and discover the*

Where lodg'd, or whither fled, or if for fight,
In motion or in alt: him soon they met

Under spred Ensignes moving nigh, in slow
But firm Battalion; back with speediest Sail
ZEPHIEL, of Cherubim the swiftest wing,

Came flying, and in mid Aire aloud thus cri'd.
Arme, Warriours, Arme for fight, the foe at hand,
Whom fled we thought, will save us long pursuit
This day, fear not his flight; so thick a Cloud
He comes, and settl'd in his face I see

Sad resolution and secure: let each
His Adamantine coat gird well, and each
Fit well his Helme, gripe fast his orbed Shield,
Born eevn or high, for this day will pour down,
If I conjecture aught, no drizling showr,

But ratling storm of Arrows barbd with fire.
So warnd he them aware themselves, and soon
In order, quit of all impediment;

Instant without disturb they took Allarm,

And onward move Embattelld; when behold
Not distant far with heavie pace the Foe

Approaching gross and huge; in hollow Cube
Training his devilish Enginrie, impal'd

On every side with shaddowing Squadrons Deep,

distant enemy,
Where he was housed, or if he had fled, if he wanted to fight,
If he was on the move or halted; they soon met him

Coming closer under raised flags, in slow
But sure battle order; back rushed Zephiel, the swiftest flyer of the Cherubim,
And while still in the air he cried out:

'Arm, warriors, arm yourselves for the fight, the enemy is here
Whom we thought had fled, he will save us having to chase
Today, don't fear that he'll flee; he comes with a great
Crowd, and fixed on his face I can see

Grim, fixed determination; all of you
Fix on your armor securely, and each
Fix his helmet on well, get a tight grip on your round shield,
For whether you are of high or low degree, this day,
If I guess rightly, will pour down no gentle drizzle

But a rattling storm of fire tipped arrows.'
So he warned them to be ready, and to quickly
Prepare for the fight, carrying nothing extra;

Straight away, without panic, they prepared

And moved on in battle order; and they saw
Not far off the slow pace with which the enemy

Was approaching, huge and coarse; they formed a hollow cube
Surrounding his devilish machinery, fenced deep

On every side with shadowing squadrons

To hide the fraud. At interview both stood

A while, but suddenly at head appeerd

SATAN: And thus was heard Commanding

Vangard, to Right and Left the Front unfould;

That all may see who hate us, how we seek

Peace and composure, and with open brest

Stand readie to receive them, if they like

Our overture, and turn not back perverse;

But that I doubt, however witness Heaven,

Heav'n witness thou anon, while we discharge
Freely our part: yee who appointed stand
Do as you have in charge, and briefly touch

What we propound, and loud that all may hear.
So scoffing in ambiguous words, he scarce

Had ended; when to Right and Left the Front
Divided, and to either Flank retir'd.
Which to our eyes discoverd new and strange,
A triple-mounted row of Pillars laid
On Wheels (for like to Pillars most they seem'd
Or hollow'd bodies made of Oak or Firr

With branches lopt, in Wood or Mountain fell'd)
Brass, Iron, Stonie mould, had not thir mouthes
With hideous orifice gap't on us wide,

Portending hollow truce; at each behind

To hide the trick. When they saw each other they both stood still
For a while, but suddenly Satan appeared at their head,
And was heard giving loud loud. *commands:*
'Front rank, split to the left and right
So that all those who hate us can see how we look for
Peace and reconciliation, and with open hearts
Stand ready to receive them, if they approve
Of our advances and do not turn away just to be awkward;
But I doubt they'll do that, however Heaven wants to witness
It may do, while we perform our part
Openly: you who have been chosen,
Do your duty, and briefly tell them what we will do
And make it loud so that all can hear it.'
He had hardly finished his mocking with ambiguous words
When to the right and left the front
Split and retired to either flank.
Then we saw something new and strange,
A triple row of pillars, mounted
On wheels (for they seemed most like pillars,
Or the hollowed out trunks of oak or fir,
With their branches trimmed, felled in woods or mountains)
They were made of brass, iron and stone and their mouths
With hideous openings gaped wide at us,
Showing talk of a truce was hollow. Behind each one

A Seraph stood, and in his hand a Reed

Stood waving tipt with fire; while we suspense,
Collected stood within our thoughts amus'd,
Not long, for sudden all at once thir Reeds

Put forth, and to a narrow vent appli'd
With nicest touch. Immediate in a flame,

But soon obscur'd with smoak, all Heav'n appeerd,
From those deep-throated Engins belcht, whose roar
Emboweld with outragious noise the Air,

And all her entrails tore, disgorging foule

Thir devillish glut, chaind Thunderbolts and Hail
Of Iron Globes, which on the Victor Host

Level'd, with such impetuous furie smote,
That whom they hit, none on thir feet might stand,
Though standing else as Rocks, but down they fell
By thousands, Angel on Arch-Angel rowl'd;

The sooner for thir Arms, unarm'd they might

Have easily as Spirits evaded swift

By quick contraction or remove; but now

Foule dissipation follow'd and forc't rout;

Nor serv'd it to relax thir serried files.

What should they do? if on they rusht, repulse
Repeated, and indecent overthrow

Doubl'd, would render them yet more despis'd,

Stood a seraph, and in his hand waved
A lighted fuse; we stood still
In our groups, confused, but not
For long, for suddenly all held their fuses out
And carefully touched them to
A narrow firing hole. There was a flash of flame,
Which was soon obscured with smoke and it seemed
All of Heaven was being belched out of those deep throated machines,
Whose roar filled the air with horrible noise
And tore through her entrails, throwing out
Their devilish material, chained shot and a hail
Of cannonballs, which flew straight at the victorious army,
And hit them with such fury
That anyone they hit, could not stay on his feet,
Though normally they were like rocks, but they fell down
In their thousands, angels rolling on archangels;
So much for their armor, for if they had been in their natural state they might
Have, as Spirits can, avoided the missiles
With quick dodging or flight into the air, but now
Foul destruction came and forced retreat;
Nor did their arms help them in breaking up their tight packed ranks.
What should they do? If they rushed on they would
Be blown back again, and their second defeat
Would make them look foolish,

And to thir foes a laughter; for in view

Stood rankt of Seraphim another row
In posture to displode thir second tire
Of Thunder: back defeated to return
They worse abhorr'd. SATAN beheld thir plight,
And to his Mates thus in derision call'd.

O Friends, why come not on these Victors proud?
Ere while they fierce were coming, and when wee,
To entertain them fair with open Front

And Brest, (what could we more?) propounded terms
Of composition, strait they chang'd thir minds,
Flew off, and into strange vagaries fell,
As they would dance, yet for a dance they seemd
Somwhat extravagant and wilde, perhaps
For joy of offerd peace: but I suppose

If our proposals once again were heard

We should compel them to a quick result.
To whom thus BELIAL in like gamesom mood.
Leader, the terms we sent were terms of weight,
Of hard contents, and full of force urg'd home,
Such as we might perceive amus'd them all,

And stumbl'd many, who receives them right,
Had need from head to foot well understand;
Not understood, this gift they have besides,

They shew us when our foes walk not upright.
So they among themselves in pleasant veine
Stood scoffing, highthn'd in thir thoughts

A joke to their enemies, for they could see
A row of Seraphim ready
To unleash their second volley
Of thunder; to turn back defeated
Would be even worse. Satan saw their quandary,
And to his comrades called out mockingly.

'Oh my friends, why don't these proud victors advance?
A while ago they were coming on fiercely, and when we
To give them a fair welcome with open ranks
And hearts (what more could we do?) gave them
Our peace terms, they changed their minds at once,
Flew off and started behaving oddly,
As if they were dancing, though their dance seemed
Rather strange and wild, perhaps
In their joy at the chance of peace; but I suppose
If we give them our proposals a second time
We'll get a quick result.'
To him Belial replied, in the same joking fashion:
'Leader, we sent them weighty terms,
With solid contents, and rammed home to them with force,
Such as we could see amused them all,
And many who received them in full stumbled
And understood them, top to toe;
Not understood, they also gave us this gift,
Showing us our enemies can't stand up straight.'
So in this humorous fashion
They stood scoffing, pleased in their

beyond All doubt of Victorie, eternal might	*thoughts* *Of a victory now beyond doubt,* *thinking it so easy*
To match with thir inventions they presum'd	*To match the eternal might with their* *own inventions*
So easie, and of his Thunder made a scorn,	*And make a mocking imitation of His* *thunder.*
And all his Host derided, while they stood	*All his army were mocked, while they* *stood*
A while in trouble; but they stood not long,	*For a while in difficulties, but not for* *long;*
Rage prompted them at length, & found them arms	*Rage spurred them on, and they soon* *found weapons*
Against such hellish mischief fit to oppose.	*Fit to fight such hellish mischief.*
Forthwith (behold the excellence, the power	*At once (see the wonder of the power*
Which God hath in his mighty Angels plac'd)	*Which God has given to his mighty* *angels)*
Thir Arms away they threw, and to the Hills	*They threw down their weapons, and* *to the hills*
(For Earth hath this variety from Heav'n	*(For these hills and valleys on Earth*
Of pleasure situate in Hill and Dale)	*Are copies of the ones in Heaven)*
Light as the Lightning glimps they ran, they flew,	*They ran and flew, quick as lightning,*
From thir foundations loosning to and fro	*They plucked all up all the hills*
They pluckt the seated Hills with all thir load,	*From their foundations, by rocking* *them to and fro,*
Rocks, Waters, Woods, and by the shaggie tops	*Rocks, water, woods, and lifting them* *by their shaggy tops*
Up lifting bore them in thir hands: Amaze,	*They carried them up in their hands;* *astonishment,*
Be sure, and terrour seis'd the rebel Host,	*You can be sure, and terror seized the* *rebel army*
When coming towards them so dread they saw	*When coming towards them so deadly* *they saw*
The bottom of the Mountains upward turn'd,	*The mountains turned upside down,*
Till on those cursed Engins triple-row	*Until on the triple row of cursed* *machines*
They saw them whelmd, and all thir confidence	*They saw them dropped, and all their* *confidence*
Under the weight of Mountains buried deep,	*Was buried deep under the weight of* *mountains.*
Themselves invaded next, and on thir heads	*They were attacked next, and on their* *heads*
Main Promontories flung, which in the Air	*Great rocky ridges were thrown,* *which cast shadows*

Came shadowing, and opprest whole Legions arm'd,	*As they fell from the sky, and smashed whole armed regiments;*
Thir armor help'd thir harm, crush't in and brus'd	*Their armor helped the damage, it crushed in and bruised them,*
Into thir substance pent, which wrought them pain	*And turned into their prisons, which gave them much pain,*
Implacable, and many a dolorous groan,	*And they had to struggle for a long time,*
Long struling underneath, ere the could wind	*With many agonized moans, before they could escape*
Out of such prison, though Spirits of purest light,	*These prisons, for though they were Spirits of pure light,*
Purest at first, now gross by sinning grown.	*Pure at first, they had become heavy with their sin.*
The rest in imitation to like Armes	*The rest, copying Heaven's army, chose the same weapons,*
Betook them, and the neighbouring Hills uptore;	*And tore up the neighboring hills,*
So Hills amid the Air encounterd Hills	*So that hill clashed against hill in the air*
Hurl'd to and fro with jaculation dire,	*Hurled to and fro with dreadful force.*
That under ground they fought in dismal shade;	*So they fought beneath the hills in dreadful shadow;*
Infernal noise; Warr seem'd a civil Game	*There was terrible noise; war seemed a polite game*
To this uproar; horrid confusion heapt	*Compared to this uproar; horrid confusion*
Upon confusion rose: and now all Heav'n	*Heaped on confusion reigned; and now all of Heaven*
Had gone to wrack, with ruin overspred,	*Would have been wrecked, overcome with ruin,*
Had not th' Almightie Father where he sits	*If the Heavenly Father, where he sat*
Shrin'd in his Sanctuarie of Heav'n secure,	*Secure in his holy sanctuary,*
Consulting on the sum of things, foreseen	*Weighing up all things had not foreseen*
This tumult, and permitted all, advis'd:	*This uproar, and allowed it to happen,*
That his great purpose he might so fulfill,	*So that he might achieve his great purpose,*
To honour his Anointed Son aveng'd	*Which was to see his anointed son revenged*
Upon his enemies, and to declare	*On his enemies, and to declare*
All power on him transferr'd: whence to his Son	*That all power was transferred to him; so he spoke*
Th' Assessor of his Throne he thus began.	*To his son, the sharer of his throne:*
Effulgence of my Glorie, Son belov'd,	*'Shining reflection of my glory,*

Son in whose face invisible is beheld
Visibly, what by Deitie I am,
And in whose hand what by Decree I doe,
Second Omnipotence, two dayes are past,

Two dayes, as we compute the dayes of
Heav'n,
Since MICHAEL and his Powers went
forth to tame
These disobedient; sore hath been thir fight,

As likeliest was, when two such Foes
met arm'd;
For to themselves I left them, and thou
knowst,
Equal in their Creation they were form'd,
Save what sin hath impaird, which yet hath

wrought
Insensibly, for I suspend thir doom;

Whence in perpetual fight they needs
must last
Endless, and no solution will be found:
Warr wearied hath perform'd what Warr
can do,
And to disorder'd rage let loose the reines,
With Mountains as with Weapons arm'd,
which makes
Wild work in Heav'n, and dangerous to the
maine.
Two dayes are therefore past, the third is
thine;
For thee I have ordain'd it, and thus farr

Have sufferd, that the Glorie may be thine

Of ending this great Warr, since none but
Thou
Can end it. Into thee such Vertue and Grace
Immense I have transfus'd, that all may k
now
In Heav'n and Hell thy Power above
compare,
And this perverse Commotion governd

beloved Son,
Son in whose face can be seen
The true nature of my Godliness,
And for whom I order all things,
The second all powerful one, two
days have passed,
Two days, as we calculate the days of
Heaven,
Since Michael and his armies went
out to tame
These rebels; they have had a terrible
battle,
As was bound to happen when two
enemies like these met in arms;
I left them to fight amongst
themselves, for you know
That they are created equal,
Except for what sin has damaged,
and that
damage
Is hardly noticeable yet, for I have
suspended their sentence;
So this fight must go on forever,

And never find an ending:
The weariness of war has done what
war can do,
And set free their blind rage,
Armed with mountains as weapons,
which causes
Great destruction in Heaven, and
danger for all.
So as two days have passed, the third
belongs to you;
I have ordered matters this way, and
have tolerated
What has happened, so that you may
have the glory
Of ending this great war, since none
but you
Can end it. I have put into you
Such great virtue and grace, so that
all will know
There is no power in Heaven or Hell
that equals you,
And once you have ended this wicked

thus,
To manifest thee worthiest to be Heir

Of all things, to be Heir and to be King

By Sacred Unction, thy deserved right.

Go then thou Mightiest in thy Fathers might,

Ascend my Chariot, guide the rapid Wheeles
That shake Heav'ns basis, bring forth all my Warr,
My Bow and Thunder, my Almightie Arms

Gird on, and Sword upon thy puissant Thigh;
Pursue these sons of Darkness, drive them out
From all Heav'ns bounds into the utter Deep:
There let them learn, as likes them, to despise
God and MESSIAH his anointed King.

He said, and on his Son with Rayes direct

Shon full, he all his Father full exprest
Ineffably into his face receiv'd,

And thus the filial Godhead answering spake.
O Father, O Supream of heav'nly Thrones,

First, Highest, Holiest, Best, thou alwayes seekst
To glorifie thy Son, I alwayes thee,

As is most just; this I my Glorie account,
My exaltation, and my whole delight,
That thou in me well pleas'd, declarst thy will
Fulfill'd, which to fulfil is all my bliss.

Scepter and Power, thy giving, I assume,

---

disturbance
They will see that you are worthy of being the Heir

Of all things, to be Heir and to be King,

By sacred anointing and by your merits.

Go then, you mightiest, take your father's strength,

Climb aboard my chariot, steer the quick wheels
That shake the foundations of Heaven, take all my weapons,
My bow and my thunder, put on my great armor,

And carry my sword by your strong side;
Chase these sons of darkness, drive them out
Of all Heaven's lands into the bottomless pit:
There let them learn, if it pleases them, to despise
God and Messiah, his appointed King.'

He said this, and his Son shone with light,

Showing in his face
All the power he had received from his Father,

And answering the Son of God spoke.
'Oh father, the greatest of Heavenly Kings,

The first, the highest, the holiest, the best, you have always sought
To glorify your Son, and I have always tried to do the same for you

As is right; this is my glory,
My praise and all my pleasure,
That you say you are pleased, and say your will
Has been done, fulfilling it is my greatest pleasure.

As you have given me the scepter and

And gladlier shall resign, when in the end

Thou shalt be All in All, and I in thee

For ever, and in mee all whom thou lov'st:

But whom thou hat'st, I hate, and can put on

Thy terrors, as I put thy mildness on,

Image of thee in all things; and shall soon,

Armd with thy might, rid heav'n of these rebell'd,
To thir prepar'd ill Mansion driven down

To chains of Darkness, and th' undying Worm,
That from thy just obedience could revolt,

Whom to obey is happiness entire.
Then shall thy Saints unmixt, and from th' impure
Farr separate, circling thy holy Mount

Unfeigned HALLELUIAHS to thee sing,
Hymns of high praise, and I among them chief.
So said, he o're his Scepter bowing, rose

From the right hand of Glorie where he sate,
And the third sacred Morn began to shine

Dawning through Heav'n: forth rush'd with whirlwind sound
The Chariot of Paternal Deitie,
Flashing thick flames, Wheele within Wheele undrawn,
It self instinct with Spirit, but convoyd

By four Cherubic shapes, four Faces each

Had wondrous, as with Starrs thir bodies all

---

the power, I take them,
And will be even happier to give them up, when at the end
You shall be all in one, and I will be in you
Forever, and in me shall be all whom you love;
But who you hate, I hate, and can put on
Your terrors, as I put on your mildness,

For I am your image in all things, and shall soon,
Armed with your weapons, rid Heaven of these rebels,
And drive them down to the horrible residence prepared for them,
To chains of darkness, and I shall defeat that snake,
Who thought he could rebel against your fair lordship,
When to obey you is total happiness.
Then your saints will be untangled, and separated far
From the impure, circling your Holy Mountain
Singing sincere hallelujahs to you,
Hymns of high praise, and I will be chief among them.'
So he spoke, bowed over his scepter, and rose
From his seat at the right hand of glory,
And the third sacred morning began to shine
Its dawn through all of Heaven; out like a whirlwind rushed
The chariot of God the Father,
Flashing thick flames, wheels within wheels, not pulled,
For it was itself filled with the Spirit, but accompanied
By four Cherubic shapes, each with four wondrous faces,
And like stars their bodies and wings

And Wings were set with Eyes, with Eyes the Wheels	*Were all covered with eyes as were the wheels*
Of Beril, and careering Fires between;	*Of beryl, and the fires in between;*
Over thir heads a chrystal Firmament,	*Over their heads was a crystal canopy,*
Whereon a Saphir Throne, inlaid with pure	*On which there was a sapphire throne, inlaid with pure*
Amber, and colours of the showrie Arch.	*Amber and all the colors of the rainbow.*
Hee in Celestial Panoplie all armd	*He, wearing armor of light,*
Of radiant URIM, work divinely wrought,	*Of radiant Urim, armor made by God,*
Ascended, at his right hand Victorie	*Climbed up, and on his right hand Victory*
Sate Eagle-wing'd, beside him hung his Bow	*Sat with her eagle wings, beside him hung his bow*
And Quiver with three-bolted Thunder stor'd,	*And quiver full of triple thunderbolts,*
And from about him fierce Effusion rowld	*And around him a great cloud boiled*
Of smoak and bickering flame, and sparkles dire;	*Of smoke and roaring flame and terrible sparks;*
Attended with ten thousand thousand Saints,	*Accompanied by ten million Saints*
He onward came, farr off his coming shon,	*He came on, and his coming could be seen shining from far off,*
And twentie thousand (I thir number heard)	*And twenty thousand (so I was told)*
Chariots of God, half on each hand were seen:	*Chariots of God were seen, ten thousand on each side:*
Hee on the wings of Cherub rode sublime	*He rode magnificent on the Cherubs' wings,*
On the Crystallin Skie, in Saphir Thron'd.	*On the crystal sky, on his sapphire throne.*
Illustrious farr and wide, but by his own	*He shone far and wide, but was first seen*
First seen, them unexpected joy surpriz'd,	*By his own side, and an unexpected joy surprised them,*
When the great Ensign of MESSIAH blaz'd	*When the great flag of Messiah flew,*
Aloft by Angels born, his Sign in Heav'n:	*Carried up by angels, his sign in Heaven:*
Under whose Conduct MICHAEL soon reduc'd	*Michael soon handed over command of his army,*
His Armie, circumfus'd on either Wing,	*Spread out on either side,*
Under thir Head imbodied all in one.	*Under their leader all fused together as one.*
Before him Power Divine his way prepar'd;	*Ahead of him Divine Power prepared his path;*
At his command the uprooted Hills retir'd	*At his word the uprooted hills went*

Each to his place, they heard his voice and went
Obsequious, Heav'n his wonted face renewd,
And with fresh Flourets Hill and Valley smil'd.
This saw his hapless Foes, but stood obdur'd,
And to rebellious fight rallied thir Powers
Insensate, hope conceiving from despair.
In heav'nly Spirits could such perverseness dwell?
But to convince the proud what Signs availe,

Or Wonders move th' obdurate to relent?

They hard'nd more by what might most reclame,
Grieving to see his Glorie, at the sight

Took envie, and aspiring to his highth,

Stood reimbattell'd fierce, by force or fraud

Weening to prosper, and at length prevaile
Against God and MESSIAH, or to fall
In universal ruin last, and now
To final Battel drew, disdaining flight,

Or faint retreat; when the great Son of God
To all his Host on either hand thus spake.

Stand still in bright array ye Saints, here stand
Ye Angels arm'd, this day from Battel rest;

Faithful hath been your Warfare, and of God
Accepted, fearless in his righteous Cause,

And as ye have receivd, so have ye don

Invincibly; but of this cursed crew

back
Each to his own place, they heard his voice and went
Obediently, Heaven reassumed its usual appearance,
And the hills and valleys were covered in fresh flowers.
His helpless enemies saw this, but stood obstinate,
And regardless rallied their armies,
Finding hope in their despair.
How could Heavenly Spirits be so obtuse?
How could we convince the proud of what is obvious,

Or what miracles would make the obstinate give in?

They were hardened more by what might soften most,
Grieving to see his Glory, they were envious
At the sight, and wanting it for themselves
Stood reorganized and fierce, hoping to prosper
By force or deceit, and at last to win
Over God and Messiah, or to fall
At last to total destruction, and now
They came to their final battle, refusing to flee
Or to surrender; the great Son of God
Spoke to all his army on either side of him:

'Stay here in your bright ranks, you Saints, stay here
You armored angels, and today rest from battle;

You have been faithful in your fighting, and acknowledging
God have been fearless in his righteous cause,

And the orders you were given you have followed

Magnificently; but the punishment of this cursed mob

The punishment to other hand belongs,	*Belongs to another hand,*
Vengeance is his, or whose he sole appoints;	*Vengeance belongs to him, or only those he chooses;*
Number to this dayes work is not ordain'd	*Numbers are not needed for this day's work,*
Nor multitude, stand onely and behold	*Nor crowds, just stand and watch*
Gods indignation on these Godless pourd	*God's indignation rained on these Godless ones*
By mee; not you but mee they have despis'd,	*By me; it was me, not you, that they hated*
Yet envied; against mee is all thir rage,	*And envied; all their anger is with me,*
Because the Father, t' whom in Heav'n supream	*Because the Father, who in highest Heaven*
Kingdom and Power and Glorie appertains,	*Allocates Kingdom and Power and Glory,*
Hath honourd me according to his will.	*Has honored me as he wished.*
Therefore to mee thir doom he hath assig'n'd;	*So he has given charge of their fate to me,*
That they may have thir wish, to trie with mee	*So that they may have their wish, to fight with me*
In Battel which the stronger proves, they all,	*In battle and see who is the stronger, all of them,*
Or I alone against them, since by strength	*Or I alone against them, since they measure everything*
They measure all, of other excellence	*By strength, they do not try to copy any other*
Not emulous, nor care who them excells;	*Virtues, or care who excels them in them,*
Nor other strife with them do I voutsafe.	*And I will not allow any other to fight with them.'*
So spake the Son, and into terrour chang'd	*So the Son spoke, and his face changed*
His count'nance too severe to be beheld	*Into a terror too awful to look upon,*
And full of wrauth bent on his Enemies.	*And full of anger he rushed on his enemies.*
At once the Four spred out thir Starrie wings	*At once the four Cherubs spread out their starry wings*
With dreadful shade contiguous, and the Orbes	*With a dreadful overlapping shade, and the wheels*
Of his fierce Chariot rowld, as with the sound	*Of his fierce chariot rolled with a sound like*
Of torrent Floods, or of a numerous Host.	*A river in torrent or a great army.*
Hee on his impious Foes right onward drove,	*He drove straight onwards at his blasphemous enemies,*

Gloomie as Night; under his burning Wheeles
The stedfast Empyrean shook throughout,
All but the Throne it self of God. Full soon
Among them he arriv'd; in his right hand

Grasping ten thousand Thunders, which he sent
Before him, such as in thir Soules infix'd

Plagues; they astonisht all resistance lost,

All courage; down thir idle weapons drop'd;

O're Shields and Helmes, and helmed heads he rode
Of Thrones and mighty Seraphim prostrate,

That wish'd the Mountains now might be again
Thrown on them as a shelter from his ire.

Nor less on either side tempestuous fell

His arrows, from the fourfold-visag'd Foure,
Distinct with eyes, and from the living Wheels,
Distinct alike with multitude of eyes,
One Spirit in them rul'd, and every eye

Glar'd lightning, and shot forth pernicious fire
Among th' accurst, that witherd all thir strength,
And of thir wonted vigour left them draind,

Exhausted, spiritless, afflicted, fall'n.

Yet half his strength he put not forth, but check'd
His Thunder in mid Volie, for he meant

Not to destroy, but root them out of Heav'n:

The overthrown he rais'd, and as a Heard

Dark as night; under his burning wheels
The solid Heaven shook,
All but the throne of God. Very soon
He arrived amongst them; in his right hand
He held ten thousand thunderbolts, which he sent
Flying ahead of him, and they brought
Sickness to their souls; astonished, they lost all resistance,
All courage, they dropped their useless weapons.
He rode over shields and helmets, the helmeted heads
Of Thrones and mighty Seraphim, lying down,
And they wished the mountains might again
Be thrown down upon them to shelter them from his anger.
No less terrible were his arrows which fell
On either side from the four faced Four,
Covered in eyes, and from the living wheels,
Also covered in eyes,
One Spirit ruled them all, and every eye
Glared lightning, and shot out vicious fire
Amongst the cursed ones, that withered their strength
And left them drained of all their usual energy,
Exhausted, spiritless, wounded, fallen.
But he did not use half his strength, but stopped
His thunder in mid volley, for he meant
Not to destroy them but to banish them from Heaven:
He lifted up the overthrown, and like

	a herd
Of Goats or timerous flock together throngd	*Of goats or timid sheep all pressed together*
Drove them before him Thunder-struck, pursu'd	*He drove them ahead of him, thunderstruck, followed*
With terrors and with furies to the bounds	*Them with terror and anger to the frontier*
And Chrystall wall of Heav'n, which op'ning wide,	*And crystal wall of Heaven, which opened wide,*
Rowld inward, and a spacious Gap disclos'd	*Rolling inward, and showed a great gap*
Into the wastful Deep; the monstrous sight	*Into the wastes of the Deep; the monstrous sight*
Strook them with horror backward, but far worse	*Made them step back in horror, but there was far worse*
Urg'd them behind; headlong themselvs they threw	*Driving them on from behind; they threw themselves headlong*
Down from the verge of Heav'n, Eternal wrauth	*Down from the edge of Heaven, with eternal anger*
Burnt after them to the bottomless pit.	*Burning after them, down into the bottomless pit.*
Hell heard th' unsufferable noise, Hell saw	*Hell heard the terrible noise, Hell saw*
Heav'n ruining from Heav'n and would have fled	*The heavenly falling from Heaven and would have fled*
Affrighted; but strict Fate had cast too deep	*In fear; but strict fate had laid*
Her dark foundations, and too fast had bound.	*Her dark foundations deep, and fixed her fast.*
Nine dayes they fell; confounded CHAOS roard,	*They fell for nine days; confused Chaos roared,*
And felt tenfold confusion in thir fall	*Feeling confusion from their fall ten times*
Through his wilde Anarchie, so huge a rout	*More than was usual in his wide anarchy, such a great retreat,*
Incumberd him with ruin: Hell at last	*Left him in ruins:Hell at last*
Yawning receavd them whole, and on them clos'd,	*Opened wide to receive them all, and closed on them.*
Hell thir fit habitation fraught with fire	*Hell, their rightful home, filled with everlasting*
Unquenchable, the house of woe and paine.	*Fire, the home of sorrow and pain.*
Disburd'nd Heav'n rejoic'd, and soon repaird	*Heaven unburdened rejoiced, and soon mended*
Her mural breach, returning whence it rowld.	*The hole in her wall, which rolled back into place.*
Sole Victor from th' expulsion of his Foes	*The solitary victor in the expulsion of*

MESSIAH his triumphal Chariot turnd:

To meet him all his Saints, who silent stood

Eye witnesses of his Almightie Acts,
With Jubilie advanc'd; and as they went,

Shaded with branching Palme, each order bright,
Sung Triumph, and him sung Victorious King,
Son, Heire, and Lord, to him Dominion giv'n,
Worthiest to Reign: he celebrated rode

Triumphant through mid Heav'n, into the Courts
And Temple of his mightie Father Thron'd

On high; who into Glorie him receav'd,
Where now he sits at the right hand of bliss.

Thus measuring things in Heav'n by things on Earth
At thy request, and that thou maist beware

By what is past, to thee I have reveal'd

What might have else to human Race bin hid;
The discord which befel, and Warr in Heav'n
Among th' Angelic Powers, and the deep fall
Of those too high aspiring, who rebelld

With SATAN, hee who envies now thy state,
Who now is plotting how he may seduce

Thee also from obedience, that with him

Bereavd of happiness thou maist partake

---

his enemies,
Messiah turned his triumphant chariot
To face all his Saints, who stood silent
As eyewitnesses to his almighty acts,
And now advanced in celebration. As they went,
Shaded with palm branches, each bright order
Sung of the triumph and sung of him as the victorious King,
Son, heir and Lord, with all power given to him,
The most deserving of rule; thus celebrated he rode
Triumphant through the middle of Heaven, into
The court and temple of his mighty Father, throned
On high; he received him into Glory,
And he sits there now at the right hand of bliss.

So, measuring things in Heaven by things on Earth
As you asked, and so you may be warned
By the events of the past, I have shown you
What might otherwise have been hidden to humans;
The disagreement which occurred, and the war in Heaven
Amongst the angels, and the great fall
Of those who were too ambitious, who rebelled
With Satan, he who now envies your happiness,
Who is now plotting how he can seduce
You from your obedience so that with him,
Stripped of happiness, you might join in

His punishment, Eternal miserie;
Which would be all his solace and revenge,

As a despite don against the most High,
Thee once to gaine Companion of his woe.

But list'n not to his Temptations, warne
Thy weaker; let it profit thee to have heard

By terrible Example the reward

Of disobedience; firm they might have
stood,
Yet fell; remember, and fear to transgress.

His punishment of eternal misery;
That would be his only comfort and
revenge,
Done to spite God,
Making you his companion in his
sorrow.
Do not listen to his temptations, warn
Your weaker half; learn from having
heard
Of the terrible example of what
disobedience
Will bring; they might have stood
firm
But they fell; remember that, and do
not disobey."

BOOK VII

THE ARGUMENT

Raphael at the request of Adam relates how and wherefore this world was first created; that God, after the expelling of Satan and his Angels out of Heaven, declar'd his pleasure to create another World and other Creatures to dwell therein; sends his Son with Glory and attendance of Angels to perform the work of Creation in six dayes: the Angels celebrate with Hymns the performance thereof, and his reascention into Heaven.

At Adam's request Raphael relates how and why this world was first created: that God, after expelling Satan and his Angels from Heaven, declared that it was his intention to create another world and other creatures to live in it. He sends his Son with his light and power and an attendance of Angels to perform the work of creation in six days. The Angels celebrate this, and his return to Heaven, with hymns.

Descend from Heav'n Urania, by that name

If rightly thou art call'd, whose Voice divine
Following, above th' Olympian Hill I soare,

Above the flight of Pegasean wing.
The meaning, not the Name I call: for thou

or of the Muses nine, nor on the top

Of old Olympus dwell'st, but Heav'nlie borne,
Before the Hills appeerd, or Fountain flow'd,
Thou with Eternal Wisdom didst converse,
Wisdom thy Sister, and with her didst play
In presence of th' Almightie Father, pleas'd

With thy Celestial Song. Up led by thee

Into the Heav'n of Heav'ns I have presum'd,
An Earthlie Guest, and drawn Empyreal Aire,
Thy tempring; with like safetie guided down
Return me to my Native Element:
Least from this flying Steed unrein'd, (as once
Bellerophon, though from a lower Clime)

Come down from Heaven, Urania, if that
Is really the name of the Divine inspiration
Which I am following, higher than the hill of Olympus,
Above the flight of Pegasus!
I'm calling on the idea, not the name, for you
Are not one of the nine ancient Muses, and you don't
Live on the peak of old Olympus but were born in heaven,
Before the land was formed or waters flowed
You lived with eternal Wisdom,
Your sister, and played with her
In the presence of the almighty Father, who was pleased
With your Heavenly song. I have been led up by you
To visit the highest of Heavens,
An earthly guest, and I have breathed the air there,
With your consent. With the same safety as you took me up,
Take me back to my own world,
In case I should be thrown from this flying horse (as Bellerophon
Once did, though from lower altitude)

Dismounted, on th' Aleian Field I fall

Erroneous there to wander and forlorne.
Half yet remaines unsung, but narrower
bound
Within the visible Diurnal Spheare;
Standing on Earth, not rapt above the Pole,

More safe I Sing with mortal voice,
unchang'd
To hoarce or mute, though fall'n on evil
dayes,
On evil dayes though fall'n, and evil t
ongues;
In darkness, and with dangers compast
round,
And solitude; yet not alone, while thou

Visit'st my slumbers Nightly, or when Morn

Purples the East: still govern thou my Song,

Urania, and fit audience find, though few.

But drive farr off the barbarous dissonance
Of Bacchus and his Revellers, the Race

Of that wilde Rout that tore the Thracian
Bard
In Rhodope, where Woods and Rocks had
Eares
To rapture, till the savage clamor dround

Both Harp and Voice; nor could the Muse
defend
Her Son. So fail not thou, who thee
implores:
For thou art Heav'nlie, shee an empty
dreame.
Say Goddess, what ensu'd when Raphael,

The affable Arch-Angel, had forewarn'd
Adam by dire example to beware

Apostasie, by what befell in Heaven

And fall in a Turkish field,

There to wander lost and ignorant.
Half my song is still to be sung, but it
takes place
In the smaller theatre of this world;
Standing on the Earth, not in rapture
above the Pole star
I can sing more safely with my mortal
voice which has not
Become rough or silent, though these
are evil days,
Evil days, which are full of evil
voices,
Surrounded by dangers in the
darkness,
Alone; but I am not really alone, as
long as you
Come to me in my sleep, or when
morning
Colors the eastern sky; you still rule
my song,
Urania, and find me proper listeners,
though few.
But drive far away the barbaric row
Of Bacchus and his drunken
followers, the people
Of that wild rabble who tore Orpheus
apart
In Rhodope, where the woods and the
rocks
Were charmed by his song, until their
savage row
Drowned out his music and his voice,
and the Muse could not
Defend her son. So do not let down
the one who is begging you,
For you are from Heaven while she is
just an illusion.
Tell, Goddess, what happened when
Raphael,
The friendly Archangel, warned
Adam to beware breaking faith with
God,
By showing him terrible examples of
what happened

To those Apostates, least the like befall

In Paradise to Adam or his Race,

Charg'd not to touch the interdicted Tree,

If they transgress, and slight that sole command,
So easily obeyd amid the choice
Of all tastes else to please thir appetite,

Though wandring. He with his consorted Eve
The storie heard attentive, and was fill'd

With admiration, and deep Muse to heare

Of things so high and strange, things to thir thought
So unimaginable as hate in Heav'n,

And Warr so neer the Peace of God in bliss
With such confusion: but the evil soon

Driv'n back redounded as a flood on those
From whom it sprung, impossible to mix

With Blessedness. Whence Adam soon repeal'd
The doubts that in his heart arose: and now

Led on, yet sinless, with desire to know

What neerer might concern him, how this World
Of Heav'n and Earth conspicious first began,
When, and whereof created, for what cause,

What within Eden or without was done

Before his memorie, as one whose drouth

Yet scarce allay'd still eyes the current streame,
Whose liquid murmur heard new thirst

---

*To those who did so in Heaven to make sure the same thing
Would not happen in Paradise to Adam or his descendants,
Ordered not to touch the forbidden tree,
And disobey that single order,*

*So easy to obey amongst the choice
Of so many other tastes to suit their appetites,
They must not be led astray. He, with his wife Eve,
Paid careful attention to the story, and was filled
With wonder and deep thoughts, to hear
Of things so holy and strange, things they
Could hardly imagine, such as hatred in Heaven,
And war in the lands of God's peace,
And so much disturbance: but the evil was soon
Driven back and rebounded on those
Who had begun it; it could not stay in Heaven
With the blessed. So Adam soon abandoned
The doubts that had arisen in his heart and now
Carried on, still without sin, wanting to know
Of things closer to him, how the world
Of sky and Earth first began;
When, and what it was made of, and why;
What, within Eden or outside, was done
Before he existed; he was like one whose thirst
Has hardly been touched, who eyes the stream,
Whose watery sounds make him feel*

Proceeded thus to ask his Heav'nly Guest.
excites,
Great things, and full of wonder in our eares,

Farr differing from this World, thou hast reveal'd
Divine interpreter, by favour sent
Down from the Empyrean to forewarne

Us timely of what might else have bin our loss,
Unknown, which human knowledg could not reach:
For which to the infinitly Good we owe
Immortal thanks, and his admonishment

Receave with solemne purpose to observe
Immutably his sovran will, the end
Of what we are. But since thou hast voutsaf't
Gently for our instruction to impart
Things above Earthly thought, which yet concernd
Our knowing, as to highest wisdom seemd,

Deign to descend now lower, and relate
What may no less perhaps availe us known,

How first began this Heav'n which we behold
Distant so high, with moving Fires adornd
Innumerable, and this which yeelds or fills

All space, the ambient Aire, wide interfus'd
Imbracing round this florid Earth, what cause
Mov'd the Creator in his holy Rest
Through all Eternitie so late to build

In Chaos, and the work begun, how soon

Absolv'd, if unforbid thou maist unfould

What wee, not to explore the secrets aske

thirsty again.
He started to question his heavenly guest.
"You have shown us great things, amazing to us,

So different from this world,

Divine messenger! Through kindness You were sent down from Heaven, to warn us
In time of what we could lose,

To tell us unknown things, beyond human knowledge;
For this we owe God
Everlasting thanks, and we receive his warning
And commit ourselves to follow
His wishes, which is the purpose
Of our lives. But since you have kindly undertaken,
To teach us, to show us things
Above human understanding,
although they were things
Which the highest wisdom thought it right for us to know,

Be so kind as to come lower, and tell Us things which it might be just as useful to know,

How this Heaven which we see, so wide and tall,
First began, decorated with so many Countless stars; and how this air was made,

Which fills all space
And wraps around this flowery Earth; what
Made the Creator, living
Through eternity, so recently decide to build

In Chaos. Once the work was begun, how soon

Was it complete? If it is permitted tell us

What we ask, not so we can get

Of his Eternal Empire, but the more

To magnifie his works, the more we know.

And the great Light of Day yet wants to run

Much of his Race though steep, suspens in Heav'n
Held by thy voice, thy potent voice he heares,
And longer will delay to heare thee tell
His Generation, and the rising Birth
Of Nature from the unapparent Deep:
Or if the Starr of Eevning and the Moon
Haste to thy audience, Night with her will bring
Silence, and Sleep listning to thee will watch,
Or we can bid his absence, till thy Song

End, and dismiss thee ere the Morning shine.
Thus Adam his illustrious Guest besought:
And thus the Godlike Angel answerd milde.

This also thy request with caution askt

Obtaine: though to recount Almightie works
What words or tongue of Seraph can suffice,
Or heart of man suffice to comprehend?

Yet what thou canst attain, which best may serve
To glorifie the Maker, and inferr

Thee also happier, shall not be withheld
Thy hearing, such Commission from above

I have receav'd, to answer thy desire
Of knowledge within bounds; beyond abstain
To ask, nor let thine own inventions hope

---

forbidden knowledge
Of his eternal empire, but so we can give greater praise
To his works, knowing more about them.
And there is still plenty of daylight left,

The sun seems to be fixed in its place in Heaven,
Held by your powerful voice, he can hear you,
And will wait longer to hear you tell
Of his creation, and the birth
Of Nature from the invisible depths:
Or if the evening star and the moon
Come rushing to hear you, then night will bring
Silence, and sleep will stand by to listen to you;
Or we can tell him to stay away, until you have

Finished your story, and you can be gone before morning."
So Adam asked his great guest,
And so the Godlike angel answered sweetly:

"As you have asked so sensibly your wish

Will be granted, though to tell of God's works
What words or language of Seraphs can do them justice,
And how can the heart of man hope to understand?

But what you can understand, things which help
You to praise your Creator, and help to make

You happier, these things will not
Be withheld from you; these are the orders I have received

From God, to satisfy your desire
For knowledge, within limits; beyond that
Do not ask, and do not try to use

Things not reveal'd, which th' invisible King,
Onely Omniscient hath supprest in Night,

To none communicable in Earth or Heaven:

Anough is left besides to search and know.

But Knowledge is as food, and needs no less
Her Temperance over Appetite, to know

In measure what the mind may well contain,
Oppresses else with Surfet, and soon turns

Wisdom to Folly, as Nourishment to Winde.

Know then, that after Lucifer from Heav'n
(So call him, brighter once amidst the Host

Of Angels, then that Starr the Starrs among)

Fell with his flaming Legions through the Deep
Into his place, and the great Son returnd
Victorious with his Saints, th' Omnipotent

Eternal Father from his Throne beheld
Thir multitude, and to his Son thus spake.

At least our envious Foe hath fail'd, who thought
All like himself rebellious, by whose aid

This inaccessible high strength, the seat
Of Deitie supream, us dispossest,

He trusted to have seis'd, and into fraud

Drew many, whom thir place knows here no more;
Yet farr the greater part have kept, I see,

Thir station, Heav'n yet populous retaines

---

guesswork
To try to understand things which the invisible King,
The only one who knows everything, has hidden in darkness
So that nobody in Heaven or Earth shall learn of them:
There is enough to learn and know of without them.

Knowledge is like food, and in the same way
One has to control one's appetite, and know
The amount that the mind can hold,
Otherwise it will become bloated with knowledge
And turn wisdom to folly, just as food turns to wind.
So know then that after Lucifer
(That is what he has been called, once brighter in the crowd
Of angels, as the morning star outshines the others)
Fell from Heaven with his burning armies through the deep
Into his place, the great Son returned
Victorious with his saints, and the all powerful
Eternal Father saw their great crowd
From his throne, and spoke to his son.
'At last our jealous enemy has been defeated, who thought
That with the help of those who were rebellious like him
This secure high place, this throne
Of the supreme God, with us overthrown,
He thought he could take from us, and into deceit
He drew many, who have no place here anymore:
But I see that the majority have remained loyal;
Heaven still has many citizens,

Number sufficient to possess her Realmes
Though wide, and this high Temple to frequent
With Ministeries due and solemn Rites:

But least his heart exalt him in the harme

Already done, to have dispeopl'd Heav'n

My damage fondly deem'd, I can repaire

That detriment, if such it be to lose

Self-lost, and in a moment will create

Another World, out of one man a Race

Of men innumerable, there to dwell,
Not here, till by degrees of merit rais'd

They open to themselves at length the way
Up hither, under long obedience tri'd,

And Earth be chang'd to Heav'n, & Heav'n to Earth,
One Kingdom, Joy and Union without end.

Mean while inhabit laxe, ye Powers of Heav'n,
And by my Word, begotten Son, by thee
This I perform, speak thou, and be it don:

My overshadowing Spirit and might with thee
I send along, ride forth, and bid the Deep

Within appointed bounds be Heav'n and Earth,
Boundless the Deep, because I am who fill

Infinitude, nor vacuous the space.

Though I uncircumscrib'd my self retire,

And put not forth my goodness, which is

---

enough
To fill her lands
Though they are wide, and to attend this high temple
With due worship and solemn ceremonies:

But in case he should rejoice in the harm

He has already done, to have depopulated Heaven,

Foolishly thinking that he has done me harm,

I can repair that loss, if it is a loss to lose

Those who are themselves lost; in an instant I will create

Another world, and out of one man I will make a race

Of countless men who will live there,
Not here; until, climbing up by degrees as they earn them,

They find for themselves the way
Up here, after they have proved their obedience through long testing,

And Earth will be changed to Heaven, Heaven to Earth,
One kingdom, with joy and union forever.

Meanwhile spread out to fill the space, you powers of Heaven;
And you, my Word, my Son, I do this Through you; speak, and it will happen!

I send my protecting Spirit and strength along
With you; ride out and command the void

Within set boundaries to become Heaven and Earth;
The void is measureless, because I fill it

And I am infinite, it is not empty space.

Although I do not directly involve myself,

And do not control my goodness,

free
To act or not, Necessitie and Chance

Approach not mee, and what I will is Fate.

So spake th' Almightie, and to what he
spake
His Word, the Filial Godhead, gave effect
Immediate are the Acts of God, more swift
Then time or motion, but to human ears
Cannot without process of speech be told,
So told as earthly notion can receave.

Great triumph and rejoycing was in Heav'n

When such was heard declar'd the
Almightie's will;
Glorie they sung to the most High, good
will
To future men, and in thir dwellings peace:

Glorie to him whose just avenging ire

Had driven out th' ungodly from his sight
And th' habitations of the just; to him

Glorie and praise, whose wisdom had
ordain'd
Good out of evil to create, in stead

Of Spirits maligne a better Race to bring
Into thir vacant room, and thence diffuse
His good to Worlds and Ages infinite.

So sang the Hierarchies: Mean while the
Son
On his great Expedition now appeer'd,

Girt with Omnipotence, with Radiance
crown'd
Of Majestie Divine, Sapience and Love

Immense, and all his Father in him shon.

About his Chariot numberless were pour'd

which
Is subject to free will,
predetermination and chance
Are not part of my plan, fate is what I
decide.
So the Almighty spoke, and what he
said
His Godly Son put into effect.
The acts of God are immediate, faster
Than time or movement, but speech
Is needed to tell them to human ears
So that they can be understood on
Earth.

There was great triumph and joy in
Heaven,
When it was heard that these were
God's orders;
'Glory,' they sang, 'to the highest,
good will
To future men, and may they have
peace in their world;

Praise to him, whose justly punishing
anger
Has driven the ungodly from his sight
And the lands of the just; glory and
praise
To him, who in his wisdom has
ordered
Good to be created from evil; to
replace
The evil Spirits with a better race
In their place, and so he will spread
His goodness through infinite worlds
and times.'
So the angels sang; meanwhile the
Son
Now appeared prepared for his great
expedition,
Dressed in infinite power, crowned
with the light
Of divine majesty; immense wisdom
and love,
And all his father's power, shone in
him.
Around his chariot there was an

	infinite number
Cherub and Seraph, Potentates and Thrones,	*Of Cherubs, Seraphs, Potentates and Thrones,*
And Vertues, winged Spirits, and Chariots wing'd,	*Virtues, winged Spirits and winged chariots*
From the Armoury of God, where stand of old	*From the armory of God; they had stood*
Myriads between two brazen Mountains lodg'd	*In reserve for a long time, stored between two great mountains*
Against a solemn day, harnest at hand,	*For an important day, harnessed and ready,*
Celestial Equipage; and now came forth	*Heavenly gear, and now they came forward*
Spontaneous, for within them Spirit livd,	*Of their own accord, for the Spirit lived within them*
Attendant on thir Lord: Heav'n op'nd wide	*And they came to wait upon their Lord: Heaven opened*
Her ever during Gates, Harmonious sound	*Her eternal gates wide with a sweet sound*
On golden Hinges moving, to let forth	*Of golden hinges, to send out*
The King of Glorie in his powerful Word	*The King of Glory with his powerful Word*
And Spirit coming to create new Worlds.	*And Spirit, coming to create new worlds.*
On heav'nly ground they stood, and from the shore	*They stood on the ground of Heaven, and from the shore*
They view'd the vast immeasurable Abyss	*They saw the great measureless abyss,*
Outrageous as a Sea, dark, wasteful, wilde,	*As stormy as a sea, dark, wasteful and wild,*
Up from the bottom turn'd by furious windes	*With furious winds and surging waves like mountains*
And surging waves, as Mountains to assault	*Rising up from the depths to assault*
Heav'ns highth, and with the Center mix the Pole.	*The heights of Heaven and mix the center with the pole.*
Silence, ye troubl'd waves, and thou Deep, peace,	*'Silence, you stormy waves, and you, depths, peace,'*
Said then th' Omnific Word, your discord end:	*Said the all-powerful Word, 'end your discord!'*
Nor staid, but on the Wings of Cherubim	*He did not stay, but lifted on the wings of angels*
Uplifted, in Paternal Glorie rode	*He rode with the glory of the Father*
Farr into Chaos, and the World unborn;	*Deep into Chaos and the uncreated world;*
For Chaos heard his voice: him all his Traine	*Chaos heard him speak, all his followers*

Follow'd in bright procession to behold	Came after in bright procession to see
Creation, and the wonders of his might.	Creation and the wonders of his power.
Then staid the fervid Wheeles, and in his hand	Then the spinning wheels paused, and in his hand
He took the golden Compasses, prepar'd	He took the golden compasses, prepared
In Gods Eternal store, to circumscribe	In God's eternal workshop, to measure out
This Universe, and all created things:	This universe and all created things:
One foot he center'd, and the other turn'd	He placed one foot of them in the center and turned the other
Round through the vast profunditie obscure,	Round through the great thick darkness,
And said, thus farr extend, thus farr thy bounds,	And said, 'This is how far you will spread, these are your boundaries,
This be thy just Circumference, O World.	This is your circumference, Oh World!'
Thus God the Heav'n created, thus the Earth,	And so God created Heaven and Earth;
Matter unform'd and void: Darkness profound	It was still empty and unformed matter, deep darkness
Cover'd th' Abyss: but on the watrie calme	Still covered the abyss: but on the calm waters
His brooding wings the Spirit of God outspred,	He spread the Spirit of God with his outstretched wings
And vital vertue infus'd, and vital warmth	And gave it vital power and vital warmth,
Throughout the fluid Mass, but downward purg'd	Right through the fluid mass; but pushed down
The black tartareous cold Infernal dregs	The black tarry dregs, which were
Adverse to life: then founded, then conglob'd	Adverse to life: then he shaped into globes
Like things to like, the rest to several place	Several similar things; the rest were scattered
Disparted, and between spun out the Air,	To various places, and between them he spun the air,
And Earth self ballanc't on her Center hung.	And the Earth hung balanced on her poles.
Let ther be Light, said God, and forthwith Light	'Let there be Light,' said God, and at once Heavenly
Ethereal, first of things, quintessence pure	Light, the first of all things, the most perfect purity,
Sprung from the Deep, and from her Native	Sprang out of the deep; and from her

East
To journie through the airie gloom began,
Sphear'd in a radiant Cloud, for yet the Sun

Was not; shee in a cloudie Tabernacle
Sojourn'd the while. God saw the Light
was good;
And light from darkness by the Hemisphere

Divided: Light the Day, and Darkness
Night He nam'd.
Thus was the first Day Eev'n and Morn:

Nor past uncelebrated, nor unsung
By the Celestial Quires, when Orient Light

Exhaling first from Darkness they beheld;

Birth-day of Heav'n and Earth; with joy
and shout
The hollow Universal Orb they fill'd,

And touch'd thir Golden Harps, and
hymning prais'd
God and his works, Creatour him they sung,

Both when first Eevning was, and when
first Morn.
Again, God said, let ther be Firmament

Amid the Waters, and let it divide
The Waters from the Waters: and God
made
The Firmament, expanse of liquid, pure,

Transparent, Elemental Air, diffus'd

In circuit to the uttermost convex
Of this great Round: partition firm and sure,

The Waters underneath from those above

Dividing: for as Earth, so he the World
Built on circumfluous Waters calme, in wide
Crystallin Ocean, and the loud misrule
Of Chaos farr remov'd, least fierce

home in the east
Began to travel through the dark air,
Surrounded with shining cloud, for
the sun

Did not yet exist; light still lived
In a cloudy dwelling. God saw the
light was good,
And light and darkness divided the
hemispheres;

He named the light Day and the
darkness Night.
So the first day, evening and
morning, passed,

And it was praised and hymned
By the Heavenly choirs, when they
first saw

The eastern light breathing out of the
darkness,

The birthday of Heaven and
Earth. With joy and shouting
They filled the hollow ball of the
universe,

And touched their golden harps, and
singing praised
God and his works; they praised him
as Creator,

Both at the first evening and the first
morning.
Again God spoke; 'Let there be a
firmament

Between the waters, and let it divide
The sea from the clouds; and God
made
The firmament, a great mass of pure,
liquid,

Transparent, elemental air, spread
round

To wrap the farthest curve
Of this great globe; it was a firm and
strong partition,

Dividing the waters below from those
above:

For as with earth, he set the world
In enclosing calm waters, in a wide
Crystal ocean, with the loud anarchy
Of Chaos kept far off, in case having

extreames
Contiguous might distemper the whole frame:
And Heav'n he nam'd the Firmament: So Eev'n
And Morning Chorus sung the second Day.

The Earth was form'd, but in the Womb as yet
Of Waters, Embryon immature involv'd,

Appeer'd not: over all the face of Earth

Main Ocean flow'd, not idle, but with warme
Prolific humour soft'ning all her Globe,
Fermented the great Mother to conceave,
Satiate with genial moisture, when God said
Be gather'd now ye Waters under Heav'n

Into one place, and let dry Land appeer.

Immediately the Mountains huge appeer

Emergent, and thir broad bare backs upheave
Into the Clouds, thir tops ascend the Skie:

So high as heav'd the tumid Hills, so low
Down sunk a hollow bottom broad and deep,
Capacious bed of Waters: thither they

Hasted with glad precipitance, uprowld

As drops on dust conglobing from the drie;

Part rise in crystal Wall, or ridge direct,
For haste; such flight the great command impress'd
On the swift flouds: as Armies at the call

Of Trumpet (for of Armies thou hast heard)

Troop to thir Standard, so the watrie throng,

Wave rowling after Wave, where way they

fierce opposites
Side by side might disturb the order of all.
He named the firmament Heaven, so evening
And morning the choirs sang through the second day.

The Earth was formed, but it was still suspended
In the waters, embryonic and immature,

And did not appear: over the whole face of the Earth

The open ocean flowed, not idle but with warm
Fertile fluid softening all the globe,
Fermenting her fertility,
Soaked in moisture; then God said,
'Gather together now, you waters under Heaven,

Into one place, and let dry land appear.'

Immediately the great mountains appeared,

Their broad bare backs rising

Into the clouds; their tops touched the sky.

As high as the hills rose, just as low
Sank hollow ground, broad and deep,
A great reservoir for the waters: there they

Rush with glad hurry, rolling together

Like drops in the dust joining together:

Some rose in a crystal wall or ridge
In their hurry, the great command had made
The floods move so fast. They were like armies

At the call of a trumpet (you have heard of armies recently),

Flocking to their flag; so the crowds of waters,

Wave after rolling wave found their

248

found,	way;
If steep, with torrent rapture, if through Plaine,	If it was steep, in a joyful torrent, if flat
Soft-ebbing; nor withstood them Rock or Hill,	Flowing softly; no rock or hill blocked them;
But they, or under ground, or circuit wide	They would go underground or wander
With Serpent errour wandring, found thir way,	In a snaky path around,
And on the washie Oose deep Channels wore;	And cut deep channels in the wet mud,
Easie, e're God had bid the ground be drie,	Which was easy, before God had ordered the Earth to dry,
All but within those banks, where Rivers now	Except within those banks, where rivers now
Stream, and perpetual draw thir humid traine.	Stream, and run their watery procession forever.
The dry Land, Earth, and the great receptacle	He called the dry land Earth and the great vessel
Of congregated Waters he call'd Seas:	Of all the joined water he called the sea;
And saw that it was good, and said, Let th' Earth	And he saw that it was good, and he said, 'Let the Earth
Put forth the verdant Grass, Herb yielding Seed,	Grow green grass, seeds for herbs,
And Fruit Tree yielding Fruit after her kind;	And fruit trees giving fruit according to their type,
Whose Seed is in her self upon the Earth.	With the seed in herself as it falls to the ground.'
He scarce had said, when the bare Earth, till then	He had hardly said this, when the bare earth, until then
Desert and bare, unsightly, unadorn'd,	Desert and brown, ugly, undecorated,
Brought forth the tender Grass, whose verdure clad	Sprouted tender grass, whose lushness
Her Universal Face with pleasant green,	Covered her whole face with pleasant green;
Then Herbs of every leaf, that sudden flour'd	Then herbs of every type suddenly flowered,
Op'ning thir various colours, and made gay	Showing their colors to brighten
Her bosom smelling sweet: and these scarce blown,	Her bosom, sweet smelling: and these, only just bloomed,
Forth flourish't thick the clustring Vine, forth crept	Put out thick grape laden vines, out crept
The smelling Gourd, up stood the cornie Reed	Swelling vegetables, up stood the corn stalks

Embattell'd in her field: and the humble Shrub,
And Bush with frizl'd hair implicit: last

Rose as in Dance the stately Trees, and spred
Thir branches hung with copious Fruit; or gemm'd
Thir blossoms: with high woods the hills were crownd,
With tufts the vallies and each fountain side,
With borders long the Rivers. That Earth now
Seemd like to Heav'n, a seat where Gods might dwell,
Or wander with delight, and love to haunt

Her sacred shades: though God had yet not rain'd
Upon the Earth, and man to till the ground

None was, but from the Earth a dewie Mist

Went up and waterd all the ground, and each
Plant of the field, which e're it was in the Earth
God made, and every Herb, before it grew

On the green stemm; God saw that it was good.
So Eev'n and Morn recorded the Third Day.

Again th' Almightie spake: Let there be Lights
High in th' expanse of Heaven to divide
The Day from Night; and let them be for Signes,
For Seasons, and for Dayes, and circling Years,
And let them be for Lights as I ordaine
Thir Office in the Firmament of Heav'n
To give Light on the Earth; and it was so.

And God made two great Lights, great for

In rows in the fields, and the humble shrubs
And bushes with their tangled hair: last of all,

As if in a dance, rose the great trees, spreading
Their branches with much fruit, or budding
With blossom. The hills were crowned with high woods,
The valleys had grass, and every spring,
And the rivers had long plant borders; Earth now
Seemed like a heaven, a place the Gods might live
Or wander with pleasure, and love to haunt

Her sacred woods: though God had not yet rained
Upon the Earth, and there were no men

To work the ground; but from the Earth a dewy mist

Rose up, and watered all the ground and every
Plant in the fields, which God had made before
He put them in the Earth, and he made every herb

Before it grew on the green stem: God saw that it was good,
And so the evening and morning of the third day passed.

Again the Almighty spoke: 'Let there be lights
High up in the sky, to divide
Day from night, and let them indicate

The passing seasons, days and years,

And let them be lamps, for I give them
This task in the sky,
To throw light on the Earth,' and it was so.

And God made two great lights, of

thir use
To Man, the greater to have rule by Day,

The less by Night alterne: and made the Starrs,
And set them in the Firmament of Heav'n
To illuminate the Earth, and rule the Day
In thir vicissitude, and rule the Night,
And Light from Darkness to divide. God saw,
Surveying his great Work, that it was good:

For of Celestial Bodies first the Sun

A mightie Spheare he fram'd, unlightsom first,
Though of Ethereal Mould: then form'd the Moon
Globose, and every magnitude of Starrs,

And sowd with Starrs the Heav'n thick as a field:
Of Light by farr the greater part he took,
Transplanted from her cloudie Shrine, and plac'd
In the Suns Orb, made porous to receive

And drink the liquid Light, firm to retaine

Her gather'd beams, great Palace now of Light.
Hither as to thir Fountain other Starrs
Repairing, in thir gold'n Urns draw Light,
And hence the Morning Planet guilds her horns;
By tincture or reflection they augment
Thir small peculiar, though from human sight
So farr remote, with diminution seen.

First in his East the glorious Lamp was seen,
Regent of Day, and all th' Horizon round

Invested with bright Rayes, jocond to run

great use
To Man; the larger was to rule over the day

And the lesser over night,
alternating; and he made the stars,
And put them in the sky
To light up the Earth, ruling over day
And night as they alternated,
And divide the light from the darkness. God saw,
Looking over his great work, that it was good:

For of the celestial bodies he first made the sun,

A mighty sphere, lightless at first

Though of ethereal matter; then he formed the moon
As a globe, and all the stars great and small

And scattered them thickly over the heavens;
He took the greatest part of light
From her containing clouds and placed
It in the ball of the sun, which was porous

So it could soak up the liquid light, and strong so she could retain
The gathered beams; she was now a great palace of light.
There other stars go, as if to a well,
Filling their golden urns with light,
And it's there the morning star polishes her horns;
By absorption or reflection they add
To their own small light, though human sight,
Being so far away, only sees them dimly.
The glorious lamp was first seen in the east,
Ruler of the day, and the horizon all round
Was lit with his bright rays as he ran

His Longitude through Heav'n's high rode: the gray
Dawn, and the Pleiades before him danc'd

Shedding sweet influence: less bright the Moon,
But opposite in leveld West was set

His mirror, with full face borrowing her Light
From him, for other light she needed none

In that aspect, and still that distance keeps

Till night, then in the East her turn she shines,
Revolvd on Heav'ns great Axle, and her Reign
With thousand lesser Lights dividual holds,
With thousand thousand Starres, that then appeer'd
Spangling the Hemisphere: then first adornd
With thir bright Luminaries that Set and Rose,
Glad Eevning and glad Morn crownd the fourth day.
And God said, let the Waters generate

Reptil with Spawn abundant, living Soule:

And let Fowle flie above the Earth, with wings
Displayd on the op'n Firmament of Heav'n.
And God created the great Whales, and each
Soul living, each that crept, which plenteously
The waters generated by thir kindes,

And every Bird of wing after his kinde;
And saw that it was good, and bless'd them, saying,
Be fruitful, multiply, and in the Seas

His happy course through the high Heavens; the gray
Dawn, and the Pleiades, danced in front of him,

Throwing sweetness; less bright was the moon,
But it was set level opposite him in the west,

His mirror, with her full face borrowing light
From him; for other light she needed none

When in that place, and stayed there until nightfall;

Then she takes her turn at shining in the east,
Revolving on Heaven's great spindle, and she rules
With a thousand lesser lights,
With a million stars that then appeared
Jewelling the hemisphere: so decorated for the first time
With their bright lamps which set and rose
Happy evening and morning marked the fourth day.
And God said, 'Let the waters generate

Reptiles with abundant spawn, living souls,

And let birds fly over the Earth, with wings
Spread in the skies of Heaven.'
And God created the great whales, and each
Living soul, each one which crept, each
Which generously populated the waters in their types,

And every type of winged bird,
And he saw that it was good, and blessed them, saying,
'Be fruitful, and multiply, and fill the seas,

And Lakes and running Streams the waters fill;	*The lakes, the running streams, all the waters;*
And let the Fowle be multiply'd on the Earth.	*And let the birds be multiplied, on the Earth.'*
Forthwith the Sounds and Seas, each Creek and Bay	*At once the channels and seas, every creek and bay,*
With Frie innumerable swarme, and Shoales	*Were swarming with fry, and shoals*
Of Fish that with thir Finns and shining Scales	*Of fish, that with their fins and shining scales*
Glide under the green Wave, in Sculles that oft	*Glide under the green waves, in schools that often*
Bank the mid Sea: part single or with mate	*Make an island in the sea: some single, some with mates*
Graze the Sea weed thir pasture, and through Groves	*Grazed their pasture, the seaweed, and wander through Groves*
Of Coral stray, or sporting with quick glance	*Groves of coral; or, playing lively,*
Show to the Sun thir wav'd coats dropt with Gold,	*Show the sun their wavy coats spotted with gold;*
Or in thir Pearlie shells at ease, attend	*Others rest in their pearly shells, taking in*
Moist nutriment, or under Rocks thir food	*Moist food, or watch their prey under the rocks,*
In jointed Armour watch: on smooth the Seale,	*Wearing jointed armor: on the calm waters seals*
And bended Dolphins play: part huge of bulk	*And arching dolphins play: some, enormous,*
Wallowing unweildie, enormous in thir Gate	*Clumsily wallowing, huge in their movements,*
Tempest the Ocean: there Leviathan	*Whip up the ocean; that is leviathan,*
Hugest of living Creatures, on the Deep	*The biggest of living creatures, who on the waters,*
Stretcht like a Promontorie sleeps or swimmes,	*Stretched out like a headland, sleeps or swims,*
And seems a moving Land, and at his Gilles	*And seems like a moving island; and he draws*
Draws in, and at his Trunck spouts out a Sea.	*In through his gills, and spouts through his blowhole, a sea.*
Mean while the tepid Caves, and Fens and shoares	*Meanwhile the tepid caves, the fens and the shorelines*
Thir Brood as numerous hatch, from the Egg that soon	*Hatch out their children, just as numerous, from eggs that soon*
Bursting with kindly rupture forth disclos'd	*Burst apart naturally and reveal*
Thir callow young, but featherd soon and fledge	*Their unfledged young; but they soon grow feathers and fly*
They summ'd thir Penns, and soaring th'	*When they have all their feathers, and*

air sublime	*soaring in the sweet air*
With clang despis'd the ground, under a cloud	*And with harsh cries spurned the ground, rising*
In prospect; there the Eagle and the Stork	*Like a cloud; there the eagle and the stork*
On Cliffs and Cedar tops thir Eyries build:	*Build their nests on clifftops and in cedar trees;*
Part loosly wing the Region, part more wise	*Some fly the skies alone, others, wiser,*
In common, rang'd in figure wedge thir way,	*Fly together arranged in a wedge,*
Intelligent of seasons, and set forth	*Knowing of the seasons they set off*
Thir Aierie Caravan high over Sea's	*With their caravan of the air, flying high*
Flying, and over Lands with mutual wing	*Over sea and land, their comradeship*
Easing thir flight; so stears the prudent Crane	*Easing their flight; so the prudent crane*
Her annual Voiage, born on Windes; the Aire,	*Goes on her annual voyage, carried on the wind; the air*
Floats, as they pass, fann'd with unnumber'd plumes:	*Shimmers as they pass, fanned by countless feathers:*
From Branch to Branch the smaller Birds with song	*From branch to branch the smaller birds calmed the woods*
Solac'd the Woods, and spred thir painted wings	*With song, and spread their colorful wings until*
Till Ev'n, nor then the solemn Nightingal	*Evening came; even then the solemn nightingale*
Ceas'd warbling, but all night tun'd her soft layes:	*Did not stop, but sang her soft song all night:*
Others on Silver Lakes and Rivers Bath'd	*Others, on silver lakes and rivers, bathed*
Thir downie Brest; the Swan with Arched neck	*Their feathered breasts; the swan with her arched neck*
Between her white wings mantling proudly, Rowes	*Carried proudly between her wings, rows*
Her state with Oarie feet: yet oft they quit	*Dignified with her oar-like feet; but often they leave*
The Dank, and rising on stiff Pennons, towre	*The damp and, rising on stiff wings, climb*
The mid Aereal Skie: Others on ground	*Into the middle sky; others walked firmly*
Walk'd firm; the crested Cock whose clarion sounds	*On the ground; the cockerel whose cry marks*
The silent hours, and th' other whose gay Traine	*Time, and the peacock whose cheerful tail*
Adorns him, colour'd with the Florid hue	*Embellishes him, colored with the bright hues*

Of Rainbows and Starrie Eyes. The Waters thus
With Fish replenisht, and the Aire with Fowle,
Ev'ning and Morn solemniz'd the Fift day.

The Sixt, and of Creation last arose

With Eevning Harps and Mattin, when God said,
Let th' Earth bring forth Foul living in her kinde,
Cattel and Creeping things, and Beast of the Earth,
Each in their kinde. The Earth obey'd, and strait
Op'ning her fertile Woomb teem'd at a Birth

Innumerous living Creatures, perfet formes,

Limb'd and full grown: out of the ground up rose
As from his Laire the wilde Beast where he wonns
In Forrest wilde, in Thicket, Brake, or Den;

Among the Trees in Pairs they rose, they walk'd:
The Cattel in the Fields and Meddowes green:
Those rare and solitarie, these in flocks

Pasturing at once, and in broad Herds upsprung.
The grassie Clods now Calv'd, now half appeer'd
The Tawnie Lion, pawing to get free

His hinder parts, then springs as broke from Bonds,
And Rampant shakes his Brinded main; the Ounce,
The Libbard, and the Tyger, as the Moale Rising, the crumbl'd Earth above them threw
In Hillocks; the swift Stag from under

Of rainbows and starry eyes. So with the waters
Filled with fish, and the air with birds,
Evening and morning celebrated the fifth day.

The sixth and last day of Creation began

With songs at evening and morning, and God said,
"Let the Earth bring forth living souls of all kinds,
Cattle, and crawling things, and beasts of the Earth,
All of their own type. The Earth obeyed, and at once
Opening her fertile womb there spilled out

Uncountable living creatures, complete forms,

With limbs and fully grown: out from the ground there rose
As he does from his lair, the wild beast where he lives
In wild forests, thickets, bushes and dens;

They appeared walking in pairs amongst the trees:
The cattle in the fields and green meadows,
Some single and alone, others in flocks

All eating together, and springing up in herds.
The clods of grass now split, now there could be seen
Half a tawny lion, struggling to get his rear half

Free, then he springs out like one released from chains,
And stands to shake his streaky mane; the lynx,
The leopard and the tiger, rising Like moles, threw the crumbled earth above them
Into mounds: the swift stag pushed

ground	*his antlered head*
Bore up his branching head: scarse from his mould	*Up from underground: out of his mould*
Behemoth biggest born of Earth upheav'd	*The elephant, largest creature of the Earth, pulled*
His vastness: Fleec't the Flocks and bleating rose,	*His great bulk; the fleecy bleating flocks rose up*
As Plants: ambiguous between Sea and Land	*Like plants; amphibious between sea and land*
The River Horse and scalie Crocodile.	*Were the hippopotamus and the scaly crocodile.*
At once came forth whatever creeps the ground,	*At once out came whatever creeps on the ground,*
Insect or Worme; those wav'd thir limber fans	*Insect or worm; they waved their supple fans*
For wings, and smallest Lineaments exact	*As wings, and their tiny features were perfect,*
In all the Liveries dect of Summers pride	*In their decoration of the colors of summer,*
With spots of Gold and Purple, azure and green:	*With spots of purple, gold, blue and green:*
These as a line thir long dimension drew,	*This sort drew their dimensions straight out,*
Streaking the ground with sinuous trace; not all	*Streaking over the ground with a weaving line; not all*
Minims of Nature; some of Serpent kinde	*Were the smallest creatures; some of the serpent type,*
Wondrous in length and corpulence involv'd	*Amazing in their length and girth, coiled*
Thir Snakie foulds, and added wings. First crept	*Their snaky folds, and added wings.For the first time*
The Parsimonious Emmet, provident	*The thrifty ant walked, storing things up for the future;*
Of future, in small room large heart enclos'd,	*A large heart in a small body;*
Pattern of just equalitie perhaps	*An example of proper equality, perhaps,*
Hereafter, join'd in her popular Tribes	*For the future, all joined in their democratic*
Of Commonaltie: swarming next appeer'd	*Tribes; next, swarming, came*
The Female Bee that feeds her Husband Drone	*The female bee, that feeds her drone husband*
Deliciously, and builds her waxen Cells	*Delicious food, and builds her wax cells*
With Honey stor'd: the rest are numberless,	*Full of honey: the rest cannot be*

And thou thir Natures know'st, & gav'st them Names,
Needless to thee repeated; nor unknown

The Serpent suttl'st Beast of all the field,

Of huge extent somtimes, with brazen Eyes

And hairie Main terrific, though to thee

Not noxious, but obedient at thy call.
Now Heav'n in all her Glorie shon, and rowld
Her motions, as the great first-Movers hand

First wheeld thir course; Earth in her rich attire
Consummate lovly smil'd; Aire, Water, Earth,
By Fowl, Fish, Beast, was flown, was swum, was walkt
Frequent; and of the Sixt day yet remain'd;

There wanted yet the Master work, the end

Of all yet don; a Creature who not prone

And Brute as other Creatures, but endu'd

With Sanctitie of Reason, might erect

His Stature, and upright with Front serene

Govern the rest, self-knowing, and from thence
Magnanimous to correspond with Heav'n,

But grateful to acknowledge whence his good
Descends, thither with heart and voice and eyes
Directed in Devotion, to adore
And worship God Supream, who made him chief
Of all his works: therefore the Omnipotent

counted,
And you know what they are and have named them,
So I don't need to repeat them to you; nor is the serpent
A stranger to you, the most cunning beast of them all,
Sometimes of great size, with metallic eyes
And a great hairy mane, though he is not poisonous to you,
And obeys your call.
Now heaven shone in all her glory, and rolled
Round her orbits, as the great first mover's hand
Set them moving for the first time. Earth, completed,
In her rich clothes smiled beautiful; air water and earth
Was swum, flown and walked by fish, bird and beast,
Thronging, and for what remained of the sixth day,
There was still needed the masterwork, the culmination
Of everything that had been done; a creature who was not low
And brutish as the other creatures, but given
The holy virtue of reason, who might stand up
Straight and upright with a serene face and
Govern the rest, having self-knowledge, and that
Will allow his soul to talk with Heaven,
Gratefully acknowledging where his good comes from
And turn his heart, voice and eyes there
With devotion, adoring
And worshipping the supreme God, who made him the best
Of all his works; so the all powerful

Eternal Father (For where is not hee
Present) thus to his Son audibly spake.
Let us make now Man in our image, Man

In our similitude, and let them rule
Over the Fish and Fowle of Sea and Aire,
Beast of the Field, and over all the Earth,

And every creeping thing that creeps the
ground.
This said, he formd thee, Adam, thee O
Man
Dust of the ground, and in thy nostrils
breath'd
The breath of Life; in his own Image hee
Created thee, in the Image of God
Express, and thou becam'st a living Soul.

Male he created thee, but thy consort

Female for Race; then bless'd Mankinde,
and said,
Be fruitful, multiplie, and fill the Earth,

Subdue it, and throughout Dominion hold

Over Fish of the Sea, and Fowle of the Aire,

And every living thing that moves on the
Earth.
Wherever thus created, for no place

Is yet distinct by name, thence, as thou
know'st
He brought thee into this delicious Grove,

This Garden, planted with the Trees of
God,
Delectable both to behold and taste;
And freely all thir pleasant fruit for food

Gave thee, all sorts are here that all th'
Earth yields,
Varietie without end; but of the Tree

*Eternal Father (for where is he not
Present?) spoke to his Son:
'Let us now make Man in our image,
Man
The same as us, and let them rule
Over the fish and birds of sea and air,
The beasts of the field, and over all
the Earth,
And every creeping thing that crawls
along the ground.'
Having said this he formed you
Adam, you, Man,
From the dust of the ground, and into
your nostrils breathed
The breath of life; he created you in
His own image, in the image of God
Directly; and you became a living
soul.
He created you male, but your
companion
Female, so that you could breed; then
he blessed mankind, and said,
'Be fruitful, multiply and fill the
Earth;
Master it, and everywhere hold
power
Over the fish of the sea, the birds of
the air,
And every living thing that moves on
the Earth.
Wherever you were created, for no
place
Has its own name yet, from there, as
you know,
He brought you to this beautiful
place,
This garden, planted with the trees of
God,
Delicious both to see and to eat;
And he freely gave you all their
wonderful food;
Here there is everything that the
Earth gives,
Endless variety; but you must not
touch the fruit*

Which tasted works knowledge of Good and Evil,	*Of the tree which, once tasted, gives knowledge of good and evil;*
Thou mai'st not; in the day thou eat'st, thou di'st;	*The day you eat that, you will die,*
Death is the penaltie impos'd, beware,	*Death is the penalty for that; be warned,*
And govern well thy appetite, least sin	*And keep control of your appetite, in case sin*
Surprise thee, and her black attendant Death.	*Should catch you unawares, with her black companion, Death.*
Here finish'd hee, and all that he had made	*God finished his work, and looked on all he had made,*
View'd, and behold all was entirely good;	*And saw that all was entirely good;*
So Ev'n and Morn accomplish't the Sixt day:	*So evening and morning completed the sixth day,*
Yet not till the Creator from his work	*But not until the Creator stopped working,*
Desisting, though unwearied, up returnd	*Although he was not tired, and returned upwards,*
Up to the Heav'n of Heav'ns his high abode,	*Up to the highest Heaven, his home,*
Thence to behold this new created World	*There to look down on his newly created world,*
Th' addition of his Empire, how it shew'd	*The new addition to his empire, to see how it looked*
In prospect from his Throne, how good, how faire,	*From his throne, how good, how beautiful,*
Answering his great Idea. Up he rode	*Fulfilling his great plan. Up he rode,*
Followd with acclamation and the sound	*Followed with praise, and the symphony*
Symphonious of ten thousand Harpes that tun'd	*Of ten thousand harps, that sung*
Angelic harmonies: the Earth, the Aire,	*Angelic harmonies: the Earth, the air*
Resounded, (thou remember'st for thou heardst)	*Resounded (you remember, because you heard it),*
The Heav'ns and all the Constellations rung,	*The skies and all the stars rang,*
The Planets in thir stations list'ning stood,	*The planets stood listening in their places,*
While the bright Pomp ascended jubilant.	*While that bright glory ascended with joy.*
Open, ye everlasting Gates, they sung,	*"Open, you everlasting gates," they sang,*
Open, ye Heav'ns, your living dores; let in	*"Open, Heavens, your everlasting doors; let in*
The great Creator from his work returnd	*The Creator returned from his work,*
Magnificent, his Six days work, a World;	*Magnificent, he has worked for six days and made a world;*

259

Open, and henceforth oft; for God will deigne
To visit oft the dwellings of just Men

Delighted, and with frequent intercourse

Thither will send his winged Messengers

On errands of supernal Grace. So sung

The glorious Train ascending: He through Heav'n,
That open'd wide her blazing Portals, led

To Gods Eternal house direct the way,
A broad and ample rode, whose dust is Gold
And pavement Starrs, as Starrs to thee appeer,
Seen in the Galaxie, that Milkie way
Which nightly as a circling Zone thou seest

Pouderd with Starrs. And now on Earth the Seventh
Eev'ning arose in Eden, for the Sun
Was set, and twilight from the East came on,

Forerunning Night; when at the holy mount

Of Heav'ns high-seated top, th' Impereal Throne
Of Godhead, fixt for ever firm and sure,

The Filial Power arriv'd, and sate him down
With his great Father (for he also went
Invisible, yet staid, such priviledge

Hath Omnipresence) and the work ordain'd,

Author and end of all things, and from work

Now resting, bless'd and hallowd the Seav'nth day,
As resting on that day from all his work,
But not in silence holy kept; the Harp

Open, and do so often from now on, for God
Will now often be pleased to visit the homes
Of just men, and there will be frequent communication
As he sends his winged messengers to Earth
On errands of Heavenly grace." So sang
The glorious procession as it rose:
He led them through Heaven,
That opened her blazing doors wide, and led them
Directly to God's eternal house,
Over a broad and roomy road, whose dust is gold
And is paved with stars, as stars appear to you,
Seen in the galaxy, the Milky Way,
That zone which you see orbiting each night,
Powdered with stars. And now on Earth the seventh
Evening began in Eden, for the sun
Had set, and twilight approached from the east,
Telling of the coming night. At the holy mountain
At the highest point of Heaven, the Imperial throne
Of God, fixed firm and strong forever,
The Son arrived and sat down
With his great father (for he had gone
With him, invisible, but also stayed in Heaven, such is the power
Of Ominpresence) and the work was done,
The maker and finisher of all things, and he was now resting
From work, and he blessed and made holy the seventh day,
As being a day to rest from all work,
But the day was not observed in holy silence; the harp

Had work and rested not, the solemn Pipe,	*Had work and did not rest, the solemn pipe*
And Dulcimer, all Organs of sweet stop,	*And dulcimer, all the sweet sounding organs,*
All sounds on Fret by String or Golden Wire	*All sounds made by plucking and pressing strings*
Temper'd soft Tunings, intermixt with Voice	*Sounded softly, mixed with voices*
Choral or Unison; of incense Clouds	*Singing harmonies or all together; the mountain was hidden*
Fuming from Golden Censers hid the Mount.	*By clouds of incense coming from golden burners.*
Creation and the Six dayes acts they sung,	*They sang of creation and the six day's work that had been done:*
Great are thy works, Jehovah, infinite	*"Your works are great, God, your power*
Thy power; what thought can measure thee or tongue	*Is infinite; what thought can comprehend you or tongue*
Relate thee; greater now in thy return	*Tell of you? You are greater now as you return*
Then from the Giant Angels; thee that day	*Than the day you fought the rebels; that day you*
Thy Thunders magnifi'd; but to create	*Strengthened your thunder, but to create*
Is greater then created to destroy.	*Is greater than making things to destroy.*
Who can impair thee, mighty King, or bound	*Who can lessen you, great King, or measure*
Thy Empire? easily the proud attempt	*Your empire? You easily overcame*
Of Spirits apostat and thir Counsels vaine	*The arrogant rebellion of the mistaken Spirits*
Thou hast repeld, while impiously they thought	*And their foolish debates, when they blasphemously thought*
Thee to diminish, and from thee withdraw	*They could lessen your glory and lower*
The number of thy worshippers. Who seekes	*The number of your worshippers. The one who tries*
To lessen thee, against his purpose serves	*To make you less only manages, against his plans,*
To manifest the more thy might: his evil	*To show even more of your strength; you use*
Thou usest, and from thence creat'st more good.	*His evil, and create more good from it.*
Witness this new-made World, another Heav'n	*See this newly made world, another Heaven*
From Heaven Gate not farr, founded in	*Not far from Heaven's gate, built*

view	*within sight*
On the cleer Hyaline, the Glassie Sea;	*On the clear glassy sea;*
Of amplitude almost immense, with Starr's	*It is almost infinte in size, with numerous*
Numerous, and every Starr perhaps a World	*Stars, and maybe every star will one day*
Of destind habitation; but thou know'st	*Be inhabited, but you know*
Thir seasons: among these the seat of men,	*What happens there. Among these stars is the home of men,*
Earth with her nether Ocean circumfus'd,	*Earth with her encircling ocean,*
Thir pleasant dwelling place. Thrice happie men,	*Their pleasant home. Men are three times blessed,*
And sons of men, whom God hath thus advanc't,	*And their sons as well; God has placed them there.*
Created in his Image, there to dwell	*Created in His image, the live there*
And worship him, and in reward to rule	*And worship him, and as their reward they rule*
Over his Works, on Earth, in Sea, or Air,	*Over his works on Earth, in the seas and in the air,*
And multiply a Race of Worshippers	*And breed a race of worshippers,*
Holy and just: thrice happie if they know	*Holy and wise; they will be three times blessed if they know*
Thir happiness, and persevere upright.	*How lucky they are, and remain righteous.'*
So sung they, and the Empyrean rung,	*So they sang, and the heavens rang*
With Halleluiahs: Thus was Sabbath kept.	*With hallelujahs: this was how the Sabbath was observed.*
And thy request think now fulfill'd, that ask'd	*And now think your question answered, you who asked*
How first this World and face of things began,	*How this world and everything in it began,*
And what before thy memorie was don	*And keep the story of this beginning*
From the beginning, that posteritie	*In your memory, so that those who come after*
Informd by thee might know; if else thou seek'st	*Will know of it, told by you; if you want to know*
Aught, not surpassing human measure, say.	*Anything else, if it's not beyond human understanding, say so.'*

BOOK VIII

THE ARGUMENT

Adam inquires concerning celestial Motions, is doubtfully answer'd, and exhorted to search rather things more worthy of knowledg: Adam assents, and still desirous to detain Raphael, relates to him what he remember'd since his own Creation, his placing in Paradise, his talk with God concerning solitude and fit society, his first meeting and Nuptials with Eve, his discourse with the Angel thereupon; who after admonitions repeated departs.	*Adam asks about the movement of the stars, receives an ambiguous answer and is encouraged to investigate things more suitable for his understanding. Adam agrees, and wishing Raphael to stay he tells him what he can remember since his own creation, his placing in Paradise, his talk with Godconcerning solitude and the right sort of companionship, his first meeting with, and marriage Eve.He talks to the Angel on this matter; the Angel gives him warnings and departs.*
THE Angel ended, and in Adams Eare	*The angel finished, and his voice echoed*
So Charming left his voice, that he a while	*So charmingly in Adam's ear that for a while*
Thought him still speaking, still stood fixt to hear;	*He thought he was still speaking, and stood listening;*
Then as new wak't thus gratefully repli'd.	*Then like one newly awoken he gratefully replied:*
What thanks sufficient, or what recompence	*'How can I thank you enough, how could I*
Equal have I to render thee, Divine	*Repay you, Heavenly*
Hystorian, who thus largely hast allayd	*Historian, who has almost quenched*
The thirst I had of knowledge, and voutsaf't	*My thirst for knowledge, and had*
This friendly condescention to relate	*The kindness to lower himself to tell*
Things else by me unsearchable, now heard	*Of things I could never discover for myself, now heard*
With wonder, but delight, and, as is due,	*With amazement and delight, and, as is right,*
With glorie attributed to the high	*With praise to the high*
Creator; something yet of doubt remaines,	*Creator; there is one thing I still don't understand,*
Which onely thy solution can resolve.	*And only you can tell me the answer.*
When I behold this goodly Frame, this World	*When I see this universe, this world*
Of Heav'n and Earth consisting, and compute,	*Made of Heaven and Earth, and calculate*
Thir magnitudes, this Earth a spot, a graine,	*Their sizes, this Earth is a spot, a grain,*
An Atom, with the Firmament compar'd	*An atom, compared with the sky*

And all her numberd Starrs, that seem to rowle	And all her many stars, that seem to travel
Spaces incomprehensible (for such	Incomprehensible distances (so one
Thir distance argues and thir swift return	Assumes, given their distance from us and their quick daily
Diurnal) meerly to officiate light	Return) just to give light
Round this opacous Earth, this punctual spot,	To this dark Earth, this little dot,
One day and night; in all thir vast survey	Giving day and night; in all their great spaces
Useless besides, reasoning I oft admire,	They are otherwise useless. Looking at them I often wonder
How Nature wise and frugal could commit	How Nature, so wise and sparing, could allow
Such disproportions, with superfluous hand	So much to do so little, unnecessarily
So many nobler Bodies to create,	Making so many greater planets,
Greater so manifold to this one use,	So much greater than needed for this one use,
For aught appeers, and on thir Orbs impose	Or so it seems, and make them
Such restless revolution day by day	Go round in their orbits day after day,
Repeated, while the sedentarie Earth,	Over and over, while the motionless Earth,
That better might with farr less compass move,	Which might be moved with far less effort,
Serv'd by more noble then her self, attaines	Is served by those greater than herself, gets
Her end without least motion, and receaves,	What she needs without any movement, and receives
As Tribute such a sumless journey brought	As a present her warmth and light, brought
Of incorporeal speed, her warmth and light;	By a measureless journey of supernatural speed;
Speed, to describe whose swiftness Number failes.	A speed which could not be described with numbers. '
So spake our Sire, and by his count'nance seemd	So our ancestor spoke, and from his face seemed
Entring on studious thoughts abstruse, which Eve	To be starting to think of academic things; seeing this Eve,
Perceaving where she sat retir'd in sight,	From where she was sitting, a little away but within sight,
With lowliness Majestic from her seat,	With majestic humility rose from her seat
And Grace that won who saw to wish her stay,	With a grace that made any who saw her want her to stay,
Rose, and went forth among her Fruits	And went out amongst her fruits and

and Flours,	*flowers,*
To visit how they prosper'd, bud and bloom,	*To see how they grew, how they budded and bloomed*
Her Nurserie; they at her coming sprung	*In her nursery; at her coming they sprang up,*
And toucht by her fair tendance gladlier grew.	*And touched with her fair tenderness grew happy.*
Yet went she not, as not with such discourse	*But she did not go because she was bored*
Delighted, or not capable her eare	*Of the talk, or incapable of understanding*
Of what was high: such pleasure she reserv'd,	*Such high matters; she enjoyed hearing such things,*
Adam relating, she sole Auditress;	*With Adam talking and she the only listener.*
Her Husband the Relater she preferr'd	*She preferred to hear the story from her husband*
Before the Angel, and of him to ask	*Rather than the angel, and decided to wait*
Chose rather: hee, she knew would intermix	*To ask him; she knew he would tell her*
Grateful digressions, and solve high dispute	*In stages, and tell her of great matters*
With conjugal Caresses, from his Lip	*Mixed with kisses, for words were not the only things*
Not Words alone pleas'd her. O when meet now	*That she enjoyed from his lips. Where are such couples*
Such pairs, in Love and mutual Honour joyn'd?	*Now, joined in love and mutual respect?*
With Goddess-like demeanour forth she went;	*With her Goddess-like appearance she went out,*
Not unattended, for on her as Queen	*Not unattended, for as if she were a queen*
A pomp of winning Graces waited still,	*A procession of charming graces went with her,*
And from about her shot Darts of desire	*And from all around her shot darts of desire*
Into all Eyes to wish her still in sight.	*In to all eyes, making them wish she would stay.*
And Raphael now to Adam's doubt propos'd	*And now Raphael replied to the question Adam raised,*
Benevolent and facil thus repli'd.	*Kindly and graciously:*
To ask or search I blame thee not, for Heav'n	*"I don't blame you for asking and seeking, for Heaven*
Is as the Book of God before thee set,	*Is like a Book of God laid out for you,*

Wherein to read his wondrous Works, and learne	*Where you can read of his wondrous works, and learn*
His Seasons, Hours, or Dayes, or Months, or Yeares:	*Of the seasons, hours, days, months or years:*
This to attain, whether Heav'n move or Earth,	*To know this, whether it is Earth or the Heavens which move,*
Imports not, if thou reck'n right, the rest	*Is of no importance, if you think about it, the rest*
From Man or Angel the great Architect	*The great Creator wisely kept from*
Did wisely to conceal, and not divulge	*Man or angels, and does not allow his secrets*
His secrets to be scann'd by them who ought	*To be pried into by those who ought*
Rather admire; or if they list to try	*To be admiring them; or if they want to try*
Conjecture, he his Fabric of the Heav'ns	*Guesswork, he has left the material of the Heavens*
Hath left to thir disputes, perhaps to move	*There for them to argue over, perhaps to make*
His laughter at thir quaint Opinions wide	*Him laugh at how wide of the mark their opinions are,*
Hereafter, when they come to model Heav'n	*In later days, when they come to describe Heaven*
And calculate the Starrs, how they will weild	*And count the stars, how they will twist*
The mightie frame, how build, unbuild, contrive	*The great structure, how they'll build, take apart, make up*
To save appeerances, how gird the Sphear	*Things to make them fit their theories, how they'll mark the universe,*
With Centric and Eccentric scribl'd o're, Cycle and Epicycle, Orb in Orb:	*Scribbling orbital paths all over it, With circles great and small, orbits within orbits;*
Alreadie by thy reasoning this I guess,	*By you asking this I can see what will happen, for you*
Who art to lead thy ofspring, and supposes	*Will be the example for your descendants, and you think*
That bodies bright and greater should not serve	*That bodies that are greater and brighter should not*
The less not bright, nor Heav'n such journies run,	*Be servants to the smaller and dimmer, and Heaven should not make such efforts*
Earth sitting still, when she alone receaves	*While the Earth sits still, and only she benefits.*
The benefit: consider first, that Great	*First of all consider that great*
Or Bright inferrs not Excellence: the Earth	*Or bright does not necessarily mean excellent; although*
Though, in comparison of Heav'n, so small,	*In comparison to the Heavens Earth*

Nor glistering, may of solid good containe

More plenty then the Sun that barren shines,
Whose vertue on it self workes no effect,

But in the fruitful Earth; there first receavd

His beams, unactive else, thir vigour find.

Yet not to Earth are those bright Luminaries

Officious, but to thee Earths habitant.

And for the Heav'ns wide Circuit, let it speak
The Makers high magnificence, who built

So spacious, and his Line stretcht out so farr;
That Man may know he dwells not in his own;
An Edifice too large for him to fill,
Lodg'd in a small partition, and the rest

Ordain'd for uses to his Lord best known.

The swiftness of those Circles attribute,

Though numberless, to his Omnipotence,

That to corporeal substances could adde
Speed almost Spiritual; mee thou thinkst not slow,
Who since the Morning hour set out from Heav'n
Where God resides, and ere mid-day arriv'd

In Eden, distance inexpressible
By Numbers that have name. But this I urge,
Admitting Motion in the Heav'ns, to shew

Invalid that which thee to doubt it mov'd;

Not that I so affirm, though so it seem

is so small
And not bright, it may contain more solid goodness
Than the sun which shines infertile,
Whose powers have no affect on itself,
But do on the fertile Earth; there its beams
First came and their strength was revealed, otherwise they'd be useless.
But all these bright lights are not servants
To Earth but to you, earth's inhabitant.
As for the great expanse of Heaven, let it tell you
Of the Maker's great magnificence, the one who built
So great, and stretched his work so far,
So that Man should know he does not live alone;
This space is too much for him to fill,
He is housed in a small part of it, and the rest
Is set aside for purposes which only God knows.
You should see the speed of those swift orbits,
Though you cannot calculate them, as a sign of his power,
Who can add to solid substances
Speed which is almost disembodied; you can see I'm not slow,
Who set out from God's home in Heaven
At dawn, and arrived in Eden before midday,
A distance which cannot be measured
With numbers which have a name.
But I'm telling you this,
Saying that the heavens move, to prove as wrong
The doubt which led you to question it;
I'm telling you it's wrong, even

To thee who hast thy dwelling here on Earth.
God to remove his wayes from human sense,
Plac'd Heav'n from Earth so farr, that earthly sight,
If it presume, might erre in things too high,

And no advantage gaine. What if the Sun

Be Centre to the World, and other Starrs

By his attractive vertue and their own
Incited, dance about him various rounds?
Thir wandring course now high, now low, then hid,
Progressive, retrograde, or standing still,
In six thou seest, and what if sev'nth to these
The Planet Earth, so stedfast though she seem,
Insensibly three different Motions move?

Which else to several Spheres thou must ascribe,
Mov'd contrarie with thwart obliquities,

Or save the Sun his labour, and that swift

Nocturnal and Diurnal rhomb suppos'd,

Invisible else above all Starrs, the Wheele

Of Day and Night; which needs not thy beleefe,
If Earth industrious of her self fetch Day

Travelling East, and with her part averse

From the Suns beam meet Night, her other part
Still luminous by his ray. What if that light

Sent from her through the wide

---

though
It may look that way to you who live on Earth.
To keep his plans beyond human comprehension
God placed Heaven so far from Earth that men,
If they presume to aim so high, will be mistaken

And gain no advantage. What if the sun

Is the centre of the universe, and other planets,
Driven by their own gravity and his,
Dance around him in various orbits?
In their wandering they are high, then low, then hidden,
Coming, going or standing still,
You see this in the six planets, so what if the seventh,
The Earth, though she seems so fixed,
Is imperceptibly moving in three different ways?

Otherwise you must give movement to several other planets,
Moving around each other in complex ways,

Or you can save the sun from moving, and suppose

That there is a swift nightly and daily orbit

Invisible up above the stars, the wheel

Of day and night. It doesn't matter what you believe,
If the earth is active and goes to fetch the day herself

From the east, and turns part of herself away

From the sun's beams to create night, with her other half
Still lit up with his rays. What if that light

Sent from her through wide

269

transpicuous aire,
To the terrestrial Moon be as a Starr

Enlightning her by Day, as she by Night
This Earth? reciprocal, if Land be there,

Fields and Inhabitants: Her spots thou seest
As Clouds, and Clouds may rain, and Rain produce
Fruits in her soft'nd Soile, for some to eate

Allotted there; and other Suns perhaps

With thir attendant Moons thou wilt descrie

Communicating Male and Femal Light,
Which two great Sexes animate the World,

Stor'd in each Orb perhaps with some that live.
For such vast room in Nature unpossest

By living Soule, desert and desolate,

Onely to shine, yet scarce to contribute
Each Orb a glimps of Light, conveyd so farr
Down to this habitable, which returnes

Light back to them, is obvious to dispute.

But whether thus these things, or whether not,
Whether the Sun predominant in Heav'n
Rise on the Earth, or Earth rise on the Sun,

Hee from the East his flaming rode begin,

Or Shee from West her silent course advance
With inoffensive pace that spinning sleeps

On her soft Axle, while she paces Eev'n,

And beares thee soft with the smooth Air

transparent air,
Is like that of a star to the moon, taking light

By day as she gives it to the Earth
At night? Then it would be possible, if there is land there,

For her to have fields and inhabitants: you see clouds
On her surface, and clouds can rain, and rain bring
Fruits from her softened soil, to make food

For those placed there; and maybe you will find

Other suns with their attendant moons,

Shining male and female light,
The two great forces which drive the universe,

Stored up in some planet where maybe others live.
For if there is so much space in Nature,

Unlived in by a living soul, deserted and desolate

Which only twinkles, just to give
Each planet a glimpse of light, carried so far
Down to this inhabited planet, which gives

Light back to them - if that's all they're for is a debatable matter.

But whether this is the case or it is not,
Whether the sun rules in Heaven
And rises on the Earth, or if the Earth rises on the sun,

Whether the sun journeys to you from the east,

Or the Earth travels to the west, moving along her silent course,
With imperceptible speed, spinning softly

Around her poles, while she travels gently

And carries you softly through the

along,
Sollicit not thy thoughts with matters hid,

Leave them to God above, him serve and feare;
Of other Creatures, as him pleases best,

Wherever plac't, let him dispose: joy thou
In what he gives to thee, this Paradise
And thy faire Eve; Heav'n is for thee too high
To know what passes there; be lowlie wise:

Think onely what concernes thee and thy being;
Dream not of other Worlds, what Creatures there
Live, in what state, condition or degree,

Contented that thus farr hath been reveal'd

Not of Earth onely but of highest Heav'n.

To whom thus Adam cleerd of doubt, repli'd.
How fully hast thou satisfi'd me, pure

Intelligence of Heav'n, Angel serene,
And freed from intricacies, taught to live

The easiest way, nor with perplexing thoughts
To interrupt the sweet of Life, from which

God hath bid dwell farr off all anxious cares,
And not molest us, unless we our selves
Seek them with wandring thoughts, and notions vain.
But apt the Mind or Fancy is to roave

Uncheckt, and of her roaving is no end;

Till warn'd, or by experience taught, she learne,

smooth air,
Don't trouble your thoughts with such hidden matters;

Leave them to God above, serve him and fear him;
Let him place other creatures wherever

It best pleases him; you enjoy
What he has given you, this Paradise
And your lovely Eve; Heaven is too high above
For you to know what happens there; be humble,

And think of only what concerns you and your existence;
Don't dream of other worlds and what creatures might
Live there, in what state, condition or order;

Be content with what has been shown to you,

Not only of Earth but of highest Heaven.

So Adam, freed from doubt, replied:

'How completely you have satisfied me, pure
Heavenly intelligence, serene Angel,
And freed me from confusion, taught me to live
In the easiest way and not to allow confusing thoughts
Disturb the sweetness of life. God has ordered
All anxious worries to stay away from us
And not interfere with us, unless we
Seek them with wandering thoughts and vain ideas.
But the mind or imagination has a tendency to wander
Uncontrolled, and her wandering is useless,
Until she is warned, or learns from experience,

271

That not to know at large of things remote

From use, obscure and suttle, but to know
That which before us lies in daily life,

Is the prime Wisdom, what is more, is fume,
Or emptiness, or fond impertinence,
And renders us in things that most concerne

Unpractis'd, unprepar'd, and still to seek.

Therefore from this high pitch let us descend
A lower flight, and speak of things at hand

Useful, whence haply mention may arise

Of somthing not unseasonable to ask

By sufferance, and thy wonted favour deign'd.
Thee I have heard relating what was don

Ere my remembrance: now hear mee relate
My Storie, which perhaps thou hast not heard;
And Day is yet not spent; till then thou seest
How suttly to detaine thee I devise,

Inviting thee to hear while I relate,
Fond, were it not in hope of thy reply:

For while I sit with thee, I seem in Heav'n,

And sweeter thy discourse is to my eare
Then Fruits of Palm-tree pleasantest to thirst
And hunger both, from labour, at the houre

Of sweet repast; they satiate, and soon fill,

Though pleasant, but thy words with Grace Divine
Imbu'd, bring to thir sweetness no satietie.

*To stop trying to learn of far off things of no use
To her, dark and hidden. To know
About the things we see in our daily life
Is the greatest wisdom, anything else is imaginary,
Empty, or irrelevant,
And makes us inexpert and unprepared in the things
Which most concern us, still uselessly asking questions.
So from this high mountain let us descend
To a lower place, and speak of the things around us,
And maybe some useful knowledge will come up
About things of which I am permitted to ask,
With your kind permission.
I have heard you tell of the things which were done
Before my time: now I'll tell you
My story, which you may not have heard;
The day is not over; until it is
You can see how I want to keep you here,
Inviting you to listen while I speak,
Which would be vain if I wasn't hoping for your reply:
For while I sit with you I seem to be in Heaven,
And your talk is sweeter to my ear
Than the coconuts are sweet for thirst
And hunger both after work, at the time
For meals; one soon has enough of them,
Though they are pleasant, but your words, filled
With divine grace, are as sweet but one can never have enough.'*

To whom thus Raphael answer'd heav'nly meek.
Nor are thy lips ungraceful, Sire of men,

Nor tongue ineloquent; for God on thee
Abundantly his gifts hath also pour'd

Inward and outward both, his image faire:
Speaking or mute all comliness and grace

Attends thee, and each word, each motion formes.
Nor less think wee in Heav'n of thee on Earth
Then of our fellow servant, and inquire
Gladly into the wayes of God with Man:

For God we see hath honour'd thee, and set

On Man his Equal Love: say therefore on;

For I that Day was absent, as befell,

Bound on a voyage uncouth and obscure,
Farr on excursion toward the Gates of Hell;

Squar'd in full Legion (such command we had)
To see that none thence issu'd forth a spie,

Or enemie, while God was in his work,
Least hee incenst at such eruption bold,

Destruction with Creation might have mixt.

Not that they durst without his leave attempt,
But us he sends upon his high behests
For state, as Sovran King, and to enure

Our prompt obedience. Fast we found, fast shut
The dismal Gates, and barricado'd strong;
But long ere our approaching heard within
Noise, other then the sound of Dance or

Raphael answered him with heavenly sweetness.
'Your lips are beautiful, father of men,
And your tongue is eloquent, for God
Has abundantly showered his gifts on you;
Outside and in you are his fair copy:
Speaking or silent all beauty and grace
Is with you, and inspires all your speech and movement.
We in Heaven think of you on Earth as nothing less
Than our fellow servant, and are glad To hear of the dealings between God and man:

For we see that God has honored you, and given
Man the same love we enjoy. So speak on,
For as it happened I was absent on that day,
Making a rough and dark journey, Travelling on a mission to the Gates of Hell;
We were in full battle order (as we had been commanded)
To see that no spies or enemies escaped
While God was at his work, In case the devils, furious at such great works,
Might have tried to mix destruction with creation.
They could not have done that without his permission,
But he sends us on his high errands To uphold his honor as the King of all, and to train us
To be obedient. We found the dismal Gates
Shut tight, and well reinforced; But from far off we heard within Noise, which was not that of dance or

273

Song,	*song;*
Torment, and loud lament, and furious rage.	*It was torture, and wailing, and furious anger.*
Glad we return'd up to the coasts of Light	*We were happy to return to Heaven*
Ere Sabbath Eev'ning: so we had in charge.	*Before the evening of the Sabbath: that was our duty then.*
But thy relation now; for I attend,	*But tell me your story now, I'm listening,*
Pleas'd with thy words no less then thou with mine.	*And I am just as pleased with your words as you are with mine."*
So spake the Godlike Power, and thus our Sire.	*So spoke the Godlike angel, and our ancestor replied.*
For Man to tell how human Life began	*"For Man to tell of how human life began*
Is hard; for who himself beginning knew?	*Is difficult; for who remembers his birth?*
Desire with thee still longer to converse	*I offered to tell from my desire to keep talking*
Induc'd me. As new wak't from soundest sleep	*To you. As if I had just woken from the deepest sleep*
Soft on the flourie herb I found me laid	*I found myself lying on the soft flowery grass,*
In Balmie Sweat, which with his Beames the Sun	*Covered in sweet sweat, which the sunbeams*
Soon dri'd, and on the reaking moisture fed.	*Soon dried, feeding on the perfumed moisture.*
Strait toward Heav'n my wondring Eyes I turnd,	*At once I turned my eyes to Heaven in wonder,*
And gaz'd a while the ample Skie, till rais'd	*And gazed for a while at the great sky, until prompted*
By quick instinctive motion up I sprung,	*By a quick instinctive motion I leapt up,*
As thitherward endevoring, and upright	*As if trying to reach the sky, and I stood upright*
Stood on my feet; about me round I saw	*On my feet; all round about me I saw*
Hill, Dale, and shadie Woods, and sunnie Plaines,	*Hills, valleys, shady woods and sunny plains,*
And liquid Lapse of murmuring Streams; by these,	*And the liquid smoothness of the murmuring streams; by these,*
Creatures that livd, and movd, and walk'd, or flew,	*Were creatures that lived, or moved, walked or flew,*
Birds on the branches warbling; all things smil'd,	*And birds warbled in the branches, all things smiled*
With fragrance and with joy my heart oreflow'd.	*And my heart was overflowing with perfumed and happiness.*
My self I then perus'd, and Limb by Limb	*I then looked over myself, limb by*

Survey'd, and sometimes went, and sometimes ran
With supple joints, as lively vigour led:

But who I was, or where, or from what cause,
Knew not; to speak I tri'd, and forthwith spake,
My Tongue obey'd and readily could name

What e're I saw. Thou Sun, said I, faire Light,
And thou enlight'nd Earth, so fresh and gay,

Ye Hills and Dales, ye Rivers, Woods, and Plaines,
And ye that live and move, fair Creatures, tell,
Tell, if ye saw, how came I thus, how here?

Not of my self; by some great Maker then,

In goodness and in power præeminent;
Tell me, how may I know him, how adore,

From whom I have that thus I move and live,
And feel that I am happier then I know.

While thus I call'd, and stray'd I knew not whither,
From where I first drew Aire, and first beheld
This happie Light, when answer none return'd,
On a green shadie Bank profuse of Flours
Pensive I sate me down; there gentle sleep

First found me, and with soft oppression seis'd
My droused sense, untroubl'd, though I thought
I then was passing to my former state
Insensible, and forthwith to dissolve:

---

limb,
And sometimes I walked, sometimes ran,
With supple joints, as the fancy took me:

But who or where I was, or why I existed,
I did not know; I tried to speak, and at once I spoke,
My tongue obeyed me and I could easily name

Whatever I saw. 'You, sun,' I said, 'You fair light,
And you shining Earth, so fresh and gay,

You hills and dales, you rivers, woods and plains,
And you that live and move, you fair creatures, tell me,
If you saw, how did I come here in this shape?

It wasn't my own doing; there must have been some great Maker,
The highest in goodness and power;
Tell me how I can know him and worship him,
The one who has given me the means to move and live,
And feel that I am happier than I know.'

While I called out this way I wandered I don't know where,
Away from the place I first drew breath, and first saw
This happy light; when nobody replied
I sat down to think on a shady green Flower covered bank; that was where gentle sleep

First found me, and with its soft heaviness seized
My drowsy senses, untroubled, though I thought
I was returning to my former state
Of unconsciousness and would then

When suddenly stood at my Head a dream,
Whose inward apparition gently mov'd

My Fancy to believe I yet had being,
And livd: One came, methought, of shape Divine,
And said, thy Mansion wants thee, Adam, rise,
First Man, of Men innumerable ordain'd

First Father, call'd by thee I come thy Guide

To the Garden of bliss, thy seat prepar'd.

So saying, by the hand he took me rais'd,

And over Fields and Waters, as in Aire

Smooth sliding without step, last led me up

A woodie Mountain; whose high top was plaine,

A Circuit wide, enclos'd, with goodliest Trees
Planted, with Walks, and Bowers, that what I saw
Of Earth before scarce pleasant seemd. Each Tree
Load'n with fairest Fruit, that hung to the Eye
Tempting, stirr'd in me sudden appetite

To pluck and eate; whereat I wak'd, and found
Before mine Eyes all real, as the dream

Had lively shadowd: Here had new begun

My wandring, had not hee who was my Guide
Up hither, from among the Trees appeer'd,

Presence Divine. Rejoycing, but with aw,

---

disappear:
When suddenly I started to dream,
And that apparition in my head gently convinced

My mind that I still existed,
Still lived: one of Divine shape came to me,
And said, 'Your dwelling is waiting for you, Adam, get up,
First man, of all countless men chosen

As the first father, called by you I come as your guide

To the garden of bliss, the place prepared for you.

Saying this, he took me by the hand and lifted me,

And took me over the fields and waters as if we flew,

Sliding smoothly without touching the ground, and at last led me up

A woody mountain; its high top was flat,

A round circle, walled in, planted with wonderful trees,
With paths and shelters, that made what I'd seen before
On Earth seem hardly pleasant. Each tree
Was loaded with the sweetest fruit, hanging
Tempting to the eye, which gave me a sudden appetite

To pick and eat; at that point I woke up, and found
That everything was in from of me, real, just as the dream

Had foretold: I would have started exploring again,

If the one who was my guide

Had not appeared from among the trees up here,

A divine presence. Rejoicing but awestruck

In adoration at his feet I fell
Submiss: he rear'd me, and Whom thou
soughtst I am,
Said mildely, Author of all this thou seest

Above, or round about thee or beneath.
This Paradise I give thee, count it thine
To Till and keep, and of the Fruit to eate:

Of every Tree that in the Garden growes

Eate freely with glad heart; fear here no
dearth:
But of the Tree whose operation brings
Knowledg of good and ill, which I have set
The Pledge of thy Obedience and thy Faith,

Amid the Garden by the Tree of Life,

Remember what I warne thee, shun to taste,

And shun the bitter consequence: for know,

The day thou eat'st thereof, my sole
command
Transgrest, inevitably thou shalt dye;
From that day mortal, and this happie State

Shalt loose, expell'd from hence into a
World
Of woe and sorrow. Sternly he pronounc'd

The rigid interdiction, which resounds
Yet dreadful in mine eare, though in my
choice
Not to incur; but soon his cleer aspect
Return'd and gracious purpose thus renew'd.
Not onely these fair bounds, but all the
Earth
To thee and to thy Race I give; as Lords
Possess it, and all things that therein live,

Or live in Sea, or Aire, Beast, Fish, and
Fowle.
In signe whereof each Bird and Beast
behold

I fell worshipping at his feet,
Submissive; he lifted me up and said
sweetly, 'I am the one
You were looking for, the one who
made all you can see,
Above, around or beneath you.
I give you this Paradise, it's yours
To keep and to work, and to eat the
fruit;
Of every tree that grows in the
garden
Eat freely and be happy; don't worry
about it running out.
But of the tree which brings
Knowledge of good and evil, which
As the pledge of your obedience and
faith
I have put in the middle of the garden
next to the tree of life,
Remember what I warn you, do not
taste it,
Do not chance the bitter
consequences: for be aware
That the day you eat from it, breaking
my only
Command, you will inevitably die;
From that day on you will be mortal,
you will lose
This happy existence, you will be
thrown from here
Into a world of sadness and
sorrow.'He sternly pronounced
This strict rule, which still rings
Dreadfully in my ear, though I do not
wish it to.
But soon his beauty returned
And he resumed his gracious speech.
'I don't only give you this fair place,
but all the Earth
To you and your kind.As lords
Rule over it, and all the things that
live on it,
Or that live in the sea or the air,
beasts, fish and birds.
To confirm your mastery, look at
each type

After thir kindes; I bring them to receave	*Of bird and beast; I bring them to you*
From thee thir Names, and pay thee fealtie	*To give them names, and so they can pay you respects*
With low subjection; understand the same	*With low obedience; the same applies to the fish*
Of Fish within thir watry residence,	*In their watery home;*
Not hither summon'd, since they cannot change	*They have not been called here, since they cannot change*
Thir Element to draw the thinner Aire.	*Their nature to breathe the thin air.'*
As thus he spake, each Bird and Beast behold	*As he spoke I saw each bird and beast*
Approaching two and two, These cowring low	*Approaching two by two, bowing low*
With blandishment, each Bird stoop'd on his wing.	*In adulation, each bird bending its wing.*
I nam'd them, as they pass'd, and understood	*I named them as they passed and understood*
Thir Nature, with such knowledg God endu'd	*Their nature; God suddenly placed*
My sudden apprehension: but in these	*This knowledge in my mind. But in all these*
I found not what me thought I wanted still;	*I could not find that which I thought I lacked,*
And to the Heav'nly vision thus presum'd.	*And presumed to speak to the heavenly vision.*
O by what Name, for thou above all these,	*'By what name do you go, for you are above all these,*
Above mankinde, or aught then mankinde higher,	*Above mankind, or anything else that is higher than mankind,*
Surpassest farr my naming, how may I	*It is far beyond me to name you, how can I*
Adore thee, Author of this Universe,	*Worship you, Creator of this Universe*
And all this good to man, for whose well being	*And all this goodness for man, for whose wellbeing*
So amply, and with hands so liberal	*You have so amply and generously*
Thou hast provided all things: but with mee	*Provided; but I do not see*
I see not who partakes. In solitude	*One to share this with. In solitude*
What happiness, who can enjoy alone,	*What happiness is there, who can find enjoyment alone,*
Or all enjoying, what contentment find?	*Or even if he finds enjoyment, what contentment?'*
Thus I presumptuous; and the vision bright,	*So I presumptuously asked, and the bright vision,*
As with a smile more bright'nd, thus repli'd.	*With his smile widening, answered.*

What call'st thou solitude, is not the Earth

With various living creatures, and the Aire

Replenisht, and all these at thy command
To come and play before thee; know'st thou not
Thir language and thir wayes? They also know,
And reason not contemptibly; with these

Find pastime, and beare rule; thy Realm is large.
So spake the Universal Lord, and seem'd

So ordering. I with leave of speech implor'd,
And humble deprecation thus repli'd.
Let not my words offend thee, Heav'nly Power,
My Maker, be propitious while I speak.

Hast thou not made me here thy substitute,

And these inferiour farr beneath me set?
Among unequals what societie
Can sort, what harmonie or true delight?

Which must be mutual, in proportion due

Giv'n and receiv'd; but in disparitie

The one intense, the other still remiss
Cannot well suite with either, but soon prove
Tedious alike: Of fellowship I speak

Such as I seek, fit to participate

All rational delight, wherein the brute

Cannot be human consort; they rejoice

Each with thir kinde, Lion with Lioness;

So fitly them in pairs thou hast combin'd;

'What are you calling solitude, is the Earth

And the air not full of living creatures,

And can you not command them
To come and entertain you? Do you not know
Their language and their habits? They also have knowledge,
And they can think to an extent; pass your time

With these, and rule them; your kingdom is large.'
So the great Lord spoke, and it seemed

To be an order. I begged permission to speak,
And humbly replied.
'Do not be offended by my words, Heavenly power,
My maker, and hear favorably what I want to say.

Have you not put me here as a substitute for you,

And put these far below me?
What sort of company can be enjoyed
Between those not equal, what harmony or true happiness?

Company must be mutual, with equal amounts

Being given or received; if there is inequality

One with more, one with less,
They cannot mix well together, but each will soon
Find the other tedious. The company I'm speaking of,

The type I'm looking for, would be fit to share

All conversation, and in that the animal

Cannot join with humans; they rejoice

In being with their own kind, lion with lioness,

You have placed them so well in their

Much less can Bird with Beast, or Fish with Fowle
So well converse, nor with the Ox the Ape;
Wors then can Man with Beast, and least of all.
Whereto th' Almighty answer'd, not displeas'd.
A nice and suttle happiness I see
Thou to thyself proposest, in the choice
Of thy Associates, Adam, and wilt taste

No pleasure, though in pleasure, solitarie.

What think'st thou then of mee, and this my State,
Seem I to thee sufficiently possest
Of happiness, or not? who am alone
From all Eternitie, for none I know
Second to mee or like, equal much less.

Who have I then with whom to hold converse
Save with the Creatures which I made, and those
To me inferiour, infinite descents
Beneath what other Creatures are to thee?
He ceas'd, I lowly answer'd. To attaine

The highth and depth of thy Eternal ways

All human thoughts come short, Supream of things;
Thou in thy self art perfet, and in thee

Is no deficience found; not so is Man,

But in degree, the cause of his desire
By conversation with his like to help,

Or solace his defects. No need that thou

Shouldst propagat, already infinite;

And through all numbers absolute,

---

pairs;
A bird cannot talk to the animals, or fish to the birds,
The ox cannot converse with the ape;
Just like them, and even worse, a man cannot speak with the beasts. '
To him the Almighty replied, not displeased:
"A nice and gentle happiness I see
You are claiming for yourself, Adam,
In your choice of companion, and I see
You will get no happiness from solitary pleasures.
What do you think of me then, and my condition?
Do you think that I have enough
Happiness, or not? I am alone
For all eternity, for I know none
Close to or even similar to me, let alone equal.
So who can I talk to

Except the creatures I have made,

Who are infinitely more below me
Than the beasts are below you.
He finished, and I humbly replied.
'To understand
The heights and depths of your eternal ways

Is not possible for humans, highest of all;
You are perfect in yourself, and there is

Nothing missing in you; it is not so for man,

Being lower, he wants
To talk to his own kind, who can help him

Or comfort him in his shortcomings. There is no need
For you to breed, as you are already infinite,
And you are present in every number,

though One;
But Man by number is to manifest

His single imperfection, and beget
Like of his like, his Image multipli'd,
In unitie defective, which requires
Collateral love, and deerest amitie.

Thou in thy secresie although alone,
Best with thy self accompanied, seek'st not

Social communication, yet so pleas'd,

Canst raise thy Creature to what highth thou wilt
Of Union or Communion, deifi'd;

I by conversing cannot these erect

From prone, nor in thir wayes complacence find.
Thus I embold'nd spake, and freedom us'd
Permissive, and acceptance found, which gain'd
This answer from the gratious voice Divine.
Thus farr to try thee, Adam, I was pleas'd,

And finde thee knowing not of Beasts alone,
Which thou hast rightly nam'd, but of thy self,
Expressing well the spirit within thee free,

My Image, not imparted to the Brute,

Whose fellowship therefore unmeet for thee

Good reason was thou freely shouldst dislike,
And be so minded still; I, ere thou spak'st,
Knew it not good for Man to be alone,

And no such companie as then thou saw'st

Intended thee, for trial onely brought,

even though one;
But Man wants to soften his solitary state
With numbers, and create
Those like him, spreading his image
Uniting in imperfection, which needs
Reciprocated love and dearest friendship.
You are alone in your perfection,
And you are best accompanied by yourself.
You don't want social intercourse, but if you did
You can raise your creature up to whatever height you want
Of union or understanding, making them a God;
By talking to these I cannot lift them up
From the ground, nor can I find happiness in their ways.'
So I boldly spoke, using the freedom I had been granted, and my points were accepted
In this answer from the gracious divine voice.
'I was pleased to test you this far, Adam,
And find you don't only know of the beasts,
Which you have properly named, but of yourself,
Giving voice to the spirit within you well.
You are my image, which was not given to the brutes,
And so their company is not fit for you.
There was good reason for you to dislike the idea,
And to still do so. Before you spoke I had already decided it was not good for Man to be alone,
And no such company as what you saw
Was meant for you, they were only

To see how thou could'st judge of fit and meet:
What next I bring shall please thee, be assur'd,
Thy likeness, thy fit help, thy other self,

Thy wish, exactly to thy hearts desire.
Hee ended, or I heard no more, for now

My earthly by his Heav'nly overpowerd,

Which it had long stood under, streind to the highth
In that celestial Colloquie sublime,
As with an object that excels the sense,

Dazl'd and spent, sunk down, and sought repair
Of sleep, which instantly fell on me, call'd

By Nature as in aide, and clos'd mine eyes.

Mine eyes he clos'd, but op'n left the Cell

Of Fancie my internal sight, by which
Abstract as in a transe methought I saw,
Though sleeping, where I lay, and saw the shape
Still glorious before whom awake I stood;

Who stooping op'nd my left side, and took

From thence a Rib, with cordial spirits warme,

And Life-blood streaming fresh; wide was the wound,
But suddenly with flesh fill'd up and heal'd:
The Rib he formd and fashond with his hands;
Under his forming hands a Creature grew,
Manlike, but different sex, so lovly faire,

That what seemd fair in all the World, seemd now

---

brought to you as a test,
To see how well you could judge what was fitting and proper:
What I shall bring you next will please you, you can be sure,
Your likeness, your helper, your other self,
Your wish, exactly what you want."
Here he stopped, or I heard no more, for now

My earthly form was overpowered by his heavenly one,

Which it had been standing under for a long time, strained to its limits
By that heavenly conversation,
As when faced with an object that is beyond comprehension.

Dazzled and exhausted I sank down and looked for the repair
Of sleep, which came to me instantly, called

By nature to help me, and closed my eyes.

It closed my eyes, but left open the eye

Of imagination, through which
I saw, as if in a trance,
Although I was asleep, where I lay,
and I saw the glorious
Shape before whom I had stood when awake;

Bending down he opened my left side, and took out

A rib, warm with the heat of my body

And streaming with my fresh blood; the wound was wide,
But suddenly it closed up and healed.
He shaped the rib with his hands,

And in his hands a creature grew,
Manlike, but of a different sex, so fair and lovely,
That what had seemed fair in the world before now seemed

Mean, or in her summ'd up, in her containd	Mean, or it was all gathered and contained within her
And in her looks, which from that time infus'd	And her looks, which from that time placed
Sweetness into my heart, unfelt before,	A sweetness in my heart which I had not felt before,
And into all things from her Aire inspir'd	And put it into all things around her,
The spirit of love and amorous delight.	The spirit of love and the joys of passion.
Shee disappeerd, and left me dark, I wak'd	She disappeared, and left me in the dark. I woke
To find her, or for ever to deplore	To look for her, or to forever mourn
Her loss, and other pleasures all abjure:	Her loss, and refuse all other pleasures.
When out of hope, behold her, not farr off,	When I had given up hope I saw her, not far off,
Such as I saw her in my dream, adornd	Just as I saw her in my dream, dressed
With what all Earth or Heaven could bestow	With all that Heaven and Earth could give
To make her amiable: On she came,	To make her sweet. On she came,
Led by her Heav'nly Maker, though unseen,	Led by her Heavenly maker, though he was invisible,
And guided by his voice, nor uninformd	And guided by his voice, and knowing
Of nuptial Sanctitie and marriage Rites:	Of the sanctity of marriage and its customs.
Grace was in all her steps, Heav'n in her Eye,	There was grace in all her steps, Heaven in her gaze,
In every gesture dignitie and love.	And every gesture was full of dignity and love.
I overjoyd could not forbear aloud	Overjoyed I could not stop myself crying aloud:
This turn hath made amends; thou hast fulfill'd	'This favor keeps your promise; you have kept
Thy words, Creator bounteous and benigne,	Your word, bounteous and kind creator,
Giver of all things faire, but fairest this	The giver of all sweet things, but this is the sweetest
Of all thy gifts, nor enviest. I now see	Of all your gifts, which you give freely. I now see
Bone of my Bone, Flesh of my Flesh, my Self	Bone made from my bone, flesh from my flesh, my self
Before me; Woman is her Name, of Man	In front of me; woman is her name, made
Extracted; for this cause he shall forgoe	From man; this is the reason he will leave

Father and Mother, and to his Wife adhere;	*His father and mother and stay with his wife,*
And they shall be one Flesh, one Heart, one Soule.	*And they shall be united in body, heart and soul.'*
She heard me thus, and though divinely brought,	*She heard me saying this, and though brought by God,*
Yet Innocence and Virgin Modestie,	*Still innocent and virginal,*
Her vertue and the conscience of her worth,	*Virtuous and knowing her worth,*
That would be woo'd, and not unsought be won,	*Knowing that she would be wooed, and be won.*
Not obvious, not obtrusive, but retir'd,	*She was not bold or forward, but retiring,*
The more desirable, or to say all,	*Which made her more desirable. To say everything,*
Nature her self, though pure of sinful thought,	*Nature, though clear of sinful thoughts,*
Wrought in her so, that seeing me, she turn'd;	*Had made her modest in herself, so that, seeing me, she turned away.*
I follow'd her, she what was Honour knew,	*I followed her, and she knew what was fitting,*
And with obsequious Majestie approv'd My pleaded reason. To the Nuptial Bowre	*And with submissive grace gave in To my pleading. I led her to*
I led her blushing like the Morn: all Heav'n,	*The wedding house, blushing like the dawn; all heaven*
And happie Constellations on that houre	*And the happy stars rained their happiness*
Shed thir selectest influence; the Earth	*Down on that moment; the Earth*
Gave sign of gratulation, and each Hill;	*Gave signs of its congratulations, so did the hills;*
Joyous the Birds; fresh Gales and gentle Aires	*The birds were joyous; fresh winds and gentle breezes*
Whisper'd it to the Woods, and from thir wings	*Whispered in the woods, and on their wings*
Flung Rose, flung Odours from the spicie Shrub,	*Carried scents of roses and spicy shrubs,*
Disporting, till the amorous Bird of Night	*Mixed, until the nightingale*
Sung Spousal, and bid haste the Eevning Starr	*Sang the wedding song, and called the evening star to hurry*
On his Hill top, to light the bridal Lamp.	*Up into the sky to light the bridal lamp.*
Thus I have told thee all my State, and brought	*So I have told you of my life, and used*
My Storie to the sum of earthly bliss	*My story to sum up the earthly bliss*
Which I enjoy, and must confess to find	*Which I enjoy, and I must admit that I find*
In all things else delight indeed, but such	*Pleasure in all other things, but*

	these,
As us'd or not, works in the mind no change,	Whether I use them or not, make no change in the mind,
Nor vehement desire, these delicacies	Do not bring on desire, these sweet things
I mean of Taste, Sight, Smell, Herbs, Fruits and Flours,	I mean of taste, sight, smell, herbs, fruits and flowers,
Walks, and the melodie of Birds; but here	Paths and birdsong; but this
Farr otherwise, transported I behold,	Was something quite different, transported I saw,
Transported touch; here passion first I felt,	Transported I touched; here I first felt passion,
Commotion strange, in all enjoyments else	A strange upheaval; in all other pleasures
Superiour and unmov'd, here onely weake	I was not disturbed, here only I was weak
Against the charm of Beauties powerful glance.	In the face of beauty.
Or Nature faild in mee, and left some part	Either nature had failed in me, and left some part unable
Not proof enough such Object to sustain,	To resist these feelings,
Or from my side subducting, took perhaps	Or taking part of me from my side, perhaps
More then enough; at least on her bestow'd	Took too much; at least she was given
Too much of Ornament, in outward shew	Too much decoration, outwardly
Elaborate, of inward less exact.	Incredible, but less so inside.
For well I understand in the prime end	I fully understand Nature's plan,
Of Nature her th' inferiour, in the mind	That she should be inferior in her mind
And inward Faculties, which most excell,	And thought, the greatest powers,
In outward also her resembling less	And externally she looked less
His Image who made both, and less expressing	Like the one who made us both, less expressive
The character of that Dominion giv'n	Of the mastery we had been given
O're other Creatures; yet when I approach	Over all other creatures; but when I come near
Her loveliness, so absolute she seems	Her loveliness, she seems so perfect
And in her self compleat, so well to know	And self-contained, to know
Her own, that what she wills to do or say,	Her self so well, that what she does or says
Seems wisest, vertuousest, discreetest, best;	Seems the wisest, most virtuous, most sensible, best;
All higher knowledge in her presence falls	In her presence all intelligence is worthless,
Degraded, Wisdom in discourse with her	Talking with her wisdom
Looses discount'nanc't, and like folly	Has no value and looks like stupidity;

shewes;	
Authority and Reason on her waite,	*She is full of authority and reason*
As one intended first, not after made	*As if she was the first one created, not made after*
Occasionally; and to consummate all,	*To fulfil a need; and to make everything prefect*
Greatness of mind and nobleness thir seat	*Greatness of mind and nobility*
Build in her loveliest, and create an awe	*Are loveliest in her, and make an aura*
About her, as a guard Angelic plac't.	*Round her like a guard of angels.'*
To whom the Angel with contracted brow.	*The angel replied with a frown,*
Accuse not Nature, she hath don her part;	*'Nature has done her part in this,*
Do thou but thine, and be not diffident	*Now you must do yours, and don't lose sight*
Of Wisdom, she deserts thee not, if thou	*Of wisdom; it won't desert you*
Dismiss not her, when most thou needst her nigh,	*Unless you send it away when you need it most,*
By attributing overmuch to things	*By giving too much praise to less perfect things,*
Less excellent, as thou thy self perceav'st.	*And you can see that they are.*
For what admir'st thou, what transports thee so,	*For what do you admire so much, what moves you?*
An outside? fair no doubt, and worthy well	*An outside? It is beautiful, no doubt, and deserves*
Thy cherishing, thy honouring, and thy love,	*To be cherished, honored and loved,*
Not thy subjection: weigh with her thy self;	*But not bowed down to: measure her against yourself*
Then value: Oft times nothing profits more	*And then assess her value; often nothing is more useful*
Then self esteem, grounded on just and right	*Than self esteem, if it's based on truth and sense*
Well manag'd; of that skill the more thou know'st,	*And is well managed; the more you practice it*
The more she will acknowledge thee her Head,	*The more she will acknowledge you as her master*
And to realities yield all her shows:	*And recognize that you are the truly perfect one:*
Made so adorn for thy delight the more,	*She is made so beautiful for your pleasure,*
So awful, that with honour thou maist love	*So it would be terrible if you let your mate*
Thy mate, who sees when thou art seen least wise.	*See you made stupid by her looks.*
But if the sense of touch whereby mankind	*But if the sensual pleasures by which*
Is propagated seem such dear delight	*Mankind breeds seems such a perfect*

	delight,
Beyond all other, think the same voutsaf't	Better than any other, remember that
To Cattel and each Beast; which would not be	The cattle and all the beasts have the same, which would not
To them made common and divulg'd, if aught	Be shared with them, if there was anything about it
Therein enjoy'd were worthy to subdue	Which was important enough to rule
The Soule of Man, or passion in him move.	The soul of man or make him passionate.
What higher in her societie thou findst	The higher things you enjoy about her company,
Attractive, human, rational, love still;	Carry on loving in a human and rational way;
In loving thou dost well, in passion not,	Love is a good thing, passion is not,
Wherein true Love consists not; love refines	And true love does not come from passion; love refines
The thoughts, and heart enlarges, hath his seat	The thoughts, enlarges the heart, has his home
In Reason, and is judicious, is the scale	In reason, is wise and makes the steps
By which to heav'nly Love thou maist ascend,	By which you can attain heavenly love.
Not sunk in carnal pleasure, for which cause	It is not buried in sexual pleasure, which is the reason
Among the Beasts no Mate for thee was found.	You were not given a partner from amongst the animals.'
To whom thus half abash't Adam repli'd.	Rather embarrassed, Adam answered him.
Neither her out-side formd so fair, nor aught	'Neither her outer beauty, nor anything
In procreation common to all kindes	In the sex which all animals perform
(Though higher of the genial Bed by far,	(Though it is a far higher thing when part of the marriage bed,
And with mysterious reverence I deem)	And I think has a mysterious holiness there)
So much delights me as those graceful acts,	Pleases me as much as those graceful acts,
Those thousand decencies that daily flow	The thousand beauties that come daily
From all her words and actions mixt with Love	From all her words and actions, mixed with love
And sweet compliance, which declare unfeign'd	And her sweet obedience, which show true
Union of Mind, or in us both one Soule;	Union of mind, both of us as one soul;
Harmonie to behold in wedded pair	Harmony between a married couple

More grateful then harmonious sound to the eare.	*Is even better than hearing harmonious music.*
Yet these subject not; I to thee disclose	*But this is irrelevant; I'm telling you*
What inward thence I feel, not therefore foild,	*What I feel inside, it doesn't mean*
Who meet with various objects, from the sense	*That when I meet with various things, although I get*
Variously representing; yet still free	*Different feelings from the senses, I am not free*
Approve the best, and follow what I approve.	*To judge what is best and act accordingly.*
To Love thou blam'st me not, for love thou saist	*You do not admonish me for loving, for you say*
Leads up to Heav'n, is both the way and guide;	*Love leads the way up to Heaven, is the path and the guide;*
Bear with me then, if lawful what I ask;	*Don't mind me asking then, if I am allowed to;*
Love not the heav'nly Spirits, and how thir Love	*Do the heavenly spirits love, and if they do then how*
Express they, by looks onely, or do they mix	*Do they express it, just by looks or do they mix*
Irradiance, virtual or immediate touch?	*Their light together, though without physical touch?'*
To whom the Angel with a smile that glow'd	*The angel replied with a smile that glowed*
Celestial rosie red, Loves proper hue,	*A heavenly rosy red, the true color of love;*
Answer'd. Let it suffice thee that thou know'st	*'Let it be enough for you to know*
Us happie, and without Love no happiness.	*That we are happy, and there can be no happiness without love.*
Whatever pure thou in the body enjoy'st	*Whatever pure enjoyment you get from your body*
(And pure thou wert created) we enjoy	*(And you were created pure), we enjoy*
In eminence, and obstacle find none	*To the highest degree, and are not encumbered*
Of membrane, joynt, or limb, exclusive barrs:	*With skin, joints, limbs and other obstacles;*
Easier then Air with Air, if Spirits embrace,	*When Spirits embrace it is easier than air mixing with air,*
Total they mix, Union of Pure with Pure	*They come together totally, wanting a union of pure with pure:*
Desiring; nor restrain'd conveyance need	*They don't need some clumsy acts as is needed*
As Flesh to mix with Flesh, or Soul with	*To mix flesh and flesh, soul and soul.*

Soul.

But I can now no more; the parting Sun	*But now I can say no more; the setting sun*
Beyond the Earths green Cape and verdant Isles	*Goes down the Cape Verde islands in the west,*
Hesperean sets, my Signal to depart.	*And that is my signal to depart.*
Be strong, live happie, and love, but first of all	*Be strong, live happily, love but love most of all*
Him whom to love is to obey, and keep	*Him who is loved by obeying, and obey*
His great command; take heed lest Passion sway	*His great command; take care in case passion persuades*
Thy Judgment to do aught, which else free Will	*Your judgment to do anything which you would not*
Would not admit; thine and of all thy Sons	*Do otherwise, and cause sorrow*
The weal or woe in thee is plac't; beware.	*To come to you and all your sons afterwards; be careful.*
I in thy persevering shall rejoyce,	*I, and all the angels, shall take pleasure in your*
And all the Blest: stand fast; to stand or fall	*Remaining obedient; to stand or fall*
Free in thine own Arbitrement it lies.	*Is left up to you.*
Perfet within, no outward aid require;	*You are perfect inside and need no outside help;*
And all temptation to transgress repel.	*Resist all temptation to disobey.'*
So saying, he arose; whom Adam thus	*Saying this he got up, and Adam spoke to him*
Follow'd with benediction. Since to part,	*In farewell. 'Since you must leave,*
Go heavenly Guest, Ethereal Messenger,	*Go heavenly guest, spiritual messenger,*
Sent from whose sovran goodness I adore.	*Sent from the one whose ruling goodness I worship.*
Gentle to me and affable hath been	*You have been polite and kind in agreeing*
Thy condescension, and shall be honour'd ever	*To talk to me, and I shall always remember it*
With grateful Memorie: thou to mankind	*With thanks; stay good and friendly*
Be good and friendly still, and oft return.	*To mankind, and come back often."*
So parted they, the Angel up to Heav'n	*So they parted, the angel went up to heaven*
From the thick shade, and Adam to his Bowre.	*From the thick shade, and Adam went to his bower.*

BOOK IX

THE ARGUMENT

Satan having compast the Earth, with meditated guile returns as a mist by Night into Paradise, enters into the Serpent sleeping. Adam and Eve in the Morning go forth to thir labours, which Eve proposes to divide in several places, each labouring apart: Adam consents not, alledging the danger, lest that Enemy, of whom they were forewarn'd, should attempt her found alone: Eve loath to be thought not circumspect or firm enough, urges her going apart, the rather desirous to make tryal of her strength; Adam at last yields: The Serpent finds her alone; his subtle approach, first gazing, then speaking, with much flattery extolling Eve above all other Creatures. Eve wondring to hear the Serpent speak, asks how he attain'd to human speech and such understanding not till now; the Serpent answers, that by tasting of a certain Tree in the Garden he attain'd both to Speech and Reason, till then void of both: Eve requires him to bring her to that Tree, and finds it to be the Tree of Knowledge forbidden: The Serpent now grown bolder, with many wiles and arguments induces her at length to eat; she pleas'd with the taste deliberates a while whether to impart thereof to Adam or not, at last brings him of the Fruit, relates what perswaded her to eat thereof: Adam at first amaz'd, but perceiving her lost, resolves through vehemence of love to perish with her; and extenuating the trespass, eats also of the Fruit: The Effects thereof in them both; they seek to cover thir nakedness; then fall to variance and accusation of one another.

Having circled the Earth, Satan returns with malice to Paradise, disguised in a night mist. He enters into the body of the serpent as it sleeps.Adam and Eve go to their work, and Eve proposes that they should work apart from each other. Adam objects, saying that the enemy they have been warned of might make an attempt on her if he finds her alone. Eve is offended that he thinks she is too weak to resist and insists she wants to go alone, wanting to prove her strength if necessary. Adam consents and the serpent finds her alone.He makes a cunning approach, looking then speaking, praising Eve above all other creatures. Eve is amazed to hear him speak and asks how he has acquired the power and human understanding. He answers answers that he gained speech and reason from eating from a tree in the tree, and finds it is the forbidden Tree of Knowledge.The serpent has now grown bolder and with many now grown bolder and with many ricks and arguments persuades her to eat.Pleased with the taste she debates whether to take the fruit to Adam or not.Eventually she brings him the fruit and tells him why she ate it. Adam is astonished, but seeing that she is lost decides, due to his love, that he will suffer the same fate as her and share her punishment; he eats the fruit.We see the effect this has; they both seek to cover their nakedness and start to argue, each blaming the other.

NO more of talk where God or Angel Guest

With Man, as with his Friend, familiar us'd

We will talk no more of when God or angelic guests

Would sit with Man as his friend,

	familiar
To sit indulgent, and with him partake	*And indulgent, and with him eat*
Rural repast, permitting him the while change	*A simple meal, allowing at the same time*
Venial discourse unblam'd: I now must	*Discourse which might be erroneous but was blameless; now I must change*
Those Notes to Tragic; foul distrust, and breach	*The tone to tragedy; horrible betrayal and*
Disloyal on the part of Man, revolt,	*Breach of trust on the part of Man, revolt*
And disobedience: On the part of Heav'n	*And disobedience; on Heaven's side,*
Now alienated, distance and distaste,	*Now estranged, distance and distaste,*
Anger and just rebuke, and judgement giv'n,	*Anger and justified rebuke, punishment*
That brought into this World a world of woe,	*That brought great sorrow into the world,*
Sinne and her shadow Death, and Miserie	*Sin and her shadow, Death, and misery,*
Deaths Harbinger: Sad task, yet argument	*Death's forerunner:this is a sad task, but it's a subject*
Not less but more Heroic then the wrauth	*Not less but more Heroic than when stern Achilles*
Of stern Achilles on his Foe pursu'd	*Unleashed his anger on his foe, chasing him three times*
Thrice Fugitive about Troy Wall; or rage	*Around the walls of Troy; or the rage*
Of Turnus for Lavinia disespous'd,	*Of Turnus when Lavinia was taken away from him,*
Or Neptun's ire or Juno's, that so long	*Or Neptune's anger or Juno's, that for so long*
Perplex'd the Greek and Cytherea's Son;	*Baffled Odysseus and Aeneas;*
If answerable style I can obtaine	*If I can write in a suitable style to suit*
Of my Celestial Patroness, who deignes	*My heavenly inspiration, who comes down*
Her nightly visitation unimplor'd,	*Nightly to make her visit, uncalled,*
And dictates to me slumb'ring, or inspires	*And dictates to me in my sleep, or gives me*
Easie my unpremeditated Verse:	*Inspiration for my spontaneous verse:*
Since first this Subject for Heroic Song	*Since I first thought of this subject for a Heroic poem,*
Pleas'd me long choosing, and beginning late;	*Chosen a long time ago but only started now;*
Not sedulous by Nature to indite	*I am not inclined by Nature to write*
Warrs, hitherto the onely Argument	*Of war, which until now was thought the only fit subject*
Heroic deem'd, chief maistrie to dissect	*For Heroic poetry, the greatest skill to analyse*

With long and tedious havoc fabl'd Knights	*With long and tedious noise the doings of mythic knights*
In Battels feign'd; the better fortitude	*And their fictional battles; the greater virtues*
Of Patience and Heroic Martyrdom	*Of patience and heroic matyrdom*
Unsung; or to describe Races and Games,	*Are left undescribed; or they write of races and games,*
Or tilting Furniture, emblazon'd Shields,	*Jousting equipment, painted shields*
Impreses quaint, Caparisons and Steeds;	*With heraldic symbols, and richly clad horses*
Bases and tinsel Trappings, gorgious Knights	*With shining decorations, gorgeous knights*
At Joust and Torneament; then marshal'd Feast	*At jousting and tournaments; then the great feast*
Serv'd up in Hall with Sewers, and Seneshals;	*Served up in a hall with servants and stewards;*
The skill of Artifice or Office mean,	*The low skills of Art or politics,*
Not that which justly gives Heroic name	*Are not the right things to give the name "heroic"*
To Person or to Poem. Mee of these	*To a person or a poem. I am not*
Nor skilld nor studious, higher Argument	*Skilled or learned in these matters, but higher matters*
Remaines, sufficient of it self to raise	*Are left for me, enough in themselves*
That name, unless an age too late, or cold	*To be called heroic, unless this is the wrong time,*
Climat, or Years damp my intended wing	*Or the cold climate or my growing age dampens my efforts,*
Deprest, and much they may, if all be mine,	*Which might well happen, if it was all down to me,*
Not Hers who brings it nightly to my Ear.	*With no help from her who brings it to my ear every night.*
The Sun was sunk, and after him the Starr	*The sun had set, and after him came*
Of Hesperus, whose Office is to bring	*The evening stars, whose task is to bring*
Twilight upon the Earth, short Arbiter	*Twilight to the Earth, the brief mediator*
Twixt Day and Night, and now from end to end	*Between day and night, and now from end to end*
Nights Hemisphere had veild the Horizon round:	*The hemisphere of night had wrapped round the horizon.*
When Satan who late fled before the threats	*That was when Satan, who had recently fled from Eden,*
Of Gabriel out of Eden, now improv'd	*Running from the threats of Gabriel, now increased*
In meditated fraud and malice, bent	*In his planned deceit and his hatred,*

On mans destruction, maugre what might hap
Of heavier on himself, fearless return'd.

By Night he fled, and at Midnight return'd.

From compassing the Earth, cautious of day,
Since Uriel Regent of the Sun descri'd
His entrance, and forewarnd the Cherubim

That kept thir watch; thence full of anguish driv'n,
The space of seven continu'd Nights he rode

With darkness, thrice the Equinoctial Line
He circl'd, four times cross'd the Carr of Night
From Pole to Pole, traversing each Colure;

On the eighth return'd, and on the Coast averse
From entrance or Cherubic Watch, by stealth
Found unsuspected way. There was a place,
Now not, though Sin, not Time, first wraught the change,
Where Tigris at the foot of Paradise

Into a Gulf shot under ground, till part

Rose up a Fountain by the Tree of Life;

In with the River sunk, and with it rose

Satan involv'd in rising Mist, then sought
Where to lie hid; Sea he had searcht and Land
From Eden over Pontus, and the Poole

Mæotis, up beyond the River Ob;
Downward as farr Antartic; and in length

West from Orontes to the Ocean barr'd

---

determined
To destroy man, disregarding the danger
Of the heavier punishment he risked, returned fearless.
He had fled at nightfall and returned at midnight.
He had been circling the Earth, hiding from the daylight
Since Uriel the Regent of the Sun saw
His entrance and warned the Cherubim
Guarding the entrance; driven from there in torment
He followed the darkness for seven nights without days,
Lapping the equator three times,
And crossing the shadow of night four times,
Going from pole to pole, crossing each quarter of the Earth;
On the eighth night he returned, and on the opposite side
From the gate and the guard of Cherubs he found
A secret entrance. There was a place
Which is now gone, though it is sin and not time which made the change,
Where the river Tigris at the foot of Paradise
Dived underground into a ravine, until part
Of it rose up in a spring by the Tree of Life;
Satan dived in with the river, and rose up
Hidden in the rising mist, then looked
For a place to hide; he searched land and sea
From Eden over the Black Sea to the Sea of Azov
And up beyond the River Ob,
Down as far as the Antarctic, and he traveled west
From the Orontes to the border of the ocean

At Darien, thence to the Land where flowes	*At Darien, then to the land where*
Ganges and Indus: thus the Orb he roam'd	*The Ganges and the Indus flowed; so he roamed the globe,*
With narrow search; and with inspection deep	*Searching closely, and he carefully inspected*
Consider'd every Creature, which of all	*Every creature, seeing which one*
Most opportune might serve his Wiles, and found	*Would best suit his plans, and he found*
The Serpent suttlest Beast of all the Field.	*The serpent was the most cunning of all the animals.*
Him after long debate, irresolute	*After long thought, unable to make up his mind,*
Of thoughts revolv'd, his final sentence chose	*He finally settled on the best*
Fit Vessel, fittest Imp of fraud, in whom	*Container, the most devious imp, for him*
To enter, and his dark suggestions hide	*To enter and hide his dark plans*
From sharpest sight: for in the wilie Snake,	*From the sharpest eyes; for in the wily snake*
Whatever sleights none would suspicious mark,	*Any cunning would not be seen as suspicious,*
As from his wit and native suttletie	*But as coming from his nature,*
Proceeding, which in other Beasts observ'd	*When if it was seen in other beasts*
Doubt might beget of Diabolic pow'r	*It might raise suspicions of devilish power*
Active within beyond the sense of brute.	*Acting inside, beyond the control of the brute.*
Thus he resolv'd, but first from inward griefe	*So he decided, but first from his inner sorrow*
His bursting passion into plaints thus pour'd:	*He burst out whining of his lot:*
O Earth, how like to Heav'n, if not preferr'd	*'Oh Earth, how like Heaven you are, if not*
More justly, Seat worthier of Gods, as built	*Even greater, more worthy of Gods, having been built*
With second thoughts, reforming what was old!	*As a second attempt, improving on the old!*
For what God after better worse would build?	*For what God would build something worse after better?*
Terrestrial Heav'n, danc't round by other Heav'ns	*An earthly heaven, danced around by other heavens*
That shine, yet bear thir bright officious Lamps,	*That shine and do their duty in bringing you light,*
Light above Light, for thee alone, as seems,	*Light above light, just for you, it appears,*

In thee concentring all thir precious beams	Concentrating all their precious beams of holy power
Of sacred influence: As God in Heav'n Is Center, yet extends to all, so thou	Onto you: as God in Heaven Is at the center and spreads everywhere, so you
Not in themselves, all thir known vertue appeers Centring receav'st from all those Orbs; in thee, Productive in Herb, Plant, and nobler birth	Are at the center and receive light from everywhere; All their powers appear in you, not in themselves, Producing herbs, plants and nobler things
Of Creatures animate with gradual life	Creatures which by degrees are animated
Of Growth, Sense, Reason, all summ'd up in Man. With what delight could I have walkt thee round, If I could joy in aught, sweet interchange	With growth, sense and reason, and Man is the pinnacle. How pleased I would have been to walk around you, If I could take pleasure in anything, the sweet mixture
Of Hill, and Vallie, Rivers, Woods and Plaines, Now Land, now Sea, and Shores with Forrest crownd, Rocks, Dens, and Caves; but I in none of these Find place or refuge; and the more I see	Of hills and valleys, rivers, woods and plains, Now land, now sea, and shores covered in forests, Rocks, dens and caves; but in none of these Can I find a home or a refuge, and the more I see
Pleasures about me, so much more I feel Torment within me, as from the hateful siege Of contraries; all good to me becomes	Beauty around me, so the more I feel Tortured with a horrible clash Of opposites; all good becomes evil to me,
Bane, and in Heav'n much worse would be my state. But neither here seek I, no nor in Heav'n	And in Heaven my condition would be much worse. But I don't want to live here, nor in Heaven,
To dwell, unless by maistring Heav'ns Supreame; Nor hope to be my self less miserable	Unless I can overcome Heaven's ruler; Nor do I hope to make myself less miserable
By what I seek, but others to make such As I, though thereby worse to me redound:	If I succeed, but to make others Like me, even though that will get me worse punishment;
For onely in destroying I find ease To my relentless thoughts; and him destroyd,	For only in destruction do I find ease For my restless thoughts; if he is destroyed,

296

Or won to what may work his utter loss,

For whom all this was made, all this will soon
Follow, as to him linkt in weal or woe,

In wo then: that destruction wide may range:
To mee shall be the glorie sole among
The infernal Powers, in one day to have marr'd
What he Almightie styl'd, six Nights and Days
Continu'd making, and who knows how long
Before had bin contriving, though perhaps

Not longer then since I in one Night freed

From servitude inglorious welnigh half

Th' Angelic Name, and thinner left the throng
Of his adorers: hee to be aveng'd,
And to repaire his numbers thus impair'd,
Whether such vertue spent of old now faild

More Angels to Create, if they at least

Are his Created, or to spite us more,

Determin'd to advance into our room
A Creature form'd of Earth, and him endow,

Exalted from so base original,
With Heav'nly spoils, our spoils: What he decreed
He effected; Man he made, and for him built
Magnificent this World, and Earth his seat,

Him Lord pronounc'd, and, O indignitie!

Subjected to his service Angel wings,
And flaming Ministers to watch and tend

Or turned to paths which will lead to his utter downfall,

The one for whom all this was made, all this
Will collapse as well, being linked to him, good or bad,
And I will make it bad. The damage will be widespread:
I shall have the sole honor, amongst
All the powers of Hell, to be the one who in one day
Wrecked what he who calls himself Almighty took six
Days and nights to make, and had spent who knows
How long in the planning, though perhaps

He's only been planning since the night when I freed

Nearly half of the angels from dishonorable service,

And left the crowds of his worshippers
Much thinner: to take revenge,
And to regain the numbers he lost,
Whether the power he had in the past has faded
So he can't create more angels (if he did
In fact create them), or just to spite us,
He decided to set up in our place
A creature made of Earth, and to give him,
Raised from such a low place,
Heavenly treasures, our treasures: what he ordered
He made happen; he made Man and for him built
This magnificent universe and Earth as his home;
He pronounced him Lord of this place and - oh the indignity! -
Gave him angels to serve him,
Flaming guards to watch and care for

Thir earthy Charge: Of these the vigilance

I dread, and to elude, thus wrapt in mist

Of midnight vapor glide obscure, and prie

In every Bush and Brake, where hap may finde
The Serpent sleeping, in whose mazie foulds
To hide me, and the dark intent I bring.
O foul descent! that I who erst contended

With Gods to sit the highest, am now constraind
Into a Beast, and mixt with bestial slime,

This essence to incarnate and imbrute,

That to the hight of Deitie aspir'd;
But what will not Ambition and Revenge
Descend to? who aspires must down as low

As high he soard, obnoxious first or last

To basest things. Revenge, at first though sweet,
Bitter ere long back on it self recoiles;
Let it; I reck not, so it light well aim'd,

Since higher I fall short, on him who next

Provokes my envie, this new Favorite
Of Heav'n, this Man of Clay, Son of despite,
Whom us the more to spite his Maker rais'd
From dust: spite then with spite is best repaid.
So saying, through each Thicket Danck or Drie,
Like a black mist low creeping, he held on

His midnight search, where soonest he might finde
The Serpent: him fast sleeping soon he found

This thing made of earth;I dread the vigilance
Of these angels, and so I wrap myself in the mist
Of midnight fogs to elude them, prying
In every bush and thicket, where I may chance to find
The serpent sleeping, and within his coils
Hide both myself and my dark plans.
What a terrible fall!That I who once contended
With God for the highest place am now forced
To become a beast, and mixed with bestial slime,
To take this Spirit and give it a brutish body,
That aspired to the title of God;
But what will ambition and revenge Not lower themselves to? He who wants them must go down as low
As he once soared high, exposed at the beginning or end
To the basest things.Revenge, though it is sweet at first,
Soon backfires bitterly on itself;
Let it, I don't care as long as it hits its target;
Since I can't hit the highest let it hit the one next
On my list in envy, this new favourite Of Heaven, this man of clay, son of spite,
Whom his maker raised from the dust To spite us more; then let spite be repaid with spite.'
Saying this he crept through each thicket, wet or dry,
Ceeping low like a black mist, he carried on
With his midnight search to where he most likely would find
The serpent: he soon found him sleeping

In Labyrinth of many a round self-rowld,
His head the midst, well stor'd with suttle wiles:
Not yet in horrid Shade or dismal Den,

Nor nocent yet, but on the grassie Herbe

Fearless unfeard he slept: in at his Mouth
The Devil enterd, and his brutal sense,

In heart or head, possessing soon inspir'd

With act intelligential; but his sleep

Disturbd not, waiting close th' approach of Morn.
Now when as sacred Light began to dawne
In Eden on the humid Flours, that breathd

Thir morning incense, when all things that breath,
From th' Earths great Altar send up silent praise
To the Creator, and his Nostrils fill

With grateful Smell, forth came the human pair
And joind thir vocal Worship to the Quire

Of Creatures wanting voice, that done, partake
The season, prime for sweetest Sents and Aires:
Then commune how that day they best may ply
Thir growing work: for much thir work outgrew
The hands dispatch of two Gardning so wide.
And Eve first to her Husband thus began.
Adam, well may we labour still to dress

This Garden, still to tend Plant, Herb and Flour,
Our pleasant task enjoyn'd, but till more

In a cave made of his own coils,
His head in the middle, full of cunning:
He did not yet sleep in dark places or dismal dens,
For he was still innocent and slept on the grass,
Unafraid: the Devil entered
In through his mouth, and took over its animal senses,
In its head and its heart, and having control of them
Would soon make it act with intelligence; but he did not

Disturb its sleep, waiting secretly for the approach of dawn.
Now, as the holy light began to dawn
In Eden, shining on the moist flowers that breathed
Out their morning perfume and all things that breathe
Sent up silent praise from the great altar of the Earth
To their Creator and filled his nostrils
With the scent of gratitude, then the human pair came out
And added their vocal worship to the choir
Of creatures lacking in voice; having done that they
Admired the morning, the best time for sweet scents and air:
Then they discussed how they might best carry out
Their growing work, for the task was outgrowing
The ability of two pairs of hands in such a wide garden.
Eve spoke to her husband first.
'Adam, we will go on trying to look after
This garden, to still attend to the plants, herbs and flowers,
The pleasant task we have been

Original	Modern
hands Aid us, the work under our labour grows,	*given, but until more hands* *Come to help us the work actually grows due to our care,*
Luxurious by restraint; what we by day	*More fruitful as it is tended; what we during the day*
Lop overgrown, or prune, or prop, or bind, One night or two with wanton growth derides Tending to wilde. Thou therefore now advise Or hear what to my minde first thoughts present,	*Lop, prune, prop or tie up,* *The frolicking growth, in a night or two, makes a mockery of it* *And returns to the wild. So you advise what to do,* *Or listen to what I think;*
Let us divide our labours, thou where choice Leads thee, or where most needs, whether to wind	*Let us divide our work; you go where* *You choose, or where you're most needed, whether it's to wind*
The Woodbine round this Arbour, or direct	*The woodbine around our shelter, or direct where*
The clasping Ivie where to climb, while I In yonder Spring of Roses intermixt	*The clasping ivy should climb, while* *In that grove over there of roses mixed*
With Myrtle, find what to redress till Noon:	*With myrtle I will find work until noon:*
For while so near each other thus all day	*When we choose tasks which put us so near each other*
Our taske we choose, what wonder if so near	*All day, is it any wonder*
Looks intervene and smiles, or object new	*That we spend time looking and smiling at each other,*
Casual discourse draw on, which intermits	*Or chatting about new things we find, and these intermissions*
Our dayes work brought to little, though begun	*Mean we do too little work in the day, even though we begin*
Early, and th' hour of Supper comes unearn'd.	*Early, and we do not earn our supper.'*
Sole Eve, Associate sole, to me beyond Compare above all living Creatures deare,	*Adam answered her mildly:* *'Unique Eve, my only companion, to me beyond*
Well hast thou motion'd, well thy thoughts imployd	*Comparison, dear above all living creatures,*
How we might best fulfill the work which here	*You have made a good suggestion, thought well*
God hath assign'd us, nor of me shalt pass Unprais'd: for nothing lovelier can be found	*About how we might best do the task* *God has given us, and I praise you for it.*

In Woman, then to studie houshold good,
And good workes in her Husband to promote.
Yet not so strictly hath our Lord impos'd

Labour, as to debarr us when we need

Refreshment, whether food, or talk between,
Food of the mind, or this sweet intercourse

Of looks and smiles, for smiles from Reason flow,
To brute deni'd, and are of Love the food,

Love not the lowest end of human life.

For not to irksom toile, but to delight

He made us, and delight to Reason joyn'd.
These paths & Bowers doubt not but our joynt hands
Will keep from Wilderness with ease, as wide
As we need walk, till younger hands ere long
Assist us: But if much converse perhaps

Thee satiate, to short absence I could yield.

For solitude somtimes is best societie,

And short retirement urges sweet returne.

But other doubt possesses me, least harm

Befall thee sever'd from me; for thou knowst
What hath bin warn'd us, what malicious Foe
Envying our happiness, and of his own

Despairing, seeks to work us woe and shame

By sly assault; and somwhere nigh at hand

Watches, no doubt, with greedy hope to find

*There is nothing lovelier
In a woman than that she thinks
about the good of the household
And works to encourage good works
in her husband.
But our Lord has not so strictly imposed
Work as to stop us from breaking for
Refreshment, whether it is food or talk,
Which is the food of the mind, or the
sweet exchanges
Of looks and smiles, for they come
from our reason
And the animals do not have them,
and they are the food of Love,
And love is not the lowest aim of
human life.
He did not make us for irksome work
But for joy, and to join reason with
that joy.
Do not doubt that together we can keep
The wilderness back from our paths
and shelters
In an area as large as we need, until
before long there will be
Younger hands to help us: but if
you've had enough
Of talk, I might agree to a short
separation.
Solitude is sometimes the best
company,
And absence makes the heart grow
fonder.
But another doubt worries me, in
case
You should come to harm on your
own, for you know
What we were warned, that a spiteful
enemy
Envies our happiness, and having
none himself
Wants to bring us to sorrow and
sadness
With sly tricks. No doubt he is*

His wish and best advantage, us asunder,
Hopeless to circumvent us joynd, where each
To other speedie aide might lend at need;

Whether his first design be to withdraw

Our fealtie from God, or to disturb
Conjugal Love, then which perhaps no bliss
Enjoy'd by us excites his envie more;

Or this, or worse, leave not the faithful side
That gave thee being, still shades thee and protects.
The Wife, where danger or dishonour lurks,

Safest and seemliest by her Husband staies,

Who guards her, or with her the worst endures.
To whom the Virgin Majestie of Eve,
As one who loves, and some unkindness meets,
With sweet austeer composure thus reply'd,
Ofspring of Heav'n and Earth, and all Earths Lord,
That such an Enemie we have, who seeks

Our ruin, both by thee informd I learne,

And from the parting Angel over-heard

As in a shadie nook I stood behind,

Just then returnd at shut of Evening Flours.

But that thou shouldst my firmness therfore doubt
To God or thee, because we have a foe

May tempt it, I expected not to hear.

His violence thou fear'st not, being such,

watching
Nearby, greedily hoping to achieve
His great wish by finding us apart;

He cannot catch us out if we are together,
Where each can help the other if needed;
His plan may be to make us withdraw
Our loyalty from God or to disturb
Our married love, which is maybe the happiness
Of ours which he envies the most;
For fear of this, or worse, do not leave the faithful company
Of the one who gave you life and still follows and protects you.
When danger or dishonor is near the best and safest. Place for a wife is at her husband's side,

So he can guard her, or share the trouble if it comes.'
The queenly innocence of Eve replied
As one who has encountered some unkindness from a lover,
With sweet but stern composure:
"Child of Heaven and Earth and Master of the Earth,
That we have such an enemy, who seeks our
Downfall I have learned both from you
And from overhearing the angel as he left
As I was standing in a shady nook just behind you,
Having come back just as evening fell.
But that you should therefore doubt my loyalty
To God or to you, just because we have an enemy
Who might test it, I didn't expect to hear that.
You cannot fear his violence as we

302

As wee, not capable of death or paine,
Can either not receave, or can repell.

His fraud is then thy fear, which plain inferrs
Thy equal fear that my firm Faith and Love

Can by his fraud be shak'n or seduc't;

Thoughts, which how found they harbour in thy brest
Adam, misthought of her to thee so dear?

To whom with healing words Adam replyd.

Daughter of God and Man, immortal Eve,

For such thou art, from sin and blame entire:
Not diffident of thee do I dissuade

Thy absence from my sight, but to avoid
Th' attempt itself, intended by our Foe.

For hee who tempts, though in vain, at least asperses
The tempted with dishonour foul, suppos'd

Not incorruptible of Faith, not proof

Against temptation: thou thy self with scorne
And anger wouldst resent the offer'd wrong,
Though ineffectual found: misdeem not then,
If such affront I labour to avert
From thee alone, which on us both at once

The Enemie, though bold, will hardly dare,

Or daring, first on mee th' assault shall light.

Nor thou his malice and false guile contemn;

---

are
Not capable of death or feeling pain,
So we can either not receive them or can repel them.

His trickery, then, is what worries you, which clearly shows
That you fear that my loyal faith and love

Can be shaken or led astray by his tricks;

How can you harbor such thoughts in your heart,
Adam, thinking so badly of the one so dear to you?"

Adam replied to her with soothing words:

"Daughter of God and Man, immortal Eve,

For that is what you are, completely free of sin and blame:
It is not because I don't trust you that I ask you

To say within my sight, but to block
The attempt which our enemy is planning.

For the one who tempts, even in vain, at least casts doubt
On the honor of the one he tries to tempt, thinking

That their faith is not incorruptible, that they could not

Resist temptation: you would be made angry
And upset by the offer of temptation,

Even though it would not be accepted; don't misunderstand then
If I try to avoid such an insult falling
On you alone, which when we are together

The enemy, though bold, will hardly dare try,

Or if he does he'll have to deal with me first.

And don't think his hatred and deceit are weak;

Suttle he needs must be, who could seduce

Angels nor think superfluous others aid.

I from the influence of thy looks receave
Access in every Vertue, in thy sight

More wise, more watchful, stronger, if
need were
Of outward strength; while shame, thou
looking on,
Shame to be overcome or over-reacht

Would utmost vigor raise, and rais'd unite.

Why shouldst not thou like sense within
thee feel
When I am present, and thy trial choose

With me, best witness of thy Vertue tri'd.

So spake domestick Adam in his care

And Matrimonial Love; but Eve, who
thought
Less attributed to her Faith sincere,

Thus her reply with accent sweet renewd.

If this be our condition, thus to dwell
In narrow circuit strait'nd by a Foe,

Suttle or violent, we not endu'd

Single with like defence, wherever met,

How are we happie, still in fear of harm?

But harm precedes not sin: onely our Foe

Tempting affronts us with his foul esteem

Of our integritie: his foul esteeme
Sticks no dishonor on our Front, but turns

Foul on himself; then wherefore shund or

He must be sly, one who could mislead

Angels, and don't think the help of others is not needed.

When you are looking at me
I am increased in all my virtues, under your gaze

I am more wise, more watchful, stronger, if

Physical strength is needed; while if you are watching

I would be so ashamed to be overcome or tricked

That I would summon up my greatest strength and win.

Why should the same not apply to you

When I am present, and make you choose to face your trial

With me, who is your best companion in that challenge?"

So spoke the husbandly Adam in his care

And love of his bride; but Eve, who thought

That her sincere faith was being doubted,

Gave back another reply in her sweet voice.

"If this is going to be our life, to live In a small space, hemmed in by our enemy,

Sly or violent, and we do not have the strength

To defend against him when on our own, wherever we meet him,

How can we be happy, if we live in fear of harm?

But harm does not lead to sin: only our enemy

By tempting us insults us with his revolting assessment

Of our integrity: his foul estimate of it Brings no dishonor on our heads, but turns

His foulness back on himself; so why

feard
By us? who rather double honour gaine

From his surmise prov'd false, find peace within,
Favour from Heav'n, our witness from th' event.
And what is Faith, Love, Vertue unassaid

Alone, without exterior help sustaind?
Let us not then suspect our happie State

Left so imperfet by the Maker wise,

As not secure to single or combin'd.

Fraile is our happiness, if this be so,

And Eden were no Eden thus expos'd.

To whom thus Adam fervently repli'd.
O Woman, best are all things as the will

Of God ordain'd them, his creating hand
Nothing imperfet or deficient left
Of all that he Created, much less Man,

Or aught that might his happie State secure,

Secure from outward force; within himself

The danger lies, yet lies within his power:

Against his will he can receave no harme.

But God left free the Will, for what obeyes

Reason, is free, and Reason he made right

But bid her well beware, and still erect,

Least by some faire appeering good surpris'd
She dictate false, and misinforme the Will

To do what God expresly hath forbid,

---

should we fear
Or avoid him? We should be wanting to gain double honor

From showing his estimate to be wrong, and inner peace
And the approval of Heaven will be our reward.
What is faith, love and virtue worth if it has not been tested

Alone, without help from outside?
Don't let us imagine that our happy state

Was left so imperfect by our wise creator,

That we are not just as safe alone as together.

Our happiness would have very weak foundations if this were so,

And Eden would be shown not to be Paradise."

Adam replied to her passionately:
"Oh woman, all things are best as the will

Of God ordered, his creating hand
Left nothing imperfect or lacking
In anything he created, least of all in Man;

He left out nothing that could make his happy state safe,

Secure from attack from outside; the danger lies

Within himself, though he can guard against it:

He can receive no harm against his will.

But God gave us free will, for following

Reason is freedom, and he made reason right,

But warned to be careful of it, and still on guard,

In case, misled by something that seems fair and good,

She leads you astray and misdirects your will

To do that which God has expressly

Not then mistrust, but tender love enjoynes,

That I should mind thee oft, and mind thou me.
Firm we subsist, yet possible to swerve,

Since Reason not impossibly may meet

Some specious object by the Foe subornd,

And fall into deception unaware,
Not keeping strictest watch, as she was warnd.
Seek not temptation then, which to avoide

Were better, and most likelie if from mee

Thou sever not: Trial will come unsought.

Wouldst thou approve thy constancie, approve
First thy obedience; th' other who can know,
Not seeing thee attempted, who attest?

But if thou think, trial unsought may finde

Us both securer then thus warnd thou seemst,
Go; for thy stay, not free, absents thee more;

Go in thy native innocence, relie
On what thou hast of vertue, summon all,
For God towards thee hath done his part, do thine.
So spake the Patriarch of Mankinde, but Eve
Persisted, yet submiss, though last, repli'd.

With thy permission then, and thus forewarnd
Chiefly by what thy own last reasoning words

forbidden.
It is not mistrust, but tender love which insists
That I should always guard you, and you me.
We are firm, but it is possible to be led astray,
Since it is not impossible for reason to meet
Some apparently good thing perverted by the enemy
And be deceived without realizing,
Not keeping the strictest watch as she had been warned to do.
Don't try and face temptation then, which is
Best avoided, and you can do that best
If you stay with me; the test will come without looking for it.
If you want to prove your loyalty, first prove
Your obedience; who can know what
The other is like, if you are not tested?
But if you think that the unlooked for trial will find
Us stronger than that warning implies,
Go; for if you stay here at my command you will be even more absent;
Go with your inbred innocence, rely
On the virtues you have, use them all,
For God has done his part, now you must do yours."
So spoke the Father of Mankind, but Eve
Persisted humbly, though having the last word, and replied.
"With your permission then, and forewarned,
Mainly by what your last words mentioned

Touchd onely, that our trial, when least sought,
May finde us both perhaps farr less prepar'd,
he willinger I goe, nor much expect

A Foe so proud will first the weaker seek,

So bent, the more shall shame him his repulse.
Thus saying, from her Husbands hand her hand
Soft she withdrew, and like a Wood-Nymph light
Oread or Dryad, or of Delia's Traine,

Betook her to the Groves, but Delia's self

In gate surpass'd and Goddess-like deport,

Though not as shee with Bow and Quiver armd,
But with such Gardning Tools as Art yet rude,
Guiltless of fire had formd, or Angels brought.
To Pales, or Pomona, thus adornd,

Likeliest she seemd, Pomona when she fled
Vertumnus, or to Ceres in her Prime,

Yet Virgin of Proserpina from Jove.
Her long with ardent look his Eye pursu'd

Delighted, but desiring more her stay.

Oft he to her his charge of quick returne

Repeated, shee to him as oft engag'd
To be returnd by Noon amid the Bowre,

And all things in best order to invite
Noontide repast, or Afternoons repose.

O much deceav'd, much failing, hapless Eve,

Only in passing, that our trial, If we do not seek it,
May catch us far more unawares,
So I go more willingly, and I don't expect
That such a proud enemy will try the weaker first,
And if he does then he shall be even more ashamed by my rejecting him."
Saying this she gently withdrew her hand
From his, and like a light wood nymph,
Of the mountains or woods, or one of Delia's attendants,
She went into the groves, but she surpassed
Delia herself in her step and her Godess-like deportment,
Though she was not armed with bow and quiver like Delia
But with such gardening tools as their basic skills,
Not having fire to forge them, had made, or the angels had brought.
She seemed like a goddess of the fields or orchards,
Like Pomona when she ran
From Vertumnus, or like Ceres in her prime,
Still a virgin of Prosperina from Jove.
He followed her with love in his eyes for a long time,
Delighted with her, but wishing she would stay.
He often repeated his order that she should return
Soon, and just as often she replied
That she would return to their home before noon
And have everything in the best order For their lunch or their afternoon's rest.
Oh how wrong you are, much failing, hapless Eve,

Of thy presum'd return! event perverse!
Thou never from that houre in Paradise

Foundst either sweet repast, or sound repose;
Such ambush hid among sweet Flours and Shades
Waited with hellish rancour imminent
To intercept thy way, or send thee back
Despoild of Innocence, of Faith, of Bliss.

For now, and since first break of dawne the Fiend,
Meer Serpent in appearance, forth was come,
And on his Quest, where likeliest he might finde
The onely two of Mankinde, but in them
The whole included Race, his purposd prey.

In Bowre and Field he sought, where any tuft
Of Grove or Garden-Plot more pleasant lay,

Thir tendance or Plantation for delight,
By Fountain or by shadie Rivulet
He sought them both, but wish'd his hap might find
Eve separate, he wish'd, but not with hope

Of what so seldom chanc'd, when to his wish,
Beyond his hope, Eve separate he spies,
Veild in a Cloud of Fragrance, where she stood,
Half spi'd, so thick the Roses bushing round

About her glowd, oft stooping to support

Each Flour of slender stalk, whose head though gay
Carnation, Purple, Azure, or spect with Gold,
Hung drooping unsustaind, them she upstaies
Gently with Mirtle band, mindless the

About your return! Terrible event!
From that time on you never in Paradise

Found either sweet food or sound sleep;
An ambush was waiting among the flowers and shadows,
Waiting with hellish spite ready
To divert your path, or send you back
Stripped of your innocence, your faith, your happiness.

For now, and since daybreak the Devil,
Just a serpent in appearance, had come out
On his hunt to where he was most likely to find
The only two humans, but they
Represented the whole race, which was his prey.

He looked for them in their shelters and the fields,
Where any piece of wood or garden looked more pleasant,

Places they had tended or planted,
By springs or shady streams
He looked for them both, but his great hope
Was to find Eve alone, though he did not have much hope

Of something that so seldom happened, when his wish
Came true, he spied Eve separate,
Cloaked in a cloud of perfume, from where she was
He could only see half of her as the rose bushes

Were glowing so thick around her as she stooped to support

Any flower that had a weak stalk, with a head that though bright
Red, purple, blue or flecked with gold

Was hanging down unsupported, then she ties them up
Gently with a piece of myrtle, not

while,	*knowing*
Her self, though fairest unsupported Flour,	*Thatshe was the fairest unsupported flower,*
From her best prop so farr, and storm so nigh.	*Far away from her support and with a storm coming.*
Neerer he drew, and many a walk travers'd	*He came nearer, and crossed many paths*
Of stateliest Covert, Cedar, Pine, or Palme,	*Through the great woodlands of cedar, pine or palm,*
Then voluble and bold, now hid, now seen	*Sometimes twisting and open, sometimes hidden, now seen*
Among thick-wov'n Arborets and Flours	*Amongst the thick shrubs and flowers*
Imborderd on each Bank, the hand of Eve:	*Decorating the bank, the work of Eve:*
Spot more delicious then those Gardens feign'd	*A more lovely spot than could be found in the stories*
Or of reviv'd Adonis, or renownd	*About Adonis' garden or that or renowned*
Alcinous, host of old Laertes Son,	*Alcinous, host of Odysseus,*
Or that, not Mystic, where the Sapient King	*Or that one, not mythical, where King Solomon*
Held dalliance with his fair Egyptian Spouse.	*Played with his fair Egyptian wife.*
Much hee the Place admir'd, the Person more.	*He admired the place very much, the person even more.*
As one who long in populous City pent,	*He was like one who has been long in a big city,*
Where Houses thick and Sewers annoy the Aire,	*With the houses close together and sewers reeking,*
Forth issuing on a Summers Morn to breathe	*Leaving on a summer morning to breathe in*
Among the pleasant Villages and Farmes	*Among the charming villages and farms*
Adjoynd, from each thing met conceaves delight,	*All around, and gets delight from everything he meets,*
The smell of Grain, or tedded Grass, or Kine,	*The smell of wheat, cut grass, cattle*
Or Dairie, each rural sight, each rural sound;	*Or the dairy, every rural sight and sound;*
If chance with Nymphlike step fair Virgin pass,	*If by chance a fair maid passes with a nymphlike step*
What pleasing seemd, for her now pleases more,	*What seems pleasant seems even more so now she is there,*
She most, and in her look summs all Delight.	*And she pleases the most, and her appearance has all the delightful things together.*

Such Pleasure took the Serpent to behold	*This was the pleasure it gave the serpent to see*
This Flourie Plat, the sweet recess of Eve	*This flowery plot, Eve's sweet retreat*
Thus earlie, thus alone; her Heav'nly forme	*So early, so alone; her divine shape*
Angelic, but more soft, and Feminine,	*Was angelic, but softer, more feminine,*
Her graceful Innocence, her every Aire	*Her graceful innocence, every movement,*
Of gesture or lest action overawd	*Gesture or least action overcame*
His Malice, and with rapine sweet bereav'd	*His spite, and with a sweet ravishing stripped*
His fierceness of the fierce intent it brought:	*His fierceness of the fierce plan it had;*
That space the Evil one abstracted stood	*For that moment the evil one was separated*
From his own evil, and for the time remaind	*From his own evil, and for that time remained*
Stupidly good, of enmitie disarm'd,	*Insensibly good, stripped of his hatred,*
Of guile, of hate, of envie, of revenge;	*Of trickery, of spite, of envy, of revenge;*
But the hot Hell that alwayes in him burnes,	*But the hot hell that always burns inside him*
Though in mid Heav'n, soon ended his delight,	*Even though he was in the middle Heaven, soon ended his delight,*
And tortures him now more, the more he sees	*And he is more tortured, the more he sees*
Of pleasure not for him ordain'd: then soon	*Of happiness forbidden him; then soon*
Fierce hate he recollects, and all his thoughts	*He remembers his fierce hate, and strengthens*
Of mischief, gratulating, thus excites.	*All his thoughts of mischief.*
Thoughts, whither have ye led me, with what sweet	*"What was I thinking, what sweet*
Compulsion thus transported to forget	*Impulse carried me away and made me forget*
What hither brought us, hate, not love, nor hope	*What brought me here, hate, not love, not hope*
Of Paradise for Hell, hope here to taste	*Of exchanging Paradise for Hell, not hoping to taste*
Of pleasure, but all pleasure to destroy,	*Pleasure here, but to destroy all pleasure.*

Save what is in destroying, other joy	*Apart from destruction there is no other joy*
To me is lost. Then let me not let pass	*Left for me. Then let me not pass up*
Occasion which now smiles, behold alone	*This lucky chance, seeing the woman*
The Woman, opportune to all attempts,	*Alone, open to attack,*
Her Husband, for I view far round, not nigh,	*Her husband, for I have looked far around, nowhere near,*
Whose higher intellectual more I shun,	*Whose higher intelligence I would rather avoid,*
And strength, of courage hautie, and of limb	*And his strength, his haughty courage*
Heroic built, though of terrestrial mould,	*And heroic build, though it is terrestrial,*
Foe not informidable, exempt from wound,	*He is a formidable foe, who cannot feel pain,*
I not; so much hath Hell debas'd, and paine	*And I can; Hell has so brought me down, and pain*
Infeebl'd me, to what I was in Heav'n.	*Weakened me, compared to what I was in Heaven.*
Shee fair, divinely fair, fit Love for Gods,	*She is lovely, divinely lovely, fit to be a lover of Gods,*
Not terrible, though terrour be in Love	*Not dangerous, though there is a danger in love*
And beautie, not approacht by stronger hate,	*And beauty, if it wasn't being approached by a stronger hate,*
Hate stronger, under shew of Love well feign'd,	*A stronger hate, well hidden under a show of love,*
The way which to her ruin now I tend.	*That's the way I shall bring about her downfall."*
So spake the Enemie of Mankind, enclos'd	*So the enemy of mankind spoke, hidden*
In Serpent, Inmate bad, and toward Eve	*In the serpent, a bad prisoner, and he made his way*
Address'd his way, not with indented wave,	*Towards Eve, not with a snaky weave*
Prone on the ground, as since, but on his reare,	*Lying on the ground as he has since, but on his end,*
Circular base of rising foulds, that tour'd	*On a circular base of rising coils that rose*
Fould above fould a surging Maze, his Head	*Coil above coil in a moving maze, his head*
Crested aloft, and Carbuncle his Eyes;	*Above, crested, and his eyes were red gems;*
With burnisht Neck of verdant Gold, erect	*With a gleaming neck of green gold, erect*
Amidst his circling Spires, that on the grass	*Amongst his circling coils, that followed*

Floted redundant: pleasing was his shape,

And lovely, never since of Serpent kind

Lovelier, not those that in Illyria chang'd

Hermione and Cadmus, or the God

In Epidaurus; nor to which transformd

Ammonian Jove, or Capitoline was seen,

Hee with Olympias, this with her who bore

Scipio the highth of Rome. With tract oblique

At first, as one who sought access, but feard

To interrupt, side-long he works his way.

As when a Ship by skilful Stearsman wrought

Nigh Rivers mouth or Foreland, where the Wind

Veres oft, as oft so steers, and shifts her Saile;

So varied hee, and of his tortuous Traine

Curld many a wanton wreath in sight of Eve,

To lure her Eye; shee busied heard the sound

Of rusling Leaves, but minded not, as us'd

To such disport before her through the Field,

From every Beast, more duteous at her call,

Then at Circean call the Herd disguis'd.

Hee boulder now, uncall'd before her stood;

But as in gaze admiring: Oft he bowd

His turret Crest, and sleek enamel'd Neck,

Unused on the grass; he was a pleasing shape,

And lovelier, lovelier than any of his kind

That followed, not those in Illyria which

Hermione and Cadmus changed into, or the God

Of healing in his temple in Epidarus, nor the one

Jupiter changed into when at Ammonia or Capitoline,

Here with Alexander's mother, here with the mother

Of Scipio, the highest in Rome. With an indirect path,

At first, like one who sought access but didn't want

To interrupt, he works his way sideways.

Like a ship brought by skilful helmsman

By the mouth of a river or a headland, where the wind

Veers often and he changes course as often, shifting the sail;

So he varied his course, and of his twisted tail

He curled many twirling coils in Eve's sight,

Hoping to catch her eye; busy, she heard the sound

Like rustling leaves, but ignored it as she was used to

Such play around her wherever she went,

From every beast; they were more keen to come to her

Than the ones who answered Circe's call and were turned to swine.

Bolder now, he stood in front of her, uncalled,

But as if he was admiring her; he often bowed

His towering crest and his sleek enameled neck,

Fawning, and lick'd the ground whereon she trod.

Fawning, and kissed the ground she walked on.

His gentle dumb expression turnd at length

Eventually his gentle dumb antics caught

The Eye of Eve to mark his play; he glad

The eye of Eve to watch his play; glad

Of her attention gaind, with Serpent Tongue

To have got her attention, using the snaky tongue

Organic, or impulse of vocal Air,
His fraudulent temptation thus began.
Wonder not, sovran Mistress, if perhaps

Of his own or hissing air,
He began his deceitful temptation.
"Do not wonder, queenly mistress, if you can,

Thou canst, who art sole Wonder, much less arm

Who are the only wonder, and do not assume

Thy looks, the Heav'n of mildness, with disdain,

A look of disdain on your face, mild as heaven,

Displeas'd that I approach thee thus, and gaze

Unhappy that I approach you like this and

Insatiate, I thus single, nor have feard

Choose you to gaze at endlessly, and I am not afraid

Thy awful brow, more awful thus retir'd.

Of your awesome forehead, more terrible when frowning like that.

Fairest resemblance of thy Maker faire,

You are the fairest copy of your fair maker,

Thee all things living gaze on, all things thine

All living things gaze upon you, all things which have been given

By gift, and thy Celestial Beautie adore

To you, and worship your heavenly beauty,

With ravishment beheld, there best beheld

Held entranced. You are seen best in heaven

Where universally admir'd; but here

Where you are universally admired, but here

In this enclosure wild, these Beasts among,

In this wild place, among these beasts,

Beholders rude, and shallow to discerne

Rough viewers, too stupid to understand

Half what in thee is fair, one man except,

Half of your beauty; apart from one man,

Who sees thee? (and what is one?) who shouldst be seen

Who sees you? (And what good is one?) You who should be seen

A Goddess among Gods, ador'd and serv'd

As a Goddess amongst the Gods, worshipped and served

By Angels numberless, thy daily Train.

By countless angels, your daily procession."

So gloz'd the Tempter, and his Proem tun'd;

So the tempter lied, playing his overture;

Into the Heart of Eve his words made way,	The words made their way into Eve's heart,
Though at the voice much marveling; at length	Though she was astonished that he could speak; at last,
Not unamaz'd she thus in answer spake.	Amazed, she gave him an answer.
What may this mean? Language of Man pronounc't	"What does this mean? The language of Man spoken
By Tongue of Brute, and human sense exprest?	With the tongue of a beast, and making human sense?
The first at lest of these I thought deni'd	I thought at least the first of these was forbidden
To Beasts, whom God on thir Creation-Day	To beasts, whom God on the day of their creation
Created mute to all articulat sound;	Made unable to let out any sound;
The latter I demurre, for in thir looks	The second I'm not sure about, for there often appears
Much reason, and in thir actions oft appeers.	To be much reason in their looks and actions.
Thee, Serpent, suttlest beast of all the field	I knew you, serpent, were the most cunning of the beasts,
I knew, but not with human voice endu'd;	But not that you had a human voice;
Redouble then this miracle, and say,	Perform this miracle again, and tell me,
How cam'st thou speakable of mute, and how	How did you go from mute to having and why
To me so friendly grown above the rest	Have you become more friendly to me than the rest
Of brutal kind, that daily are in sight?	Of the beasts, that I see every day?
Say, for such wonder claims attention due.	Tell me, for these strange things deserve attention."
To whom the guileful Tempter thus reply'd.	The cunning tempter answered her:
Empress of this fair World, resplendent Eve,	"Empress of this fair world, wonderful Eve,
Easie to mee it is to tell thee all	It is easy for me to answer all your questions
What thou commandst and right thou shouldst be obeyd:	And right that I should do do:
I was at first as other Beasts that graze	I was at first like the other beasts
The trodden Herb, of abject thoughts and low,	That graze on the grass, with low ean thoughts,
As was my food, nor aught but food discern'd	And my food was the same, and I thought of nothing but food
Or Sex, and apprehended nothing high:	Or sex, and had no notion of higher things:
Till on a day roaving the field, I chanc'd	Until one day as I roamed in the fields lady gaga song donl happened

314

A goodly Tree farr distant to behold	*To see a handsome tree in the distance*
Loaden with fruit of fairest colours mixt,	*Loaded with fruit in a mixture of the loveliest colors,*
Ruddie and Gold: I nearer drew to gaze;	*Red and gold: I went nearer to see,*
When from the boughes a savorie odour blow'n,	*And from the branches came a savory scent*
Grateful to appetite, more pleas'd my sense,	*Which sharpened my appetite and pleased my senses,*
Then smell of sweetest Fenel or the Teats	*More than the smell of sweet fennel or the teats*
Of Ewe or Goat dropping with Milk at Eevn,	*Of a ewe or a goat full of milk in the evening,*
Unsuckt of Lamb or Kid, that tend thir play.	*Unsuckled by a lamb or kid, that are off playing.*
To satisfie the sharp desire I had	*I resolved to satisfy the sharp desire I had*
Of tasting those fair Apples, I resolv'd	*For a taste of those fair apples,*
Not to deferr; hunger and thirst at once,	*At once; hunger and thirst together,*
Powerful perswaders, quick'nd at the scen	*Powerful persuaders, sharpened at the scent*
Of that alluring fruit, urg'd me so keene.	*Of that tempting fruit, calling to me.*
About the mossie Trunk I wound me soon,	*I soon wound myself around the mossy trunk,*
For high from ground the branches would require	*For the high branches would be at the edge*
Thy utmost reach or Adams: Round the Tree	*Of you reach or Adam's: round the tree*
All other Beasts that saw, with like desire	*Stood all the other beasts watching with the same desire,*
Longing and envying stood, but could not reach.	*Full of longing and envy, but they could not reach.*
Amid the Tree now got, where plenty hung	*I was now well in the tree, where there was plenty of fruit*
Tempting so nigh, to pluck and eat my fill	*Hanging temptingly, so I did not hesitate*
I spar'd not, for such pleasure till that hour	*To pluck and eat my fill, for until that time*
At Feed or Fountain never had I found.	*I had never had so much pleasure from food or drink.*
Sated at length, ere long I might perceive	*Full at last, it was not long before I found*
Strange alteration in me, to degree	*That I was strangely changed, having a degree*
Of Reason in my inward Powers, and Speech	*Of reason in my mind, and speech*

Wanted not long, though to this shape retain'd.
Thenceforth to Speculations high or deep

I turnd my thoughts, and with capacious mind
Considerd all things visible in Heav'n,

Or Earth, or Middle, all things fair and good;
But all that fair and good in thy Divine

Semblance, and in thy Beauties heav'nly Ray
United I beheld; no Fair to thine

Equivalent or second, which compel'd
Mee thus, though importune perhaps, to come
And gaze, and worship thee of right declar'd
Sovran of Creatures, universal Dame.

So talk'd the spirited sly Snake; and Eve

Yet more amaz'd unwarie thus reply'd.

Serpent, thy overpraising leaves in doubt

The vertue of that Fruit, in thee first prov'd:

But say, where grows the Tree, from hence how far?
For many are the Trees of God that grow
In Paradise, and various, yet unknown

To us, in such abundance lies our choice,
As leaves a greater store of Fruit untoucht,
Still hanging incorruptible, till men

Grow up to thir provision, and more hands

Help to disburden Nature of her Bearth.
To whom the wilie Adder, blithe and glad.

Empress, the way is readie, and not long,

Came shortly afterwards, although I kept this shape.
From then on I turned my mind to thoughts
High or deep, and with an ample mind
Considered all the things visible in Heaven,
Or Earth, or the air between, all the good and fair things;
But I saw all those good and fair things
United in your Godlike shape

And the heavenly rays of your beauty; there was nothing
Equal or close, which forced me,
Though bothersome perhaps, to come as I have
And look, and worship you rightly called
The queen of creatures, first lady of all."

So the possessed sly snake spoke, and Eve,

Even more amazed, unsuspecting, replied.

"Serpent, your excessive praise makes me doubt,

How much wisdom that fruit really gives that you tried:

But tell me, where does this tree grow, how far from here?
For many of God's trees grow
In Paradise, of different types, but that we don't know,

As we have such a great choice,
We leave most of the fruit untouched,
Hanging unpicked, until the number of men

Increases to match what is available, and more hands

Help to collect Nature's bounty."
To whom the cunning adder, cheery and happy, said,

"Empress, the path is ready, and not

Beyond a row of Myrtles, on a Flat,

Fast by a Fountain, one small Thicket past
Of blowing Myrrh and Balme; if thou accept
My conduct, I can bring thee thither soon.

Lead then, said Eve. Hee leading swiftly rowld
In tangles, and made intricate seem strait,

To mischief swift. Hope elevates, and joy

Bright'ns his Crest, as when a wandring Fire

Compact of unctuous vapor, which the Night
Condenses, and the cold invirons round,

Kindl'd through agitation to a Flame,

Which oft, they say, some evil Spirit attends
Hovering and blazing with delusive Light,

Misleads th' amaz'd Night-wanderer from his way
To Boggs and Mires, and oft through Pond or Poole,
There swallow'd up and lost, from succour farr.
So glister'd the dire Snake, and into fraud

Led Eve our credulous Mother, to the Tree

Of prohibition, root of all our woe;
Which when she saw, thus to her guide she spake.
Serpent, we might have spar'd our coming hither,
Fruitless to mee, though Fruit be here to excess,
The credit of whose vertue rest with thee,
Wondrous indeed, if cause of such effects.

---

long,
Beyond a row of myrtles, on a flat piece of ground,

Right by a spring, past a small thicket
Of blooming myrrh and balm; if you will have me
As your guide I can bring you there soon."

"Lead on," said Eve. Leading her he swiftly rolled
In his tangles, and made the twisted seem straight,

Leading quickly to trouble. Hope lifts him, and joy

Shines in his crest, as when a will-o-the-wisp,

Made of strong gases, which the night
And the cold surroundings condenses down,

And it is kindled through its agitation into flame,

Which often, they say, some evil Spirit attends,
Hovering and blazing with cheating light,

Which misleads the bewildered night traveler from his path
Into swamps or marshes, and often into a pond or pool,
Where they are swallowed up and lost, far from help.
So the terrible snake shone, and into error

Led Eve, our gullible mother, to the banned tree,

The root of all our sorrow;
When she saw what it was she spoke to her guide.
"Serpent, we might have been saved the bother of coming here,
Which is useless to me, though there is plenty of fruit here,
The proof of whose power is in you,
Truly incredible, if it is indeed the

	cause.
But of this Tree we may not taste nor touch;	But we may not taste or touch the fruit of this tree;
God so commanded, and left that Command	God commanded it, and left that order,
Sole Daughter of his voice; the rest, we live	The only law he made; in everything else
Law to our selves, our Reason is our Law.	We make our own laws, our reason is our law."
To whom the Tempter guilefully repli'd. Indeed? hath God then said that of the Fruit	The tempter cunningly answered her: "Indeed? Has God said that you cannot eat Fruit
Of all these Garden Trees ye shall not eate,	From any of these trees in the garden,
Yet Lords declar'd of all in Earth or Aire?	Even though you are called Lords of all that's on Earth or in the air?"
To whom thus Eve yet sinless. Of the Fruit	Eve, still sinless, answered him: "We may eat the fruit
Of each Tree in the Garden we may eate, But of the Fruit of this fair Tree amidst	Of every tree in the garden, Except for the fruit of this fair tree in the middle,
The Garden, God hath said, Ye shall not eate Thereof, nor shall ye touch it, least ye die.	God said, 'You shall not eat it, Nor shall you touch it, or you will die.'"
She scarse had said, though brief, when now more bold The Tempter, but with shew of Zeale and Love	She had hardly said this short speech when the tempter, Now more bold and pretending to show passion and love
To Man, and indignation at his wrong,	For man and to be indignant at the wrong done to him
New part puts on, and as to passion mov'd,	Puts on new acts, and as if he was shaken by anger
Fluctuats disturbd, yet comely and in act	Ripples disturbed, though still handsome and looking
Rais'd, as of som great matter to begin.	Noble, as if he was about to talk of some great matter.
As when of old som Orator renound	It was like ancient times when some famous orator
In Athens or free Rome, where Eloquence	In Athens or the Roman Republic, where eloquence
Flourishd, since mute, to som great cause addrest,	Flourished but has since vanished, spoke of some great cause,
Stood in himself collected, while each part,	Standing in control of himself, while each part,

Motion, each act won audience ere the tongue,
Somtimes in highth began, as no delay

Of Preface brooking through his Zeal
of Right.
So standing, moving, or to highth upgrown

The Tempter all impassiond thus began.
O Sacred, Wise, and Wisdom-giving Plant,

Mother of Science, Now I feel thy Power

Within me cleere, not onely to discerne
Things in thir Causes, but to trace the ways

Of highest Agents, deemd however wise.

Queen of this Universe, doe not believe
Those rigid threats of Death; ye shall not Die:
How should ye? by the Fruit? it gives you Life
To Knowledge, By the Threatner, look on mee,
Mee who have touch'd and tasted, yet both live,
And life more perfet have attaind then Fate

Meant mee, by ventring higher then my Lot.
Shall that be shut to Man, which to the Beast
Is open? or will God incense his ire

For such a petty Trespass, and not praise

Rather your dauntless vertue, whom the pain
Of Death denounc't, whatever thing Death be,
Deterrd not from atchieving what might leade
To happier life, knowledge of Good and Evil;
Of good, how just? of evil, if what is evil

Movement or action won over the audience before the tongue
Began right at the middle, as if he could not allow the delay
Of a prologue to obstruct his righteous passion.
So, standing, moving, or drawing himself up to his full height,
The tempter passionately began.
"Oh sacred, wise and wisdom giving plant,
Mother of Knowledge, now I can feel your power
Clearly within me, not only seeing
The causes of things but understanding the thoughts
Of the very highest, however wise they are thought.
Queen of this universe, do not believe
These stern threats of death; you shall not die:
How could you? From the fruit? It gives you life
Through knowledge! Look at the one who threatens you, look at me,
Who has both touched and tasted, and we both live,
And I have gained a life more perfect than Fate
Meant for me, by aiming higher than my place.
Shall humans not have that which is available
To the beasts? Or will God become angry
At such a tiny transgression? Won't he rather praise
Your bravery at rejecting the pain
Of death, whatever that is,

Undeterred from trying something which might lead
To a happier life, a knowledge of good and evil;
How right would it be to know of

	good? Of evil,
Be real, why not known, since easier shunnd?	If that exists, why should you not know, so it would be easier to avoid?
God therefore cannot hurt ye, and be just;	God would not be fair in punishing you;
Not just, not God; not feard then, nor obeyd:	And if he is not fair he is not God; then he would not be feared or obeyed:
Your feare it self of Death removes the feare.	You fear of death takes away the fear.
Why then was this forbid? Why but to awe,	Then why was this forbidden? Why except to awe you,
Why but to keep ye low and ignorant,	To keep you low and ignorant,
His worshippers; he knows that in the day	Worshipping him; he knows that the day
Ye Eate thereof, your Eyes that seem so cleere,	You eat from the tree, your eyes, which you think are so clear
Yet are but dim, shall perfetly be then	But are actually dim, shall be perfectly
Op'nd and cleerd, and ye shall be as Gods,	Opened and cleared, and you shall be like Gods,
Knowing both Good and Evil as they know.	Knowing both good and evil as they do.
That ye should be as Gods, since I as Man,	That you should be Gods is only keeping things in order,
Internal Man, is but proportion meet,	Since I am a man, inside at least;
I of brute human, yee of human Gods.	I am a brute become human, so you as humans should become Gods.
So ye shall die perhaps, by putting off	So perhaps you will die, by stopping being human
Human, to put on Gods, death to be wisht,	And becoming Gods. You are threatened with death;
Though threat'nd, which no worse then this can bring.	If that's the worst it can bring then you should wish for it.
And what are Gods that Man may not become	And what are Gods that man should not become like them,
As they, participating God-like food?	Sharing in the food of the Gods?
The Gods are first, and that advantage use	The Gods were here first, and they use that adavantage
On our belief, that all from them proceeds;	To manipulate out belief, saying all comes from them;
I question it, for this fair Earth I see,	I question that, for I see this fair Earth,
Warm'd by the Sun, producing every kind,	Warmed by the sun, producing everything
Them nothing: If they all things, who	While they produce nothing; if they

enclos'd
Knowledge of Good and Evil in this Tree,

That whoso eats thereof, forthwith attains

Wisdom without their leave? and wherein lies
Th' offence, that Man should thus attain to know?
What can your knowledge hurt him, or this Tree

Impart against his will if all be his?

Or is it envie, and can envie dwell
In Heav'nly brests? these, these and many more
Causes import your need of this fair Fruit.

Goddess humane, reach then, and freely taste.
He ended, and his words replete with guile

Into her heart too easie entrance won:
Fixt on the Fruit she gaz'd, which to behold

Might tempt alone, and in her ears the sound
Yet rung of his perswasive words, impregn'd
With Reason, to her sccming, and with Truth;
Mean while the hour of Noon drew on, and wak'd
An eager appetite, rais'd by the smell
So savorie of that Fruit, which with desire,
Inclinable now grown to touch or taste,

Sollicited her longing eye; yet first

Pausing a while, thus to her self she mus'd.

Great are thy Vertues, doubtless, best of Fruits.
Though kept from Man, and worthy to be admir'd,

made everything, who
Put knowledge of good and evil in this tree,
So that whoever eats from it at once gains
Wisdom without their permission?
And why is it wrong
That man should want to gain knowledge?
How can your knowledge do God any harm, or this tree

Give it against his will, if he made everything?
Or is it envy, and can envy live
In Heavenly hearts? These, and many more, arguments
Show that you should have this fair fruit.
Human Goddess, reach out and taste freely."
He ended, and his words, loaded with trickery,
Sneaked into her heart too easily:
She stared at the fruit, just the sight of which
Was enough to tempt, and in her ears

His persuasive words rang, packed

With logic, it seemed to her, and with truth;
Meanwhile noon approached, and awoke
A sharp hunger in her, made worse
By the savory smell of the fruit,
Which she was now much inclined to touch or taste,
And which called to her longing gaze; but first
She paused for a while, and thought to herself.
"You have great powers, no doubt, best of fruits,
Though you have been kept from Man, and are worthy of admiration.

Whose taste, too long forborn, at first assay

Gave elocution to the mute, and taught
The Tongue not made for Speech to speak thy
praise:
Thy praise hee also who forbids thy use,
Conceales not from us, naming thee the Tree
Of Knowledge, knowledge both of good and evil;
Forbids us then to taste, but his forbidding

Commends thee more, while it inferrs the good
By thee communicated, and our want:

For good unknown, sure is not had, or had

And yet unknown, is as not had at all.

In plain then, what forbids he but to know,

Forbids us good, forbids us to be wise?

Such prohibitions binde not. But if Death

Bind us with after-bands, what profits then
Our inward freedom? In the day we eate

Of this fair Fruit, our doom is, we shall die.

How dies the Serpent? hee hath eat'n and lives,
And knows, and speaks, and reasons, and discerns,
Irrational till then. For us alone

Was death invented? or to us deni'd
This intellectual food, for beasts reserv'd?

For Beasts it seems: yet that one Beast which first
Hath tasted, envies not, but brings with joy

Your taste, too long unknown, at the first try,

*Gave speech to the mute, and taught
The tongue not made for speech to
praise you.*

*He who forbids us to taste you
Does not hide you goodness, calling you the Tree
Of Knowledge, knowledge of both good and evil;
He forbids us to taste, but his forbidding*

*Makes you more attractive, as it speaks of the good
Which you can bring, and how we need it;*

*For if we don't know we are given good things, then there is no good,
Or if we do have them and don't know it, then it's as if we don't really have them.*

Put simply then, what is he forbidding us but knowledge?

Is he forbidding us good, forbidding us to be wise?

Such rules cannot be binding. But if death

*Captures us afterwards, what use will
Our inner freedom be then? The day we eat*

This fair fruit it is fated that we shall die.

*But is the serpent dead? He has eaten from the tree and lives,
And knows, speaks, reasons and has perception,
And he was without reason before.
Was death invented*

*Just for us? Or to keep us from
This brain enhancing food, saved for beasts?*

*It seems it is for beasts, but the first beast
To taste it does not become selfish but*

The good befall'n him, Author unsuspect,

Friendly to man, farr from deceit or guile.

What fear I then, rather what know to feare

Under this ignorance of good and Evil,
Of God or Death, of Law or Penaltie?

Here grows the Cure of all, this Fruit
Divine,
Fair to the Eye, inviting to the Taste,
Of vertue to make wise: what hinders then

To reach, and feed at once both Bodie and
Mind?
So saying, her rash hand in evil hour

Forth reaching to the Fruit, she pluck'd,
she eat:
Earth felt the wound, and Nature from her
seat
Sighing through all her Works gave signs
of woe,
That all was lost. Back to the Thicket slunk

The guiltie Serpent, and well might, for Eve

 Intent now wholly on her taste, naught else

Regarded, such delight till then, as seemd,

In Fruit she never tasted, whether true

Or fansied so, through expectation high

Of knowledg, nor was God-head from her
thought.
Greedily she ingorg'd without restraint,
And knew not eating Death: Satiate at
length,
And hight'nd as with Wine, jocond and
boon,
Thus to her self she pleasingly began.

happily shares
The good which has come to him,
with the creator ignorant,
Friendly to man, far from lies or
trickery.
What should I be afraid of then? I
don't know what to fear
In my ignorance of good and evil,
Of God or death, of law and
punishments.
Here is the cure for this, this
heavenly fruit,
Lovely to the eye, inviting to taste,
With the power of giving wisdom:
what's to stop me

Picking it, and feeding the body and
mind at the same time?"
Saying this, her foolish hand, in that
evil moment,
Reached out for the fruit, she picked
it, she ate it:
Earth felt pain, and Nature in her
home
Sighed through all her works with
signs of sorrow
That all was lost. Back to the thicket
crept
The guilty serpent, which he did
unstopped as Eve,
Thinking only about what she tasted,
disregarded
Everything else. It seemed she had
never found such
Taste in any fruit before, whether this
was true or
She just imagined it, because of her
expectations
Of knowledge, and she was still
thinking of becoming Godlike.
She gobbled greedily, uncontrolled,
And did not know she was eating
death: full at last,
And lifted as if with wine, jolly and
cheerful,
She thought to herself, pleased,

O Sovran, vertuous, precious of all Trees

In Paradise, of operation blest
To Sapience, hitherto obscur'd, infam'd,

And thy fair Fruit let hang, as to no end

Created; but henceforth my early care,

Not without Song, each Morning, and due praise
Shall tend thee, and the fertil burden ease

Of thy full branches offer'd free to all;
Till dieted by thee I grow mature
In knowledge, as the Gods who all things know;

Though others envie what they cannot give;
For had the gift bin theirs, it had not here

Thus grown. Experience, next to thee I owe,

Best guide; not following thee, I had remaind
In ignorance, thou op'nst Wisdoms way,

And giv'st access, though secret she retire.

And I perhaps am secret; Heav'n is high,

High and remote to see from thence distinct
Each thing on Earth; and other care perhaps

May have diverted from continual watch
Our great Forbidder, safe with all his Spies

About him. But to Adam in what sort
Shall I appeer? shall I to him make known

As yet my change, and give him to partake
Full happiness with mee, or rather not,

But keep the odds of Knowledge in my power

"Oh King, powerful, most precious of all the trees
In Paradise, blessed with the power
To give wisdom, which was before hidden and wronged,
And your fair fruit was left to hang, as if made
For nothing; but from now on the first thing
I do each morning, with song and due praise,
Will be to care for you, and I shall take the weight
Off your full branches, offered to all,
Until fed by you I grow full
Of knowledge, like the Gods who know everything;
They might be jealous of what they don't have the power to give,
For if it had been theirs to give it would not
Have grown here. Experience, I am in your debt,
The best guide; if I hadn't followed you I would still
Be ignorant; you opened up the path of wisdom
And let me in, though she is well hidden.
Perhaps I am hidden too; Heaven is high,
High and too far off to see clearly
Every thing on Earth; maybe other cares
Have distracted our great forbidder
From his continual watch, secure with all his spies
Around him. But how shall I appear to Adam? Shall I let him now how I've changed
Straight away, and let him join in
Full happiness with me, or keep it back,
And keep the power of knowledge for myself

324

Without Copartner? so to add what wants	*Without sharing? That way I could add to what is lacking*
In Femal Sex, the more to draw his Love,	*In females, to make him love me more,*
And render me more equal, and perhaps,	*And make me more equal, and maybe,*
A thing not undesireable, somtime	*Something which is not undesirable, at some point*
Superior: for inferior who is free?	*Superior; for who is free if they are inferior?*
This may be well: but what if God have seen	*This is all good, but what if God has seen*
And Death ensue? then I shall be no more,	*And death follows? Then I shall be gone,*
And Adam wedded to another Eve,	*And Adam will marry another Eve*
Shall live with her enjoying, I extinct;	*And be happy in his life with her, while I am extinct;*
A death to think. Confirm'd then I resolve,	*It's like death to even think of. So I am decided:*
Adam shall share with me in bliss or woe:	*Adam will share with me in joy or sorrow;*
So dear I love him, that with him all deaths	*I love him so much that I could face all deaths*
I could endure, without him live no life.	*With him, and without him I could not face life."*
So saying, from the Tree her step she turnd,	*Saying this, she turned away from the tree,*
But first low Reverence don, as to the power	*First bowing low to it, as if to the power*
That dwelt within, whose presence had infus'd	*Inside it, whose presence had filled*
Into the plant sciential sap, deriv'd	*That plant with the sap of knowledge, made*
From Nectar, drink of Gods. Adam the while	*From nectar, the drink of the Gods. Meanwhile Adam,*
Waiting desirous her return, had wove	*Waiting fondly for her return, had woven her*
Of choicest Flours a Garland to adorne	*A garland of the best flowers to decorate*
Her Tresses, and her rural labours crown,	*Her hair, and reward her gardening work,*
As Reapers oft are wont thir Harvest Queen.	*Just as peasants often crown their Harvest Queen.*
Great joy he promis'd to his thoughts, and new	*He promised himself that great happiness was coming*

Solace in her return, so long delay'd;

Yet oft his heart, divine of somthing ill,

Misgave him; hee the faultring measure felt;

And forth to meet her went, the way she took

That Morn when first they parted; by the Tree

Of Knowledge he must pass, there he her met,

Scarse from the Tree returning; in her hand

A bough of fairest fruit that downie smil'd,

New gatherd, and ambrosial smell diffus'd.

To him she hasted, in her face excuse

Came Prologue, and Apologie to prompt,

Which with bland words at will she thus addrest.

Hast thou not wonderd, Adam, at my stay?

Thee I have misst, and thought it long, depriv'd

Thy presence, agonie of love till now

Not felt, nor shall be twice, for never more

Mean I to trie, what rash untri'd I sought,

The pain of absence from thy sight. But strange

Hath bin the cause, and wonderful to heare:

This Tree is not as we are told, a Tree

Of danger tasted, nor to evil unknown

Op'ning the way, but of Divine effect

To open Eyes, and make them Gods who taste;

And hath bin tasted such: the Serpent wise,

In the sweetness of her return which had been put off for so long;

But often his heart, which had an inkling that something was wrong,

Worried him; he felt its nervous beat

And went out to meet her, taking the way she had

That morning when they parted for the first time; he had to pass

By the Tree of Knowledge, and he met her there,

Just coming back from the tree; in her hand

Was a branch of that fairest fruit softly gleaming,

Newly picked and spreading its heavenly scent.

She hurried up to him, with an excuse showing in her face,

The forerunner of an apology,

Which she began with bland words:

"Did you wonder, Adam, why I was away so long?

I have missed you, and the time dragged without

You, a pain of love which I never felt

Until now, and never will again, for I shall never

Suffer again what I foolishly suffered in my ignorance,

The pain of being without you. But there is a strange

Cause for my absence, wonderful to hear of:

This tree is not the thing we were told it was,

A tree dangerous to taste; it doesn't open the way

To unknown evil, but it has the divine effect

Of opening the eyes, and making those who taste into Gods;

This has been proved by tasting; the

Or not restraind as wee, or not obeying,
Hath eat'n of the fruit, and is become,

Not dead, as we are threatn'd, but thenceforth

Endu'd with human voice and human sense,

Reasoning to admiration, and with mee
Perswasively hath so prevaild, that I
Have also tasted, and have also found
Th' effects to correspond, opener mine Eyes

Dimm erst, dilated Spirits, ampler Heart,

And growing up to Godhead; which for thee
Chiefly I sought, without thee can despise.

For bliss, as thou hast part, to me is bliss,

Tedious, unshar'd with thee, and odious soon.
Thou therefore also taste, that equal Lot

May joyne us, equal Joy, as equal Love;

Least thou not tasting, different degree

Disjoyne us, and I then too late renounce

Deitie for thee, when Fate will not permit.

Thus Eve with Countnance blithe her storie told;
But in her Cheek distemper flushing glowd.

On th' other side, Adam, soon as he heard

The fatal Trespass don by Eve, amaz'd,

Astonied stood and Blank, while horror chill
Ran through his veins, and all his joynts relax'd;

serpent, wiser
Or bolder than us, or less obedient,
Has eaten the fruit and has not suffered
Death, as we were told would happen, but from then on

He was given a human voice and human senses,
Impressive powers of reason, and he
Worked on me so persuasively that I
Have also tasted, and had
The same results; my eyes are opened wider,
That were dim before; my Spirits have risen, my heart is more full
And I am becoming like a God; I looked for this
Mainly for you; without you I wouldn't want it.
For bliss shared with you is bliss for me,
Not shared with you it is dull and soon hateful.
So you taste as well, so that we are joined
With equal shares, with equal joy, equal love.
If you will not taste then we will be parted
By being of different levels, and then it will be too late
To renounce my Godship for you, Fate will not allow it."
This is how Eve told her story with a happy face,
But on her cheek there was a furious blush.
On the other hand Adam, as soon as he heard
Of the terrible sin committed by Eve, stood shocked
And horrified, stunned, while cold terror
Ran through his veins, and all his joints trembled;

From his slack hand the Garland wreath'd for Eve	*From his limp hand the garland he had made for Eve*
Down drop'd, and all the faded Roses shed:	*Dropped down and shed its faded roses:*
Speechless he stood and pale, till thus at length	*He stood speechless and pale, until at last*
First to himself he inward silence broke.	*He first broke his silence by speaking to himself:*
O fairest of Creation, last and best	*"Oh fairest of creation, the last and best*
Of all Gods works, Creature in whom excell'd	*Of all God's works, the creature who was the peak*
Whatever can to sight or thought be formd,	*Of everything that can be made of sight or thought,*
Holy, divine, good, amiable, or sweet!	*Holy, divine, good amiable or sweet!*
How art thou lost, how on a sudden lost,	*How have you fallen, so suddenly,*
Defac't, deflourd, and now to Death devote?	*Defaced, deflowered, and now marked out for death?*
Rather how hast thou yeelded to transgress	*How were you persuaded to disobey*
The strict forbiddance, how to violate	*That strict injunction, to violate*
The sacred Fruit forbidd'n! som cursed fraud	*That sacred forbidden fruit! Some cursed trick*
Of Enemie hath beguil'd thee, yet unknown,	*Of the enemy, not yet known, has seduced you,*
And mee with thee hath ruind, for with thee	*And has ruined me with you, for I am determined*
Certain my resolution is to Die;	*That I shall die with you;*
How can I live without thee, how forgoe	*How can I live without you, do without*
Thy sweet Converse and Love so dearly joyn'd,	*Your sweet conversation and the love so sweetly united*
To live again in these wilde Woods forlorn?	*To live alone again in these wild woods?*
Should God create another Eve, and I	*If God created another Eve, and I*
Another Rib afford, yet loss of thee	*Could spare another rib, the loss of you*
Would never from my heart; no no, I feel	*Would never leave my heart; no, no, I feel*
The Link of Nature draw me: Flesh of Flesh,	*The ties of Nature leading me; you are flesh of my flesh,*
Bone of my Bone thou art, and from thy State	*Bone of my bone, and from your condition*
Mine never shall be parted, bliss or woe.	*Mine shall never be separated, whether happiness or sorrow."*
So having said, as one from sad dismay	*Having said this he seemed as one who is comforted*

Recomforted, and after thoughts disturbd	*Again after sad dismay, and who after disturbed thoughts*
Submitting to what seemd remediless,	*Gives in to what seems incurable,*
Thus in calm mood his Words to Eve he turnd.	*And so he turned to Eve in a calm mood.*
Bold deed thou hast presum'd, adventrous Eve	*"You have done a bold deed, adventurous Eve,*
And peril great provok't, who thus hath dar'd	*And anyone who dares this risks great danger*
Had it been onely coveting to Eye	*Even if it had only been coveting by looking*
That sacred Fruit, sacred to abstinence,	*At that holy fruit, which God commands cannot be eaten,*
Much more to taste it under banne to touch.	*And it's much worse to taste it when we were banned from even touching.*
But past who can recall, or don undoe?	*But who can call back the past or undo what's done?*
Not God Omnipotent, nor Fate, yet so	*Not all powerful God, nor fate, but maybe*
Perhaps thou shalt not Die, perhaps the Fact	*You won't die, perhaps the deed*
Is not so hainous now, foretasted Fruit,	*Is not so terrible now after the fruits was already tasted,*
Profan'd first by the Serpent, by him first	*Polluted first by the serpent, maybe he made it*
Made common and unhallowd ere our taste;	*Common and unholy before we tasted it;*
Nor yet on him found deadly, he yet lives,	*And it hasn't proved deadly to him, he still lives,*
Lives, as thou saidst, and gaines to live as Man	*Lives, as you said, and gains a life like man's,*
Higher degree of Life, inducement strong	*A higher life, a strong temptation for us,*
To us, as likely tasting to attaine	*As we would be likely to rise up*
Proportional ascent, which cannot be	*To the same degree, which could only mean*
But to be Gods, or Angels Demi-gods.	*That we would become Gods, or angels, demigods.*
Nor can I think that God, Creator wise,	*And I cannot believe that God, the wise creator,*
Though threatning, will in earnest so destroy	*Although he threatened it, will really destroy*
Us his prime Creatures, dignifi'd so high,	*His most important creatures, given such high position,*
Set over all his Works, which in our Fall,	*Ruling over all his works, and if we fall*
For us created, needs with us must faile,	*They must collapse too,*

Dependent made; so God shall uncreate,

Be frustrate, do, undo, and labour loose,

Not well conceav'd of God, who though his Power
Creation could repeate, yet would be loath

Us to abolish, least the Adversary
Triumph and say; Fickle their State whom God
Most Favors, who can please him long; Mee first
He ruind, now Mankind; whom will he next?
Matter of scorne, not to be given the Foe,

However I with thee have fixt my Lot,
Certain to undergoe like doom, if Death

Consort with thee, Death is to mee as Life;

So forcible within my heart I feel
The Bond of Nature draw me to my owne,

My own in thee, for what thou art is mine;

Our State cannot be severd, we are one,

One Flesh; to loose thee were to loose my self.
So Adam, and thus Eve to him repli'd.
O glorious trial of exceeding Love,

Illustrious evidence, example high!

Ingaging me to emulate, but short
Of thy perfection, how shall I attaine,
Adam, from whose deare side I boast me sprung,
And gladly of our Union heare thee speak,

One Heart, one Soul in both; whereof good proof
This day affords, declaring thee resolvd,

For they were made dependent on us; so God shall unmake,

Be frustrated, do, undo and lose his work,

Which he won't want to do, for although he could remake
Creation through his powers he would hate to

Abolish us, in case the enemy
Should claim victory, saying, 'Those God favors are

On shaky ground, who can keep him pleased for long? First
He ruined me, now mankind; who will suffer next?'
This is ammunition which shouldn't be given to the enemy.

However, I have tied myself to you
And am certain to suffer the same fate if death

Comes to you; death and life are the same to me,

So strongly within my heart do I feel
The bonds of Nature calling out to myself,

I am within you and what you are is mine;

Our natures cannot be separated, we are one,

One flesh; if I lost you I would lose myself."

So Adam said, and Eve answered:
"Oh what an exhibition of the greatness of love,

A shining example, wonderful evidence!

I must try to copy it, but without
Your perfection how can I do so,
Adam, from whose dear side I am proud to have come,

And I am glad to hear you talk of our union,

One heart, one soul in both; this day

Gives true proof of that, as you

330

Rather then Death or aught then Death more dread
Shall separate us, linkt in Love so deare,

To undergoe with mee one Guilt, one Crime,
If any be, of tasting this fair Fruit,

Whose vertue, for of good still good proceeds,
Direct, or by occasion hath presented

This happie trial of thy Love, which else

So eminently never had bin known.

Were it I thought Death menac't would ensue
This my attempt, I would sustain alone

The worst, and not perswade thee, rather die
Deserted, then oblige thee with a fact
Pernicious to thy Peace, chiefly assur'd

Remarkably so late of thy so true,

So faithful Love unequald; but I feel

Farr otherwise th' event, not Death, but Life

Augmented, op'nd Eyes, new Hopes, new Joyes,
Taste so Divine, that what of sweet before

Hath toucht my sense, flat seems to this, and harsh.
On my experience, Adam, freely taste,

And fear of Death deliver to the Windes.

So saying, she embrac'd him, and for joy

Tenderly wept, much won that he his Love

declare
That death, or anything worse than death,
Cannot separate us, joined in such great love,
That you will participate with me in this guilty crime –
If it is a crime – of tasting this fair fruit,
Which has power, for good still comes from it,
Directly, or by the events it has inspired,
This happy trial of your love, which otherwise
Could never have been shown so clearly.
If I really thought that terrible death
Would follow from my actions, I would face the worst
Alone, and not persuade you, I would rather die
Alone than involve you in a crime
Which would damage your peace, particularly
As you have just shown such remarkable proof
Of your unrivalled faithful love; but I feel
That this will not happen, it's not death but
A better life, clearer vision, new hopes, new joys,
With such a divine taste that what I tried
That seemed sweet before now seems flat and harsh.
Follow my example, Adam, freely taste,
And throw fear of death to the winds."
Saying this she embraced him and tenderly wept
With joy, so pleased that he valued his love

Had so enobl'd, as of choice to incur	*So highly that he would choose to incur*
Divine displeasure for her sake, or Death.	*The wrath of God, or death, for her sake.*
In recompence (for such compliance bad	*To repay him (for such wrong agreement*
Such recompence best merits) from the bough	*Deserves such repayment) she gave him*
She gave him of that fair enticing Fruit	*That fair enticing fruit from the branch,*
With liberal hand: he scrupl'd not to eat	*Generously; he ate, not*
Against his better knowledge, not deceav'd,	*Against his better knowledge, not tricked,*
But fondly overcome with Femal charm.	*But sweetly overcome with female charm.*
Earth trembl'd from her entrails, as again	*Earth was shaken to her core, seeming in agony*
In pangs, and Nature gave a second groan,	*Again, and nature gave a second groan,*
Skie lowr'd, and muttering Thunder, som sad drops	*The sky lowered, thunder grumbled and some sad drops*
Wept at compleating of the mortal Sin	*Wept at the commission of Original Sin.*
Original; while Adam took no thought,	*Adam was thoughtless,*
Eating his fill, nor Eve to iterate	*Eating his fill, and Eve was not frightened*
Her former trespass fear'd, the more to soothe	*Of repeating her former sin and joined in*
Him with her lov'd societie, that now	*So that he would be soothed by her loved company, so now*
As with new Wine intoxicated both	*As if they were both drunk on new wine*
They swim in mirth, and fansie that they feel	*They rolled in pleasure, and imagined they felt*
Divinitie within them breeding wings	*Divinity within them, sprouting wings*
Wherewith to scorne the Earth: but that false Fruit	*With which they could reject the Earth; but that false fruit*
Farr other operation first displaid,	*Showed quite a different effect,*
Carnal desire enflaming, hee on Eve	*Inflaming bodily desires, he began to look*
Began to cast lascivious Eyes, she him	*At Eve with lustful eyes, and she looked*
As wantonly repaid; in Lust they burne:	*Just the same; they burned with lust:*
Till Adam thus 'gan Eve to dalliance move,	*Adam began to talk persuasively to Eve,*
Eve, now I see thou art exact of taste,	*"Eve, I see you have perfect taste,*

And elegant, of Sapience no small part,	*And elegance, plenty of wisdom,*
Since to each meaning savour we apply,	*Since we taste all those things*
And Palate call judicious; I the praise	*And find them good; I give the praise*
Yeild thee, so well this day thou hast purvey'd.	*To you, you have brought them to us so well today.*
Much pleasure we have lost, while we abstain'd	*We missed much pleasure while we abstained*
From this delightful Fruit, nor known till now	*From this delightful fruit, and until now we did not know*
True relish, tasting; if such pleasure be	*True flavor in taste; if there is such pleasure for us*
In things to us forbidden, it might be wish'd,	*In forbidden things then we might wish*
For this one Tree had bin forbidden ten.	*That instead of one forbidden tree there were ten.*
But come, so well refresh't, now let us play,	*But come, now we're so well refreshed, let's play,*
As meet is, after such delicious Fare;	*As we should after such delicious food;*
For never did thy Beautie since the day	*For you beauty has never, since the day*
I saw thee first and wedded thee, adorn'd	*I first saw and married you, decorated*
With all perfections, so enflame my sense	*With all perfection, so lit up my sense*
With ardor to enjoy thee, fairer now	*With desire to enjoy you, lovlier now*
Then ever, bountie of this vertuous Tree.	*Than ever, thanks to the power of this tree."*
So said he, and forbore not glance or toy	*So he spoke, and he did not hold back from looks and gestures*
Of amorous intent, well understood	*Which showed his desire, which was well understood*
Of Eve, whose Eye darted contagious Fire.	*By Eve, whose eyes burned with infectious heat.*
Her hand he seis'd, and to a shadie bank,	*He grabbed her hand and led her, unresisting,*
Thick overhead with verdant roof imbowr'd	*To a shady bank with a thick green roof;*
He led her nothing loath; Flours were the Couch,	*Flowers were the bed,*
Pansies, and Violets, and Asphodel,	*Pansies, violets and asphodel,*
And Hyacinth, Earths freshest softest lap.	*And hyacinth, the freshest and softest cushion on Earth.*
There they thir fill of Love and Loves disport	*There they greedily enjoyed love and the games*
Took largely, of thir mutual guilt the Seale,	*Of love, the seal of their mutual guilt*

The solace of thir sin, till dewie sleep

Oppress'd them, wearied with thir amorous play.
Soon as the force of that fallacious Fruit,
That with exhilerating vapour bland
About thir spirits had plaid, and inmost powers
Made erre, was now exhal'd, and grosser sleep
Bred of unkindly fumes, with conscious dreams
Encumberd, now had left them, up they rose
As from unrest, and each the other viewing,

Soon found thir Eyes how op'nd, and thir minds
How dark'nd; innocence, that as a veile

Had shadow'd them from knowing ill, was gon,
Just confidence, and native righteousness

And honour from about them, naked left

To guiltie shame hee cover'd, but his Robe

Uncover'd more, so rose the Danite strong

Herculean Samson from the Harlot-lap
Of Philistean Dalilah, and wak'd

Shorn of his strength, They destitute and bare
Of all thir vertue: silent, and in face

Confounded long they sate, as struck'n mute,
Till Adam, though not less then Eve abasht,

At length gave utterance to these words constraind.
O Eve, in evil hour thou didst give eare

Which soothed their sin, until heavy sleep

Came over them, tired out by their lovemaking.
Soon the strength of that false fruit
That with its exhilarating scent
Had played with their spirits, and given them
Inner powers, was breathed out, and troubled sleep,
Bred from unnatural fumes and with guilty dreams,
Fell upon them. It left them, and they rose
As if they had never slept, and looking at each other
Soon found that with their eyes opened their minds were
Darkened; innocence, which had been like a veil
Stopping them from seeing ill, was gone,
And so was simple honesty and natural piety
And honor, all gone and they were left naked.
Adam covered himself up in guilty shame, but his robe
Showed more; just as the Danite Samson, strong
As Hercules, had risen from the lap
Of the Philistine harlot Delilah, and woken
Stripped of all his strength, so they were stripped
Of all their virtue: they were silent, and with confused
Looks they sat for a long time, as if struck dumb,
Until Adam, though no less ashamed than Eve,
Finally spoke these forced words:
"Oh Eve, it was an evil hour when you listened

334

To that false Worm, of whomsoever taught

To counterfet Mans voice, true in our Fall,

False in our promis'd Rising; since our
Eyes
Op'nd we find indeed, and find we know

Both Good and Evil, Good lost, and Evil
got,
Bad Fruit of Knowledge, if this be to know,

Which leaves us naked thus, of
Honour void,
Of Innocence, of Faith, of Puritie,
Our wonted Ornaments now soild and
staind,
And in our Faces evident the signes

Of foul concupiscence; whence evil store;

Even shame, the last of evils; of the first

Be sure then. How shall I behold the face

Henceforth of God or Angel, earst with joy

And rapture so oft beheld? those heav'nly
shapes
Will dazle now this earthly, with thir blaze

Insufferably bright. O might I here

In solitude live savage, in some glade
Obscur'd, where highest Woods
impenetrable
To Starr or Sun-light, spread thir umbrage
broad,
And brown as Evening: Cover me ye Pines,

Ye Cedars, with innumerable boughs

Hide me, where I may never see them
more.
But let us now, as in bad plight, devise

---

*To that false worm, taught by
somebody*

*To imitate the voice of Man, truthful
in saying we would fall,*

*Lying about our promised rise; since
our eyes*

*Have been opened we have indeed
discovered that we know*

*Both good and evil; good lost and
evil found.*

*The fruit of knowledge is harmful, if
this is what it means to know,*

Leaving us naked, stripped of honor,

Of innocence, faith, purity,
*Our usual decorations which are now
soiled and stained,*

*And in our faces you can see the
signs*

*Of foul longings, a great store of
them,*

*And you can see shame, the last of
evils, so you can be sure*

*What the first one was. How can I
look on the face*

*Of God or an angel from now on, that
I used to see*

*With such joy and rapture? Those
heavenly shapes*

*Will dazzle this earthly one, with their
blaze*

*Insufferably bright. I wish I could live
here*

*Alone, like a savage, in some hidden
Clearing, where the highest woods,
impenetrable*

*By star or sunlight, spread their wide
shadows,*

*And it is dark as evening; cover me
you pines,*

*You cedars, with numberless
branches*

*Hide me, so I never have to see them
again.*

But let us now, in this awful position,

	devise
What best may for the present serve to hide	*Something which can for the present serve*
The Parts of each from other, that seem most	*To hide our parts from each other, they seem*
To shame obnoxious, and unseemliest seen,	*In our shame to be the most horrid and immodest.*
Some Tree whose broad smooth Leaves together sowd,	*If we take the broad smooth leaves of some tree and sew them together*
And girded on our loyns, may cover round	*And tie them round our waists, that may cover*
Those middle parts, that this new commer, Shame,	*These middle parts so that we do not feel this new emotion, shame,*
There sit not, and reproach us as unclean	*Reproaching us for being unclean."*
So counsel'd hee, and both together went	*So he advised, and they went together*
Into the thickest Wood, there soon they chose	*Into the thickest wood, where they soon settled on*
The Figtree, not that kind for Fruit renown'd,	*The fig tree, not the kind that is known for its fruit*
But such as at this day to Indians known	*But the type that is known in our times to Indians,*
In Malabar or Decan spreds her Armes	*That spreads its branches in Malabar or Decan,*
Braunching so broad and long, that in the ground	*So broad and long that the bended twigs*
The bended Twigs take root, and Daughters grow	*Take root in the ground, and daughters grow*
About the Mother Tree, a Pillard shade	*Around the mother tree, making a pillared roof*
High overarch't, and echoing Walks between;	*In a high arch, with echoing paths between;*
There oft the Indian Herdsman shunning heate	*There often the Indian herdsman, shunning heat,*
Shelters in coole, and tends his pasturing Herds	*Shelters in the cool, and cares for his grazing herds*
At Loopholes cut through thickest shade: Those Leaves	*Through holes cut in the thickest shade; these were the leaves*
They gatherd, broad as Amazonian Targe,	*They gathered, as broad as the shields of Amazons,*
And with what skill they had, together sowd,	*And with what skill they had they sewed them together*
To gird thir waste, vain Covering if to hide	*To go round their waists, a vain covering if they thought*
Thir guilt and dreaded shame; O how unlike	*It could hide their guilt and shame; how different*

To that first naked Glorie. Such of late

Columbus found th' American so girt

With featherd Cincture, naked else and wilde
Among the Trees on Iles and woodie Shores.
Thus fenc't, and as they thought, thir shame in part
Coverd, but not at rest or ease of Mind,

They sate them down to weep, nor onely Teares
Raind at thir Eyes, but high Winds worse within
Began to rise, high Passions, Anger, Hate,

Mistrust, Suspicion, Discord, and shook sore
Thir inward State of Mind, calm Region once
And full of Peace, now tost and turbulent:

For Understanding rul'd not, and the Will

Heard not her lore, both in subjection now

To sensual Appetite, who from beneathe

Usurping over sovran Reason claimd

Superior sway: From thus distemperd brest,

Adam, estrang'd in look and alterd stile,

Speech intermitted thus to Eve renewd.
Would thou hadst heark'nd to my words, and stai'd
With me, as I besought thee, when that strange
Desire of wandring this unhappie Morn,

I know not whence possessd thee; we had then

To their original naked glory. This was how in our time

Columbus found the native Americans dressed,

With girdles of feathers, otherwise naked and wild
Amongst the trees on their islands and woody shores.
So dressed, and thinking that they had at least partly covered
Their shame, but restless and troubled in mind

They sat down to weep, and it was not only that tears
That ran from their eyes, but inside them worse storms
Were brewing, high passions, anger, hate,

Mistrust, suspicion, discord, which shook
Their inner minds, once such a calm region,
So full of peace, now tossed and stormy:

Understanding was not in command, and the will

Did not hear her wisdom, they were both now enslaved

To the sensual appetites, which came from below

And overthrew ruling reason, claiming

Superior power; from his disturbed heart

Adam, different in his look and his bearing,

Renewed his halting speech to Eve. "I wish you had listened to me, and stayed
With me, as I asked you to, when that strange
Desire to go wandering possessed you this unhappy morning;

I don't know where it came from. Then we could have

Remaind still happie, not as now, despoild
Of all our good, sham'd, naked, miserable.

Let none henceforth seek needless cause to approve
The Faith they owe; when earnestly they seek
Such proof, conclude, they then begin to faile.
To whom soon mov'd with touch of blame thus Eve.
What words have past thy Lips, Adam severe,
Imput'st thou that to my default, or will

Of wandring, as thou call'st it, which who knows
But might as ill have happ'nd thou being by,

Or to thy self perhaps: hadst thou been there,
Or here th' attempt, thou couldst not have discernd
Fraud in the Serpent, speaking as he spake;

No ground of enmitie between us known,

Why hee should mean me ill, or seek to harme.
Was I to have never parted from thy side?

As good have grown there still a liveless Rib.
Being as I am, why didst not thou the Head

Command me absolutely not to go,
Going into such danger as thou saidst?

Too facil then thou didst not much gainsay,
Nay, didst permit, approve, and fair dismiss.
Hadst thou bin firm and fixt in thy dissent,

Neither had I transgress'd, nor thou with mee.

Stayed happy, not, as now, stripped
Of all our good, shamed, naked and miserable.

Let no-one from now on needlessly try to test
Their beliefs; we can see that when they start
To look for proof then their downfall begins."
Eve replied, having been blamed,

"The words that have passed your lips, severe Adam,
Show that you are blaming me and my desire
To wander, as you call it, but who can say
The same thing wouldn't have happened if you had been there with me,

Or on your own, perhaps: if you had been there
Or heard what happened, you would not have seen
The serpent's trickery, the way he spoke;

There was no animosity between us, I had no reason to think
He meant anything bad or to do me harm.
Should I never have left your side ever?

I may as well have stayed there as a lifeless rib.
Being who I am, why didn't you, as the ruler,
Absolutely order me not to go
If you thought there was as much danger as you've said?

You didn't resist much at the time,
No, you allowed it, approved and gave me a sweet farewell,
If you had been firm and unmoving in your disagreement,
I would not have sinned and nor would you with me."

To whom then first incenst Adam repli'd,
Is this the Love, is this the recompence
Of mine to thee, ingrateful Eve, exprest

Immutable when thou wert lost, not I,

Who might have liv'd and joyd immortal
bliss,
Yet willingly chose rather Death with thee:

And am I now upbraided, as the cause
Of thy transgressing? not enough severe,

It seems, in thy restraint: what could I
more?
I warn'd thee, I admonish'd thee, foretold

The danger, and the lurking Enemie
That lay in wait; beyond this had bin force,

And force upon free Will hath here no
place.
But confidence then bore thee on, secure

Either to meet no danger, or to finde

Matter of glorious trial; and perhaps

I also err'd in overmuch admiring
What seemd in thee so perfet, that I
thought
No evil durst attempt thee, but I rue

That errour now, which is become my
crime,
And thou th' accuser. Thus it shall befall

Him who to worth in Women overtrusting

Lets her Will rule; restraint she will not
brook,
And left to her self, if evil thence ensue,

Shee first his weak indulgence will accuse.

Thus they in mutual accusation spent

Furious, Adam answered her,
"Is this the love I get in return
For the love I give you, ungrateful
Eve, which you said
Was unchangeable when you were
lost and I wasn't,
I who could have lived and enjoyed
immortal bliss,
But willingly chose death with you
instead:
Am I now blamed as the cause
Of your sin? You claim I was not stern
enough
In holding you back; what else should
I have done?
I warned you, I scolded you,
predicted
The danger and the lurking enemy
That lay in wait; the only other thing
would have been to use force,
And force cannot be used against free
will here.
But your cockiness carried you on,
sure
That you would either face no danger
or would find
A chance for a glorious trial; and
perhaps
I was wrong to admire so much
What seemed so perfect in you, so I
thought
No evil would dare come near you,
but I regret
My error now, the error which has
become my crime
With you as my accuser. This is what
happens
To him who trusts women's strength
too much
And so lets her have her way; she will
not be told,
But if she's left to herself and
something bad happens
The first thing she does is call him
weak for giving in."
So they spent useless hours accusing

The fruitless hours, but neither
self-condemning,
And of thir vain contest appeer'd no end.

*Each other, but neither blamed
themselves,
And it seemed the pointless contest
would never end.*

BOOK X

THE ARGUMENT

Mans transgression known, the Guardian Angels forsake Paradise, and return up to Heaven to approve thir vigilance, and are approv'd, God declaring that The entrance of Satan could not be by them prevented. He sends his Son to judge the Transgressors, who descends and gives Sentence accordingly; then in pity cloaths them both, and reascends. Sin and Death sitting till then at the Gates of Hell, by wondrous sympathie feeling the success of Satan in this new World, and the sin by Man there committed, resolve to sit no longer confin'd in Hell, but to follow Satan thir Sire up to the place of Man: To make the way easier from Hell to this World to and fro, they pave a broad Highway or Bridge over Chaos, according to the Track that Satan first made; then preparing for Earth, they meet him proud of his success returning to Hell; thir mutual gratulation. Satan arrives at Pandemonium, in full of assembly relates with boasting his success against Man; instead of applause is entertained with a general hiss by all his audience, transform'd with himself also suddenly into Serpents, according to his doom giv'n in Paradise; then deluded with a shew of the forbidden Tree springing up before them, they greedily reaching to take of the Fruit, chew dust and bitter ashes. The proceedings of Sin and Death; God foretells the final Victory of his Son over them, and the renewing of all things; but for the present commands his Angels to make several alterations in the Heavens and Elements. Adam more and more perceiving his fall'n condition heavily bewailes, rejects the condolement of Eve; she persists and at length appeases him: then to evade the Curse likely to fall on thir Ofspring, proposes to Adam violent wayes which

Man's transgression having been discovered, the guardian Angels Angels leave Paradise and return to Heaven to explain, and are told they are not to blame, God saying that they could not have done anything to prevent Satan entering. He sends his Son to judge the transgressors. He descends and gives sentence, then out of pity he clothes them and returns. Sin and Death, sitting at the Gates of Hell, through their connection to Satan feel that he has succeeded in the new world, and feeling that man has sinned they resolve to leave Hell and make their way to the world of men. To make the journey to and from Hell easier they build a great bridge over the abyss of Chaos, following the path Satan first took. They meet him returning from Earth and they congratulate each other. Satan arrives at Pandemonium and boasts of his great success; instead of applause he is greeted by a hiss, as he and all the others are transformed into serpents, as Heaven had decreed. Then they are tricked by an illusion of the forbidden tree appearing in from of them, with fruit which turns to dust and ashes as they try to eat it. We see the proceedings of Sin and Death. God foretells the final victory of the Son over them, and the renewing of all things. For the present he orders the angels to make several alterations in the Heavens and the Elements. Adam becomes more aware of his fallen condition and complains of his fate, rejecting Eve's attempts to console him. She persists and appeases him at last, then proposes that they commit

he approves not, but conceiving better hope, puts her in mind of the late Promise made them, that her Seed should be reveng'd on the Serpent, and exhorts her with him to seek Peace of the offended Deity, by repentance and supplication.

suicide to avoid the curse which will fall on their children. He rejects this and offers a better plan, reminding her that they were promised their children would be revenged on the the serpent, and encourages her, with him, to seek peace with God through repentance and prayer.

Meanwhile the hainous and despightfull act
Of Satan done in Paradise, and how

Hee in the Serpent, had perverted Eve,

Her Husband shee, to taste the fatall fruit,

Was known in Heav'n; for what can scape the Eye
Of God All-seeing, or deceave his Heart

Omniscient, who in all things wise and just,
Hinder'd not Satan to attempt the minde

Of Man, with strength entire, and free will arm'd,
Complete to have discover'd and repulst

Whatever wiles of Foe or seeming Friend.

For still they knew, and ought to have still remember'd
The high Injunction not to taste that Fruit,
Whoever tempted; which they not obeying,

Incurr'd, what could they less, the penaltie,

And manifold in sin, deserv'd to fall.

Up into Heav'n from Paradise in haste
Th' Angelic Guards ascended, mute and sad
For Man, for of his state by this they knew,
Much wondring how the suttle Fiend had stoln
Entrance unseen. Soon as th' unwelcome

Meanwhile the horrible and spiteful act
Committed by Satan in Paradise, and how

Disguised as the serpent he had led Eve astray,
And her husband with her, to taste the fatal fruit,
Was known in Heaven, for what escapes the eye of
All seeing God, or deceives his all knowing heart?

Just and wise in all things,
He did not stop Satan from testing the mind
Of Man, with his full strength and armed with free will,
Fully able to have discovered and rejected
Any tricks of an enemy or apparent friend.

For they knew, and should not have forgotten,
The high order not to taste that fruit,
Whoever tempted them; they did not obey
And so incurred (what less could they expect?) the penalty,
And having committed many sins, deserved to fall.

Up to Heaven, silent and sad
For Man, for by this time they knew what had happened,
And were perplexed as to how the cunning fiend
Had sneaked in. As soon as the

news
From Earth arriv'd at Heaven Gate, displeas'd

All were who heard, dim sadness did not spare
That time Celestial visages, yet mixt

With pitie, violated not thir bliss.

About the new-arriv'd, in multitudes

Th' ethereal People ran, to hear and know
How all befell: they towards the Throne Supream
Accountable made haste to make appear
With righteous plea, thir utmost vigilance,

And easily approv'd; when the most High

Eternal Father from his secret Cloud,

Amidst in Thunder utter'd thus his voice.
Assembl'd Angels, and ye Powers return'd

From unsuccessful charge, be not dismaid,

Nor troubl'd at these tidings from the Earth,
Which your sincerest care could not prevent,
Foretold so lately what would come to pass,
When first this Tempter cross'd the Gulf from Hell.
I told ye then he should prevail and speed

On his bad Errand, Man should be seduc't

And flatter'd out of all, believing lies

Against his Maker; no Decree of mine
Concurring to necessitate his Fall,
Or touch with lightest moment of impulse
His free Will, to her own inclining left
In eevn scale. But fall'n he is, and now

unwelcome news
From Earth arrived at Heaven's gate, all

Who heard were displeased, the cloud of sadness
Was over their heavenly faces, and it was mixed

With pity, though it did not disturb their heavenly bliss.

The people of Heaven ran to the new arrivals

In crowds, to hear and to know
What had happened; they made haste towards
The highest throne to tell,
With righteous pleading, how they had been completely vigilant,

And they were quickly exonerated; the most high

Eternal Father spoke in a voice like thunder

From inside his covering cloud.
"Assembled angels, and you forces returned

From your unsuccessful mission, do not be dismayed

Or troubled by this news from Earth.
Your best efforts could not have prevented it,
For it was recently foretold that this would happen,
When the tempter first crossed the abyss from Hell.
I told you then that he would prevail and succeed

On his bad errand, that Man would be seduced

And enticed away from everything, believing lies

Against his maker; no decree of mine
Forced him to fall,
Or in the slightest way interfered with
His free will, which was left balanced
To tip as it chose. But he has fallen, and now

What rests but that the mortal Sentence pass
On his transgression Death denounc't that day,
Which he presumes already vain and void,

Because not yet inflicted, as he fear'd,

By some immediate stroak; but soon shall find
Forbearance no acquittance ere day end.

Justice shall not return as bountie scorn'd.

But whom send I to judge them? whom but thee
Vicegerent Son, to thee I have transferr'd

All Judgement whether in Heav'n, or Earth, or Hell.
Easie it might be seen that I intend

Mercie collegue with Justice, sending thee
Mans Friend his Mediator, his design'd

Both Ransom and Redeemer voluntarie,

And destin'd Man himself to judge Man fall'n.
So spake the Father, and unfoulding bright

Toward the right hand his Glorie, on the Son
Blaz'd forth unclouded Deitie; he full
Resplendent all his Father manifest

Express'd, and thus divinely answer'd milde.
Father Eternal, thine is to decree,
Mine both in Heav'n and Earth to do thy will
Supream, that thou in mee thy Son belov'd

Mayst ever rest well pleas'd. I go to judge
On Earth these thy transgressors, but thou knowst,

All that is left is that we pass on him the mortal sentence
Of death for his transgression, that he disregarded
And thinks is empty and invalid,

Because it has not happened yet, as he feared it would,

With some immediate blow; but he will soon find
Before the end of the day, that the delay does not mean acquittal.

Justice will come to them and cannot be denied.

But who shall I send to judge them? Who else but you,
My viceregent Son, I have transferred all powers
Of judgement to you, whether in Heaven, on Earth or in Hell.

This way it will be easy to see that I intend
To join mercy to justice, sending you,
Man's friend and mediator, the one chosen

Voluntarily as his ransom and redeemer,

The one who will become a man judging Man fallen."
So the Father spoke, and uncovering his light

Towards his right hand side he shone
The full light of God upon the Son; he
Was shining and showed all his father's glory

In himself, and so he divinely answered sweetly.
"Eternal Father, it is for you to order
And for me to do your high bidding on Heaven and on Earth,
So that you will always be pleased with me

Your beloved Son. I will go to judge
These wrongdoers on Earth, but you know

Whoever judg'd, the worst on mee must light,	*That whoever is punished, the worst of it shall fall on me,*
When time shall be, for so I undertook	*When the time comes, for this is what I promised*
Before thee; and not repenting, this obtaine	*In front of you; and as I do not repent, then this*
Of right, that I may mitigate thir doom	*Is my right, that I can soften their punishment*
On me deriv'd, yet I shall temper so	*By taking it on myself, but I shall soften*
Justice with Mercie, as may illustrate most	*Justice with mercy in a way which will be*
Them fully satisfied, and thee appease.	*Best for them, and please you.*
Attendance none shall need, nor Train, where none	*I shall need no servants or retinue, there shall be none*
Are to behold the Judgement, but the judg'd,	*To see the judgment but those two who are*
Those two; the third best absent is condemn'd,	*Being judged. The third, who does well to stay away, is condemned,,*
Convict by flight, and Rebel to all Law	*And convicted by his flight, and a rebel against all law.*
Conviction to the Serpent none belongs.	*The serpent cannot be convicted. "*
Thus saying, from his radiant Seat he rose	*Saying this he rose from his shining throne*
Of high collateral glorie: him Thrones and Powers,	*Of great reflected glory; the Thrones and Powers,*
Princedoms, and Dominations ministrant	*Princedoms and Dominations serving him*
Accompanied to Heaven Gate, from whence	*Accompanied him to Heaven's Gate, from where*
Eden and all the Coast in prospect lay.	*Eden and all the coast could be seen.*
Down he descended strait; the speed of Gods	*He flew down straight away; the speed of the Gods*
Time counts not, though with swiftest minutes wing'd.	*Cannot be measured by time, however quickly it flies.*
Now was the Sun in Western cadence low	*Now the sun was sinking low in the west*
From Noon, and gentle Aires due at thir hour	*From its height of noon, and the gentle breezes of that hour*
To fan the Earth now wak'd, and usher in	*Now came to fan the Earth and bring in*
The Eevning coole, when he from wrauth more coole	*The cool evening, when there came with even cooler wrath*
Came the mild Judge and Intercessor both	*The one who was both mild judge and mediator*
To sentence Man: the voice of God they	*To sentence Man: they heard the*

heard
Now walking in the Garden, by soft windes

Brought to thir Ears, while day declin'd, they heard,
And from his presence hid themselves among
The thickest Trees, both Man and Wife, till God

Approaching, thus to Adam call'd aloud.

Where art thou Adam, wont with joy to meet
My coming seen far off? I miss thee here,

Not pleas'd, thus entertaind with solitude,

Where obvious dutie erewhile appear'd unsaught:
Or come I less conspicuous, or what change

Absents thee, or what chance detains?
Come forth.
He came, and with him Eve, more loth, though first
To offend, discount'nanc't both, and discompos'd;
Love was not in thir looks, either to God

Or to each other, but apparent guilt,
And shame, and perturbation, and despaire,
Anger, and obstinacie, and hate, and guile.
Whence Adam faultring long, thus answer'd brief.
I heard thee in the Garden, and of thy voice

Affraid, being naked, hid my self.

To whom

The gracious Judge without revile repli'd.
My voice thou oft hast heard, and hast not fear'd,
But still rejoyc't, how is it now become
So dreadful to thee? that thou art naked,

voice of God
As they walked in he garden, brought to their ears
By soft breezes at the day's end. They heard,
And hid themselves from him amongst

The thickest trees, both man and wife, until God

Approached, and called aloud to Adam:

"Where are you Adam, who usually comes to meet me with joy
When you see me coming from far off? I can't see you,
And am not pleased to be welcomed with solitude,
When I am used to you coming to me uncalled:
Can I not be seen, or what has changed

To make you absent, what keeps you? Come forward."
He came, and with him Eve, less willing though she was the first
To offend, both of them looking out of sorts;
There was no love in their faces, not for God

Nor for each other, but obvious guilt,
And shame, disturbance, despair,
Anger, obstinacy, hatred and slyness.
So Adam paused for a long time, and answered briefly.
"I heard you in the garden, and I was afraid
Of your voice, being naked, so I hid myself."
The gracious judge answered him without reproach.
"You have often heard my voice and not been afraid,

But were happy, why is it now
So terrifying for you? Who told you

who
Hath told thee? hast thou eaten of the Tree

Whereof I gave thee charge thou shouldst not eat?
To whom thus Adam sore beset repli'd.
O Heav'n! in evil strait this day I stand

Before my Judge, either to undergoe

My self the total Crime, or to accuse
My other self, the partner of my life;
Whose failing, while her Faith to me remaines,
I should conceal, and not expose to blame

By my complaint; but strict necessitie
Subdues me, and calamitous constraint
Least on my head both sin and punishment,

However insupportable, be all
Devolv'd; though should I hold my peace, yet thou
Wouldst easily detect what I conceale.
This Woman whom thou mad'st to be my help,
And gav'st me as thy perfet gift, so good,

So fit, so acceptable, so Divine,
That from her hand I could suspect no ill,

And what she did, whatever in it self,
Her doing seem'd to justifie the deed;

Shee gave me of the Tree, and I did eate.

To whom the sovran Presence thus repli'd.
Was shee thy God, that her thou didst obey

Before his voice, or was shee made thy guide,
Superior, or but equal, that to her

Thou did'st resigne thy Manhood, and the Place
Wherein God set thee above her made

that
You were naked? Have you eaten from the tree
Which I ordered you should not eat from?"
Adam, in turmoil, answered him.
"Oh Heaven! I am in an evil position today, standing
Before my judge; either I can take the whole blame
For the crime myself, or I can accuse
My other half, my life partner;
While she is still loyal to me I should conceal
Her failing, and not expose her to blame
By accusing her; but strict necessity
Stops me, and terrible fear
In case both the sin and the punishment,
However terrible, should all
Fall on me; if I did say nothing then you
Would quickly see what I was hiding.
The woman you made to be my help,
And gave to me as your perfect gift, so good,
So right, so acceptable, so divine
That I could never suspect any harm from her hand,
And all she did, whatever it was,
The fact that it was her doing it seemed to make it good;
She gave me fruit from the tree, and I ate it."
The ruling presence answered him.
"Was she your God, so that you obeyed her
Instead of him, or was she made your guide,
Superior to you, or even just equal, so you
Gave up your manhood to her, and the place
God gave you, above her who was

348

of thee,
And for thee, whose perfection farr excell'd

Hers in all real dignitie: Adornd

She was indeed, and lovely to attract
Thy Love, not thy Subjection, and her Gifts

Were such as under Government well seem'd,
Unseemly to beare rule, which was thy part

And person, hadst thou known thy self aright.
So having said, he thus to Eve in few:

Say Woman, what is this which thou hast done?
To whom sad Eve with shame nigh overwhelm'd,
Confessing soon, yet not before her Judge

Bold or loquacious, thus abasht repli'd.

The Serpent me beguil'd and I did eate.
Which when the Lord God heard, without delay
To Judgement he proceeded on th' accus'd

Serpent though brute, unable to transferre

The Guilt on him who made him instrument
Of mischief, and polluted from the end
Of his creation; justly then accurst,

As vitiated in Nature: more to know

Concern'd not Man (since he no further knew)
Nor alter'd his offence; yet God at last

To Satan first in sin his doom apply'd
Though in mysterious terms, judg'd as then best:
And on the Serpent thus his curse let fall.

made from you,
And for you, whose perfection was far greater

Than hers in all important aspects: she was

Decorated, indeed, and made lovely
To attract your love, not your subjection, and her gifts

Were of a type that would serve well under rule,
They were not made to rule, which was your role

And character, if you had known yourself properly."

Having said this, he spoke a few words to Eve:

"Tell me woman, what is this thing that you've done?"

Sad Eve, almost overwhelmed with shame,

Quickly confessed, but she was not bold or wordy

Before her judge, and replied, abashed:

"The serpent seduced me and I ate."
When the Lord God heard this he proceeded

Without delay to pass judgment on the accused

Serpent, though he was an animal and he could not transfer

The guilt onto him from the one who had made him a tool

Of his mischief, and polluted all Of his creation; then he was justifiably cursed,

As one who had had his nature spoiled: he did not need to know

About the fate of Man (since he knew no more)

And it did not change the nature of his offence; but God at last

Passed sentence on Satan's sin,
Though in mysterious terms, as he judged best at the time:

And he let his curse fall upon the

	serpent.
Because thou hast done this, thou art accurst	*"Because you have done this, you are cursed*
Above all Cattle, each Beast of the Field;	*Above all the cattle and each beast of the field;*
Upon thy Belly groveling thou shalt goe,	*You shall go crawling on your belly*
And dust shalt eat all the dayes of thy Life.	*And eat dust all the days of your life.*
Between Thee and the Woman I will put	*I will put hatred between you and the woman*
Enmitie, and between thine and her Seed;	*And between your children and hers;*
Her Seed shall bruise thy head, thou bruise his heel.	*Her children shall hurt your head, yours shall hurt his heels."*
So spake this Oracle, then verifi'd	*So the judge spoke, and the prediction came true*
When Jesus son of Mary second Eve,	*When Jesus, the son of Mary, the second Eve,*
Saw Satan fall like Lightning down from Heav'n,	*Saw Satan fall like lightning down from Heaven,*
Prince of the Aire; then rising from his Grave	*A prince of the air; then he rose from his grave,*
Spoild Principalities and Powers, triumph	*Defeated Principalities and Powers, triumphed*
In open shew, and with ascension bright	*In plain view, and with his bright ascension*
Captivity led captive through the Aire,	*Led captivity as a prisoner through the air,*
The Realm it self of Satan long usurpt,	*The realm of Satan long overthrown,*
Whom he shall tread at last under our feet;	*Whom he shall at last tread under our feet.*
Eevn hee who now foretold his fatal bruise,	*He who now predicted this fatal bruise*
And to the Woman thus his Sentence turn'd.	*Turned to pass sentence on the woman.*
Thy sorrow I will greatly multiplie	*"I will make the pain of childbirth*
By thy Conception; Children thou shalt bring	*Far greater for you; you shall bear children*
In sorrow forth, and to thy Husbands will	*With sorrow, and you will submit your will*
Thine shall submit, hee over thee shall rule.	*To your husband's, he shall be your ruler."*
On Adam last thus judgement he pronounc'd.	*He pronounced his judgment on Adam last of all.*
Because thou hast heark'nd to the voice of thy Wife,	*"Because you listened to the voice of your wife,*
And eaten of the Tree concerning which	*And ate from the tree which I*

I charg'd thee, saying: Thou shalt not eate thereof,	*ordered you* *Not to eat from,*
Curs'd is the ground for thy sake, thou in sorrow	*The ground is cursed for you, and in sorrow*
Shalt eate thereof all the days of thy Life;	*You shall eat from it all the days of your life;*
Thorns also and Thistles it shall bring thee forth	*It shall bring forth thorns and thistles*
Unbid, and thou shalt eate th' Herb of th' Field,	*Unasked, and you shall eat the grass of the fields,*
In the sweat of thy Face shalt thou eat Bread,	*And you will have to work to make your own food,*
Till thou return unto the ground, for thou	*Until you return to the ground, for you*
Out of the ground wast taken, know thy Birth,	*Were taken from the ground, know how you were born,*
For dust thou art, and shalt to dust returne.	*For you come from dust and you shall return to it."*
So judg'd he Man, both Judge and Saviour sent,	*So he judged Man, sent as both judge and savior,*
And th' instant stroke of Death denounc't that day	*And took away the instant sentence of death*
Remov'd farr off; then pittying how they stood	*Announced that day; then taking pity on how they stood*
Before him naked to the aire, that now	*Before him, naked in the open air, that would now*
Must suffer change, disdain'd not to begin	*Be at the mercy of the seasons, he did not turn away*
Thenceforth the form of servant to assume,	*From assuming the role of a servant,*
As when he wash'd his servants feet so now	*As when he washed the feet of his disciples so now*
As Father of his Familie he clad	*As the Father of his family he dressed*
Thir nakedness with Skins of Beasts, or slain,	*Them in the skins of beasts, either killed*
Or as the Snake with youthful Coate repaid;	*Or with ones that shed their coats like the snake,*
And thought not much to cloath his Enemies:	*And he did not act as though he was clothing his enemies:*
Nor hee thir outward onely with the Skins	*He not only clad their outsides with the skin*
Of Beasts, but inward nakedness, much more	*Of beasts, but clad their inner nakedness,*
Opprobrious, with his Robe of righteousness,	*Which was far worse, with his Robe of Righteousness,*

Araying cover'd from his Fathers sight.

To him with swift ascent he up returnd,
Into his blissful bosom reassum'd

In glory as of old, to him appeas'd

All, though all-knowing, what had past
with Man
Recounted, mixing intercession sweet.
Meanwhile ere thus was sin'd and judg'd
on Earth,
Within the Gates of Hell sate Sin and
Death,
In counterview within the Gates, that now

Stood open wide, belching outrageous
flame
Farr into Chaos, since the Fiend pass'd
through,
Sin opening, who thus now to Death began.

O Son, why sit we here each other viewing

Idlely, while Satan our great Author thrives

In other Worlds, and happier Seat provides

For us his ofspring deare? It cannot be

But that success attends him; if mishap,

Ere this he had return'd, with fury driv'n

By his Avengers, since no place like this

Can fit his punishment, or their revenge.

Methinks I feel new strength within me
rise,
Wings growing, and Dominion giv'n me
large
Beyond this Deep; whatever drawes me on,

Or sympathie, or som connatural force

*Covering them from his father's
sight.*

*He swiftly returned up to the Father,
And was taken back into his blissful
heart, reassuming*

*His former glory and explained to
him*

*(Though he was all knowing) all that
had happened with Man,*
Mixing in sweet pleas for mercy.
*Meanwhile, before there was sin and
judgement on Earth,*
*Sin and Death sat at the Gates of
Hell,*
*Opposite each other within the gates,
that now*

*Stood open wide, belching huge
flames*
*Far into Chaos, since the fiend had
passed through;*
*They were opened by Sin, who now
spoke to Death.*

*"Oh Son, why do we sit here idly
looking*

*At each other, while Satan, our great
Author, thrives*

*In other worlds, and provides a
happier home*

*For us, his dear children? It must be
the case*

*That he has met with success; if he
had failed*

*He would have returned before this,
driven by fury,*

*By his Avengers, for there is no better
place than this*

*To suit his punishment, or their
revenge.*

*I think I can feel a new strength
rising within me,*
*Wings growing, and a great
kingdomgiven to me*
*Far beyond this pit; something leads
me on,*

*Whether it is sympathy or some
special force*

352

Powerful at greatest distance to unite

With secret amity things of like kinde

By secretest conveyance. Thou my Shade

Inseparable must with mee along:
For Death from Sin no power can separate.

But least the difficultie of passing back

Stay his return perhaps over this Gulfe
Impassable, Impervious, let us try

Adventrous work, yet to thy power and mine
Not unagreeable, to found a path
Over this Maine from Hell to that new World
Where Satan now prevailes, a Monument
Of merit high to all th' infernal Host,

Easing thir passage hence, for intercourse,

Or transmigration, as thir lot shall lead.

Nor can I miss the way, so strongly drawn

By this new felt attraction and instinct.

Whom thus the meager Shadow answerd soon.
Goe whither Fate and inclination strong

Leads thee, I shall not lag behinde, nor erre

The way, thou leading, such a sent I draw

Of carnage, prey innumerable, and taste
The savour of Death from all things there that live:
Nor shall I to the work thou enterprisest

Be wanting, but afford thee equal aid,

So saying, with delight he snuff'd the smell

Which has the power to unite over great distances

Things of the same spirit through secret kinship,

In secret ways. You, my inseparable shadow,

Must come along with me:
No power can separate Death from Sin.

But in case the difficulty of the return journey

Delays his return over this abyss
Which is impassable, impenetrable, let us try

Some bold work, which is agreeable to your power and
To mine, to build a path
Over this sea of Chaos from Hell to that new world
Where Satan now rules, a great Monument to all the Host of Hell

That can ease their journey there, so they can come and go

Or emigrate permanently, as their fate decides.

I cannot lose the way, as I am so strongly drawn

By this new attraction and instinct I feel."

The thin shadow soon answered.
"Go wherever fate and strong inclination

Lead you, I shall not lag behind or lose

The way, with you leading, for I can smell such a scent

Of carnage, countless prey, and taste The smell of Death on all the things that live there:
Nor shall I be found wanting in the work you

Are going to try, but I shall give you equal help."

Saying this, he sniffed with delight the

Of mortal change on Earth. As when a flock flock
Of ravenous Fowl, though many a League remote,
Against the day of Battel, to a Field,

Where Armies lie encampt, come flying, lur'd
With sent of living Carcasses design'd

For death, the following day, in bloodie fight.
So sented the grim Feature, and upturn'd

His Nostril wide into the murkie Air,
Sagacious of his Quarry from so farr.
Then Both from out Hell Gates into the waste
Wide Anarchie of Chaos damp and dark

Flew divers, and with Power (thir Power was great)

Hovering upon the Waters; what they met

Solid or slimie, as in raging Sea

Tost up and down, together crowded drove

From each side shoaling towards the mouth of Hell.
As when two Polar Winds blowing adverse

Upon the Cronian Sea, together drive

Mountains of Ice, that stop th' imagin'd way

Beyond Petsora Eastward, to the rich
Cathaian Coast. The aggregated Soyle
Death with his Mace petrific, cold and dry,

As with a Trident smote, and fix't as firm

As Delos floating once; the rest his look

smell
Of the death that had fallen on Earth. It was like when a flock
Of ravenous vultures, though many miles away,
Anticipating the day of battle will come flying

To a field where armies lie in their camps, lured
By the scent of living bodies that are destined

To die, the next day, in a bloody fight.
This is what the grim shape smelled, and lifted

His nostril high into the murky air,
Aware of his quarry from so far off.
Then they both flew out from the Gates of Hell into
The wastelands of Chaos' wide anarchy, damp and dark,

And with their power (their power was great)

Hovered over the waters; whatever they met,

Solid or slimy, they tossed up and down

As if they were a raging sea, and herding them together

Drove them up into a causeway towards the mouth of Hell.
It was as though when two polar winds blowing against each other

Upon the Arctic Ocean between them drive up

Mountains of Ice, that block the imagined way

Eastward over Siberia to the rich Coast of Cathay. This gathered soil
Death, with his fossilized club, cold and dry,

Smashed as with a great spear and fixed it as firm

As the island of Delos, which also once floated; the rest

Bound with Gorgonian rigor not to move,

And with Asphaltic slime; broad as the Gate,

Deep to the Roots of Hell the gather'd beach

They fasten'd, and the Mole immense wraught on

Over the foaming deep high Archt, a Bridge

Of length prodigious joyning to the Wall

Immovable of this now fenceless world

Forfeit to Death; from hence a passage broad,

Smooth, easie, inoffensive down to Hell.

So, if great things to small may be compar'd,

Xerxes, the Libertie of Greece to yoke,

From Susa his Memnonian Palace high

Came to the Sea, and over Hellespont

Bridging his way, Europe with Asia joyn'd,

And scourg'd with many a stroak th' indignant waves.

Now had they brought the work by wondrous Art

Pontifical, a ridge of pendent Rock

Over the vext Abyss, following the track

Of Satan, to the self same place where hee

First lighted from his Wing, and landed safe

From out of Chaos to the out side bare

Of this round World: with Pinns of Adamant

And Chains they made all fast, too fast they made

And durable; and now in little space

The confines met of Empyrean Heav'n

And of this World, and on the left hand Hell

He ordered with a gorgon like look not to move,

And bound it with a tarry slime; as wide as the gate

And deep down to the roots of Hell they fastened

What they had gathered, and on this great foundation

Built over the foaming deep a high arched bridge

Of astonishing length joined to the solid wall

Of this now defenceless world

Which was given over to Death; from there there was

A wide passage, smooth and easy, without obstacles, down to Hell.

So, if great things may compared with small,

Xerxes, to enslave Greece,

Came from Susa his great Memnonian palace

To the sea, and made a bridge over the Hellespont

Joining Europe and Asia,

And whipped the indignant waves.

Now they had brought to the work, with wondrous

Bridge building art, a ridge of hanging rock

Over the stormy abyss, following the tracks

Of Satan to the same place where he

First landed from his flight, safe

Out of Chaos on the bare frontiers

Of this round world: they made it fast

With pins of adamant and chains, they made it all too solid

And lasting; and now in a small space

The edges met of Heaven

And of this world, and on the left hand Hell

With long reach interpos'd; three sev'ral ways	*Reached out its long arm in between; there were three ways*
In sight, to each of these three places led.	*Visible, leading to these three places.*
And now thir way to Earth they had descri'd,	*And now they had seen their path to Earth*
To Paradise first tending, when behold	*They were looking towards Paradise when they saw*
Satan in likeness of an Angel bright	*Satan in the guise of a bright Angel*
Betwixt the Centaure and the Scorpion stearing	*Between the constellations of Sagittarius and Scorpio, steering*
His Zenith, while the Sun in Aries rose:	*On high while the sun rose in Aries:*
Disguis'd he came, but those his Children dear	*He came disguised but these dear children of his*
Thir Parent soon discern'd, though in disguise.	*Soon recognized their parent.*
Hee after Eve seduc't, unminded slunk	*After he had seduced Eve he, forgotten, had slunk*
Into the Wood fast by, and changing shape	*Into the nearby wood, and changing shape*
To observe the sequel, saw his guileful act	*To observe the sequel he saw his cunning trap*
By Eve, though all unweeting, seconded	*Passed on by Eve, though unaware,*
Upon her Husband, saw thir shame that sought	*To her husband, saw their shame that looked*
Vain covertures; but when he saw descend	*To cover itself; but when he saw the Son of God*
The Son of God to judge them terrifi'd	*Descend to judge them he fled terrified,*
Hee fled, not hoping to escape, but shun	*Not thinking he could escape but to put off*
The present, fearing guiltie what his wrauth	*Punishment, fearing in his guilt what his anger*
Might suddenly inflict; that past, return'd	*Might suddenly inflict on him; that past he returned*
By Night, and listening where the hapless Paire	*By night, and eavesdropping where the unhappy pair*
Sate in thir sad discourse, and various plaint,	*Sat talking sadly of various things*
Thence gatherd his own doom, which understood	*He learned of his own punishment, which he understood*
Not instant, but of future time. With joy	*Was not to be instant but happen in the future. With joy*
And tidings fraught, to Hell he now return'd,	*And full of news he now returned to Hell,*
And at the brink of Chaos, neer the foot	*And on the edge of Chaos, near the*

Of this new wondrous Pontifice, unhop't	*foot* *Of this wondrous new bridge, he unexpectedly*
Met who to meet him came, his Ofspring dear.	*Met those who came to meet him, his dear children.*
Great joy was at thir meeting, and at sight	*There was great joy at their meeting, and at the sight*
Of that stupendious Bridge his joy encreas'd.	*Of that stupendous bridge his joy increased.*
Long hee admiring stood, till Sin, his faire	*He stood long admiring it, until Sin, his fair*
Inchanting Daughter, thus the silence broke.	*Bewitching daughter, broke the silence.*
O Parent, these are thy magnific deeds,	*"Oh parent, these things which you do not view as your own*
Thy Trophies, which thou view'st as not thine own,	*Are your trophies, your magnificent deeds,*
Thou art thir Author and prime Architect:	*You are their creator and architect:*
For I no sooner in my Heart divin'd,	*For no sooner had I felt in my heart,*
My Heart, which by a secret harmonie	*(Which is joined by secret harmonies*
Still moves with thine, join'd in connexion sweet,	*To still move with yours, joined in a sweet connection)*
That thou on Earth hadst prosper'd, which thy looks	*That you had succeeded on Earth, which your looks*
Now also evidence, but straight I felt	*Also show, straight away I felt,*
Though distant from thee Worlds between, yet felt	*Though you were worlds away,*
That I must after thee with this thy Son;	*That I must come after you with your son;*
Such fatal consequence unites us three:	*We are all so closely tied together*
Hell could no longer hold us in her bounds,	*That Hell could not keep us within her boundaries*
Nor this unvoyageable Gulf obscure	*Nor could this uncrossable dark abyss*
Detain from following thy illustrious track.	*Stop us from following your glorious path.*
Thou hast atchiev'd our libertie, confin'd	*You have won our freedom, we were confined*
Within Hell Gates till now, thou us impow'rd	*Within the gates of Hell until now, you empowered us*
To fortifie thus farr, and overlay	*To build this far and lay*
With this portentous Bridge the dark Abyss.	*This ill-omened bridge over the dark abyss.*
Thine now is all this World, thy vertue hath won	*All this world is now yours, your strength has won*
What thy hands builded not, thy Wisdom	*What your hands did not build, your*

357

gain'd
With odds what Warr hath lost, and fully aveng'd
Our foile in Heav'n; here thou shalt Monarch reign,
There didst not; there let him still Victor sway,
As Battel hath adjudg'd, from this new World
Retiring, by his own doom alienated,
And henceforth Monarchie with thee divide

Of all things parted by th' Empyreal bounds,
His Quadrature, from thy Orbicular World,

Or trie thee now more dang'rous to his Throne.
Whom thus the Prince of Darkness answerd glad.
Fair Daughter, and thou Son and Grandchild both,
High proof ye now have giv'n to be the Race
Of Satan (for I glorie in the name,
Antagonist of Heav'ns Almightie King)

Amply have merited of me, of all
Th' Infernal Empire, that so neer Heav'ns dore
Triumphal with triumphal act have met,

Mine with this glorious Work, and made one Realm
Hell and this World, one Realm, one Continent
Of easie thorough-fare. Therefore while I

Descend through Darkness, on your Rode with ease
To my associate Powers, them to acquaint
With these successes, and with them rejoyce,
You two this way, among these numerous Orbs

wisdom got back
What war had lost and more, and you have fully avenged
Our defeat in Heaven; here you shall rule as King,
Which you did not there; let him stay there as winner,
As judged by battle, keeping out of this new world,
Excluded by his own orders.
From now on he must share kingship of all things with you,

Kingdoms divided by the frontiers of the sky,
He having his flat square kingdom and you your round one,

Or he will find you a greater danger to his throne."
The Prince of Darkness answered her, happy.
"My fair daughter, and you both my son and grandchild,
You have given great proof that you are related
To Satan (for I glory in the name,
The fighter of the almighty King of Heaven).

I thoroughly deserve this, out of all
The empire of Hell, that so near Heaven's door
A triumphal arch should meet a triumphal act,

My act and this glorious work, making one kingdom
Out of Hell and this world, one kingdom, one continent
That can be travelled across easily. And so while I

Descend through the darkness on your easy road
To my comrades, to tell them of
These successes, and rejoice with them,
You two go this way, amongst all these stars

358

All yours, right down to Paradise descend;	*Which are all yours, and descend right down to Paradise;*
There dwell and Reign in bliss, thence on the Earth	*Live there and reign in bliss, have mastery*
Dominion exercise and in the Aire,	*Over the Earth and the skies,*
Chiefly on Man, sole Lord of all declar'd,	*And as for Man, declared the sole Lord of all,*
Him first make sure your thrall, and lastly kill.	*First make him your captive and lastly kill him.*
My Substitutes I send ye, and Create	*I send you as my representatives, and give you*
Plenipotent on Earth, of matchless might	*My full authority; you shall be of matchless strength*
Issuing from mee: on your joynt vigor now	*Which comes from me; on your joint efforts*
My hold of this new Kingdom all depends,	*My grip on this whole kingdom depends;*
Through Sin to Death expos'd by my exploit.	*Through my actions it is exposed to Sin and Death.*
If your joynt power prevailes, th' affaires of Hell	*If your power rules there, the business of Hell*
No detriment need feare, goe and be strong.	*Need never fear failure; go and be strong."*
So saying he dismiss'd them, they with speed	*Saying this he dismissed them and they rushed*
Thir course through thickest Constellations held	*On a path through the thickest constellations,*
Spreading thir bane; the blasted Starrs lookt wan,	*Spreading their evil; the blasted stars looked pale,*
And Planets, Planet-strook, real Eclips	*And the planets, malignly influenced, suffered*
Then sufferd. Th' other way Satan went down	*Real eclipse. Satan went down the other way,*
The Causey to Hell Gate; on either side	*Down the causeway to the gate of Hell; on either side*
Disparted Chaos over built exclaimd,	*Parted Chaos, built over, complained*
And with rebounding surge the barrs assaild,	*And threw itself against the bridge,*
That scorn'd his indignation: through the Gate,	*Which scorned his complaints; through the Gate,*
Wide open and unguarded, Satan pass'd,	*Wide open and unguarded, Satan passed,*
And all about found desolate; for those	*And found all around was empty; those*
Appointed to sit there, had left thir charge,	*Appointed to sit there had left their*

Flown to the upper World; the rest were all

Farr to the inland retir'd, about the walls
Of Pandæmonium, Citie and proud seate

Of Lucifer, so by allusion calld,
Of that bright Starr to Satan paragond.

There kept thir Watch the Legions, while the Grand
In Council sate, sollicitous what chance

Might intercept thir Emperour sent, so hee

Departing gave command, and they observ'd.
As when the Tartar from his Russian Foe

By Astracan over the Snowie Plaines
Retires, or Bactrian Sophi from the hornes
Of Turkish Crescent, leaves all waste beyond
The Realm of Aladule, in his retreate

To Tauris or Casbeen. So these the late

Heav'n-banisht Host, left desert utmost Hell

Many a dark League, reduc't in careful Watch
Round thir Metropolis, and now expecting
Each hour thir great adventurer from the search
Of Forrein Worlds: he through the midst unmarkt,
In shew Plebeian Angel militant
Of lowest order, past; and from the dore

Of that Plutonian Hall, invisible
Ascended his high Throne, which under state
Of richest texture spred, at th' upper end

Was plac't in regal lustre. Down a while

station,
Flown to the upper world; the rest had all
Retired far inside, around the walls
Of Pandemonium, the city and proud seat
Of Lucifer, he was once nicknamed,
With that bright star compared to Satan.
There the armies kept watch, while the Great
Sat in council, waiting to hear if anything
Might intercept their Emperor; this he
Had ordered as he left, and they obeyed.
As when the Tartar retreats from his Russian enemy
Over the snowy plains by Astrakhan,
Or the Persian Shah from the horns
Of the Turkish crescent, leaving everything ruined
In his retreat beyond the lands of Armenia,
To Tabriz or Kazbin, this was how the host
Lately banished from Heaven, had left outer Hell a desert
For many dark miles, falling back to a careful watch
Around their city, now expecting
Every hour their great explorer back from the search
Of foreign worlds: he walked through the guards unnoticed,
Looking like a plebian angel soldier
Of the lowest order; and from the door
Of that hall of Pluto, invisible,
He climbed onto his high throne, which was under a canopy
Of the richest material, shining in regal glory
At the top end.He sat down for a while

He sate, and round about him saw unseen: / *And looked about him, unseen:*
At last as from a Cloud his fulgent head / *At last, as from behind a cloud his shining head*

And shape Starr bright appeer'd, or brighter, clad / *And shape appeared, bright as a star, or brighter,*
With what permissive glory since his fall / *Dressed in what glory he had been permitted*

Was left him, or false glitter: All amaz'd / *To keep after his fall, or else false glitter; all astonished*

At that so sudden blaze the Stygian throng / *At that sudden blaze, the Hellish throng*

Bent thir aspect, and whom they wish'd beheld, / *Turned to look, and saw what they had hoped for,*
Thir mighty Chief returnd: loud was th' acclaime: / *The return of their mighty chief: the cheers were loud,*
Forth rush'd in haste the great consulting Peers, / *And the council of Peers rushed forward,*
Rais'd from thir dark Divan, and with like joy / *Raised from their dark couches, and with the same joy*
Congratulant approach'd him, who with hand / *Approached him with congratulations; he got*
Silence, and with these words attention won. / *silence with a wave of his hand, and attention with these words:*
Thrones, Dominations, Princedoms, Vertues, Powers, / *"Thrones, Dominions, Princedoms, Virtues, Powers,*
For in possession such, not onely of right, / *For I can now call you those names as owners,*

I call ye and declare ye now, returnd / *Not just as titles; I have returned*
Successful beyond hope, to lead ye forth / *Successful beyond hope, to lead you*
Triumphant out of this infernal Pit / *Triumphant out of this hellish pit,*
Abominable, accurst, the house of woe, / *Horrible, cursed, the house of sorrow*
And Dungeon of our Tyrant: Now possess, / *And the dungeon of the tyrant.We now own,*

As Lords, a spacious World, to our native Heaven / *As Lords, a spacious world, not much inferior*
Little inferiour, by my adventure hard / *To our native Heaven, gained with great peril*

With peril great atchiev'd. Long were to tell / *By my hard adventures.It would take long*
What I have don, what sufferd, with what paine / *To tell you all I have done, with what pain*
Voyag'd th' unreal, vast, unbounded deep / *I crossed the unreal, vast, boundless abyss*

Of horrible confusion, over which / *Of horrible confusion, over which*
By Sin and Death a broad way now is pav'd / *Sin and Death have now paved a*

To expedite your glorious march; but I
Toild out my uncouth passage, forc't to ride
Th' untractable Abysse, plung'd in the womb
Of unoriginal Night and Chaos wilde,
That jealous of thir secrets fiercely oppos'd
My journey strange, with clamorous uproar
Protesting Fate supreame; thence how I found
The new created World, which fame in Heav'n
Long had foretold, a Fabrick wonderful
Of absolute perfection, therein Man
Plac't in a Paradise, by our exile
Made happie: Him by fraud I have seduc'd
From his Creator, and the more to increase
Your wonder, with an Apple; he thereat
Offended, worth your laughter, hath giv'n up
Both his beloved Man and all his World,
To Sin and Death a prey, and so to us,
Without our hazard, labour, or allarme,
To range in, and to dwell, and over Man
To rule, as over all he should have rul'd.
True is, mee also he hath judg'd, or rather
Mee not, but the brute Serpent in whose shape
Man I deceav'd: that which to mee belongs,
Is enmity, which he will put between
Mee and Mankinde; I am to bruise his heel;

broad way
To help your glorious march; but I
Struggled on my unknown way, forced to ride
Over the unmapped abyss, plunged into the womb
Of uncreated darkness and wild Chaos,
Who guarding their secrets fiercely opposed
My strange journey, with a great clamor
Shouting against destiny; from there I found
The newly created world, which had long been
Foretold in Heaven, a wonderful creation
Of absolute perfection, and within it Man
Placed in a Paradise, profiting from
Our exile. By fraud I have led him astray
From his creator, and, to increase wonder
Still further, with an apple; that caused God to
Be offended, it's worth laughing at, and he has given up
Both his beloved Man and his whole World
As a target for Sin and Death, and so to us,
Without any risk, work or danger,
To walk over and to live in, and to rule
Over Man, as he should have ruled over all.
True, he has judged me as well, or rather
Not me, but the brute serpent in whose shape
I deceived Man; hatred belongs to me
And he has put it between
Me and mankind; I am to bruise his heel;

His Seed, when is not set, shall bruise my head:
A World who would not purchase with a bruise,
Or much more grievous pain? Ye have th' account
Of my performance: What remains, ye Gods,
But up and enter now into full bliss.

So having said, a while he stood, expecting

Thir universal shout and high applause
To fill his eare, when contrary he hears

On all sides, from innumerable tongues
A dismal universal hiss, the sound
Of public scorn; he wonderd, but not long

Had leasure, wondring at himself now more;
His Visage drawn he felt to sharp and spare,

His Armes clung to his Ribs, his Leggs entwining
Each other, till supplanted down he fell
A monstrous Serpent on his Belly prone,

Reluctant, but in vaine: a greater power

Now rul'd him, punisht in the shape he sin'd,
According to his doom: he would have spoke,
But hiss for hiss returnd with forked tongue

To forked tongue, for now were all transform'd
Alike, to Serpents all as accessories

To his bold Riot: dreadful was the din

Of hissing through the Hall, thick swarming now
With complicated monsters head and taile,

His children (he doesn't say when) shall bruise my head:
Who wouldn't swap a bruise, or much worse pain,
For a whole world? You have the story
Of my deeds; nothing remains, you Gods,
But for us to rise up and enter into full happiness."

Having said this he stood for a while, expecting

Their great shout and applause
To fill his ear, when he hears the opposite

On all sides, from countless tongues
A dismal universal hiss, the sound
Of public scorn; he was confused, but did not have

Much time to think, being now more confused by himself;
He felt his face becoming sharp and thin,

His arms clamped to his ribs, his legs wrapped round
Each other, until he tripped and fell,
A monstrous serpent lying on his belly,

Unwilling, but powerless: a greater power

Controlled him and punished him by giving him the shape in which
He had sinned, according to his sentence: he would have spoken,
But the forked tongues answered each other,

Hiss for hiss, for now all alike had been changed,
They were all serpents as his accomplices

In his bold rebellion; now there was a dreadful din

Of hissing through the hall, now swarming thickly
With monsters entwined head and tail,

Scorpion and Asp, and Amphisbæna dire,	*Scorpions, asps, terrible Amphisbaena,*
Cerastes hornd, Hydrus, and Ellops drear,	*Horned Cerastes, Hydrus and dreary Ellops,*
And Dipsas (not so thick swarm'd once the Soil	*And Dipsas (thicker than once swarmed on the soil*
Bedropt with blood of Gorgon, or the Isle	*Soaked with Gorgon's blood, or the island of*
Ophiusa) but still greatest hee the midst,	*Ophiusa) but still he was the greatest in the middle,*
Now Dragon grown, larger then whom the Sun	*Now turned into a dragon, larger than the one the sun*
Ingenderd in the Pythian Vale on slime,	*Grew from the mud in the Pythian vale,*
Huge Python, and his Power no less he seem'd	*The huge python, and he seemed to keep*
Above the rest still to retain; they all	*His power as greater than the rest; they all*
Him follow'd issuing forth to th' open Field,	*Followed him out into the open field,*
Where all yet left of that revolted Rout	*Where all that were left of the defeated rebellion,*
Heav'n-fall'n, in station stood or just array,	*Fallen from Heaven, stood on parade,*
Sublime with expectation when to see	*Full of excitement at the thought*
In Triumph issuing forth thir glorious Chief;	*Of their glorious chief exiting in triumph;*
They saw, but other sight instead, a crowd	*But they saw another sight instead, a crowd*
Of ugly Serpents; horror on them fell,	*Of ugly serpents, horror fell on them,*
And horrid sympathie; for what they saw,	*And a horrid sympathy, for what they saw*
They felt themselvs now changing; down thir arms,	*They felt themselves changing into; they dropped*
Down fell both Spear and Shield, down they as fast,	*Their weapons, their spears and shields, they fell with them*
And the dire hiss renew'd, and the dire form	*And they copied the dreadful hiss, and were infected*
Catcht by Contagion, like in punishment,	*By the same awful shape, suffering the same punishment*
As in thir crime. Thus was th' applause they meant,	*For the same crime. So the applause they had meant to give*
Turn'd to exploding hiss, triumph to shame	*Turned into a thundering hiss, their triumph became a shame,*
Cast on themselves from thir own mouths. There stood	*Insulted by their own mouths. There was a grove*

A Grove hard by, sprung up with this thir change,
His will who reigns above, to aggravate

Thir penance, laden with Fruit like that

Which grew in Paradise, the bait of Eve

Us'd by the Tempter: on that prospect strange
Thir earnest eyes they fix'd, imagining
For one forbidden Tree a multitude

Now ris'n, to work them furder woe or shame;
Yet parcht with scalding thurst and hunger fierce,
Though to delude them sent, could not abstain,
But on they rould in heaps, and up the Trees

Climbing, sat thicker then the snakie locks
That curld Megæra: greedily they pluck'd
The Frutage fair to sight, like that which grew
Neer that bituminous Lake where Sodom flam'd;
This more delusive, not the touch, but taste

Deceav'd; they fondly thinking to allay

Thir appetite with gust, instead of Fruit
Chewd bitter Ashes, which th' offended taste
With spattering noise rejected: oft they assayd,
Hunger and thirst constraining, drugd as oft,
With hatefullest disrelish writh'd thir jaws

With soot and cinders fill'd; so oft they fell

Into the same illusion, not as Man
Whom they triumph'd once lapst. Thus were they plagu'd

Right by them, sprung up at as they changed,
Ordered by he who reigns above, to worsen
Their punishment, loaded with fruit like that
Which had grown in Paradise, Eve's bait
As used by the tempter; on that strange sight
They fixed their eyes, imagining
That instead of one forbidden tree a multitude
Had grown up, to cause them further sorrow and shame;
But they were were parched with scalding thirst and fierce hunger,
But although they were sent to trick them they could not resist,
And they rolled on in heaps, and climbed up
The trees, thicker than the snaky hair
On Megaera; greedily they picked
The beautiful looking fruit, which was like that which grew
Near the Dead Sea where Sodom burned;
This was more deceptive, not in the touch
But in taste; imagining that they could stop
Their hunger easily, instead of fruit
They found they were chewing bitter ashes, which their mouths
Gaggingly rejected; they tried again and again,
Forced by hunger and thirst, and were as often sickened,
And with horrible distaste their jaws twisted,
Filled with soot and cinders; so often they fell
Into the same trap, not like Man,
Whom they beat with just one lapse.So they were tormented

And worn with Famin, long and ceasless hiss,
Till thir lost shape, permitted, they resum'd,

Yearly enjoynd, some say, to undergo

This annual humbling certain number'd days,
To dash thir pride, and joy for Man seduc't.

However some tradition they dispers'd
Among the Heathen of thir purchase got,

And Fabl'd how the Serpent, whom they calld
Ophion with Eurynome, the wide-
Encroaching Eve perhaps, had first the rule
Of high Olympus, thence by Saturn driv'n

And Ops, ere yet Dictæan Jove was born.

Mean while in Paradise the hellish pair

Too soon arriv'd, Sin there in power before,

Once actual, now in body, and to dwell

Habitual habitant; behind her Death

Close following pace for pace, not mounted yet
On his pale Horse: to whom Sin thus began.
Second of Satan sprung, all conquering Death,
What thinkst thou of our Empire now, though earnd
With travail difficult, not better farr
Then stil at Hels dark threshold to have sate watch,
Unnam'd, undreaded, and thy self half starv'd?
Whom thus the Sin-born Monster answerd soon.
To mee, who with eternal Famin pine,

And worn with famine, with long ceaseless hissing,
Until they were permitted to resume their former shape,
And some say they are forced each year to suffer
This annual punishment for a certain number of days,
To keep them humble and pay them for Man's seduction.
However some say they spread
Amongst the heathen they had turned to their cause
And tell stories of how the serpent, whom they called
The wide ruling one, a copy
Of Eve perhaps, was the first ruler
Of high Olympus, driven from there by Saturn
And Rhea before the ruler Jupiter was born.
Meanwhile, too soon, the hellish pair arrived
In Paradise; Sin's power had been there before,
As a concept and was there now in body
To live there forever; behind her Death
Shadowed her footsteps, not yet mounted
On his pale horse: Sin spoke to him;

"Second child of Satan, all conquering Death,
What do you think of our empire now, though it was earned
With great labor, is it not far better
Than sitting watch at the Gate of Hell,
Unnamed, unfeared, and you half starving?"
The sin-born monster soon answered her:
"To me whose hunger can never be satisfied

Alike is Hell, or Paradise, or Heaven,

There best, where most with ravin I may meet;

Which here, though plenteous, all too little seems

To stuff this Maw, this vast unhide-bound Corps.

To whom th' incestuous Mother thus repli'd.

Thou therefore on these Herbs, and Fruits, Flours

Feed first, on each Beast next, and Fish, and Fowle,

No homely morsels, and whatever thing

The Sithe of Time mowes down, devour unspar'd,

Till I in Man residing through the Race,

His thoughts, his looks, words, actions all infect,

And season him thy last and sweetest prey.

This said, they both betook them several wayes,

Both to destroy, or unimmortal make

All kinds, and for destruction to mature

Sooner or later; which th' Almightie seeing,

From his transcendent Scat the Saints among,

To those bright Orders utterd thus his voice.

See with what heat these Dogs of Hell advance

To waste and havoc yonder World, which I

So fair and good created, and had still

Kept in that State, had not the folly of Man

Let in these wastful Furies, who impute

Folly to mee, so doth the Prince of Hell

And his Adherents, that with so much ease

Hell, Paradise or Heaven are all the same,

I like it best where I can get the most prey;

Although there's plenty here it's not enough

To fill this mouth, this great body which is not limited by its skin."

The incestuous mother replied to him thus:

"So first prey on these herbs, fruits and and flowers,

Then on each animal, fish and bird,

They're no little snacks, and whatever

The scythe of time mows down, do not spare it,

Until I, living in Man right through all the race,

Infect all his thoughts, his looks, words and actions,

Preparing him as your last and sweetest victim."

Having spoken they went their separate ways,

Both to destroy or make mortal

All kinds, and to make them ready for destruction

Sooner or later; God, seeing this

From his high seat amongst the saints,

Spoke to his bright cohorts:

"See the eagerness with which these dogs of Hell rush

To bring waste and chaos to that world, which I

Created so fair and good, and which would still

Be kept in that state, if Man's folly had not

Let in these destroying Furies, who think

That I am foolish, as does the Prince of Hell

And his followers, because I allow

I suffer them to enter and possess
A place so heav'nly, and conniving seem

To gratifie my scornful Enemies,
That laugh, as if transported with some fit

Of Passion, I to them had quitted all,

At random yielded up to their misrule;

And know not that I call'd and drew them thither
My Hell-hounds, to lick up the draff and filth
Which mans polluting Sin with taint hath shed
On what was pure, till cramm'd and gorg'd, burst
With suckt and glutted offal, at one sling

Of thy victorious Arm, well-pleasing Son,

Both Sin, and Death, and yawning Grave at last
Through Chaos hurld, obstruct the mouth of Hell
For ever, and seal up his ravenous Jawes.

Then Heav'n and Earth renewd shall be made pure
To sanctitie that shall receive no staine:

Till then the Curse pronounc't on both precedes.
He ended, and the Heav'nly Audience loud

Sung Halleluia, as the sound of Seas,

Through multitude that sung: Just are thy ways,
Righteous are thy Decrees on all thy Works;
Who can extenuate thee? Next, to the Son,

Destin'd restorer of Mankind, by whom

---

them so easily
To enter and take possession
Of such a heavenly place, and seem to want

To please my scornful enemies,
Who laugh, as if they think that in a fit

Of anger I have given up everything to them,

Given over to their powers at random;

They don't know that I called them there,
My hellhounds, to lick up the filthy dregs
Which Man's polluting sin has spewed
Over what was pure, until, stuffed and nigh *swollen, nearly bursting*
With the offal they have gorged on, with one swing

Of your victorious arm, always pleasing Son,

Both Sin and Death and the yawning grave shall finally
Be thrown through Chaos and block the mouth of Hell
Forever, and seal up his ravenous jaws.

Then Heaven and Earth will be renewed and made pure
With a sanctity that cannot be stained:

Until then the curse sentenced on both continues."
He finished, and the Heavenly audience sung

Loud praises, like the sound of the sea,

Sung through the whole crowd:
"Your ways are just,
And your rule over all your works is righteous;
Who can refuse to praise you? And we praise the Son,

Destined to be the Savior of Mankind,

New Heav'n and Earth shall to the Ages rise,
Or down from Heav'n descend. Such was thir song,

While the Creator calling forth by name

His mightie Angels gave them several charge,
As sorted best with present things. The Sun

Had first his precept so to move, so shine,

As might affect the Earth with cold and heat
Scarce tollerable, and from the North to call
Decrepit Winter, from the South to bring

Solstitial summers heat. To the blanc Moone
Her office they prescrib'd, to th' other five

Thir planetarie motions and aspects
In Sextile, Square, and Trine, and Opposite,

Of noxious efficacie, and when to joyne

In Synod unbenigne, and taught the fixt
Thir influence malignant when to showre,

Which of them rising with the Sun, or falling,
Should prove tempestuous: To the Winds they set
Thir corners, when with bluster to confound
Sea, Aire, and Shoar, the Thunder when to rowle
With terror through the dark Aereal Hall.

Some say he bid his Angels turne ascanse
The Poles of Earth twice ten degrees and more
From the Suns Axle; they with labour

---

through whom
A new eternal Earth and skies shall rise
Or be lowered down from Heaven."
This was their song,

While the Creator called his mighty angels
By their names and gave them different orders,
As suited the present state of things. The sun
Was given his first orders to move and shine in such a way
That the Earth would be affected with almost unbearable
Cold and heat, and from the north to call down
Dead winter, from the south to bring up
The boiling heat of summer. To the white moon
They gave her orders, to the other five planets
They told them how to travel
Through the different angles of the skies,
Having evil influence, and telling them when to join
In a malign meeting, and taught them
When to rain down their evil influence,
Which of them rising or falling with the sun
Should cause trouble; they put the winds
In their corners, telling them when with gales they should confuse
The sea, air and land, told the thunder when to crash
With terror through the dark halls of sky.

Some say he told his angels to turn
The poles of the earth twenty degrees and more away
From the sun's axle; they worked to

push'd
Oblique the Centric Globe: Som say the Sun
Was bid turn Reines from th' Equinoctial Rode
Like distant breadth to Taurus with the Seav'n

Atlantick Sisters, and the Spartan Twins

Up to the Tropic Crab; thence down amaine

By Leo and the Virgin and the Scales,
As deep as Capricorne, to bring in change

Of Seasons to each Clime; else had the Spring
Perpetual smil'd on Earth with vernant Flours,
Equal in Days and Nights, except to those

Beyond the Polar Circles; to them Day
Had unbenighted shon, while the low Sun

To recompence his distance, in thir sight
Had rounded still th' Horizon, and not known
Or East or West, which had forbid the Snow
From cold Estotiland, and South as farr

Beneath Magellan. At that tasted Fruit

The Sun, as from Thyestean Banquet, turn'd
His course intended; else how had the World
Inhabited, though sinless, more then now,

Avoided pinching cold and scorching heate?
These changes in the Heav'ns, though slow, produc'd
Like change on Sea and Land, sideral blast,

Vapour, and Mist, and Exhalation hot,

push
The centred globe off straight: some say the sun
Was told to turn away from the path of the equator
To weave from Taurus and the Seven Sisters

Of the Atlantic, from the Spartan Twins

Up to the Tropic of Cancer, then down

Through Leo, Virgo and Libra
As low as the Tropic of Capricorn, to bring the change

Of seasons to all lands; otherwise spring
Would have smiled on Earth forever with blooming flowers,
With equal lengths of day and night, except for those

Beyond the polar circles; to them day
Had shone without night, while the low sun,

Because of his distance, to their view
Was still lying on the horizon, and they did not know
How he was in the east or west, banning the snow
From cold Estostiland and south as far

As the Magellan Straits. When the fruit had been tasted

The sun turned away in horror, moving
His intended course; otherwise how would the inhabited
World, though more sinless then than now,

Have avoided pinching cold and scorching heat?
These changes in the Heavens, though slow, produced
The same change on land and sea, evil influence from the stars,

Vapors, mists, and hot winds,

Corrupt and Pestilent: Now from the North	*Corrupt and diseased; now from the north*
Of Norumbega, and the Samoed shoar	*Of America, and the Siberian shore*
Bursting thir brazen Dungeon, armd with ice	*The winds burst from their captivity, armed with ice*
And snow and haile and stormie gust and flaw,	*And snow and hail and storms and squalls.*
Boreas and Cæcias and Argestes loud	*All the different winds loudly*
And Thrascias rend the Woods and Seas upturn;	*Ripped through the woods and whipped up the seas;*
With adverse blast up-turns them from the South	*With a counterblast up from the south*
Notus and Afer black with thundrous Clouds	*Come Notus and Afer black thunderous clouds*
From Serraliona; thwart of these as fierce	*From Sierra Leone; across these just as fierce*
Forth rush the Levant and the Ponent Windes	*Out rush the East and West winds*
Eurus and Zephir with thir lateral noise,	*Eurus and Zephyr with their cross winds*
Sirocco, and Libecchio.	*Sirocco and Libecchio.*
Thus began	*So began*
Outrage from liveless things; but Discord first	*Violence from lifeless things, but first Discord,*
Daughter of Sin, among th' irrational,	*The daughter of Sin, was introduced into the confusion*
Death introduc'd through fierce antipathie:	*By Death due to his fierce hatred;*
Beast now with Beast gan war, and Fowle with Fowle,	*Beasts began fighting beasts, birds with birds,*
And Fish with Fish; to graze the Herb all leaving,	*And fish with fish; they stopped grazing the grass*
Devourd each other; nor stood much in awe	*And began eating each other; nor did they stand and admire*
Of Man, but fled him, or with count'nance grim	*Man, but fled from him, or glared at him as he passed*
Glar'd on him passing: these were from without	*With grim faces: these were the growing miseries*
The growing miseries, which Adam saw	*Outside, which Adam already saw*
Alreadie in part, though hid in gloomiest shade,	*Part of, though hiding in the deepest shadow,*
To sorrow abandond, but worse felt within,	*Given over to sorrow, but he felt worse inside,*
And in a troubl'd Sea of passion tost,	*Tossed in agony on a sea of troubles,*
Thus to disburd'n sought with sad complaint.	*And he poured out his sorrows thus:*
O miserable of happie! is this the end	*"Oh what misery has come from*

	happiness! Is this the end
Of this new glorious World, and mee so late	*Of this glorious new World, and me who was so recently*
The Glory of that Glory, who now becom	*The pinnacle of that glory, now become*
Accurst of blessed, hide me from the face	*Cursed instead of blessed, hiding from the face*
Of God, whom to behold was then my highth	*Of God, whom it used to be my greatest pleasure*
Of happiness: yet well, if here would end	*To look upon: all would still be well if the misery*
The miserie, I deserv'd it, and would beare	*Would end here; I deserved death, and would face*
My own deservings; but this will not serve;	*My deserved punishment; but this will not do;*
All that I eat or drink, or shall beget,	*All that I eat or drink, or shall father,*
Is propagated curse. O voice once heard	*Is under a curse. The voice that was once delightful to hear*
Delightfully, Encrease and multiply,	*Saying, 'Increase and multiply'*
Now death to hear! for what can I increase	*Is now death to hear! For what can I increase*
Or multiplie, but curses on my head?	*Or multiply, except for the curses on my head?*
Who of all Ages to succeed, but feeling	*In all the ages to come, anyone feeling*
The evil on him brought by me, will curse	*The evil brought to him through me, will curse*
My Head, Ill fare our Ancestor impure,	*My head, 'Bad cess to our impure ancestor!*
For this we may thank Adam; but his thanks	*We can thank Adam for this!' But his thanks*
Shall be the execration; so besides	*Will be the curse; so besides*
Mine own that bide upon me, all from mee	*The curses I give myself those of all my descendants*
Shall with a fierce reflux on mee redound,	*Will with a fierce instinct fall on me*
On mee as on thir natural center light	*As a natural target, heavily,*
Heavie, though in thir place. O fleeting joys	*Though well deserved. Oh fleeting joy*
Of Paradise, deare bought with lasting woes!	*Of Paradise, bought at such a cost with eternal sorrow!*
Did I request thee, Maker, from my Clay	*Did I ask you, Makers, to make me*
To mould me Man, did I sollicite thee	*A man out of the dust? Did I ask you*
From darkness to promote me, or here place	*To bring me out of the darkness or put me here*
In this delicious Garden? as my Will	*In this delicious garden? As I had*

Concurd not to my being, it were but right

And equal to reduce me to my dust,
Desirous to resigne, and render back
All I receav'd, unable to performe
Thy terms too hard, by which I was to hold

The good I sought not. To the loss of that,

Sufficient penaltie, why hast thou added

The sense of endless woes? inexplicable

Thy Justice seems; yet to say truth, too late,

I thus contest; then should have been refusd

Those terms whatever, when they were propos'd:
Thou didst accept them; wilt thou enjoy the good,
Then cavil the conditions? and though God

Made thee without thy leave, what if thy Son
Prove disobedient, and reprov'd, retort,

Wherefore didst thou beget me? I sought it not
Wouldst thou admit for his contempt of thee
That proud excuse? yet him not thy election,
But Natural necessity begot.
God made thee of choice his own, and of his own
To serve him, thy reward was of his grace,

Thy punishment then justly is at his Will.

Be it so, for I submit, his doom is fair,
That dust I am, and shall to dust returne:
O welcom hour whenever! why delayes

His hand to execute what his Decree

---

no say
In my being made, it would only be fair

And just to turn me back to dust,
For I wish to resign, give back
Everything I was given, I could not keep to
Your too strict conditions, by which I was meant

To keep the good I had not looked for. Why have you added

To the loss of that, punishment enough,

Endless sorrow? Your justice seems

Inexplicable; to speak truthfully though too late

This is what I feel. But then you should have refused

Those terms, when they were proposed:
You did accept them, are you going to accept the rewards
But argue over the conditions? And though God

Made you without permission, what would you do if your son
Proved to be disobedient, and when you told him off he answered,

'Why then did you father me? I didn't ask you to.'
Would you allow that as an excuse
For his disobedience? But you did not father him by choice
But by the demands of Nature.
God made you with free will, and you had a free choice
To serve him. Your reward was given from his love,

And so it's right your punishment should be his choice.

So be it, I
I shall return to dust:
A welcome hour when it comes! Why does he

Hold back his hand from carrying out the sentence

Fixd on this day? why do I overlive,

Why am I mockt with death, and length'nd out

To deathless pain? how gladly would I meet

Mortalitie my sentence, and be Earth

Insensible, how glad would lay me down

As in my Mothers lap! There I should rest

And sleep secure; his dreadful voice no more

Would Thunder in my ears, no fear of worse

To mee and to my ofspring would torment me

With cruel expectation. Yet one doubt

Pursues me still, least all I cannot die,

Least that pure breath of Life, the Spirit of Man

Which God inspir'd, cannot together perish

With this corporeal Clod; then in the Grave,

Or in some other dismal place who knows

But I shall die a living Death? O thought

Horrid, if true! yet why? it was but breath

Of Life that sinn'd; what dies but what had life

And sin? the Bodie properly hath neither.

All of me then shall die: let this appease
The doubt, since humane reach no further knows.

For though the Lord of all be infinite,

Is his wrauth also? be it, man is not so,

But mortal doom'd. How can he exercise

Passed on this day? Why do I still live,

Why I am taunted with death and made to go on living

In deathless pain? How glad I would be to meet

My sentence of mortality, and become unfeeling

Earth, how glad I would be to lie down

As if in my mother's lap! I should rest there

And sleep soundly; his dreadful voice would no longer

Thunder in my ears, I would have no fear of worse

Tormenting me, expecting it to fall upon me

And my children. But there is one doubt

Which still follows me, fearing that I cannot die,

That the pure breath of life, the spirit of Man,

Created by God, cannot completely die

With this earthy body; then in the grave

Or in some other dismal place how can I know

That I won't suffer eternal damnation? What a horrible

Thought, if it comes true! But why should it? It was only

The soul which sinned; what dies but that which had life

And sin? The body does not have either.

All of me then shall die: let this calm The doubts, because this is all that humans can know.

For although the Lord of all is infinite,

Is his anger infinite too? Even if it is, man is not,

But doomed to die. How can he

Wrath without end on Man whom Death must end?
Can he make deathless Death? that were to make
Strange contradiction, which to God himself
Impossible is held, as Argument
Of weakness, not of Power. Will he draw out,
For angers sake, finite to infinite

In punisht man, to satisfie his rigour
Satisfi'd never; that were to extend

His Sentence beyond dust and Natures Law,

By which all Causes else according still

To the reception of thir matter act,
Not to th' extent of thir own Spheare. But say
That Death be not one stroak, as I suppos'd,

Bereaving sense, but endless miserie

From this day onward, which I feel begun

Both in me, and without me, and so last

To perpetuitie; Ay me, that fear
Comes thundring back with dreadful revolution
On my defensless head; both Death and I

Am found Eternal, and incorporate both,
Nor I on my part single, in mee all

Posteritie stands curst: Fair Patrimonie

That I must leave ye, Sons; O were I able

To waste it all my self, and leave ye none!

So disinherited how would ye bless

---

perform
Eternal punishment on Man, who death must bring to an end?
Can he make Death deathless? That would make
A strange contradiction, which is impossible
For God to do, for it would prove
His weakness, not his power. Will he extend,
For the sake of his anger, finite to infinite

In punishing man, to satisfy his anger
By never stopping? That would be to extend

His sentence beyond that of dust and the law of Nature,

Which everything else is still obeying according

To their construction, not influenced
By things from outside their world. But what
If death is not a single blow as I imagined,

Taking away all feeling, but instead endless misery

From this day onwards, which I can feel has begun

Both in me and in the world and will last

Forever; ah me, that fear
Comes thundering back with dreadful regularity
On my defenceless head; that Death and I

Are eternal and live in the same body,
And this won't just apply to me, but all

Posterity will be cursed through me; what an inheritance

I leave you, my sons; if only I were able

To spend it all myself and leave you none!

Disinherited, how you would bless me

Me now your curse! Ah, why should all mankind
For one mans fault thus guiltless be condemn'd,
If guiltless? But from mee what can proceed,
But all corrupt, both Mind and Will deprav'd,
Not to do onely, but to will the same

With me? how can they then acquitted stand
In sight of God? Him after all Disputes

Forc't I absolve: all my evasions vain

And reasonings, though through Mazes, lead me still
But to my own conviction: first and last

On mee, mee onely, as the sourse and spring
Of all corruption, all the blame lights due; thou
So might the wrauth. Fond wish! couldst support
That burden heavier then the Earth to bear
Then all the World much heavier, though divided
With that bad Woman? Thus what thou desir'st,
And what thou fearst, alike destroyes all hope
Of refuge, and concludes thee miserable
Beyond all past example and future,

To Satan only like both crime and doom.

O Conscience, into what Abyss of fears

And horrors hast thou driv'n me; out of which
I find no way, from deep to deeper plung'd!
Thus Adam to himself lamented loud
Through the still Night, not now, as ere

Instead of cursing me! Ah, why should all mankind,
Guiltless, be condemned for one man's fault,
If they are without guilt? But what can come from me
But corrupt offspring, perverted in mind and will,
Not to only do the same but to want the same

As me? How can they then be acquitted
In the eyes of God? After all these arguments

I am forced to admit God is right: all my vain excuses

And reasoning, twist it as I might, lead me still
Back to my own belief: first and last

On me, only me, as the source and fount
Of all corruption, all the blame falls,

And so should the punishment. Foolish hope! Could you support
That burden, heavier than the Earth,
Heavier than the universe, even if it was shared
With that bad woman? So what you hope
And what you fear both alike destroy all hope
Of shelter and leave you miserable
Beyond anything known in the past or future,

With only Satan as your equal in crime and punishment.

Oh conscience, what a pit of fear and horror
You have driven me into, and I can find
No way out, but plunge deeper and deeper."
So Adam lamented loudly all through
The still night, which was not now, as

man fell,
Wholsom and cool, and mild, but with black Air
Accompanied, with damps and dreadful gloom,
Which to his evil Conscience represented

All things with double terror: On the ground
Outstretcht he lay, on the cold ground, and oft
Curs'd his Creation, Death as oft accus'd

Of tardie execution, since denounc't

The day of his offence.
Why comes not Death,
Said hee, with one thrice acceptable stroke

To end me? Shall Truth fail to keep her word,
Justice Divine not hast'n to be just?
But Death comes not at call, Justice Divine

Mends not her slowest pace for prayers or cries.
O Woods, O Fountains, Hillocks, Dales and Bowrs,
With other echo late I taught your Shades
To answer, and resound farr other Song.
Whom thus afflicted when sad Eve beheld,
Desolate where she sate, approaching nigh,

Soft words to his fierce passion she assay'd:

But her with stern regard he thus repell'd.
Out of my sight, thou Serpent, that name best
Befits thee with him leagu'd, thy self as false
And hateful; nothing wants, but that thy shape,
Like his, and colour Serpentine may shew
Thy inward fraud, to warn all Creatures from thee
Henceforth; least that too heav'nly form,

it was before his fall,
Wholesome and cool, and mild, but it was full
Of black cloud, with mists and dreadful gloom,
Which made everything twice as frightening
To his guilty conscience: he lay outstretched
On the ground, on the cold ground, and often
Cursed his birth, cursed death as often
For not carrying out sentence of execution
On the day of his offence.
"Why does death not come,"
He asked, 'To finish me with one welcome blow?
Shall truth not keep her word,
Shall divine justice fail to be just?
But death does not come when it is called, and divine justice
Does not speed up her slow pace in answer to prayers or pleas.
Oh woods, fountains, hillocks, dales, bowers,
I recently made your echoes ring
With a far different song than this."
In this torment sad Eve saw him,
Desolate where she sat, and she drew near,
Trying to soothe his passion with soft words:
But he rejected her with a stern look.
"Get out of my sight, you serpent, that's the name that best
Suits you, the same name as the one you teamed up with. You're
Just as false and hateful; you're missing nothing but his shape
And snaky color to show
The deceit inside, so that all other creatures could be warned
To guard against you from now on;

pretended
To hellish falshood, snare them. But for thee
I had persisted happie, had not thy pride

And wandring vanitie, when lest was safe,

Rejected my forewarning, and disdain'd

Not to be trusted, longing to be seen

Though by the Devil himself, him overweening
To over-reach, but with the Serpent meeting
Fool'd and beguil'd, by him thou, I by thee,

To trust thee from my side, imagin'd wise,

Constant, mature, proof against all assaults,
And understood not all was but a shew

Rather then solid vertu, all but a Rib
Crooked by nature, bent, as now appears,
More to the part sinister from me drawn,
Well if thrown out, as supernumerarie

To my just number found. O why did God,
Creator wise, that peopl'd highest Heav'n

With Spirits Masculine, create at last

This noveltie on Earth, this fair defect

Of Nature, and not fill the World at once

With Men as Angels without Feminine,

Or find some other way to generate
Mankind? this mischief had not then befall'n,
And more that shall befall, innumerable

Disturbances on Earth through Femal snares,
And straight conjunction with this Sex:

---

then that gorgeous form,
Laid out for hellish deceit, won't trap them. But for you
I could have stayed happy, if your pride

And wandering vanity, at the most dangerous time,

Hadn't rejected my warning and insisted that

You could be trusted, longing to show yourself off

Even to the Devil himself, arrogantly thinking
You could beat him, but when you met the serpent
You were fooled and seduced, you by him and I by you.

I trusted you as being made from me, I thought you were wise,

Faithful, mature, immune to attack,
And did not understand it was all a show,

Not real virtue, just a rib,
Twisted by nature, bent, it now seems,
Drawn from the most evil part of me,
And well thrown out, as superfluous to my

true self. Oh why did God,
The wise Creator, that filled the highest Heaven

With masculine Spirits, make as his last thing

This novelty on Earth, this fair perversion

Of Nature, why did he not fill the world

With Men who were like angels, without female influence,

Or find some other way for Mankind
To breed? Then this mischief would not have happened,
Nor the consequences that are coming, numberless

Disturbances on Earth through women's traps,
And our mixing with this sex; for Man

for either
He never shall find out fit Mate, but such
As some misfortune brings him, or mistake,
Or whom he wishes most shall seldom gain
Through her perversness, but shall see her gaind
By a farr worse, or if she love, withheld
By Parents, or his happiest choice too late
Shall meet, alreadie linkt and Wedlock-bound
To a fell Adversarie, his hate or shame:
Which infinite calamitie shall cause
To Humane life, and houshold peace confound.
He added not, and from her turn'd, but Eve
Not so repulst, with Tears that ceas'd not flowing,
And tresses all disorderd, at his feet
Fell humble, and imbracing them, besought
His peace, and thus proceeded in her plaint.
Forsake me not thus, Adam, witness Heav'n
What love sincere, and reverence in my heart
I beare thee, and unweeting have offended,
Unhappilie deceav'd; thy suppliant
I beg, and clasp thy knees; bereave me not,
Whereon I live, thy gentle looks, thy aid,
Thy counsel in this uttermost distress,
My onely strength and stay: forlorn of thee,
Whither shall I betake me, where subsist?
While yet we live, scarse one short hour perhaps,
Between us two let there be peace, both

shall either
Never find a suitable partner, only the one
Some misfortune brings him, or a mistake.
Often the one he wants most he will not get
Through her perversity, but will see her won
By a far worse partner, or if she loves him her parents
Will forbid it, or he'll meet the perfect woman too late,
Already engaged and heading for marriage
To a horrible enemy, one he hates.
All this will cause infinite upheaval
In human life, and ruin household peace."
He spoke no more, and turned away, but Eve
Would not be rejected, and with incessant tears
And her hair all awry, fell humbly at his feet,
Hugging them, begging his forgiveness,
And made her plea.
"Do not forsake me like this, Adam, as Heaven is my witness
I have sincere love and reverence for you
In my heart, and I offended unwittingly,
Unhappily tricked; I make a humble plea,
I beg you and hug your knees; don't take from me
That which I live for, your gentle looks, your help,
Your advice in this terrible situation,
My only strength and comfort: stripped of you,
Where shall I go, how shall I live?
While we still live, which might be perhaps just another hour,
Let there be peace between us two,

joyning,
As joyn'd in injuries, one enmitie

Against a Foe by doom express assign'd us,

That cruel Serpent: On me exercise not
Thy hatred for this miserie befall'n,

On me alreadie lost, mee then thy self

More miserable; both have sin'd, but thou

Against God onely, I against God and thee,

And to the place of judgment will return,

There with my cries importune Heaven,
that all
The sentence from thy head remov'd may
light
On me, sole cause to thee of all this woe,

Mee mee onely just object of his ire.

She ended weeping, and her lowlie plight,

Immovable till peace obtain'd from fault

Acknowledg'd and deplor'd, in Adam
wraught
Commiseration; soon his heart relented

Towards her, his life so late and sole
delight,
Now at his feet submissive in distress,
Creature so faire his reconcilement seeking,

His counsel whom she had displeas'd,
his aide;
As one disarm'd, his anger all he lost,

And thus with peaceful words uprais'd
her soon.
Unwarie, and too desirous, as before,

So now of what thou knowst not, who

---

both joining
As we are joined in injury, in our
hatred

For the enemy whom fate assigned
us,

That cruel serpent: don't take out
Your hatred for all this misery which
has come

On me, who is already lost, and so
make me

Even more miserable than you. We
have both sinned,

But you only against God, I against
both God and you,

And I will go back to the place of
judgment

And with my cries I will beg Heaven
to take

All punishment away from you and let
it all fall

On me, the one cause of all your
sorrows,

I shall ask him to justly make me the
one object of his anger."

She finished, weeping, and her lowly
plight,

Which could not be soothed until
forgiveness was obtained for the fault

Which she acknowledged and
deplored, made Adam

Feel sorry for her. Soon his heart
relented

Towards she who was so recently his
whole life and only pleasure,

Now begging at his feet in distress,

Such a fair creature asking for
reconciliation

And the advice and help of the one
she had displeased;

He was disarmed, he lost all his
anger,

And lifted her up with peaceful
words.

"You are as reckless as before and
too willing

To become involved with things of

desir'st
The punishment all on thy self; alas,

Beare thine own first, ill able to sustaine

His full wrauth whose thou feelst as yet
lest part,
And my displeasure bearst so ill. If Prayers

Could alter high Decrees, I to that place

Would speed before thee, and be louder
heard,
That on my head all might be visited,

Thy frailtie and infirmer Sex forgiv'n,

To me committed and by me expos'd.
But rise, let us no more contend, nor blame

Each other, blam'd enough elsewhere,
but strive
In offices of Love, how we may light'n

Each others burden in our share of woe;

Since this days Death denounc't, if ought
I see,
Will prove no sudden, but a slow-pac't evill,

A long days dying to augment our paine,

And to our Seed (O hapless Seed!) deriv'd.

To whom thus Eve, recovering heart,
repli'd.
Adam, by sad experiment I know
How little weight my words with thee can
finde,
Found so erroneous, thence by just event
finde,
Found so unfortunate; nevertheless,

Restor'd by thee, vile as I am, to place

Of new acceptance, hopeful to regaine

which you know nothing,
When you ask for all the punishment
to fall on you; alas,

Bear your own first, you will not cope
with

His full anger, of which you have
only so far felt the smallest part;
You have not even been able to bear
my displeasure. If prayers

Could alter the orders of Heaven I
would rush

To that place ahead of you, and be
heard louder,
Asking that all punishment should fall
on me,

That your weakness and frail sex
should be forgiven,

With everything blamed on me.
But get up, let us stop arguing and
not blame

Each other, for we have been blamed
enough by others, we should

Work at our love, and see how we can
lighten

Each others' burden in the sadness
we share,

Since today's sentence of death, if I
see rightly,
Will not come suddenly, but is a slow
paced evil,

A long day of dying to add to our
pain,

And it will fall upon our unhappy
children."

Eve, gaining heart, answered.

"Adam, by sad experience I know
How little weight you give my words,

Which you thought so wrong and you
were proved
Right by the unfortunate events;
nevertheless,

Forgiven by you, vile as I am, and
given your

Renewed acceptance, hoping to

	regain
Thy Love, the sole contentment of my heart	*Your love, the sole pleasure of my heart*
Living or dying, from thee I will not hide	*In life or death, I will not hide from you*
What thoughts in my unquiet brest are ris'n,	*The thoughts that rise in my disturbed heart,*
Tending to some relief of our extremes,	*Thinking of some relief for our torment,*
Or end, though sharp and sad, yet tolerable,	*Or an end, though sharp and sad, but tolerable*
As in our evils, and of easier choice.	*In such a desperate situation, and an easier choice.*
If care of our descent perplex us most,	*If care for our descendants is our biggest worry,*
Which must be born to certain woe, devourd	*For they must be born to certain sorrow, eaten*
By Death at last, and miserable it is	*By death at last, and it is miserable*
To be to others cause of misery,	*To be the cause of misery in others,*
Our own begotten, and of our Loines to bring	*Our own flesh and blood. From our loins we will bring*
Into this cursed World a woful Race,	*Into this world a sorrowful race,*
That after wretched Life must be at last	*That after a wretched life will become*
Food for so foule a Monster, in thy power	*Food for such a foul monster, but it lies*
It lies, yet ere Conception to prevent	*In your power, before conception,*
The Race unblest, to being yet unbegot.	*To stop that unblessed race from being started.*
Childless thou art, Childless remaine:	*You are childless, you should remain so:*
So Death shall be deceav'd his glut, and with us two	*So Death will be cheated of his feast, and be forced*
Be forc'd to satisfie his Rav'nous Maw.	*To satisfy his ravenous mouth with just us two.*
But if thou judge it hard and difficult,	*But if you think it will be difficult,*
Conversing, looking, loving, to abstain	*Being together, looking, loving, to abstain*
From Loves due Rites, Nuptial imbraces sweet,	*From the rites of love, sweet marital embraces,*
And with desire to languish without hope,	*And to suffer with unfulfilled desire*
Before the present object languishing	*Before me, feeling the same desire,*
With like desire, which would be miserie	*Which would be a misery*
And torment less then none of what we dread,	*And punishment as great as all the others we dread,*
Then both our selves and Seed at once to free	*Then let us free ourselves and our children*

From what we fear for both, let us make short,
Let us seek Death, or he not found, supply

With our own hands his Office on our selves;
Why stand we longer shivering under feares,
That shew no end but Death, and have the power,
Of many ways to die the shortest choosing,

Destruction with destruction to destroy.

She ended heer, or vehement despaire
Broke off the rest; so much of Death her thoughts
Had entertaind, as di'd her Cheeks with pale.
But Adam with such counsel nothing sway'd,
To better hopes his more attentive minde

Labouring had rais'd, and thus to Eve repli'd.
Eve, thy contempt of life and pleasure seems
To argue in thee somthing more sublime

And excellent then what thy minde contemnes;
But self-destruction therefore saught, refutes

That excellence thought in thee, and implies,
Not thy contempt, but anguish and regret

For loss of life and pleasure overlov'd.

Or if thou covet death, as utmost end
Of miserie, so thinking to evade
The penaltie pronounc't, doubt not but God

Hath wiselier arm'd his vengeful ire then so

From what we fear for us both: let us cut it short,
Let us look for Death, or if we cannot find him
Then do his job ourselves.

Why should we stand any longer quaking at a future
Which shows no end but death, when we have the power
To choose the shortest of the many ways to die,
To destroy destruction with destruction?"

Here she ended, or great despair Stopped her finishing; she had thought so much
Of death that her cheeks paled as if she was actually dead.
But Adam would not be swayed by such advice,
For his greater intelligence had given him
Better hopes, and so he answered Eve.
"Eve, your contempt for life and pleasure seems
To argue that there is within you something more noble
And excellent than you believe.

But looking for suicide like this argues against

That excellence, and implies

Not that you have contempt but you have anguish and regret
For the loss of life and pleasure you loved too much.
Or if you seek death as the final end
To misery, thinking that is a way to avoid
The sentence that has been passed, do not doubt that God
Has made his plan of punishment too wisely to

To be forestall'd; much more I fear least Death
So snatcht will not exempt us from the paine
We are by doom to pay; rather such acts

Of contumacie will provoke the highest

To make death in us live: Then let us seek
Some safer resolution, which methinks

I have in view, calling to minde with heed
Part of our Sentence, that thy Seed shall bruise
The Serpents head; piteous amends, unless

Be meant, whom I conjecture, our grand Foe
Satan, who in the Serpent hath contriv'd

Against us this deceit: to crush his head
Would be revenge indeed; which will be lost
By death brought on our selves, or childless days
Resolv'd, as thou proposest; so our Foe

Shall scape his punishment ordain'd, and wee
Instead shall double ours upon our heads.
No more be mention'd then of violence
Against our selves, and wilful barrenness,

That cuts us off from hope, and savours onely

Rancor and pride, impatience and despite,

Reluctance against God and his just yoke

Laid on our Necks. Remember with what mild
And gracious temper he both heard and judg'd
Without wrauth or reviling; wee expected
Immediate dissolution, which we thought

Be cheated like that; I would be more worried that death
Grabbed like that will not exempt us from the pain
That we are sentenced to pay; rather such acts

Of disobedience will provoke the highest

To make death live in us. Let us seek
Some safer plan, which I think I can see,

Thinking carefully about
Part of our sentence, that our descendants shall bruise
The serpent's head; small consolation, unless

As I conjecture by serpent was meant our great enemy
Satan, who in the shape of a serpent devised

All our downfall; to crush his head
Would indeed be revenge; this will be lost
If we bring death on ourselves, or choose to be
Childless, as you have proposed; so our enemy

Will escape his sentence and we
Shall double ours upon ourselves.
Say no more then of violence
Against ourselves, or chosen infertility,

That cuts us off from hope, and looks only like

Resentment and pride, impatience and spite,

Reluctance to accept God's order and the just punishment

He has laid on our necks. Remember with what a sweet
And gracious temper he heard and judged us,
Without anger or abuse; we expected
To be eliminated at once, which we

Was meant by Death that day, when lo, to thee
Pains onely in Child-bearing were foretold,
And bringing forth, soon recompenc't with joy,
Fruit of thy Womb: On mee the Curse aslope
Glanc'd on the ground, with labour I must earne
My bread; what harm? Idleness had bin worse;
My labour will sustain me; and least Cold

Or Heat should injure us, his timely care

Hath unbesaught provided, and his hands

Cloath'd us unworthie, pitying while he judg'd;
How much more, if we pray him, will his ear
Be open, and his heart to pitie incline,

And teach us further by what means to shun

Th' inclement Seasons, Rain, Ice, Hail and Snow,
Which now the Skie with various Face begins
To shew us in this Mountain, while the Winds
Blow moist and keen, shattering the graceful locks
Of these fair spreading Trees; which bids us seek
Som better shroud, som better warmth to cherish
Our Limbs benumm'd, ere this diurnal Starr
Leave cold the Night, how we his gather'd beams
Reflected, may with matter sere foment,

Or by collision of two bodies grinde
The Air attrite to Fire, as late the Clouds

Was coming with instant death, when suddenly, for you,
Pain only in childbirth was predicted,
And those would soon be repaid with happiness as you brought forth
Your children; on me the curse glanced off
Onto the ground, that I must earn my bread
Through work; what harm is that? It would be worse to be idle;
My work will keep me strong, and in case cold
Or heat should harm us, his well timed care
Has provided help unasked for, and his hands
Clothed us, unworthy, pitying while he judged;
How much more, if we pray to him, will his ear
Be open, and his heart lean towards pity,
And he will teach us further ways in which we can shun
The inclement seasons, rain, ice, hail and snow,
Which the sky with various appearances begins
To show us in this mountain, while the winds
Blow wet and harsh, stripping the leaves
Of these fair trees. This warns us to find
Some better covering, some better warmth to heat
Our numbed limbs before the sun
Leaves the night cold. We may be able to reflect
His gathered rays onto some dry matter,
Or by grinding two objects together
To make friction to start a fire, as recently the clouds

Justling or pusht with Winds rude in thir shock	*Pushed by the winds clash with each other and in the shock*
Tine the slant Lightning, whose thwart flame driv'n down	*Kindle the slanting lightning, whose jagged flame is driven down*
Kindles the gummie bark of Firr or Pine,	*And lights the oily bark of fir or pine,*
And sends a comforttable heat from farr,	*And sends a comfortable heat from far off,*
Which might supplie the Sun: such Fire to use,	*Which might be a replacement for the sun: how to use such fire*
And what may else be remedie or cure	*And whatever else might be a remedy or cure*
To evils which our own misdeeds have wrought,	*For the evils which our own misdeeds have created,*
Hee will instruct us praying, and of Grace	*He will tell us when we pray, and we will ask*
Beseeching him, so as we need not fear	*For his grace, so we will be able*
To pass commodiously this life, sustain'd	*To pass this life comfortably, sustained*
By him with many comforts, till we end	*By him with many comforts, until we finish*
In dust, our final rest and native home.	*As dust, our final rest and our homeland.*
What better can we do, then to the place	*What better can we do than go to the place*
Repairing where he judg'd us, prostrate fall	*Where he judged us and fall prostrate*
Before him reverent, and there confess	*Before him in worship, humbly confess*
Humbly our faults, and pardon beg, with tears	*Our faults and beg for forgiveness,*
Watering the ground, and with our sighs the Air	*With tears watering the ground and filling the air*
Frequenting, sent from hearts contrite, in sign	*With our sighs, sent from our remorseful hearts,*
Of sorrow unfeign'd, and humiliation meek.	*A sign of our genuine regret and meek submission.*
Undoubtedly he will relent and turn	*Undoubtedly he will relent and turn away*
From his displeasure; in whose look serene,	*From his anger; in his serene look,*
When angry most he seem'd and most severe,	*When he seemed most angry and severe,*
What else but favor, grace, and mercie shon?	*What else could be seen but favor, grace and mercy?"*
So spake our Father penitent, nor Eve	*So spoke our Father, repentant, nor did Eve*
Felt less remorse: they forthwith to the place	*Feel any less remorse: they went straight to the place*

386

Repairing where he judg'd them prostrate
fell
Before him reverent, and both confess'd

Humbly thir faults, and pardon beg'd,
with tears
Watering the ground, and with thir sighs
the Air
Frequenting, sent from hearts contrite,
in sign
Of sorrow unfeign'd, and humiliation meek.

Where he had judged them and fell
prostrate
Before him, worshipping, and both
humbly
Confessed their faults, and begged
for forgiveness, with
Their tears watering the ground, and
with sighs
Filling the air, sent from their
remorseful hearts,
A sign of their genuine regret and
meek submission.

BOOK XI

THE ARGUMENT

The Son of God presents to his Father the Prayers of our first Parents now repenting, and intercedes for them: God accepts them, but declares that they must no longer abide in Paradise; sends Michael with a Band of Cherubim to dispossess them; but first to reveal to Adam future things: Michaels coming down. Adam shews to Eve certain ominous signs; he discerns Michaels approach, goes out to meet him: the Angel denounces thir departure. Eve's Lamentation. Adam pleads, but submits: The Angel leads him up to a high Hill, sets before him in vision what shall happ'n till the Flood.

The Son of God presents his Father with the prayers of our first parents who are now repentant, and intercedes for them. God accepts them but declares that they may no longer live in Paradise. He sends Michael with a band of Cherubim to dispossess them, telling him to reveal things of the future to Adam first. Michael descends to Paradise. Adam shows Eve certain ominous signs. He sees Michael approaching and goes to meet him. The Angel announces that they must depart. Eve Eve laments. Adam pleads but submits. The Angel takes Adam to the top of a high hill and gives him a vision of what will happen until the Flood comes.

Thus they in lowliest plight repentant stood

So, in their humble trouble, they stood

Praying, for from the Mercie-seat above

Praying, for from the Heavenly seat of mercy

Prevenient Grace descending had remov'd

Specail grace had descended and removed

The stonie from thir hearts, & made new flesh

The stone from their hearts and made new flesh

Regcncrate grow instead, that sighs now breath'd

Grow again instead, that now breathed wordless

Unutterable, which the Spirit of prayer Inspir'd, and wing'd for Heav'n with speedier flight

Sighs, inspired by the spirit of prayer, And flew to Heaven quicker

Then loudest Oratorie: yet thir port

Than the loudest speech; but their attitude

Not of mean suiters, nor important less

Was not that of beggars, nor did their plea

Seem'd thir Petition, then when th' ancient Pair

Seem less important than when the ancient pair

In Fables old, less ancient yet then these,

Of old stories (though less ancient than these two)

Deucalion and chaste Pyrrha to restore

Deucalion and chaste Pyrrah, to restore

The Race of Mankind drownd, before the

The human race which had been

Shrine	drowned stood
Of Themis stood devout. To Heav'n thir prayers	Praying at the shrine of Themis. Their prayers flew
Flew up, nor missd the way, by envious windes	Up to Heaven, and were not blown off course
Blow'n vagabond or frustrate: in they passd	By jealous winds; they passed,
Dimentionless through Heav'nly dores; then clad	Pure spirit, through the doors of Heaven; then perfumed
With incense, where the Golden Altar fum'd,	With incense, where the golden altar burned,
By thir great Intercessor, came in sight	By their great mediator, appeared
Before the Fathers Throne: Them the glad Son	Before the Father's throne: the glad Son
Presenting, thus to intercede began.	Presented them, and began his intervention.
See Father, what first fruits on Earth are sprung	"You see, Father here are the first fruits grown on Earth
From thy implanted Grace in Man, these Sighs	From the grace you place in man, these sighs
And Prayers, which in this Golden Censer, mixt	And prayers, which in this golden censer, mixed
With Incense, I thy Priest before thee bring,	With incense, I bring before you as your priest.
Fruits of more pleasing savour from thy seed	These are fruits of better taste, grown from the seed
Sow'n with contrition in his heart, then those	Of remorse you sowed in his heart, than could
Which his own hand manuring all the Trees	Have been produced by his own hand
Of Paradise could have produc't, ere fall'n	Tending all the trees in Paradise, before he fell
From innocence. Now therefore bend thine eare	From innocence. So now lend your ear
To supplication, heare his sighs though mute;	To their pleas, hear his wordless sighs;
Unskilful with what words to pray, let mee	As he is not skilled in choice of words for prayer let me
Interpret for him, mee his Advocate	Interpret for him, let me be his representative
And propitiation, all his works on mee	And sacrifice, make me responsible for all he does,
Good or not good ingraft, my Merit those	Good or bad, and my merits shall make
Shall perfet, and for these my Death shall pay.	The good perfect, and I shall pay for the bad with my death.
Accept me, and in mee from these receave	Accept me, and receiving these prayers through me

The smell of peace toward Mankinde, let him live

Give peace to Mankind, let him live

Before thee reconcil'd, at least his days

Reconciled with you, even if sad, at least for

Numberd, though sad, till Death, his doom (which I

The days of his life, until death, his sentence (which I

To mitigate thus plead, not to reverse)

Am asking you to soften, not to reverse)

To better life shall yeeld him, where with mee

Shall lead him to a better life, where he will live

All my redeemd may dwell in joy and bliss,

With me and all my redeemed in joy and bliss,

Made one with me as I with thee am one.

Made a part of me as I am a part of you."

To whom the Father, without Cloud, serene.

To whom the Father, in open view, serenely replied.

All thy request for Man, accepted Son,

"All your requests for man, welcome Son,

Obtain, all thy request was my Decree:

Are granted, all you ask was in my plan;

But longer in that Paradise to dwell,

But they cannot live longer in Paradise,

The Law I gave to Nature him forbids: Those pure immortal Elements that know

The natural laws I made forbid it. Those pure eternal elements do not know

No gross, no unharmoneous mixture foule, Eject him tainted now, and purge him off

Any unpleasant or clashing mixture And they reject him now as tainted, and as

As a distemper, gross to aire as gross,

An infection, he must breathe normal air,

And mortal food, as may dispose him best For dissolution wrought by Sin, that first

Eat mortal food as best he can, Due to the destruction done by sin, that first

Distemperd all things, and of incorrupt Corrupted. I at first with two fair gifts Created him endowd, with Happiness And Immortalitie: that fondly lost,

Infected all things, and corrupted The pure. In the beginning I gave him Two fair gifts, happiness And immortality: with happiness foolishly lost

This other serv'd but to eternize woe;

Immortality only served to make his sorrow eternal,

Till I provided Death; so Death becomes

Until I gave him death; so death becomes

His final remedie, and after Life Tri'd in sharp tribulation, and refin'd By Faith and faithful works, to second Life,

His final cure, and after a life Of trials and trouble, and bettered By faith and the work of faith, he

Wak't in the renovation of the just,

Resignes him up with Heav'n and Earth renewd.
But let us call to Synod all the Blest

Through Heav'ns wide bounds; from them I will not hide
My judgments, how with Mankind I proceed,
As how with peccant Angels late they saw;

And in thir state, though firm, stood more confirmd.
He ended, and the Son gave signal high
To the bright Minister that watchd, hee blew
His Trumpet, heard in Oreb since perhaps

When God descended, and perhaps once more
To sound at general Doom. Th' Angelic blast
Filld all the Regions: from thir blissful Bowrs
Of Amarantin Shade, Fountain or Spring,

By the waters of Life, where ere they sate

In fellowships of joy: the Sons of Light
Hasted, resorting to the Summons high,

And took thir Seats; till from his Throne supream
Th' Almighty thus pronouncd his sovran Will.
O Sons, like one of us Man is become

To know both Good and Evil, since his taste
Of that defended Fruit; but let him boast
His knowledge of Good lost, and Evil got,

Happier, had suffic'd him to have known

gives himself up
To a second life, awoken by the restoration of the just,
And arrives at Heaven and Earth reborn.
But let us call to meeting all the blessed
In Heaven's wide lands; I will not keep
My judgments from them as to how I will deal with mankind,
As they saw me recently deal with the sinful angels,
Who were condemned even though they were of the highest."
He ended, and the son signaled
To the angelic minister who watched, he blew
His trumpet, in later times maybe heard in Oreb
When God came down to Moses, and perhaps will be heard
Again on the Day of Judgment.The angelic blast
Filled all the lands: from their lovely bowers
Shaded by Amaranth, fountain or spring,
By the waters of life, wherever they sat
In joyful fellowship, the sons of light
Hurried in response to the high summons
And took their seats, and from the highest throne
The Almighty pronounced his royal will.
"Oh sons, man has come to be like one of us,
Knowing both good and evil since he tasted
That forbidden fruit; but he has found
He has lost his knowledge of good, and found evil.
He would have been happier if he'd been satisfied

Original	Modern
Good by it self, and Evil not at all.	With good alone, and not known evil at all.
He sorrows now, repents, and prayes contrite,	He grieves now, repents, and prays with remorse.
My motions in him, longer then they move,	My spirit moves more in him now,
His heart I know, how variable and vain	For I know his heart, how variable and vain it is
Self-left. Least therefore his now bolder hand	If left to itself.In case his now bolder hand
Reach also of the Tree of Life, and eat,	Should also reach for the tree of life and eat
And live for ever, dream at least to live	And live for ever, or at least imagine he would live
For ever, to remove him I decree,	Forever, I rule that he shall be moved
And send him from the Garden forth to Till	From the garden and sent out to work
The Ground whence he was taken, fitter soile.	The ground from which he was taken, better soil for him.
Michael, this my behest have thou in charge,	Michael, I give you my order to carry out;
Take to thee from among the Cherubim	Take with you from amongst the Cherubim
Thy choice of flaming Warriours, least the Fiend	Your choice of fiery warriors, in case the fiend,
Or in behalf of Man, or to invade	Either on behalf of Man, or to invade
Vacant possession som new trouble raise:	The empty land, tries to start some new trouble.
Hast thee, and from the Paradise of God	Hurry, drive the sinful pair out
Without remorse drive out the sinful Pair,	Of the Paradise of God without pity,
From hallowd ground th' unholie, and denounce	Forbid the sacred ground to the unholy and announce
To them and to thir Progenie from thence	That they are banished forever, them
Perpetual banishment. Yet least they faint	And their children.But in case they faint
At the sad Sentence rigorously urg'd,	At this sad sentenced being enforced
For I behold them softn'd and with tears	(For I see they are softened and regretting
Bewailing thir excess, all terror hide.	Their behavior with tears) then take away their fears.
If patiently thy bidding they obey,	If they do as they are told,
Dismiss them not disconsolate; reveale	Don't send them away downhearted; tell
To Adam what shall come in future dayes,	Adam what will happen in the future,
As I shall thee enlighten, intermix	As I shall tell you, let them know
My Cov'nant in the womans seed renewd;	How my promise will be renewed in the woman's seed;
So send them forth, though sorrowing,	So send them away in peace, though

yet in peace:
And on the East side of the Garden place,
Where entrance up from Eden easiest climbes,
Cherubic watch, and of a Sword the flame
Wide waving, all approach farr off to fright,

And guard all passage to the Tree of Life:

Least Paradise a receptacle prove

To Spirits foule, and all my Trees thir prey,

With whose stol'n Fruit Man once more to delude.
He ceas'd; and th' Archangelic Power prepar'd
For swift descent, with him the Cohort bright
Of watchful Cherubim; four faces each

Had, like a double Janus, all thir shape

Spangl'd with eyes more numerous then those
Of Argus, and more wakeful then to drouze,
Charm'd with Arcadian Pipe, the Pastoral Reed
Of Hermes, or his opiate Rod. Mean while

To resalute the World with sacred Light
Leucothea wak'd, and with fresh dews imbalmd
The Earth, when Adam and first Matron Eve
Had ended now thir Orisons, and found,
Strength added from above, new hope to spring
Out of despaire, joy, but with fear yet linkt;

Which thus to Eve his welcome words renewd.
Eve, easily may Faith admit, that all

---

sad,
And on the east side of the garden,
Where it is easiest to gain entry from Eden,
Place a guard of Cherubs and a flaming sword
Waving far and wide, to deter all approaches from far away.

And guard all access to the Tree of Life,

In case Paradise should become a home

For foul spirits, all preying on my trees,

Using their stolen fruit to trick Man again."
He finished, and the archangel prepared
For a swift descent with a group
Of bright Cherubim guards. They each had four faces,
Like a double Janus, and their shapes were covered
With more eyes than Argos, and more watchful
Than to fall asleep
Charmed by the Aracadian pipe, the pastoral reed
Of Hermes or his magic wand. Meanwhile,

To refill the world with holy light,
The goddess of the morning woke, and with fresh dews anointed
The Earth, so that when Adam and the first mother Eve
Had finished their prayers they found
New strength sent from above, new hope springing
From despair, joy, but it was still linked with fear,
Which he spoke of to her with his welcome words.
"Eve, it is easy, with faith, to believe that all

The good which we enjoy, from Heav'n descends;
But that from us ought should ascend to Heav'n
So prevalent as to concerne the mind

Of God high-blest, or to incline his will,

Hard to belief may seem; yet this will Prayer,

Or one short sigh of humane breath, up-borne
Ev'n to the Seat of God. For since I saught

By Prayer th' offended Deitie to appease,

Kneel'd and before him humbl'd all my heart,
Methought I saw him placable and mild,

Bending his eare; perswasion in me grew

That I was heard with favour; peace returnd

Home to my brest, and to my memorie

His promise, that thy Seed shall bruise our Foe;
Which then not minded in dismay, yet now

Assures me that the bitterness of death

Is past, and we shall live. Whence Haile to thee,
Eve rightly call'd, Mother of all Mankind,

Mother of all things living, since by thee

Man is to live, and all things live for Man.

To whom thus Eve with sad demeanour meek.
Ill worthie I such title should belong
To me transgressour, who for thee ordaind

The good which we enjoy comes down from Heaven;
But that anything from us should rise up to Heaven
Would be important enough to concern the mind

Of great God, or make him change his actions,

Seems hard to believe; but prayer can do this,

Just one small sigh of human breath can be carried up
Even to the throne of God. For since I tried

To appease the angered Deity with prayer,

Kneeled and humbly spread my heart before him,
I thought I saw him peaceful and mild,

Bending down to listen; I became convinced

That I was heard favorably; peace returned

To my heart, and to my memory returned

His promise, that your offspring shall bruise our enemy.
At the time I did not pay any attention to it in my despair, but now

It assures me that the bitterness of death

Is past, and we shall live. So hail to you,
Eve who is rightly called Mother of all Mankind,

Mother of all living things, since Man will live

Through you, and all things live for man."

Eve said to him, with a sad and humble face,
"I do not deserve to have such a title,
Me, the sinner, who was made for you as a help

A help, became thy snare; to mee reproach	*And instead became a trap; to me reproach*
Rather belongs, distrust and all dispraise:	*Belongs, distrust and censure.*
But infinite in pardon was my Judge,	*But my judge showed infinite mercy,*
That I who first brought Death on all, am grac't	*So that I who first brought death on all am graced*
The sourse of life; next favourable thou,	*With the source of life; you are next to him in mercy,*
Who highly thus to entitle me voutsaf'st,	*Giving me such a high title*
Farr other name deserving. But the Field	*When I deserve a very different one. But the field*
To labour calls us now with sweat impos'd,	*Calls us to our punishment of sweaty labor,*
Though after sleepless Night; for see the Morn,	*Though we have had a sleepless night.See the morning,*
All unconcern'd with our unrest, begins	*Not concerned with our restlessness, begins*
Her rosie progress smiling; let us forth,	*Her rosy journey all smiling.Let us go out*
I never from thy side henceforth to stray,	*(And I will never again stray from your side)*
Wherere our days work lies, though now enjoind	*To where our day's work waits, although it is now*
Laborious, till day droop; while here we dwell,	*To be laborious, until the day's end. While we are living here,*
What can be toilsom in these pleasant Walkes?	*How hard could work be in these pleasant paths?*
Here let us live, though in fall'n state, content.	*Let us live here, and though fallen, be content."*
So spake, so wish'd much-humbl'd Eve, but Fate	*So much humbled Eve spoke of her wishes, but fate*
Subscrib'd not; Nature first gave Signs, imprest	*Would not allow it; Nature first gave signs, marked*
On Bird, Beast, Aire, Aire suddenly eclips'd	*On the birds, beasts and the air, air that was suddenly dark*
After short blush of Morn; nigh in her sight	*After the first blush of morning; Eve saw*
The Bird of Jove, stoopt from his aerie tour,	*The eagle dive from his journey in the sky,*
Two Birds of gayest plume before him drove:	*Driving two peacocks ahead of him:*
Down from a Hill the Beast that reigns in Woods,	*Down from the hill came a lion,*
First hunter then, pursu'd a gentle brace,	*Now the first hunter, chasing a hart and a hind,*
Goodliest of all the Forrest, Hart and Hinde;	*The gentle pair, best of all the forest;*

<table>
<tr><td>

Direct to th' Eastern Gate was bent thir flight.
Adam observ'd, and with his Eye the chase

Pursuing, not unmov'd to Eve thus spake.
O Eve, some furder change awaits us nigh,

Which Heav'n by these mute signs in Nature shews
Forerunners of his purpose, or to warn

Us haply too secure of our discharge

From penaltie, because from death releast

Some days; how long, and what till then our life,
Who knows, or more then this, that we are dust,
And thither must return and be no more.

Why else this double object in our sight

Of flight pursu'd in th' Air and ore the ground
One way the self-same hour? why in the East
Darkness ere Dayes mid-course, and Morning light
More orient in yon Western Cloud that draws
O're the blew Firmament a radiant white,
And slow descends, with somthing heav'nly fraught.
He err'd not, for by this the heav'nly Bands

Down from a Skie of Jasper lighted now

In Paradise, and on a Hill made alt,
A glorious Apparition, had not doubt

And carnal fear that day dimm'd Adams eye.
Not that more glorious, when the Angels met
Jacob in Mahanaim, where he saw

</td><td>

They ran straight towards the eastern gate.
Adam saw this, and following the chase with his eyes
Spoke to Eve, disturbed.
"Oh Eve, some further punishment is coming for us,
Which Heaven shows through these signs in Nature,
Demonstrating his plan, or maybe they are
To warn us not to think that we have escaped
All punishment, just because we have been released from death
For a while; how long for, and what until then our life will be,
Who knows? All we can be certain of is that we are dust
And will return there and cease existing.
Why else would we be shown this double sign
Of flight in the air and over the ground,
Both at the same time? Why is it dark in the east
Before day is half over, and the morning light
Shines more in that western cloud that's drawing
A shining white over the blue sky
And slowly descending, carrying something from Heaven."
He was right, for as he said this the Heavenly band
Landed in Paradise from a sky of jasper
And stopped on a hill.
It would have been glorious to see, if doubt
And mortal fear had not dimmed Adam's eye that day.
It was more glorious than when the angels met
Jacob in Mahanaim, where he saw

</td></tr>
</table>

The field Pavilion'd with his Guardians bright;
Nor that which on the flaming Mount appeerd
In Dothan, cover'd with a Camp of Fire,

Against the Syrian King, who to surprize
One man, Assassin-like had levied Warr,

Warr unproclam'd. The Princely Hierarch
In thir bright stand, there left his Powers to seise
Possession of the Garden; hee alone,

To find where Adam shelterd, took his way,
Not unperceav'd of Adam, who to Eve,

While the great Visitant approachd, thus spake.
Eve, now expect great tidings, which perhaps
Of us will soon determin, or impose
New Laws to be observ'd; for I descrie
From yonder blazing Cloud that veils the Hill
One of the heav'nly Host, and by his Gate

None of the meanest, some great Potentate

Or of the Thrones above, such Majestie

Invests him coming? yet not terrible,

That I should fear, nor sociably mild,

As Raphael, that I should much confide,

But solemn and sublime, whom not to offend,
With reverence I must meet, and thou retire.

He ended; and th' Arch-Angel soon drew nigh,
Not in his shape Celestial, but as Man

Clad to meet Man; over his lucid Armes

The field covered in the tents of his bright guardians,
More glorious than those that appeared on the flaming mountain
In Dothan, covered with a camp of fire

Against the Syrian king, who to trap
One man had gone to war like an assassin,

Making war by ambush.Michael
Left his forces in that place to take

Possession of the garden; he went alone

To find where Adam was sheltering,
Who saw him coming, and spoke to Eve

As the great visitor approached.

"Eve, now expect great news, which perhaps
Will tell us of our fate, or impose
New laws for us to obey; for I see
One of the Heavenly host coming from the blazing cloud
That veils that hill, and from his bearing I see

He is not one of the low ones, he is some great power,

Or is he even from one of the thrones of Heaven,

He has such majesty in his approach?But he is not terrible,

Like one I should fear, nor friendly and kind

Like Raphael, so that I would chat with him.

He is solemn and spiritual, and so as not to offend him
I must meet him with reverence, and you must withdraw."

He finished, and the archangel soon came near,
Not in his Heavenly shape but as a man,

Dressed to meet Man; over his

A militarie Vest of purple flowd
Livelier then Meliboean, or the graine

Of Sarra, worn by Kings and Hero's old

In time of Truce; Iris had dipt the wooff;

His starrie Helme unbuckl'd shew'd him prime
In Manhood where Youth ended; by his side
As in a glistering Zodiac hung the Sword,

Satans dire dread, and in his hand the Spear.

Adam bowd low, hee Kingly from his State

Inclin'd not, but his coming thus declar'd.

Adam, Heav'ns high behest no Preface needs:
Sufficient that thy Prayers are heard, and Death,
Then due by sentence when thou didst transgress,
Defeated of his seisure many dayes

Giv'n thee of Grace, wherein thou may'st repent,
And one bad act with many deeds well done

Mayst cover: well may then thy Lord appeas'd
Redeem thee quite from Deaths rapacious claime;
But longer in this Paradise to dwell
Permits not; to remove thee I am come,

And send thee from the Garden forth to till

The ground whence thou wast tak'n, fitter Soile.
He added not, for Adam at the newes

shining armor
Was a robe of military purple,
Brighter than one dyed with
Meliboean dye or the dye
Of Tyre, worn by the ancient kings
and heroes
In peacetime, for the cloth had been
dipped in the rainbow.
When he took off his starry helmet he
could be seen as in the prime
Of manhood, where youth ended; by
his side
His sword hung as one does from
Orion's belt,
The sword which Satan dreaded, and
his spear was in his hand.
Adam bowed low, but he, having the
status of a King

Did not return it, but announced his
coming thus.
"Adam, heaven's high orders need no
preamble:
It is enough to say that your prayers
are heard, and death,
The proper sentence due for your
sins,
Has been cheated of his prey for
many days
Given to you by grace, which you
may use to repent
And cover the one bad deed with
many good ones.
Then your Lord may well be
appeased
And free you from death forever;

But you are no longer permitted
To live in Paradise; I have come to
remove you
And send you from the garden to
work
The earth from which you were taken,
fitter soil."
He spoke no further, for at the news
Adam

Heart-strook with chilling gripe of sorrow stood,
That all his senses bound; Eve, who unseen

Yet all had heard, with audible lament

Discover'd soon the place of her retire.
O unexpected stroke, worse then of Death!

Must I thus leave thee Paradise? thus leave
Thee Native Soile, these happie Walks and Shades,
Fit haunt of Gods? where I had hope to spend,
Quiet though sad, the respit of that day

That must be mortal to us both. O flours,

That never will in other Climate grow,

My early visitation, and my last

At Eev'n, which I bred up with tender hand

From the first op'ning bud, and gave ye Names,
Who now shall reare ye to the Sun, or ranke
Your Tribes, and water from th' ambrosial Fount?
Thee lastly nuptial Bowre, by mee adornd

With what to sight or smell was sweet; from thee
How shall I part, and whither wander down

Into a lower World, to this obscure
And wilde, how shall we breath in other Aire
Less pure, accustomd to immortal Fruits?

Whom thus the Angel interrupted milde.
Lament not Eve, but patiently resigne

What justly thou hast lost; nor set thy heart,

Stood thunderstruck, gripped with a chilling sorrow
That seized all his sense; Eve, although invisible

Had heard all, and soon gave away her hiding place

With an audible lament:
"Oh unexpected blow, worse than death!

Must I leave you, Paradise? Leave You, my native soil, these happy walks and glades,
A place fit for Gods? The place I had hoped to spend,
Quietly but sadly, the remains of the day

That must end in death for us both. Oh flowers,

That will never grow in another climate,

That I visited in the morning and last thing

In the evening, which I raised with a tender hand

From the first opening bud, and gave you names,
Who shall now raise you to the sun, or plant you
In rows, and water you from the heavenly spring?
You lastly, marriage bower, decorated by me

With all that was sweet to sight and smell; how can I
Leave you, and how can I wander down

Into a lower world, dark and wild,
How shall we breathe in less pure air,
When we are accustomed to eternal fruits?"

The angel, interrupted her, softly.
"Do not complain, Eve, but give up with resignation
The things which you have rightly

	lost; do not set your heart,
Thus over-fond, on that which is not thine;	*Too fond, on things which are not yours.*
Thy going is not lonely, with thee goes	*You do not go alone; with you goes*
Thy Husband, him to follow thou art bound;	*Your husband, and you are bound to follow him;*
Where he abides, think there thy native soile.	*Where he lives, that then is your native soil."*
Adam by this from the cold sudden damp	*Adam recovered from this sudden cold shock,*
Recovering, and his scatterd spirits returnd,	*And he gathered his spirits together*
To Michael thus his humble words addressd.	*And addressed Michael with these humble words.*
Celestial, whether among the Thrones, or nam'd	*"Heavenly, whether you are one of the Thrones or named*
Of them the Highest, for such of shape may seem	*One of the highest, for being of such a shape*
Prince above Princes, gently hast thou tould	*You seem to be a Prince above Princes, you have given us*
Thy message, which might else in telling wound,	*Your message gently, which otherwise might have wounded us,*
And in performing end us; what besides	*And killed us in its execution; what else*
Of sorrow and dejection and despair	*Do your tidings bring, apart from sorrow and dejection and despair,*
Our frailtie can sustain, thy tidings bring,	*As much as our frail forms can bear?*
Departure from this happy place, our sweet	*We must leave this happy place, our sweet*
Recess, and onely consolation left	*Shelter and the only consolation we have left.*
Familiar to our eyes, all places else	*It is familiar to our eyes, and all other places*
Inhospitable appeer and desolate,	*Appear inhospitable and desolate,*
Nor knowing us nor known: and if by prayer	*Unknown to us as we are unknown to them; and if*
Incessant I could hope to change the will	*By constant prayer I could hope to change the will*
Of him who all things can, I would not cease	*Of he who can change anything, I would not cease*
To wearie him with my assiduous cries:	*To tire him with my constant pleas;*
But prayer against his absolute Decree	*But prayer against his absolute rulings*
No more availes then breath against the winde,	*Are as useless as blowing into the wind,*
Blown stifling back on him that breaths it	*Where the breath blows back to*

forth:
Therefore to his great bidding I submit.
This most afflicts me, that departing hence,

As from his face I shall be hid, deprivd

His blessed count'nance; here I could frequent,
With worship, place by place where he voutsaf'd
Presence Divine, and to my Sons relate;

On this Mount he appeerd, under this Tree
Stood visible, among these Pines his voice

I heard, here with him at this Fountain talk'd:
So many grateful Altars I would reare

Of grassie Terfe, and pile up every Stone

Of lustre from the brook, in memorie,
Or monument to Ages, and thereon

Offer sweet smelling Gumms and Fruits and Flours:
In yonder nether World where shall I seek

His bright appearances, or foot step-trace?

For though I fled him angrie, yet recall'd

To life prolongd and promisd Race, I now

Gladly behold though but his utmost skirts

Of glory, and farr off his steps adore.

To whom thus Michael with regard benigne.
Adam, thou know'st Heav'n his, and all the Earth.
Not this Rock onely; his Omnipresence fills

Land, Sea, and Aire, and every kinde that

choke the one who breathed it:
So I submit to his great orders.
What afflicts me most is that leaving here

I shall be hidden from his sight, deprived

Of seeing his blessed face; here I could frequent,
With worship, each place were he revealed
The divine presence, and say to my sons,

'On this hill he appeared, I saw him
Under this tree, I heard his voice amongst these pines,

I talked with him by this spring:

I would have raised so many thanksgiving altars
On the grassy turf, and piled up every shiny stone

From the streams as a memorial
Or monument for all time, and on them I would have placed

Offerings of sweet smelling gums and fruits and flowers:
In that world down there where can I remember
His bright appearances, or trace his footsteps?
For although I fled his anger, now recalled
To longer life and the promise of descendants
I would gladly see him even at the outer edge of
His glory, and worship his steps from far off."
Michael replied to him gently.

"Adam, you know that Heaven and all the Earth is his,
Not just this place. He is ever present on
Land, in the sea, in the air and in

402

lives,
Fomented by his virtual power and warmd:

All th' Earth he gave thee to possess and rule,
No despicable gift; surmise not then

His presence to these narrow bounds confin'd
Of Paradise or Eden: this had been

Perhaps thy Capital Seate, from whence had spred
All generations, and had hither come

From all the ends of th' Earth, to celebrate
And reverence thee thir great Progenitor.
But this præeminence thou hast lost, brought down
To dwell on eeven ground now with thy Sons:
Yet doubt not but in Vallie and in Plaine

God is as here, and will be found alike

Present, and of his presence many a signe

Still following thee, still compassing thee round
With goodness and paternal Love, his Face

Express, and of his steps the track Divine.

Which that thou mayst beleeve, and be confirmd
Ere thou from hence depart, know I am sent
To shew thee what shall come in future dayes
To thee and to thy Ofspring; good with bad

Expect to hear, supernal Grace contending
With sinfulness of Men; thereby to learn

True patience, and to temper joy with fear

every living thing,
Nurtured by his holy power and warmed:

He gave you the whole Earth to own and rule,
No mean gift; do not think then that his

Presence is confined to these narrow boundaries
Of Paradise or Eden: this was to have been

Perhaps your capital, from where all the generations
Would spread, and would have come here

From all over the Earth, to celebrate
And respect you as their great father.
But you have lost this high position, brought down
To live on lower ground with your children:
But do not doubt that in the valleys and plains

God is as he is here, and will be found

Just the same, and he will give many signs

That he still follows you, still wraps you
In his goodness and paternal love, his face

Will show it and so will the divine footsteps.

You may believe this, and it will be proved
Before you leave here; know that I am sent
To show you what will come in the future
To you and your offspring; expect to hear good and bad,

Heavenly grace battling
With Man's sinfulness; from what I tell you you shall learn

True patience, and to temper joy with

And pious sorrow, equally enur'd
By moderation either state to beare,
Prosperous or adverse: so shalt thou lead

Safest thy life, and best prepar'd endure

Thy mortal passage when it comes. Ascend

This Hill; let Eve (for I have drencht her eyes)
Here sleep below while thou to foresight wak'st,
As once thou slepst, while Shee to life was formd.
To whom thus Adam gratefully repli'd.
Ascend, I follow thee, safe Guide, the path
Thou lead'st me, and to the hand of Heav'n submit,
However chast'ning, to the evil turne

My obvious breast, arming to overcome

By suffering, and earne rest from labour won,
If so I may attain. So both ascend
In the Visions of God: It was a Hill

Of Paradise the highest, from whose top
The Hemisphere of Earth in cleerest Ken

Stretcht out to amplest reach of prospect lay.
Not higher that Hill nor wider looking round,
Whereon for different cause the Tempter set
Our second Adam in the Wilderness,
To shew him all Earths Kingdomes and thir Glory.
His Eye might there command wherever stood
City of old or modern Fame, the Seat

Of mightiest Empire, from the destind Walls

fear
And pious sorrow, prepared
By moderation to bear either state,
Good or bad: so you will lead your life
In the safest way, and be best prepared
To meet your death when it comes. Climb
This hill; let Eve (for I have closed her eyes)
Sleep here below while you wake to the future,
Just as you once slept while she was brought to life."
Adam replied with gratitude:
"Climb, I will follow you, safe guide,
On the path you lead me over and I will submit
My exposed heart to the hand of Heaven,
However painful it will be, I am ready to
Be overcome with suffering, and so earn rest from labor,
If I may." So both climbed up
In the sight of God: it was the highest hill
In Paradise, from the top of which
The earth's hemisphere showed in clearest sight,
Stretched out as far as the eye could see.
That hill was as tall and had as wide a view
As the hill where for a different reason the Tempter placed
Jesus in the wilderness,
To how him all the kingdoms of Earth and their glory.
His eye might have commanded all

The cities of ancient or modern times, the seat
Of the mightiest empire, from the walls

404

Of Cambalu, seat of Cathaian Can	*Of Cambalu, seat of the Khan of Cathay,*
And Samarchand by Oxus, Temirs Throne,	*And Samarkand by Oxus, ruled by Temir,*
To Paquin of Sinæan Kings, and thence	*To Peking of the Chinese kings,*
To Agra and Lahor of great Mogul	*To Agra and Lahore, the seats of the great Moguls,*
Down to the golden Chersonese, or where	*Down to the gold of Thailand, or where*
The Persian in Ecbatan sate, or since	*The Persian sat in Ecbatana, or since then*
In Hispahan, or where the Russian Ksar	*In Hispahan, or where the Russian Tsar*
In Mosco, or the Sultan in Bizance,	*Ruled in Moscow, or the Sultan in Byzantium,*
Turchestan-born; nor could his eye not ken	*Born in Turkey; he could also see*
Th' Empire of Negus to his utmost Port	*The Empire of Abyssinia to the farthest port*
Ercoco and the less Maritim Kings	*Of Arkiko, and the lesser maritime kingdoms*
Mombaza, and Quiloa, and Melind,	*Of Mobassa, Quiloa and Melind,*
And Sofala thought Ophir, to the Realme	*And Sofala thought to be Ophir, to the realm*
Of Congo, and Angola fardest South;	*Of Congo, and Angola farthest south;*
Or thence from Niger Flood to Atlas Mount	*Or from there from the River Niger to the Atlas mountains,*
The Kingdoms of Almansor, Fez and Sus,	*The Kingdoms of Almansor, Fez and Sus,*
Marocco and Algiers, and Tremisen;	*Morrocco and Algiers, and Tremisen;*
On Europe thence, and where Rome was to sway	*Then on to Europe, where Rome was to rule*
The World: in Spirit perhaps he also saw	*The world; spiritually perhaps he also saw*
Rich Mexico the seat of Motezume,	*Rich Mexico, the land of Montezuma,*
And Cusco in Peru, the richer seat	*And Cusco in Peru, the richer seat*
Of Atabalipa, and yet unspoil'd	*Atahuallpa, and not yet spoiled*
Guiana, whose great Citie Geryons Sons	*Guinea, whose great city the Spanish*
Call El Dorado: but to nobler sights	*Called El Dorado: but Michael took the film from Adam's eyes*
Michael from Adams eyes the Filme remov'd	*That the false fruit had put there*
Which that false Fruit that promis'd clearer sight	*when promising clearer sight,*
Had bred; then purg'd with Euphrasie and Rue	*And showed him nobler sights.*
The visual Nerve, for he had much to see;	*Then he cleaned his eyes with Euphrasie and Rue, For there was much for him to see;*

And from the Well of Life three drops instill'd.
So deep the power of these Ingredients pierc'd,
Eevn to the inmost seat of mental sight,
That Adam now enforc't to close his eyes,

Sunk down and all his Spirits became intranst:
But him the gentle Angel by the hand
Soon rais'd, and his attention thus recall'd.

Th' effects which thy original crime hath wrought
In some to spring from thee, who never touch'd
Th' excepted Tree, nor with the Snake conspir'd,
Nor sinn'd thy sin, yet from that sin derive

Corruption to bring forth more violent deeds.
His eyes he op'nd, and beheld a field,
Part arable and tilth, whereon were Sheaves

New reapt, the other part sheep-walks and foulds;
Ith' midst an Altar as the Land-mark stood

Rustic, of grassie sord; thither anon

A sweatie Reaper from his Tillage brought

First Fruits, the green Eare, and the yellow Sheaf,
Uncull'd, as came to hand; a Shepherd next

More meek came with the Firstlings of his Flock
Choicest and best; then sacrificing, laid

The Inwards and thir Fat, with Incense strew'd,
On the cleft Wood, and all due Rites perform'd.
His Offring soon propitious Fire from

He put three drops from the well of life in here.
The power of these ingredients went so deep,
Even into the brain and imagination,
That Adam was forced to close his eyes,

He sank down and his spirits were in a trance:
But the gentle angel soon lifted him By the hand, and called him back to sense:

"Adam, now open your eyes, and see The effects your original crime had On some of your descendants, who never touched The forbidden tree, nor conspired with the snake,
Nor committed your sin, but they are corrupted

By that sin and commit more violent deeds."
His eyes opened and he saw a field, Partly arable and cultivated, on which there were newly

Cut sheaves of corn, on the other part were sheep paths and pens;
There was an altar like a landmark in the middle,

Rustic, made from grassy turf; soon a sweaty reaper

Brought there from his work

The first fruits, the green ear and the yellow sheaf,
Chosen randomly as they came to hand; next came

A shepherd, more humble, with the first born of his flock,
The choicest and best; sacrificing them he laid

Their innards and their fat, covered in incense
On the cleft wood, and performed all the correct rites.
Soon his offering was consumed by

406

Heav'n	*favorable fire*
Consum'd with nimble glance, and grateful steame;	*From Heaven, quickly and with appreciative smoke;*
The others not, for his was not sincere;	*The other offering was not, for his was not sincere;*
Whereat hee inlie rag'd, and as they talk'd,	*He raged inwardly at this and as they talked*
Smote him into the Midriff with a stone	*Hit the other in the stomach with a stone*
That beat out life; he fell, and deadly pale	*That beat out his life; he fell, and deadly pale*
Groand out his Soul with gushing bloud effus'd.	*He groaned out his soul with his gushing blood.*
Much at that sight was Adam in his heart	*At that sight Adam was much disturbed in his heart,*
Dismai'd, and thus in haste to th' Angel cri'd.	*And called quickly to the angel:*
O Teacher, some great mischief hath befall'n	*"Oh teacher, some terrible thing has happened*
To that meek man, who well had sacrific'd;	*To that humble man, who had made his sacrifice so well!*
Is Pietie thus and pure Devotion paid?	*Is this how piety and pure devotion is repaid?"*
T' whom Michael thus, hee also mov'd, repli'd.	*Michael, also disturbed, replied:*
These two are Brethren, Adam, and to come	*"These two are brothers, Adam, and spring*
Out of thy loyns; th' unjust the just hath slain,	*From your loins; the unjust has slain the just,*
For envie that his Brothers Offering found	*Out of jealousy because his brother's offering*
From Heav'n acceptance; but the bloodie Fact	*Was accepted by Heaven; but the bloody act*
Will be aveng'd, and th' others Faith approv'd	*Will be punished, and the other's accepted faith*
Loose no reward, though here thou see him die,	*Will be rewarded, though you see him die here,*
Rowling in dust and gore.	*Rolling in dust and gore."*
To which our Sire.	*Our sire responded,*
Alas, both for the deed and for the cause!	*"Alas, both for the deed and the cause!*
But have I now seen Death? Is this the way	*But have I now seen death? Is this the way*
I must return to native dust? O sight	*I shall return to my native dust? This is a terrible*
Of terrour, foul and ugly to behold,	*Sight, foul and ugly to see,*

Horrid to think, how horrible to feel!

To whom thus Michael. Death thou hast seen
In his first shape on man; but many shapes
Of Death, and many are the wayes that lead
To his grim Cave, all dismal; yet to sense
More terrible at th' entrance then within.
Some, as thou saw'st, by violent stroke shall die,
By Fire, Flood, Famin, by Intemperance more
In Meats and Drinks, which on the Earth shall bring
Diseases dire, of which a monstrous crew
Before thee shall appear; that thou mayst know
What miserie th' inabstinence of Eve
Shall bring on men.
Immediately a place
Before his eyes appeard, sad, noysom, dark,
A Lazar-house it seemd, wherein were laid
Numbers of all diseas'd, all maladies
Of gastly Spasm, or racking torture, qualms
Of heart-sick Agonie, all feavorous kinds,
Convulsions, Epilepsies, fierce Catarrhs,

Intestin Stone and Ulcer, Colic pangs,

Dæmoniac Phrenzie, moaping Melancholie
And Moon-struck madness, pining Atrophie
Marasmus and wide-wasting Pestilence,
Dropsies, and Asthma's, and Joint-racking Rheums.
Dire was the tossing, deep the groans,

It's horrid to think of, how horrid it must be to feel!"

Michael answered, "You have seen Death
In its first attack on man, but there are many types
Of death, and there are many paths leading
To his grim cave, all dismal; but to the mind
The entrance is more terrible than the inside.
Some, as you saw, shall die by violence,
By fire, flood, famine, more shall die by gluttony
In meat and drink, which on Earth shall bring
Awful diseases, of which a monstrous crew
Shall now appear before you, so you shall know
What misery Eve's gluttony
Shall bring on men."
Immediately a place
Appeared before his eyes, sad, smelly and dark.
It seemed like a leper hospital, where there were
Crowds suffering from all known diseases, all illnesses
Of terrible spasms, racking torture, attacks
Of heart sick agony, all types of fever,
Convulsions, epilepsies, fierce inflammations,

Intestinal stones and ulcers, pangs of colic,

Demonic possession, depression,
And moonstruck madness, malnutrition,
Wide spreading disease,
Dropsy, asthma and joint racking rheumatism.
There was terrible tossing, deep

despair
Tended the sick busiest from Couch to Couch;
And over them triumphant Death his Dart

Shook, but delaid to strike, though oft invokt
With vows, as thir chief good, and final hope.
Sight so deform what heart of Rock could long
Drie-ey'd behold? Adam could not, but wept,
Though not of Woman born; compassion quell'd
His best of Man, and gave him up to tears

A space, till firmer thoughts restraind excess,
And scarce recovering words his plaint renew'd.
O miserable Mankind, to what fall

Degraded, to what wretched state reserv'd!

Better end heer unborn. Why is life giv'n

To be thus wrested from us? rather why Obtruded on us thus? who if we knew

What we receive, would either not accept

Life offer'd, or soon beg to lay it down, Glad to be so dismist in peace. Can thus Th' Image of God in man created once

So goodly and erect, though faultie since,

To such unsightly sufferings be debas't Under inhuman pains? Why should not Man,
Retaining still Divine similitude

In part, from such deformities be free, And for his Makers Image sake exempt?

groans and despair
Waited on the sick at every bed.

Over them triumphant Death was shaking his arrow,
But he delayed striking, though he was often
Begged to, as their chief good and final hope.
At the sight of so much pain what stony heart
Could remain dry eyed? Adam could not, and he wept,
Though he was not born of woman; compassion suppressed
His manly strength and he gave himself up to tears
For a time, until firmer thoughts controlled him,
And as soon as he could speak he renewed his complaint.
"Oh miserable mankind, fallen so low,
What a wretched state you have come to!
It would be better to end the race here. Why is life given
To us to be taken away like this? Why Is it forced on us like this? Who, if they knew
What was coming, would either not accept
Life, or would soon ask to give it up, Glad to leave it in peace? Can
The image of God created in man, once
So good and proud, though faulty since,
Be reduced to such terrible suffering, Such inhuman pain? Why should man not,
Still keeping part of his divine resemblance,
Be kept free from such deformities, And kept exempt for the sake of his maker's image?"

Thir Makers Image, answerd Michael, then
Forsook them, when themselves they villifi'd
To serve ungovern'd appetite, and took
His Image whom they serv'd, a brutish vice,
Inductive mainly to the sin of Eve.
Therefore so abject is thir punishment,
Disfiguring not Gods likeness, but thir own,
Or if his likeness, by themselves defac't
While they pervert pure Natures healthful rules
To loathsom sickness, worthily, since they
Gods Image did not reverence in themselves.
I yield it just, said Adam, and submit.
But is there yet no other way, besides
These painful passages, how we may come
To Death, and mix with our connatural dust?
There is, said Michael, if thou well observe
The rule of not too much, by temperance taught
In what thou eatst and drinkst, seeking from thence
Due nourishment, not gluttonous delight,
Till many years over thy head return:
So maist thou live, till like ripe Fruit thou drop
Into thy Mothers lap, or be with ease
Gatherd, not harshly pluckt, for death mature:
This is old age; but then thou must outlive
Thy youth, thy strength, thy beauty, which

"Their maker's image," answered Michael,
"Left them when they turned to evil,
Letting their appetites run unchecked, and replaced
The image of the one they served with brutish vice,
Leading on from Eve's sin.
That is why they have this terrible punishment,
Disfiguring not God's likeness, but their own,
Or if it is God's likeness they deface it themselves
By perverting the pure rules of nature
To horrible disease, which they deserve, since they
Did not respect God's image in themselves."
"I admit it is just," said Adam, "and accept it.
But is there no other way, apart from
These painful ones, by which we may come
To death, and return to our dusty origins?"
"There is," said Michael, "If you follow carefully
The rule of moderation, be temperate
In what you eat and drink, taking from it
Proper nourishment, not greedy pleasure,
So many years will pass in your life;
So you may live, until you fall like ripe fruit
Into the lap of Mother Earth, or you will be
Gently picked, not harshly torn down, for death in maturity;
This is old age; but then you must outlive
Your youth, your strength, your

will change
To witherd weak and gray; thy Senses then

Obtuse, all taste of pleasure must forgoe,

To what thou hast, and for the Aire of youth
Hopeful and cheerful, in thy blood will reigne
A melancholly damp of cold and dry
To weigh thy spirits down, and last consume
The Balme of Life.
To whom our Ancestor.
Henceforth I flie not Death, nor would prolong
Life much, bent rather how I may be quit

Fairest and easiest of this combrous charge,

Which I must keep till my appointed day

Of rendring up, and patiently attend
My dissolution.
Michael repli'd,
Nor love thy Life, nor hate; but what thou livst
Live well, how long or short permit to Heav'n:
And now prepare thee for another sight.
He lookd and saw a spacious Plaine, whereon
Were Tents of various hue; by some were herds
Of Cattel grazing: others, whence the sound
Of Instruments that made melodious chime

Was heard, of Harp and Organ; and who moovd
Thir stops and chords was seen: his volant touch

Instinct through all proportions low and high
Fled and pursu'd transverse the resonant

---

beauty, which will change
To withered weakness and greyness; your senses
Will be dumb, you will have pleasure in nothing
That you have, and in place of the spirit of youth,
Hopeful and cheerful, in your blood will reign
A melancholy misery of cold and dry
To weigh your spirits down and at last devour
The sweetness of life."
Our Ancestor replied:
"From now on I shall not run from death, nor try
To prolong my life much, thinking more about how
I might lose most easily this heavy weight of life,
Which I must bear until my appointed day
Of dying, and I shall wait patiently
For my extinction."
Michael replied,
"Neither love nor hate your life, but as you live
Then live well, leave the length of your life to Heaven:
And now prepare for another sight."
He looked and saw a wide plain, on which
Were tents of various colors; by some there were herds
Of cattle grazing: from others was heard the sound
Of instruments which made melodious music,
Harp and organ, and the one who played
The keys and strings could be seen; his flying touch

Moved through all the notes, low and high,
Trying to find the chords which

Original	Modern
fugue.	would match the song of the universe.
In other part stood one who at the Forge	In another part one stood laboring at the forge.
Labouring, two massie clods of Iron and Brass	Having melted two great lumps of iron and brass
Had melted (whether found where casual fire	(Either found where a forest fire
Had wasted woods on Mountain or in Vale,	Had stripped the woods on a mountain or in a valley,
Down to the veins of Earth, thence gliding hot	Down to the veins of the Earth, which then glided hot
To som Caves mouth, or whether washt by stream	To some cave's mouth, or else washed from underground by
From underground) the liquid Ore he dreind	Some stream)he drained the liquid metal
Into fit moulds prepar'd; from which he formd	Into prepared moulds, from which he first made
First his own Tooles; then, what might else be wrought	His own tools, then afterwards he made other things
Fusil or grav'n in mettle. After these,	That can be cast or beaten from metal. After these
But on the hether side a different sort	Men of a different type came down
From the high neighbouring Hills, which was thir Seat,	From their homes in the neighboring hills,
Down to the Plain descended: by thir guise	Down to the plain; by their bearing
Just men they seemd, and all thir study bent	They seemed to be good men, and all their efforts were devoted
To worship God aright, and know his works	To worshipping God correctly, and they did not avoid
Not hid, nor those things last which might preserve	Knowing his works, and especially those things which might bring
Freedom and Peace to men: they on the Plain	Freedom and peace to men: they had not been walking
Long had not walkt, when from the Tents behold	On the plain for long, when from the tents there came
A Beavie of fair Women, richly gay	A group of fair women, gaudy
In Gems and wanton dress; to the Harp they sung	In jewels and revealing clothes; they sang soft songs
Soft amorous Ditties, and in dance came on:	Of love to the harp, and danced as they came:
The Men though grave, ey'd them, and let thir eyes	The men, though serious, eyed them, and let their eyes
Rove without rein, till in the amorous Net	Stray without control, until they were caught
Fast caught, they lik'd, and each his liking	In the net of lust; they liked, and each

412

chose;
And now of love they treat till th'Eevning Star
Loves Harbinger appeerd; then all in heat

They light the Nuptial Torch, and bid invoke
Hymen, then first to marriage Rites invok't;
With Feast and Musick all the Tents resound.
Such happy interview and fair event
Of love and youth not lost, Songs, Garlands, Flours,
And charming Symphonies attach'd the heart
Of Adam, soon enclin'd to admit delight,

The bent of Nature; which he thus express'd.
True opener of mine eyes, prime Angel blest,
Much better seems this Vision, and more hope
Of peaceful dayes portends, then those two past;
Those were of hate and death, or pain much worse,
Here Nature seems fulfilld in all her ends.

To whom thus Michael. Judg not what is best
By pleasure, though to Nature seeming meet,
Created, as thou art, to nobler end

Holie and pure, conformitie divine.
Those Tents thou sawst so pleasant, were the Tents
Of wickedness, wherein shall dwell his Race
Who slew his Brother; studious they appere

Of Arts that polish Life, Inventers rare,

Unmindful of thir Maker, though his Spirit

---

one chose his favorite.
And now they talked of love until the Evening Star,
Love's messenger, appeared; then all in heat
They light the wedding torch and pray
To Hymen, then the God of marriage;
All the tents rang to the sound of music and feasting.
Such happy sights and events
Of love and youth still thriving,
songs, garlands and flowers
And charming symphonies caught the heart
Of Adam, who was soon ready to take pleasure,
Which is our way of worshipping Nature, and he spoke of it.
"True opener of my eyes, first blessed angel,
This vision seems much better, and gives more hope
Of peaceful future days, than those last two;
Those were of hate and death, or much worse pain,
Here Nature seems to be filling her true purpose."
Michael answered him: "Do not judge what is best
By the pleasure it gives, though it seems the purpose of Nature.
You are created for a more noble purpose,
Holy and pure, matching God.
Those tents you thought were so pleasant were the tents
Of wickedness, where the offspring of the one who killed
His brother shall live; you can see they are devoted
To the arts that improve life, great inventors,
Not thinking of their maker; though his spirit

Taught them, but they his gifts acknowledg'd none.	Taught them, they did not acknowledge his influence.
Yet they a beauteous ofspring shall beget;	But they shall give birth to beautiful offspring;
For that fair femal Troop thou sawst, that seemd	That fair female group you saw, that looked like
Of Goddesses, so blithe, so smooth, so gay,	Goddesses, so jolly, so smooth, so happy,
Yet empty of all good wherein consists	But empty of all the good which makes up
Womans domestic honour and chief praise;	Woman's domestic honor and most praiseworthy feature;
Bred onely and completed to the taste	Bred only, and decorated, to fulfil the taste
Of lustful appetence, to sing, to dance,	Of lustful appetites, to sing, to dance,
To dress, and troule the Tongue, and roule the Eye.	To dress, and chatter, and to catch the eye.
To these that sober Race of Men, whose lives	That sober race of men, whose religious
Religious titl'd them the Sons of God,	Lives gave them the title of Sons of God,
Shall yield up all thir vertue, all thir fame	Will give up all their virtue, their fame,
Ignobly, to the traines and to the smiles	Shamefully, to the tricks and smiles
Of these fair Atheists, and now swim in joy,	Of these fair atheists, and now swim in joy,
(Erelong to swim at large) and laugh; for which	(Before long they shall be swimming in reality) and laugh; for this
The world erelong a world of tears must weepe.	Before long the world will endure a flood of tears."
To whom thus Adam of short joy bereft.	Adam, his short lived joy taken from him, said,
O pittie and shame, that they who to live well	"Oh pity and shame, that they who started off living so well
Enterd so faire, should turn aside to tread	Should turn aside to tread
Paths indirect, or in the mid way faint!	Twisted paths, or falter in the middle of their journey!
But still I see the tenor of Mans woe	But still I see that the root of men's sorrow
Holds on the same, from Woman to begin.	Is still the same, it comes from women."
From Mans effeminate slackness it begins,	"It comes from man's effeminate laziness,"
Said th' Angel, who should better hold his place	Said the angel, "He should stand by

By wisdome, and superiour gifts receav'd.

His wisdom and the superior talents he is given.

But now prepare thee for another Scene.

But now prepare yourself for another scene."

He lookd and saw wide Territorie spred

He looked and saw a wide territory spread

Before him, Towns, and rural works between,

In front of him, towns, and cultivated land between,

Cities of Men with lofty Gates and Towrs,

Cities of men with high gates and towers,

Concours in Arms, fierce Faces threatning Warr,

Jostling in arms, fierce faces threatening war,

Giants of mightie Bone, and bould emprise;

Giants of great size and bold daring;

Part wield thir Arms, part courb the foaming Steed,

Some flourish their arms, some tame their foaming horses,

Single or in Array of Battel rang'd

Arranged singly or in battle order,

Both Horse and Foot, nor idely mustring stood;

Both on horse and on foot, not standing in idle crowds;

One way a Band select from forage drives

In one place a band drives away from their grazing

A herd of Beeves, faire Oxen and faire Kine

A herd of cattle, fair oxen and calves,

From a fat Meddow ground; or fleecy Flock,

From a fertile pasture, or a fleecy flock,

Ewes and thir bleating Lambs over the Plaine,

Ewes and their bleating lambs over the plain,

Thir Bootie; scarce with Life the Shepherds flye,

Their booty; the shepherds barely escape with their lives,

But call in aide, which makes a bloody Fray;

But they call in help, which causes a bloody fight.

With cruel Tournament the Squadrons joine;

The armies join in cruel contest;

Where Cattle pastur'd late, now scatterd lies

Where cattle recently grazed the bloody field

With Carcasses and Arms th'ensanguind Field

Is scattered with bodies and weapons,

Deserted: Others to a Citie strong

Deserted; others lay siege, encamped outside

Lay Seige, encampt; by Batterie, Scale, and Mine,

A great city, assaulting it with cannons, ladders

Assaulting; others from the Wall defend

And mines; the defenders on the wall use

With Dart and Jav'lin, Stones and sulfurous Fire;

Darts and javelins, stones and burning fire;

On each hand slaughter and gigantic deeds.

Everywhere is slaughter and great deeds.

In other part the scepter'd Haralds call
To Council in the Citie Gates: anon

Grey-headed men and grave, with Warriours mixt,
Assemble, and Harangues are heard, but soon
In factious opposition, till at last
Of middle Age one rising, eminent
In wise deport, spake much of Right and Wrong,
Of Justice, of Religion, Truth and Peace,
And Judgment from above: him old and young
Exploded, and had seiz'd with violent hands,
Had not a Cloud descending snatch'd him thence
Unseen amid the throng: so violence

Proceeded, and Oppression, and Sword-Law
Through all the Plain, and refuge none was found.
Adam was all in tears, and to his guide

Lamenting turnd full sad;
O what are these,
Deaths Ministers, not Men, who thus deal Death
Inhumanly to men, and multiply
Ten thousandfould the sin of him who slew

His Brother; for of whom such massacher

Make they but of thir Brethren, men of men?
But who was that Just Man, whom had not Heav'n
Rescu'd, had in his Righteousness bin lost?

To whom thus Michael. These are the product
Of those ill mated Marriages thou saw'st:

---

*In another part the official heralds call
People to a council at the city gates; soon*

*Grey haired serious men assemble, mixed
With warriors, and speeches are heard, but soon
There is quarreling, until at last
One of middle age arose, dignified
And of wise appearance. He spoke much of right and wrong,
Justice, religion, truth and peace,
And the judgment of God; old and young
Jeered him, and would have seized him with violence,
If a cloud had not come down and snatched him from the place,
Unseen amidst the throng: so violence*

*Continued, and oppression, and the rule of the sword
Across all the plain, and there was no refuge for any.
Adam was in tears, and turned to his guide*

*Lamenting, and said sadly;
"Oh who are these,
Death's servants, not men, who deal out death
Inhumanely to men, and multiply
Ten thousand times the sin of the one who killed*

His brother; for who are they massacring

*If it is not their own brothers, men the same as them?
But who was that just man, who would have been lost
For his righteousness if Heaven had not rescued him?"*

*Michael said to him: "These men are the result
Of those mismatched marriages you*

416

Where good with bad were matcht, who of themselves
Abhor to joyn; and by imprudence mixt,

Produce prodigious Births of bodie or mind.
Such were these Giants, men of high renown;
For in those dayes Might onely shall be admir'd,
And Valour and Heroic Vertu call'd;

To overcome in Battle, and subdue

Nations, and bring home spoils with infinite

Man-slaughter, shall be held the highest pitch
Of human Glorie, and for Glorie done

Of triumph, to be styl'd great Conquerours,

Patrons of Mankind, Gods, and Sons of Gods,
Destroyers rightlier call'd and Plagues of men.
Thus Fame shall be atchiev'd, renown on Earth,
And what most merits fame in silence hid.

But hee the seventh from thee, whom thou beheldst
The onely righteous in a World perverse,

And therefore hated, therefore so beset
With Foes for daring single to be just,

And utter odious Truth, that God would come
To judge them with his Saints: Him the most High
Rapt in a balmie Cloud with winged Steeds

Did, as thou sawst, receave, to walk with God

---

saw,
Where good with bad were joined, who normally
Avoid mixing; and by this unwise mixing

They produced offspring with monstrous bodies or minds.
These were the Giants, men of great fame,
For in those days strength was the only thing admired,
And called bravery and Heroic virtue;

To overcome in battle, and subdue nations,

And bring home treasures with infinite

Slaughter, was thought of as the height
Of human glory, and they were given glory

For their triumphs, to be called great conquerors,

Patrons of mankind, gods and sons of gods,
When they should have been called destroyers and a plague on men.
So fame shall be achieved, renown on Earth,
And what most deserves fame is hidden in silence.

But he you saw is of the seventh generation after you,
The only righteous one in a perverse world,

And so is hated, surrounded
With enemies for daring, alone, to be just,

And tell them what they don't want to hear, that God
Would come with his saints to judge them; the Almighty
Wrapped him in a sweet cloud and with winged horses

Took him to walk with God,

High in Salvation and the Climes of bliss,

Exempt from Death; to shew thee what reward
Awaits the good, the rest what punishment?

Which now direct thine eyes and soon behold.

He look'd, and saw the face of things quite chang'd;
The brazen Throat of Warr had ceast to roar,
All now was turn'd to jollitie and game,
To luxurie and riot, feast and dance,

Marrying or prostituting, as befell,

Rape or Adulterie, where passing faire

Allurd them; thence from Cups to civil Broiles.
At length a Reverend Sire among them came,
And of thir doings great dislike declar'd,

And testifi'd against thir wayes; hee oft
Frequented thir Assemblies, whereso met,

Triumphs or Festivals, and to them preachd

Conversion and Repentance, as to Souls

In prison under Judgments imminent:

But all in vain: which when he saw, he ceas'd
Contending, and remov'd his Tents farr off;
Then from the Mountain hewing Timber tall,
Began to build a Vessel of huge bulk,
Measur'd by Cubit, length, and breadth, and highth,
Smeard round with Pitch, and in the side a dore

High in the list of saved and the lands of Heaven,
Exempt from death; this shows you the reward
Awaiting the good; what punishment do the rest have?
Look down and you will soon see."

He looked, and saw things were quite changed;
The brazen noise of war had ceased,
And now all was fun and games,
Luxury and debauchery, feasting and dancing,
Marriage and prostitution as it suited,
Rape or adultery as any passing woman
Attracted them, which led to drunken brawling.
At length Noah came among them,
And declared his hatred of their behavior,
And spoke out against their habits;
He often went to their meetings, wherever they were held,
Triumphs or festivals, and to them he preached
Conversion and repentance, as if they were souls
In prison, shortly to receive their sentence.
But it was all in vain; when he saw this he stopped
Arguing, and took his household far away;
Then he began cutting down tall trees on the mountain
To make a huge boat,
Measured in cubits, length, breadth and height,
Covered in tar, and in the side he made

Contriv'd, and of provisions laid in large

For Man and Beast: when loe a wonder strange!
Of every Beast, and Bird, and Insect small
Came seavens, and pairs, and enterd in, as taught
Thir order; last the Sire, and his three Sons

With thir four Wives; and God made fast the dore.
Meanwhile the Southwind rose, and with black wings
Wide hovering, all the Clouds together drove
From under Heav'n; the Hills to their supplie
Vapour, and Exhalation dusk and moist,
Sent up amain; and now the thick'nd Skie
Like a dark Ceeling stood; down rush'd the Rain
Impetuous, and continu'd till the Earth

No more was seen; the floating Vessel swum
Uplifted; and secure with beaked prow

Rode tilting o're the Waves, all dwellings else
Flood overwhelmd, and them with all thir pomp
Deep under water rould; Sea cover'd Sea,

Sea without shoar; and in thir Palaces

Where luxurie late reign'd, Sea-monsters whelp'd
And stabl'd; of Mankind, so numerous late,

All left, in one small bottom swum imbark't.
How didst thou grieve then, Adam, to behold
The end of all thy Ofspring, end so sad,
Depopulation; thee another Floud,

Of tears and sorrow a Floud thee also

A door, and laid in a large store of provisions
For men and animals: then there was a strange sight!
Every beast, bird and small insect
Came in sevens or in pairs and entered in, as
They were ordered; last came Noah, with his three sons
And their four wives, and God sealed up the door.
Meanwhile the south wind rose, and with their black wings
Hovering wide, all the clouds of the sky drove together.
The hills sent up all their vapor
And dark moist steam,
And now the thickened sky
Was like a dark ceiling; down rushed the rain
With great force, and continued until the earth
Could no longer be seen; the floating vessel swam,
Lifted up, and safe with a beaked prow
Rode rolling over the waves; all other dwellings
Were overwhelmed with the flood, and all their luxury
Sank deep underwater; sea covered sea,
A sea without a shore, and in their palaces,
Where luxury had recently ruled, sea monsters bred
And lived. All that was left of mankind, that had been so numerous,
Was in that one small boat.
How sad you were then, Adam, to see the end
Of all your offspring, an end so sad,
Depopulation; you made another flood
Of tears, and a flood of sorrow

drown'd,
And sunk thee as thy Sons; till gently reard

By th' Angel, on thy feet thou stoodst at last,
Though comfortless, as when a Father mourns
His Children, all in view destroyd at once;

And scarce to th' Angel utterdst thus thy plaint.
O Visions ill foreseen! better had I

Liv'd ignorant of future, so had borne

My part of evil onely, each dayes lot
Anough to bear; those now, that were dispenst
The burd'n of many Ages, on me light

At once, by my foreknowledge gaining Birth
Abortive, to torment me ere thir being,
With thought that they must be. Let no man seek
Henceforth to be foretold what shall befall

Him or his Childern, evil he may be sure,

Which neither his foreknowing can prevent,

And hee the future evil shall no less

In apprehension then in substance feel

Grievous to bear: but that care now is past,

Man is not whom to warne: those few escapt
Famin and anguish will at last consume
Wandring that watrie Desert: I had hope

When violence was ceas't, and Warr on Earth,
All would have then gon well, peace would have crownd

drowned you
And sank you as your sons had been;
until gently lifted
By the angel you stood on your feet again,
Though comfortless, a father mourning
His children, with all in view destroyed in an instant,
And could hardly speak to lament to the angel:
"Oh, these are terrible visions! It would have been better
If I had lived ignorant of the future, and had to bear
Only my part of evil, each day's lot
Is enough to bear; these evils, which were handed
Out to be carried by many ages, now all land
On me at once, gaining false birth through my foreknowledge,
Tormenting me before they happen
With the thought that they will come to pass. Let no man
From now on seek foreknowledge of what will happen
To him or his children; he may be sure it will be evil
And his foreknowledge cannot prevent it,
And he shall now feel the evil in imagination
No less painfully than if it was happening
To him. But that care has now passed,
Man cannot be warned, and those few escaped
Will die of famine and grief
Wandering in that watery desert: I had hoped
That when violence and war ended on Earth
All would have gone well, peace would have given

420

With length of happy dayes the race of man;
But I was farr deceav'd; for now I see

Peace to corrupt no less then Warr to waste.

How comes it thus? unfould, Celestial Guide,
And whether here the Race of man will end

To whom thus Michael. Those whom last thou sawst
In triumph and luxurious wealth, are they

First seen in acts of prowess eminent
And great exploits, but of true vertu void;

Who having spilt much blood, and don much waste
Subduing Nations, and achievd thereby

Fame in the World, high titles, and rich prey,
Shall change thir course to pleasure, ease, and sloth,
Surfet, and lust, till wantonness and pride
Raise out of friendship hostil deeds in Peace.
The conquerd also, and enslav'd by Warr

Shall with thir freedom lost all vertu loose

And fear of God, from whom thir pietie feign'd
In sharp contest of Battel found no aide

Against invaders; therefore coold in zeale
Thenceforth shall practice how to live secure,
Worldlie or dissolute, on what thir Lords

Shall leave them to enjoy; for th' Earth shall bear
More then anough, that temperance may be tri'd:
So all shall turn degenerate, all deprav'd,

Ages of happy days to the race of men;
But I was greatly mistaken; for now I see

That peace corrupts no less than war destroys.

How does this happen? Tell me, heavenly guide,
And tell me if this is the end of mankind."

Michael answered him: "Those who you last saw
In triumph, with luxurious wealth, are the same

You first saw in great acts of skill
And daring exploits, but they were lacking true virtue;

Having spilt so much blood, and destroyed so much in
Subduing nations, and by doing so achieved

Fame in the world, high titles and great booty,
Will change their lives to pleasure, ease and laziness,
Greed and lust, until excess and pride
Turn friendship into hostility in days of peace.
The conquered also, and those enslaved by war,

Shall lose all their virtue along with their freedom,

And also their fear of God, who gave them no help
In battle against the invaders, as all their piety

Was fake; so they lost their courage
And learned how to live in safety,
Wordly or immoral, on what their Lords

Left them to enjoy; for the Earth shall grow
More than enough for man's self control to be tested.
So all shall become degenerate, all

Justice and Temperance, Truth and Faith
forgot;
One Man except, the onely Son of light
In a dark Age, against example good,
Against allurement, custom, and a World

Offended; fearless of reproach and scorn,

Or violence, hee of wicked ways
Shall them admonish, and before them set

The paths of righteousness, how much
more safe,
And full of peace, denouncing wrauth to
come

On thir impenitence; and shall returne

Of them derided, but of God observd
The one just Man alive; by his command

Shall build a wondrous Ark, as thou
beheldst,
To save himself and houshold from amidst

A World devote to universal rack.

No sooner hee with them of Man and
Beast
Select for life shall in the Ark be lodg'd,

And shelterd round, but all the Cataracts

Of Heav'n set open on the Earth shall
power
Raine day and night, all fountains of the
Deep
Broke up, shall heave the Ocean to usurp
Beyond all bounds, till inundation rise
Above the highest Hills: then shall this
Mount
Of Paradise by might of Waves be moovd

Out of his place, pushd by the horned floud,

---

depraved,
And forget justice, temperance, truth
and faith;
Only one man, the only son of light
In a dark age, good unlike all others,
Stands against temptation, custom
and a world
Which hated him; fearless of
reproach or scorn
Or violence, he shall admonish them
For their wicked ways, and set before
them
The way of righteousness, so much
safer
And full of peace, foretelling the
punishment which will come
For their Godlessness; he shall get
derision
In return, but God will see him
As the one just man alive; by his
command
He shall build a wondrous Ark, as
you saw,
To save himself and his household
from
A world which suffers universal
destruction.
No sooner will he be embarked on the
Ark
With those men and beasts chosen to
live,
And all in shelter, but all the
waterfalls
Of Heaven will pour down on the
Earth
Rain, day and night, all the fountains
of the deep
Will erupt, heaving the ocean beyond
All boundaries, until the flood rises
Above the highest hills; then this
mountain
Of Paradise shall be pushed by the
strength of the waves
Out of place, pushed by the boiling
flood,

With all his verdure spoil'd, and Trees adrift

With all his greenery ruined, and trees will drift

Down the great River to the op'ning Gulf,
And there take root an Iland salt and bare,

*Down the great river to the gulf,
And there will grow up an island salty and barren,*

The haunt of Seales and Orcs, and Sea-mews clang.

The home of seals and orcs and seagulls.

To teach thee that God attributes to place

This teaches you that God counts no place

No sanctitie, if none be thither brought

As holy, if no holiness is not brought to it

By Men who there frequent, or therein dwell.

By the men who go there, or live there.

And now what further shall ensue, behold.

And now, what happened next, watch."

He lookd, and saw the Ark hull on the floud,

He looked, and saw the Ark drift on the flood,

Which now abated, for the Clouds were fled,

Which now abated, for the clouds had fled,

Drivn by a keen North- winde, that blowing drie

Driven by a keen north wind, that blew dry

Wrinkl'd the face of Deluge, as decai'd;

And wrinkled the face of the flood, as if it rotted;

And the cleer Sun on his wide watrie Glass

And the bright sun shone hot on the wide watery

Gaz'd hot, and of the fresh Wave largely drew,

Glass, and drew much water from the fresh waves,

As after thirst, which made thir flowing shrink

As if it was thirsty, and it made their flow lessen

From standing lake to tripping ebbe, that stole

From the standing lake to a gentle tide, that stole

With soft foot towards the deep, who now had stopt

Softly off towards the deep, which had now closed

His Sluces, as the Heav'n his windows shut.

Its sluices, as Heaven had closed his windows.

The Ark no more now flotes, but seems on ground

The Ark now floats no more but seems aground

Fast on the top of som high mountain fixt.

Fixed high on the top of some mountain.

And now the tops of Hills as Rocks appeer;

And now the tops of the hills appear like rocks;

With clamor thence the rapid Currents drive

With great noise the rapid currents drive

Towards the retreating Sea thir furious tyde.

Their furious tide towards the retreating sea.

Forthwith from out the Arke a Raven flies,

A raven flies out from the Ark,

And after him, the surer messenger,
A Dove sent forth once and agen to spie

Green Tree or ground whereon his foot
may light;
The second time returning, in his Bill

An Olive leafe he brings, pacific signe:
Anon drie ground appeers, and from his
Arke
The ancient Sire descends with all his
Train;
Then with uplifted hands, and eyes devout,

Grateful to Heav'n, over his head beholds

A dewie Cloud, and in the Cloud a Bow

Conspicuous with three listed colours gay,
Betok'ning peace from God, and Cov'nant
new.
Whereat the heart of Adam erst so sad

Greatly rejoyc'd, and thus his joy broke
forth.
O thou that future things canst represent

As present, Heav'nly instructer, I revive

At this last sight, assur'd that Man shall live

With all the Creatures, and thir seed
preserve.
Farr less I now lament for one whole
World
Of wicked Sons destroyd, then I rejoyce

For one Man found so perfet and so just,

That God voutsafes to raise another World

From him, and all his anger to forget.
But say, what mean those coloured streaks
in Heavn,
Distended as the Brow of God appeas'd,

And after him, the surer messenger,
A dove, sent out once and again to
find
A green tree or ground on which he
can land;
Coming back the second time he
carries in his beak
An olive leaf, a sign of peace;
Soon dry ground appears, and from
his Ark
The ancient ancestor descends with
all his crew.
Then with uplifted hands and
worshipping eyes,
Grateful to Heaven, he sees over his
head
A misty cloud, and in the cloud a
bow,
Shining with three bright colours,
A sign of peace from God, and of a
new covenant.
At this, the heart of Adam, which had
been so sad,
Greatly rejoiced, and he in his joy
burst out:
"Oh you that can show the future as
if
It was the present, Heavenly teacher,
I recover
At this last sight, assured that man
shall live
And all the creatures, and life shall
go on.
Now I feel far less sadness for a
whole world
Of wicked sons destroyed than I feel
happiness
For one man found so perfect and
just
That God promises to raise a new
world
From him, and to forget all his anger.
But tell me, what do those colored
streaks in the sky mean?
They look like the face of God,
satisfied,

Or serve they as a flourie verge to binde
The fluid skirts of that same watrie Cloud,
Least it again dissolve and showr the Earth?
To whom th' Archangel. Dextrously thou aim'st;
So willingly doth God remit his Ire,

Though late repenting him of Man deprav'd,
Griev'd at his heart, when looking down he saw
The whole Earth fill'd with violence, and all flesh
Corrupting each thir way; yet those remoov'd,
Such grace shall one just Man find in his sight,
That he relents, not to blot out mankind,

And makes a Covenant never to destroy

The Earth again by flood, nor let the Sea

Surpass his bounds, nor Rain to drown the World
With Man therein or Beast; but when he brings
Over the Earth a Cloud, will therein set

His triple-colour'd Bow, whereon to look

And call to mind his Cov'nant: Day and Night,
Seed time and Harvest, Heat and hoary Frost
Shall hold thir course, till fire purge all things new,
Both Heav'n and Earth, wherein the just shall dwell.

Or are they a flowery border binding
The edges of that watery cloud,
To stop it dissolving again and raining on the Earth?"
The archangel said, "You have hit the mark;
It shows how willing God is to soften his anger,

Though recently he was so grieved by the depravity of man,
Hurt to the heart, when he looked down to see
The whole Earth filled with violence, and all flesh
Corrupted in their different ways; but with those removed
One just man shall find such grace from him
That he relents his decision to wipe out mankind,

And makes a covenant that he will never again destroy

The Earth by flood, nor shall he let the sea

Break its boundaries, nor let the rain drown the world
Or the man and beasts within it. So when he puts
A cloud over the earth, he will place in it

His triple colored bow, for men to look on

And remember his promise; day and night,
Seed time and harvest, heat and gray frost,
Shall hold their right places, until fire shall clean all things again,
Both Heaven and Earth, where the just shall live.

BOOK XII

THE ARGUMENT

The Angel Michael continues from the Flood to relate what shall succeed; then, in the mention of Abraham, comes by degrees to explain, who that Seed of the Woman shall be, which was promised Adam and Eve in the Fall; his Incarnation, Death, Resurrection, and Ascension; the state of the Church till his second Coming. Adam greatly satisfied and recomforted by these Relations and Promises descends the Hill with Michael; wakens Eve, who all this while had slept, but with gentle dreams compos'd to quietness of mind and submission. Michael in either hand leads them out of Paradise, the fiery Sword waving behind them, and the Cherubim taking thir Stations to guard the Place.

The Angel Michael continues to explain what will happen following the flood. At the mention of Abraham he explains by steps who the Seed of Woman shall be that was promised to them in the fall, his birth, death, resurrection and ascension. He tells of the state of the Church until the second coming. Adam I greatly comforted and much satisfied with these stories and predictions and descends the hill with Michael. He wakes Eve, who had slept all through, having gentle dreams which lead her to be obedient and quiet in her mind. Michael takes them by the hand and leads them out of Paradise with the fiery sword waving behind them, and the Cherubim set up a guard around the place.

As one who in his journey bates at Noone,

Like someone who breaks his journey at noon

Though bent on speed, so heer the Archangel paus'd

Even though in a hurry, so here the Archangel paused

Betwixt the world destroy'd and world restor'd,

Between the world destroyed and the world restored

If Adam aught perhaps might interpose;
Then with transition sweet new Speech resumes.

*To see if Adam had any questions,
Then moving on he resumed his sweet speech.*

Thus thou hast seen one World begin and end;
And Man as from a second stock proceed.

*"You have seen one world begin and end,
And Man continue from a second root.*

Much thou hast yet to see, but I perceive

There is still much for you to see, but I notice

Thy mortal sight to faile; objects divine

Your mortal sight is failing; divine matters

Must needs impaire and wearie human sense:
Henceforth what is to com I will relate,

*Inevitably tire and impair human senses,
So from now on I'll just tell you about the future,*

Thou therefore give due audience, and attend.
This second sours of Men, while yet but

So listen, and pay attention.

This second source of Men still only

few;	*numbered a few,*
And while the dread of judgement past remains	*And while the dreadful judgment just given remains*
Fresh in thir mindes, fearing the Deitie,	*Fresh in their minds, so that they fear God,*
With some regard to what is just and right	*And pay some attention to right and wrong*
Shall lead thir lives and multiplie apace,	*In the way they lead their lives and will multiply quickly,*
Labouring the soile, and reaping plenteous crop,	*Working the soil and reaping abundant crops,*
Corn wine and oyle; and from the herd or flock,	*Corn, wine and oil; and from the herd or flock*
Oft sacrificing Bullock, Lamb, or Kid,	*They will often sacrifice a bullock, lamb or kid,*
With large Wine-offerings pour'd, and sacred Feast,	*With large offerings of wine and sacred feasting.*
Shal spend thir dayes in joy unblam'd, and dwell	*They shall spend their lives untroubled in joy, and live*
Long time in peace by Families and Tribes	*A long time in peace in families and tribes*
Under paternal rule; till one shall rise	*Under paternal rule; until one shall rise*
Of proud ambitious heart, who not content	*With a proud ambitious heart, who not content*
With fair equalitie, fraternal state,	*With fair equality and a brotherly society*
Will arrogate Dominion undeserv'd	*Will give himself undeserved Lordship*
Over his brethren, and quite dispossess	*Over his brothers, and completely remove*
Concord and law of Nature from the Earth,	*Harmony and the law of Nature from the Earth,*
Hunting (and Men not Beasts shall be his game)	*Hunting (and Men, not beasts, will be his quarry)*
With Warr and hostile snare such as refuse	*With war and hostile traps those who refuse*
Subjection to his Empire tyrannous:	*To become subjects of his tyrannous empire:*
A mightie Hunter thence he shall be styl'd	*A mighty hunter, he shall be named in their lists*
Before the Lord, as in despite of Heav'n,	*Before God, as if to fight against Heaven*
Or from Heav'n claming second Sovrantie;	*Or claiming his kingship derives from Heaven;*

And from Rebellion shall derive his name,	*He shall take his name from rebellion,*
Though of Rebellion others he accuse.	*Although he will accuse others of being rebels.*
Hee with a crew, whom like Ambition joyns	*He, with a gang who have the same ambition and join*
With him or under him to tyrannize,	*Him, or act as tyrants under his orders,*
Marching from Eden towards the West, shall finde	*Will find, as they march from Eden into the west,*
The Plain, wherein a black bituminous gurge	*The Plain of Shinar, where a black tarry whirlpool*
Boiles out from under ground, the mouth of Hell;	*Boils out from underground, the mouth of Hell;*
Of Brick, and of that stuff they cast to build	*They will use that stuff with bricks to build*
A Citie and Towre, whose top may reach to	*A city and a tower, planning to reach right up*
Heav'n;	*to Heaven;*
And get themselves a name, least far disperst	*They wanted to make a name for themselves*
In foraign Lands thir memorie be lost,	*So they would be remembered even in foreign lands,*
Regardless whether good or evil fame.	*And they did not care whether the name was good or evil.*
But God who oft descends to visit men	*But God, who often comes down to visit men*
Unseen, and through thir habitations walks	*Unseen, and walks through their settlements*
To mark thir doings, them beholding soon,	*To observe their actions, soon saw them*
Comes down to see thir Citie, ere the Tower	*And came down to see their city, before the tower*
Obstruct Heav'n Towrs, and in derision sets	*Could tangle with the towers of Heaven. To mock them*
Upon thir Tongues a various Spirit to rase	*He put a spell on their tongues to erase*
Quite out thir Native Language, and instead	*Their native language, and instead*
To sow a jangling noise of words unknown:	*To start a jangling racket of unknown words:*
Forthwith a hideous gabble rises loud	*At once a hideous loud babble begins*
Among the Builders; each to other calls	*Among the builders; what each said to the other*
Not understood, till hoarse, and all in rage,	*Was not understood until they were all hoarse and all in a rage,*
As mockt they storm; great laughter was in	*As they rampaged, mocked; there was*

Heav'n	*great laughter in Heaven*
And looking down, to see the hubbub strange	*When they looked down to see the strange hubbub*
And hear the din; thus was the building left	*And hear the din; so the building became*
Ridiculous, and the work Confusion nam'd.	*Absurd, and it was named Confusion."*
Whereto thus Adam fatherly displeas'd.	*Adam the father was displeased by this.*
O execrable Son so to aspire	*"Oh terrible Son to have ambitions*
Above his Brethren, to himself assuming	*To be higher than his brothers, taking authority*
Authoritie usurpt, from God not giv'n:	*For himself, not being given it by God:*
He gave us onely over Beast, Fish, Fowl	*He only gave us rule over beasts, fish and birds;*
Dominion absolute; that right we hold	*We have that right from his gift,*
By his donation; but Man over men	*But Man cannot be Lord over men,*
He made not Lord; such title to himself	*He kept that title for himself*
Reserving, human left from human free.	*And left humans free from humans.*
But this Usurper his encroachment proud	*But this usurper is not content just to rule*
Stayes not on Man; to God his Tower intends	*Over Man; his tower is intended to besiege and defy*
Siege and defiance: Wretched man! what food	*God: wretched man! What food*
Will he convey up thither to sustain	*Will he carry up there to sustain*
Himself and his rash Armie, where thin Aire	*Himself and his foolish army, where the thin air*
Above the Clouds will pine his entrails gross,	*Above the clouds will make his innards ache*
And famish him of Breath, if not of Bread?	*And starve him of breath, if not of bread?"*
To whom thus Michael. Justly thou abhorr'st	*Michael said to him, "You are right to hate*
That Son, who on the quiet state of men	*That son, who brought such trouble on*
Such trouble brought, affecting to subdue	*The quiet state of men, trying to suppress*
Rational Libertie; yet know withall,	*Man's freedom; but you should know*
Since thy original lapse, true Libertie	*That since your original sin true freedom*
Is lost, which alwayes with right Reason dwells	*Is lost, which must always be joined to reason,*
Twinn'd, and from her hath no dividual	*And cannot exist without her;*

being:

Reason in man obscur'd, or not obeyd,	*When reason in man is hidden, or disobeyed,*
Immediately inordinate desires	*At once excessive desires*
And upstart Passions catch the Government	*And boiling passions start to rule*
From Reason, and to servitude reduce	*Instead of reason, and they reduce the free man*
Man till then free. Therefore since hee permits	*To slavery. So, since he allows*
Within himself unworthie Powers to reign	*Unworthy powers within himself to rule*
Over free Reason, God in Judgement just	*Over free reason, God, in fair judgment,*
Subjects him from without to violent Lords;	*Makes him suffer violent Lords on the outside,*
Who oft as undeservedly enthral	*Who often just as wrongly enslave*
His outward freedom: Tyrannie must be,	*His physical freedom; tyranny must exist,*
Though to the Tyrant thereby no excuse.	*Though that does not excuse the tyrant.*
Yet somtimes Nations will decline so low	*But sometimes nations will get so far away*
From vertue, which is reason, that no wrong,	*From virtue, which is reason, that no wrongdoing*
But Justice, and some fatal curse annext	*Deprives them of their physical freedom*
Deprives them of thir outward libertie,	*But Justice and some curse on their race,*
Thir inward lost: Witness th' irreverent Son	*With their inner freedom lost; you can see the irreverent son*
Of him who built the Ark, who for the shame	*Of the one who built the Ark, who, for the shame*
Don to his Father, heard this heavie curse,	*He had forced on his father, was given the heavy curse*
Servant of Servants, on his vitious Race.	*That he and all his vicious race would be forever slaves.*
Thus will this latter, as the former World,	*Just like the former world so this second one*
Still tend from bad to worse, till God at last	*Will go from bad to worse, until God at last,*
Wearied with their iniquities, withdraw	*Tired of their wickedness, shall withdraw*
His presence from among them, and avert	*His presence from them, and avert*
His holy Eyes; resolving from thenceforth	*His holy eyes, resolving from then on*
To leave them to thir own polluted wayes;	*To leave them to their polluted habits,*

And one peculiar Nation to select	*And to choose just one tribe*
From all the rest, of whom to be invok'd,	*Above all the rest, whose prayers he would answer,*
A Nation from one faithful man to spring:	*A nation that will spring from a single faithful man,*
Him on this side Euphrates yet residing,	*Who lived on this side of the Euphrates,*
Bred up in Idol-worship; O that men	*Who was brought up on idol worship; Oh that men*
(Canst thou believe?) should be so stupid grown,	*(Can you believe it) had grown so stupid*
While yet the Patriark liv'd, who scap'd the Flood,	*That while the Patriarch who escaped the flood was still alive*
As to forsake the living God, and fall	*They abandoned the living God and started*
To worship thir own work in Wood and Stone	*To worshipping their own works of wood and stone*
For Gods! yet him God the most High voutsafes	*As Gods! But God the most high decided*
To call by Vision from his Fathers house,	*To call him with a vision from his father's house,*
His kindred and false Gods, into a Land	*From his family and his false Gods, into a land*
Which he will shew him, and from him will raise	*Which he will show him, and from him he will raise*
A mightie Nation, and upon him showre	*A mighty nation, and give him such*
His benediction so, that in his Seed	*Blessing that in his descendants*
All Nations shall be blest; he straight obeys	*All nations shall be blessed; he obeys at once,*
Not knowing to what Land, yet firm believes:	*Not knowing the land he is being taken to but having faith:*
I see him, but thou canst not, with what Faith	*I can see him, though you cannot, with what faith*
He leaves his Gods, his Friends, and native Soile	*He leaves his Gods, his friends, his natice land,*
Ur of Chaldæa, passing now the Ford	*Ur of Chaldaea, now passing the ford, going on*
To Haran, after a cumbrous Train	*To Haran, followed by a great procession*
Of Herds and Flocks, and numerous servitude;	*Of cattle and sheep, and many servants;*
Not wandring poor, but trusting all his wealth	*He did not wander as a beggar, but took all his wealth, trusting God,*
With God, who call'd him, in a land unknown.	*Who called him, in an unknown land.*

Canaan he now attains, I see his Tents

Pitcht about Sechem, and the neighbouring Plaine
Of Moreh; there by promise he receaves

Gift to his Progenie of all that Land;

From Hamath Northward to the Desert South
(Things by thir names I call, though yet unnam'd)
From Hermon East to the great Western Sea,
Mount Hermon, yonder Sea, each place behold
In prospect, as I point them; on the shoare
Mount Carmel; here the double-founted stream
Jordan, true limit Eastward; but his Sons

Shall dwell to Senir, that long ridge of Hills.

This ponder, that all Nations of the Earth

Shall in his Seed be blessed; by that Seed

Is meant thy great deliverer, who shall bruise
The Serpents head; whereof to thee anon

Plainlier shall be reveald. This Patriarch blest,
Whom faithful Abraham due time shall call,
A Son, and of his Son a Grand-childe leaves,
Like him in faith, in wisdom, and renown;

The Grandchilde with twelve Sons increast, departs
From Canaan, to a land hereafter call'd

Egypt, divided by the River Nile;
See where it flows, disgorging at seaven mouthes

Now he reaches Canaan, I see his tents

Gathered around Sechem, and on the neighboring plain
Of Moreh; there as he was promised he was given

A gift of all that land for himself and his descendants;

Stretching from Hamath in the north to the southern desert
(I call these things by their names, though they had none then),
From Hermon in the East to the great Western Sea,
Mount Hermon, that sea, see each place
As I point to them; there on the shore
Is Mount Carmel, here the double springed stream
Of Jordan, the true eastern border; but his sons

Shall live in Shenir, that long ridge of hills.

Think of all this, that all the nations of the Earth

Shall be blessed by his seed; by that seed

I mean your great deliverer, who shall bruise
The head of the serpent, about whom soon

I shall tell you more. This blessed patriarch,
Who when his time comes will be called Abraham,
Will leave a son, and from the son a grandchild,
The same as him in wisdom, faith and fame;

The grandchild will be blessed with twelve sons and will leave
Canaan for a land which will come to be called

Egypt, divided by the River Nile;
See where it flows, disgorging at seven mouths

Into the Sea: to sojourn in that Land
He comes invited by a yonger Son
In time of dearth, a Son whose worthy deeds
Raise him to be the second in that Realme
Of Pharao: there he dies, and leaves his Race
Growing into a Nation, and now grown

Suspected to a sequent King, who seeks

To stop thir overgrowth, as inmate guests

Too numerous; whence of guests he makes them slaves
Inhospitably, and kills thir infant Males:
Till by two brethren (those two brethren call
Moses and Aaron) sent from God to claime

His people from enthralment, they return

With glory and spoile back to thir promis'd Land.
But first the lawless Tyrant, who denies

To know thir God, or message to regard,
Must be compelld by Signes and Judgements dire;
To blood unshed the Rivers must be turnd,
Frogs, Lice and Flies must all his Palace fill
With loath'd intrusion, and fill all the land;

His Cattel must of Rot and Murren die,

Botches and blaines must all his flesh imboss,
And all his people; Thunder mixt with Haile,
Haile mixt with fire must rend th' Egyptian Skie
And wheel on th' Earth, devouring where it rouls;
What it devours not, Herb, or Fruit, or

Into the sea: he is invited to stay
In that land by a younger son
In a time of famine, a son whose worthy deeds
Elevated him to second in command
In the Pharaoh's kingdom; he dies there, leaving his race
Growing into a nation, and now a later Pharaoh

Becomes suspicious of them and wants to stop

Their spread, thinking that his guests are

Too numerous; so he makes his guests into slaves,
And kills their male children:
Until two brothers (by name
Moses and Aaron) were sent by God to take

His people out of slavery and they return

With glory and booty to their promised land.
But first the lawless tyrant, who does not recognize

Their God or his message
Must be warned with terrible signs and judgments;
The rivers must be turned to blood,
Frogs, lice and flies must fill his palace
With horrible invasion, and fill all the land;

His cattle must die of foot and mouth disease,
Boils and swellings must cover his flesh
And that of all his people; thunder mixed with hail
And hail mixed with fire must tear the Egyptian sky
And fall down on the Earth, destroying as it goes;
What it does not destroy, herb, or

Graine,
A darksom Cloud of Locusts swarming down
Must eat, and on the ground leave nothing green:
Darkness must overshadow all his bounds,
Palpable darkness, and blot out three dayes;
Last with one midnight stroke all the first-born
Of Egypt must lie dead. Thus with ten wounds
The River-dragon tam'd at length submits
To let his sojourners depart, and oft

Humbles his stubborn heart, but still as Ice
More hard'nd after thaw, till in his rage
Pursuing whom he late dismissd, the Sea
Swallows him with his Host, but them lets pass
As on drie land between two christal walls,
Aw'd by the rod of Moses so to stand
Divided, till his rescu'd gain thir shoar:
Such wondrous power God to his Saint will lend,
Though present in his Angel, who shall goe
Before them in a Cloud, and Pillar of Fire,
By day a Cloud, by night a Pillar of Fire,
To guide them in thir journey, and remove
Behinde them, while th' obdurat King pursues:
All night he will pursue, but his approach
Darkness defends between till morning Watch;
Then through the Firey Pillar and the Cloud

fruit, or grain,
A dark cloud of locusts will swarm down
And eat, and leave nothing green on the ground:
Darkness will overshadow all his lands,
Thick darkness which will blot out three days;
At last one day on the stroke of midnight all the first born
Of Egypt will die. So, tamed with ten wounds,
The Pharaoh at last allows
His guests to leave, and often

Humbles his stubborn heart, but it remains
Like ice, which is harder when it refreezes after a thaw,
Until in his rage he pursues those he just let go and the sea
Swallows him and his army, but lets the others pass
As if they were on dry land, between two crystal walls,
Ordered by the rod of Moses to stand
Apart until those he was rescuing reached the shore;
God will lend these wondrous powers to his saints,
Though here he was only present through his angel,
Who will go ahead of them in a cloud, and a pillar of fire,
By day a cloud, by night a pillar of fire,
To guide them on their journey and cover
Their tracks, while the stubborn King pursues them;
All night he will chase, but they are Safe under cover of darkness until morning;
Then through the fiery pillar and cloud

God looking forth will trouble all his Host

And craze thir Chariot wheels: when by command

Moses once more his potent Rod extends

Over the Sea; the Sea his Rod obeys;

On thir imbattelld ranks the Waves return,

And overwhelm thir Warr: the Race elect

Safe towards Canaan from the shoar advance

Through the wilde Desert, not the readiest way,

Least entring on the Canaanite allarmd

Warr terrifie them inexpert, and feare

Return them back to Egypt, choosing rather

Inglorious life with servitude; for life
To noble and ignoble is more sweet

Untraind in Armes, where rashness leads not on.
This also shall they gain by thir delay
In the wide Wilderness, there they shall found
Thir government, and thir great Senate choose
Through the twelve Tribes, to rule by Laws ordaind:
God from the Mount of Sinai, whose gray top
Shall tremble, he descending, will himself
In Thunder Lightning and loud Trumpets sound
Ordaine them Lawes; part such as appertaine
To civil Justice, part religious Rites
Of sacrifice, informing them, by types

And shadowes, of that destind Seed to bruise

God will look out and disturb all his army

And shatter their chariot wheels; then by order

Moses once more raises his powerful staff

Over the sea; the sea obeys his staff, and

The waves roll back in on the fighting ranks

And overwhelm their army: the chosen people

Advance safely towards Canaan from the shore

Through the wild desert, not taking the easiest way,

In case their coming should provoke the Canaanites

To war, at which they were not expert, and their fear

Would make them return to Egypt, choosing

An inglorious life of slavery; for life
To both noble and the common is more sweet

If not trained to fight, so they don't rush in as soldiers would.
They shall also gain by their delay
In the wilderness, where they shall establish
Their government and choose their leaders
From the twelve tribes, to rule by the laws they are given;
God shall descend to Mount Sinai, whose gray top
Will tremble and he will himself,
With thunder, lightning and loud trumpets
Give them laws, some referring to

Civil laws, some to religious rites
Of sacrifice, telling them with theology

And hints of that seed that is destined to bruise

The Serpent, by what meanes he shall achieve	The serpent, and how he shall achieve
Mankinds deliverance. But the voice of God	Mankind's deliverance.But the voice of God
To mortal eare is dreadful; they beseech	Is painful to mortal ears; they beg
That Moses might report to them his will,	That Moses might pass on his message
And terror cease; he grants what they besought	And so the terror would end.He gives them what they asked,
Instructed that to God is no access	Ordering that there is no access to God
Without Mediator, whose high Office now	Without a mediator, whose great office now
Moses in figure beares, to introduce	Moses assumes, the forerunner
One greater, of whose day he shall foretell,	Of a greater one, whose coming he will predict,
And all the Prophets in thir Age the times	And all the prophets of the age
Of great Messiah shall sing. Thus Laws and Rites	Will sing of the coming Messiah.So laws and rites
Establisht, such delight hath God in Men	Are established, and God is so pleased
Obedient to his will, that he voutsafes	With Man's obedience that he permits them
Among them to set up his Tabernacle,	To set up his tabernacle among them,
The holy One with mortal Men to dwell:	A place where the holy one can live amongst mortal man:
By his prescript a Sanctuary is fram'd	By his order a sanctuary is built
Of Cedar, overlaid with Gold, therein	Of cedar, overlaid with gold, and inside
An Ark, and in the Ark his Testimony,	An Ark, and inside the Ark his laws,
The Records of his Cov'nant, over these	The record of his covenant, and over these
A Mercie-seat of Gold between the wings	A throne of gold between the wings
Of two bright Cherubim, before him burn	Of two bright cherubs, and before him burn
Seaven Lamps as in a Zodiac representing	Seven lamps as in a sky map, each one representing
The Heav'nly fires; over the Tent a Cloud	The Heavenly fires; over the tent a cloud
Shall rest by Day, a fiery gleame by Night,	Will float by day, a fiery gleam by night,
Save when they journie, and at length they come,	Except when they travel.At last they arrive,
Conducted by his Angel to the Land	Led by the angel to the land
Promisd to Abraham and his Seed: the rest	Promised to Abraham and his tribe:

	the rest
Were long to tell, how many Battels fought,	*Would take long to tell, how many battles were fought,*
How many Kings destroyd, and Kingdoms won,	*Kings destroyed, kingdoms won,*
Or how the Sun shall in mid Heav'n stand still	*Or how the sun will stand still in Heaven*
A day entire, and Nights due course adjourne,	*For a whole day, postponing night's normal entrance,*
Mans voice commanding, Sun in Gibeon stand,	*A man's voice commanding it; 'Sun, wait in Gibeon,*
And thou Moon in the vale of Aialon,	*And you moon wait in the Vale of Aialon,*
Till Israel overcome; so call the third	*Until Jacob triumphs.'This will be said by the third*
From Abraham, Son of Isaac, and from him	*Descendant from Abraham, son of Isaac, and from him*
His whole descent, who thus shall Canaan win.	*All will descend, who in this way shall win the land of Canaan."*
Here Adam interpos'd. O sent from Heav'n,	*Here Adam interrupted."Oh messenger from Heaven,*
Enlightner of my darkness, gracious things	*Who brings light to my darkness, you have revealed*
Thou hast reveald, those chiefly which concerne	*Wonderful things, mainly those concerning*
Just Abraham and his Seed: now first I finde	*Just Abraham and his descendants: for the first time I find*
Mine eyes true op'ning, and my heart much eas'd,	*My eyes are truly open, and my heart is much eased,*
Erwhile perplext with thoughts what would becom	*Which before was tormented with thoughts of what*
Of mee and all Mankind; but now I see	*Would become of me and all mankind; but now I see*
His day, in whom all Nations shall be blest,	*The light, that He shall bless all the nations,*
Favour unmerited by me, who sought	*A favor I do not merit, I who sought to get*
Forbidd'n knowledge by forbidd'n means.	*Forbidden knowledge by forbidden means.*
This yet I apprehend not, why to those	*But I still do not understand this: why does God*
Among whom God will deigne to dwell on Earth	*Give so many and such complex laws*
So many and so various Laws are giv'n;	*To those he favors on Earth?*

So many Laws argue so many sins

Among them; how can God with such reside?
To whom thus Michael. Doubt not but that sin
Will reign among them, as of thee begot;

And therefore was Law given them to evince
Thir natural pravitie, by stirring up

Sin against Law to fight; that when they see

Law can discover sin, but not remove,
Save by those shadowie expiations weak,

The bloud of Bulls and Goats, they may conclude
Some bloud more precious must be paid for Man,
Just for unjust, that in such righteousness

To them by Faith imputed, they may finde
Justification towards God, and peace
Of Conscience, which the Law by Ceremonies
Cannot appease, nor Man the moral part

Perform, and not performing cannot live.

So Law appears imperfet, and but giv'n

With purpose to resign them in full time

Up to a better Cov'nant, disciplin'd
From shadowie Types to Truth, from Flesh to Spirit,
From imposition of strict Laws, to free
Acceptance of large Grace, from servil fear

To filial, works of Law to works of Faith.

And therefore shall not Moses, though of God
Highly belov'd, being but the Minister

To have so many laws argues that there is much sin

Amongst them: how then can God live with them?"
Michael answered, "Do not doubt that sin
Will be there with them, as they are born of you,

So law was given to them to show them
Their natural wickedness, by stirring up

Sin to fight against law; so when they see

Law can punish sin, but not forgive it,
Which can only be done by these shadowy weak payments,

With the blood of bulls and goats, they may see
That some more precious blood must be paid for Man,
Just for unjust, so that in the righteousness

Given to them by faith they may find
A way to speak with God, and peace
Of conscience, which the law cannot achieve
With ceremonies, and it cannot help man

To live morally, and without morals he cannot live.

So the law is not perfect, and is only given

To fill the time until they exchange it in the end

For a better covenant, moving
From obscure theology to truth, from flesh to spirit,
From rule by strict law to free
Acceptance of great mercy, from servile fear

To respect for our parent, from works of law to works of faith.

And so Moses, though greatly loved by God,
Being only the Minister of the Law,

Of Law, his people into Canaan lead;	*Shall not lead his people into Canaan;*
But Joshua whom the Gentiles Jesus call,	*That shall be done by Joshua, whom the Gentiles call Jesus,*
His Name and Office bearing, who shall quell	*Taking his title and office, and he will crush*
The adversarie Serpent, and bring back	*The enemy, the serpent, and bring back*
Through the worlds wilderness long wanderd man	*Through all the world's wilderness from his long wanderings*
Safe to eternal Paradise of rest.	*Man safe to the eternal Paradise of rest.*
Meanwhile they in thir earthly Canaan plac't	*Meanwhile in their Earthly Canaan*
Long time shall dwell and prosper, but when sins	*They shall live and prosper for a long time, but when*
National interrupt thir public peace,	*General wickedness disturbs the public peace*
Provoking God to raise them enemies:	*God will send enemies;*
From whom as oft he saves them penitent	*Just as often he will save them when they repent,*
By Judges first, then under Kings; of whom	*First through Judges and then through Kings;*
The second, both for pietie renownd	*The second king, who will be famous both for piety*
And puissant deeds, a promise shall receive	*And bravery, will receive an unbreakable promise*
Irrevocable, that his Regal Throne	*That the royal throne*
For ever shall endure; the like shall sing	*Shall last forever; all prophecies*
All Prophecie, That of the Royal Stock	*Will sing that from the royal line*
Of David (so I name this King) shall rise	*Of David (so I call this King) there shall rise*
A Son, the Womans Seed to thee foretold,	*A son, the seed of Woman prophesied to you,*
Foretold to Abraham, as in whom shall trust	*Predicted to Abraham, to be handed down to*
All Nations, and to Kings foretold, of Kings	*All nations, and predicted to Kings, for he will be the*
The last, for of his Reign shall be no end	*Last King, and his reign shall never end.*
But first a long succession must ensue,	*But first there is a long line of succession.*
And his next Son for Wealth and Wisdom fam'd,	*The next son was famous for his wealth and wisdom,*
The clouded Ark of God till then in Tents	*And he will take the mysterious Ark of God, kept in*

Wandring, shall in a glorious Temple enshrine.
Such follow him, as shall be registerd

Part good, part bad, of bad the longer scrowle,
Whose foul Idolatries, and other faults
Heapt to the popular summe, will so incense
God, as to leave them, and expose thir Land,
Thir Citie, his Temple, and his holy Ark

With all his sacred things, a scorn and prey

To that proud Citie, whose high Walls thou saw'st
Left in confusion, Babylon thence call'd.

There in captivitie he lets them dwell
The space of seventie years, then brings them back,
Remembring mercie, and his Cov'nant sworn
To David, stablisht as the dayes of Heav'n.

Returnd from Babylon by leave of Kings

Thir Lords, whom God dispos'd, the house of God
They first re-edifie, and for a while

In mean estate live moderate, till grown

In wealth and multitude, factious they grow;
But first among the Priests dissension springs,
Men who attend the Altar, and should most

Endeavour Peace: thir strife pollution brings
Upon the Temple it self: at last they seise

The Scepter, and regard not Davids Sons,

Tents until then, and enshrine it in a glorious temple.
Those who follow him will be written down

As some good, some bad – the bad being the longer list,
Whose foul idolatry, and other faults Piled up against the nation, will so incense
God that he will abandon them, and expose their land,
Their city, his Temple and his holy Ark,

With all his sacred things, a joke and a victim

For the proud city, that you last saw with its walls
Throne into confusion, then called Babylon.

He lets them live in captivity there For seventy years, then brings them back,
Remembering his mercy and the promise he made
To David, as unshakeable as Heaven itself.

Returned from Babylon with the permission of the Kings,

Their rulers, whom God made willing, they first
Rededicate the house of God, and for a while

They live modestly and humbly, until grown

In wealth and numbers they become argumentative;
First among the priests dissent begins,
The men who look after the altar, who should be

The ones promoting peace.Their strife brings pollution
To the temple itself: at last they seize power,

And ignore the claims of the sons of

Then loose it to a stranger, that the true

Anointed King Messiah might be born

Barr'd of his right; yet at his Birth a Starr

Unseen before in Heav'n proclaims him com,
And guides the Eastern Sages, who enquire
His place, to offer Incense, Myrrh, and Gold;
His place of birth a solemn Angel tells

To simple Shepherds, keeping watch by night;
They gladly thither haste, and by a Quire

Of squadrond Angels hear his Carol sung.
A Virgin is his Mother, but his Sire
The Power of the most High; he shall ascend
The Throne hereditarie, and bound his Reign
With earths wide bounds, his glory with the Heav'ns.
He ceas'd, discerning Adam with such joy

Surcharg'd, as had like grief bin dew'd in tears,

Without the vent of words, which these he breathd.
O Prophet of glad tidings, finisher

Of utmost hope! now clear I understand

What oft my steddiest thoughts have searcht in vain,
Why our great expectation should be call'd
The seed of Woman: Virgin Mother, Haile,

High in the love of Heav'n, yet from my Loynes
Thou shalt proceed, and from thy Womb the Son

David,
Then they lose it to a stranger, so the true
Annointed King Messiah might be born
Without his rights; but at his birth a star
Never before seen in the sky
announces his coming,
And guides the wise men, who ask for
His location, to offer him incense,
myrrh and gold;
His place of birth is told by a solemn angel
To simple shepherds, keeping watch by night;
They gladly rush there, and hear his praises
Sung by a massed choir of angels.
His mother is a virgin, but his father
Is God; he shall climb

Onto the hereditary throne, and his kingdom
Will be the Earth and his glory will be in Heaven."
He stopped, seeing that Adam was so full of joy
That he was wet with tears as if sad,

Beyond words, but now he spoke.
"Oh prophet of glad tidings, ending your story
With the greatest hope!Now I clearly understand
What my deepest thoughts have not revealed,
Why our great hope should be called
The seed of woman: hail to you, virgin mother,
High in the love of Heaven, but from my loins
You shall come, and from your womb shall come the son

Of God most High; So God with man
unites.
Needs must the Serpent now his capital
bruise
Expect with mortal paine: say where and
when
Thir fight, what stroke shall bruise the
Victors heel
To whom thus Michael. Dream not of
thir fight,
As of a Duel, or the local wounds

Of head or heel: not therefore joynes the
Son
Manhood to God-head, with more strength
to foil
Thy enemie; nor so is overcome

Satan, whose fall from Heav'n, a deadlier
bruise,
Disabl'd not to give thee thy deaths wound:

Which hee, who comes thy Saviour, shall
recure,
Not by destroying Satan, but his works

In thee and in thy Seed: nor can this be,

But by fulfilling that which thou didst want,

Obedience to the Law of God, impos'd

On penaltie of death, and suffering death,

The penaltie to thy transgression due,
And due to theirs which out of thine will
grow:
So onely can high Justice rest appaid.

The Law of God exact he shall fulfil

Both by obedience and by love, though
love
Alone fulfill the Law; thy punishment

---

*Of God Almighty; so God unites with
man.*
*Now the serpent must expect to get
his bruised head*
*With mortal pain; tell me where and
when*
*They will fight, and what blow will
bruise the victor's heel.*
*Michael answered, "Don't think of
their fight*
*As being like a duel, or of causing
local wounds*
*To heads or heels; this is not why the
Son*
*Joins Man and God, with more
strength to beat*
*Your enemy; nor can Satan be so
easily overcome,*
*The one whose fall from Heaven, a
far deadlier bruise,*
*Did not stop him giving you your
fatal wound:*
*The wound which he who comes as
your savior shall cure,*
*Not by destroying Satan but by
destroying his works*
*In you and your children; and this
cannot happen*
*Unless man sticks to that which you
could not,*
*Obedience to the law of God,
imposed*
*On penalty of death, and suffering
death,*
The sentence due for your sin
And due to all who descend from you:
*This is the only way God's justice can
be satisfied.*
*He shall completely follow the law of
God*
*Through obedience and love, though
love*
*Is enough to follow the law; he shall
endure*

He shall endure by coming in the Flesh	*Your punishment by coming in the flesh*
To a reproachful life and cursed death,	*To hatred in life and a cursed death,*
Proclaiming Life to all who shall believe	*Offering life to all who believe*
In his redemption, and that his obedience	*In his forgiveness, and that his obedience*
Imputed becomes theirs by Faith, his merits	*Becomes theirs if they believe in him, and that*
To save them, not thir own, though legal works.	*It is his merit, not their own, which will save them.*
For this he shall live hated, be blasphem'd,	*For this he shall live hated, be cursed,*
Seis'd on by force, judg'd, and to death condemnd	*Seized by force, judged and condemned to death,*
A shameful and accurst, naild to the Cross	*A shameful and cursed death, nailed to the cross*
By his own Nation, slaine for bringing Life;	*By his own people, killed for bringing life;*
But to the Cross he nailes thy Enemies,	*But he nails your enemies to the cross,*
The Law that is against thee, and the sins	*The punishment that hangs over you, and the sins*
Of all mankinde, with him there crucifi'd,	*Of all mankind, are crucified with him,*
Never to hurt them more who rightly trust	*And will never more hurt those who truly believe*
In this his satisfaction; so he dies,	*That he has paid the price for them. So he will die*
But soon revives, Death over him no power	*But soon come back to life, as Death has no power*
Shall long usurp; ere the third dawning light	*To hold him for long; before the third morning*
Returne, the Starres of Morn shall see him rise	*He will come back, the stars of the morning will see him rise*
Out of his grave, fresh as the dawning light,	*Out of his grave, fresh as the morning light,*
Thy ransom paid, which Man from death redeems,	*Your ransom will be paid and Man will be freed from death;*
His death for Man, as many as offerd Life	*His dying for Man, for all of those who were ever born,*
Neglect not, and the benefit imbrace	*Do not forget, and give thanks for it*
By Faith not void of workes: this God-like act	*With faith and deeds: this Godlike act*
Annuls thy doom, the death thou shouldst	*Cancels your sentence, the death you*

have dy'd,
In sin for ever lost from life; this act

Shall bruise the head of Satan, crush his
strength
Defeating Sin and Death, his two maine
armes,
And fix farr deeper in his head thir stings

Then temporal death shall bruise the
Victors heel,
Or theirs whom he redeems, a death like
sleep,
A gentle wafting to immortal Life.
Nor after resurrection shall he stay
Longer on Earth then certaine times to
appeer
To his Disciples, Men who in his Life

Still follow'd him; to them shall leave in
charge
To teach all nations what of him they
learn'd
And his Salvation, them who shall believe

Baptizing in the profluent streame, the signe
Of washing them from guilt of sin to Life
Pure, and in mind prepar'd, if so befall,

For death, like that which the redeemer
dy'd.
All Nations they shall teach; for from
that day
Not onely to the Sons of Abrahams Loines
Salvation shall be Preacht, but to the Sons

Of Abrahams Faith wherever through the
world;
So in his seed all Nations shall be blest.

Then to the Heav'n of Heav'ns he shall
ascend
With victory, triumphing through the aire

Over his foes and thine; there shall surprise

---

should have died,
When your sin should have brought
you death; this act
Will bruise the head of Satan, crush
his power
By defeating Sin and Death, his two
main weapons,
And cause him far more pain in his
head
Than brief physical death shall bruise
the victor's heel,
Or those of whom he redeems, for
that shall be a death just like sleep,
A gentle drifting to immortal life.
After resurrection he shall not stay
Longer on Earth except to appear a
few times
To his disciples, Men who had
followed him
In his life; he shall leave orders with
them
That they are to teach all nations
what they learned from him,
And also his salvation, baptizing
those who believe
In running water, the sign of washing
Away the guilt of sin and making life
Pure, and making them prepared in
their minds for death
If it comes, a death such as the
redeemer died.
They shall teach all nations; for from
that day
Salvation shall not only be preached
To the descendants of Abraham but to
the sons
Of Abraham's faith throughout the
world,
So in his seed all nations shall be
blessed.
Then he shall ascend to the highest
Heaven,
Victorious, triumphing through the
air
Over his enemies and yours; there he
shall ambush

The Serpent, Prince of aire, and drag in Chaines
Through all his Realme, and there confounded leave;
Then enter into glory, and resume

His Seat at Gods right hand, exalted high

Above all names in Heav'n; and thence shall come,
When this worlds dissolution shall be ripe,

With glory and power to judge both quick and dead
To judge th' unfaithful dead, but to reward

His faithful, and receave them into bliss,

Whether in Heav'n or Earth, for then the Earth
Shall all be Paradise, far happier place

Then this of Eden, and far happier daies.

So spake th' Archangel Michael, then paus'd,
As at the Worlds great period; and our Sire

Replete with joy and wonder thus repli'd.
O goodness infinite, goodness immense!

That all this good of evil shall produce,

And evil turn to good; more wonderful

Then that which by creation first brought forth
Light out of darkness! full of doubt I stand,

Whether I should repent me now of sin

By mee done and occasiond, or rejoyce

Much more, that much more good thereof

The serpent, the Prince of Air, and drag him in chains
All through his kingdom, and leave him there defeated;
Then he shall enter into glory and take up

His seat at God's right hand, exalted high

Above all others in Heaven. He will come from there,
When it is time for this world to be dissolved,

With power and glory to judge the living and the dead,
To judge the unfaithful dead, but to reward

His faithful, and to receive them into bliss,

Whether in Heaven or on Earth, for then the Earth
Shall all be Paradise, a far happier place

Than this Eden, and it will see far happier days."

So spoke the archangel Michael, then paused,
As he reached the end of the world; and our ancestor

Answered, full of joy and wonder.
"Oh infinte goodness, immense goodness!

That all this evil shall come from this goodness,

Which will then be turned back to good; more wonderful

Than the power which in creation first brought
Light from the darkness! I am now full of doubt,

Not knowing whether I should repent of the sin

Done by me which caused all this, or rejoice

Much more, that much more good

shall spring,
To God more glory, more good will to Men

From God, and over wrauth grace shall abound.
But say, if our deliverer up to Heav'n

Must reascend, what will betide the few

His faithful, left among th' unfaithful herd,

The enemies of truth; who then shall guide

His people, who defend? will they not deale

Wors with his followers then with him they dealt?
Be sure they will, said th' Angel; but from Heav'n
Hee to his own a Comforter will send,
The promise of the Father, who shall dwell

His Spirit within them, and the Law of Faith
Working through love, upon thir hearts shall write,
To guide them in all truth, and also arme

With spiritual Armour, able to resist

Satans assaults, and quench his fierie darts,

What Man can do against them, not affraid,

Though to the death, against such cruelties

With inward consolations recompenc't,

And oft supported so as shall amaze

Thir proudest persecuters: for the Spirit
Powrd first on his Apostles, whom he sends

To evangelize the Nations, then on all

Baptiz'd, shall them with wondrous gifts

---

will spring from it;
To God more glory, to Men more good will
From God, and forgiveness shall triumph over anger.
But tell me, if our redeemer must go back
To Heaven, what will happen to the few,
His faithful, left amongst the unfaithful herd
With the enemies of truth? Who will guide
His people and defend them? Will they not treat
His followers worse than they treated him?"
"You can be sure they will," said the angel, "But he will send
A comfort to them from Heaven,
The promise of the Father, who shall place
The Holy Spirit within them, and the law of faith
Working through love will be written on their hearts,
To guide them towards the truth, and to arm them
With spiritual armour which can resist
Satan's assaults, and extinguish his fiery darts.
They are not afraid of what men can do to them,
Even if it leads to death, for they are consoled
Against such cruelties by their inner faith,
And with that support their hardiness will often amaze
Their cruelest persecutors. The Spirit
Landed first on his Apostles, whom he sends
To teach the Nations, and then it fell on all
Baptized and it will give the

endue
To speak all Tongues, and do all Miracles,

As did thir Lord before them. Thus they win
Great numbers of each Nation to receave

With joy the tidings brought from Heav'n:

Thir Ministry perform'd, and race well run,

Thir doctrine and thir story written left,

They die; but in thir room, as they forewarne,
Wolves shall succeed for teachers, grievous Wolves,
Who all the sacred mysteries of Heav'n

To thir own vile advantages shall turne

Of lucre and ambition, and the truth

With superstitions and traditions taint,

Left onely in those written Records pure,

Though not but by the Spirit understood.
Then shall they seek to avail themselves of names,
Places and titles, and with these to joine

Secular power, though feigning still to act

By spiritual, to themselves appropriating

The Spirit of God, promisd alike and giv'n

To all Beleevers; and from that pretense,
Spiritual Lawes by carnal power shall force

On every conscience; Laws which none shall finde
Left them inrould, or what the Spirit within

wondrous gifts,
To speak all languages and to perform miracles
As their Lord did before them. So they will win
Great numbers of each Nation over to receiving

With joy the tidings brought from at length Heaven. Eventually,
With their Ministry performed and their job well done,
Their theology and their stories written down,

They die; but in their place, as they warned,
Will come wolves for teachers, terrible wolves,
Who will take all the holy mysteries of Heaven

And turn them to serve their own vile desires

For money and fame, and they will taint
The truth and traditions with superstition,

And the traditions shall only be pure in the written records,

Though only understood by the Spirit.
Then they will try to get names,

Places and titles, and with these they will take
Secular power, even though they will pretend that
They are still spiritual, claiming only they have
The Spirit of God, which was promised and given to all
Believers alike. From that pretence
They shall force spiritual laws on everyone
Through physical power; laws which none shall feel
Leave them close to God, and not what the Spirit

Shall on the heart engrave. What will they then
But force the Spirit of Grace it self, and binde
His consort Libertie; what, but unbuild

His living Temples, built by Faith to stand,
Thir own Faith not anothers: for on Earth

Who against Faith and Conscience can be heard
Infallible? yet many will presume:
Whence heavie persecution shall arise
On all who in the worship persevere
Of Spirit and Truth; the rest, farr greater part,
Well deem in outward Rites and specious forms
Religion satisfi'd; Truth shall retire
Bestuck with slandrous darts, and works of Faith
Rarely be found: so shall the World goe on,

To good malignant, to bad men benigne,
Under her own waight groaning till the day

Appeer of respiration to the just,
And vengeance to the wicked, at return

Of him so lately promiss'd to thy aid

The Womans seed, obscurely then foretold,

Now amplier known thy Saviour and thy Lord,
Last in the Clouds from Heav'n to be reveald
In glory of the Father, to dissolve
Satan with his perverted World, then raise

From the conflagrant mass, purg'd and refin'd,
New Heav'ns, new Earth, Ages of endless date
Founded in righteousness and peace and love

Will write on the heart. Then they will
Enslave the Spirit of Grace itself, and tie up
His companion, liberty; they shall destroy

His living temples, built with faith,
Their own faith, not another's; for on Earth

Who, who has faith and conscience, would call themselves
Infallible? But many will try:
And so great persecution will start
Of all who in their worship keep
To Spirit and Truth; the rest, the far greater part,
Will be happy with the external shows and superficial
Forms of religion; truth shall retreat,
Stuck with lying darts, and works of faith
Will rarely be found: so the world will go on,

Bad to the good and good to the bad,
Groaning under her own weight until the day

Comes of reward for the just
And punishment for the wicked, at the return

Of him so recently promised for your help,

The woman's seed, foretold obscurely then,

Now more openly known as your Savior and Lord,
At last revealed in the clouds from Heaven
In the glory of the father, to destroy
Satan and his perverted world, then raise

From the great fire, cleaned and refined,
New Heavens, a new Earth, never-ending ages
Of righteousness and peace and love,

To bring forth fruits Joy and eternal Bliss.

He ended; and thus Adam last reply'd.

How soon hath thy prediction, Seer blest,

Measur'd this transient World, the Race of time,
Till time stand fixt: beyond is all abyss,

Eternitie, whose end no eye can reach.
Greatly instructed I shall hence depart.

Greatly in peace of thought, and have my fill
Of knowledge, what this Vessel can containe;
Beyond which was my folly to aspire.

Henceforth I learne, that to obey is best,

And love with feare the onely God, to walk

As in his presence, ever to observe

His providence, and on him sole depend,
Merciful over all his works, with good
Still overcoming evil, and by small

Accomplishing great things, by things deemd weak
Subverting worldly strong, and worldly wise
By simply meek; that suffering for Truths sake
Is fortitude to highest victorie,
And to the faithful Death the Gate of Life;
Taught this by his example whom I now

Acknowledge my Redeemer ever blest.

To whom thus also th' Angel last repli'd:

This having learnt, thou hast attained the summe
Of wisdom; hope no higher, though all the

Creating joy and eternal bliss."

He finished, and Adam gave his last reply.
"How quickly your prophecies, blessed seer,
Have measured this passing world, this race of time,
Until time stands still: beyond that is an abyss,
Eternity, whose end no eye can reach.
I will leave here having learned much,
And I will leave with great peace of mind, I am full
Of knowledge, all this vessel can hold;
It was foolish of me to try and get more than this.
From now on I know that to obey is best
And to love with fear the only God, to walk
As if in his presence, always remembering
His care, and only depending on him,
Who is merciful above all, with good
Still overcoming evil, and with small things
Accomplishing great things, with things thought weak
Beating the world strong and worldly wise
Simply through their meekness; suffering for truth
Brings the greatest victory,
And the way to life after death;
I learn this from the example of the one
Whom I now acknowledge as my blessed redeemer."
And the angel also gave his last words to him:
"Having learnt this you have achieved the highest
Wisdom; you can hope for no higher,

450

Starrs	*even if you knew*
Thou knewst by name, and all th' ethereal Powers,	*The names of all the stars and of all the Heavenly powers,*
All secrets of the deep, all Natures works,	*All the secrets of the deep, all Nature's works,*
Or works of God in Heav'n, Aire, Earth, or Sea,	*Or works of God in Heaven, Air, Earth or Sea,*
And all the riches of this World enjoydst,	*And enjoyed all the riches of this world,*
And all the rule, one Empire; onely add	*And ruled over it all as Emperor; you must add*
Deeds to thy knowledge answerable, add Faith,	*Deeds influenced by your knowledge, faith,*
Add vertue, Patience, Temperance, add Love,	*Virtue, patience, temperance, love,*
By name to come call'd Charitie, the soul	*Which in future will be called charity, the soul*
Of all the rest: then wilt thou not be loath	*Of all the rest. Then you will not hate*
To leave this Paradise, but shalt possess	*To leave this Paradise, for you shall have*
A Paradise within thee, happier farr.	*A Paradise within you, far greater.*
Let us descend now therefore from this top	*Now let us climb down from this viewing peak,*
Of Speculation; for the hour precise	*For it is the hour*
Exacts our parting hence; and see the Guards,	*Set for our leaving; and you see the guards*
By mee encamp on yonder Hill, expect	*Placed by me on that hill, waiting for*
Thir motion, at whose Front a flaming Sword,	*Their orders, with a flaming sword in front of them*
In signal of remove, waves fiercely round,	*Which is waving fiercely to signal you to go.*
We may no longer stay: go, waken Eve;	*We can stay no longer; go and wake Eve;*
Her also I with gentle Dreams have calm'd	*I have calmed her with gentle dreams,*
Portending good, and all her spirits compos'd	*Promising future good and making her spirit*
To meek submission: thou at season fit	*Meekly submissive: at the right time*
Let her with thee partake what thou hast heard,	*Tell her what you have heard,*
Chiefly what may concern her Faith to know,	*Especially what specifically concerns her,*
The great deliverance by her Seed to come	*The great redemption to come from her seed*
(For by the Womans Seed) on all Mankind.	*(For from the seed of woman) to all*

	mankind.
That ye may live, which will be many dayes,	And so you can live for many days,
Both in one Faith unanimous though sad,	Together in one faith, though sad,
With cause for evils past, yet much more cheer'd	Rightly so, thinking of past evils, but more happy
With meditation on the happie end.	Thinking about the happy end."
He ended, and they both descend the Hill;	He finished, and they both came down the hill;
Descended, Adam to the Bowre where Eve	Adam ran to the bower where Eve
Lay sleeping ran before, but found her wak't;	Lay sleeping, but found her awake,
And thus with words not sad she him receav'd.	And she welcomed him with words which were not sad.
Whence thou returnst, and whither wentst, I know;	"Where you have come from and where you went, I know;
For God is also in sleep, and Dreams advise,	For God can be found in sleep, and advice in dreams,
Which he hath sent propitious, some great good	Which he has sent with great favor, foretelling
Presaging, since with sorrow and hearts distress	Some great good, because I fell asleep worn out
Wearied I fell asleep: but now lead on;	With sorrow and heart's distress: but now lead on.
In mee is no delay; with thee to goe,	I will not delay; to go with you
Is to stay here; without thee here to stay,	Is like staying here; to stay here without you
Is to go hence unwilling; thou to mee	Would be like going out unwillingly; you to me
Art all things under Heav'n, all places thou,	Are the whole world, you are all places,
Who for my wilful crime art banisht hence.	You who are banished from here by my willful crime.
This further consolation yet secure	And I carry a further consolation with me
I carry hence; though all by mee is lost,	As I leave; though all is lost through me,
Such favour I unworthie am voutsaft,	I have been given a great gift I do not deserve,
By mee the Promis'd Seed shall all restore.	That through me the Promised Seed shall restore everything."
So spake our Mother Eve, and Adam heard	So our mother Eve spoke, and Adam heard,
Well pleas'd, but answer'd not; for now too nigh	Well pleased, but he did not answer, for now
Th' Archangel stood, and from the other	The archangel stood close, and from

452

Hill
To thir fixt Station, all in bright array

The Cherubim descended; on the ground
Gliding meteorous, as Ev'ning Mist
Ris'n from a River o're the marish glides,

And gathers ground fast at the Labourers heel
Homeward returning. High in Front advanc't,
The brandisht Sword of God before them blaz'd
Fierce as a Comet; which with torrid heat,

And vapour as the Libyan Air adust,

Began to parch that temperate Clime; whereat
In either hand the hastning Angel caught

Our lingring Parents, nd to th' Eastern Gate

Led them direct, and down the Cliff as fast

To the subjected Plaine; then disappeer'd.

They looking back, all th' Eastern side beheld
Of Paradise, so late thir happie seat,

Wav'd over by that flaming Brand, the Gate

With dreadful Faces throng'd and fierie Armes:
Som natural tears they drop'd, but wip'd them soon;
The World was all before them, where to choose
Thir place of rest, and Providence thir guide:
They hand in hand with wandring steps and slow,
Through Eden took thir solitarie way.

the other hill
To their posts the Cherubim descended,
All in shining armor; they glided fast
Over the ground, like an evening mist
Rising from a river, gliding over the marshes,

Snapping at the heels of the laborers

On their way home. High in front of them

The brandished sword of God blazed,

Fierce as a comet, and its burning heat

And steam like the scorching Libyan air

Began to parch that moderate place, and
The hurrying angel caught our lingering parents,
One in each hand, and led them directly
To the eastern gate, and just as quickly down the cliff
To the lower plain, and then disappeared.
Looking back they saw all the eastern side
Of Paradise, so recently their happy home,
Waved over by that flaming sword, the gate
Was crowded with dreadful faces and fiery weapons.
They naturally shed some tears, but soon wiped them away;
The world was set out before them, from which they could choose
Their place of rest, with the kindness of God guiding them:
Hand in hand, with wandering slow steps,
They made their lonely way through Eden.

453

Paradise Regainged

BOOK I

I, Who erewhile the happy Garden sung	*I, who a while ago sang of the happy garden,*
By one man's disobedience lost, now sing	*Lost by one man's disobedience, now sing*
Recovered Paradise to all mankind,	*To all mankind of Paradise regained,*
By one man's firm obedience fully tried	*Through one man's obedience being tested*
Through all temptation, and the Tempter foiled	*With every temptation, and the tempter beaten,*
In all his wiles, defeated and repulsed,	*With all his cunning, beaten and thrown back,*
And Eden raised in the waste Wilderness.	*And Eden created again in the empty wilderness.*
Thou Spirit, who led'st this glorious Eremite	*You spirit, who led this glorious hermit*
Into the desert, his victorious field	*Into the desert, the place he defeated*
Against the spiritual foe, and brought'st him thence 10	*His spiritual enemy, and brought him from there*
By proof the undoubted Son of God, inspire,	*Having been proved to be undoubtedly the son of God, inspire,*
As thou art wont, my prompted song, else mute,	*As you always do, the song I ask for, which would otherwise be silent,*
And bear through highth or depth of Nature's bounds,	*And carry me through the heights and depths of nature's world,*
With prosperous wing full summed, to tell of deeds	*With your great wings spread out fully, to tell of acts*
Above heroic, though in secret done,	*More than heroic, although done in secret,*
And unrecorded left through many an age:	*That have not been recorded for many ages:*
Worthy to have not remained so long unsung.	*They deserve to have been sung about.*
Now had the great Proclaimer, with a voice	*Now the great announcer, with a voice*
More awful than the sound of trumpet, cried	*More dreadful than the loudest trumpet, shouted*
Repentance, and Heaven's kingdom nigh at hand 20	*That it was time to repent and that the kingdom of heaven was ready*
To all baptized. To his great baptism flocked	*For all who had been baptised. From*

	far and wide they rushed
With awe the regions round, and with them came	*To his great baptism, and with them came*
From Nazareth the son of Joseph deemed	*The one called the son of Joseph, from Nazareth,*
To the flood Jordan—came as then obscure,	*To the River Jordan; he came in secret,*
Unmarked, unknown. But him the Baptist soon	*Unnoticed and unknown. But the Baptist soon*
Descried, divinely warned, and witness bore	*Recognised him, having been alerted by an angel, and said*
As to his worthier, and would have resigned	*That this one was greater, and would have handed over*
To him his heavenly office. Nor was long	*His divine task to him. And it wasn't long*
His witness unconfirmed: on him baptized	*Before the truth of this was shown; when he was baptised*
Heaven opened, and in likeness of a Dove 30	*Heaven opened, and the spirit came down*
The Spirit descended, while the Father's voice	*In the shape of a dove, while the father's voice*
From Heaven pronounced him his beloved Son.	*From heaven announced that this was his beloved son.*
That heard the Adversary, who, roving still	*The enemy heard this, as he was still wandering*
About the world, at that assembly famed	*The world, and had not been the last to come*
Would not be last, and, with the voice divine	*To that great gathering, and was thunderstruck*
Nigh thunder-struck, the exalted man to whom	*To hear the divine voice; he looked with amazement*
Such high attest was given a while surveyed	*For a while at the blessed man to whom*
With wonder; then, with envy fraught and rage,	*Such high praise was given; then, torn with envy and rage,*
Flies to his place, nor rests, but in mid air	*He flies to his home, and does not rest but calls*
To council summons all his mighty Peers, 40	*All his mighty lords to council in mid-air,*
Within thick clouds and dark tenfold involved,	*Inside thick clouds and great darkness,*
A gloomy consistory; and them amidst,	*A dismal meeting; and in the middle,*
With looks aghast and sad, he thus bespake:—	*Looking horrified and serious, he spoke to them:*
"O ancient Powers of Air and this wide World	*"You ancient rulers of air and this wide world*

(For much more willingly I mention Air,	*(I am much happier to mention air,*
This our old conquest, than remember Hell,	*Our earliest territory, than remember hell,*
Our hated habitation), well ye know	*Our hated home), you are well aware*
How many ages, as the years of men,	*Of how many ages, counted in the years of men,*
This Universe we have possessed, and ruled	*We have owned this universe, and had*
In manner at our will the affairs of Earth, 50	*Free rule over the affairs of Earth,*
Since Adam and his facile consort Eve	*Since Adam and his simple wife Eve*
Lost Paradise, deceived by me, though since	*Lost paradise, tricked by me, although ever since*
With dread attending when that fatal wound	*I have been dreading the time when*
Shall be inflicted by the seed of Eve	*The descendants of Eve will inflict that fatal wound*
Upon my head. Long the decrees of Heaven	*Upon my head. The justice of heaven waits for a long time,*
Delay, for longest time to Him is short;	*For to him the longest time is short;*
And now, too soon for us, the circling hours	*And now, too soon for us, the hands of the clock*
This dreaded time have compassed, wherein we	*Have come round to this dreaded time, when we*
Must bide the stroke of that long-threatened wound	*Must suffer the blow of that long ago predicted wound*
(At least, if so we can, and by the head 60	*(At least if we can, and if our broken head*
Broken be not intended all our power	*Does not mean that all our power*
To be infringed, our freedom and our being	*Is broken, or our freedom and existence*
In this fair empire won of Earth and Air)—	*In this wonderful Empire we won of earth and air is taken from us)–*
For this ill news I bring: The Woman's Seed,	*For I bring this bad news: the woman's seed,*
Destined to this, is late of woman born.	*Which is going to do this, has recently been born from a woman.*
His birth to our just fear gave no small cause;	*His birth certainly justifies our fears;*
But his growth now to youth's full flower, displaying	*But the fact that he has now reached the height of youth, showing*
All virtue, grace and wisdom to achieve	*The virtue, grace and wisdom to achieve*
Things highest, greatest, multiplies my fear.	*The highest and greatest things; this makes my fear even worse.*
Before him a great Prophet, to proclaim 70	*A great prophet comes ahead of him, to announce*

His coming, is sent harbinger, who all

Invites, and in the consecrated stream
Pretends to wash off sin, and fit them so
Purified to receive him pure, or rather

To do him honour as their King. All come,

And he himself among them was baptized—

Not thence to be more pure, but to receive

The testimony of Heaven, that who he is
Thenceforth the nations may not doubt.
I saw
The Prophet do him reverence; on him,
rising 80
Out of the water, Heaven above the clouds
Unfold her crystal doors; thence on his head

A perfet Dove descend (whate'er it meant);

And out of Heaven the sovraign voice I
heard,
'This is my Son beloved,—in him am
pleased.'
His mother, than, is mortal, but his Sire
He who obtains the monarchy of Heaven;
And what will He not do to advance his
Son?
His first-begot we know, and sore have felt,

When his fierce thunder drove us to the
Deep; 90
Who this is we must learn, for Man he
Seems
In all his lineaments, though in his face
The glimpses of his Father's glory shine.

Ye see our danger on the utmost edge
Of hazard, which admits no long debate,

But must with something sudden be opposed

(Not force, but well-couched fraud,
well-woven snares),

---

*His coming, he is the forerunner, who
calls*
Everyone, and in the holy stream
Pretends to wash off sin, and purify
*Them to welcome the pure one, or
rather*
*To worship him as their king. They
all come,*
*And he himself was baptised with
them–*
*Not so he could be more pure, but to
receive*
*Proof from heaven so that the world
Could no longer doubt who he is. I
saw*
*The prophet worship him; when he
rose*
*Out of the water, highest heaven
Opened her crystal doors, and from
there to his head*
*A perfect dove came down (whatever
that meant);*
*And from heaven I heard the voice of
the King saying,*
*"This is my beloved son with whom I
am well pleased."*
*So his mother is mortal, but his father
Is the one who rules in heaven;
What will he not do to help his son?*
*We know his firstborn, and felt the
pain,*
*When he drove us into hell with his
fierce thunder.*
*We must find out who this is, for he is
a man*
*In his shape, though in his face
One can see glimpses of his father's
glory.*
*You see that we are on the edge
Of a precipice, and cannot spend
long arguing,*
*And must produce our defence at
once*
*(Not force, but cunning tricks and
well laid traps),*

Ere in the head of nations he appear,	*Before he appears to all the nations*
Their king, their leader, and supreme on Earth.	*As their king, their leader, and the greatest on earth.*
I, when no other durst, sole undertook 100	*When no one else dared I alone took on*
The dismal expedition to find out	*The hard journey to discover*
And ruin Adam, and the exploit performed	*And ruin Adam, and I completed the task*
Successfully: a calmer voyage now	*Successfully: this time the journey*
Will waft me; and the way found prosperous once	*Will be easier; and the way which worked once*
Induces best to hope of like success."	*Is the best hope of a second success.*
He ended, and his words impression left	*He finished, and his words left*
Of much amazement to the infernal crew,	*His hellish crew dumbfounded,*
Distracted and surprised with deep dismay	*Confused and amazed with deep distress*
At these sad tidings. But no time was then	*At this sad news. But there was no time then*
For long indulgence to their fears or grief: 110	*To wallow in their fears or grief:*
Unanimous they all commit the care	*They unanimously voted to hand the planning*
And management of this main enterprise	*And management of this great Endeavour*
To him, their great Dictator, whose attempt	*To him, their great dictator, whose first*
At first against mankind so well had thrived	*Attack on mankind had worked so well*
In Adam's overthrow, and led their march	*With Adam's fall, and who had led them*
From Hell's deep-vaulted den to dwell in light,	*From the depths of hell to live in the light,*
Regents, and potentates, and kings, yea gods,	*Regents, potentates, Kings, even gods,*
Of many a pleasant realm and province wide.	*Of many lovely countries and wide regions.*
So to the coast of Jordan he directs	*So he directs his soft steps, full of snaky cunning*
His easy steps, girded with snaky wiles, 120	*Towards the coast of Jordan,*
Where he might likeliest find this new-declared,	*Where he is most likely to find this newly revealed*
This man of men, attested Son of God,	*Greatest of men, sworn son of God,*
Temptation and all guile on him to try—	*To test him with temptation and all deceptions–*

So to subvert whom he suspected raised

To end his reign on Earth so long enjoyed:

But, contrary, unweeting he fulfilled

The purpose counsel, pre-ordained and fixed,

Of the Most High, who, in full frequence bright

Of Angels, thus to Gabriel smiling spake:—

"Gabriel, this day, by proof, thou shalt behold, 130

Thou and all Angels conversant on Earth

With Man or men's affairs, how I begin

To verify that solemn message late,

On which I sent thee to the Virgin pure

In Galilee, that she should bear a son,

Great in renown, and called the Son of God.

Then told'st her, doubting how these things could be

To her a virgin, that on her should come

The Holy Ghost, and the power of the Highest

O'ershadow her. This Man, born and now upgrown, 140

To shew him worthy of his birth divine

And high prediction, henceforth I expose

To Satan; let him tempt, and now assay

His utmost subtlety, because he boasts

And vaunts of his great cunning to the Throng

Of his Apostasy. He might have learnt

Less overweening, since he failed in Job,

Whose constant perseverance overcame

Whate'er his cruel malice could invent.

And so to undermine the one he suspected had come

To end the reign on earth he had so long enjoyed:

But it was otherwise, he unwittingly carried out

The preordained and fixed plan

Of the highest one who, surrounded by all

His bright angels, smiled and said this to Gabriel:

"Gabriel, today you shall see it proved,

You and all the angels on earth who know

About man or men's affairs, how I begin

To make true that recent solemn message

Which I sent you with to the pure virgin

In Galilee, saying that she should have a son,

Who would be of great fame, and called the son of God.

You told her, when she doubted how this could happen

To her, a virgin, that the Holy Ghost

Would come to her, and the power of God

Would hang over her. This man, born and now grown-up,

I am now going to expose

To Satan, to show him worthy of

His divine birth and the great predictions made for him.

Let Satan tempt him, and try

His best tricks, because he boasts

And brags of his great cunning to his Treacherous mob. He might have Learnt

To be less proud, as he failed with Job,

Whose never failing patience

overcame whatever his wicked
cruelty could invent.

     "Gabriel, this day, by proof,
thou shalt behold, 130
Thou and all Angels conversant on Earth

With Man or men's affairs, how I begin

To verify that solemn message late,

On which I sent thee to the Virgin pure

In Galilee, that she should bear a son,

Great in renown, and called the Son of God.

Then told'st her, doubting how these things could be
To her a virgin, that on her should come
The Holy Ghost, and the power of the Highest
O'ershadow her. This Man, born and now upgrown, 140
To shew him worthy of his birth divine
And high prediction, henceforth I expose
To Satan; let him tempt, and now assay

His utmost subtlety, because he boasts
And vaunts of his great cunning to the throng
Of his Apostasy. He might have learnt
Less overweening, since he failed in Job,

Whose constant perseverance overcame

Whate'er his cruel malice could invent.

     He now shall know I can produce a man, 150
Of female seed, far abler to resist

All his solicitations, and at length
All his vast force, and drive him back to Hell—
Winning by conquest what the first man lost

"Gabriel, today
you shall see it proved,
You and all the angels on earth who know
About man or men's affairs, how I begin
To make true that recent solemn message
Which I sent you with to the pure virgin
In Galilee, saying that she should have a son,
Who would be of great fame, and called the son of God.
You told her, when she doubted how this could happen
To her, a virgin, that the Holy Ghost
Would come to her, and the power of God
Would hang over her. This man, born and now grown-up,
I am now going to expose
To Satan, to show him worthy of
His divine birth and the great predictions made for him.
Let Satan tempt him, and try
His best tricks, because he boasts
And brags of his great cunning to his Treacherous mob. He might have learnt
To be less proud, as he failed with Job,
Whose never failing patience overcame whatever his wicked cruelty could invent.
Now he will know that I can produce a man,
Born of woman, far better able to resist
All his invitations, and in the end
All his great armies, and drive him back to hell—
Winning through war what the first

By fallacy surprised. But first I mean

To exercise him in the Wilderness;
There he shall first lay down the rudiments
Of his great warfare, ere I send him forth

To conquer Sin and Death, the two grand foes.
By humiliation and strong sufferance 160

His weakness shall o'ercome Satanic strength,
And all the world, and mass of sinful flesh;

That all the Angels and aethereal Powers—

They now, and men hereafter—may discern
From what consummate virtue I have chose
This perfect man, by merit called my Son,

To earn salvation for the sons of men."

       So spake the Eternal Father, and all Heaven
Admiring stood a space; then into hymns

Burst forth, and in celestial measures moved, 170
Circling the throne and singing, while the hand
Sung with the voice, and this the argument :—

       "Victory and triumph to the Son of God,
Now entering his great duel, not of arms,

But to vanquish by wisdom hellish wiles!

The Father knows the Son; therefore secure

Ventures his filial virtue, though untried,

       Against whate'er may tempt, whate'er seduce,
Allure, or terrify, or undermine.

man lost
Through his wrong ideas. But first I intend
To test him in the wilderness;
There he shall begin the preparations
For his great war, before I send him out
To conquer sin and death, the two great enemies.
Through humiliation and great suffering
His weakness will overcome the strength of Satan,
And all the world, and all the sins of the flesh;
So that all the angels and heavenly powers–
Them now, and men later–will see
How wise I was to choose
This perfect man, who deserves to be called my son,
To win salvation for the sons of men."
This is what the eternal Father said, and all of Heaven
Stood for a while admiring him; then they burst
Out singing and moved to the rhythm of the stars,
Circling the throne and singing, while the Instruments
Played in accompaniment, and these were their words:
"May the son of God have a triumphant victory,
As he begins this great fight, not with weapons,
But to defeat hell's cunning with his wisdom!
The father knows the son; and so he feels safe
In risking his son's virtue, though it has yet to be tested,
Against whatever may tempt him, whatever may seduce him,
Attract, or terrify, or undermine him.

Be frustrate, all ye stratagems of Hell, 180	*May all the plans of hell be frustrated,*
And, devilish machinations, come to nought!"	*And may all devilish schemes come to nothing!"*
So they in Heaven their odes and vigils tuned.	*This was how they sang and played in heaven.*
Meanwhile the Son of God, who yet some days	*Meanwhile the son of God, who for some days*
Lodged in Bethabara, where John baptized,	*Had been staying in Bethabara, where John had baptised him,*
Musing and much revolving in his breast	*Was thinking and turning over in his mind*
How best the mighty work he might begin	*The best way to begin his great work*
Of Saviour to mankind, and which way first	*Of saving mankind, and how he should first*
Publish his godlike office now mature,	*Announce his holy mission now he was full-grown.*
One day forth walked alone, the Spirit leading	*One day he walked out alone, following the spirit*
And his deep thoughts, the better to converse 190	*And his deep thoughts, feeling he could think better*
With solitude, till, far from track of men,	*Alone, until, far from the paths of men,*
Thought following thought, and step by step led on,	*Following thought after thought and step after step*
He entered now the bordering Desert wild,	*He now entered the surrounding wild desert,*
And, with dark shades and rocks environed round,	*And, surrounded by dark shadows and rocks*
His holy meditations thus pursued:—	*He continued his holy meditations:*
"O what a multitude of thoughts at once	*"Oh what a great number of thoughts suddenly*
Awakened in me swarm, while I consider	*Appear thronging in my head, while I think*
What from within I feel myself, and hear	*About what I can feel inside, and hear*
What from without comes often to my ears,	*What comes to me from outside,*
Ill sorting with my present state compared! 200	*None of which matches my present state!*
When I was yet a child, no childish play	*When I was still a child, no childish games*
To me was pleasing; all my mind was set	*Pleased me; my whole mind was devoted*
Serious to learn and know, and thence to do,	*To learning and to know, and then to do,*

What might be public good; myself I thought	*What was best for mankind; I thought that*
Born to that end, born to promote all truth,	*Was the purpose I was born for, to promote truth,*
All righteous things. Therefore, above my years,	*And all things holy. And so, precociously,*
The Law of God I read, and found it sweet;	*I read the law of God, and found it wonderful;*
Made it my whole delight, and in it grew	*I made it my only pleasure, and became*
To such perfection that, ere yet my age	*So knowledgeable that before I was*
Had measured twice six years, at our great Feast 210	*Twelve years old, at our great feast,*
I went into the Temple, there to hear	*I went into the temple to hear*
The teachers of our Law, and to propose	*The teachers of law, and to put forward*
What might improve my knowledge or their own,	*Ideas to improve their knowledge or my own,*
And was admired by all. Yet this not all	*And I was admired by everyone. But this was not all*
To which my spirit aspired. Victorious deeds	*My spirit hoped for. Great deeds*
Flamed in my heart, heroic acts—one while	*Burned in my heart, heroic acts–I wanted*
To rescue Israel from the Roman yoke;	*To rescue Israel from Roman rule;*
Then to subdue and quell, o'er all the earth,	*Then to defeat, everywhere on earth,*
Brute violence and proud tyrannic power,	*Senseless violence and the proud power of tyrants,*
Till truth were freed, and equity restored: 220	*Until truth and equality reigned:*
Yet held it more humane, more heavenly, first	*But I thought it was more humane, and more divine, to first*
By winning words to conquer willing hearts,	*Win over those who were willing with words,*
And make persuasion do the work of fear;	*And to use persuasion instead of threats,*
At least to try, and teach the erring soul,	*At least to try and teach the mistaken soul,*
Not wilfully misdoing, but unware	*Who was not deliberately doing wrong but was misled*
Misled; the stubborn only to subdue.	*Through ignorance. Only the stubborn would I fight.*
These growing thoughts my mother soon perceiving,	*My mother soon noticed these growing thoughts,*
By words at times cast forth, inly rejoiced,	*Sometimes shown in my words, and rejoiced inwardly,*

And said to me apart, 'High are thy thoughts,
O Son! but nourish them, and let them soar 230
To what highth sacred virtue and true worth
Can raise them, though above example high;
By matchless deeds express thy matchless Sire.
For know, thou art no son of mortal man;
Though men esteem thee low of parentage,
Thy Father is the Eternal King who rules
All Heaven and Earth, Angels and sons of men.
A messenger from God foretold thy birth
Conceived in me a virgin; he foretold
Thou shouldst be great, and sit on David's throne, 240
And of thy kingdom there should be no end.
At thy nativity a glorious quire
Of Angels, in the fields of Bethlehem, sung
To shepherds, watching at their folds by night,
And told them the Messiah now was born,
Where they might see him; and to thee they came,
Directed to the manger where thou lay'st;
For in the inn was left no better room.
A Star, not seen before, in heaven appearing,
Guided the Wise Men thither from the East, 250
To honour thee with incense, myrrh, and gold;
By whose bright course led on they found the place,

And said to me privately, " Your thoughts are heavenly,
My son! Feed them, and let them soar
To the heights which holy goodness and true worth
Can raise them, though they are high beyond comparison;
By unrivalled deeds do the will of your unrivalled father.
You should know that you are no son of a mortal man,
Though men think you are of low birth;
Your father is the eternal King who rules
All of heaven and earth, angels and the sons of men.
The messenger from God predicted your birth
To me, a virgin; he predicted
That you would be great, and sit on the throne of David,
And that your kingdom would never fall.
At your birth a glorious choir
Of angels sang to shepherds who were watching
Their flocks by night in the fields of Bethlehem,
And told them the Messiah was born
And where they might see him. They came to you
Directed to the manger where you were lying,
Because that was all the inn had to offer.
"A star which had never been seen before appeared in heaven,
And guided the wise men there from the East,
Bringing you tributes of incense, myrrh, and gold;
By following its bright course they found a place,

Affirming it thy star, new-graven in heaven,
By which they knew thee King of Israel born.
Just Simeon and prophetic Anna, warned
By vision, found thee in the Temple, and spake,
Before the altar and the vested priest,
Like things of thee to all that present stood.'
This having heart, straight I again revolved
The Law and Prophets, searching what was writ 260
Concerning the Messiah, to our scribes
Known partly, and soon found of whom they spake
I am—this chiefly, that my way must lie

Through many a hard assay, even to the death,
Ere I the promised kingdom can attain,
Or work redemption for mankind, whose sins'
Full weight must be transferred upon my head.
Yet, neither thus disheartened or dismayed,
The time prefixed I waited; when behold
The Baptist (of whose birth I oft had heard, 270
Not knew by sight) now come, who was to come
Before Messiah, and his way prepare!
I, as all others, to his baptism came,
Which I believed was from above; but he

Confirming that it was your star, newly made in heaven,
Which showed them that the king of Israel was born.
Just Simeon and prophetic Anna, alerted
By visions, found you in the temple, and spoke
In front of the altar and the robed priest,
Telling everyone there the same things about you."
"Having heard this, I went straight back to search
The law and the prophets, studying what was written
About the Messiah, which was partly known
To our scribes, and I soon found that I was the one
They spoke of. I found that my path leads me

Through many hard tests, even to death,
Before I can get to the promised kingdom,
Or gain forgiveness for mankind, the full weight of whose
Sins must be put upon my head.
But this did not dishearten or dismay me,
I awaited the appointed time; then I saw
The Baptist (whose birth I had often heard of,
But did not know by sight) had now come, the one who was to come
Before the Messiah, and prepare the way for him!
I came, like all the others, to be baptised by him,
Which I believed meant being baptised by heaven; but he

Straight knew me, and with loudest voice proclaimed	*Knew me at once, and in his loudest voice announced*
Me him (for it was shewn him so from Heaven)—	*That I was the one (because heaven had showed him so),*
Me him whose harbinger he was; and first	*The one whose forerunner he was; and at first*
Refused on me his baptism to confer,	*He refused to give me his baptism*
As much his greater, and was hardly won.	*Saying I was so much greater, and I had to work to persuade him.*
But, as I rose out of the laving stream, 280	*But, as I rose out of the cleansing stream,*
Heaven opened her eternal doors, from whence	*Heaven opened her eternal doors, and the spirit*
The Spirit descended on me like a Dove;	*Came down upon me in the shape of a dove;*
And last, the sum of all, my Father's voice,	*And last, the greatest thing of all, my father's voice,*
Audibly heard from Heaven, pronounced me his,	*Could be heard from heaven, announcing that I was his*
Me his beloved Son, in whom alone	*Beloved son, the only one with whom*
He was well pleased: by which I knew the time	*He was completely pleased. This showed me that this time*
Now full, that I no more should live obscure,	*Had come, that I should no longer live in secret,*
But openly begin, as best becomes	*But begin in the open to do whatever is best*
The authority which I derived from Heaven.	*With the power which heaven has given me.*
And now by some strong motion I am led 290	*And now some powerful feeling leads me*
Into this wilderness; to what intent	*Into this wilderness; for what reason*
I learn not yet. Perhaps I need not know;	*I have not yet learnt. Perhaps I need not know;*
For what concerns my knowledge God reveals."	*God tells me everything I need to know."*
So spake our Morning Star, then in his rise,	*This is how our morning Star, who was then rising, spoke,*
And, looking round, on every side beheld	*And looking round he saw on every side*
A pathless desert, dusk with horrid shades.	*A pathless desert, dark with horrible shadows.*
The way he came, not having marked return,	*The way he went, without thinking of the way back,*
Was difficult, by human steps untrod;	*Was difficult, and had never been walked by man;*

And he still on was led, but with such thoughts
Accompanied of things past and to come 300
Lodged in his breast as well might recommend
Such solitude before choicest society.
Full forty days he passed—whether on hill

Sometimes, anon in shady vale, each night

Under the covert of some ancient oak
Or cedar to defend him from the dew,
Or harboured in one cave, is not revealed;

Nor tasted human food, nor hunger felt,

Till those days ended; hungered then at last

Among wild beasts. They at his sight grew mild, 310
Nor sleeping him nor waking harmed; his walk
The fiery serpent fled and noxious worm;

The lion and fierce tiger glared aloof.

But now an aged man in rural weeds,

Following, as seemed, the quest of some stray ewe,
Or withered sticks to gather, which might serve
Against a winter's day, when winds blow keen,
To warm him wet returned from field at eve,
He saw approach; who first with curious eye
Perused him, then with words thus uttered spake:— 320
        "Sir, what ill chance hath brought thee to this place,
So far from path or road of men, who pass

In troop or caravan? for single none

Still he was led on, but with such thoughts
Of things past and future

In his mind that he preferre

Such loneliness to the best company.
He spent fully forty days– whether on a hillside,

Or sometimes in a shady valley, each night

Under the shelter of some ancient oak
Or cedar to protect him from the dew,
Or if he sheltered in a cave we do not know;

He did not taste mortal food, nor felt hunger

Until those days were over; then at last he was hungry

And among wild beasts. Seeing him they grew peaceful,
And did not harm him, sleeping or waking;
The fiery serpent and poisonous snake fled from his footsteps;

The lion and fierce tiger gave him uninterested stares.

But now he saw an old man in peasant clothes approaching,

Who seemed to be searching for some stray sheep,
Or gathering dry sticks, which might help
On a winter's day, when the cold winds blow,
To warm him when he came home wet from the fields at dusk;
At first he looked over him curiously
And then said these words to him:

" Sir, what bad luck has brought you to this place,
So far from the path or road of the men who pass

In groups or convoys? For nobody has ever

Durst ever, who returned, and dropt not here
His carcass, pined with hunger and with droughth.
I ask the rather, and the more admire,

For that to me thou seem'st the man whom late
Our new baptizing Prophet at the ford
Of Jordan honoured so, and called thee Son
Of God. I saw and heard, for we sometimes 330
Who dwell this wild, constrained by want, come forth
To town or village nigh (nighest is far),
Where aught we hear, and curious are to hear,
What happens new; fame also finds us out."

   To whom the Son of God:—"Who brought me hither
Will bring me hence; no other guide I seek."

   "By miracle he may," replied the swain;
"What other way I see not; for we here

Live on tough roots and stubs, to thirst inured
More than the camel, and to drink go far— 340
Men to much misery and hardship born.
But, if thou be the Son of God, command
That out of these hard stones be made thee bread;
So shalt thou save thyself, and us relieve

With food, whereof we wretched seldom taste."

   He ended, and the Son of God replied:—

Come back who has come out here alone,
They have all left their bodies, dead of hunger and thirst.
I ask especially, and am more amazed,
As you seem to me to be the man who recently
Our new baptising Prophet honoured so much
At the Ford of Jordan, calling you the son
Of God. I saw and heard, for we who live
In this wilderness sometimes, forced by need, come out
To the nearest town or village (the nearest is far away),
Where we like to hear about
Anything new; we know about notable people too."
The son of God answered him: "The one who brought me here
Will take me back; I need no other guide."
" He might if he can work miracles," the shepherd answered;
" I can't see any other way; for we who live here
Survive on tough roots and stumps, less affected by thirst
Than the camels, and we have to go far for water—
We have a hard and miserable life.
But, if you are the son of God, order
That one of these hard stones turn into bread;
So you will save yourself, and comfort us
With food, which we wretched people seldom taste."
He finished, and the son of God replied:

"Think'st thou such force in bread? Is it not written
(For I discern thee other than thou seem'st),
Man lives not by bread only, but each word
Proceeding from the mouth of God, who fed
350
Our fathers here with manna? In the Mount
Moses was forty days, nor eat nor drank;
And forty days Eliah without food
Wandered this barren waste; the same I now.
Why dost thou, then, suggest to me distrust
Knowing who I am, as I know who thou art?"
       Whom thus answered the Arch-Fiend, now undisguised:—
"'Tis true, I am that Spirit unfortunate
Who, leagued with millions more in rash revolt,
Kept not my happy station, but was driven
360
With them from bliss to the bottomless Deep—
Yet to that hideous place not so confined
By rigour unconniving but that oft,
Leaving my dolorous prison, I enjoy
Large liberty to round this globe of Earth,
Or range in the Air; nor from the Heaven of Heavens
Hath he excluded my resort sometimes.
I came, among the Sons of God, when he
Gave up into my hands Uzzean Job,
To prove him, and illustrate his high worth;
370
And, when to all his Angels he proposed
To draw the proud king Ahab into fraud,

"Do you think bread is that powerful? Is it not written
(For I see that you are not what you seem)
That man cannot live by bread alone, but by the words
Coming from the mouth of God, who fed
Our fathers here with manna? Moses was on
The mountain for forty days, without food or drink,
And Elijah wandered this barren waste without food
For forty days; I am doing the same now.
Why then do you suggest that I don't have faith,
Knowing who I am, as I know who you are?"
The devil, now undisguised, answered him:
"It's true that I am that unfortunate spirit
Who, allied with millions more in foolish rebellion
Lost my happy place, and was driven
With them from heaven to the pit of hell–
But I am not so rigourously confined
To that hideous place that I cannot often
Leave my sad prison and enjoy
The freedom of walking the earth
Or flying in the air; at times he has not even
Barred me from the highest heaven.
I came there, amongst the Angels, when he
Gave me Job, from Uz,
To test him, and prove his great worth;
And when he told all his angels
That he was going to trick the proud King Ahab into a fraud,

That he might fall in Ramoth, they demurring,
I undertook that office, and the tongues

Of all his flattering prophets glibbed with lies
To his destruction, as I had in charge:

For what he bids I do. Though I have lost

Much lustre of my native brightness, lost
To be beloved of God, I have not lost
To love, at least contemplate and admire,
380
What I see excellent in good, or fair,

Or virtuous; I should so have lost all sense.
What can be then less in me than desire
To see thee and approach thee, whom I know
Declared the Son of God, to hear attent

Thy wisdom, and behold thy godlike deeds?

Men generally think me much a foe

To all mankind. Why should I? they to me

Never did wrong or violence. By them

I lost not what I lost; rather by them 390

I gained what I have gained, and with them dwell
Copartner in these regions of the World,
If not disposer—lend them oft my aid,

Oft my advice by presages and signs,

And answers, oracles, portents, and dreams,

Whereby they may direct their future life.
Envy, they say, excites me, thus to gain

Companions of my misery and woe!

So he might lose the kingdom of Ramoth, they disagreed,
And I took the job on, and gave the tongues
Of all his flattering prophets lies which led
To his destruction, as I had been ordered:
What he orders I do. Though I have lost
The shine of my natural brightness,
Lost the love of God, I have not lost
The power to love, at least to look upon and admire,
What I see is excellent in goodness, beauty,
Or virtue; I would be mad if I had.
So how can I help wanting
To see you and approach you, when I know
You have been declared the son of God, to listen carefully
To your wisdom, and see your godlike deeds?
Men generally think that I'm a great enemy
Of all mankind. Why should I be? They have never
Done me wrong or harm. It was not them
Who made me lose what I have lost; rather through them
I gained what I have gained, and live with them,
Sharing these lands of the world,
If not ruling them. I often give them my help,
And advise them through warnings and signs,
Answers, oracles, portents and dreams,
To help them plan their way in future.
They say I am motivated by envy, trying to get
Others to share in my misery and sorrow!

At first it may be; but, long since with woe

Nearer acquainted, now I feel by proof 400

That fellowship in pain divides not smart,

Nor lightens aught each man's peculiar load;

Small consolation, then, were Man adjoined.

This wounds me most (what can it less?) that Man,

Man fallen, shall be restored, I never more."

      To whom our Saviour sternly thus replied:—

"Deservedly thou griev'st, composed of lies

From the beginning, and in lies wilt end,

Who boast'st release from Hell, and leave to come

Into the Heaven of Heavens. Thou com'st, indeed, 410

As a poor miserable captive thrall

Comes to the place where he before had sat

Among the prime in splendour, now deposed,

Ejected, emptied, gazed, unpitied, shunned,

A spectacle of ruin, or of scorn,

To all the host of Heaven. The happy place

Imparts to thee no happiness, no joy—

Rather inflames thy torment, representing

Lost bliss, to thee no more communicable;

So never more in Hell than when in Heaven. 420

But thou art serviceable to Heaven's King!

Wilt thou impute to obedience what thy fear

It might have been the case at first;
but I have known sorrow

Close up for a long time now, and
now I can see

That sharing pain does not lessen the
hurt

Or lighten each man's individual
load;

So it would be little consolation, if I
made man join in.

What hurts me most is (can you
blame me?) that man,

Man who has fallen, will be lifted up
again, but I will never be."

Our Saviour sternly answered to him:

"You deserve your grief, you were
made of lies

From the beginning, and you will end
with lies,

You who boast of your release from
hell, and claim permission to come

Into the highest heaven. You do
indeed come,

As a miserable bound prisoner

Who comes to the place where once
he sat

In glory amongst the highest, now
thrown down,

Ejected, emptied, stared at, unpitied,
rejected,

An example of destruction, or of
contempt,

To all the angels. The happy place
Gives you no happiness, no joy—
It actually increases your agony,
showing

The lost happiness you can no longer
have;

So you are never more in hell than
when you are in heaven.

But the King of Heaven still has uses
for you!

Will you claim that you are obeying
when you do

Extorts, or pleasure to do ill excites?
What but thy malice moved thee to misdeem
Of righteous Job, then cruelly to afflict him
With all inflictions? but his patience won.
The other service was thy chosen task,
To be a liar in four hundred mouths;
For lying is thy sustenance, thy food.
Yet thou pretend'st to truth! all oracles 430
By thee are given, and what confessed more true
Among the nations? That hath been thy craft,
By mixing somewhat true to vent more lies.

But what have been thy answers? what but dark,
Ambiguous, and with double sense deluding,
Which they who asked have seldom understood,
And, not well understood, as good not known?
      Who ever, by consulting at thy shrine,
Returned the wiser, or the more instruct
To fly or follow what concerned him most, 440
And run not sooner to his fatal snare?

For God hath justly given the nations up
To thy delusions; justly, since they fell
Idolatrous. But, when his purpose is
Among them to declare his providence,

To thee not known, whence hast thou then thy truth,
But from him, or his Angels president

Things through fear, or the pleasure of doing evil?
What was it except your hatred which caused you to mistreat
Righteous Job, and then cruelly assault him
With all those trials? But his patience won.
That other service was chosen for you
To be a liar in four hundred mouths;
Lying is your nutrition, your food.
And yet you pretend to tell the truth! All oracles
Are run by you, and are thought to be true
By all men. That has been your task,
Giving a little bit of truth so you can add more lies.

But how have you answered? Your answers have been dark,
Ambiguous, and tricking people with double meaning,
So that they who have asked rarely understood,
And if they didn't understand well, wasn't it as bad as not knowing?
Who has ever consulted your shrine
And come back wiser, or better able
To fly or follow what was best for him,
Didn't they all just reach their deadly ends sooner?

For God has rightly given up men
To your tricks; rightly because they became
Idolatrous. But, when he means
To show them his care,

Which is unknown to you, where do you get your truth from
Except from him or his angels who rule

In every province, who, themselves disdaining
To approach thy temples, give thee in command
What, to the smallest tittle, thou shalt say 450
To thy adorers? Thou, with trembling fear,

Or like a fawning parasite, obey'st;
Then to thyself ascrib'st the truth foretold.

But this thy glory shall be soon retrenched;
No more shalt thou by oracling abuse

The Gentiles; henceforth oracles are ceased,

And thou no more with pomp and sacrifice

Shalt be enquired at Delphos or elsewhere—
At least in vain, for they shall find thee mute.
God hath now sent his living Oracle 460
Into the world to teach his final will,

And sends his Spirit of Truth henceforth to dwell
In pious hearts, an inward oracle
To all truth requisite for men to know."

      So spake our Saviour; but the subtle Fiend,
Though inly stung with anger and disdain,

Dissembled, and this answer smooth returned:—
      "Sharply thou hast insisted on rebuke,
And urged me hard with doings which not will,
But misery, hath wrested from me. Where 470
Easily canst thou find one miserable,

And not inforced oft-times to part from truth,

In every land, who, not wanting to approach
Your temples themselves, give you orders
Down to the last detail of what you should say
To your worshippers? You, trembling with fear,

Like a grovelling insect, obey;
Then you say that the predicted truth came from you.

But you will soon lose this glory;
You shall no longer abuse the Gentiles

With your predictions. From now on oracles are banned

And no one will question you at Delphi or elsewhere

With ceremony and sacrifices—
Or at least it will be in vain, for they will find you silent.
God has now sent his living oracle
Into the world to teach his final wishes,

And is sending his spirit of truth to live from now on
In pious hearts, an internal oracle
That will tell all the truth it is suitable for men to know."

So our saviour spoke, but the subtle demon,
Though burning inside with anger and hatred,

Disguised his feelings and smoothly answered:
"You have been quick to rebuke me,

And criticise me harshly for things I didn't want to do
But was forced to through misery. It's easy
For you to criticise people as miserable

When you haven't often been forced to part from the truth,

If it may stand him more in stead to lie,
Say and unsay, feign, flatter, or abjure?

But thou art placed above me; thou art Lord;

From thee I can, and must, submiss, endure
Cheek or reproof, and glad to scape so quit.

Hard are the ways of truth, and rough to
walk,
Smooth on the tongue discoursed, pleasing
to the ear,
And tunable as sylvan pipe or song; 480

What wonder, then, if I delight to hear

Her dictates from thy mouth? most men
admire
Virtue who follow not her lore. Permit me
To hear thee when I come (since no man
comes),
And talk at least, though I despair to attain.

Thy Father, who is holy, wise, and pure,

Suffers the hypocrite or atheous priest

To tread his sacred courts, and minister

About his altar, handling holy things,
Praying or vowing, and voutsafed his voice
490
To Balaam reprobate, a prophet yet

Inspired: disdain not such access to me."

To whom our Saviour, with unaltered
brow:—
"Thy coming hither, though I know thy
scope,
I bid not, or forbid. Do as thou find'st

Permission from above; thou canst not
more."
He added not; and Satan, bowing low

For some it is necessary to lie,
Say and don't say, fake, flatter and
renounce.

But you have a higher place than me;
you are God;

I have to submit to you, endure
Cheek and reprimands, and be glad
to escape so lightly.

The paths of truth are hard and rough
to walk,
But it is smooth when heard from
your tongue, and pleasing to the ear,
As tuneful as a shepherd's pipe or
song;

Is it any wonder then that it pleases
me to hear

The truth from your mouth? Most
men who are not virtuous
Still admire virtue. Allow me
To hear you as I have come (since no
man comes),
And talk at least, even if I cannot
copy you.

Your father, who is holy, wise and
pure,

Allows the hypocritical or atheist
priest

To walk in his sacred temples, and
officiate

At his altar, handling holy things,
Praying or promising, and he gave
his orders

To the reprobate Balaam, inspired
him

Like a prophet: do not bar me from
similar favor."

Our saviour said to him, with an
unchanged expression:
"Although I know what you get up to
I did not
Ask you to come here or forbid you.
Do what you have

Permission for from above; that's all
you can do."

He spoke no more; and Satan bowed
low

His gray dissimulation, disappeared,
Into thin air diffused: for now began
Night with her sullen wing to double-shade 500
The desert; fowls in their clay nests were couched;
And now wild beasts came forth the woods to roam.

In his grey disguise then disappeared,
Vanishing into thin air: for now night
With her dark wings began thickly to cover
The desert; the birds slept in their mud nests,
And now wild beasts came out of the woods to explore.

BOOK II

Meanwhile the new-baptized, who yet remained
At Jordan with the Baptist, and had seen

Him whom they heard so late expressly called
Jesus Messiah, Son of God, declared,

And on that high authority had believed,

And with him talked, and with him lodged—I mean
Andrew and Simon, famous after known,

With others, though in Holy Writ not named

Now missing him, their joy so lately found,

So lately found and so abruptly gone, 10

Began to doubt, and doubted many days,

And, as the days increased, increased their doubt.
Sometimes they thought he might be only shewn,
And for a time caught up to God, as once

Moses was in the Mount and missing long,

And the great Thisbite, who on fiery wheels
Rode up to Heaven, yet once again to come.

Therefore, as those young prophets then with care
Sought lost Eliah, so in each place these

Nigh to Bethabara—in Jericho 20
The city of palms, AEnon, and Salem old,

---

*Meanwhile the newly baptised, who were still
By the Jordan with the Baptist, and had seen*

*The one whom they had so recently heard called
Jesus Messiah, son of God, confirmed,*

And on that high authority they had believed in him,

*And had talked with him and lived with him—I refer
To Andrew and Simon, famous afterwards,*

With others, though they are not named in holy writings—

Now they missed him, the happiness they had so lately discovered,

Lately discovered and so quickly gone.

They began to doubt, and doubted for many days,

*And as time went by their doubt increased.
Sometimes they thought he had only been shown to them
And then taken back up to God, like the occasion when*

Moses was missing on the mountain for a long time,

*Or when Elijah went up to heaven
In his fiery chariot, but then came back again.*

*So, just as those young prophets then ceaselessly
Looked for lost Elijah these ones looked in each place,*

*Going to Bethabara, Jericho
The city of palms, Ænon and old Salem,*

Machaerus, and each town or city walled

On this side the broad lake Genezaret,

Or in Peraea—but returned in vain.

Then on the bank of Jordan, by a creek,

Where winds with reeds and osiers whispering play,
Plain fishermen (no greater men them call),

Close in a cottage low together got,
Their unexpected loss and plaints outbreathed:—
"Alas, from what high hope to what relapse 30
Unlooked for are we fallen! Our eyes beheld

Messiah certainly now come, so long

Expected of our fathers; we have heard

His words, his wisdom full of grace and truth.
'Now, now, for sure, deliverance is at hand;
The kingdom shall to Israel be restored:'

Thus we rejoiced, but soon our joy is turned

Into perplexity and new amaze.
For whither is he gone? what accident
Hath rapt him from us? will he now retire 40
After appearance, and again prolong

Our expectation? God of Israel,
Send thy Messiah forth; the time is come.

Behold the kings of the earth, how they oppress
Thy Chosen, to what highth their power unjust
They have exalted, and behind them cast

All fear of Thee; arise, and vindicate

Machaerus, and each major town or city

On this side of the great Lake of Galilee,

Or in Peraea–but came back empty-handed.

Then on the bank of the Jordan, by a creek,

Where the winds whisper amongst the reeds and willows,
Simple fishermen (there is no greater name)

Met together in a lowly cottage
And spoke of their unexpected loss and sorrows
Alas, how we have gone from such a high hope
To such an unexpected fall! Our eyes saw

The Messiah, definitely come, who was so long

Expected by our fathers; we have heard

His words, his wisdom full of grace and truth.
' Now certainly we shall be saved,
Israel shall be given back its kingdom. '

That is how we rejoiced, but now our joy has turned

To confusion and new astonishment.
Where has he gone? What misfortune
Has carried him away from us? Will he now go away
After his appearance, and make us wait

Still longer? God of Israel,
Send us your messiah; the time has come.

Look at the kings of the earth, and how they oppress
Your chosen people, see what a high position
They have taken for themselves, throwing off

All fear of you; arise, and show

Thy glory; free thy people from their yoke!
But let us wait; thus far He hath performed
Sent his Anointed, and to us revealed him
50
By his great Prophet pointed at and shown
In public, and with him we have conversed.
Let us be glad of this, and all our fears
Lay on his providence; He will not fail,
Nor will withdraw him now, nor will recall
—
Mock us with his blest sight, then snatch him hence:
Soon we shall see our hope, our joy, return."
      Thus they out of their plaints new hope resume
To find whom at the first they found unsought.
But to his mother Mary, when she saw 60
Others returned from baptism, not her Son,
Nor left at Jordan tidings of him none,
Within her breast though calm, her breast though
Motherly cares and fears got head, and raised
Some troubled thoughts, which she in sighs thus clad:—
      "Oh, what avails me now that honour high,
To have conceived of God, or that salute,
'Hail, highly favoured, among women blest!'
While I to sorrows am no less advanced,
And fears as eminent above the lot 70
Of other women, by the birth I bore:
In such a season born, when scarce a shed

Your glory; free your people from slavery!
But let us wait; so far he has done what he said he would-
He sent his chosen one, who was revealed to us
By his great prophet, pointing him out
In public, and we have spoken with him.
Let us be glad of this, and forget our fears
By trusting in his goodness; he will not fail us
Nor take him away from us now;
He would not mock us with the blessed vision then snatch him away:
Soon our hope and joy will return."
So from their sorrows they took new hope
That they would find the one whom they had first found without looking.
But his mother Mary, when she saw
The others coming back from their baptism, but not her son,
And heard there was no news of him at Jordan,
Although her heart stayed calm and pure
Her motherly anxiety took over, and gave rise
To some troubled thoughts, which she spoke of, sighing:
"Oh, what use to me now is that high honor
Of bearing God's child, or that greeting,
'Hail highly favoured one, blessed amongst women!'
I have no less sorrow than other women,
And my fears are far greater
Due to the baby I carried:
Born at a time when we could hardly get

Could be obtained to shelter him or me	*A shed to shelter him or me*
From the bleak air? A stable was our warmth,	*From the cold air. A stable was our shelter,*
A manger his; yet soon enforced to fly	*A manger his; but soon we were forced to fly*
Thence into Egypt, till the murderous king	*From there into Egypt, until the murderous King*
Were dead, who sought his life, and, missing, filled	*Was dead, the one who tried to kill him, who not finding him filled*
With infant blood the streets of Bethlehem.	*The streets of Bethlehem with children's blood.*
From Egypt home returned, in Nazareth	*Having come home from Egypt, we lived*
Hath been our dwelling many years; his life 80	*In Nazareth for many years; his life*
Private, unactive, calm, contemplative,	*Has been private, quiet, calm, contemplative,*
Little suspicious to any king. But now,	*Nothing to make any king suspicious. But now,*
Full grown to man, acknowledged, as I hear,	*He is a full-grown man, recognised, as I hear,*
By John the Baptist, and in public shewn,	*By John the Baptist and appearing in public,*
Son owned from Heaven by his Father's voice,	*Acknowledged as his son from heaven by his father's voice,*
I looked for some great change. To honour? no;	*I thought there would be some great change. For glory? No;*
But trouble, as old Simeon plain foretold,	*But trouble, as old Simeon plainly predicted,*
That to the fall and rising he should be	*That he should be the saviour and destroyer*
Of many in Israel, and to a sign	*Of many in Israel, and there is a thing*
Spoken against—that through my very soul 90	*Predicted, that will run a sword*
A sword shall pierce. This is my favoured lot,	*Right through my soul. This is my great fortune,*
My exaltation to afflictions high!	*I have been lifted up to great pain!*
Afflicted I may be, it seems, and blest!	*It seems I am to be blessed with suffering!*
I will not argue that, nor will repine.	*I won't argue with that, or grumble.*
But where delays he now? Some great intent	*But where has he gone now? Some great plan*
Conceals him. When twelve years he scarce had seen,	*Makes him hide. When he was hardly twelve years old*
I lost him, but so found as well I saw	*I lost him, but when I found him I saw*

He could not lose himself, but went about
His Father's business. What he meant I mused—
Since understand; much more his absence now 100

Thus long to some great purpose he obscures.
But I to wait with patience am inured;
My heart hath been a storehouse long of things
And sayings laid up, pretending strange events."
     Thus Mary, pondering oft, and oft to mind
Recalling what remarkably had passed

Since first her Salutation heard, with thoughts
Meekly composed awaited the fulfilling:

The while her Son, tracing the desert wild,

Sole, but with holiest meditations fed, 110

Into himself descended, and at once

All his great work to come before him set—

How to begin, how to accomplish best

His end of being on Earth, and mission high.

For Satan, with sly preface to return,

Had left him vacant, and with speed was gone
Up to the middle region of thick air,

Where all his Potentates in council sate.

There, without sign of boast, or sign of joy,

Solicitous and blank, he thus began:— 120

*That he could never be lost, but was doing
His father's work. I wondered what he meant—
I now understand; so I know that his absence now*

*Means that he is following some great unspoken purpose.
But I am used to waiting patiently;
My heart has long been a storehouse of things
And sayings which prophesy strange events."
So spoke Mary, often wondering, and often
Remembering the remarkable things that happened*

*Since she first was greeted by the angel, her thoughts
Humbly ordered waiting for the prophesies to be fulfilled:*

Meanwhile her son, wandering the wild desert,

Alone, but full of the holiest meditations,

Looked into himself, and straight away

He saw all of his great work laid out before him—

How he should begin, the best way to fulfil

The purpose for which he was put on earth and his great mission.

Satan, with cunning intentions to return,

Had left him alone, and had flown

Up to the middle region of the air,

Where all his noblemen sat in Council.

There, without boasting or showing happiness,

Respectful and neutral, he began to speak:

"Princes, Heaven's ancient Sons, AEthereal Thrones—	*"Princes, ancient sons of heaven, celestial Princes–*
Daemonian Spirits now, from the element	*Demon spirits now, each given an element*
Each of his reign allotted, rightlier called	*To rule over, more properly called*
Powers of Fire, Air, Water, and Earth beneath	*Rulers of fire, air, water and earth below*
(So may we hold our place and these mild seats	*(May we keep our place and these quiet thrones*
Without new trouble!)—such an enemy	*Without new trouble!)–There is an enemy*
Is risen to invade us, who no less	*Who has come forward to challenge us, who threatens*
Threatens than our expulsion down to Hell.	*Nothing less than to send us back to hell. I, as*
I undertook, and with the vote	*I, as I said I would, and with a unanimous*
Consenting in full frequence was impowered, 130	*Vote of the full assembly empowering me*
Have found him, viewed him, tasted him; but find	*Have found him, looked at him, tested him; but I find*
Far other labour to be undergone	*That he will be much harder work*
Than when I dealt with Adam, first of men,	*Than when I dealt with Adam, the first man;*
Though Adam by his wife's allurement fell,	*Adam was led astray by his wife,*
However to this Man inferior far—	*However he is far inferior to this man–*
If he be Man by mother's side, at least	*He may be a man on his mother's side, but he*
With more than human gifts from Heaven adorned,	*Has been given more than human gifts from heaven,*
Perfections absolute, graces divine,	*Absolute perfection, divine grace,*
And amplitude of mind to greatest deeds.	*And a greatness of spirit capable of the greatest things.*
Therefore I am returned, lest confidence 140	*So I have come back, in case the memory*
Of my success with Eve in Paradise	*Of my success with Eve in Paradise*
Deceive ye to persuasion over-sure	*Makes you overconfident that*
Of like succeeding here. I summon all	*I can do the same here. I warn all of you*
Rather to be in readiness with hand	*To be ready to help with actions*
Or counsel to assist, lest I, who erst	*Or advice, in case I, who once*
Thought none my equal, now be overmatched."	*Thought I had no equal, have now met my master."*
So spake the old Serpent, doubting, and from all	*This is how the old Serpent spoke, doubtfully,*

With clamour was assured their utmost aid
At his command; when from amidst them rose
Belial, the dissolutest Spirit that fell, 150
The sensualest, and, after Asmodai,
The fleshliest Incubus, and thus advised:—

      "Set women in his eye and in his walk,
Among daughters of men the fairest found.
Many are in each region passing fair
As the noon sky, more like to goddesses
Than mortal creatures, graceful and discreet,
Expert in amorous arts, enchanting tongues
Persuasive, virgin majesty with mild
And sweet allayed, yet terrible to approach, 160
Skilled to retire, and in retiring draw
Hearts after them tangled in amorous nets.
Such object hath the power to soften and tame
Severest temper, smooth the rugged'st brow,
Enerve, and with voluptuous hope dissolve,
Draw out with credulous desire, and lead
At will the manliest, resolutest breast,
As the magnetic hardest iron draws.
Women, when nothing else, beguiled the heart
Of wisest Solomon, and made him build, 170

And they all loudly promised him that they
Were at his service; from amongst them Belial
Stood up, the most immoral spirit that fell,
The most sexual, and, apart from Asmodai,
Most lustful demon, and he gave his advice:

"Give him women to look at, put them in his path,
The loveliest you can find amongst the daughters of men.
There are many in every land as beautiful
As the noonday sky, more like goddesses
Than mortal creatures, graceful and subtle,
Experts in love, with enchanting persuasive
Voices, their virgin Majesty softened with mild
Sweetness, but they are fearsome in their attack,
Skilful in retreat, and when they retreat they pull
Hearts after them tangled in the nets of love.
These ones have the power to calm and tame
The worst anger, smooth the sternest frown,
Weaken, and dissolve with lustful hopes,
Trap with foolish desire, and lead
The manliest strongest heart
Like a magnet pulling the hardest iron.
Women enchanted the heart of wisest Solomon
When nothing else could, and made him build temples,

And made him bow, to the gods of his wives."
              To whom quick answer Satan thus returned:—
"Belial, in much uneven scale thou weigh'st

All others by thyself. Because of old

Thou thyself doat'st on womankind, admiring
Their shape, their colour, and attractive grace,
None are, thou think'st, but taken with such toys.
Before the Flood, thou, with thy lusty crew,

False titled Sons of God, roaming the Earth,

Cast wanton eyes on the daughters of men, 180
And coupled with them, and begot a race.

Have we not seen, or by relation heard,
In courts and regal chambers how thou lurk'st,
In wood or grove, by mossy fountain-side,

In valley or green meadow, to waylay
Some beauty rare, Calisto, Clymene, Daphne, or Semele, Antiopa,
Or Amymone, Syrinx, many more

Too long—then lay'st thy scapes on names adored,
Apollo, Neptune, Jupiter, or Pan, 190
Satyr, or Faun, or Silvan? But these haunts

Delight not all. Among the sons of men

How many have with a smile made small account
Of beauty and her lures, easily scorned

All her assaults, on worthier things intent!

And made him bow, to the gods of his wives."
Satan quickly gave him back this answer:
"Belial, you are mistakenly judging everyone
By your own standards. Because you have always
Been obsessed with women, loving
Their shape, their colour, and attractive grace,
You think that everyone must feel the same.
Before the flood you, and your lusty comrades,
Falsely titled the sons of God, roamed the Earth
And looked lustfully at the daughters of men,
And mated with them and started a race.
Haven't we seen, or heard the stories,
How you look around courts and palaces,
In woods or groves, by the side of springs,
In valleys or green meadows, to catch
Some rare beauty, Calisto, Clymene, Daphne, or Semele, Antiopa,
Or Amymone, Syrinx, the list is too long
To mention them all; then you blame your escapades on beloved names,
Apollo, Neptune, Jupiter or Pan,
Satyr, Faun or Silvian? But these games
Don't please everyone. Among the sons of men
How many have smiled and paid no attention
To beauty and her traps, easily rebuffed
All her attacks, with their minds on higher things!

Remember that Pellean conqueror,	*Remember Alexander when he was young,*
A youth, how all the beauties of the East	*How he looked uninterestedly at all the beauties*
He slightly viewed, and slightly overpassed;	*Of the East, and passed them all up,*
How he surnamed of Africa dismissed,	*And remember how Scipio Africanus,*
In his prime youth, the fair Iberian maid. 200	*In the prime of youth, passed up that lovely Spanish girl.*
For Solomon, he lived at ease, and, full	*As for Solomon, he lived comfortably, and stuffed*
Of honour, wealth, high fare, aimed not beyond	*With honour, wealth, good food, did not want*
Higher design than to enjoy his state;	*Anything better than to enjoy his life;*
Thence to the bait of women lay exposed.	*So he was easy meat for the traps of women.*
But he whom we attempt is wiser far	*But the one we want to trap now is far wiser*
Than Solomon, of more exalted mind,	*Than Solomon, with a greater mind,*
Made and set wholly on the accomplishment	*Completely devoted to achieving*
Of greatest things. What woman will you find,	*The greatest things. Where will you find a woman,*
Though of this age the wonder and the fame,	*Even if she was the wonder of the age,*
On whom his leisure will voutsafe an eye 210	*Whom he will spend a moment looking at*
Of fond desire? Or should she, confident,	*With desire? Or if she, confident*
As sitting queen adored on Beauty's throne,	*In the power of her beauty,*
Descend with all her winning charms begirt	*Should come with all her charms ready*
To enamour, as the zone of Venus once	*To attract him, as the girdle of Venus once*
Wrought that effect on Jove (so fables tell),	*Attracted Jove (so the fables say),*
How would one look from his majestic brow,	*Imagine how one frown from his kingly brow,*
Seated as on the top of Virtue's hill,	*Showing him as being a paragon of virtue,*
Discountenance her despised, and put to rout	*Would throw her into confusion, brush away*
All her array, her female pride deject,	*All her decoration, humble her female pride,*
Or turn to reverent awe! For Beauty stands 220	*Or turn her to reverent worship! For beauty*
In the admiration only of weak minds	*Only works on weak minds*
Led captive; cease to admire, and all her plumes	*Which are trapped; stop admiring, and her feathers*
Fall flat, and shrink into a trivial toy,	*Fall flat, and become mere trinkets,*

486

At every sudden slighting quite abashed.	*Ashamed by every criticism.*
Therefore with manlier objects we must try	*So we must test his loyalty with more manly things,*
His constancy—with such as have more shew	*Those which have promises*
Of worth, of honour, glory, and popular praise	*Of wealth, honour, glory and fame*
(Rocks whereon greatest men have oftest wrecked);	*(the rocks on which great men are most often wrecked);*
Or that which only seems to satisfy	*Or things which seem only to fulfil*
Lawful desires of nature, not beyond. 230	*Lawful natural desires, not more.*
And now I know he hungers, where no food	*And I know that he is now hungry, and there is no food*
Is to be found, in the wide Wilderness:	*To be found in the wide wilderness:*
The rest commit to me; I shall let pass	*Leave the rest to me; I shall not miss*
No advantage, and his strength as oft assay."	*Any chance, and I'll test him as often as I can.*
He ceased, and heard their grant in loud acclaim;	*He finished, and heard their approval in their loud applause;*
Then forthwith to him takes a chosen band	*Then at once he gathered a select group*
Of Spirits likest to himself in guile,	*Of spirits most close to him in cunning,*
To be at hand and at his beck appear,	*To be ready to appear when he ordered,*
If cause were to unfold some active scene	*If there was a reason to show some scene*
Of various persons, each to know his part; 240	*With several people in, then each one would know his part;*
Then to the desert takes with these his flight,	*Then they fly together to the desert,*
Where still, from shade to shade, the Son of God,	*Where the son of God still, day and night,*
After forty days' fasting, had remained,	*Had remained after forty days fasting,*
Now hungering first, and to himself thus said:—	*Now felt hungry for the first time, and said to himself:*
"Where will this end? Four times ten days I have passed	*"Where will this end? I have spent forty days*
Wandering this woody maze, and human food	*Wandering in this woody maze, and have not tasted*
Nor tasted, nor had appetite. That fast	*Human food, nor have I wished for it. I do not*
To virtue I impute not, or count part	*Think of that fast as virtuous, or see*
Of what I suffer here. If nature need not,	*It as part of my sufferings. If one is not hungry,*
Or God support nature without repast, 250	*Or God supports one without food,*

Though needing, what praise is it to endure?	*How is it praiseworthy to endure that?*
But now I feel I hunger; which declares	*But now I am hungry, which shows*
Nature hath need of what she asks. Yet God	*That nature demands what she needs. But God*
Can satisfy that need some other way,	*Can satisfy that need in other ways,*
Though hunger still remain. So it remain	*Although one will still be hungry. As long as I can go on*
Without this body's wasting, I content me,	*Without my body dying I am happy,*
And from the sting of famine fear no harm;	*And do not fear the pain of hunger;*
Nor mind it, fed with better thoughts, that feed	*Nor do I mind it, I am fed with better thoughts,*
Me hungering more to do my Father's will."	*That give me a hunger to do my father's bidding."*
It was the hour of night, when thus the Son 260	*It was nighttime when the Son*
Communed in silent walk, then laid him down	*Had these thoughts on his silent walk, then laid down*
Under the hospitable covert nigh	*Under the welcoming shelter*
Of trees thick interwoven. There he slept,	*Of overhanging branches. There he slept,*
And dreamed, as appetite is wont to dream,	*And dreamed, as the hungry usually do,*
Of meats and drinks, nature's refreshment sweet.	*Of meat and drink, nature's sweet refreshment.*
Him thought he by the brook of Cherith stood,	*He thought he stood by the stream of Cherif,*
And saw the ravens with their horny beaks	*And saw the ravens with their horny beaks*
Food to Elijah bringing even and morn—	*Bringing Elijah food night and morning–*
Though ravenous, taught to abstain from what they brought;	*Though they were hungry he had taught them not to eat what they brought;*
He saw the Prophet also, how he fled 270	*He saw the Prophet as well, how he escaped*
Into the desert, and how there he slept	*Into the desert, and how he slept there*
Under a juniper—then how, awaked,	*Under a juniper bush, and how, when he woke,*
He found his supper on the coals prepared,	*He found his supper waiting on the fire,*
And by the Angel was bid rise and eat,	*And was told by the angel to get up and eat,*
And eat the second time after repose,	*Then to eat again after his rest,*

The strength whereof sufficed him forty days:	*And the strength that gave him lasted for 40 days:*
Sometimes that with Elijah he partook,	*Sometimes he dreamt he ate with Elijah,*
Or as a guest with Daniel at his pulse.	*Or as a guest with Daniel over his beans.*
Thus wore out night; and now the harald Lark	*So the night wore out, and now the announcing lark*
Left his ground-nest, high towering to descry 280	*Left his nest on the ground, flying up high to see*
The Morn's approach, and greet her with his song.	*The approach of morning, and greet her with his song.*
As lightly from his grassy couch up rose	*Just as quickly our saviour rose up*
Our Saviour, and found all was but a dream;	*From his grassy bed, and found it had all been a dream;*
Fasting he went to sleep, and fasting waked.	*Starving he went to sleep, and starving he woke up.*
Up to a hill anon his steps he reared,	*Soon he walked up a hill,*
From whose high top to ken the prospect round,	*To take a look around from its summit,*
If cottage were in view, sheep-cote, or herd;	*To see if he could see a cottage, sheep pen or a herd,*
But cottage, herd, or sheep-cote, none he saw—	*But there were none of these to be seen.*
Only in a bottom saw a pleasant grove,	*But in a hollow he saw a pleasant grove*
With chaunt of tuneful birds resounding loud. 290	*Ringing with the song of tuneful birds.*
Thither he bent his way, determined there	*He walked there, deciding that it was where*
To rest at noon, and entered soon the shade	*He would rest at noon, and he soon got into the*
High-roofed, and walks beneath, and alleys brown,	*High roofed shade, and walked under it, on the brown paths*
That opened in the midst a woody scene;	*That lead him to a woody scene;*
Nature's own work it seemed (Nature taught Art),	*It seemed to be the work of nature (nature taught art),*
And, to a superstitious eye, the haunt	*And, to a superstitious person, the home*
Of wood-gods and wood-nymphs. He viewed it round;	*Of wood gods and wood nymphs. He looked all around;*
When suddenly a man before him stood,	*Suddenly he saw a man in front of him,*
Not rustic as before, but seemlier clad,	*Not a peasant like before, but better dressed,*

As one in city or court or palace bred, 300

And with fair speech these words to him addressed:—

    "With granted leave officious I return,

But much more wonder that the Son of God

In this wild solitude so long should bide,

Of all things destitute, and, well I know,

Not without hunger. Others of some note,

As story tells, have trod this wilderness:

The fugitive Bond-woman, with her son,
Outcast Nebaioth, yet found here relief
By a providing Angel; all the race 310

Of Israel here had famished, had not God

Rained from heaven manna; and that Prophet bold,
Native of Thebez, wandering here, was fed
Twice by a voice inviting him to eat.
Of thee those forty days none hath regard,

Forty and more deserted here indeed."

    To whom thus Jesus:—"What conclud'st thou hence?
They all had need; I, as thou seest, have none."
"How hast thou hunger then?" Satan replied.

"Tell me, if food were now before thee set, 320
Wouldst thou not eat?" "Thereafter as I like

the giver," answered Jesus. "Why should that
Cause thy refusal?" said the subtle Fiend.

"Hast thou not right to all created things?

Like one who grew up in a city, court or palace.

With elegant speech he spoke these words to him:

" I have been given official permission to come back,

But I am astonished that the son of God

Should spend so long in this wild loneliness,

Lacking everything, and, as I well know

Hungry. There are other notable ones,

So the story tells, who have walked this wilderness:

Hagar and her son,
Exiled but finding relief here
From a providing angel; the whole nation

Of Israel would have starved here, if God

Had not rained manna from heaven; and the bold prophet
Elijah, wandering here, was fed
Twice by a voice inviting him to eat.
For you, nobody has paid attention to you for forty days,

You have been abandoned here for forty days and more."

Jesus answered him: "What conclusions are you drawing?
They were all in need; as you can see I am not."
"Why are you hungry then?" Satan replied.

"Tell me, if food was put before you now,
Would you eat it?" "That would depend on who

Offered it," answered Jesus." Why would that
Make you refuse?" said the cunning devil.

"Don't you have a right to everything in creation?

Owe not all creatures, by just right, to thee | *Don't all creatures by law owe you*
Duty and service, nor to stay till bid, | *Duty and service, and should not wait*
| *until asked,*

But tender all their power? Nor mention I | *But should offer everything they can?*
| *I'm not talking about*

Meats by the law unclean, or offered first | *Meat that the law says is unclean, or*
| *has been offered*

To idols—those young Daniel could refuse; | *To idols–young Daniel refused those;*
Nor proffered by an enemy—though who | *Nor meat offered by an enemy,*
330 | *though who*
Would scruple that, with want oppressed? | *Would turn that down if they were in*
Behold, | *need? Look,*
Nature ashamed, or, better to express, | *Nature is ashamed, or, to put it*
| *better,*

Troubled, that thou shouldst hunger, hath | *Troubled, that you should be hungry,*
purveyed | *and has brought*
From all the elements her choicest store, | *You all her best things to treat you*
To treat thee as beseems, and as her Lord | *In the proper fashion, to honour you*
| *as her Lord.*

With honour. Only deign to sit and eat." | *All you have to do is sit and eat.*
      He spake no dream; for, as his | *This was not idle talk, for when he*
words had end, | *finished speaking*
Our Saviour, lifting up his eyes, beheld, | *Our saviour, looking up, saw,*
In ample space under the broadest shade, | *In a wide space under the largest tree*
A table richly spread in regal mode, 340 | *A table laid out fit for a king,*
With dishes piled and meats of noblest sort | *Piled high with dishes and meat of*
| *the best sort*

And savour—beasts of chase, or fowl of | *And taste–animals from the hunt, or*
game, | *game fowl,*
In pastry built, or from the spit, or boiled, | *Wrapped in pastry, or roasted on the*
| *spit, or boiled,*

Grisamber-steamed; all fish, from sea or | *Scented with perfume; all sorts of*
shore, | *fish, from the sea*
Freshet or purling brook, of shell or fin, | *Or from streams and running brooks,*
| *with shells or fins,*

And exquisitest name, for which was | *The most lovely of all, for which men*
drained | *scoured*
Pontus, and Lucrine bay, and Afric coast. | *The Black Sea, the lagoon of Naples,*
| *and the African coast.*

Alas! how simple, to these cates compared, | *Alas! How simple compared to these*
| *dishes,*

Was that crude Apple that diverted Eve! | *Was the ordinary apple that led Eve*
| *astray!*
And at a stately sideboard, by the wine, 350 | *And on a rich sideboard, by the wine,*

That fragrant smell diffused, in order stood	*That gave off a beautiful aroma, stood waiting*
Tall stripling youths rich-clad, of fairer hue	*Tall strapping lads, richly dressed, better looking*
Than Ganymed or Hylas; distant more,	*Than Ganymede or Hylas; in the distance under the trees*
Under the trees now tripped, now solemn stood,	*More sometimes danced, sometimes stood to attention,*
Nymphs of Diana's train, and Naiades	*Nymphs from Diana's court, and water nymphs*
With fruits and flowers from Amalthea's horn,	*With fruits and flowers from the horn of plenty,*
And ladies of the Hesperides, that seemed	*And ladies from the garden of Hersperus, who seemed*
Fairer than feigned of old, or fabled since	*More lovely than the stories of them in the past,*
Of faery damsels met in forest wide	*Or the stories since of fairy ladies met in the wide forests*
By knights of Logres, or of Lyones, 360	*By Arthur's knights,*
Lancelot, or Pelleas, or Pellenore.	*Lancelot, Pelleas or Pellenore.*
And all the while harmonious airs were heard	*And all the time sweet music was heard*
Of chiming strings or charming pipes; and winds	*Of ringing strings or charming pipes; and*
Of gentlest gale Arabian odours fanned	*Gentle breezes wafted around Arabian perfumes*
From their soft wings, and Flora's earliest smells.	*And the sweet smells of flowers.*
Such was the splendour; and the Tempter now	*This was the splendid sight, and the tempter now*
His invitation earnestly renewed:—	*Strongly repeated his invitation:*
"What doubts the Son of God to sit and eat?	*"Why won't the son of God sit and eat?*
These are not fruits forbidden; no interdict	*These are not forbidden fruit; no ban*
Defends the touching of these viands pure; 370	*Stops you from touching these pure foods;*
Their taste no knowledge works, at least of evil,	*Their taste gives no knowledge, at least of evil,*
But life preserves, destroys life's enemy,	*But preserves life, banishes life's enemy,*
Hunger, with sweet restorative delight.	*Hunger, with the sweet joy of fulfilment.*
All these are Spirits of air, and woods, and springs,	*All of these people are spirits of the air, woods and springs,*
Thy gentle ministers, who come to pay	*Your gentle servants who've come to pay*

Thee homage, and acknowledge thee their Lord.
What doubt'st thou, Son of God? Sit down and eat."

　　　　To whom thus Jesus temperately replied:—
"Said'st thou not that to all things I had right?
And who withholds my power that right to use? 380
Shall I receive by gift what of my own,

When and where likes me best, I can command?
I can at will, doubt not, as soon as thou,

Command a table in this wilderness,
And call swift flights of Angels ministrant,

Arrayed in glory, on my cup to attend:
Why shouldst thou, then, obtrude this diligence
In vain, where no acceptance it can find
And with my hunger what hast thou to do?

Thy pompous delicacies I contemn, 390
And count thy specious gifts no gifts, but guiles."
　　　　To whom thus answered Satan, male-content:—
"That I have also power to give thou seest;

If of that power I bring thee voluntary
What I might have bestowed on whom I pleased,
And rather opportunely in this place
Chose to impart to thy apparent need,
Why shouldst thou not accept it? But I see

What I can do or offer is suspect.

Of these things others quickly will dispose, 400
Whose pains have earned the far-fet spoil."
With that

Their respects and acknowledge you as their Lord.
Why do you doubt, son of God? Sit down and eat."
Jesus calmly replied to him:

"Didn't you say that I had a right to everything?
And who is there stopping me using that power?
Shall I be given as a gift things that I can order
For myself when and where I prefer?

Do not doubt that I can summon up a table
In this wilderness just as well as you,
And call swift flights of angel servants,
Dressed in glory, to wait on me:
So why do you keep trying to please me
In vain, when I will never accept?
What has my hunger got to do with you?

I reject your extravagant delicacies,
And see your misleading gifts for the traps that they are."
Satan answered him, disgruntled:

"You can see that I also have the power to give;
If I bring you voluntarily the things I might have given to whomever I pleased,
And, fortunately for you in this place,
Choose to fulfil your obvious needs
Why would you not accept it? But I can see
That you suspect everything I offer or do.

There are others who will be glad of these things,
Whose efforts deserve these exotic foods." With that

Both table and provision vanished quite,	*The table and food completely vanished,*
With sound of harpies' wings and talons heard;	*To the sound of harpies' wings and claws;*
Only the importune Tempter still remained,	*Only the persistent tempter remained,*
And with these words his temptation pursued:—	*And carried on his temptation with these words:*
"By hunger, that each other creature tames,	*"Hunger, which can be used to tame any other creature,*
Thou art not to be harmed, therefore not moved;	*Does not harm you, and so you can't be persuaded;*
Thy temperance, invincible besides,	*Your self restraint cannot be overcome*
For no allurement yields to appetite;	*And no temptation makes you give in to your appetite;*
And all thy heart is set on high designs, 410	*All of your heart is set on higher things*
High actions. But wherewith to be achieved?	*And higher actions. But how will you achieve these?*
Great acts require great means of enterprise;	*Great acts require great powers;*
Thou art unknown, unfriended, low of birth,	*You are unknown, friendless, lowborn,*
A carpenter thy father known, thyself	*Known to be the son of a carpenter, you*
Bred up in poverty and straits at home,	*Grew up in poverty and need at home,*
Lost in a desert here and hunger-bit.	*And are now lost in the desert and racked with hunger.*
Which way, or from what hope, dost thou aspire	*In what way, from what source, do you hope*
To greatness? whence authority deriv'st?	*To achieve greatness? Where does your authority come from?*
What followers, what retinue canst thou gain,	*What followers, what servants can you get,*
Or at thy heels the dizzy multitude, 420	*How can you hold on to the changeable crowds*
Longer than thou canst feed them on thy cost?	*Longer than you can feed them at your expense?*
Money brings honour, friends, conquest, and realms.	*Money brings honor, friends, victory and kingdoms.*
What raised Antipater the Edomite,	*What gave Antipater the Edomite his position*
And his son Herod placed on Juda's throne,	*And got the throne of Judaea (your throne) for his son Herod,*
Thy throne, but gold, that got him puissant friends?	*If not money, that got him strong friends?*

Therefore, if at great things thou wouldst
Get riches first, get wealth, and treasure heap—
Not difficult, if thou hearken to me.
Riches are mine, fortune is in my hand;
They whom I favour thrive in wealth amain,
430
While virtue, valour, wisdom, sit in want."

   To whom thus Jesus patiently replied:—
"Yet wealth without these three is impotent

To gain dominion, or to keep it gained—
Witness those ancient empires of the earth,

In highth of all their flowing wealth dissolved;
But men endued with these have oft attained,
In lowest poverty, to highest deeds—

Gideon, and Jephtha, and the shepherd lad
Whose offspring on the throne of Juda sate
440
So many ages, and shall yet regain
That seat, and reign in Israel without end.

Among the Heathen (for throughout the world
To me is not unknown what hath been done

Worthy of memorial) canst thou not remember
Quintius, Fabricius, Curius, Regulus?

For I esteem those names of men so poor,

Who could do mighty things, and could contemn
Riches, though offered from the hand of kings.
And what in me seems wanting but that I
450

So if you want to do great things,
First get riches, wealth and treasure–

Easily done if you listen to me.
I have riches to give, I hold fortunes in my hand;
Those whom I favour are rolling in money
While virtue, bravery, and wisdom sit in poverty."

Jesus patiently replied to him:

"But wealth without these things cannot

Gain power, or hold onto it–
Look at those great empires of the Earth,

Which fell at the height of all their wealth;
But men who have those virtues have often achieved,
Even in great poverty, the highest things–

Gideon, and Jepatha, and David
Whose descendants sat on the throne of Judaea
For so many ages, and shall regain
That seat again, and rule in Israel forever.

Among the heathens (for there is nothing
In the world worth remembering that I

Do not know about) have you forgotten
Quintius, Fabricius, Curius, Regulus?

I respect the names of men who were so poor

But still did mighty things, and could reject
Riches, even though they were offered by Kings."
What do you think is lacking in me that I

May also in this poverty as soon

Accomplish what they did, perhaps and more?
Extol not riches, then, the toil of fools,

The wise man's cumbrance, if not snare; more apt
To slacken virtue and abate her edge

Than prompt her to do aught may merit

What if with like aversion I reject
Riches and realms! Yet not for that a crown,

Golden in shew, is but a wreath of thorns,

Brings dangers, troubles, cares, and sleepless nights, 460
To him who wears the regal diadem,

When on his shoulders each man's burden lies;
For therein stands the office of a king,
His honour, virtue, merit, and chief praise,

That for the public all this weight he bears.

Yet he who reigns within himself, and rules

Passions, desires, and fears, is more a king—
Which every wise and virtuous man attains;

And who attains not, ill aspires to rule

Cities of men, or headstrong multitudes, 470

Subject himself to anarchy within,
Or lawless passions in him, which he serves.
But to guide nations in the way of truth

By saving doctrine, and from error lead

To know, and, knowing, worship God aright,

Could not accomplish as much as they did
In poverty, and perhaps more?
Do not praise riches, the thing fools work for,

The burden of the wise man, if not his trap; it's better
To be less virtuous and soften virtue's efforts

Than ask her to do things in order to get praise.

So for the same reason I reject
Riches and kingdoms! For a crown which

Appears to be gold is just a crown of thorns,

Bringing danger, trouble, care and sleepless nights,
To the one who wears the Royal Crown,

Carrying each man's words on his shoulders;
That is the duty of the King,
His honour, virtue, merit and most praiseworthy duty,

That he carries all this weight for his people.

But the one who rules over himself, and controls

His passions, desires and fears, is greater than a king—
And every wise and good man can attain this;

The one who cannot do this should not hope to rule

The cities of men, or headstrong crowds,

When he is ruled by anarchy within,
Or is serving his own lawless desires.
But to lead nations in the ways of truth

Through the doctrine of redemption, to show them the error of their ways,

To know God and knowing him to worship him correctly,

Is yet more kingly. This attracts the soul,

Governs the inner man, the nobler part;

That other o'er the body only reigns,
And oft by force—which to a generous mind
So reigning can be no sincere delight. 480
Besides, to give a kingdom hath been thought

Greater and nobler done, and to lay down

Far more magnanimous, than to assume.

Riches are needless, then, both for themselves,
And for thy reason why they should be sought—
To gain a sceptre, oftest better missed."

Is more kingly. This draws in the soul,

Governs over the inner man, which is the nobler part;

The other only rules over the body,
Often by force–and to a good mind
Ruling like that can give no pleasure.
Besides, to give a kingdom is thought

A greater and nobler deed and to give it up

Is far more high-minded than to take it.

Riches are useless then, both in themselves
And in the reasons why men strive for them–
It is often better to lose power than to gain it."

So spake the Son of God; and Satan stood	*So said the son of God; and Satan stood*
A while as mute, confounded what to say,	*For a while as if dumb, not knowing what to say,*
What to reply, confuted and convinced	*How to reply, confused and convinced*
Of his weak arguing and fallacious drift;	*Of the weakness and foolishness of his arguments.*
At length, collecting all his serpent wiles,	*Eventually, gathering up all his serpent cunning,*
With soothing words renewed, him thus accosts:—	*He went back on the attack with soothing words:*
"I see thou know'st what is of use to know,	*"I can see that you know the things it's good to know,*
What best to say canst say, to do canst do;	*You can say what is best to say, do what's best to do;*
Thy actions to thy words accord; thy words	*Your actions match your words, your words*
To thy large heart give utterance due; thy heart 10	*Truly reflect your great heart; your heart*
Contains of good, wise, just, the perfect shape.	*Contains the perfect amounts of goodness, wisdom and justice.*
Should kings and nations from thy mouth consult,	*If kings and nations asked for your advice*
Thy counsel would be as the oracle	*Your counsel would be like the wisdom of*
Urim and Thummim, those oraculous gems	*Urim and Thummim, those oracular gems*
On Aaron's breast, or tongue of Seers old	*In Aaron's breastplate, of the infallible tongues*
Infallible; or, wert thou sought to deeds	*Of ancient seers; or if you were called to actions*
That might require the array of war, thy skill	*Which might require the use of armies, your generalship*
Of conduct would be such that all the world	*Would be so great that nothing in the world*
Could not sustain thy prowess, or subsist	*Could resist you, or survive*
In battle, though against thy few in arms. 20	*In battle, even if you only had a few soldiers.*
These godlike virtues wherefore dost thou	*So why are you hiding these godlike*

hide?
Affecting private life, or more obscure

In savage wilderness, wherefore deprive

All Earth her wonder at thy acts, thyself

The fame and glory—glory, the reward

That sole excites to high attempts the flame
Of most erected spirits, most tempered pure
AEthereal, who all pleasures else despise,

All treasures and all gain esteem as dross,
And dignities and powers, all but the highest? 30
Thy years are ripe, and over-ripe. The son

Of Macedonian Philip had ere these

Won Asia, and the throne of Cyrus held

At his dispose; young Scipio had brought down
The Carthaginian pride; young Pompey quelled
The Pontic king, and in triumph had rode.

Yet years, and to ripe years judgment mature,
Quench not the thirst of glory, but augment.

Great Julius, whom now all the world admires,
The more he grew in years, the more inflamed 40
With glory, wept that he had lived so long
Ingloroious. But thou yet art not too late."

       To whom our Saviour calmly thus replied:—
"Thou neither dost persuade me to seek wealth
For empire's sake, nor empire to affect

virtues?
In living a secluded life, or hiding yourself

In the savage wilderness, why do you deprive

Earth the privilege of wondering at your deeds,

And deprive yourself of the fame and glory–glory, the reward

Which so inspires the greatest spirits,
The most pure and heavenly
Who have contempt for all other pleasures,

Regard treasures and money as dirt,
Reject all titles and powers, except for this highest one?
You are old enough, more than old enough. Before he was

Your age Alexander had conquered Asia

And held the throne of Persia in his hands.

Young Scipio had already defeated

The Carthaginians; Young Pompey had beaten

The King of Greece and ridden in triumph.

But age, with its maturing judgements,
Does not calm the urge for glory but adds to it.

Great Julius, whom all the world now admires,

Wanted more glory the older he got

And wept that he had lived so long
Without it. But it is not too late for you."

Our saviour replied to him calmly:

"You have not persuaded me to look for wealth
To get an empire, nor to look for an empire

For glory's sake, by all thy argument.	*To get glory, despite all your arguments.*
For what is glory but the blaze of fame,	*For what is glory but a blaze of fame,*
The people's praise, if always praise unmixed?	*The people's praise, if that is ever unanimous?*
And what the people but a herd confused,	*And what are the people but a confused herd,*
A miscellaneous rabble, who extol 50	*A miscellaneous rabble who worship*
Things vulgar, and, well weighed, scarce worth the praise?	*Things that are vulgar, that in the end are worthless?*
They praise and they admire they know not what,	*They don't know what they are praising and admiring*
And know not whom, but as one leads the	*Or who, they just follow each other;*
And what delight to be by such extolled,	*What pleasure is there in being praised by these,*
To live upon their tongues, and be their talk?	*To live on their tongues and be spoken of by them?*
Of whom to be dispraised were no small praise—	*To be criticised by them would be great praise,*
His lot who dares be singularly good.	*And is the lot of him who dares to be unusually good.*
Th'intelligent among them and the wise	*There are few among them who are intelligent*
Are few, and glory scarce of few is raised.	*And wise, and few of them are given glory.*
This is true glory and renown—when God, 60	*The true glory and fame is when God*
Looking on the Earth, with approbation marks	*Looks down on earth and notices with approval*
The just man, and divulges him through Heaven	*The just man and shows him throughout heaven*
To all his Angels, who with true applause	*To all his angels, who with true applause*
Recount his praises. Thus he did to Job,	*Sing his praises. This is what he did with Job, when,*
When, to extend his fame through Heaven and Earth,	*To spread his fame through heaven and earth,*
As thou to thy reproach may'st well remember,	*As to your shame you may well remember,*
He asked thee, 'Hast thou seen my servant Job?'	*He asked you, "Have you seen my servant Job?"*
Famous he was in Heaven; on Earth less known,	*He was famous in heaven; less well-known on earth*
Where glory is false glory, attributed	*Where glory is false, and given*
To things not glorious, men not worthy of fame. 70	*To inglorious things, and men who don't deserve fame*

500

They err who count it glorious to subdue

By conquest far and wide, to overrun

Large countries, and in field great battles win,

Great cities by assault. What do these worthies
But rob and spoil, burn, slaughter, and enslave
Peaceable nations, neighbouring or remote,
Made captive, yet deserving freedom more

Than those their conquerors, who leave behind
Nothing but ruin wheresoe'er they rove,
And all the flourishing works of peace destroy; 80
Then swell with pride, and must be titled Gods,
Great benefactors of mankind, Deliverers,
Worshipped with temple, priest, and sacrifice?
One is the son of Jove, of Mars the other;

Till conqueror Death discover them scarce men,
Rowling in brutish vices, and deformed,

Violent or shameful death their due reward.

But, if there be in glory aught of good;

It may be means far different be attained,

Without ambition, war, or violence— 90
By deeds of peace, by wisdom eminent,

By patience, temperance. I mention still

Him whom thy wrongs, with saintly patience borne,
Made famous in a land and times obscure;

Who names not now with honour patient

Those who think it is glorious to oppress
Through conquest far and wide, to overrun
Large countries, and to win great battles in the field,

Great cities by assault, are wrong.
What do these people do
Except rob and spoil, burn, slaughter and enslave
Peaceful nations, close or far away,
They are made prisoners, but deserve freedom more

Than the ones who conquer them, who leave behind
Nothing but ruin wherever they go,
And destroy all the growing works of peace;
They are puffed up with pride, and insist on being called gods,
Benefactors of mankind, saviours,
And want to be worshipped in the temples with priests and sacrifices.
One is the son of Jove, the other of Mars.

Death will come and show them to be hardly men at all,
Wallowing in animal vices, and twisted,

Violence or shameful death will be their just deserts.

But if there is anything at all good about glory,

It can be gained in very different ways,

Without ambition, war, or violence–
Through peaceful deeds, through great wisdom,

With patience and sobriety. I mention again

The one who became famous in a forgotten land and time
By tolerating your assaults, bearing them with saintly patience;

Who now does not speak the name of

Job?	*Job with admiration?*
Poor Socrates, (who next more memorable?)	*Poor Socrates (who else is more memorable?)*
By what he taught and suffered for so doing,	*Through his teaching, and what he suffered for teaching,*
For truth's sake suffering death unjust, lives now	*Suffering an unjust death for the sake of truth, is now*
Equal in fame to proudest conquerors.	*As famous as the proudest conquerors.*
Yet, if for fame and glory aught be done, 100	*But if everything is done for fame and glory,*
Aught suffered—if young African for fame	*Anything suffered–if young Scipio had freed his country*
His wasted country freed from Punic rage—	*From Hannibal for the sake of fame—*
The deed becomes unpraised, the man at least,	*The deed becomes worthless, at least the man does,*
And loses, though but verbal, his reward.	*And he loses his reward, even if it is only for people to speak well of him.*
Shall I seek glory, then, as vain men seek,	*Shall I seek glory then, as vain men seek it,*
Oft not deserved? I seek not mine, but His	*Often undeserved? I am not looking for my glory but for the glory*
Who sent me, and thereby witness whence I am."	*Of the one who sent me, which I bear witness to.*
To whom the Tempter, murmuring, thus replied:—	*Murmuring, the tempter answered him:*
"Think not so slight of glory, therein least Resembling thy great Father. He seeks glory, 110	*"Don't think so little of glory, in this You are very unlike your great father. He looks for glory,*
And for his glory all things made, all things	*And he made everything for his glory, and orders and governs*
Orders and governs; nor content in Heaven, By all his Angels glorified, requires	*All things. He's not happy in heaven, Being glorified by all his angels, he wants*
Glory from men, from all men, good or bad,	*Glory from men, from all men good or bad,*
Wise or unwise, no difference, no exemption.	*Wise or unwise, he sees no difference, makes no exemption.*
Above all sacrifice, or hallowed gift, Glory he requires, and glory he receives,	*He values glory above all sacrifices Or holy gifts, and he gets it,*
Promiscuous from all nations, Jew, or Greek,	*He wants it from every nation, Jews, Greeks,*
Or Barbarous, nor exception hath declared;	*Or barbarians, and does not turn any down;*
From us, his foes pronounced, glory he exacts." 120	*He even asks for glory from us, his sworn enemies."*

To whom our Saviour fervently replied:
"And reason; since his Word all things produced,
Though chiefly not for glory as prime end,
But to shew forth his goodness, and impart

His good communicable to every soul
Freely; of whom what could He less expect
Than glory and benediction—that is, thanks—
The slightest, easiest, readiest recompense

From them who could return him nothing else,
And, not returning that, would likeliest render 130
Contempt instead, dishonour, obloquy?
Hard recompense, unsuitable return

For so much good, so much beneficience!
But why should man seek glory, who of his own
Hath nothing, and to whom nothing belongs

But condemnation, ignominy, and shame—

Who, for so many benefits received,

Turned recreant to God, ingrate and false,

And so of all true good himself despoiled;

Yet, sacrilegious, to himself would take 140

That which to God alone of right belongs?

Yet so much bounty is in God, such grace,

That who advances his glory, not their own,

Them he himself to glory will advance."
So spake the Son of God; and here again
Satan had not to answer, but stood struck

Our Saviour passionately answered him:
"And with reason; since he created everything,
Though not primarily for glory
But to show his own goodness, and show

That he gives it freely to every soul,
So what so what should he expect
From them less than the glory and praise– that is, thanks–
The smallest, easiest, most available payment

From those who have nothing else to give,
And who, if they did not give that, might instead give
Contempt, dishonor, and abuse?
This would be a harsh payment, an unsuitable return

For so much good, so much kindness!
But why would man look for glory, when he has
None of his own, and nothing belongs to him

But condemnation, disgrace and shame–

The one who, for all the good things he received

Became a traitor to God, ungrateful and false,

And so polluted all the true good in himself;

But, blasphemously, he now wants to take

The thing which only God has a right to?

Yet God is so generous, so full of grace,

That anyone who works for his glory, not their own,

Will be given glory by him."
So spoke the son of God, and once again
Satan had no answer, but stood stunned,

With guilt of his own sin—for he himself,

Guilty at the knowledge of his own sin--for he himself

Insatiable of glory, had lost all;

Greedy for glory, had lost everything;

Yet of another plea bethought him soon:—

But he soon thought of another argument:

      "Of glory, as thou wilt," said he, "so deem; 150

"Say what you like about glory, you can think

Worth or not worth the seeking, let it pass.

It is worth seeking or not, let it go.

But to a Kingdom thou art born—ordained

But you are born to rule a kingdom, destined

To sit upon thy father David's throne,

To sit upon your ancestor David's throne—

By mother's side thy father, though thy right

He is your ancestor on your mother's side, though your inheritance

Be now in powerful hands, that will not part

Is now in powerful hands, which will not easily

Easily from possession won with arms.

Give up what they won through force.

Judaea now and all the Promised Land,

Now Judea and the whole promised land

Reduced a province under Roman yoke,

Are just a Roman province, which obeys

Obeys Tiberius, nor is always ruled

Tiberius, and is not always ruled

With temperate sway: oft have they violated 160

With sound justice; they have often gone against

The Temple, oft the Law, with foul affronts,

The Temple and the Law, with foul insults,

Abominations rather, as did once

In fact blasphemies, as Antiochus

Antiochus. And think'st thou to regain

Once did. Do you think you will regain

Thy right by sitting still, or thus retiring?

Your rightful place by sitting still or retreating like this?

So did not Machabeus. He indeed

This was not what Machabeus did. Yes he did

Retired unto the Desert, but with arms;

Go into the desert, but armed;

And o'er a mighty king so oft prevailed

He came out to beat a mighty king so often

That by strong hand his family obtained,

That his family got by force,

Though priests, the crown, and David's throne usurped,

Though they were priests, the Crown and the throne of David,

With Modin and her suburbs once content. 170

They who were once content with Modin and its suburbs.

If kingdom move thee not, let move thee zeal

If you are not bothered about ruling, let passion

And duty—zeal and duty are not slow,

And duty rule you—passion and duty do not delay,

But on Occasion's forelock watchful wait:	*But are always watching for their opportunity:*
They themselves rather are occasion best—	*These are the things that should drive you on;*
Zeal of thy Father's house, duty to free	*Passion for your father's house, and your duty*
Thy country from her heathen servitude.	*To free your country from the slavery to heathens.*
So shalt thou best fulfil, best verify,	*That's the best way for you to fulfil, and to prove right,*
The Prophets old, who sung thy endless reign—	*The ancient prophets, who predicted your never-ending rule–*
The happier reign the sooner it begins.	*And the sooner that rule begins the better.*
Reign then; what canst thou better do the while?" 180	*So rule; do you have something better to do in the meantime?"*
To whom our Saviour answer thus returned :—	*Our saviour answered him in this fashion:*
"All things are best fulfilled in their due time;	*"All things are best done at their proper time;*
And time there is for all things, Truth hath said.	*And the Word has said that there is a time for all things.*
If of my reign Prophetic Writ hath told	*If the prophets have written*
That it shall never end, so, when begin	*That my rule shall never end then when it begins*
The Father in his purpose hath decreed—	*Is when the father decides–*
He in whose hand all times and seasons rowl.	*The one who controls time and the seasons.*
What if he hath decreed that I shall first	*What if he has ordered that I should first*
Be tried in humble state, and things adverse,	*Be tested in a humble situation, by hardships,*
By tribulations, injuries, insults, 190	*Trials, injuries, insults,*
Contempts, and scorns, and snares, and violence,	*Contempt, scorn, traps and violence,*
Suffering, abstaining, quietly expecting	*Suffering, not fighting back, quietly waiting,*
Without distrust or doubt, that He may know	*Trusting without doubt, so that he can know*
What I can suffer, how obey? Who best	*How I'm suffering and how I obey him? The person*
Can suffer best can do, best reign who first	*Who can bear suffering is greatest, the one*
Well hath obeyed—just trial ere I merit	*Who has learnt obedience is the best ruler.*

My exaltation without change or end.

But what concerns it thee when I begin
My everlasting Kingdom? Why art thou

Solicitous? What moves thy inquisition? 200

Know'st thou not that my rising is thy fall,

And my promotion will be thy destruction?"

       To whom the Tempter, inly racked,
replied :—
"Let that come when it comes. All hope is
lost
Of my reception into grace; what worse?

For where no hope is left is left no fear.

If there be worse, the expectation more

Of worse torments me than the feeling can.
I would be at the worst; worst is my port,

My harbour, and my ultimate repose, 210
The end I would attain, my final good.

My error was my error, and my crime
My crime; whatever, for itself condemned,

And will alike be punished, whether thou

Reign or reign not—though to that gentle
brow
Willingly I could fly, and hope thy reign,

From that placid aspect and meek regard,

Rather than aggravate my evil state,
Would stand between me and thy Father's
ire
(Whose ire I dread more than the fire of
Hell) 220
A shelter and a kind of shading cool
Interposition, as a summer's cloud.

*I will undergo a proper trial before I
deserve*
But what do you care when I begin
*My eternal reward, never-ending,
never changing. My everlasting rule?
Why are you*
*So concerned? Why are you
questioning me?*
*Do you not know that my triumph will
be your defeat,*
*And my promotion will be your
destruction?"*

*The tempter, tortured inside,
answered:*
*"When it happens it happens. I have
no hope*
*Of being forgiven; what else have I to
lose?*
*When there is no hope there is no
fear.*
*If there is worse to come, the wait for
it*
Is worse torture than the thing itself.
*I want to get to the worst, the worst is
my port,*
My harbor, and my final rest,
*That's where I want to get to, that's
my goal.*
*My error was my error, and my crime
Was my crime; whatever happens I
have been judged for it,*
*And will be punished in any case,
whether you*
*Rule or not–though I would gladly
run*
*To that sweet face, and hope, from
your calm*
*And humble appearance that your
rule,*
Rather than make my evil state worse,
*Would intervene between me and
your father's anger*
*(The anger that I dread more than the
fire of hell),*
*A shelter and a cooling
Intervention, like a cloud in summer.*

If I, then, to the worst that can be haste,
Why move thy feet so slow to what is best?

Happiest, both to thyself and all the world,

That thou, who worthiest art, shouldst be their King!
Perhaps thou linger'st in deep thoughts detained
Of the enterprise so hazardous and high!

No wonder; for, though in thee be united

What of perfection can in Man be found, 230
Or human nature can receive, consider

Thy life hath yet been private, most part spent
At home, scarce viewed the Galilean towns,

And once a year Jerusalem, few days'

Short sojourn; and what thence couldst thou observe?
The world thou hast not seen, much less her glory,
Empires, and monarchs, and their radiant courts—
Best school of best experience, quickest in sight
In all things that to greatest actions lead.
The wisest, unexperienced, will be ever 240

Timorous, and loth, with novice modesty

(As he who, seeking asses, found a kingdom)
Irresolute, unhardy, unadventrous.
But I will bring thee where thou soon shalt quit
Those rudiments, and see before thine eyes

The monarchies of the Earth, their pomp and state—

So if I can rush towards the worst,
Why are you so slow to head for what is best?

The best thing, for itself and the whole world,

Is that you, who deserve it most, should be their king!
Perhaps you are waiting because you're thinking about
The risks and magnitude of such an enterprise!

It's no wonder, for although in you there is

All the perfection that can be found in man,
Or that can be given to human nature, think

That your life has been quiet so far, mostly spent
At home, you have hardly seen the towns of Galilee,

And have come once a year to Jerusalem, for a few days'

Short stay; what could you see in that time?
You have not seen the world, still less her glory,
Empires, Kings and their glorious courts–
The best places to learn, easiest to see
All the things that lead to greatness.
Without experience even the wisest will always be
Scared and cautious, with the backwardness of the novice
(like Saul who, when looking for asses, gained a kingdom)
Indecisive, weak and unadventurous.
But I will bring you where you will soon learn
The basics, you will see before your eyes

The kingdoms of the Earth, their glory and power–

Sufficient introduction to inform	*This will be enough to show you*
Thee, of thyself so apt, in regal arts,	*The arts of kingship, so necessary for you,*
And regal mysteries; that thou may'st know	*And the secrets of Kings, so you will know best*
How best their opposition to withstand." 250	*How to oppose them."*
With that (such power was given him then), he took	*With that (this was the power he had been given then) he took*
The Son of God up to a mountain high.	*The son of God up to a high mountain.*
It was a mountain at whose verdant feet	*It was a mountain at the wooded foot of which*
A spacious plain outstretched in circuit wide	*A great plain stretched round in a circle,*
Lay pleasant; from his side two rivers flowed,	*Beautiful; two rivers flowed from its slopes,*
The one winding, the other straight, and left between	*One winding, the other straight, and between them*
Fair champaign, with less rivers interveined,	*There was lovely countryside, woven with smaller rivers,*
Then meeting joined their tribute to the sea.	*Then they met to give their waters to the sea.*
Fertil of corn the glebe, of oil, and wine;	*The soil was fertile with corn, olives and wine;*
With herds the pasture thronged, with flocks the hills; 26	*The fields were full of cattle, the hills full of sheep;*
Huge cities and high-towered, that well might seem	*There were great cities with high towers, that might well have been*
The seats of mightiest monarchs; and so large	*The thrones of the greatest kings; and the view*
The prospect was that here and there was room	*Was so wide that here and there there was room*
For barren desert, fountainless and dry.	*For barren desert, dry without springs.*
To this high mountain-top the Tempter brought	*The tempter brought our savior to this high mountaintop*
Our Saviour, and new train of words began:—	*And began a new speech:*
"Well have we speeded, and o'er hill and dale,	*"We have travelled well, over hills and valleys,*
Forest, and field, and flood, temples and towers,	*Forest, fields, rivers, temples and towers,*
Cut shorter many a league. Here thou behold'st	*Taking many shortcuts. Here you can see*

Assyria, and her empire's ancient bounds, 270
Araxes and the Caspian lake; thence on

As far as Indus east, Euphrates west,

And oft beyond; to south the Persian bay,

And, inaccessible, the Arabian drouth:
Here, Nineveh, of length within her wall

Several days' journey, built by Ninus old,
Of that first golden monarchy the seat,

And seat of Salmanassar, whose success

Israel in long captivity still mourns;
There Babylon, the wonder of all tongues, 280
As ancient, but rebuilt by him who twice

Judah and all thy father David's house

Led captive, and Jerusalem laid waste,
Till Cyrus set them free; Persepolis,

His city, there thou seest, and Bactra there;

Ecbatana her structure vast there shews,

And Hecatompylos her hunderd gates;

There Susa by Choaspes, amber stream,

The drink of none but kings; of later fame,

Built by Emathian or by Parthian hands, 290

The great Seleucia, Nisibis, and there

Artaxata, Teredon, Ctesiphon,
Turning with easy eye, thou may'st behold.

All these the Parthian (now some ages past

Assyria, and the ancient borders of her empire,
Araxes and the Caspian lake; further on

You can see as far as the Indus in the east, Euphrates in the west,

And often beyond that; there is the Persian gulf to the south

And the inaccessible Arabian desert;
Here is Nineveh, whose walls took several days

To walk around, built by Ninus of old,
The throne of that first golden monarchy,

The seat of Salmanassar, whose triumph

The captive Israel still regrets;
There is Babylon, which astonishes everyone,
Just as old, but rebuilt by the one who twice

Enslaved Judea and all your ancestor David's descendants

And destroyed Jerusalem,
Until Cyrus freed them; there you can see

Persepolis, his city, and there is Bactra;

Ecbatana is over there with her great buildings

And Hecatompylos with her hundred gates;

There is Shushan by Chospaes, the golden stream,

That is the only water kings would drink; famous later

Built by Emathian or by Parthian hands,

The great Seleucia, Nisibis, and there are

Artaxata, Terdon, Ctesiphon,
Which you can see easily just by turning your head.

All of these the Parthians (led some ages ago

By great Arsaces led, who founded first

That empire) under his dominion holds,
From the luxurious kings of Antioch won.

And just in time thou com'st to have a view
Of his great power; for now the Parthian king

In Ctesiphon hath gathered all his host 300

Against the Scythian, whose incursions wild

Have wasted Sogdiana; to her aid

He marches now in haste. See, though from far,
His thousands, in what martial equipage

They issue forth, steel bows and shafts their arms,
Of equal dread in flight or in pursuit—
All horsemen, in which fight they most excel;
See how in warlike muster they appear,

In rhombs, and wedges, and half-moons, and wings."
            He looked, and saw what numbers numberless 310
The city gates outpoured, light-armed troops

In coats of mail and military pride.

In mail their horses clad, yet fleet and strong,
Pra;ncing their riders bore, the flower and choice
Of many provinces from bound to bound—
From Arachosia, from Candaor east,

And Margiana, to the Hyrcanian cliffs

Of Caucasus, and dark Iberian dales;

From Atropatia, and the neighbouring plains

By great Arsaces, the one who founded

That empire) have under their power,
Taken from the depraved kings of Antioch.

And you come just in time to see
His great power; from now the Parthian King

Has mustered all his army in Ctesiphon

To fight the Scythians, whose terrible invasions

Have laid Sogdiana to waste; he is now marching

Quickly to help her. Even though we are far away
You can see his thousands, going out dressed

In their battle gear, with steel bows and spears,
As fearsome attacking or retreating–
All horsemen, experts in cavalry battles;
See how they are lined up ready for war,

In their different military formations."

He looked and saw what countless numbers

Poured out of the city gates, lightly armed soldiers

Wearing chainmail and full of military pride.

Their horses were also in mail, but fast and strong,
Prancing they carried their riders, the best ones
From all provinces of that empire–
From Arachosia, from Candaor in the east,

And Margiana, from the Hyrcanian cliffs

Of the Caucasus and dark Spanish valleys;

From Atropatia and the neighboring plains

Of Adiabene, Media, and the south 320	*Of Adiabene, Media and the south*
Of Susiana, to Balsara's haven.	*Of Susiana and the harbor of Balsara.*
He saw them in their forms of battle ranged,	*He saw them in their battle order*
How quick they wheeled, and flying behind them shot	*How quickly they wheeled, and shot backwards*
Sharp sleet of arrowy showers against the face	*A sharp rain of arrows into the faces*
Of their pursuers, and overcame by flight;	*Of their pursuers, winning by running;*
The field all iron cast a gleaming brown.	*The field was covered in shining brown iron.*
Nor wanted clouds of foot, nor, on each horn,	*And they weren't lacking footsoldiers, nor, on each flank*
Cuirassiers all in steel for standing fight,	*Cavalry in steel armor waiting for the fight,*
Chariots, or elephants indorsed with towers	*Chariots, or elephants carrying towers full*
Of archers; nor of labouring pioners 330	*Of archers; they also had a multitude*
A multitude, with spades and axes armed,	*Of engineers, armed with spades and axes,*
To lay hills plain, fell woods, or valleys fill,	*To make hills flat, cut down woods, fill valleys,*
Or where plain was raise hill, or overlay	*Or build a hill on flat ground, or cross*
With bridges rivers proud, as with a yoke:	*Great rivers with bridges, as if enslaving them:*
Mules after these, camels and dromedaries,	*These were followed by mules, camels and dromedaries,*
And waggons fraught with utensils of war.	*And carts packed with the weapons of war.*
Such forces met not, nor so wide a camp,	*Such armies did not meet, nor were there such camps,*
When Agrican, with all his northern powers,	*When Agrican, with all the powers of the North,*
Besieged Albracea, as romances tell,	*Besieged Albracaea, so the romances tell us,*
The city of Gallaphrone, from thence to win 340	*And the city of Gallaphrone, to get back*
The fairest of her sex, Angelica,	*The most beautiful of all, Angelica,*
His daughter, sought by many prowest knights,	*His daughter, wanted by many of the greatest knights,*
Both Paynim and the peers of Charlemane.	*Muslims and Charlemagne's lords.*
Such and so numerous was their chivalry;	*This was how these vast numbers were assembled;*

At sight whereof the Fiend yet more presumed,	*The sight of them made the devil more bold,*
And to our Saviour thus his words renewed :—	*And he carried on talking to our savior:*
"That thou may'st know I seek not to engage	*"So you know that I'm not trying to undermine*
Thy virtue, and not every way secure	*Your goodness, and can see that I'm trying*
On no slight grounds thy safety, hear and mark	*In every way to do what's best for you, listen and see*
To what end I have brought thee hither, and shew 350	*The reason for which I have brought you here, and am showing you*
All this fair sight. Thy kingdom, though foretold	*These wonderful sights. You will never inherit your kingdom, even though it was predicted*
By Prophet or by Angel, unless thou Endeavour, as thy father David did,	*By prophets or angels, unless you Fight, as your ancestor David did,*
Thou never shalt obtain: prediction still In all things, and all men, supposes means;	*You will never get it: predictions In everything, and for all men, assume you have the means;*
Without means used, what it predicts revokes.	*Without them, the predictions are worthless.*
But say thou wert possessed of David's throne	*But say you were seated on David's throne*
By free consent of all, none opposite,	*With the agreement of all, nobody opposing,*
Samaritan or Jew; how couldst thou hope	*Samaritan or Jew; how could you hope*
Long to enjoy it quiet and secure 360	*To enjoy it in peace and safety for long,*
Between two such enclosing enemies,	*Trapped between two such armies,*
Roman and Parthian? Therefore one of these	*The Roman and the Parthian? So you must*
Thou must make sure thy own: the Parthian first,	*Take control of one of them: my advice would be*
By my advice, as nearer, and of late	*The Parthian first, as it is nearer, and recently*
Found able by invasion to annoy	*Was shown able to harm your country*
Thy country, and captive lead away her kings,	*Through invasion, and take away her kings,*
Antigonus and old Hyrcanus, bound,	*Antigonus and old Hyrcanus in chains*
Maugre the Roman. It shall be my task	*To the pleasure of the Romans. It will be my task*

To render thee the Parthian at dispose,

Choose which thou wilt, by conquest or by league. 370
By him thou shalt regain, without him not,

That which alone can truly reinstall thee

In David's royal seat, his true successor—

Deliverance of thy brethren, those Ten Tribes
Whose offspring in his territory yet serve

In Habor, and among the Medes dispersed:

The sons of Jacob, two of Joseph, lost

Thus long from Israel, serving, as of old

Their fathers in the land of Egypt served,

This offer sets before thee to deliver. 380

These if from servitude thou shalt restore
To their inheritance, then, nor till then,

Thou on the throne of David in full glory,

From Egypt to Euphrates and beyond,

Shalt reign, and Rome or Caesar not need fear."
To whom our Saviour answered thus, unmoved:—
"Much ostentation vain of fleshly arm
And fragile arms, much instrument of war,

Long in preparing, soon to nothing brought,

Before mine eyes thou hast set, and in my ear 390
Vented much policy, and projects deep
Of enemies, of aids, battles, and leagues,

To hand the Parthians over to your control,
You choose the method, conquest or alliance.
Through them you will be victorious, without them you will not,
They are the only ones who can achieve
Your restoration to David's throne as his true successor
And the freedom of your brothers, those ten tribes
Whose children are still slaves in their lands
In Habor and dispersed amongst the Medes:
The sons of Jacob, two of Joseph, missing
From Israel for so long, servants, as in olden times
Their fathers were servants in the land of Egypt;
I offer you the chance to set them free.
If you free them from their slavery
And give them back their inheritance then, and only then,
Will you reign on the throne of David in full glory,
From Egypt to the Euphrates and beyond,
And you will not need to fear Rome or Caesar."
Our savior, unmoved, answered him:

"You have shown me a vain display
Of muscle and frail weapons, many machines of war,
Which take long to prepare, and are soon smashed to nothing,
And in my ear you have whispered

Many plans and cunning intrigues
Of enemies, help, battles and alliances,

Plausible to the world, to me worth naught.

Means I must use, thou say'st; prediction else
Will unpredict, and fail me of the throne!

My time, I told thee (and that time for thee

Were better farthest off), is not yet come.
When that comes, think not thou to find me slack
On my part aught endeavouring, or to need

Thy politic maxims, or that cumbersome
400
Luggage of war there shewn me—argument

Of human weakness rather than of strength.
My brethren, as thou call'st them, those Ten Tribes,
I must deliver, if I mean to reign
David's true heir, and his full sceptre sway

To just extent over all Israel's sons!

But whence to thee this zeal? Where was it then
For Israel, or for David, or his throne,
When thou stood'st up his tempter to the pride
Of numbering Israel—which cost the lives
410
of threescore and ten thousand Israelites
By three days' pestilence? Such was thy zeal

To Israel then, the same that now to me.

As for those captive tribes, themselves were they
Who wrought their own captivity, fell off

From God to worship calves, the deities

Of Egypt, Baal next and Ashtaroth,
And all the idolatries of heathen round,

Which seem good to the world, and are worthless to me.

You say I must use these things, otherwise
Prophesies will fail, and I will not gain the throne!

I told you that my time (and you should wish

That it is far off) has not yet come.
When it does come don't think you'll find me
Slow to do anything necessary, and I won't need

Your politics or all the clumsy

Gear of war that you have shown me— they show

Human weakness, not strength.
My brothers, as you call them, those ten tribes,
I must free if I want to rule
As the true heir of David and have the right

To have power over all the sons of Israel.

But what makes you so keen on this? Where was this concern
For Israel, for David, or his throne,
When you tempted him into the proud act
Of counting Israel—which cost the lives

Of seventy thousand Israelites
In a three-day plague? That was how you cared

For Israel then, and that's how you care for me now.

As for the captive tribes, they brought

Their captivity on themselves, by falling away

From God to worship calves, the deities

Of Egypt, Baal and then Ashtaroth,
And practised the idolatry of the heathens,

Besides their other worse than heathenish crimes;
Nor in the land of their captivity 420
Humbled themselves, or penitent besought
The God of their forefathers, but so died
Impenitent, and left a race behind
Like to themselves, distinguishable scarce
From Gentiles, but by circumcision vain,
And God with idols in their worship joined.
Should I of these the liberty regard,
Who, freed, as to their ancient patrimony,
Unhumbled, unrepentant, unreformed,
Headlong would follow, and to their gods perhaps 430
Of Bethel and of Dan? No; let them serve
Their enemies who serve idols with God.
Yet He at length, time to himself best known,
Remembering Abraham, by some wondrous call
May bring them back, repentant and sincere,
And at their passing cleave the Assyrian flood,
While to their native land with joy they haste,
As the Red Sea and Jordan once he cleft,
When to the Promised Land their fathers passed.
To his due time and providence I leave them." 440
      So spake Israel's true King, and to the Fiend
Made answer meet, that made void all his wiles.

As well as their other even worse crimes;
And when they were in the land of their captivity
They did not humble themselves, or repentantly seek
The God of their forefathers, but died Unrepentant, and left behind descendants
Like themselves, hardly distinguishable
From gentiles except by pointless circumcision,
Who worshipped both god and the idols.
Why should I care about the freedom of these,
Who, if they were given back their ancient inheritance,
Would, arrogant, unrepentant, unreformed
Still follow their gods
Of Bethel and of Dan? No; let them serve
Their enemies who treat idols as God.
But He may, at some time best known to himself,
Remember Abraham, and bring them back
With some miraculous summons, repentant and sincere
And will part the Assyrian River to let them pass
As they hurry joyfully to their native land,
Just as he once parted the Red Sea and the Jordan,
To let their fathers go to the promised land.
I leave them to his own chosen time and his goodness."
This is how Israel's true King spoke, giving the devil
An answer which undermined all his cunning.

So fares it when with truth falsehood contends.

This is what happens when lies try to take on the truth.

BOOK IV

Perplexed and troubled at his bad success	*Confused and troubled by his lack of success*
The Tempter stood, nor had what to reply,	*The tempter stood, and had no answer,*
Discovered in his fraud, thrown from his hope	*With his tricks uncovered, cheated of his hopes*
So oft, and the persuasive rhetoric	*So often, and the persuasive speeches*
That sleeked his tongue, and won so much on Eve,	*Which rolled off his tongue, and had so completely triumphed over Eve,*
So little here, nay lost. But Eve was Eve;	*Meant so little here, were wasted. But Eve was Eve;*
This far his over-match, who, self-deceived	*He was way out of his depth, self-deluded*
And rash, beforehand had no better weighed	*And careless, he had not considered the strength*
The strength he was to cope with, or his own.	*Of his opponent or his own.*
But—as a man who had been matchless held 10	*But he was like a man who had been thought*
In cunning, over-reached where least he thought,	*The most cunning, beaten when he least expected it,*
To salve his credit, and for very spite,	*Who, to save face, and out of spite,*
Still will be tempting him who foils him still,	*Will carry on assaulting the one who beat him*
And never cease, though to his shame the more;	*And never stop, however foolish he looks;*
Or as a swarm of flies in vintage-time,	*Or like a swarm of flies at the winemaking,*
About the wine-press where sweet must is poured,	*Thronging round the press where the grapes are crushed,*
Beat off, returns as oft with humming sound;	*When they are beaten off they return with the same humming;*
Or surging waves against a solid rock,	*Or like surging waves against a solid rock,*
Though all to shivers dashed, the assault renew,	*Though they are split to smithereens, they attack again*
(Vain battery!) and in froth or bubbles end— 20	*(pointless assault!) and end in froth or bubbles—*
So Satan, whom repulse upon repulse	*This was what Satan was like, who was met with rejection after rejection*
Met ever, and to shameful silence brought,	*And reduced to an ashamed silence,*

Yet gives not o'er, though desperate of success,	*But he did not give up, though he had little hope of success,*
And his vain importunity pursues.	*And he continued his vain attempts at persuasion.*
He brought our Saviour to the western side	*He brought our Savior round to the western side*
Of that high mountain, whence he might behold	*Of that high mountain, from where he could see*
Another plain, long, but in breadth not wide,	*Another plain, long but narrow,*
Washed by the southern sea, and on the north	*Washed by the Southern Sea, and to the north*
To equal length backed with a ridge of hills	*There ran a ridge of hills*
That screened the fruits of the earth and seats of men 30	*That sheltered the crops and the homes of men*
From cold Septentrion blasts; thence in the midst	*From the cold northerly winds; it was divided*
Divided by a river, off whose banks	*Down the middle by a river, and on the banks*
On each side an Imperial City stood,	*On each side an imperial city stood,*
With towers and temples proudly elevate	*With towers and temples proudly raised*
On seven small hills, with palaces adorned,	*On seven small hills, covered with palaces,*
Porches and theatres, baths, aqueducts,	*Porticos and theatres, baths, aqueducts,*
Statues and trophies, and triumphal arcs,	*Statues and trophies, and triumphal arches,*
Gardens and groves, presented to his eyes	*Gardens and woods, shown to him*
Above the highth of mountains interposed—	*Even though there were mountains in between—*
By what strange parallax, or optic skill 40	*It is curious to think of what strange optical illusion*
Of vision, multiplied through air, or glass	*Or skill with lenses could have this effect*
Of telescope, were curious to enquire.	*Of enlarging the vision as if through the glass of a telescope.*
And now the Tempter thus his silence broke:—	*And now the tempter broke his silence.*
"The city which thou seest no other deem	*The city you can see is none other*
Than great and glorious Rome, Queen of the Earth	*Than great and glorious Rome, queen of the earth,*
So far renowned, and with the spoils enriched	*So famous and decorated with the plunder*
Of nations. There the Capitol thou seest,	*Of all countries. You can see the Capitol there,*

Above the rest lifting his stately head	*Raising its noble head above everything*
On the Tarpeian rock, her citadel	*On the Tarpeian rock, her impregnable*
Impregnable; and there Mount Palatine, 50	*Citadel; and there is the Palatine Hill,*
The imperial palace, compass huge, and high	*The imperial palace covering masses of ground,*
The structure, skill of noblest architects,	*And built so high, showing the skills of the greatest architects,*
With gilded battlements, conspicuous far,	*With gilded battlements which can be seen from afar,*
Turrets, and terraces, and glittering spires.	*Turrets, terraces and glittering spires.*
Many a fair edifice besides, more like	*There are many other beautiful buildings besides, more like*
Houses of gods—so well I have disposed	*The houses of gods–I have set up my magnifier*
My aerie microscope—thou may'st behold,	*So well that you can see*
Outside and inside both, pillars and roofs	*Both the interiors and exteriors, pillars and roofs,*
Carved work, the hand of famed artificers	*Carvings that are the work of famous craftsmen*
In cedar, marble, ivory, or gold. 60	*In cedar, marble, ivory or gold.*
Thence to the gates cast round thine eye, and see	*Then look round to the gates, and see*
What conflux issuing forth, or entering in:	*What a great crowd goes out and comes in:*
Praetors, proconsuls to their provinces	*Magistrates, the governors of provinces,*
Hasting, or on return, in robes of state;	*Hurrying out or returning in their official robes*
Lictors and rods, the ensigns of their power;	*With their underlings carrying the symbols of their power;*
Legions and cohorts, turms of horse and wings;	*Battalions and regiments, squadrons of cavalry and infantry;*
Or embassies from regions far remote,	*Ambassadors from far off regions,*
In various habits, on the Appian road,	*In different clothes, on the Appian Way*
Or on the AEmilian—some from farthest south,	*Or on the Via Ameilia–some come from the farthest south,*
Syene, and where the shadow both way falls, 70	*Aswan on the equator,*
Meroe, Nilotic isle, and, more to west,	*From Ethiopia and, more to the west,*
The realm of Bocchus to the Blackmoor sea;	*From Morocco in the southern Mediterranean;*

From the Asian kings (and Parthian among these),
From India and the Golden Chersoness,
And utmost Indian isle Taprobane,

Dusk faces with white silken turbants wreathed;
From Gallia, Gades, and the British west;
Germans, and Scythians, and Sarmatians north
Beyond Danubius to the Tauric pool.
All nations now to Rome obedience pay—
80 To Rome's great Emperor, whose wide domain,
In ample territory, wealth and power,
Civility of manners, arts and arms,
And long renown, thou justly may'st prefer

Before the Parthian. These two thrones except,
The rest are barbarous, and scarce worth the sight,
Shared among petty kings too far removed;

These having shewn thee, I have shewn thee all
The kingdoms of the world, and all their glory.
This Emperor hath no son, and now is old, 90
Old and lascivious, and from Rome retired

To Capreae, an island small but strong
On the Campanian shore, with purpose there
His horrid lusts in private to enjoy;
Committing to a wicked favourite
All public cares, and yet of him suspicious;

Hated of all, and hating. With what ease,

Endued with regal virtues as thou art,
Appearing, and beginning noble deeds,

Might'st thou expel this monster from his throne, 100

From the kings of Asia (with Parthians amongst them),
From India and Malaysia
And the farthest Indian island of Sri Lanka,

Dark faces wrapped with white silk turbans;
From France, Cadiz and Brittany;
There are Germans, Scythians and Sarmatians from north
Of the Danube by the Sea of Azov.
Now all nations pay tribute to Rome—
To Rome's great Emperor, whose wide realm
Of great land, wealth and power,
Culture of manners, arts and arms,
And great fame you may rightly prefer

To the Parthians. Apart from these two empires
The rest are barbarian, hardly worth looking at,
Shared amongst insignificant kings and too far away;

Having shown you these, I have shown you all
The kingdoms of the world, and all the glory.
The Emperor is old and has no son,
He is old and immoral and has retired from Rome

To Capri, a small but strong island
Off the shore of Campania, meaning
To enjoy his obscene lusts in private;
He has given a wicked henchman
Charge of all public affairs, and yet is suspicious of him;

He is hated by all, and hates them. How easy it would be,

Full of kingly virtues as you are,
To appear and begin your great adventure

By throwing this monster from his throne

Now made a sty, and, in his place ascending,	*Which he has made into a pigsty, and taking his place;*
A victor-people free from servile yoke!	*You would free this ruling nation from slavery!*
And with my help thou may'st; to me the power	*And with my help you can; I have that power*
Is given, and by that right I give it thee.	*And I have the right to give it to you.*
Aim, therefore, at no less than all the world;	*Aim for nothing less than the whole world;*
Aim at the highest; without the highest attained,	*Aim at the highest; if you do not win the highest prize,*
Will be for thee no sitting, or not long,	*You will not sit, or anyway not for long,*
On David's throne, be prophesied what will."	*On David's throne, whatever has been prophesied."*
To whom the Son of God, unmoved, replied:—	*The son of God, unmoved, answered him:*
"Nor doth this grandeur and majestic shew 110	*"None of this greatness and majestic show*
Of luxury, though called magnificence,	*Of indulgence, though it's called magnificence,*
More than of arms before, allure mine eye,	*Attracts my eye any more than that show of arms did before,*
Much less my mind; though thou should'st add to tell	*And it attracts my mind still less; you should*
Their sumptuous gluttonies, and gorgeous feasts	*Stories of their great feasts and elaborate stuffing on*
On citron tables or Atlantic stone	*Tables of citron wood or stone from Mount Atlas,*
(For I have also heard, perhaps have read),	*For I have also heard, maybe I read about,*
Their wines of Setia, Cales, and Falerne,	*Their wines from Setia, Cales and Falerne,*
Chios and Crete, and how they quaff in gold,	*Chios and Crete, and how they swig from gold,*
Crystal, and myrrhine cups, imbossed with gems	*Crystal and fine porcelain cups, studded with jewels*
And studs of pearl—to me should'st tell, who thirst 120	*And pearls—you should tell me, who is still thirsty*
And hunger still. Then embassies thou shew'st	*And hungry. Then you show me embassies*
From nations far and nigh! What honour that,	*From nations far and near! What honor is there in that,*
But tedious waste of time, to sit and hear	*That tedious waste of time, to sit and hear*
So many hollow compliments and lies,	*So many empty compliments and lies,*

Outlandish flatteries? Then proceed'st to talk	*Far-fetched flatteries? Then you start to talk*
Of the Emperor, how easily subdued,	*About the Emperor, how easily I can beat him,*
How gloriously. I shall, thou say'st, expel	*How gloriously. You say I shall get rid of*
A brutish monster: what I withal	*A brutish monster: how about if at the same time*
Expel a Devil who first made him such?	*I get rid of the devil that made him that way?*
Let his tormentor, Conscience, find him out; 130	*Let conscience be his torturer, and find him out;*
For him I was not sent, nor yet to free	*I wasn't sent for him, or these people,*
That people, victor once, now vile and base,	*Once triumphant, now vile and low,*
Deservedly made vassal—who, once just,	*They deserve to be slaves–once they were just,*
Frugal, and mild, and temperate, conquered well,	*Frugal, humble, and sober, they were good conquerors,*
But govern ill the nations under yoke,	*But they are bad governors of the nations under their thumb,*
Peeling their provinces, exhausted all	*Stripping their provinces bare, all exhausted*
By lust and rapine; first ambitious grown	*By greed and plunder; first they became ambitious*
Of triumph, that insulting vanity;	*For triumphs, those empty things;*
Then cruel, by their sports to blood inured	*Then they became cruel, through their games they did not care*
Of fighting beasts, and men to beasts exposed; 140	*About the blood of fighting beasts, or that of men exposed to the beasts;*
Luxurious by their wealth, and greedier still,	*They became indulgent through their wealth, and still greedier,*
And from the daily Scene effeminate.	*And got soft from seeing this sort of thing daily.*
What wise and valiant man would seek to free	*What wise and brave man would want to free*
These, thus degenerate, by themselves enslaved,	*These ones, so degenerate, who made themselves slaves;*
Or could of inward slaves make outward free?	*How could you set them free when they are slaves inside?*
Know, therefore, when my season comes to sit	*You should know that when it comes my time to sit*
On David's throne, it shall be like a tree	*On the throne of David, it shall be like a tree*
Spreading and overshadowing all the earth,	*Spreading over and shading all the earth,*

Or as a stone that shall to pieces dash

All monarchies besides throughout the world; 150
And of my Kingdom there shall be no end.
Means there shall be to this; but what the means
Is not for thee to know, nor me to tell."

      To whom the Tempter, impudent, replied:—
"I see all offers made by me how slight

Thou valuest, because offered, and reject'st.

Nothing will please the difficult and nice,

Or nothing more than still to contradict.

On the other side know also thou that I

On what I offer set as high esteem, 160
Nor what I part with mean to give for naught,
All these, which in a moment thou behold'st,
The kingdoms of the world, to thee I give

(For, given to me, I give to whom I please),

No trifle; yet with this reserve, not else—
On this condition, if thou wilt fall down,

And worship me as thy superior Lord
(Easily done), and hold them all of me;

For what can less so great a gift deserve?"

      Whom thus our Saviour answered with disdain:— 170
"I never liked thy talk, thy offers less;

Now both abhor, since thou hast dared to utter
The abominable terms, impious condition.

Or like a rock on which all other monarchies
Throughout the world will be wrecked,
And my kingdom will never end.
There are ways in which this shall be achieved;
But these are not for you to know or for me to tell you."

The tempter arrogantly answered him:
"I see how little store you set by the offers I make
Because I offer them and you reject them.
Nothing will please those who are awkward and precious,
Or anyway, the only thing which pleases them is to argue.
So, for my part you should also know that I
Set a high value on what I offer,
And I'm not giving this away for nothing,
All these, which you see all at once,
The kingdoms of the world, I am giving to you
(for they have been given to me and I can give them to whom I please),
No small thing; but only
On this condition—that you will kneel before me,
And worship me as your lord
(an easy thing to do), and rule them in my name;
Surely such a great gift deserves no less?"

Our savior answered him contemptuously:
"I never liked your talk, and I liked your offers less;
Now I hate both, since you have dared to speak
The disgraceful terms, the blasphemous condition.

But I endure the time, till which expired

Thou hast permission on me. It is written,

The first of all commandments, 'Thou shalt worship
The Lord thy God, and only Him shalt serve.'
And dar'st thou to the Son of God propound

To worship thee, accursed? now more accursed

For this attempt, bolder than that on Eve, 180
And more blasphemous; which expect to rue.
The kingdoms of the world to thee were given!
Permitted rather, and by thee usurped;

Other donation none thou canst produce.

If given, by whom but by the King of kings,

God over all supreme? If given to thee,

By thee how fairly is the Giver now

Repaid! But gratitude in thee is lost
Long since. Wert thou so void of fear or shame
As offer them to me, the Son of God— 190

To me my own, on such abhorred pact,

That I fall down and worship thee as God?

Get thee behind me! Plain thou now appear'st
That Evil One, Satan for ever damned."

        To whom the Fiend, with fear abashed, replied:—

But I will tolerate you until the time allocated
For you to be with me is finished. It is written
As the first commandment, 'you shall worship
The lord your God, and will serve only him.'
Do you dare to propose to the son of God
That he should worship you, the damned? Now you're even more damned

For making this attempt, more audacious than the one on Eve,
And more blasphemous; expect to regret this.
You say the kingdoms of the world were given to you!
You were allowed to enter them, and you stole them;
You cannot show proof that they were given to you.
Who but the king of kings, God over all supreme,
Could have given them to you? If he gave them to you,
How charmingly you are thanking the giver now!
But you lost your gratitude long ago.
Are you so devoid of fear and shame
As to offer them to me, the son of God—
Offering me what belongs to me, with the filthy deal
That I fall down and worship you as a god?
Get behind me! Now I can see you clearly for who you are,
The evil one, Satan eternally damned."
The devil, ashamed and fearful, answered:

"Be not so sore offended, Son of God—

Though Sons of God both Angels are and Men—
If I, to try whether in higher sort

Than these thou bear'st that title, have proposed
What both from Men and Angels I receive, 200
Tetrarchs of Fire, Air, Flood, and on the Earth
Nations besides from all the quartered winds—
God of this World invoked, and World beneath.
Who then thou art, whose coming is foretold

To me most fatal, me it most concerns.

The trial hath indamaged thee no way,

Rather more honour left and more esteem;

Me naught advantaged, missing what I aimed.
Therefore let pass, as they are transitory,

The kingdoms of this world; I shall no more 210
Advise thee; gain them as thou canst, or not.

And thou thyself seem'st otherwise inclined
Than to a worldly crown, addicted more

To contemplation and profound dispute;
As by that early action may be judged,

When, slipping from thy mother's eye, thou went'st
Alone into the Temple, there wast found

Among the gravest Rabbies, disputant
On points and questions fitting Moses' chair,

"Don't be so greatly offended, son of god—

Though angels and men are sons of god as well—
If I, to test whether you deserve that title

More than these others, have offered

What I have been given by men and angels,

Rule over fire, air, water and on earth also

Rule over nations at all points of the compass—

Called god of this world and the underworld.

So it is my business to find out who you are,

Whose coming is predicted to be fatal for me.

This trial has not damaged you in any way,

In fact it has left you with more honor and greater esteem;

I have gained nothing, missing my target.

So let the kingdoms of the world go by,

As they do not last; I shall no longer

Advise you; get them if you can, or not.

And you yourself seem uninterested
In a worldly crown, being more addicted

To meditation and deep debate;
We can see that from your early actions,

When you slipped away from your mother and went
Alone into the temple, where you were found

Amongst the wisest rabbis, arguing
Points and questions regarding who should fill Moses' chair,

Teaching, not taught. The childhood shews the man, 220	*You were teaching, not being taught. The child was the forerunner of the man,*
As morning shews the day. Be famous, then,	*As morning is forerunner of the day. Be famous then*
By wisdom; as thy empire must extend,	*For your wisdom; as your empire spreads*
So let extend thy mind o'er all the world	*So let your mind spread over the world*
In knowledge; all things in it comprehend.	*In its knowledge; understand everything in it.*
All knowledge is not couched in Moses' law,	*Not all knowledge is to be found in the laws of Moses,*
The Pentateuch, or what the Prophets wrote;	*The Pentateuch or the writings of the prophets;*
The Gentiles also know, and write, and teach	*The Gentiles also know, write and teach*
To admiration, led by Nature's light;	*Very well, following the guidance of nature.*
And with the Gentiles much thou must converse,	*You must talk much with the Gentiles,*
Ruling them by persuasion, as thou mean'st. 230	*Persuading them to accept you, as you mean to.*
Without their learning, how wilt thou with them,	*If you don't know their learning how will you hold*
Or they with thee, hold conversation meet?	*Proper conversations with them, or them with you?*
How wilt thou reason with them, how refute	*How will you reason with them, how will you show*
Their idolisms, traditions, paradoxes?	*That their idolatry, traditions and paradoxes are wrong?*
Error by his own arms is best evinced.	*Error is best shown through its own techniques.*
Look once more, ere we leave this specular mount,	*Before we leave this viewing point, look once more*
Westward, much nearer by south-west; behold	*To the west, closer to the south-west; you see*
Where on the AEgean shore a city stands,	*Where a city stands on the Aegean shore,*
Built nobly, pure the air and light the soil—	*Nobly built, with pure air and light soil—*
Athens, the eye of Greece, mother of arts 240	*Athens, the centre of Greece, the mother of the arts*
And Eloquence, native to famous wits	*And eloquence, home of famous geniuses,*

Or hospitable, in her sweet recess,

City or suburban, studious walks and shades.
See there the olive-grove of Academe,

Plato's retirement, where the Attic bird
Trills her thick-warbled notes the summer long;
There, flowery hill, Hymettus, with the sound
Of bees' industrious murmur, oft invites

To studious musing; there Ilissus rowls

His whispering stream. Within the walls then view 250
The schools of ancient sages—his who bred

Great Alexander to subdue the world,

Lyceum there; and painted Stoa next.

There thou shalt hear and learn the secret power
Of harmony, in tones and numbers hit

By voice or hand, and various-measured verse,
AEolian charms and Dorian lyric odes,
And his who gave them breath, but higher sung,
Blind Melesigenes, thence Homer called,

Whose poem Phoebus challenged for his own. 260
Thence what the lofty grave Tragedians taught
In chorus or iambic, teachers best

Of moral prudence, with delight received
In brief sententious precepts, while they treat
Of fate, and chance, and change in human life,
High actions and high passions best describing.

Welcoming in the sweet shade of her paths
In the city or the suburbs.
There you can see the olive grove of Academe,
Plato's shelter where the Greek bird
Sings her rich notes all summer;
There is the flowery hill, Hymettus, with the sound
Of the industrious murmur of bees, which often inspires
Study and philosophising; there the whispering stream
Of Ilissus flows. Within the walls you can see
The schools of the ancient wise men, the Lyceum
Of Aristotle who taught the great Alexander
To conquer the world; there is painted Stoa.
There you shall learn and hear the secret power
Of harmony, in tones and numbers played
By the voice or hand, and verse of different rhythms,
Aeolian songs and Doric odes,
And the words of the one who inspired them all,
Blind Melesigenes, so they call Homer,
Whose poetry challenged that of Apollo.
Then you will see what the high serious tragedians taught
In choruses or iambics, the best teachers
Of moral values, who took delight
In concise moral instructions while they dealt with
Fate, chance and the changes in human life,
The best describers of great actions and great passions.

Thence to the famous Orators repair,
Those ancient whose resistless eloquence

Wielded at will that fierce democraty,
Shook the Arsenal, and fulmined over Greece 270
To Macedon and Artaxerxes' throne.

To sage Philosophy next lend thine ear,

From heaven descended to the low-roofed house
Of Socrates—see there his tenement—

Whom, well inspired, the Oracle pronounced
Wisest of men; from whose mouth issued forth
Mellifluous streams, that watered all the schools
Of Academics old and new, with those
Surnamed Peripatetics, and the sect

Epicurean, and the Stoic severe. 280
These here revolve, or, as thou likest, at home,
Till time mature thee to a kingdom's weight;

These rules will render thee a king complete

Within thyself, much more with empire joined."
    To whom our Saviour sagely thus replied:—
"Think not but that I know these things; or, think
I know them not, not therefore am I short

Of knowing what I ought. He who receives

Light from above, from the Fountain of Light,
No other doctrine needs, though granted true; 290
But these are false, or little else but dreams,

Then go and see the famous orators,
The ancient ones whose irresistible speech
Ruled over that strict democracy,
Shook the military, and their protests were heard over Greece
All the way to Macedon and the throne of Artaxerxes.
Next you should listen to wise philosophy,
That came down from heaven to the low roofed house
Of Socrates–you can see his lodging there–
The one whom the oracle, getting it right, judged
To be the wisest of men; from his mouth there came
Sweet streams that refreshed all the branches
Of academia, old and new, the ones
Called Peripatetics, and the Epicurean sect,
And the severe Stoics.
Explore these here, or at home if you wish,
Until in time you grow strong enough to bear the weight of a kingdom;
These rules will make you a complete king
Within yourself, so you will be even more so when joined with an empire."
Our savior wisely replied to him:
"Don't think that I do not know these things,
Or that if I do not know them that I lack
Knowledge that I ought to have. He who receives
Light from above, from the fountain of light,
Needs no other theories, even if they are right;
But these are false, or just dreams,

Conjectures, fancies, built on nothing firm.	*Speculation, fantasies, castles in the air.*
The first and wisest of them all professed	*The first and wisest of them all admitted*
To know this only, that he nothing knew;	*That the only thing he knew was that he knew nothing;*
The next to fabling fell and smooth conceits;	*The next resorted to making things up and cunning stories;*
A third sort doubted all things, though plain sense;	*A third doubted everything, even what was obvious;*
Others in virtue placed felicity,	*Others put their faith in virtue,*
But virtue joined with riches and long life;	*But virtue backed with riches and a long life;*
In corporal pleasure he, and careless ease;	*In the pleasures of the flesh, and unworried leisure.*
The Stoic last in philosophic pride, 300	*The stoic has the greatest pride in his philosophy,*
By him called virtue, and his virtuous man,	*Which he calls virtue and his virtuous man*
Wise, perfect in himself, and all possessing,	*Is wise, perfect to himself, self-possessed,*
Equal to God, oft shames not to prefer,	*Equal to God, and shamefully often won't choose between the two,*
As fearing God nor man, contemning all	*The fear of God or man, he condemns everything,*
Wealth, pleasure, pain or torment, death and life—	*Wealth, pleasure, pain or torment, death and life–*
Which, when he lists, he leaves, or boasts he can;	*When he mentions them he boasts that he can take them or leave them;*
For all his tedious talk is but vain boast,	*All his tedious talk is just boasting,*
Or subtle shifts conviction to evade.	*Or cunning words to avoid having to commit to a belief.*
Alas! what can they teach, and not mislead,	*Alas! What can they teach, without misleading;*
Ignorant of themselves, of God much more, 310	*They don't even know themselves, much less God,*
And how the World began, and how Man fell,	*Or how the world began, and how man fell,*
Degraded by himself, on grace depending?	*Brought down by himself, falling from grace?*
Much of the Soul they talk, but all awry;	*They talk a lot about the soul, but get it all wrong;*
And in themselves seek virtue; and to themselves	*They look for virtue in themselves, and give themselves*
All glory arrogate, to God give none;	*All the glory, they give God none;*

Rather accuse him under usual names,	*Instead they give him the names of fortune*
Fortune and Fate, as one regardless quite	*And fate, and accuse him, as if he were quite unaware*
Of mortal things. Who, therefore, seeks in these	*Of mortal things. So anyone who looks to these men*
True wisdom finds her not, or, by delusion	*For true wisdom will not find her or, with a worse delusion*
Far worse, her false resemblance only meets, 320	*Only finds a false imitation of her,*
An empty cloud. However, many books,	*An empty cloud. However, wise men have said*
Wise men have said, are wearisome; who reads	*That too many books will wear you out; the one who is always*
Incessantly, and to his reading brings not	*Reading, and doesn't apply a matching or greater amount*
A spirit and judgment equal or superior,	*Of sense and judgment*
(And what he brings what needs he elsewhere seek?)	*(and if he has that why does he need to look*
Uncertain and unsettled still remains,	*Will remain uncertain and unsettled,*
Deep-versed in books and shallow in himself,	*Well read but unlearned,*
Crude or intoxicate, collecting toys	*Rough or reeling, thinking that ribbons*
And trifles for choice matters, worth a sponge,	*And bows are weighty things; he sucks words up like a sponge,*
As children gathering pebbles on the shore. 330	*Like children gathering pebbles on the shore.*
Or, if I would delight my private hours	*Or, if I want to spend my leisure*
With music or with poem, where so soon	*With music or with poetry, where better*
As in our native language can I find	*To find that comfort than in*
That solace? All our Law and Story strewed	*Our first text? All our law and story is full*
With hymns, our Psalms with artful terms inscribed,	*Of hymns, our psalms are full of poetry,*
Our Hebrew songs and harps, in Babylon	*Our Hebrew songs and music that were so pleasing*
That pleased so well our victor's ear, declare	*To our conqueror in Babylon show*
That rather Greece from us these arts derived—	*That these arts came from us not from Greeks—*
Ill imitated while they loudest sing	*Poorly copied while they sing loudly*
The vices of their deities, and their own, 340	*About the vices of their gods, and their own,*
In fable, hymn, or song, so personating	*In story, hymn or song, depicting*

Their gods ridiculous, and themselves past shame.	*Their absurd gods, and themselves without shame.*
Remove their swelling epithetes, thick-laid	*Take away their poetic language, laid on as thick*
As varnish on a harlot's cheek, the rest,	*As makeup on a whore's cheek, the rest*
Thin-sown with aught of profit or delight,	*Has very little that teaches or pleases,*
Will far be found unworthy to compare	*And cannot be compared*
With Sion's songs, to all true tastes excelling,	*With the songs of Zion, which all real taste finds greatest,*
Where God is praised aright and godlike men,	*Where God is given proper praise as well as godlike man*
The Holiest of Holies and his Saints	*The holiest of holies and his saints*
(Such are from God inspired, not such from thee); 350	*(these are inspired by God, not by*
Unless where moral virtue is expressed	*The only works of theirs worth anything are where*
By light of Nature, not in all quite lost.	*Moral virtue is shown through nature.*
Their orators thou then extoll'st as those	*You praise their orators as being*
The top of eloquence—statists indeed,	*The greatest speakers–indeed they are patriots*
And lovers of their country, as may seem;	*And lovers of their country, it appears;*
But herein to our Prophets far beneath,	*But they are far below our prophets,*
As men divinely taught, and better teaching	*Who are men taught by god, who can better teach*
The solid rules of civil government,	*The fundamental rules of civil government*
In their majestic, unaffected style,	*In their majestic unpretentious manner*
Than all the oratory of Greece and Rome. 360	*Than all the flowery words of Greece and Rome.*
In them is plainest taught, and easiest learnt,	*They give the clearest teaching, easiest to learn,*
What makes a nation happy, and keeps it so,	*They say what makes a nation happy, and keeps it that way,*
What ruins kingdoms, and lays cities flat;	*What destroys kingdoms and brings cities to the ground;*
These only, with our Law, best form a king."	*Along with our law this is all a king needs."*
So spake the Son of God; but Satan, now	*So the son of God spoke; but Satan, now*
Quite at a loss (for all his darts were spent),	*Completely baffled (as he was out of ammunition),*

Thus to our Saviour, with stern brow,
replied:—
　　　　"Since neither wealth nor honour,
arms nor arts,
Kingdom nor empire, pleases thee, nor
aught
By me proposed in life contemplative 370
Or active, tended on by glory or fame,
What dost thou in this world? The
Wilderness
For thee is fittest place: I found thee there,
And thither will return thee. Yet remember
What I foretell thee; soon thou shalt have
cause
To wish thou never hadst rejected, thus
Nicely or cautiously, my offered aid,
Which would have set thee in short time
with ease
On David's throne, or throne of all the
world,
Now at full age, fulness of time, thy season,
380
When prophecies of thee are best fulfilled.
Now, contrary—if I read aught in heaven,
Or heaven write aught of fate—by what the
stars　　　Voluminous, or single characters
In their conjunction met, give me to spell,
Sorrows and labours, opposition, hate,
Attends thee; scorns, reproaches, injuries,
Violence and stripes, and, lastly, cruel death.
A kingdom they portend thee, but what
kingdom,
Real or allegoric, I discern not; 390
Nor when: eternal sure—as without end,
Without beginning; for no date prefixed

Frowned and answered our savior:

*"Since neither wealth nor honor,
war nor art,
Kingdom nor Empire, pleases you,
nor anything
Which I have proposed in terms of an
intellectual
Or active life, which would bring you
glory or fame,
Then what are you doing in this
world? The wilderness
Is the best place for you: I found you
there,
And will take you back there. But
remember
What I predict for you; soon you will
wish
That you had never rejected so
Preciously or timidly the help I
offered,
Which could have quickly and easily
set you up
On the throne of David, or the throne
of all the world,
At this good age, at the right time,
your time,
The time when the predictions of you
should come true.
Now things will be different—if I can
read the stars
Or the stars show anything of fate—
Together or singly lining up
They are showing me
That you will face sorrow and trials,
opposition and hate,
Scorn, criticism, injury,
Violence and whipping, and, lastly, a
cruel death.
They predict a kingdom for you, but
what kingdom,
Real or metaphorical, I cannot see,
Or know when it will come: it will
certainly be eternal—without an end,
As it is without a beginning; for I can
see no date*

Directs me in the starry rubric set."
       So saying, he took (for still he knew his power
Not yet expired), and to the Wilderness
Brought back, the Son of God, and left him there,
Feigning to disappear. Darkness now rose,
As daylight sunk, and brought in louring Night,
Her shadowy offspring, unsubstantial both,
Privation mere of light and absent day. 400
Our Saviour, meek, and with untroubled mind
After his aerie jaunt, though hurried sore,
Hungry and cold, betook him to his rest,
Wherever, under some concourse of shades,
Whose branching arms thick intertwined might shield
From dews and damps of night his sheltered head;
But, sheltered, slept in vain; for at his head
The Tempter watched, and soon with ugly dreams
Disturbed his sleep. And either tropic now
'Gan thunder, and both ends of heaven; the clouds 410
From many a horrid rift abortive poured
Fierce rain with lightning mixed, water with fire,
In ruin reconciled; nor slept the winds
Within their stony caves, but rushed abroad
From the four hinges of the world, and fell

Written in the stars."
Saying this he picked up (for his power had not
Yet run out) and returned to the wilderness
The son of God, and left him there,
Pretending to disappear. Darkness now came
To replace the daylight and bring in gathering night,
Her dark child, both of them insubstantial,
Just being the deprivation of light and the absence of day.
Our savior, humble, and with an untroubled mind
After his trip through the air, though exhausted,
Hungry and cold, looked for a place to sleep,
Wherever he could find branches twined together thick enough to protect
His sleeping head from the dew and damp of the night;
But although he found shelter he did not sleep well; for the tempter
Watched at his head and soon disturbed his sleep
With ugly dreams. And both ends of the earth now
Began to thunder, and both ends of heaven, from many
Horrible clefts in the clouds there poured
Fierce rain mixed with lightning, water with fire,
Together in destruction; nor did the winds
Sleep in their stony caves, but rushed around
The four corners of the world, and swooped
On the tortured wilderness, whose tallest pines

On the vexed wilderness, whose tallest pines,

Though rooted deep as high, and sturdiest oaks,
Bowed their stiff necks, loaden with stormy blasts,
Or torn up sheer. Ill wast thou shrouded then,
O patient Son of God, yet only stood'st 420

Unshaken! Nor yet staid the terror there:

Infernal ghosts and hellish furies round
Environed thee; some howled, some yelled, some
Some bent at thee their fiery darts, while thou

Sat'st unappalled in calm and sinless peace.

Thus passed the night so foul, till Morning fair
Came forth with pilgrim steps, in amice grey,
Who with her radiant finger stilled the roar

Of thunder, chased the clouds, and laid the winds,
And griesly spectres, which the Fiend had raised 430
To tempt the Son of God with terrors dire.

And now the sun with more effectual beams

Had cheered the face of earth, and dried the wet

From drooping plant, or dropping tree; the birds,
Who all things now behold more fresh and green,
After a night of storm so ruinous,
Cleared up their choicest notes in bush and spray,

Though their roots went down as deep as their height, and the sturdiest oaks,
Bowed their stiff necks, pressed down with the stormy gusts
Or completely blown over. You were poorly sheltered then,
Oh patient son of god, but you were the only one who stood
Unshaken! But the terror did not end there:
You were surrounded by devilish ghosts and
Hellish demons; some howled,
Some yelled, some shrieked,

Some aimed their fiery arrows at you, while you

Sat unworried in calm and sinless peace.
So the foul night passed, until lovely morning
Came forward like a pilgrim, in clerical grey,
And with her shining fingers stopped the roar
Of thunder, chased away the clouds, calmed the winds
And fearsome ghosts which the devil had summoned
To attack the son of God with dire terror.
And now the sun with its stronger rays
Put a smile on the face of Earth, and burned the water

Off the drooping plants and bowed trees; the birds,
Who now saw everything fresher and greener,
After such a destructive stormy night,
Sang their sweetest songs in the bushes and on the branches,

To gratulate the sweet return of morn.

Nor yet, amidst this joy and brightest morn,

Was absent, after all his mischief done, 440

The Prince of Darkness; glad would also seem
Of this fair change, and to our Saviour came;
Yet with no new device (they all were spent),
Rather by this his last affront resolved,

Desperate of better course, to vent his rage

And mad despite to be so oft repelled.

Him walking on a sunny hill he found,

Backed on the north and west by a thick wood;
Out of the wood he starts in wonted shape,

And in a careless mood thus to him said :— 450

  "Fair morning yet betides thee, Son of God,
After a dismal night. I heard the wrack,

As earth and sky would mingle; but myself

Was distant; and these flaws, though mortals fear them
As dangerous to the pillared frame of Heaven,
Or to the Earth's dark basis underneath,

Are to the main as inconsiderable
And harmless, if not wholesome, as a sneeze

To man's less universe, and soon are gone.

Yet, as being ofttimes noxious where they light 460

To welcome the sweet return of morning.

However, amidst all this joy and bright morning,

The Prince of Darkness was not absent,

After all the mischief he had done; he also looked
Glad to see this lovely change, and he came to our savior;
He had no new tricks (he had used them all),
But he had decided, with no better thing to do,

To make one last attack, to spill out his rage

And frustration at being so often defeated.

He found him walking on a sunny hill,

With thick woods to the north and west;
He came out of the wood in his true shape,

And lightly said to him:

"The fair morning has come to you, son of God,
After a dismal night. I heard the storm,

As if Earth and sky would crash together; but I

Was far away; and these upsets, though feared by mortals
Who think that they will bring down the sky,
Or shake the foundations of the Earth,

Are in general as unimportant
And harmless, if not as healthy, as a sneeze

In man's little universe, and they soon disappear.

But as they can often do damage when they land

On man, beast, plant, wasteful and turbulent, *On man, beast or plants, destructive and stormy,*

Like turbulencies in the affairs of men, *Like storms in the affairs of men,*
Over whose heads they roar, and seem to point, *Whose heads they roar over, seeming to give signs,*
They oft fore-signify and threaten ill. *They are often predictors of bad things.*

This tempest at this desert most was bent; *This storm was aimed directly at this desert;*

Of men at thee, for only thou here dwell'st. *It was aiming at you, for you are the only one here.*

Did I not tell thee, if thou didst reject *Didn't I tell you that would happen if you rejected*

The perfect season offered with my aid *My help, at this perfect time,*
To win thy destined seat, but wilt prolong *In winning your destined throne, and want to*

All to the push of fate, pursue thy way 470 *String out the course of fate, following your way*

Of gaining David's throne no man knows when *Of gaining David's throne at a time unknown*
(For both the when and how is nowhere told), *(for neither the time or the method have been announced),*
Thou shalt be what thou art ordained, no doubt; *You will get what has been predicted for you, no doubt;*
For Angels have proclaimed it, but concealing *For Angels have announced it, but have hidden*
The time and means? Each act is rightliest done *The time and means. The proper time to do something*
Not when it must, but when it may be best. *Is not when you are forced to, but when it is best.*

If thou observe not this, be sure to find *If you can't see this then you will get*
What I foretold thee—many a hard assay *What I predicted for you—many hard trials,*

Of dangers, and adversities, and pains, *Dangers, suffering and pain*
Ere thou of Israel's sceptre get fast hold; 480 *Before you get a grip on Israel's sceptre;*

Whereof this ominous night that closed thee round, *This ominous night which surrounded you*
So many terrors, voices, prodigies, *With so many terrors, voices and marvels*

May warn thee, as a sure foregoing sign." *Is a warning to you that these things are coming."*

    So talked he, while the Son of God went on, *So he spoke, while the son of God walked on*
And staid not, but in brief him answered thus:— *Without stopping but answered him briefly:*

"Me worse than wet thou find'st not; other har
Those terrors which thou speak'st of did me none.
I never feared they could, though noising loud
And threatening nigh: what they can do as

Betokening or ill-boding I contemn 490
As false portents, not sent from God, but thee;
Who, knowing I shall reign past thy preventing,
Obtrud'st thy offered aid, that I, accepting,

At least might seem to hold all power of thee,
Ambitious Spirit! and would'st be thought my God;
And storm'st, refused, thinking to terrify

Me to thy will! Desist (thou art discerned,

And toil'st in vain), nor me in vain molest."

    To whom the Fiend, now swoln with rage, replied:—
"Then hear, O Son of David, virgin-born! 500
For Son of God to me is yet in doubt.

Of the Messiah I have heard foretold

By all the Prophets; of thy birth, at length
Announced by Gabriel, with the first I knew,
And of the angelic song in Bethlehem field,

On thy birth-night, that sung thee Saviour born.
From that time seldom have I ceased to eye

Thy infancy, thy childhood, and thy youth,

"All that happened to me is I got wet; those terrors
Which you speak of did me no other harm.
I never thought that they would, though they crashed loudly
And came close, threatening: their powers of prediction

Whether good or bad I reject
As false signs, not coming from God, but from you;
You, who, knowing that you cannot stop me from reigning,
Pushed forward your offers of help so that if I accepted

It would at least look as though I had been given the power by you,
Ambitious spirit! You want to be thought of as my God;
And as you were rebuffed you created the storm thinking you would

Terrify me into complying with you! Stop (I can see your plans

And you work in vain) these pointless attacks on me."

The fiend, now swollen with rage, answered him:
"Then listen to me, son of David, born of a virgin!
I still doubt whether you are the son of God.

I have heard of the coming of the Messiah

From all the prophets; of your birth, Announced by Gabriel, I was among the first to know,
As well as hearing the angelic song in the fields of Bethlehem

On the night of your birth, that praised you as the savior.
From that time I have always kept an eye

On your infancy, your childhood, your adolescence,

Thy manhood last, though yet in private bred;

Till, at the ford of Jordan, whither all 510
Flocked to the Baptist, I among the rest
(Though not to be baptized), by voice from Heaven
Heard thee pronounced the Son of God beloved.
Thenceforth I thought thee worth my nearer view
And narrower scrutiny, that I might learn
In what degree or meaning thou art called
The Son of God, which bears no single sense.
The Son of God I also am, or was;
And, if I was, I am; relation stands:
All men are Sons of God; yet thee I thought 520
In some respect far higher so declared.
Therefore I watched thy footsteps from that hour,
And followed thee still on to this waste wild,
Where, by all best conjectures, I collect
Thou art to be my fatal enemy.

Good reason, then, if I beforehand seek

To understand my adversary, who

And what he is; his wisdom, power, intentl;

By parle or composition, truce or league,

To win him, or win from him what I can. 530
And opportunity I here have had
To try thee, sift thee, and confess have found thee
Proof against all temptation, as a rock
Of adamant and as a centre, firm

And last of all your adulthood,
though you were still being brought up in private;
Until, at the ford of Jordan, when everyone
Flocked to the Baptist, I went along with the rest
(though not to be baptised) and heard a voice from heaven
Announcing that you were the beloved son of God.
From then on I thought you were worth a closer look
And more detailed examination, so I could learn
What exactly is meant by you being called
The son of God, as that can mean more than one thing.
I am also the son of God, or was;
And if I was, I am; you cannot erase a relationship:
All men are sons of God; but I thought you
Were in some way rated far higher.
And so I watched your footsteps from that time,
And followed you into this wasteland,
And my best guess is
That you are going to be my fatal enemy.
So I have good reason to try to understand
My opponent before the battle begins, who
And what he is; his wisdom, power and intentions;
I want to win him over, or get from him what I can,
By talking or debate, truce or alliance.
I have had the opportunity here
To test you, examine you, and I admit I found you
Resistant to all temptation, like a rock
Of diamond and as unshakeable

To the utmost of mere man both wise and good,
Not more; for honours, riches, kingdoms, glory,
Have been before contemned, and may again.
Therefore, to know what more thou art than man,
Worth naming the Son of God by voice from Heaven,
Another method I must now begin." 540
       So saying, he caught him up, and, without wing
Of hippogrif, bore through the air sublime,

Over the wilderness and o'er the plain,

Till underneath them fair Jerusalem,

The Holy City, lifted high her towers,
And higher yet the glorious Temple reared
Her pile, far off appearing like a mount

Of alablaster, topt with golden spires:
There, on the highest pinnacle, he set
The Son of God, and added thus in scorn
:— 550
       "There stand, if thou wilt stand; to stand upright
Will ask thee skill. I to thy Father's house
Have brought thee, and highest placed:
highest is best.

Now shew thy progeny; if not to stand,

Cast thyself down. Safely, if Son of God;

For it is written, 'He will give command

Concerning thee to his Angels; in their hands
They shall uplift thee, lest at any time
Thou chance to dash thy foot against a stone.'"
       To whom thus Jesus: "
Also it is written, 560

As the strongest of wise and good men,
But no more than this; honors, riches, kingdoms, glory,
Have been rejected before, and maybe will be again.
So, to know in what way you are more than a man,
Worth naming as the son of God by the voice from heaven,
I must now try another method."
Saying this he snatched him up, and, without using
A hippogriff, carried him through the empty air,
Over the wilderness and over the plain,
Until fair Jerusalem was beneath them,
The holy city, with her high towers
And still higher the glorious temple
Thrusting upwards, from far off seeming like a mountain
Of marble, topped with golden spires:
There on the highest point, he put
The son of God, and scornfully added:
"Stand up there, if you will; to stand upright
Will demand skill. I have brought you
To your father's house, and put you in the highest place: the highest is the best.
Now show your ancestry; if you will not stand,
Throw yourself down. If you are the son of God you can do this safely;
For it is written, 'he will give his orders
About you to all his angels; they will lift you up
In their hands, to prevent you
From stumbling. '"
Jesus answered him: "it is also written,

'Tempt not the Lord thy God.'" He said, and stood;
But Satan, smitten with amazement, fell.

As when Earth's son, Antaeus (to compare

Small things with greatest), in Irassa strove

With Jove's Alcides, and, oft foiled, still rose,

Receiving from his mother Earth new strength,
Fresh from his fall, and fiercer grapple joined,
Throttled at length in the air expired and fell,
So, after many a foil, the Tempter proud,

Renewing fresh assaults, amidst his pride 570
Fell whence he stood to see his victor fall;

And, as that Theban monster that proposed

Her riddle, and him who solved it not devoured,
That once found out and solved, for grief and spite
Cast herself headlong from the Ismenian steep,

So, strook with dread and anguish, fell the Fiend,
And to his crew, that sat consulting, brought

Joyless triumphals of his hoped success,

Ruin, and desperation, and dismay,
Who durst so proudly tempt the Son of God. 580
So Satan fell; and straight a fiery globe

Of Angels on full sail of wing flew nigh,

'Do not tempt the Lord your God.'"
He spoke, and stood up;
But Satan, stunned with astonishment, fell.

It was as when the son of Earth, Antaeus (to compare

Small things with the greatest), fought in Irassa

With Hercules, son of Jupiter, and, being often knocked down, still rose again,

Gaining fresh strength from his mother, the Earth,
And rejoined the battle even more fiercely,
But was eventually throttled, died in the air and fell;
So after many rebuttals the proud tempter,

Trying a fresh attack, in his pride

Fell from the place where he had hoped to see his opponent fall;

It was as when the Sphinx put forward

Her riddle, and did not eat the one who solved it;
Once she had been discovered and the riddle solved
She threw herself, through grief and pite, straight down from the Ismenian Heights;

So, stricken with fear and pain, down the devil fell,
And brought his crew, that sat debating,

Unhappy news of his hoped-for success,

Ruin, desperation and dismay
For the one who so arrogantly dared to tempt the son of God.
So Satan fell; and at once a flaming body

Of angels with their wings spread flew past,

Who on their plumy vans received Him soft	*And with their feathered wings plucked Jesus softly*
From his uneasy station, and upbore,	*From his wobbly perch and carried him up,*
As on a floating couch, through the blithe air;	*As if on a floating couch, through the happy air;*
Then, in a flowery valley, set him down	*Then they put him down in a flowery valley,*
On a green bank, and set before him spread	*On a green bank, and laid out before him*
A table of celestial food, divine	*A table of heavenly food, divine*
Ambrosial fruits fetched from the Tree of Life,	*Sweet fruits taken from the tree of life,*
And from the Fount of Life ambrosial drink, 590	*And sweet drink from the fountain of life,*
That soon refreshed him wearied, and repaired	*That soon took away his tiredness and repaired*
What hunger, if aught hunger, had impaired,	*Any damage that hunger, if there had been hunger, or thirst*
Or thirst; and, as he fed, Angelic quires	*Had done; and as he ate, angelic choirs*
Sung heavenly anthems of his victory	*Sang heavenly anthems about his victory*
Over temptation and the Tempter proud:—	*Over temptation and the arrogant tempter:*
"True Image of the Father, whether throned	*"You are the true image of the father, whether on your throne*
In the bosom of bliss, and light of light	*In the heart of happiness, amidst the light of light,*
Conceiving, or, remote from Heaven, enshrined	*Or far away from heaven, placed*
In fleshly tabernacle and human form,	*In a vessel of flesh and in human shape,*
Wandering the wilderness—whatever place, 600	*Wandering the wilderness–wherever you are,*
Habit, or state, or motion, still expressing	*However dressed, in what state, or place, you are still*
The Son of God, with Godlike force endued	*The son of God, full of Godlike force*
Against the attempter of thy Father's throne	*Against the one who tried to take your father's throne*
And thief of Paradise! Him long of old	*The one who stole paradise! You tamed him*
Thou didst debel, and down from Heaven cast	*Long ago, and threw him down from heaven*
With all his army; now thou hast avenged	*With all his army; now you have avenged*

Supplanted Adam, and, by vanquishing	*The exiled Adam, and by defeating*
Temptation, hast regained lost Paradise,	*Temptation you have regained the lost paradise,*
And frustrated the conquest fraudulent.	*And blocked his fraudulent attempts.*
He never more henceforth will dare set foot 610	*He will never dare again to set foot*
In paradise to tempt; his snares are broke.	*In Paradise to try temptation; his traps are broken.*
For, though that seat of earthly bliss be failed,	*For, although that home of earthly bliss has gone,*
A fairer Paradise is founded now	*A greater Paradise has now been built*
For Adam and his chosen sons, whom thou,	*For Adam and his chosen sons, whom you,*
A Saviour, art come down to reinstall;	*A savior, have come down to lead back.*
Where they shall dwell secure, when time shall be,	*When the time comes they shall live there safely,*
Of tempter and temptation without fear.	*Without fearing temptation or the tempter.*
But thou, Infernal Serpent! shalt not long	*But you, you infernal Serpent! You shall not*
Rule in the clouds. Like an autumnal star,	*Rule the clouds for long. Like a shooting star,*
Or lightning, thou shalt fall from Heaven, trod down 620	*Or lightning, you shall fall from heaven, crushed*
Under his feet. For proof, ere this thou feel'st	*Under his feet. To prove it, before this happens*
Thy wound (yet not thy last and deadliest wound)	*You are feeling the wound (but this is not your last and deadliest wound)*
By this repulse received, and hold'st in Hell	*That this defeat has given you, and cannot hold*
No triumph; in all her gates Abaddon rues	*Your triumph in hell; all through the underworld*
Thy bold attempt. Hereafter learn with awe	*They regret your bold challenge. From now on learn with awe*
To dread the Son of God. He, all unarmed,	*To dread the son of God. He, completely unarmed,*
Shall chase thee, with the terror of his voice,	*Will chase you, with the terror of his voice*
From thy demoniac holds, possession foul—	*From your demonic possessions, your foul home—*
Thee and thy legions; yelling they shall fly,	*You and your armies; they will run screaming*
And beg to hide them in a herd of swine, 630	*And beg you to hide them in a herd of pigs,*

Lest he command them down into the Deep, *In case he sends them down into the pit,*

Bound, and to torment sent before their time. *Bound, sent to torture before their time.*

Hail, Son of the Most High, heir of both Worlds, *We salute you, son of the highest, heir to both worlds,*

Queller of Satan! On thy glorious work *Crusher of Satan! Now start your glorious work*

Now enter, and begin to save Mankind." *And begin to save mankind."*

       Thus they the Son of God, our Saviour meek, *So they sang a victory song for the son of God,*

Sung victor, and, from heavenly feast refreshed, *Our gentle savior, and, refreshed from the heavenly feast,*

Brought on his way with joy. He, unobserved, *They sent him on his way with joy. He, unobserved,*

Home to his mother's house private returned. *Secretly returned home to his mother's house.*

Made in United States
Orlando, FL
02 May 2023

32705027R00300